Warhost of Vastmark

Janny Wurts is the author of several successful
fantasy novels including the Cycle of Fire trilogy
(*Stormwarden*, *The Keeper of the Keys* and
Shadowfane) and the *Master of Whitestorm*. She
is also the author, with Raymond E. Feist, of the
Empire series (*Daughter of the Empire*, *Servant
of the Empire* and *Mistress of the Empire*).

Her skill as a horsewoman, offshore sailor and
musician is reflected in her novels. She is also a
talented artist and has recently been awarded the
Chesley Award for illustration. The cover of
Warhost of Vastmark is one of her own paint-
ings. She lives in Florida, USA.

Voyager

JANNY WURTS

Warhost of Vastmark

The Wars of Light and Shadows
Volume 3

HarperCollins*Publishers*

Voyager
An Imprint of HarperCollins*Publishers*
77–85 Fulham Palace Road,
Hammersmith, London W6 8JB

www.voyager-books.com

This paperback edition 1996
10

First published in Great Britain by
HarperCollins*Publishers* 1988

ISBN 0 00 648207 4

Set in Linotron Trump Mediaeval by
Rowland Phototypesetting Ltd,
Bury St Edmunds, Suffolk

Printed in Great Britain by
Clays Ltd, St Ives plc

Acknowledgments

My thanks to the sales force at HarperCollins whose
efforts make all the difference:
and to those who work in the bookshops,
who handle the dreams of authors.

For Jane Johnson,
for the grand leap of faith –
thanks is too small a word.

Contents

In Werpoints wide harbour, beside Minderl Bay
the Master's spun shadow drowned out the new day
The Prince of the West raised his gift of white light
Cry Justice! For brave ships burned, and doomed men
drowned, one shadow-binding criminal goes unfound.

Lay for the Stranded Warhost
Third Age Year 5645

I. *SECOND CONVOCATION*

Sethvir of Althain soaked in his hip bath those rare times when he suffered glum spirits. Lapped like a carp in warm water, his hair frizzled over the sculptured bones of thin shoulders, he sulked with his chin in his fists while the steam whorled up through the hanks of his beard and dripped off the white combs of his brows. Misted and half-closed with melancholy, his eyes seemed to cast their brooding focus on his gnarled toes, now perched in a row on the tub's rim.

The nails curled in neglected need of trimming.

Of more telling concern to Sethvir, Prince Arithon's brilliant strike at Minderl Bay had still failed the wider scope of his intent. If the allied northern war host recruited to hound him had been dismantled with lightest losses, Lysaer s'Ilessid's misled following had not awakened to perceive the stark truth: that what had destroyed their sea fleet at Werpoint had been less a bloody ploy of the Shadow Master's than the mishandled force of Lysaer's own gift of light, maligned by Desh-thiere's curse.

The one ship's captain lent the insight to know differently lay slain, beset in a dingy dockside alley. The

1

footpads who knifed him had been hired by Avenor's Lord Commander for political expediency, Sethvir knew beyond doubt. As Arithon's sole witness, and a man who had viewed the unalloyed directive of the Mistwraith's geas firsthand, the seaman had been killed before he could cast any pall of public doubt upon Prince Lysaer's judgment in defence. Remanned by a crew of less-questionable loyalty, his benighted brig would sail south with the tide for Alestron, Lysaer s'Ilessid and the pick of his officers on board.

The sorry conclusion weighed like a stone in the heart.

If Arithon had just demonstrated his fullest under-standing of the curse that shackled his will, if this second encounter at Minderl Bay had increased his respect for its fearful train of ill consequence, his half-brother Lysaer owned no such searching self-awareness. Misconstrued by the gift of the s'Ilessid royal line, which bound his relentless pursuit of justice, Tysan's lost prince remained the sad puppet of circumstance. To the root of his conscience, he stayed righteously assured that he held to honourable principles. He believed his born cause was to hunt down and eliminate a confirmed minion of evil.

Sethvir glowered into the soap-scummed surface of his bathwater, then blinked, as if for the barest, fragmentary second he had thought to see stars in the suds clinging about his knobby knees.

Stars; idle musing sharpened into farsight. The muddled distance in the Sorcerer's blue-green eyes snapped into sudden, sharp focus. His wet skin stabbed into gooseflesh, Sethvir bolted from his tub. Water splashed jagged stains in his abused scarlet carpet. He snatched up his robe, burrowed it over his wet head, then paused through a drawn-out, prickling shudder as dread raked through him once again.

Grazed against the limits of his awareness, beyond the world's wind-spun cloak of living air, an event of chilling wrongness carved a line. Its fire-tailed passage jostled the harmonics of the stars into thin and jangling discord.

Sethvir took only an instant to confirm that the upset was bound to an associate Sorcerer's Name and signature. Kharadmon of the Fellowship was at long last returning from the interdicted worlds beyond South Gate, and an immediate crisis came with him.

The Warden of Althain rushed barefoot from his personal chambers. He slapped wet footprints up the spiral stair to reach the library in the tower's topmost chamber. Even as his hand tripped the latch and flung wide the oaken door, his cry of distress rang out to summon his disparate colleagues.

Ranged over vast distance, the call roused Luhaine from his sojourn to settle the ghosts drawn back across the veil of the mysteries by the doings of a necromancer, who then abandoned them to winnow in lost patterns over the frost-burned waste of Scarpdale.

Asandir was in Halwythwood, reconsecrating the old Paravian standing stones that held and warded the earthforce; he would ride in driving haste to reach the power focus at Caith-al-Caen, but not in time to trap the dawn sun surge for a spell transfer.

The raven which flew partnered with Traithe sailed on the air currents above Vastmark. Its master tested the fault lines in the slopes, that shepherds too poor to survive losses not pen their flocks through the winter in valleys prone to shale slides. The pair, bird and Sorcerer, were too distant from Atainia to help. No recourse existed. The sense of pending danger grew in Sethvir, sharper and more pressing by the second.

He needed the particulars of what was wrong, and quickly, but Kharadmon proved too beleaguered to send details. The door from the stairwell at Althain had barely slammed shut when Sethvir flung open the casement. Autumn wind sheared fresh chill over his soggy beard and dripping skin, crisp with the musk of dying bracken. The Sorcerer shivered again, hounded by urgency. Before he raised wards and grand conjury against disaster, he could have done with a scalding mug of tea.

The speed of events left no time. An icier vortex of air laced through the wet tails of his beard: vexed as always by the untimely nature of emergencies, Luhaine blew in on a huffed breeze of inquiry.

'It's Kharadmon, coming home,' Sethvir explained. His attention stayed pinned on the white points of stars, strung between flying scraps of cloud. 'Before you ask, he's brought trouble along with him.'

'That's his born nature,' Luhaine snapped. 'Like the dissonance in a cracked crystal, some things in life never sweeten.'

Sethvir maintained polite silence, then spoiled all pretence to dignity by gathering his draggled beard and wringing the soggy hanks like a rag. Soapy runnels slid down his wrists and dampened the rucked hems of his sleeves. While the catspaw gusts of his colleague's irritation riffled the pages of his books, he held his face tipped skyward. Starshine imprinted the glassy surface of his eyes through long and listening minutes.

Then the last tinge of colour drained from his wizened cheeks.

Luhaine's presence resolved into concentrated stillness. 'Ath have mercy, what is it?'

Sethvir whirled in an agitated squall of shed droplets. 'Wards,' he cried, terse. 'Two sets, concentric. We must circle all Athera for protection, then ring this tower as haven and catchpoint for a spirit under threat of possession.'

'*Kharadmon! Under siege!*' Luhaine exclaimed.

Sethvir nodded, speechless. Three steps impelled him to the table's edge. He ploughed a clear space among his clutter of parchments. Two candlestands toppled. A tea mug rocked out into air, spell-caught before it shattered against the stone floor by Luhaine's fussy penchant for tidiness.

Amid a pelting storm of flung papers, Sethvir set up the black iron brazier and ignited its pan, cold blue with the current of the third lane. Too pressed to trifle with marking his presence with an image, Luhaine immersed his whole being into the lane's quickened flow, then channelled his awareness through the old energy paths that past Paravian dancers had scribed across the earth to interlink the world's magnetic flux at each solstice. His task was made difficult by rites fallen into disuse. Everywhere the tracery was reduced to faint glimmers. Many lines were snarled, or severed by obstructions where migrant herders had unknowingly built sheep-folds, or significant trees had been cut, creating sharp breaks in continuity. Meadows long harrowed by the ploughshare's cold iron contorted the energy flow. The powers Luhaine laced in patterns across the land resisted and sought to bleed from his grasp, to dissipate in useless bursts of static, except in convergence around Jaelot, where Arithon's past meddling with music at the crux of a lane tide had scoured the paths to clean operancy.

Kharadmon's straits would not wait for perfection. Forced against his grain to rely upon hurried handiwork, Luhaine was scarcely ready as Sethvir murmured, 'Now.'

Crowded to the edge of a chair already occupied by a tipsy stack of books, Sethvir tucked his chin in cupped palms. His china-bright eyes glazed and went sightless as he plunged into the throes of deep trance.

Luhaine felt the Warden's consciousness twine through the lane-spark in the brazier, then beyond to access the earth net. Now interlinked with the broad-scale scope of Sethvir's specialized vision, he, too, could sense the white-orange fireball which scored the black deeps toward Athera. At firsthand, he grasped the peril drawn in from the worlds sealed past South Gate. The measure of its virulence lay beyond spoken language to express. Whatever fearsome, coiling presence had become attached in pursuit of Kharadmon, it carried a malevolence to stun thought.

Far too methodical for volatile emotion, Luhaine matched effort with Althain's Warden and cast his whole resource into a call to raise the earth's awareness into guard.

Not unlike the consciousness of stone, the balanced mesh of forces which comprised the disparate qualities of bedrock, and rich loam, and the fiery heartcore of magma danced to their own staid pace. Ath Creator's living stamp upon the land owned no concept for desperate necessity. Sluggish to rouse, slower still to catalyse into change from within, the deepest dreams of the earth counted the passage of years and seasons little more than an animal might mark the singular sum of its own heartbeats. Seas and shore noted the trials of men and sorcerers less than the wild deer took stock of biting insects.

To pierce through that current of quiescence, Sethvir and Luhaine rewove the third lane's bright forces into a chord that framed Name. Attuned to their effort, long leagues to the east, Asandir linked the hoofbeats of the horse who galloped under him into a tattoo of distress. The rhythm struck down through topsoil and stone there, to resound the full length of the fourth lane.

Hours passed before the earth heeded. More minutes, before deep-laid energies quickened in response. In paired, reckless speed, the Fellowship Sorcerers sited at Althain conjoined the roused charge of the world's two dozen major power lanes.

They took small care to shield their efforts. Any outside mind attuned to the mysteries could not fail to overhear the cry as primal elements sparked awake to the play of meddled mystery. Koriani enchantresses reached for spell crystals to gauge the pulse of change, while mariners shot awake as the winds whined and gusted

6

in unnatural key through their rigging. Sailors on deck cowered and gripped lucky amulets in fear, for across the broad deeps of the oceans, flared lines the blued tinge of lightning sheared beneath the foam of the wavecrests.

In Halwythwood, the grey, lichened standing stones just blessed by Asandir discharged a purple corona of wild power. Along the old roads and on the hillcrests revered in the time-lost rites of First Age ceremony, the spirit imprints of Paravians shone like wisps drawn in silver point and starlight. The bones of forsaken ruins keened in pitched tones of harmonics. An uprooted jumble of carved rock by the fired brick walls of Avenor moaned aloud, though no breeze at all combed through its exposed nooks and crannies.

At Althain Tower, as the last of the energy paths joined, Sethvir pushed erect and scrabbled through his books to find a sliver of white chalk. Within the pooled glow from the brazier, he scribed runes in parallel columns; in circles; in triangles; in counterlocked squares, the symbols of guard and of ward. He bordered the whole with a blessing of protection. Then he added the tracery which framed the tidal surge of life, renewed year to year, century to century, age to age, each thread wound and strengthened to a brilliance of diversity on the natural loom of storm, disease, and calamity.

He sketched the symbols of beginning and ending that, entwined, formed the arc of eternity. He added the patience of stone and the endurance of air, that flowed through all change without resistance; then the blind grace of trees, that reached for the light despite trials of weather and ice.

The widening scrawl of the Warden's symbols glimmered in pale phosphor against the obsidian tabletop. His fingernails snapped sparks like the clash of flint to steel where power bled through his written tapestry. Minutes passed and stars turned. Nightfall silvered dew on the stems of wild grasses. Sethvir felt these things and weighed them as precious, while his labours tuned and channelled the ozone torrent of raw force; until his wet hair fanned dry, then raised and crackled with static, and the tower's slate roof sang, each shingle in singular counterpoint.

'Hurry,' Luhaine whispered through a thundering gust that swooped in to rattle the unlatched casements. The currents poised between him and Sethvir were fast cresting to the cusp of explosion. To stay them in containment for any span of time demanded more than two Sorcerers' paired strength. Luhaine dared not slacken his grip. If his control slipped in the slightest degree, the unbalance would trip off an elemental backlash. The rampage of spilled energy could unleash a cyclone of ruin to lash up the ire of the earth. Should natural order be cast into chaos, storms would run riot; whole strips of coastline would be torn into change. Great quakes would shake the dry land and the seas. From the volcanoes that fumed like sleeping dragons in Northstrait to the dormant cauldrons crowning the clouded peaks of the Tiriacs, the great continent itself might crack corner to corner in a seam of burst fault lines, to vent steam and boulders, or spew lava in swathes of destruction.

Sethvir dashed sweat from the tip of his nose and scribed the last flourish on a cipher. 'Now,' he whispered into air drawn so taut, the word seemed snapped from strung wire.

Like magma poured from a crucible, Luhaine bent the poised powers of the earth through the construct formed by Sethvir's rune seals. The ancient stone tabletop rang out like mallet-struck iron. White chalk lines glimmered green, then blazed into light fierce enough to blast untrained sight into blindness.

Sethvir cried out, his outline immolated by a burn of wild radiance too intense for breathing flesh to encompass. He dared not succumb to the flood of bodily sensation. Every faculty he possessed fought to master the influx, then deflect its blind torrent to imprint defence wards in figured arcs across the heavens.

Outside the tower window, the sky flared a fleeting, raw orange. Then lines crossed the stars, tuned in strict mirror image from the arcane markings scribed upon the table. A spiked scent of ozone whetted the winds, and a thunderous report slammed and rumbled above the frost-rimed wastes surrounding Althain.

Then the glow of grand conjury dimmed and faded. Chalked lines of fire subsided to the dull glare of cinders, then dissipated, febrile as blown wisps of ash. Peace remained. The land spread quiet under untrammelled starlight; but to any with mage-sight to witness, the cloak of the night lay patterned across with a spidery blue tracery of guard spells.

Barefoot and rumpled in his water-stained robe, his hair a thatched nest of tangles, Sethvir of Althain regarded his handiwork and muttered a prayer to Ath that his stopgap effort was sufficient. Luhaine was too distressed to grumble recriminations. Already withdrawn from communion with the earth, he weighed the most expedient means by which the wards over Althain Tower could be realigned to aid Kharadmon in his predicament.

Scant seconds remained before the problem came to roost in their midst.

Luhaine demanded more facts. 'I presume our colleague is beset by wraiths of the same sort and origin as the ones that grant the Mistwraith its sentience.'

Sethvir grunted an assent, his knuckles latched white in his beard. Once again, his eyes were wide open and blank as his awareness ranged outward to track the inbound progress of Kharadmon. A minute passed before he voiced the worst of all possible conclusions. 'The creatures in pursuit are free wraiths not embodied in any shell of mist.'

Which meant a binding would be needed that was

every bit as potent as the one which sealed the jasper
flask prisoned inside Rockfell Pit. Luhaine asked a permission, then made a change to Althain's outer wards
that crackled the air beyond the casements. He added in
acerbic disapproval, 'Kharadmon shouldered an unspeakable risk to draw such entities to Athera.'

'He had no choice.' Sethvir seemed suddenly as fragile
as a figure cast in porcelain as he recovered his chalk stub
and scribbled a fresh round of ciphers on the windowsill.
'Rather, the beacon spell Asandir and I sent to rescue
him became the turn of ill luck to force his hand.'

The implications behind that admission were broad-
scale and laced with ironies enough to seed tragedy.
Wordless in his anguish, Sethvir passed on what he
knew: that Kharadmon had heard every call, every
thought, every entreaty dispatched from Althain Tower
to urge him home. He had been unable to answer, locked
as he was into conflict against hostile entities. These
had been bent on his destruction from the instant he was
recognized for an emissary from Athera, and a Sorcerer of
the Fellowship of Seven. The wraiths cut off beyond
South Gate desired to assimilate his knowledge of grand
conjury for their own ends. In stealth, in patience, Kharadmon had fought to outwit them. Adversity had only
reconfirmed the gravity of his quest, to unriddle the
Name of the Mistwraith incarcerated back at Rockfell
Peak, that its tormented spirits could be redeemed and
two princes be freed from its curse.

'That beacon held the signature map of all Athera,'
Sethvir ended in a stripped whisper. 'We used the very
trees to tie its binding.'

Luhaine absorbed the ripples of wider quandary like a
thunderclap. Long years in the past, at the hour of the
Mistwraith's first incursion, Traithe had sealed South
Gate to close off its point of entry at hideous personal
cost. Now, through the conjury sent to recall Kharadmon, the main body of the mists once thwarted from

10

the crossing were offered another means to trace Athera. Until every tree, every sapling and seed that had lent its vibration to the homing spell had lived out its allotted span of days, a tenuous tie would remain, a ghost imprint of the mighty ward dispatched across the void to recontact those sundered worlds. The threat remained in force, that those truncated spirits once a part of Deshthiere's autonomy might seek to rejoin their fellows still precariously sealed alive in Rockfell Pit.

'Dharkaron's black vengeance!' Luhaine burst out, a shattering departure for a spirit well-known to condemn his colleagues' oaths as a mannerless lack of imagination. The fear behind his outburst stayed unspoken, that the Fellowship's covenant with the Paravian races might be thrown irredeemably into jeopardy.

'Quite,' Sethvir said in sour summary. Any outside chance of renewed conflict with the Mistwraith meant the Fellowship might need their princes' irreplaceable talents with light and shadow once again. The scope of fresh setback staggered thought. For as long as the lives of the royal half brothers lay entangled into enmity by the curse, its ever-tightening spiral would drive them toward a final annihilating conflict. The risks would but increase over time.

The Warden of Althain bent a furrowed scowl toward his sprawl of runes and seals. 'Let us pray that Kharadmon has brought us back answers and a Name for this terror from the gate worlds.'

Luhaine drifted in from a point poised in air beyond the window. 'Your hope is premature.' Ever the pessimist, he keyed a seal into power, and, with a flaring crack, a blue net of light enmeshed the tower's high battlement. 'First, we have to rescue the rash idiot from his latest tangle with calamity.'

A bone-chilling gust tinged with ozone flayed a sudden gap through the clouds. The wards above Althain flared purple and sealed in a white effusion of sparks. Sethvir laid down his chalk, bemused to dismay, while disturbed breezes settled, riming the windowsill next to his elbow with diamond crystals of ice.

'Don't act so virtuous, Luhaine,' retorted the Fellowship spirit just returned. A peppery insouciance clipped his speech. 'I recall the days when you did little but sit about eating muffins and leaving smears of butter on the books. To hear you pontificate now, one can't help but feel sorry. Such windy bouts of language make a sorrowful substitute for the binges you can't manage as a ghost.'

While Luhaine was left at flustered odds for rejoinder, Sethvir twisted in his seat to face the turbid patch of air inside his library. A pixie's bright smile flexed his lips. 'Welcome home to Althain Tower, Kharadmon.'

A riffle like a snort crossed the chamber. 'I daresay you won't think so when you see what's tagged a ride on my coattails.' The Sorcerer just arrived resumed in flippant phrasing at odds with his predicament. 'I hate to be the bore to wreck the party, but don't be startled if the earth wards you've set fail to stand up under trial.'

Urgency pressed him too closely to share the premise behind his bleak forecast. In a fiery flourish of seals, Kharadmon configured an unfamiliar chain of runes and safeguards. These meshed into the primary protections already laid over the tower to receive the hate-driven entities he had battled and failed to outrun.

'As a last resort, the wraiths dislike the stink of sulphur,' he finished off in crisp haste.

Ever intolerant of his colleague's provocations, Luhaine retuned the balance of a sigil the sudden change had tipped awry. 'I suggest we don't allow the wretched creatures any liberty to need tactics of such flimsy desperation.'

'Luhaine! From you, an enchanting understatement!' Kharadmon's quick turn around the chamber masked a trepidation like vibrations struck off tempered steel. For should the wraiths which trailed him across the deeps of space escape Fellowship confinement here at Althain, they would gain access to all of Athera. Set loose, their potential for havoc could unleash horrors beyond all imagining.

After all, they were an unfettered aspect drawn here from the original body of the Mistwraith, an entity created from a misguided meddling with the Law of the Major Balance. Its works had driven the Paravians to vanish in despair; in defeat, its dire vengeance had twisted the lives of two princes.

While Luhaine's ghost churned through brown thoughts over Kharadmon's tasteless humour, the wards crisscrossing the darkened sky outside flared active with a scream of raw light. Sethvir shouted a binding cantrip, then gave way to alarm as Kharadmon's hunch was borne through. A burst hurtled down like a meteor storm, in angry red arcs curdling holes through every ward and guard he and Luhaine had shaped from roused earthforce.

'Ath's infinite pity!' Althain's Warden cried, his fingers wrung through his beard.

'No,' Kharadmon interjected, his insouciance torn away by exhaustion that verged on impairment. 'These wraiths won't fall on the defenceless countryside. Not yet. They'll besiege us here first. Incentive will draw them. *They desire to steal knowledge from our Fellowship.* We'll be under attack, and if any one of us falls as a victim, there will be no limit to our sorrow.' His warning fell into a dread stillness, since he alone could gauge the threat now descending upon Althain Tower.

'Don't try to close with them. Don't let them grapple,' he added in hurried, last caution. 'Their bent is possession. They can slip traps through time. The best chance we have is to keep out of reach, use this tower's primary defences for containment, then try to snare the creatures in ring wards.'

The mirror-loop spells to entrap a hostile consciousness back into itself were a simple enough undertaking, provided a mage knew the aura pattern of the spirit appointed for restraint. To Luhaine's high-browed flick of inquiry, Kharadmon showed tart disgust. 'I'd hardly have needed to flee the fell creatures if I'd held command of their Names.'

And then the wraiths were upon them in a swirling, unseen tide of spite. They poured through the casements to winnow the unshielded spark in the brazier, and cause Sethvir's scattered tomes to clap shut like trap jaws on bent pages and loose sheaves of quill pens.

Through the last battle to confine Desh-thiere, Paravian defence wards alone had been impervious to the wraiths' aberrant nature. Even as Asandir had once done in desperation atop another beleaguered tower nine years past, Luhaine fired a charge through a spell net held ready. A power more ancient than any sorcerer's tenancy surged in response to his need. A deep-throated rumble shook the old stonework as the wards over Althain slammed fast.

The pack of free wraiths bent in hate against the Fellowship were now sealed inside Sethvir's library. If Kharadmon had resisted their malevolence alone through an exhaustive toll of years, he was now left too worn from his trials to offer much fight to help stay them. Bare hope must suffice that the Paravian safeguards laid within the tower's walls would prove as potent against these invaders as the wards once reconfigured against Desh-thiere.

Yet in this hour of trial, the attacking entities inhabited no body spun from mist. These free wraiths held no fleshly tie to life, nor were they subject to any physical law. They could not be lured through illusions framed to malign or confuse the senses. Not being fogbound, no gifted command of light and shadow would suffice to turn them at bay. Lent the knife-edged awareness that no power in the land might contain these fell creatures should they slip Althain's wards and escape, three Sorcerers stewed inside with them had no option at all but to try and evade their deadly grasp. They must seek to subdue and enchain them without falling prey to possession.

The peril was extreme and the risk beyond thought, for should they fail to contain this threat here and now, the very depths of their knowledge and craft would be turned against the land their Fellowship was sworn and charged to guard.

To surface appearance, there seemed no present enemy to fight. Limned in sheeting flares thrown off by the disrupted fields in the tower wards, the metal clasps of books bit corners of reflection through the gloom. The third lane spark in the brazier recovered its steady blue to cast harsh illumination over the massive black table with its scrawled chalk ciphers and its empty chairs left arrayed at jutted angles. As unkempt as the caches upon his fusty aumbries, Sethvir stood poised, his hair and beard raked up into tufts and his fingers interlaced beneath the threadbare shine of his cuffs. His gaze sieved the air to pick out sign of the hostile motes of consciousness which lurked in the crannies and the shelves.

Unlike his spirit-formed colleagues, he was hampered, his perception tied to mortal senses. The earth link that enabled him to track simultaneous world events out of half trance was no help in a direct encounter. Its use slowed his reflexes. Unlike his discorporate colleagues, he could not see behind to guard his back. To the refined sensitivity of his mage-sight, the wraiths would show as spirit light, brighter if they moved or tried to exert their influence over anything alive. Were they stilled or stalking, poised beyond his peripheral vision, he must rely on hearing, for their auras would be traceless through the air. Yet eyes had to blink; fleshly senses fell prey to fatigue.

And the danger was present and closing.

'Beware,' warned Luhaine. 'I count nine hostile vortices.'

Engrossed in the throes of tuned awareness, Sethvir made them out with more difficulty. Twined amid the jumble of his possessions, the faint, coiling currents of the wraiths seemed sketched against the dimness like strayed dust motes, stroked to clinging eddies by weak static. Ephemeral as they seemed, translucent as the steam wisps off his tea mugs, he was not fooled. The broadened span of his perception could detect their unrest, hazed in vibrations of hatred. These entities cast their essence in the forms of leering faces, yawling mouths, in glass-clear, skeletal fingers that plucked and clawed and pricked like jabbing needles in quest of the barest chink in his defences.

'Sethvir, don't let them flank you.' Thin drawn under stress as the wraiths themselves, Luhaine stood guard by the library door, his stance set opposite Kharadmon's. For with frightful intent in those first, passing minutes, the victim the wraiths had chosen was the Warden of Althain himself.

Of them all, Sethvir alone owned the talent for splitting his mind into multiple awareness. He was Althain's Warden, the earth's tried link, and through him flowed all events to influence the fate of Athera. Were the wraiths to possess him, they could access at will any aspect they chose within the world. They would grasp the last particular concerning the ward-bound fragments of the Mistwraith held captive in Rockfell Pit, even the means to key their freedom.

Sethvir pushed back the shabby maroon velvet of his cuffs. He hooked his stub of chalk from the table rim, then spoke a word in sharp, staccato syllables that snagged the wild force of the elements. The clear air before him turned brittle and hard, sheer as a pane of sheet ice. Onto that enspelled, glassine surface, he scribed a fresh line of ciphers. Each rune as written flared

16

into lines of fire. While the wraiths roiled back, gnashing silent teeth and flailing clawed fists, and fleering fanged snarls at the punitive pinch of bristled energy, the Warden of Althain murmured a litany of unbinding.

Spell-cast air reclaimed its natural state with a cry like rending crystal. The construct traced out in chalk lines stayed adrift, fanned and winnowed on the draughts as burning oil might ride on a water current. To reach Sethvir, the hostile entities must cross through them, or else try to permeate the spell-tempered stone that formed the wall at his back.

One moment the wraiths coiled in an agitated swirl of frustration. Then they vanished.

Sethvir shouted. Behind his ward of spelled air, he shrank a step, cornered by the table, while around him, a roiled press like heat waves off brick, the spirit forms attacked.

'They've breached his defences across time!' cried Luhaine.

But Kharadmon was forewarned. His counterstrike sheeted around Sethvir's body. The wraiths frothed in thrashing retreat. Above their heaving moil, a rune blazed, then dissolved to spread a stench like rotten eggs over the space they inhabited.

'Sulphur,' said Kharadmon. 'It's bought us a handful of seconds.'

'I shouldn't act smug,' Luhaine huffed. 'Such stopgap measures build no measure of permanence, but only waste what remains of your strength.' Self-righteously immersed, he undertook to build a vessel of confinement in the prior style used against Desh-thiere.

'What use to build jars?' Kharadmon stabbed back in rejoinder. 'We can scarcely sweep these beings into captivity if we can't force them back in retreat.'

The quandary held far-reaching implications since a free wraith without Name could not be grappled. These had already defied the Wheel's passage into natural

17

death. To destroy the unclothed spirit was to unweave a strand of Ath's creation, a misuse of grand conjury and a direct intervention against the prime vibration that no Fellowship tenet could sanction. The Sorcerers were committed to harm no being, nor to unbind or inhibit any spark of self-awareness, even at the cost of their very lives.

While the entities seethed to renew their assault, Luhaine conjoined his spirit essence in painstaking care with the seals spread across the surface of the tabletop. A moment passed as he asked free consent from the stone. Then curtains of sparks fountained around the bronze tripod of the brazier. In a torrent of force borrowed from the third lane, the discorporate Sorcerer melted the dark rock and reshaped its gold magma to form a canister.

His work singed the air into stinging, dry wind. Unbound sheets of parchment thrashed in scraping distress across the floor to catch on the chair legs and hang on the carved Khadrim that formed the table's massive pedestal. The wraiths winnowed through like floss caught in current, bent once again on Althain's Warden. Their caustic contempt rang in dissonance against mage-tuned awareness. Prolonged years of battle against Kharadmon had taught these enemies too well. They understood the limitations of their prey: provoke how they might, twist life as they would, no Fellowship mage would spurn Ath's trust and the Law of the Major Balance to fling spells of unmaking against them.

The Sorcerers who protected Athera were guardians. Their strength of constraint could be used against them as a weapon to breach their steadfast self-command and turn moral force into weakness.

Whether the powers Sethvir could have raised on a thought to negate any threat to his autonomy tormented him to temptation, none could know as the wraiths closed upon him. He watched their advance with pale, narrowed eyes, his wiry shoulders bowed as if the drag of his robes bore him down. The ink stains showed stark against knuckles bleached and gnarled as stranded driftwood. In a move that looked like a vagary of nerves, he exchanged his chalk stick for two dusty bits of river stone, plucked in haste from the clutter by the windowsill.

'Don't try a field charge to corner them.' Bled from the effort of his own defences, Kharadmon's voice was a wisp of its usual rich timbre. 'That sort of energy feeds them.'

'I saw,' Sethvir said. His empty hand gripped the table edge. The wraiths fanned about him, less substantial than half-glimpsed puffs of spent smoke. Before their poised menace, he seemed a wizened grandfather, reduced by senility to threatening thrown pebbles to halt the rise of a flood.

'There's another way to draw them,' Sethvir offered. 'Above anything they want to seize control of my gifts.'

Luhaine responded in fraught fear, 'Don't try. You cannot think to risk baiting them!'

But the Warden already chanted a musical phrase in Paravian. The pebbles radiated a kindly warmth through his palm, then chimed back a note of assurance. His binding immediately paired them one to another in tuned resonance.

In the instant the wraiths closed, Sethvir cast the first stone into the obsidian cylinder Luhaine had fashioned from the table slab. The second he pitched to the floor. His throw held no apparent force; yet the river rock struck and shattered into a thousand tiny fragments. These scattered as though life and will lent them impetus to lodge in every cranny of the library.

The same moment, Sethvir's knees gave way. He slumped against the table, then slid unconscious into a rumpled heap of robes. His sunken cheek lay pillowed in his beard and hair, entangled as a mass of washed fleeces.

'Ath, the grand idiot!' Luhaine cried on a shocked snap of breeze. 'He's split his consciousness and fused each part into the shards of the rock!'

But the tactic had succeeded. Already the wraiths were diverted, divided and quartering every square inch of floor to retrieve the prize within the pebble's sundered pieces. Each one of these contained, like a puzzle, a scrap of Sethvir's awareness. Entirely without fight, the entities could have stolen his emptied flesh. But since access to the earth link was their coveted aim, the body was a useless container to them without the Warden's talents and spirit. In the predictable arrogance of wraith forms, they spurned the physical housing and pressed in greed to gather and conquer each disparate bit of the Sorcerer's essence.

'Will you whine, or will you stand strong?' Kharadmon exhorted. For the wraiths would possess what they recovered from the stone shards. The only help for Sethvir now lay in two colleagues' readiness to back his desperate ploy.

Nine hostile entities and a thousand slivers of stone to seek out; the spirits prowled the flagstones, searching hungrily, spinning like unspooled thread between the chair legs and through the dust-clogged mesh of old spiderwebs spanning the feet of the cupboards. Their trackless passage breathed draughts across Sethvir's slackened knuckles and combed through every moth-hole in his sleeves.

Eyeless, senseless, lured on by the singing glints of spirit light that formed the sundered slivers of their prey, the wraiths were doubly guided in their hunt by the pewter dance of energies which framed the prosaic signature of river stone. They skimmed like gleaners on a threshing floor and claimed their offered prize.

Too late, they sensed the hook and trap the Warden

had set in his subtlety, which tied the broken pebble with its whole twin, thrown to rest inside Luhaine's container. When Sethvir called on that binding and knit the flung fragments of his awareness back into one cohesive whole, the wraiths were pulled with him. Attached, all nine, to a split portion of himself, but not yet allowed full possession to inflict total mastery over him, they found themselves upended and sucked without volition to home with their victim's conscious will. The spell-forged link to the second pebble, where the Sorcerer now fled, drew the entities to follow in blind compulsion through the neck of the slate flask.

Their collective cry seemed to harrow the air and shiver the books on the shelves.

'Now!' Kharadmon's shout melded with Luhaine's response. Incandescent spells bathed the cylinder on the table, searing its outline seamless white.

Tired as he was, worn to a shadow of his strength, Kharadmon etched the first seal over the wraiths to imprison them.

'Let be,' Luhaine chided. 'Would you waste yourself to a mute shade?' Since Kharadmon was ever the sort to spurn sense, he balanced his energies and joined in.

Night mist beyond the casements blazed like spilled oil to the out-flood of light from sparked power. The raised aura of Fellowship spellcraft flung off a mighty corona until the chamber keened in shared tension, and the slates in the floor hummed in stressed resonance to the flux of tempered force.

With time the lights died, leaving the lane-spark in the brazier a needle of blue light in velvet darkness. Draught through the opened shutters stirred through a faint stench of sulphur, tainted with ozone and an ashy miasma of singed dust. The wraiths' prison rested on the dimpled slab of the tabletop, an obsidian cylinder that tapped and pinged through the stresses of natural cooling.

On the floor, wax still, limp flesh devoid of spirit, Sethvir's body sprawled in the blood-dark puddle of his robes. The white curve of his lashes never flickered. He did not dream; his breathing was shallow and imperceptibly slow, except to the eyes of another mage.

Across heavy silence, through sorrowful, shared awareness and a stillness that presaged false peace, two discorporate Fellowship Sorcerers steeled themselves to wait. They exchanged no speech. Their fear loomed wide as sky itself. For although the wraiths lay safely contained, the spirit of their colleague was trapped also.

Inside the flask, alone against nine, Sethvir now battled for his life.

'We cannot abandon him in there,' Luhaine said at last in a slow, careful phrase of masked pain.

Kharadmon swirled from his place by the casement, to his colleague's sight a moiled patch of shade that wore spirit light in flecks like fogged stars. 'No, we can't. The wraiths will devour his identity.' A sigh of breeze raised frost on the book spines as he roved in restless currents through the chamber. 'That's what became of the people who inhabited the worlds beyond South Gate. The same tragedy would have repeated itself here, had Traithe not spared us all by checking Desh-thiere's invasion at the outset.'

Had Luhaine still worn flesh, he would have swallowed back the coppery taste of fear. 'You're saying the fell mists held intent to enslave our whole world?'

'They still could,' Kharadmon pronounced in bleak fact. 'Were its two sundered portions ever to be rejoined, there's no doubt left of its strength. All Athera would be laid to waste.' He need not repeat that the beacon spell set on the solstice had seeded the opening to admit just such a horrid possibility. Forewarned at the time of the danger, he had unwound the spell sent to call him, even exposed himself to attack in the doing. But the clean, fine signature of Fellowship power could not fully be erased without imprint.

A tracery leading back to the spell's point of origin would linger for several centuries to be tracked. The stakes of the nightmare had widened. Now the wraiths confined at Rockfell Peak were just the bitter edge of a greater peril.

But for now future worries must defer to the weight of present crisis. Inside the sealed flask the battle still raged. Mage-sight could cross the ward boundaries to trace Sethvir's tactics as he twisted and zigzagged like a hunted hare through the maze of the river pebble's structure. Attached to him were the wraiths, striving ever to complete their possession.

To aid him, the two colleagues left free must build spells of frightful complexity.

In partnered concentration, they embraced the contours that comprised the black flagon, then softened the bonding of its structure. The wailing resonance of the wraiths inside dragged at the Sorcerers' focus and struck hurtful harmonics through their auras. They stood fast. Of necessity, they ignored even the rending awareness of Sethvir's tortured flight. In care, with infinite patience, they crooned a litany to the river pebble and coaxed its solid, round contour to meld its structure with that of the flask.

Like a teardrop in a puddle, the grained bit of granite ceded its separate nature to pool into the obsidian's denser matrix. Kharadmon and Luhaine paused in slack silence, their rivalry stilled into listening. If luck held and Sethvir had not weakened, he could have preserved his tie to inanimate stone and followed the river pebble's transmutation. The way had been opened for him to fly in retreat. He could attempt to sieve his beleaguered consciousness through the guard spells borrowed from Althain's grand warding that Luhaine had affixed in the flask. The conjury itself was a welded amalgamation of

Paravian magics and his own wary knitting of defences. Theory held that the pattern of the Warden's spirit Name should be recognized, mazed as it was with the stamp of the Ilitharis Paravians' own blessing. The great centaurs themselves had ceded the earth link to Sethvir's care in the hour when the last of their race had abandoned their post at Althain Tower.

But fear and guessed odds made small footing for hope as the seconds sang by, and Kharadmon and Luhaine held in wait for their fellow to seize his chance.

Sethvir had no reprieve to test his hunches, no moment to hesitate and think. If his choice stood in error, the effects would become irreversible.

His first step was made unsupported and alone, with his two colleagues helpless to lend him guidance. In his passage through the coiled sigils which cross-linked to form the guard spells' mighty seals, the Warden would hope that the parasitic wraiths would be strained away. Only then could his self-awareness emerge whole and unsullied.

If he misjudged, he could be annihilated by the countersurge of his own defences; or he might be held as the prisoner of his very tower's fell guard spells, trapped inside a pebble and smothered for all time inside a tomb of warded slate. Worse, perhaps, and most frightening, the wraiths could seize upon some clever delusion, might turn some trick to corrupt the wards and slip by. Should this transpire, the Sorcerer who awakened would be changed from the dear colleague who had entered, an evil too ruinous to contemplate.

Distress drove Kharadmon to unwonted sympathy. 'Sethvir is most wise and clever enough in his ways to fool even Daelion Fatemaster. An ugly truth will not deter him. He would disperse his very spirit to oblivion before ever he let such a risk walk abroad to harm Athera.'

Luhaine for once had no words. Coiled into tight

worry, he maintained a tortured stillness, as if to acknowledge his colleague's restless movement might cause him to abandon his dignity and fidget.

Hours passed without sign. Breezes off the desert funnelled through the casement, sharp with the bite of autumn frost. The unlatched shutters swung to the gusts and thumped odd tattoos on the window jambs. On a floor gritted with the shattered remains of what had been a blameless river pebble, moonlight sliced oblate patterns.

In time the new dawn masked the stars in leaden grey. The stilled form sprawled upon the chill flagstone regained a flush of rose about the nostrils. One wiry, veined hand curled closed.

'Tea,' Sethvir sighed in a wistful, weak whisper. 'Khar-admon, do you think you might dredge up a spark to kindle the fire? If my memory isn't damaged, I believe the cauldron's filled and ready.'

The Warden of Althain was himself; two colleagues withdrew from close inspection of his aura pattern, while a fired ray of sun lit the clouds and etched a blush of leaf gold against the lichened stone of the east casement.

In response to Luhaine's furious and silent burst of censure, Sethvir propped himself on one elbow and scrubbed at wisps of beard that had hung themselves up in his eyebrows. 'What else could we do?' He said in cold conclusion, 'I couldn't let these free wraiths come to be mewed up in Rockfell alongside Desh-thiere's captive consciousness.' If mishap occurred and the two halves of this monster should ever chance to recombine, there could be no end to the world's suffering. 'It's all right,' he added, then looked up and blinked, a smear of dust on his nose. Unshed tears glistened in his eyes. 'At least through the course of a partial possession I've recovered true Name for these nine. It's a pitiful start. But we now have the means to unravel the wickedness that binds them. Shall we not make an end and restore their lost path to Ath's peace?'

By noon, restored by hot tea and a catnap, Sethvir sat huddled in furled robes in the windy niche of a window seat. Daylight mapped the whorled distortion in the grain of the tabletop where Luhaine had reconfigured the stone to create the warded flask.

The container itself stood empty beside a porcelain mug with spiderwork cracks through the glaze.

After harrowing labour, the nine enchained spirits had been given their redemption and release. The books had been tidied, the ink flasks set right, but Sethvir had not bothered with sweeping. His library floor still lay scattered with river sand, the cobwebs in the corners caught with small twists of parchment last pressed into use as his pagemarks.

Luhaine's groomed image inhabited the apron by the hearth, unstirred by the draughts from the chimney. Kharadmon appeared as a wan, slender form perched on the stuffing of a chair. His posture was all dapper angles and elegant, attenuated bones. His spade point beard and piebald hair and narrow nose appeared as foxy as ever, but his green cloak with its ruddy orange lining tended to drift through intervals of transparency. Despite a clear outline, the force of him seemed washed and faded.

In pared, quiet phrases, the discorporate Sorcerer related what befell on his quest to the splinter worlds cut away from their link to Athera. 'On the other side, Desh-thiere's essence is stronger than our most dismal estimate,' he said. 'I'm left humbled by the power Traithe faced, to his ruin, on the day he sealed off the South Gate. I say now with certainty that he spared all life on Athera.'

Kharadmon went on to tell of Marak, where the Fellowship had once exiled those people whose curiosity prompted them to pursue the knowledge proscribed by the compact between mankind and the Paravians. In a lightless search, through a suffocating mist that shrouded that far place into darkness and an ice-ridden, desolate wasteland, no living thing had breathed or moved.

'I narrowed my search in the gutted shells of the libraries,' Kharadmon resumed. 'I found records there, fearful maps of what was done.' His image chafed its thin fingers as if to bring warmth to lost flesh. 'As we guessed, Desh-thiere was created by frightened minds as a weapon of mass destruction. A faction on Marak built on the laws of physical science, then meddled in theories that came to unbalance the axis of prime life force. The intent was to interweave spirit with machine. These men desired to create the ultimate synergy between the human mind and a physical construct, and transcend the limits of the flesh. Well, their works went wrong. The ionized fields of mists that contained the captive spirits over time drifted their awareness out of self-alignment. The experiment turned on its creators. I can only conclude that those sorry entities tied outside of Daelion's Wheel became warped and vicious and insane.'

The result laid two entire worlds to white waste; then the hundreds of thousands of dead from that carnage, subverted and entrapped in brutal turn.

'I have failed in my mission,' Kharadmon summed up in drawn sorrow. 'No roll list of Names could I find for the original set of wraiths that comprised Desh-thiere's first sentience. And now, those prime spirits have been joined by every other casualty they have caused. They react as a body, their mad purpose to devour life. The strength of them is deadly and far too vast for our Fellowship to grapple without help.'

Sethvir tapped the knuckle of his thumb against his teeth. 'We'll need the aid of the Paravians,' he ventured.

'Their resonance with prime power could perhaps turn those lost entities to recall their forgotten humanity.'

'A masterbard's talents might do the same, had we the means to isolate each individual victim from the pull of collective consciousness,' Luhaine said.

The Warden of Althain was silent. His turquoise eyes locked on Kharadmon in recognition of the annihilating truth left unmentioned. 'The mist sublimates away under vacuum,' he surmised.

'Exactly.' Kharadmon shot upright and stalked a soundless circuit of the chamber. 'Free wraiths result, as you saw. If the ones still fogbound on Marak can unriddle the guidance traces left by that beacon spell of summoning, we could find ourselves beset beyond all recourse.'

Silence ate the seconds as the three mages pondered. The quandary of the Mistwraith had expanded to fearful dimensions. Its threat would not end with the creatures mewed up under wards in Rockfell Pit. Indeed, Athera would never be safe from predation until the trapped, damned spirits from both worlds beyond South Gate could be drawn under bindings, then redeemed.

The royal half-brothers already set in jeopardy by the curse might yet be needed to right the balance.

Recent events at Minderl Bay had effectively shown that Lysaer held no vestige of control over Desh-thiere's aberrant geas.

Which left Arithon once again at the critical crux of responsibility.

Sethvir sighed, his crown tipped back against the tower's chisel-cut window. In tones hammered blank by a burden just extended through trials enough to stop the heart, he said, 'Asandir will reach the focus at Caith-al-Caen by the advent of tonight's sundown. He can transfer to Athir's ruin on the east shore and flag down the sloop *Talliarthe*. He will treat with the Shadow Master there and charge him, for the world's sake, to stay alive.

At any cost, by whaever means, the Prince of Rathain must survive until this threat beyond South Gate can be resolved.'

Beside the table, thinned to wan imprint against the varnished tiers of the bookshelves, Kharadmon blinked like a cat. 'Not enough,' he said in his old, stinging curtness. 'Have Asandir bind our crown prince to his promise by blood oath.'

Luhaine stiffened to indignance and Sethvir looked aghast. 'He is s'Ffalenn and compelled by his birth line to compassion,' they protested in clashing chorus.

The Warden of Althain finished. 'Since Torbrand, no scion of Rathain has *ever* required more than his royal promise!'

Kharadmon's image vanished into a wisp of gloom that fanned a chill through the chamber. 'You didn't experience what lies behind South Gate. Heed my warning. Who can say what lengths may be necessary to save us all before this disaster is played out.'

Tharrick

Dakar the Mad Prophet snapped awake from the tail of
a nightmare that involved the loss of his best spirits into
the gawping jaws of a fish. The lap of wavelets against
wood reminded him that he inhabited a musty berth
aboard *Talliarthe*. He cracked open one eye and immediately groaned as light speared into his pupil from a scald
of reflection which danced on the deck beams overhead.

'Is it sunset or daybreak?' he bellowed, then stuffed
his face like a turtle back into the dark refuge of his
blankets.

From his place by the stays in the stern, Arithon
merely kept whistling a threnody with an odd, glancing
dissonance that went ill with the aches of a hangover.

'Ath,' Dakar grumped. He shrugged off the suffocating
layers of salt-damp wool, his pudgy hands stretched to
cover his eyes and his ears, and successfully managing
neither. 'Your tune sounds like a damned fiend
bane.'

Arithon nodded. His screeling measures stayed
unbroken. He had seen iyats in the waves at the turn of
the tide and preferred to keep his rigging unmolested.
He had yet to change the ripped shirt he had worn

through the affray at Minderl Bay. Bathed in the ruddy gold light that washed the misted shoreline at Athir, where his little sloop lay at anchor, he twisted the cork from the neck of another flask, then upended it over the stern rail.

Dakar screamed and shot upright as a stream of neat whisky splashed with a gurgle into the brine. The night-mare that had wakened him had been no prank of imagination, after all. 'Dharkaron rip off your cursed bol-locks!' he howled, and added a damning string of epithets that curdled the quiet of new morning. 'You're dumping my last stock of spirits into the Ath-forsaken sea!'

Arithon never paused in his pursuit. 'I wondered how long you'd take to notice.' That icy note of warning in his tone was unmistakable to anyone who knew him.

Dakar paused in the companionway to catch his breath, take stock, and indulge in a long, thoughtful scratch at his crotch. 'What's changed?'

In the days since the discharge of his hired seamen, then Earl Jieret's landing ashore for return to Caolle and his clans, the Shadow Master's brittle temper had seemed to ease. With Lysaer's warhost disbanded, the intolerable mood he had affected since the massive strike at Werpoint had settled out. Left to his preferred state of solitude, the Shadow Master plied the helm and set *Talliarthe*'s course gently south.

By the drilling intensity his green eyes held now, something had happened since last night's sunset to upset his plans yet again.

Too sore for subtlety before balking silence, Dakar repeated his question a plaintive half pitch higher.

Arithon stabbed the cork back into the emptied crock, teeth bared in a wince as the movement troubled some hurt beneath a bandage on his forearm. The injury had not existed the day before. 'We're going on to Perdith to visit the forges, and here forward you'll need to stay sober.'

The reference took a muddled moment to resolve through a headache into sense.

'Fiends!' Dakar cried, scaring up the gulls who had just folded wings and settled back into the waves. 'Don't say. It's those Sithaer-begotten brigantines again. *You promised you weren't going to arm them!*'

'Complain, if you like, to Asandir,' said the Master of Shadow, succinct. 'If I thought it would help, I'd back you.'

The Mad Prophet opened his mouth to speak, then poised, still agape. He swelled in a gargantuan breath of disbelief, and stopped again, jabbed back to furious thought by the stained strip of linen tied over his adversary's left wrist. 'Ath Creator!' His eyes bulged as he exhaled a near-soundless whistle. 'Asandir *was* here. Whatever have you done to require a blood oath before the almighty Fellowship of Seven? No such strong binding has ever been asked, and you a sanctioned crown prince!'

Arithon shot back a glare like a rapier, hooked the last crock by his feet, and ripped the cork from the neck.

Dakar turned desperate. 'Have a care for your health! At least save one flask. It might be helpful, for need, in case that knife wound turns septic.'

Awarded the Shadow Master's cool indifference at its worst, the Mad Prophet knew when to desist. If he gave in to fury, his head would explode and, from nasty past experience, he knew better than to provoke the s'Ffalenn temper while emerging from the throes of a hangover. He would seek a patch of shade and sleep off the worst before he shouldered the risk of having his own whisky crocks thrown at him.

He awakened much later to the bone-jarring crash of *Talliarthe* beating to windward. Her topsails carved in dizzy circles against a clouded sky, while winter-cold spray sheeted over him at each rearing plunge through the swell. Green in the face and long since soaked to his underclothes, Dakar groaned. He rolled, clawed upright, and staggered to the rail to be sick. The horizon showed an unbroken bar of grey and the wind in his nose was scoured salt.

The Mad Prophet closed his eyes and retched, too miserable to curse his companion's entrenched preference for the rigours of deep-water sailing.

At the helm, far from cheerful, Arithon s'Ffalenn whistled a ballad about a wicked stepson who murdered to steal an inheritance. The tune held a dissonance to unravel thought. By the arrowed force behind each bar and note, Dakar resigned himself: he had no case left to argue. The renowned royal temper already burned fierce enough to singe any man in close quarters. To cross a s'Ffalenn prince in that sort of mood was to invite a retaliation in bloodshed.

The wind scudded through a change and blew from the north, and the rains came and made passage miserable. Dakar lay below decks, too wrung to move, while the sloop ran south, her brick-coloured sails bent taut. At Perdith, Arithon concluded his business with the weapon smiths in haste. The respite in sheltered waters was too brief to allow Dakar a proper recovery. *Talliarthe* was under canvas and bound back offshore before he could prop himself up and crawl on all fours to find a bawdy house.

Arithon manned the helm like a creature possessed, urgent to reach the south latitudes. He slept wrapped in oilskins beside his lashed tiller. Dakar grew inured to the thump of his step on the cabin top as he tied in fresh reefs, or shook them out at every slight shift in the breeze. The clouds loomed lower each day, until the whitecaps seemed to graze their black, swollen bellies. Rain fell in wind-whirled, spitting drizzle, barbed at times with flecks of ice. The season had turned with cruel vengeance. Hammering squalls joined forces and bred gales; in her run down the eastshore, *Talliarthe* weathered several that howled through two days and nights.

The incessant cold water stung Arithon's hands angry red. His hair tangled to white ends from dried deposits of blown salt.

Dakar lived like a snail, crawling over the bucking deck from his berth to the sloop's tiny galley. He brewed peppermint tea to help ease his nausea and nibbled hardtack and salt pork and cheese. When the weather blew roughest, he stayed in a prone sprawl and groaned like a man with the ague.

Talliarthe carved into tropical waters two weeks shy of the winter solstice.

Arithon by then was a scarecrow figure, sea-beaten and haunted hollow around the eyes. Too much wetting had infected his cut wrist. The gash scabbed and peeled, saltwater sores caused by the chafe of linen dressings swelled sullen purple underneath. Shirtless, driven, pressured sleepless by some tie to conscience that involved his recent oath to Asandir, the Shadow Master leaned on the weather shroud, a silhouette against thin, morning sunlight, his hand at his brow to cut the glare.

Emerged from his lair to relieve himself, Dakar noted the strung tension in his adversary's back. He spoke for the first time in days. 'What's amiss? If it's whales, I wish they'd stove in this filthy bucket's keel. Since a bath ashore at a tavern is too much to ask, I'm going to wish with all my heart to get us shipwrecked.'

'Getting skewered on a beach by Alestron's best mercenaries is by far the more likely fate.' Arithon drummed his fingers in an irritable tattoo on the sloop's rail. 'We should see half-rigged masts by now. What can the labourers in my shipyard have been doing to while away three months' time?'

Busy with his trouser points, Dakar looked up and realized that the coast of Scimlade Tip loomed off the bow. The sloop would be moored at Merior by noon, and he could get blissfully drunk. A sigh of content eased from him, cut short by the prickling awareness that the Shadow Master glared at his back.

'No.' Clear as a glass edge, a masterbard's voice, like a blade through the calls of white gulls and the softer susurrance of the sloop's wake. 'You will not indulge yourself senseless.'

Dakar's jerk of outrage mistimed with a gust; he swore as he almost wet his knuckles. Stuffing himself back into his trousers, hands shaking as he hurried the lacing, he spun toward the cockpit in a rage. 'Since when are you appointed as guardian of my fate?'

Back at the sloop's tiller, Arithon threw her helm down. His apparent attention stayed fixed on the heading as her bow bore up and all manner of tackle slatted loose to a rattle of blocks that defied all attempt at speech. As the headsails caught aback and pressed the *Talliarthe*'s painted bow past the eye of the wind, the gaff-rigged main slammed taut on the opposite tack. Arithon freed the jib sheets from their cleats. The thunder as thrashed canvas bellied to the breeze finally muted to a driving sheet of spray as he hardened the lines alee.

'I am master of nothing,' he answered then on a queer, wrung note of exhaustion. 'My own fate least of all.'

He spent the next hour on the foredeck with a bucket of seawater, a fish knife for shaving, and soap. While he sluiced himself clean and aired out dry clothes, Dakar blistered his hands at the helm, by turns immersed in sulking, or else scowling as he weighed inveigling plots to slip beer or neat spirits past his adversary's vigilance.

By midday the weather turned gloomy. Winter rains curtained the beachhead at Merior like dirty, layered gauze and pocked the leaden troughs of the breakers. Soaked to the skin, the twins Fiark and Feylind quiet at his heels, their ebullience subdued by disaster, Arithon s'Ffalenn stood still as deadwood and regarded the wreckage of his shipyard.

Of the brigantine which should have been launched and by now rigged to completion, nothing remained but a straggle of crooked ribs, scabbed to black charcoal by fire. The planked-over hull that lay adjacent gaped like a cave, her stem and forequarter burned away. The stacks of new lumber for her finishing were all charred to ash in the sand. The ropewalk was gone, a snarl of gutted boards amid the puddled runoff shed by dunes tarnished dark with rinsed carbon.

Aghast, his face white and his frame racked to shivers, Arithon looked stricken by a deathblow as he regarded the ruin of his hope to make clean escape to blue water.

Feylind reached up and squeezed his dripping, cold fingers. 'Mother asked you to come home with us. She made a pot of fish soup.'

Fiark blew plastered blond hair from his lips and chimed in, 'You can borrow my blanket from the loft.'

Arithon forced himself to stir. 'Thank you. And thank Jinesse, too, for her kindness. Say that I'll visit her cottage later. Now go home. She'll greet me with scolding if she finds out I've let you get wet.'

The children hared off, screaming in delight as they kicked and splashed through the puddles.

Ignored where he waited, growing soggy in a tunic that reeked of unwashed sweat, Dakar slapped the crimped locks behind his neck to dam the water that dribbled down his collar. 'Are we just going to stand here until we grow roots in the damp?'

The chart loft still stood. To judge by the cries of raucous laughter ringing in muffled bursts through the boards, and the woodsmoke which trailed from the chimney, the labourers inside would at least be warm, if the beer that made them blithe had run out.

Arithon's stillness cracked into a purposeful stride that carried him up to the doorway. He lifted the latch, crashed the panel inward, and stood stiff-armed against the silver splash of runoff that poured off the palm-thatched roof.

Blocked in the entry behind him, Dakar saw the uproarious company of the yard's workers rock into stupefied stillness. Calloused hands drifted in midair, crockery beer mugs forgotten; bare feet shifted under bench boards and table. Like the rasp of a hornet's nest disturbed in dry grass, Ivel the blind splicer chuckled in malice from his perch on a nail barrel in the corner. 'It's himself come back, and early, too. What else could shrivel the tongues in yer mouths? I'd warrant a visit by Dharkaron's Chariot would be given a saucier welcome.'

'I want to know what happened,' Arithon cut in, his bard's trained diction never sharper. 'Let the master ship-wright stay and tell me. The steam box is whole, still. So are the tools and the sawpit. If the new wood's a loss, the one hull not decked yet can be taken apart and used to patch up the holed one. By Ath, I don't pay any man silver to sit on his rump sucking down beer 'til he's witless!'

A galvanic stir swept the crowded tables as benches rumbled back from plank trestles. The labourers arose in guilt-fed haste and pressed to be first to crowd the doorway. Arithon stepped aside to let them pass, his burning gaze merciless on every man's face. Only when the last cringing layabout had passed did he move to enter the sail loft. Stale air and dampness and the smell of sour lager hung heavy in the stifling heat. Reprieved at last from the misery of the rain, Dakar sidled to the stove to warm his fingers, eyes darting in prayerful search for a tankard and a broached cask.

'No beer left,' rasped Ivel from his cranny. Scathelessly smug before Arithon's flicked glance, and crafty enough to anticipate, he tipped his grizzled beard toward the tread that advanced and shrugged his bony shoulders.

His large, seamed hands with their thumbs worn shiny from years of twining hemp gleamed red against shadow as Dakar fiddled open the gate of the iron stove and prodded the embers inside.

'Rope store's full burnt,' the splicer quipped in brassy cheer. 'Can't make me work in yon rain without materials.' He tilted his narrow head, impertinent as a gossip. 'What'll ye do? That gold store of yers, lad, she's bound to be played right low.'

Arithon swept aside a litter of sticky crockery, kicked a bench closer, and sat. 'I'll thank you not to comment until the master shipwright has explained himself.'

Ivel leaned aside and shot a neat stream of spit at a bowl on the trestle by his elbow. 'Master shipwright's run off. He feared to face yer temper, and some lass in Shaddorn took him in. You want to know what happened, I'll tell it. Else you can try out yer touch with the wretch who torched the yard. The men hazed him like butchers. He won't talk.'

Arithon straightened, his wet fingers clenched and his eyes icy sparks in the gloom. 'One man?'

'Aye.' Ivel's grin revealed gapped, yellow teeth. 'Hates yer living guts. Hid in the brush till the lads all got drunk, then launched on his merry bit of sabotage.'

'He knows who I am?' Arithon asked in a dead, level voice. 'He told the labourers?'

A cracking, high cackle split from Ivel's throat. He hugged his knees to his chest on his barrel, a dried-up, corded little monkey of a man who lived and breathed to stir up malice. 'He told the men nothing, for all the hide they singed off him. What I ken, I got because I took him water when he raved. But your secret's full safe with me, prince.'

Arithon snapped up a chipped flagon and hurled it. The smash of unglazed crockery against the board floor raised a storm of clay dust and chinking fragments. 'Secret?' He laughed in a brittle, thin irony more bitter than the splicer could match. 'The whole of the north knows precisely where I am, and *I find my ships burned to ashes.*'

Still by the stove, polished ruddy by the coals, Dakar rubbed sweaty knuckles over his rumpled tunic. 'You say the man who did this is held captive?'

Ivel rocked off a nod. 'Aye, he is. Bound and locked in the boiler shed. The master joiner guards the key.'

The wood fire had been lit to heat the steam box again. Aware of the rain as a drummed, liquid trickle off the thatch and the erratic, spaced hiss as a leak dripped onto the hot copper vat, the prisoner curled on his side in abject misery. The damp, sand floor made him shiver. Hungry, thirsty, fevered down to his bones, at first he presumed the footsteps outside meant a labourer had come to fuel the stove.

Since such were wont to kick him as they passed, he wormed into the gap behind the log stores. If he feigned sleep and stayed out of sight, sometimes his presence was forgotten. Today, the mere hope made him pitiful. The sweeping chills that seized through his frame made him unable to keep still.

The footsteps outside came closer, overlaid by agitated talk. Then a stranger's voice blistered across rising argument like tempered steel through threshed straw. 'Enough! I'll hear no excuses. Stay out here until you're called.' Keys chimed sour notes through a patter of hurried strides, and the new arrival spoke again. 'No, Dakar. You will wait.'

The bar in the lock grated and gave; the door jerked open. A flood of rain-washed air swirled through the heat and a small, lithe man stepped inside. He stood a moment, eyes searching the darkness, while the fiery glare from the furnace lined his sharp profile and the lip he curled up at the stench.

Snapped to a scourge of clear anger, he said, 'You claim he's in here?'

The master joiner's south shore drawl filtered back, uncertain through the silvered splash of water. 'Master, he's there. My heart's blood as surety. We'd never let him escape.'

Without any fumbling, the man found the lamp and the striker kept ready on the shelf by the doorway. His hands shook as he lit the spill. The trembling flare of illumination as he touched flame to wick shed gold over finely made knuckles. He raised the lamp and hung its iron ring from a nail in the rafters.

Through vision impaired to slits by bruises and swelling, the prisoner saw him fully, centred beneath the yellow glow. Thin and well-knit, he looked like a wraith in dark breeches, his white shirt slathered to his shoulders by the rain. His hair was black. Wet strands stuck like ink to his temples and jaw. The features they framed were pale granite, all chipped angles and fury, the eyes now shadowed by lamplight.

Wind riffled through the portal at his back. The lantern flame wavered and failed to a spark, then leaped back in dazzling recovery. Swept by a chill that chattered his teeth, the prisoner shrank into his cranny.

The man spun toward the noise like a predator. He could not miss the lashed pair of ankles that protruded from the wood stores, livid and blackened with scabs.

'*Merciful Ath!*' He lilted a fast phrase in the old tongue that resounded with appalled shock. Then in a rage to freeze the falling rain itself, he changed language and commanded, 'Strike his bonds.'

'But, my lord,' protested the master joiner through the sizzle as the leak let fall another droplet on the boiler. 'The wretch came intending to murder y —'

In fearful speed, the man in authority cut him off. 'Do it now! Are you deaf or a fool, to defy me?'

While the joiner entered, chastened to cowering, the

black-haired man sank to his knees and laid his own icy hands over the prisoner's roped ankles. 'Give me the knife. I'll do this myself. Then send for a litter and some sort of tarp to cut the rain.' In the same distilled tone of venom he added, 'Dakar and I will serve as bearers.'

The prisoner flinched in agony as his leg was grasped and steadied and the knife touched against the crusted cord.

'Easy,' soothed the speaker in a murmured change of register. As the bonds fell away, the same fingers explored the swelling cuts and burns, gentle despite their marring tremor and the slowed reflex of deep chill. 'We'll have to ease him out before I can reach to free his wrists.'

Worked clear of his cranny with the aid of a fat man he recognized, the captive forced open the grazed, bloodied pulp that clogged his eyelids. The presence of the gem-dealing imposter last seen tied for questioning in the Duke of Alestron's private study cleared his wits. At close quarters the identity of the other could be guessed.

Such sharp-angled features and green eyes must surely belong to the Master of Shadow, who had ruined his name in the duke's guard and brought him to ignominy and exile.

'You!' he ground out, half-choked by bile and hatred. 'You're the dread sorcerer who enspelled my lord's armoury the day it burned. I swore in cold blood to see you dead!' He wrenched his strapped arms with such force that the stout, bearded henchman scrambled back in sceptical alarm.

'You see who he is? You're sure you want him freed?' The Mad Prophet clasped his fat fists in trepidation. 'He's sure to fly at your throat.'

Arithon s'Ffalenn simply sat down. Already white, his face looked like paper soaked over bone from the impact of pity and shock. 'I said I want his bonds struck. Have you eyes? Ath Creator, the man's out of his mind with

41

pain, and feverish to the point where a fair weather breeze could knock him down.'

'At your service, with pleasure, your Grace, except for one thorny problem.' Dakar's round face furrowed in sly sarcasm as he accepted the knife to slice ropes. 'When this brutish fellow gets up and cuts your heart out, I'll be forced to explain. The Fellowship of Seven will hold me to blame when they hear how your line met its end.'

A small movement; the Master of Shadow turned his head.

Dakar sucked in a sharp breath. 'You win, as always. Dharkaron show mercy, forget I ever spoke!'

Awash in dizziness and quick hatred, the captive gritted his teeth. Such reversal of fate lay beyond even dreams, that he might snatch back his chance to avenge his honour. He endured the frightful pain as his enemies raised his shoulder and turned him over. 'I was never careless,' he ground out in mulish acrimony. 'Your black sorcery allowed you entrance to that keep. A vixen's cunning got you out alive. Ath's Avenger bear me witness, you shall get what you deserve.'

Behind and above him, Arithon s'Ffalenn regarded the older grid of scars that marked the captive's naked back. 'Your duke made you pay sorely for what was, at most, a lapse of attention. What brought you here? A need to strike back for injustice?'

Stubborn in pride, the exiled guardsman held silent, his cheek pressed to damp sand until his cuts stung. The grate of broken ribs stitched his side in red fire and spasmed his muscles at each breath. He squeezed his eyes closed, clinging to patience, but the close heat and the sweat that ran from him in his agony made him light-headed and sick. His senses upended into vertigo. Long before the ropes that tied his wrists were sawn through, his awareness had unreeled into dark.

* * *

He awakened raving, deep in the night. A vision tormented him, of clean sheets and the astringent scent of poultice herbs. He thrashed against the touch that restrained him and railed aloud at the woman's voice that implored an unseen demon for assistance. Then he cursed as other hands reached down in diabolical force to restrain him.

'Is there no end?' someone cried in distress. 'He's started the bleeding again.'

Over his head loomed the face of the antagonist he had ached and endured horrors for the chance to kill. He shivered. His nerves an inferno of thwarted rage, he tried to strike out with his fist.

Bandages stopped him; then the sorcerer's features, haggard with an incomprehensible pity.

'Mountebank,' gasped the guardsman, reduced to frustration and tears. His enemy's dread shadows and his darkness were real enough. They spun him in their web once again and swallowed his struggles. Pinned helpless and moaning, he lost his thoughts into starless, lightless night.

Later he heard someone weeping his name. The harsh accents sounded like his own. Sunlight burned his eyes and branded hot bands at his naked wrists and ankles. He remembered the prison and the post. Again he tasted the fire of the whip, as Duke Bransian s'Brydion's master-at-arms flayed open the skin of his back. 'I'm no traitor, to beg like a dog to be forgiven,' he said, and then retched, sickened by his weakness. 'Why can't you believe me? I opened no doors. I met no Master of Shadow!'

But the whip fell and fell. The accusatory voice of Dharkaron Avenger seemed to roll like thunder through his dreams. 'If you suffered a flogging harsh enough to scar for failing to secure a locked passage, then what shall be your lot for setting fire to the ships of a sorcerer?'

The bed where he lay underwent a mad spin, like the

turn of Daelion's Wheel. The pain in his flesh swelled and drowned him. He heard water splash from a bowl and then music. Notes tapped and pried against his fevered senses like slivers flung off breaking crystal. Their sweetness conspired to weave a rolling pattern of freed beauty that scalded a breach through his hatred. Again he wept. The purity of song left him chilled like white rain, then threatened to break his laboured heart. He fell back, gasping against a soft pillow that swelled around his head until he died.

Or thought so, until he opened his eyes, limp and lucid, to a gloom gently lit by a candle. Rain chapped against the shutters of a cottage which smelled of oiled oak and dried lavender. He moved his head, aware by the softened prickle beneath his cheek that someone had washed and trimmed his hair. The strands were tarnished gold again, and shining on the linen, combed neat as in the days before his beggary.

'He's awakened,' said a woman in a shy, cautious whisper.

Someone else in the shadows responded. 'Leave us, Jinesse.' Light steps creaked against the floorboards. A man's outline swept across the candleflame, etched in brief light before he pulled up a wicker stool and sat down. 'Your name is Tharrick?'

The guard captain condemned to an unkind exile opened bruised eyelids and discovered his enemy at his bedside.

He swallowed, whipped dry from the aftermath of fever and a pathetic, languid weakness that required all his will to turn his head. Echoes from delirium rang back out of memory to haunt him: *What would be his lot for setting fire to the ships of a sorcerer?*

Terrified by the kindness that had nursed his cruel injuries, he swept the stilled features of his benefactor with a scorching, searching gaze. 'Why?' he croaked at last.

Restored reason could no longer deny the compassion in the man, whose very hands had bandaged and poulticed, and whose masterful playing upon the lyranthe had spiralled tortured thoughts into sleep.

'I came here to kill you,' said Tharrick. 'Why not make me suffer?' He reddened at the memory of the curses he had uttered to speed this man's spirit off to Sithaer.

Arithon stared down at his fingers, loosely cradled on his knees. His calm was all pretence. His masked spark of urgency lay so perfectly damped, his presence became a statement wound in patience. Whatever had unnerved him in the boiler shed, the emotion had washed clean and passed.

A faint frown tucked his upswept brows as the Master of Shadow weighed his answer. The lacings at his cuffs hung still as pen strokes, unmoved by the draught that teased the candleflame. 'When a man has been handled like an animal, it should come as no surprise when, from mistreatment, he's finally driven to desperation. What happened at Alestron was no fault of yours. The spell that brought the keep's destruction was not mine, but your duke's, that I was sent in by the Fellowship to help disarm. The plan went sadly wrong, for all of us. But I am not as Lord Bransian of Alestron, to hold you to blame out of temper.'

'Temper! I wanted a sword in your heart!' Tharrick gave a riled push at the blankets. Only sour luck had let him strike at a time when the victim he came to assassinate had been absent on business in the north.

'Don't.' Arithon caught the guardsman's shoulder, pressed him back. 'Your broken rib could be jostled to nick a lung. The leg wound is serious. If you stir, you'll restart the bleeding.'

'*I burned your brigantine!*' Tharrick gasped, anguished. 'All your cut timber. Your ropewalk.'

Quiet on the stool, Arithon released his hold and

looked at him. He said nothing. His face showed regret, but not anger.

Tharrick shut his eyes. His bruises throbbed. Under the ache of linen bindings, he felt as though his chest would tear and burst. Then remorse shredded even his last hold on pride. He wept, while the Master of Shadow stayed at his bedside and withheld comment like a brother.

'Get well, with my blessing,' said Arithon finally in that tone that could hurt for its sympathy. 'Jinesse will give you shelter in her cottage while you heal. After that, by my word, you go free. Return to your loved ones and live out your days without fear. For if in truth I were the sorcerer you believed, your life in my hands would be sacrosanct.'

But Tharrick had no family, nor any place left to call home. His post in the duke's guard had been his whole life until this man, who meant no malice, had ruined him. Desire for revenge had sustained him ever since. Denied that, he was an honourless exile, lost without purpose and cast adrift.

Duke and Prince

The hour after the brig *Savrid* dropped anchor behind the chain in Alestron's inner harbour, Duke Bransian and two brothers s'Brydion prepared to fare out hunting. The formal messenger sent by Lysaer of Tysan to request an audience reached them in the stable yard, just then a commotion of running grooms and glossy horses plunging and snorting at their leads. Underfoot, through the puddles seized black in the frost, the stag hounds yapped and cavorted.

Even while coursing for pleasure on his lands, the duke preferred to wear mail. Planted spraddle-legged over an upset trestle that had spilled its overweighted load of horse trappings, Lord Bransian turned the snarled frown begun by his servant's incompetence upon the harried royal dignitary. 'The timing's a cursed inconvenience!' His shout boomed across the milling chaos in the bailey. 'I shan't hold a war council without the attendance of my family. That's a problem, since Mearn hates to hunt.'

Lysaer's greying seneschal clasped his cloak in his fists before a gust ripped it up around his throat. A slender, quiet man who disliked being dishevelled, he fought the odds to maintain diplomacy and dignity, and ignored the puppy which crouched to gnaw his ankle.

Lord Bransian overshadowed him, a tower of a man in cowl and surcoat, who fumed in impatience until his groom scuttled up in breathless deference to retrieve the scattered ducal horsecloths.

'My lord, our news involves bloodshed,' pressed the seneschal.

The huntsman by the kennels chose that moment to try his horn; Lysaer's statesman pitched his plea above the bugle. 'His Grace of Avenor bid me say that the Master of Shadow who laid waste to your armoury has burned the trade fleet in the harbour at Werpoint.'

Framed in steel links, the scowl on Bransian's square features knitted to thunderous disgust. 'Dharkaron's avenging Spear and Chariot! His Grace petitioned us to withhold our assault against the meddling little criminal last summer. Just like kissing idiots, see what we get for our waiting! I suppose the royal army's been land-locked?'

While the seneschal hunched like a turtle in his cloak and lace collars in mute affirmation of bad news, Bransian raised a mailed fist to flag down the pageboy who raced past with both arms looped in bridles. 'Tell the master of horse to saddle Mearn's gelding!'

The boy bobbed a bow, dragging reins. 'Yes, my lord.'

'And kick my brother's narrow arse out of bed!' Bransian's bellowed order sent a massive black stud in a clattering shy across the cobbles. Its bunched, dappled haunches set two carter's lads to flight, while a lone, honking gander, escaped from its crate in the kitchen yard, flapped in distress through the fracas. 'Say he's to attend me, however late he's stayed out to gamble, and bedamned to his disdain for blooding stags.'

The ducal displeasure fastened back on Avenor's skinny seneschal. 'Does your master ride a palfrey or a war-horse? Speak fair. Our destriers want for exercise, but I won't spare your prince the rough side of my temper if his mount slips the bit and kicks a hound.'

Midday saw the four brothers s'Brydion reined up in the softened, grey slush on a hillside. They had taken no stag, but not for want of trying. Mud splashed and boisterous astride their foam flecked mounts, they groused in rough play, and derided Keldmar for his temerity. An exchange of dares had led him to jump over a wall in a shortcut through a crofter's hog pen. The landing had mired his mount to his knees in a wallow overflowing with a shrieking sow and her farrow.

'Ath, I'll split,' chuckled Parrien, his battle braid fallen undone and his hair whipped in crimped hanks across his shoulders. 'That piglet that fell in your boot cuff –'

'Shut up!' Keldmar snapped, his eyes creased with malice. Reminder enough, the tassels on his horsecloths were crusted with dirt that reeked of faeces. 'Your turn will come. Remember that stream with the sink pool, last season?'

Rain misted through the trees, nipping Bransian's cheeks to clash pink against his beard, and chilling the thinner Mearn ghost white beneath the black velvet band of his cap. Still clad in the ribboned doublet he had chosen in expectation of a quiet morning minding the accounts, the youngest of the brothers tipped his head in cool courtesy toward the royal guest. The only one likely to commiserate with a foreigner dragged headlong through raw weather and winter fields, he apologized for the barren hunt.

'We don't use beaters. That's a mayor's habit, and shame on the man who kills a beast without due respect for its honour, its pride and wild strength.' He combed nervous fingers through his mount's burr-caught mane and flicked up one shoulder in a shrug. 'I never liked coursing stag. Too much sweat and ploughing through briars. But the sorcerer you chase. He's another matter. I should like to feed his heart to my falcon.'

Resplendent despite the soil on his blue-and-gold cloak, his hand in skilled quiet holding a mettlesome bay charger in check, Lysaer s'Ilessid at last gained the moment to address the subject which had brought him. 'I'm here to join our efforts to that end.'

'You mean you're here to beg for ships,' Parrien cut in, the humour erased from his face.

In the dark gash of the draw, cross-laced with winter trees, a hound bayed on a false scent. The huntsman shouted and winded his horn. Reduced to a toy figurine by the distance, he wheeled his horse and cantered, his pack fanned over the sere ground ahead like shadows streamered in a current.

Bransian grunted in disgust, backed his rawboned mount from the hillcrest, and reined around to rejoin his brothers. Faced to the wind, his beard whipped like a lion's mane across his faded surcoat, he regarded the Prince of the West with eyes the gritted grey of filed iron. 'This hunt's a shambles. We may as well discuss the other.' Never one to trouble over niceties, he plunged headlong to the point. 'An entire fleet was scuttled. Excuses won't restore your burned ships. I want to know if the loss was due to incompetence.'

Lysaer met the duke's glare, his back straight, and his hands square and steady on his reins. 'Let me tell you how a pirate who works sorcery and shadow goes about butchering the innocent.'

Keldmar snorted and scuffed a gob of dirt off the steel-studded knuckles of his gauntlet. 'The trade fleet was anchored off Werpoint for the purpose of moving your war host. A fool might call that innocent. Your s'Ffalenn enemy's proved he's not stupid, that's all.'

Parrien glared at the brother near enough in looks to be his birth twin. 'You jabber like a woman at her laundry tub.'

Keldmar returned a smile rowed with teeth. 'Say that again across my sword. Words are for ninnies. Let's determine who's a woman with bare steel.'

Duke Bransian shouldered his horse between the pair, effectively strangling their rivalry. To the prince interrupted by the family style of bickering, he said, 'We have our ships snugged down and our mercenaries on leave for the season, as they should be. Winter's no time to pursue war. Men sicken and die from disease. They desert from poor spirits. I hate this Master of Shadow full well and yet, on your counsel, we held our strike against him last summer. Now you've gone and made a bungle of things, bedamned if I'll campaign in unfavourable weather to make amends for the lapse! Nor will I rise to arms in alliance for anything short of a cause to stir Dharkaron's Chariot from Athlieria.'

'We have that,' Lysaer said, unsmiling. 'Time's gone against us since Werpoint. The Master of Shadow will pull out of Merior. He knows we're aware of his intentions there. The best chance we have is to close on him now, before he dismantles his shipyard.'

Bransian regarded the blond prince before him, silent, unbending, and as powerful as the trained war-horse beneath him, who awaited his command in taut stillness.

Lysaer matched that dagger steel gaze. 'You're quick to ask of incompetence. Tell me straight, and mean what you say, that on the day your armoury went to ashes and smoke at the hand of Arithon s'Ffalenn, you never felt duped, or a fool.'

The duke's grey destrier flung its head hard as the fist on its reins snapped the bit. State visitors who came to Alestron to importune on the heels of a grossly misspent favour were wont to cajole, or flatter, or bring some rich offering to ease relations. This unvarnished honesty was unprecedented, its impact as stunningly unpleasant as an unveiled insult or a threat. Mearn dragged a hissed breath between his teeth, while Parrien and Keldmar fixed the Prince of the West with expressions of matched admiration.

Straight against the icy, winter whine of the wind, Bransian flushed irate red. A hound in the distant stream bottom yipped. The huntsman's whip cracked in swift reprimand. On the ridgetop, the more dangerous challenge brought stillness, until the duke's war-horse sidled and slashed its thick tail in an ear-flattened response to its rider's temper.

Then Bransian threw back his coiffed head and succumbed to a deep, belly laugh. 'You have bollocks, prince. I'll give you that. Yes. I felt like the world's born fool. If you were incompetent at Werpoint, so was I that day our secret armoury was ruined. You've made your point. This Shadow Master's far too wily to be permitted to live and run abroad. But if I'm going to muster Alestron's troops to march against him, I'm not going to waste my hours of comfort. Our plans should be discussed underneath a dry roof, over wine and a table of hot food.'

Lane Imprints

In Whitehold, the Koriani Prime broods over two image spheres whose significance stymies all conjecture: in one, the flare of mighty wards conceals some momentous event in Althain Tower; the next shows the Master of Shadow on a windy beach, a knife at his wrist as he kneels to swear blood oath at the feet of a Fellowship Sorcerer; and resigned to frustration, the Prime Matriarch curses timing, that First Enchantress Lirenda's trial to regain the order's Great Waystone cannot take place any sooner than spring equinox . . .

In a windy pass in Vastmark, the discorporate Sorcerer Luhaine waylays a black-clad colleague in the company of a circling raven to relate ill news from Althain Tower: 'The knowledge Kharadmon sought from the worlds beyond South Gate has eluded his grasp. The Mistwraith's curse over the royal half-brothers cannot be tried at this time. Its latent evils are far worse than we feared, a danger too dire to provoke . . .'

* * *

Soon after Prince Lysaer and Duke Bransian shake hands to seal an armed alliance, and the mercenary camps at Alestron muster to cross Shand to stage an attack on Merior, the clansmen under Erlien, *caithdein* of the realm, engage his given order to strip every farmstead in the path of the army of horses and cattle, and to hamper their advance as they can . . .

II. *SHIPS OF MERIOR*

In the quiet back room of the widow Jinesse's cottage, the exiled guard captain lay on his cot in recovery, while the wind through the opened casement beside him carried the distant beat of hammers. Their frenetic rhythm did not slacken for rain showers, nor for the onset of dark. Had Tharrick still burned to inflict his revenge upon the Master of Shadow, the desperate hurry implied by the pace would have rung sweet to his ears.

The balm of his victory instead left him hollow and distressed. The undaunted resumption of activity on the sandspit abraded the satisfaction from his achievement until he felt shamed to puzzled anguish. His single-handed attack had fairly ruined a man's hopes, and yet, no one close to Arithon stepped forth to berate him for the damage. The widow named his friend did not stint her hospitality. She did not speak out in censure. If her twin children were more aggressive in their loyalties, the morning she caught them paired at his bedside, accusing voices raised in a shocking turn of language, she scolded their mannerless tongues and packed them off on an errand to the fish market.

While brother and sister raced in barefoot escape down

the lane, their shouts washed into the tireless thunder
of surf, Tharrick turned his face to the wall and closed
his eyes. For hours he listened to the gusts through the
palm fronds and the swish of the rush broom the widow
used to tidy her floors. Left ill from his wounds, he
skirted the dizzy brink of delirium. At cruel and fickle
moments, his ears remade sound into the high, whining
slash of the braided leather whip that stung him still in
bad dreams.

Weak as a husk swathed in dressings and poultices,
he counted the knots in the ceiling beams, while the
diced square of sun let in through the casement crept its
daily arc across the floor.

Afternoons, as the room cooled into shadow, Arithon
came with a satchel of herbs to brew simples in the
widow's cramped kitchen. Her murmur beyond the
inside door carried overtones of worry as she asked after
progress at the shipyard.

'The work goes well enough.' Through the splash of
well water poured from bucket to pot, Arithon explained
how his craftsmen were breaking up the worn hulk of a
lugger to ease the shortage of planking. 'Dakar needs the
use of your trestle table by tomorrow,' he added in a
brisk change of subject. 'Would you mind? I've asked
him to copy some nautical charts. He'll stay sober. The
twins have been offered three coppers to watch him.
They've promised to fetch me running if he tries to sneak
out to buy spirits.'

Jinesse gave the delighted, little fluttery laugh she
seemed to hoard for the Master of Shadow. 'They'll be
like small fiends on his case. Won't you pity him?'

'Dakar?' Visible through the narrow doorway, Arithon
settled with his shoulder against the brick by the hob.
His gaze stayed fixed on the water in defiance of the
adage that insisted a watched pot never boiled. 'The
man's been deadweight on my hands long enough. If he
moans over-much, or his manners get crude, I'll send

two of my caulkers to sit on him while you sew his offensive mouth shut.'

'I doubt I'll notice his swearing,' Jinesse admitted. 'Dakar's grumbles are no match for my twins when they're shouting.'

The astringency of steeping remedies wafted on the steam that trailed from the kitchen. From the back room, Tharrick made out the rim of the pot on the fire as Arithon crouched alongside. Sorcerer though he was, he made no spell passes over the brew. In Alestron, to treat whip weals, even the wizened herb witch had done as much while she mixed her powders and unguents. The Master of Shadow sometimes phrased a catchy bar of notes over the burble of hot water. All but plain song lay beyond him. The fingers that clasped the wooden spoon to stir were grained in dirt and callus, the split nails too work-worn to handle his exquisite lyranthe.

'Too much tar on my knuckles again,' he murmured, the struck resonance of his voice despair overlaid by chagrin.

'Don't you mind.' The widow rummaged in her closet, found a tattered shirt of her late husband's, and tore the clean linen into strips. 'I changed the dressings yesterday. I can do the same again.' She pushed a wisp of hair off her cheek with the back of a spidery hand. 'If you need to be at the yard, you should go.'

'I'll thank you to handle the bandages. But I won't leave until I've seen how Tharrick's cuts are closing.' Arithon swung the pot off the hob, arose, and tipped his raven head for Jinesse to pass ahead of him.

The pair entered the sickroom, the widow with her face flushed pink above her blouse and her unburdened hands given to fidgeting with her skirts. Through his days of convalescence, Tharrick had taken quiet pleasure in her presence. She had a certain shy grace in those moments when she believed no one watched. But Arithon set her on edge. His quick, light movement and contained self-command hurled her off course like a moth thrown into strong light.

The bandages provided the excuse she needed to steady herself. Despite her retiring nature, her handling was firm as she lifted the bedclothes to attend her battered charity case. The number and severity of Tharrick's burns and cuts made even small movement unpleasant. Soothed by her touch, grateful for her gentle care as she used the herb infusion to soak and soften the scabs before she peeled the crusted linen, Tharrick sweated through the undignified process in silence.

Jinesse was not alone in feeling unnerved before the intensity of Arithon's regard. With the window at his back, his face looked drawn to hollows, the eyes like sharp points sunk in pits. His tone held the edge of a burr, struck from impatience or exhaustion as he said, Stay with the red clover for the burns. That gash on the thigh still looks inflamed. Along with elecampane and coneflower, let's add wild thyme, and of course, keep on with the betony.'

He began a step to fetch the pastes for the poultices, swayed, and snatched at the windowsill to steady himself.

Jinesse rounded on him, as near as she ever came to scolding. 'You can't continue on like this!'

A stunned second passed. Dismayed by her inadvertent boldness, Jinesse trapped a breath behind closed lips. As if to hold off an attack by wild wolves, she clutched the snarl of fouled linen to her breast.

Too tired for temper, stung by her wary fear, Arithon gave way to wide surprise. 'What choice do I have?'

'Sit!' Jinesse snapped. As if the half-naked presence of the invalid on her sheets were of no more account than cut wood, she cast the linens into her laundry hamper, yanked the high-backed chair from beyond the clothes chest, and plunked it on the boards by the windowsill. 'If you're too pressed and dirty to attend this job yourself, the very least you'll do for me is to spend a few minutes off your feet.'

To everyone's astonishment, most of all his own, the Prince of Rathain did her bidding. Up close, he looked drawn beneath his tan. His hair was caught in pitchy tangles at the temples where he had raked it back with knuckles still smeared from green planks. The thumbnail on his left hand was swollen black, perhaps from a mis-struck mallet. Unable to bear his appearance straight on, the widow threw open the curtains to flush out the cloying reek of herbs.

Breezes off the ocean fingered the loosened laces of Arithon's shirt. The impersonal touch relaxed him, or else the flood of fresh air. He tipped his crown to rest against the chair back and almost instantly fell asleep.

Tharrick surrendered his chafed wrist to the widow for dressing, and pondered the incongruity; how unlikely it seemed, that a sorcerer of such black reputation could behave in mild, trusting innocence.

To his dismay, he found he had mused his thought aloud.

Jinesse slapped a heated strip of linen over the applied layer of poultice paste brusquely enough to raise a sting. 'Arithon's driving himself half to death in that shipyard!' At Tharrick's subdued flinch, she gentled her touch with the wrapping. 'They say he's not slept in two days beyond catnaps, and Ath show him mercy, just look at his hands! He's Athera's own Masterbard, and criminal indeed, to dare risk his gift to common labour!'

Which was near enough to outright accusation. Already miserable, caught vulnerably naked before a benefactor he had not wanted and unable to turn away for the lacerations still open to the air, the burly exile could do nothing else but tip his chin to the wall and shut his eyes.

Jinesse smoothed a wrinkle in the linen, ashamed. 'I'm sorry.' She tucked the bandage into itself and spread her hands loose in her lap. 'Arithon insisted you weren't at fault, but the setback has gone very hard. Those ships that you burned were the dream of his heart, and now he scarcely speaks for disappointment.'

'Is he not, then, the felon he is named?' Tharrick swallowed. 'Do you think him innocent of all charges?'

The ticking in the mattress whispered as Jinesse sat down. Steam from the pot by her ankle sieved a backdrop like gauze against a profile as thin-skinned and fair. Tendrils of blond hair wisped out of the coiled braid at her nape, atremble in the breeze as she darted a glance at the prince sprawled asleep in her chair. 'I don't know.'

Tharrick propped himself on one elbow.

'How can I tell?' Jinesse admitted, her divided opinion a palpable weight upon shoulders too frail for harsh judgment. 'Arithon once charged me to measure him by his behaviour. The villagers here respect him. They might not know him for the Master of Shadow, but they don't give their trust lightly. Arithon never cheated anyone. Nor has he sheltered behind lies. Except for the music he draws from his heart, no one has seen him work spellcraft.'

She trailed off, her lip pinched between small, tight teeth.

Flat on his back with cracked ribs, and never in his life more helpless, Tharrick was swept by a sharp, sudden urge to protect her. She seemed so slender and torn, alone in this house with no trusted mate to share the rearing of her twins, nor this moment's pained indecision.

Arithon, perhaps, was perceptive enough to take advantage. Moved to a queer stab of jealousy, Tharrick said, 'The sorcery that burned Alestron's armoury killed seven men. I was there.'

The light brushed without sparkle over plain wooden hairpins as Jinesse quickly shook her head. 'I don't say he's blameless, of that or any other accusation laid against him. He's never made excuses or tried to deny his past actions. His silence is so strict on the subject, if I dared, I would challenge him in frustration.'

'What do you think?' pressed Tharrick.

The widow bent, wrung out another dressing, and scooped up a dollop of herb paste. 'I think this village need not become involved. The Shadow Master took pains to set no roots here. Quite the contrary. He wishes himself at sea to the point where he's desperate. If he were some dread sorcerer or a minion of evil, I'm doubting he'd need to drive himself to the edge for the sake of a half-built brace of ships.'

The shadow of a gull flicked past the window. Chilled by its passage, Tharrick said, 'What if he wishes such ships to disrupt the trade of honest men?'

'Piracy?' Jinesse looked up, her cupped hands filled with remedies, to stare at Tharrick in shock. 'Is that what you believe? If it's true, there's no thread of evidence. These brigantines weren't planned for armament. I held the impression they were Arithon's hope to outrun the bloodshed loosed upon him by the armies from the north.'

The bandaging resumed in stiff silence. Arithon slept on, pliant as a scarecrow, his head tipped aslant and his blistered palms slack against the soiled thighs of his breeches. Jinesse proceeded on her own to mix the tisane from valerian and poppy to dull her invalid's pain and let him sleep. Warmed and eased by her ministrations, Tharrick watched through half-closed eyelids as she hooked the basket of soiled linens on one arm and collected the herb jar and pot from the side table. As comfort returned and he slipped into drugged reverie, he noticed she took extreme care not to disturb the other sleeper as she passed.

Before he dozed off, Tharrick pondered this reserve, in his quiet way relieved. If she were corrupted by the

Shadow Master, or sheltered him in collusion, she acted without ties to the heart.

In time, the wounded guardsman drifted into dreams. When he roused, much later, and Jinesse brought him bread and gruel, the chair was vacant and Arithon long gone.

The days passed, the schedule of the widow's attentions interspersed between drug-soaked sleep and hours spun into muddled awareness. Impressions not hazed by possets and fever stood out like cut crystal: of the twins' boisterous contention over which last fetched water from the well; of a killdeer crying in the deeps of the night; of storm rains pattering the beachhead, and once, Arithon's voice in a whipcrack inflection berating the Mad Prophet for shoddy penmanship on the charts.

'I don't care blazes if an iyat has warped all your quill pens! If you're too fat and slack to chalk out a simple bane-ward, then buy a tin talisman for the purpose! Either way, your copies had better be up to my standards.'

'To Sithaer with all that!' Dakar plunged on in scathing hatred. 'Alestron's joined forces with Lysaer to kill you. I saw the duke swear alliance in a dream . . .'

Another night, held restless and awake by the throb of the leg wound that had festered, Tharrick overheard the end of another discussion, Arithon's diction muted by concern. 'Well yes, the coffers are low. The outlay to the forges at Perdith was never planned. I've got enough silver left to keep the workers on, period. No more funds for wood. None for new canvas. If the hull that's least damaged gets launched at all, she'll have to leave Merior under tow. The point's likely moot. Ath knows there's no coin to charter a vessel to drag her.'

A chair scraped on brick as Jinesse arose to set water on the hob for tea. Some other stranger with a sailor's broad drawl murmured commiseration, then finished off in dry warning. 'The rumour's true enough. Alestron's troops of mercenaries are mustering. War galleys refitted to put to sea. You'd better pray Ath sends in storms black enough to close the harbours, because if the season holds fair, the sands of Scimlade Tip could soon grow too hot to hold you.'

Then Dakar cut in, carping, 'If you had a firkin of sense, man, you'd give up the yard. Take what silver you have left and sail out on the tide in your sloop.'

Arithon replied in a timbre to raise sudden chills. 'I have no intention of letting my efforts get scuttled in Merior's harbour. That means you're not only going to stay sober, you'll stir off your backside and help. I want a lane scrying daily at noon, and each time you fail me, by my oath to Asandir, I'll see you starve without dinner.'

The back-and-forth volley of argument extended long into the night. When Jinesse entered late, her pale face lit by the flutter of a hand-carried candle, Tharrick struggled up from his pillow. 'Why doesn't the Shadow Master take better care? I can eavesdrop on all of his plans.'

'If you ask him yourself, he would tell you straight out that he hasn't got anything to hide.' Jinesse set her light on the nightstand, bent over, and laid a tentative palm on his brow. 'Your fever's abated. How goes the pain? The posset should be stopped, if you can bear it. Poppy's unsafe, over time. Arithon won't have you grow addicted.'

'Why ever should he care?' Tharrick cried, and flopped back, his large hands bunched in the sheets the way a castaway might cling to a reef. 'What am I to him but an enemy?'

His dread had recurred more than once in his night-mares, that a sorcerer might cosset an assassin back to health for some lingering, spell-turned revenge.

Jinesse tugged the linen free of Tharrick's fists and smoothed the ruched bedclothes across his chest. She looked tired. The dry lines of crow's-feet around her eyes were made harsh in the upslanting glow of the candle as she gave a tight shake of her head. 'The prince means you no harm. He's said, if you wanted, he would arrange for a cart to bear you to take sanctuary in the hostel with Ath's adepts. The moment you're well enough to travel, you can leave.'

Tharrick dragged in a hissed breath and said in bleak pain through locked teeth, 'When I go, I shall walk, and not be asking that bastard for his royal charity.'

A timid, pretty smile bowed the widow's mouth. 'Ask mine, then. You're welcome here. By my word, his coin never paid for your soup.'

Tharrick sank back into sheets that smelled faintly of lavender, his cheeks stained to colour by embarrassment. 'You know I have no prospects.'

Against habit, the widow's smile broadened. 'My dear man, forgive me. But you're going to have to be back up and walking before that becomes anybody's worry.'

Denied cause for outrage, reft of every justification for his enmity against the Shadow Master, Tharrick exerted his last, stubborn pride to arise from his bed and recover. From his faltering first steps across the widow's cottage, his progress seemed inextricably paired with the patching of the damaged brigantine his act of revenge had holed through.

A fit man, conditioned to a life of hard training, he pressed his healing strength with impatience. Reclad in castoffs from Jinesse's drowned husband, Tharrick limped through the fish market. His path skirted mud between bait casks and standing puddles left from the showers that swept off the wintry, slate sea. The snatches of talk he overheard among the women who salted down fish for the barrels made uneasy contrast with the nighttime discussions over the widow's kitchen trestle. Here, the strident squabbles as the gulls snatched after offal seemed the only stressed note. Engrossed in homey gossip, Merior's villagers appeared utterly oblivious to the armed divisions bound south to storm their peninsula.

Tharrick maintained a stiff silence, set apart by his awareness of the destruction Duke Bransian's style of war could unleash. The fishwives' inimical, freezing quiet disbarred him from conversation. Already an outsider, his assault upon Arithon's shipyard made him outcast. Disapproval shuttered the villagers' dour faces and pressured him to move on. Tharrick felt just as uneasy in their company, uninformed as they were of Dakar's noon scryings, which showed an outbreak of clan livestock raids intended to hamper Alestron's crack mercenaries in their passage down the coast.

Such measures would yield small delay. Once on the march, s'Brydion war captains were a force inexorable as tide, as Tharrick well knew from experience. A fleet pulled out of dry dock converged to blockade, manned by cautious captains who took care to snug down in safe harbours at night. This was not the fair weather trade season, when passage to Scimlade Tip might be made without thought in a fortnight. Through the uneasy winds before each winter's solstice, no galleyman worth his salt dared the storms that could sweep in without warning. Years beyond counting, ships had been thrashed to wreckage as they hove into sight of sheltered waters. The passage between Ishlir and Elssine afforded small protection, where the grass flats spread inland and mighty winds roared off the Cildein Ocean. Even Selkwood's tall pines could gain no foothold to root. What oaks could survive grew stunted by breakage, skeletal and hunched as old men.

Bound in its tranquil spell of ignorance, unwarned by

the cracking pace of Arithon's work shifts, the folk of Merior walked their quiet lanes, while their rows of whitewashed cottages shed the rains in a mesmerized, whispered fall of droplets. For a rootless, directionless man accustomed to armed drills and activity, the fascination with the herons that fished the shallows of Garth's pond paled through one solitary hour. Tharrick startled the birds into ungainly flight on an oath spat out like flung stone. Like Jinesse's twins with their penchant for scrapes, he felt himself drawn beyond reason to wander up the spit toward the racketing industry of the shipyard.

There, under firm-handed discipline, the craftsmen his fires had caught slacking laboured to rectify their lapse. He strolled among them. Brazen as nails, even daring retaliation for their master's hand in his recovery, Tharrick meandered through the steam fanned from the boiler-shack chimney. The crunch of shavings beneath his boot soles and his conspicuous, clean linen shirt drew the eyes of the men, stripped to the waist, sweaty skins dusted by chaff from the sawpits as they cut and shaped smooth reworked planks. His trespass was noted by unembarrassed glances, then just as swiftly forgotten.

Even the master joiner, who had ordered his beatings and tried unspeakable means to force his silence, showed no rancour at his presence. Arithon's will had made itself felt. Enemy though he was, none dared to raise word or hand against him. All were ruled by their master's ruthless tongue and his fever-pitched driving purpose. The salvage effort on the damaged brigantine already showed a near-complete patch at her bow; the one still in frames on her bedlogs lay changed, half-cannibalized for her wood, then lessened in length and faired ready for planking. A less-ambitious vessel with a shorter sheerline took shape, fitted here and there between the yellow of new spruce with the odd checked timber fished together from the derelict lugger.

In three weeks of mulish, unswerving effort, Arithon s'Ffalenn had rechannelled his loss into what skirted the edge of a miracle.

Struck by a stabbing, unhappy urge to weep, Tharrick held his chin in stiff pride. He would not bend before awe, would not spin and run to the widow's cottage to hide his face in shame. The man who had forgiven his malice in mercy would be shown the qualities which had earned his past captaincy in Alestron. In hesitant steps on the fringes, Tharrick began to lend his help. If his mending ribs would not let him wheel a handcart, or his palms were too tender to wield a pod auger to drill holes for treenails in hardened oak, he could steady a plank for the plane on the trestles, or run errands, or turn dowels to pin timbers and ribs. He could stoke the fire in the boiler shed, and maybe, for his conscience, regain a small measure of the self-respect he had lost to disgrace and harsh exile.

On the third day, when he returned to the widow's with his shirt and hair flecked with shavings, he found silver on the table, left in his name by the Shadow Master.

Tharrick's unshaven face darkened in a ruddy burst of temper.

Drawn by the bang as he hurled open the casement, Jinesse caught his wrist and stopped his attempt to fling the coins into the fallow tangle of her garden. 'Tharrick, no. What are you thinking? Arithon doesn't run a slave yard. Neither does he give grown men charity. He said if you can't be bothered to collect your pay with the others, this was the last time he'd cover for your mistakes.'

'Mistakes?' Poised with one brawny wrist imprisoned in her butterfly clasp, Tharrick shook off a stab of temper. The widow's tipped-up features implored him. Her hair wisped at her temples like new floss, and her wide, worried eyes were a delicate, dawn-painted blue. He swallowed. His grip on the coins relaxed from its white-knuckled tension.

'Mistakes,' he repeated. This time the word rang bitter. He slanted his cheek against the window frame, eyes shut in racking distaste. 'By Daelion Fatemaster, yon one's a demon for forcing a man to think.'

'More than just men.' Jinesse gave a nervous, soft laugh and let him go.

His lids still squeezed closed, Tharrick asked her, 'What did he do for you, then?'

She stepped back, swung the basket of carrots brought up from the market onto the table, and rummaged through a drawer for a knife. 'He once took me sailing to Innish.' In a confidence shared with nobody else, she told what that passage had meant.

Evening stole in. The kitchen lay purpled in shadow, cut by fiery, glancing sparkles from the bowl of Falgaire crystal which sat, unused, in the dish cupboard. Tharrick progressed from helping to peel vegetables to holding Jinesse's cool hands as she finished her careful account. They sat together without speaking, until the twins clambered through the outside doorway and startled the pair of them apart.

The storm struck before dawn to a mean snarl of wind that flattened the sea oats and hurled breakers like bulwarks against the strand. Men rushed with lanterns through the rain-torn dark to drag exposed dories into shelter behind the dunes, and supplement moorings with anchor and cable. The brunt of the gale howled in from the north, more trouble to shipping upcoast, the widow insisted, clad in a loose cotton robe as she set the pot on the hob to make soup.

If she rejoiced in the delay of the war galleys or the army, she had the restraint not to gloat.

The shutters creaked and slammed against their

fastenings, and their sharp, random bangs as the gusts changed direction caused Tharrick to flinch from edged nerves. 'What of Arithon's shipyard?'

The widow sighed and pushed back the hair that unreeled down her shoulders like limp flax. 'There could be damage if the wind veers. A storm surge could ride the high tide. Should the gale blow through first, the beached hulls will be safe. The luggers may run aground off the Scimlade, where sandbars have shifted from their beds, but the hook in the coastline here usually shelters us. Just pray the wind stays northeast.'

Morning broke yellow-grey as an old bruise above the eastern horizon. Cold light revealed a cove racked and littered with palm fronds and the flaccid, corpse fingers of stranded kelp. Two cottages had lost their thatched roofs. Against the whining gusts, the ragged beat of hammers resumed.

Yet when Tharrick picked his way around puddles and downed sticks to the yard on its wind-racked spit, he found no joiners at work on the framing. He was told all three shifts had been sent to make repairs in the village.

Arithon was immersed in sweating industry, restoking the stove beneath the boiler.

Quiet to one side, his hair newly trimmed and yesterday's stubble shaven clean, Tharrick ventured the first comment he had dared since making his own way at the shipyard. 'It's likely your generosity has doomed the last hull.'

Arithon crammed another billet into the stove, then yanked back his hand as the sparks flew. 'If so, that was my choice to make.'

'I'm not a green fool.' Tharrick envied the neat, practised speed that hurled each split piece of kindling over the heat-rippled bed of hot ash. 'I've led men. Your example makes them work until their hearts burst to meet an impossible standard.'

A slick, cold laugh wrung from the Shadow Master's

throat as he clashed the fire door closed. 'You're mistaken.' He straightened, reduced to lean contours sketched out in a silverpoint gleam of wet skin. His eyes were derisive and heavy with fatigue as he regarded the former guardsman who offered his tentative respect. 'I happen to have employed every wood-sawyer and carpenter inside of thirty leagues. Had I not sent the joiners, we'd have gotten every fishwife and her man's favourite marlinespike fouling the works here by noon. In case you hadn't noticed, the framing's all done. It's the caulkers I can't spare, and I needed some excuse to keep the fasteners overtime with the planking.'

Unapologetic, ill-tempered, Arithon sidestepped and slipped past. Abandoned to an eddied whirl of air, Tharrick swallowed back humiliation. The widow's observation was borne out with sharp vengeance, that if the Shadow Master's generosity could be held beyond reproach, it was not to be mistaken for his friendship.

The day wore away in grey drizzle and a murderous round of hard work. The ragged thunder of the caulkers' mallets as hot oakum was forced between the gaps in the brigantine's decking winnowed the stink of melting tar on winds left tainted with storm wrack. At nighfall, the pace did not relent. Planks were run out of the steam box and forced tight against the ship's timbers. Still hot, they were fastened with treenails of locust to lie below the waterline, oak above. Torches spilled a hellish, flickering light across the naked shoulders of the labourers, slicked through the dirt where sweat and cold water channelled in runnels off their bodies.

The joiners returned in grumbling small groups. Their senior craftsman sought Arithon to call him aside. Pressed by his mulish, exhausted reluctance, the stout-bellied journeyman who checked the yard's measuring gave in to necessity and shouldered the end of the plank the Shadow Master had been carrying.

'It's only a ship,' the master joiner exhorted to the

spare, tired figure that confronted him. 'Does losing her matter so much that you ruin yourself and break the very hearts of the men?'

Scathing in anger, Arithon said, 'You brought me away *just for that*?'

'No.' The master joiner braced rangy shoulders against the urgency of those green eyes upon him. 'You're losing your sense of propriety. This morning Tharrick admired your judgment and you threw back his words in his face.'

Arithon's lips thinned into instant contempt. 'In case you'd failed to notice, Tharrick's all too quick to carve life up into absolutes. I can do very well without his worshipful admiration. Not when the reckoning is likely as not to get him killed by the hand of his own duke!'

'Very well.' The master joiner shrugged. 'If you're Sithaer bent on wearing yourself out with work, I'll not stand and watch with only my good sense for company.' An easy-natured spirit when his handiwork was not being kindled by vengeance-bent arsonists, he stripped off his shirt and ordered his journeyman to hand him his heaviest mallet.

A question rang back through the darkness. The master joiner returned his most irritable bellow. 'Bedamned to my supper! I asked for a tool to shoulder a shift with the fasteners.'

The next day brought news, called across choppy water to a fishing lugger from a Telzen trader blown off her course by the storm. A troop of mercenaries north of the city had come to grief when the plank span of the river bridge in Selkwood had collapsed beneath their marching weight.

'Barbarian work,' the fisherman related. 'No lives were lost, but the delay caused an uproar. The duke's captains were short-tempered when they reached the city markets to resupply.'

If Merior's villagers never guessed the identity of the man Alestron's army joined forces with Prince Lysaer to eradicate, Arithon continued his pursuits in brazen defiance of the odds. Undaunted by logic, that his enemies would board galleys to cross Sickle Bay to shorten the long march through Southshire, he faced this fresh setback without flinching.

The fleet he had burned in Werpoint harbour to buy respite had won him precious little leeway. Alestron's troops would be hounding his heels well ahead of the advent of spring.

Clad in a shirt for the first time in weeks, the light in his hair like spilled ink, Arithon stood to one side of the hull of his sole salvaged brigantine. Her new decking caulked and made watertight only that morning, she wore the strong reek of oakum and tar, and a linseed aroma of new paint. In sheer, smooth lines, an axe forged to cleave through deep waters, she seemed to strain toward the surface of the bay. The yard workers who crowded in excitement by the strand could not help but feel proud of their accomplishment. If any of them knew of the warhost days away, none broached the subject to Tharrick.

The man who replaced the master shipwright and another one chosen for fast reflexes knelt beneath a keel sheathed in gleaming copper. They pounded now to split out the blocks that braced the craft on her ways. The high cries of gulls, and the clangour of steel mauls marked the moment as the hull shifted, her birth pang a creak like the stretched joints of a wrestler.

Fiark's shout rang down from his perch on the bowsprit. Content to hang in Arithon's shadow, Feylind flung both arms around his waist in a hug of elfin delight.

Rankly sweating in a tunic too hot for the tropics, Dakar observed the proceedings in glowering sobriety. 'Their faith is vast,' he said, and sniffed down his nose, as the eighty-foot vessel shifted and squealed on her ways. Her quivering hesitancy marked the start of her plunge toward her first kiss of salt waters. 'I wouldn't be caught under that thing. Not drunken, insane, nor for the gold to founder a trade galley.'

From his place in deep shadow, arrested between mallet strokes, the shipwright cracked a dry laugh. 'And well might you worry, at that! A fat sot like you, down here? First off, if you'd fit, the Fatemaster would as likely snatch at his chance to turn your lazy bones beneath the Wheel.'

Dakar's outraged epithet became lost as the hull gave way into motion with a slide of wood on wood. She splashed onto the aquamarine breast of the shallows, adrift, to the twins' paired shrieks of exuberance.

While sailhands recruited from the south shore taverns waded after, to catch lines and launch longboats to warp the floated hull to a mooring, Tharrick was among the first to approach and offer his congratulations. Arithon returned a quick, brilliant smile that faded as the former guardsman's gaze shifted to encompass the smaller hull still poised forlorn on her ways.

Understanding flashed wordless between them. Of ten ships planned at the outset, one brigantine in the water might be all that Arithon's best effort could garner. As fishermen said, his luck neared the shoals; the hour was too late to save the second.

Whatever awaited in the uncertain future, the workers were spared trepidation. A beer cask was rolled out and broached in the yard to celebrate the launching of *Khetienn*, named in the old tongue for the black-and-gold leopard renowned as the s'Ffalenn royal arms. While the mean schedule slackened and men made merry to the pipe of a sailor's tin whistle, Arithon, and most notably, Dakar, were conspicuous for their early absence. If the new vessel's master pleaded weariness, the Mad Prophet was parted from the beer cask in vociferous, howling disagreement. Too careful to drink in the company of men his earlier rancour had injured, Tharrick slipped away the moment he drained his first tankard.

The boom of winter breakers rolled like thunder down the sleepy village lanes. Slanted in afternoon shadows through the storm-stripped palms, he strode past the fishnets hung out to dry and entered the widow's cottage. The day's homey smell of fish stew and bacon was cut by a disquieting murmur of voices.

The twins were not in their place by the hob, shelling peas and squalling in argument. In a quiet unnatural for their absence, a meeting was in progress around the trestle in Jinesse's kitchen.

'Tonight,' Arithon was saying, his tone subdued to regret, 'I'll slip *Talliarthe*'s mooring on the ebb tide and sail her straight offshore. No trace will be left to follow. The workers are paid through the next fortnight. Ones loyal to me will ship out one by one, the last out to scuttle the little hull. When the Prince of the West arrives with his galleys, he'll find no sign of my presence, and no cause to engage bloody war.'

'What of the *Khetienn*?' the widow protested. 'You can't just abandon her. Not when she's cost all you own to get launched.'

Arithon flipped her a sweet, patient smile. 'We've made disposition.' Across a glower of palpable venom from the Mad Prophet, he added, 'Dakar held a dicing debt over a trader captain out of Innish. His galley lies off Shaddorn to slip in by night and take my new vessel under tow. Her sails, her mastcaps and chain are crated and packed in her hold along with the best of the yard's tools. The riggers at Southshire will complete her on credit against a share of her first run's cargo. With luck, I'll stay free to redeem her.'

A board creaked to Tharrick's shifted weight. Arithon started erect, noted whose presence blocked the doorway, then settled back in maddening complacence.

'You dare much to trust me,' said the exiled captain. 'Should you not show alarm? It's my own duke's army inbound toward this village. A word from me and that hull could be impounded at Southshire.'

'Will you speak, then?' challenged Arithon. Coiled and still as the leopard his brigantine honoured, the calm he maintained as he waited for answer built to a frightening presence. In the widow's cosy kitchen, the quiet felt isolate, a bubble blown out of glass. The sounds outside the window, of surf and crying gulls and the distant shouts of fishermen snatched by the wind from the decks of a lugger, assumed the unreality of a daydream.

Tharrick found himself unable to sustain the blank patience implied by those level, green eyes. 'Why should you take such a risk?'

Arithon's answer surprised him. 'Because your master abandoned all faith in you. The least I can do as the cause of your exile is to leave you the chance to prove out your duke's unfair judgment.'

'You'd allow me to ruin you in truth,' Tharrick said.

'Once, that was everything you wanted.' Motionless Arithon remained, while the widow at his shoulder held her breath.

The appeal in Jinesse's regard made Tharrick speak out at last. 'No.' He had worked himself to blisters seeing that brigantine launched. Respect before trust tempered his final decision. 'Dharkaron Avenger bear witness, you've treated me nothing but fairly. Betrayal of your interests will not be forthcoming from me.'

Arithon's taut brows lifted. He smiled. The one word of thanks, the banal platitude he instinctively avoided served to sharpen the impact of his pleasure. His honest emotion struck and shattered the reserve of the guardsman who had set out to wrong him.

Tharrick straightened his shoulders, restored to dignity and manhood.

Then the widow's shy nod of approval vaulted him on

to rash impulse. 'Don't scuttle the other brigantine. I could stay on, see her launched. If Alestron's galleys are delayed a few days, she could be jury-rigged out on a lugger's gear.'

Arithon pushed to his feet in astonishment. 'I would never on my life presume to ask so much!' He embarked on a scrutiny that seemed to burn Tharrick through to the marrow, then finally shrugged, embarrassed and caught at a loss. 'I need not give warning. You well know the odds you must face, and the risk.'

Tharrick agreed. 'I could fail.'

Arithon was curt. 'You could find yourself horribly compromised.' Small need to imagine how Duke Bransian might punish what would be seen as a second betrayal.

'Let me try,' the former guardsman begged. He suddenly felt the recovery of his honour hung on the strength of the sacrifice. 'I give you my oath, I'll do all I can to save what my pride set in jeopardy.'

'You'll not swear to me,' Arithon said, his rebuff fallen shy of the vehemence his cornered straits warranted. 'I'll be far offshore and beyond Lysaer's reach. No. If you swear, you'll bind your promise to the widow Jinesse. She's the only friend I have in this village who's chosen to stay with the risk of knowing my identity.'

'Demon!' Amazed to near anger by the trap that would hold him to the absolute letter of loyalty, Tharrick asked, 'Have you always weighed hearts like the Fatemaster?' For of all spirits living, he would not see the widow let down.

The white flash of a grin, as Arithon caught his hand in a firm clasp of amity. 'I judge no one. Your duke in Alestron was a man blind to merit. If the labourers in the yard will support your mad plan, I'd bless my good luck and be grateful.'

Sealed to undertake the adventure on a handshake, Tharrick stepped back. The Master of Shadow gave a nod in salute to Jinesse, who hung back in mute anguish by the hob. With no more farewell than that, he turned in neat grace toward the doorway.

Dakar heaved to his feet and followed after, plaintive and resigned as a cur snapped on a short leash. 'We could at least stay for supper,' he lamented. 'Jinesse spreads a much better table than you do.'

His entreaty raised no reply.

The last Merior saw of Rathain's prince was his spare silhouette as he launched *Talliarthe's* tiny dory against the silver-laced breakers on the strand. His bright, pealing laugh carried back through the rush of the tide's ebb.

'Very well, Dakar. I've laid in spirits to ease your sick stomach on the voyage. But you'll broach the cask *after* we've rowed to the mooring. Once aboard the sloop, you can drink yourself senseless. But damned if I'll strain myself hauling your deadweight over the rail on a halyard.'

Fugitives

The twins stowed away. No one discovered their absence until dawn, when the luggers sailed out to fish. By then, the bayside mooring that had secured the *Khetienn* bobbed empty. The line of the horizon cut the sea's edge in an unbroken band, Arithon's sloop *Talliarthe* long gone.

The widow's tearful questions raised no answers. No one had seen the children slip into the water by moonlight the previous night. No small, dripping forms had been noticed, climbing the wet length of a mooring chain, and no dory was missed from the beach.

'They could be anywhere,' Jinesse cried, her thin shoulders cradled in Tharrick's burly arms and her face pressed against his broad chest. Memories of Innish's quayside impelled her to jagged edged grief. 'Ten years of age is far too young to be out and about in the world.'

Tharrick stroked the blonde hair she had been too distraught to bind up. 'They're not alone,' he assured her. 'If they hid in the sloop, they'll come to no harm. Arithon cares for them like an older brother.'

'What if they stowed aboard the *Khetienn*?' Jinesse's

voice split. 'Ath preserve them, Southshire's a sailor's port! Even so young, Fiark could be snatched and sold to a trade galley! And Feylind –' She ran out of nerve to voice her anxieties over brothels.

'No.' Tharrick grasped her tighter and gave her a gentle shake. 'Arithon's two most trusted hands sailed with that brigantine. Think soundly! His discipline's forthright. His men fear his temper like Dharkaron himself, or believe this, I'd have found my throat slit on the first dark night since he freed me.'

Every labourer in the yard knew their master's fondness for the twins. The measure of his censure when rules were transgressed, or a mob grew unruly with drink, was an experience never to be forgotten. Arithon's response to Tharrick's rough handling had been roundly unpleasant, had left joiners twice his size and strength cowed and cringing. It would be worth a man's life to misuse the widow's children, or allow any harm to befall them.

While Jinesse's composure crumpled into sobs, Tharrick bundled her close and swept her out of the fog and back to the snug comfort of her cottage.

'It's eighty leagues overland to Southshire!' he cried as she lunged to snatch her shawl and chase the fish wagon. 'You won't make it off the Scimlade peninsula before that army's sealed the roads.'

Which facts held an unkindly truth. Made by plodding oxcart, such a journey would take weeks. A fishing lugger might reach the south-coast in a fortnight, but to seek out the *Khetienn* with an army infesting Alland was to jeopardize Arithon's anonymity. Jinesse sank down at her kitchen table, her face muffled in her hands and her shoulders bowed in despair. If the twins were away with the *Talliarthe*, their position with the Shadow Master would become the more endangered through a search to attempt their recovery.

Tharrick's large hands rubbed the nape of her neck. 'I

share your concern. You won't be alone. Once the little brigantine's launched, I'll take it upon myself to sail to Southshire.' The promise felt right, once made. 'Whether your young ones have gone there with *Khetienn*, or if they've thrust their bothersome presence upon Arithon, I'll track them both down and see them safe.'

The days after solstice passed in an agony of worry for Jinesse. She could not confide the extent of her distress to the villagers, who knew Arithon only as a respectable outsider with a talent for music and well-founded interests in shipbuilding.

The boardinghouse landlady awarded her moping short shrift. 'Yon man is no fool, never mind the fat drunk who keeps his company. He'll bring your twins back, well scolded and chastened, and they'll be none the worse for their escapade.'

Tharrick, who knew the dire facts behind her fear, lent whatever comfort he could. Through the labour that consumed him day and night at the shipyard, he took his meals at the widow's, and sat up over candlelight in the hours before dawn when the ceaseless tension spoiled her sleep.

They spoke of the lives they had led, Jinesse married to a man too spirited for her retiring nature to match, and the emptiness of the house since his boisterous presence had been claimed untimely by the sea. Tharrick sharpened her carving knives, flame light playing over knuckles grown scarred from his former years of armed service. The blades across the whetstone slid in natural habit, as sword steel often had before battle. Yet his voice held very little of regret as he talked about a girl who had married a rival, then the heartbreak that led him to enrol in the duke's guard. Summer campaigns against Kalesh or Adruin had kept him too busy for homelife after that.

They discussed the twins, who had inherited their father's penchant for wider horizons. Often as not, the conversation ended with the widow shedding tears on Tharrick's shoulder.

The shortened winter days passed in swift succession to the ring of caulker's hammers; and then in a rush that allowed neither respite nor relief, the small hull was complete and afloat. She was named the *Shearfast*. In a ferocious hurry that hazed the villagers to unease, the few men still employed at the shipyard fitted her out with the temporary masts and rigging to ready her for blue water.

The grey, rainy morning her sails were bent on, the first war galleys breasted the northern horizon.

Ashore, like wasps stirred up by the onset of cataclysm, the four hired men still caught on the Scimlade spit raced in grim haste to carry through their master's intent to fire what remained of his shipworks. Damp weather hampered them. Even splashed in pitch and turpentine, the thatch on the sheds was slow to catch. By the time the last outbuilding shot up in flames, the oncoming fleet drew in close. The eye could distinguish their banners and blazons, the devices of Avenor and Alestron in stitched gold, on fields red as rage, and ice blue. The clarion cry of trumpets and shouted orders from the officers pealed over the wind-borne boom of drums. The oarsmen on the galleys quickened stroke to battle speed, thrashing spray in cold drifts on the gusts.

Thigh-deep by the shoreline with a longboat held braced against the combers, the nimble little sailhand hired in to captain *Shearfast* screamed to hurry the men who sprinted down the strand and threw themselves splashing through the shallows. Tharrick had time to notice the widow's forlorn figure, bundled in black shawls by the dunes, as he hurled himself over the gunwales and grabbed up oars.

He knew Jinesse well enough to guess the depth of her misery, and to ache in raw certainty she was weeping.

'Stroke!' yelled the grizzled captain. He balanced like a monkey in the stern seat as the longboat surged ahead to the timed dig of her crew. 'Didn't flay my damned knuckles patching leftover canvas to see our spars get flamed in the cove!'

A crewman who muscled the craft toward deep water cursed a skinned wrist, then flung a harried look behind. The galleys had gained with a speed that left him wide-eyed. 'Must have demons rowing.'

Tharrick dragged hard on his loom. 'Those are Duke Bransian's warships. His oarsmen won't be a whipped bunch of convicts, but mercenaries standing short shifts.'

'Rot them,' the hired captain gasped through snatched breaths. 'Just row and beg luck sends a squall line.'

The newly launched hull wore a lugger's rig. In dimmed visibility, half-seen through dirty weather, she might be passed over as a fishing craft. Distance offered a slim hope to save her. Once she lay hull down over the horizon, the duke's fleet would see scant reason to turn and pursue what would look like a hard-run fishing smack.

Tharrick shut his eyes and threw all his weight into the pull of his oar. Better than his fugitive companions, he knew the efficiency of Alestron's training and assault tactics. Cold horror spurred his incentive. He might suffer a fate more ruinous than flogging should his former commanders retake him. This time he would be caught beyond doubt in collusion with Arithon s'Ffalenn.

By the time the longboat slewed under the *Shearfast*'s sleek side, the burn scars on Tharrick's palms were broken open with blisters. He winced through the sting as he clambered on board, then snarled curses with the seamen as he shouldered his share and caught hemp slivers hauling on halyards. The temporary masts carried no head-sails, only two yards rigged fore and aft with an unwieldy, loose-footed lugsail. The sorry old canvas made over from a wreck was patched and dingy with mildew.

The captain summed up *Shearfast*'s prospects with language that damned in rich epithets. 'Bitch'll hide herself roundly in a fogbank or storm, but lumber like a spitted pig to weather. Shame that. Hull's built on glorious lines. Rig her out decent, she'd fly.'

'She'll need to fly,' groused the deckhand who returned at speed from unshackling the mooring chain. 'They're onto us, busy as sharks to bloody meat.'

As the yards were hauled around squealing to brace full to the wind, Tharrick saw the oncoming galleys deploy in smooth formation, one group to give chase and harry, and a second to turn wide and flank them. In a straight race of speed, *Shearfast* was outmatched.

The grizzled little captain bounded aft to the helm, a whipstaff that, given time and skilled carpentry, would be replaced by cables and wheel. 'We've got one advantage,' he said, then spat across the rail in madcap malice. 'We know the reefs. They don't. Fiends take the hindmost. Stay their course to sound the mark, and they've lost us.'

Wind cracked loose canvas, then kicked sails in taut curves with a whump. *Shearfast* bore off and gathered way, a pressure wave of wrinkled water forced against her lee strakes as the lugsails began sluggishly to draw. The quiet, cove harbour of Merior fell behind, while east gusts spat rain through the rigging. Tharrick did not look back, nor allow himself to think of other chases in the past, when he had held a captaincy among the troops aboard the galleys.

A hare before wolves, *Shearfast* wore ship and spread her patched rig on a reach to drive downcoast. The men Arithon had entrusted to crew his last vessel owned the nerve to stand down Dharkaron's Chariot. On guts and desperation, they shouldered the challenge of an untried hull, shook her down in an ill-balanced marriage with ungainly sails, set at odds with her keel and the free-running grace of her lines. The drag of the whipstaff to hold her on course would have daunted the strength of most helmsmen. Her captain bared teeth and muscled her brute pull. Mastered through wits and determination, and an unerring gut instinct for seamanship, *Shearfast* danced a dainty course through the reefs. She flirted with the wind and courted the lee shore like a rich maid in rags, caught slumming in dangerous company.

Behind her, voracious, the galleys chewed away her lead in a flying white thrash of timed oars.

The first of them ran aground on a coral head in a grinding, grating screech of smashed timbers. Like a back-broken insect, her looms waved and splashed in clacking disunity, then snarled in misdirected stroke. Shouts re-echoed across the open water. A bugle wailed a frantic call for aid.

'Hah!' *Shearfast*'s captain loosed a wicked laugh. 'There's one belly-up and another bogged down to tend her.'

In the waist, the one crewman not busy easing sheet-lines strung a bow and began wrapping tips onto fire arrows. His stripped palms bound in cloth, Tharrick passed lint and short lengths of twine to tie the wisps in place. Fitful drizzle added drops to the sweat misted over his face. Cold water fingered runnels down his collar. He leaned to the buck of the deck. The captain steered to headings as gnarled and tortuous as any chased prey, with the galleys relentlessly gaining.

A curtain of rainfall dusted hazed mercury over the narrowing span of sea left between them. The captain shot a hurried, wild glance at the clouds, leaden and low-bellied as a strumpet's hiked petticoats above the snapped crests of the whitecaps. The squall which struck now would bring no salvation. Any gain through reduced visibility would come offset by increased risk. Under-waters frayed to froth by driving bands of precipitation, the reefs *Shearfast* skirted would be treacherously hidden, the greener shallows that warned of submerged sandbars and coral hammered out into uniform grey.

Rising winds slewed and heeled her, close-hauled. The heavy, broad lugsails made her sloppy, and the rooster tails clawed by sideslip at each gust showed the *Shearfast* could not maintain leeway against the coast. The mazed shoals that granted her marginal protection would turn forces and present renewed hazard. If she wrecked or ran aground, no man aboard held false hope. To be stranded ashore was to die, first run down by tracking dogs, then butchered on the swords of Skannt's headhunters.

A second galley struck with a thud against a sandbar, this one near enough to savour the chaos as the consternation of her crewmen resounded in shrill oaths across the water. A horn pealed in warning. The ship just behind her backwatered her stroke, then glanced off her exposed side in screaming collision. Oarshafts sheared off, to the cries of crushed men as leaded beech stove their chests like so many rows of burst barrels. Blood painted streaks down the oarports, and the drummers abandoned their beat.

'Just hope she's beached hard enough they'll lighten the chase manning windlasses and kedging her off,' said the captain, licking salt off his teeth in a bent of incurable optimism.

Of fifteen galleys packed with troops that converged to tear into *Shearfast*, three left disabled was scarcely a change in bad odds.

'Well, what good is moping,' snapped the captain to the crewman who pointed this out. 'Have to find some joy to cheer about. Not for any stinking galleyman's fun will I pass the Fatemaster's Wheel with a stupid, glum look on my mug.'

The pursuit had slowed behind, fleet captains warned by the two crippled vessels to thread the narrow channel with more care; the strike force split off on an oblique angle to flank and then intercept were far enough away that the blurring, heavy deluge had dulled their rapacious outlines.

'I'd take that squall now and chance the damned reefs,' confided one crewman to Tharrick above the hissed spray off the waves.

In blind answer, the cloudburst redoubled and drummed the decks silver. For the first moment since the galleys turned their course to give chase, there seemed a faint glimmer of hope.

Then a horn call blared above the thunder of strained canvas. Through splashing spindrift thrown off the forecastle, a shouted challenge hailed the *Shearfast*. 'Heave to and surrender all hands!'

'Over my still bleedin' carcass,' cracked Arithon's game captain from the helm. 'Old storm's going to hide us, and those poor harried bastards hard-set on our tail have to know it.' He yelled for the men at the braces to belay their lines and move forward. 'Jump lively! I want bearings on every shoal you can see off our bow.'

Even as the pair raced up the forward companionway, a light bolt arced out. It scribed from the rambade of the hindmost galley, a line that unreeled like incandescent wire to a shriek of hissed protest through the thickened fall of rain.

'It's the Prince of the West, curse him!' *Shearfast*'s helmsman dragged the whipstaff alee in last-ditch, defiant evasion.

The vessel slewed, mired by her yards and too sluggish. Lysaer's light-cast assault struck the straining canvas of the stern lugsail and seeded a starburst of fire.

The foresail still left whole to draw wind veered the *Shearfast* off heading to starboard, and stempost and rudder and the timbers of her quarter slammed with a crunch into coral. Sparks showered the deck and spat answering flame from fresh oakum. Then the evil, swollen clouds opened up and unburdened. The downpour unleashed in a thundering cascade and thrashed out the burgeoning conflagration.

Through smoke and white water, the captain leaped from the helm, one arm pressed to bruised ribs. The whipstaff had taken charge upon impact and dealt him a buffeting clout. Half-stunned and labouring, he grunted phrases of blistering invective. Then, above the whining howl of wind and the battering of the squall, he dispatched swift instructions to his men. 'She's a loss! No use but to fire her, and damn the weather now. We'll have to use pitch flares and torch her sorry timbers belowdecks.'

Tharrick stumbled as a crewman blundered into him and shoved the guard of a cutlass in his hand. 'You'll need this. It'll be hand-to-hand when they board us. Do as you like for yourself. The rest of us agree, we don't fancy being taken alive.'

Appalled to chills through the cataract of water, Tharrick shouted, 'Ath in his pity! The duke's men aren't merciful, but hope isn't lost. While the hull burns, the storm could still hide your escape.'

The sailhand paused, eyes narrowed with anger. 'Won't risk a capture. I'd rather die fighting on open water then running like a dog through the briar.'

'If you had cover,' Tharrick broke in, 'if I gave you the means to delay them, you might row for the beachhead. Claim sanctuary at the hostel of Ath's Brotherhood and no enemy of Arithon's could touch you.'

'Speak your piece and fast,' snapped the captain, arrived that moment in the waist. 'We have only minutes. I'll burn this blighted vessel to her waterline with all of us aboard before she's risked to enemies as a prize.'

So simple, Tharrick thought; the hoodwink he

proposed should be obvious. He steeled his resolve and explained. 'I was the duke's man. I wrecked your master's shipyard. Who could believe I would be here alive, except as Arithon's bound prisoner?'

'Right, aye.' The captain grinned through the stumps of front teeth, chipped in some past scrap in a brothel. His levity faded. 'Ye'd do this for us? It's fair risky. The hull's to be left blazing regardless.'

'Do it.' Tharrick forced reason over fear, though his nerves felt dissolved into jelly. 'Who's to know my loyalty ever changed? If the duke's men find me before I burn, there's every likely chance I can mislead them long enough for the Brotherhood to grant you Ath's protection.'

'Right aye, belowdecks we go, then.' The captain snapped out his rigging knife and slashed off a sheetline for binding the volunteer victim. Like all blue-water seamen, he could tie knots in his sleep. Over his ongoing rattle of orders, and the crackle of pitch flares, and the hellish, drowning pound of rain on wooden decking, Tharrick found himself thrust down a companionway and lashed in total helplessness to a hatch ring over his head.

'All right, listen up!' cracked the captain. 'I stay, and one other. We'll draw straws to see who bids for shore leave.'

Tharrick voiced an immediate protest, cut silent as the captain yanked the sash off his waist to twist into use as a gag. 'There has to be a sacrifice,' he said as he tied off the cloth in desperation. 'If we leave an empty ship, your place will be questioned. Then they're sure to mount a search for survivors.'

A brisk hand clapped his shoulder, while the sailhands drew lots for the longboat. 'Off we go, mate, and Dharkaron avenge.' The captain threw Tharrick a bright-eyed, fierce wink. 'We'll send prayers from Ath's sanctuary, and me from past the Wheel. Bless you for bravery. It's grand luck ye'll need. Ye've charted fair course fer bad waters.'

Shearfast's crewman raced light-footed from the hold. Behind, for cold necessity, they left the whispered lick of flame and a poisonous, pitch-fed haze of smoke. Tharrick coughed. His throat closed and his eyes ran. The thick fumes sickened him to dizziness. He felt as though he were falling headlong through the very gates of Sithaer. Driven senseless by the metallic taste of fear, dazed beyond reason by poisoned air, he did not remember giving way to terrified screams, muffled to whimpers by the gag. Nor did he keep any shred of raw courage as he wrenched like a beast at the rope ties.

Awareness became wrapped in an inferno. Skin knew again the blistering kiss of agony as the red snap of fire chewed through the planks overhead. The thumps of a distant scuffle made no sense, nor the mazed clang of steel, followed by the defiant last shout of the gamecock captain. 'Kill the prisoner!'

The cry that bought Tharrick his chance for salvation rang through the steel clash of weapons. A fallen body thudded, kicking in nerve-fired death throes. Then a dying man choked out a rattling gasp and slammed through the companionway door, the blade through his chest a glistening reflection doused in fresh running blood.

'Merciful Ath, hurry on!' someone cried with the bite of authority. 'They've got some wretch lashed in the hold!'

Two officers in gold braid kicked past the downed corpse. They staggered across canted decking and barked into bulkheads, fumbling through the murky, coiled smoke to cut his bonds. Tharrick scarcely felt the hands that grasped and steadied him onto his feet. Cramped double and choking, he lost consciousness as they dragged him like a gutted fish up a reeling companion-way into clear air and rainfall.

Whether he lay in the hands of the duke's officers or those of the Prince of the West, he had no awareness left to care.

Landfall

Lysaer s'Ilessid set foot on the damp sands of Merior, still dissatisfied over the report sent back from the galley which had run down the fugitive vessel. Of an unknown number of enemy crewmen, two had been slain in the mêlée of boarding. The sole survivor brought back for questioning was himself a prisoner of the Shadow Master, notched in scars from recent cruel handling, and unconscious from fresh burns and smoke poisoning.

Duke Bransian's crack captains had been too busy sparing the one life to mount a search of the waters for longboats.

Thwarted from gaining the informant he required to dog his enemy's trail, Lysaer clenched his jaw to rein back a savage bout of temper. Since the strike force under his personal banner was land-bound to close off the peninsula, Alestron's mercenaries had done the boarding, a setback he lacked sovereignty to reverse. His own officers had been trained on no uncertain terms to expect the vicious style of Arithon's pirate forebears. Seldom, if ever, had the men they commanded surrendered their vessels with crewmen still alive to be captured.

A salt-laden gust parted Lysaer's fair hair as he trained

his stormy regard up the beachhead. The rain had stopped. Mid-afternoon light shafted through broken clouds. The puddles wore a leaden sheen, and a shimmer of dipped silver played over the drenched crowns of the palm groves. Nestled in gloom as though uninhabited, the whitewashed cottages of Merior greeted his landing with wooden plank doors and pegged shutters shut fast.

The harbour stretched grey and empty as the land, choppy waters peppered with vacant moorings. The local fishing fleet would return with the dusk, as on any ordinary day. Up the strand, a sullen, black streamer of smoke spiralled on the wind from the site of Arithon's shipyard. No fugitives had sought to cross the cordon of mercenaries that blocked Scimlade Tip from the mainland; the single lugger found setting fish traps in the bay had offered no hostilities when flagged down for questioning.

The name of the Master of Shadow had drawn a blank reaction from the crew. Also from every man and woman in the trade port of Shaddorn to the south, that advance scouts had waylaid for inquiry.

'I wonder how long he prepared for our coming?' Lysaer mused as Diegan strode up behind him.

The Lord Commander's best boots were soaked from the landing, his demeanour as bleak as the surrounding landscape above chain mail and black-trimmed surcoat. 'You know we won't find anything. The shipworks will be a gutted ruin.'

A thorough search was conducted anyway, a party of foot troops sent to poke through the steaming embers of collapsed sheds under Diegan's direction. Lysaer waited to one side, his royal finery concealed beneath a seaman's borrowed oilskins, while the breakers rolled and boomed in sullen rhythm against the headland and the wind riffled wrinkles in the puddles.

'The withdrawal was well planned,' Avenor's Lord Commander confirmed at length. 'No tools were abandoned. These buildings were emptied before they were fired. We can send officers house to house through Merior all you like, but I'd lay sand to diamonds that Arithon left nothing to clue us of his intentions.'

Lysaer kicked the charred fragment of a corner post amid the rubble that remained of the sail loft. Scarcely audible, he said, 'He left the village.'

'You think he'll be back?' Prepared to disagree, Diegan pushed up his helm to scrape his damp hair off his brow.

'No.' Lysaer spun in a flapping storm of oilcloth and stalked to the edge of the tidemark. 'The fugitive ship which burned before our eyes was the easiest chance we had to track him. Now that option's lost, he'll have the whole ocean in which to take cover. We're balked, but not crippled. The stamp of his design can never be mistaken for merchant shipping. Wherever the Shadow Master plans to make landfall, I'll find the means to be waiting.'

At twilight, when the fishing luggers sailed homeward to find their cove patrolled by war galleys and their shores cluttered with encampments of mercenaries, knots of shouting men and a congregation of goodwives converged upon the beaten earth of the fish market. A groomed contingent of Avenor's senior officers turned out and met them to assure their prince would answer their complaints. By the fluttered, ruddy light of pitch torches, on a dais constructed of fish barrels and planks, the Prince of the West awaited in a surcoat edged in braided bullion. In token of royal rank he wore only a gold circlet. Against all advice, he was not armed. His bodyguard remained with the longboats, and only Alestron's fleet admiral and two officers attended at his right hand.

Lord Diegan stood at the edge of the crowd. Surrounded by a plainly clad cadre of men-at-arms, his strict orders were to observe without interference. The restraint left him uneasy since the crowd showed defiance. Grumbles from the fringes held distinct, unfriendly overtones concerning the presumption of outsiders.

Lysaer gave such talk small chance to blossom into strife. 'We are gathered here to begin a celebration,' he announced.

The background buzz of speculation choked off in stiff outrage. 'Yer war galleys scarcely be welcomed here!' cried one of the elders from the boardinghouse.

Other men called gruff agreement. Lysaer waited them out in elegant stillness while the piped cry of a killdeer sliced the soughing snap of the torch flames, and the air pressed rain-laden gusts to flap sullen folds in the standards of Alestron and Avenor that flanked his commanding stance upon the dais. 'The cask for the occasion shall be provided from my stores.'

'We had peace before ye set foot here!' called a goodwife. 'When our fish wagon to Shaddorn's turned back by armed troops, I'd say that's muckle poor cause for dancing!'

Again Lysaer waited for the shouts to die down. 'Your village has just been spared from the designs of great evil, and the grasp of a man of such resource and cunning, none here could know the extent of his ill intentions. I speak of the one you call Arithon, known in the north as Teir's'Ffalenn and the Master of Shadow.'

This time when hubbub arose, Lysaer cut clearly through the clamour. 'During his years among you, he has exploited your trust, lured blameless craftsmen into dishonest service, and spent stolen funds to outfit a fleet designed and intended for piracy. I'm here tonight to expose his bloody history, and to dispel without question every doubt to be raised against the criminal intent he sought to hide.'

The quiet at this grew profound. Muscular men in

patched oilskins and their goodwives in their aprons spangled with cod scales packed into a solid and threatening body. Before the ranks of inimical faces, Lysaer resumed unperturbed. In clear, magisterial elegance, he presented his case, beginning with the wrongs done his family on his homeworld of Dascen Elur. There, the s'Ffalenn bent for sea raids had been documented by royal magistrates for seven generations. The toll of damaged lives was impressive. Stirred to forceful resolve, the fair-haired prince related his eyewitness account of the slaughter at Deshir Forest. Other transgressions at Jaelot and Alestron were confirmed by Duke Bransian's officer. He ended with the broad-scale act of destruction which had torched the trade fleet at Minderl Bay.

The villagers remained unconvinced.

A few in the front ranks crossed their arms in disgust, unimpressed with foreign news that held little bearing upon the daily concerns of their fishing fleet.

'Is it possible you think the man who sheltered here was not one and the same person?' Lysaer asked. 'Let me say why that fails to surprise me.' He went on to describe the Shadow Master's appearance and habits in a damning array of detail. He spoke of innocents diabolically corrupted, small children taught to cut the throats of the wounded lying helpless in their blood on the field. His description was dire and graphic enough to wring any parent to distress.

Before Lysaer's forthright and painful self-honesty, Arithon, in retrospect, seemed shady as a night thief. Natural reticence felt like dishonest concealment, and leashed emotion, the mark of a cold, scheming mind.

'This is a man whose kindness is drawn in sharp calculation, whose every word and act masks a hidden motive. Pity does not move him. His code is base deceit. The people he befriends are as game pieces, and if violent death suits the stripe of his design, not even babes are exempt.'

'Now that's a foul lie!' objected the boardinghouse landlady. 'The shipyard master we knew here had as much compassion for children as any man gifted with fatherhood. The young ones adored him. Jinesse there will say as much.'

Lysaer focused where the matron pointed, and picked out the figure in the dark shawl who shrank at the mention of her name: a woman on the fringes, faceless in the gloom except for the wheaten coil of hair pinned over her blurred, oval features.

'Lady, come here,' Lysaer commanded. He stepped down from the dais. His instinctive, lordly grace caused the villagers to part and give him way. At her evident reluctance, he waved to his officer to unsocket a torch and bring it forward. Trapped isolate amid a sudden, brilliant ring of light, the widow could do naught else but confront him.

Golden, majestic, the Prince of the West did not address her on the level of the crowd. He caught her bird-boned hand in a sure, warm grip, and as if she were wellborn and precious, drew her up the plank step to the dais. He gave her no chance for embarrassed recrimination. His gaze, blue as unflawed sky, stayed direct and fixed on her face. 'I'm grieved indeed to see a man with no scruples delude an upright goodwife such as you.'

Jinesse heaved a tight breath, her fingers grown damp and starting to tremble. She searched the heart-stopping, beautiful male features beneath the circlet and cap of pale hair. She found no reassurance, no trace of the charlatan in the square, honest line of his jaw and the sculptured slope of his cheekbones. His unclouded eyes reflected back calm concern and unimpeachable sincerity.

'Forgive me,' said the prince in a gentleness very different than the mettlesome, biting irony of the Shadow Master. 'I see I've struck hurtfully close to the mark. I never intended to grieve you.'

Jinesse pushed away the uneasy recollection of green eyes, heavy with shadows too impenetrably deep to yield their mystery. 'Master Arithon showed only kindness to my twins. I cannot believe he'd cause them harm.'

'Young children?' Lysaer probed. 'Lady, hear my warning, Arithon's past is a history of misdirection. He may indeed have shown only his finest intentions in your presence. But where are your little ones now?' Informed by the small jerk of the hand he still clasped, Lysaer returned a squeeze of commiseration. 'The man has succeeded in luring your offspring from your side, I see. You were very right to say children love him. They are as clay in his hands. I can see I need not say more.'

Jinesse clenched her lip to stop a fierce quiver. She did not trust herself to speak.

'It may not be too late,' the prince reassured, his voice pitched as well for the villagers gathered beneath the dais. The people, all unwitting, had crowded closer to hang on each word as he spoke. 'I have an army and Alestron's fleet of war galleys. We are highly mobile, well supplied, and most able to mount swift pursuit. I only need know where the Master of Shadow has gone. Prompt action could restore your lost twins to your side.'

Jinesse recovered the courage to draw back. 'What you offer is a war! That could as easily drown them in Ath's oceans to share a grave in the deeps with their father.'

'Perhaps,' Lysaer said equably. 'Would you rather Dharkaron Avenger should meet and judge their spirits first? If the Wheel's turning took them in some machination of the Shadow Master's, they could find their damnation as well.'

'How dramatic,' Jinesse said in a stiff-backed distaste that deplored his choice of public venue. 'We've known Arithon as a fair-minded man for the better part of a year. On your word, in just one afternoon, we're to accept the greater mercy of your judgment?'

Yet her composure crumbled just enough for Lysaer

to glean a ruler's insight: if the villagers of Merior had sheltered Arithon in ignorance, this one woman had been aware of his identity beforetime. An added depth of grief pinched her features as she challenged, 'What of the crew who manned the *Shearfast*? Where was your vaunted pity when your galleys ran them down and let them burn?'

'Your husband was aboard?' Lysaer probed softly.

Jinesse jerked her fingers from his clasp. Her wide-eyed flash of resentment transformed to dismay as she spun and flounced off of the dais.

'Go with her,' Lysaer said in swift order to the officer at the base of the stair. 'See her home safely and stay there until I can send someone to console her. There were survivors from that vessel. I don't know how many, but her loved one could possibly be among them.'

Mollified by the kindness shown to one of their own, the villagers of Merior gave way to a grudging, gruff patience as Lysaer concluded his speech. 'I've scarcely touched on the danger this conniving pirate presents. If you never saw him work shadows or sorcery, you will be shown that his gifts are no tale without substance. Among you stand my officers, who saw the sunlight over Minderl Bay become strangled into darkness. They will stay and hear your questions. Lord Diegan will tell of the massacre he survived on the banks of Tal Quorin in Deshir. We have a man from Jaelot and another from Alestron, who witnessed the felonies there. But lest what they say turn your hearts to rank fear, I would have you understand you're not alone.'

Lysaer raised his arms. His full, embroidered sleeves fell away from his wrists as he stretched his hands wide and summoned the powers of his birth gift. A flood of golden light washed the fish market. It rinsed through the flames in the torches, and built, blinding, dazzling, until the eye could not separate the figure of the prince from the overwhelming, miraculous glare.

Lysaer's voice rolled over the dismayed gasps of the awestruck fisherfolk at his feet. 'My gift of light is a full match for the Master of Shadow! Be assured I shall not rest until this land is safe, and his evil designs are eradicated.'

From the boardinghouse landlady, who called with a basket of scones, Jinesse learned how opinion had turned once Prince Lysaer had left the villagers to enjoy his hospitality. The beer and the wine had flowed freely, while talk loosened. The old gossip concerning the *Black Drake* and the widow's past voyage on *Talliarthe* were resurrected and bandied about with fresh fervour. Most telling of all was Arithon's reticence. The fact he had no confidant, that he never shared the least clue to his intentions became the most damning fact against him. Paired with first-hand accounts of his atrocities in the north, such self-possessed privacy in hindsight became the quiet of a secret, scheming mind.

By roundabout means, the landlady reached the news she had been appointed to deliver. 'When the galley's crew boarded and took *Shearfast*, they insist only two of Arithon's sailors met them. Those refused quarter and fought to the death, but not to save their command. They had already fired the new hull to scuttle her. Despite the flames, the duke's officers searched the hold. They found a bound man held captive below decks. He was cut loose while unconscious, and is now in the care of Prince Lysaer's personal healer.'

Jinesse looked up from the skirt she had been mending, her needle poised at an agonized angle between stitches she had jerked much too tight. The name of Tharrick hung unspoken as she said, 'But Arithon kept no one prisoner.'

The boardinghouse landlady sniffed and drizzled honey over one of the pastries. 'I said so. The Prince of the West showed no opinion on the matter, but looked me through as though I were a child in sad want of wisdom.'

Unbleached homespun crumpled under Jinesse's knuckles. She, too, kept her thoughts to herself. For the ruinous delay which Tharrick's retribution had inflicted on the works at the shipyard, it seemed entirely plausible that *Shearfast*'s doomed crew might have seized their belated revenge. To ask the next question required all the courage she possessed. 'What did you say to his Grace?'

'Why, nothing.' The landlady flicked crumbs from her blouse and gave a shrug as dour as a fisherman's. 'Let these outsiders untangle their own misadventures. We're not traderfolk, to hang our daily lives upon rumours. The mackerel won't swim to the net any better should we buy and sell talk like informants. If Arithon's evil, that's his own affair. He tried no foul acts in our village.' But her forceful, brusque note as she ended spoke of doubts irrevocably seeded.

The landlady folded the linen she had used to pack the scones. 'With only two bodies found to be counted, Prince Lysaer wished you to hear there may have been other survivors.' As she arose and smoothed her skirts over her ample thighs, she added on afterthought, 'His Grace seems anxious to know the number of *Shearfast*'s crew. They were Arithon's people, I told him.'

Miserable and mute, Jinesse watched the other woman sweep past the pantry to let herself out. Paused at the threshold on departure, her full-lipped, cattiest smile as much for Lysaer's young officer, listening at his post outside the doorway, the landlady concluded her last line. 'I said, why ever should we care?'

The following morning, the Prince of the West presented himself at the widow's cottage for a visit. By then, he had made enough inquiries to know that her husband had drowned a year past in a fishing accident. Whatever her attachment to the men who had crewed the lost *Shearfast*, he came prepared to treat her grief with compassion. As his escort, he brought a pair of neatly appointed guardsmen to relieve the one on duty in the yard.

The elegance and manners of old blood royalty should not have upset her poise, Jinesse thought. Arithon's disconcerting, satirical directness had never made her feel embarrassed for unrefined origins, nor had his bearing afflicted her with apologetic confusion over whether or not she should curtsy.

Resplendent in glossy silk, and a chain of gold and matched sapphires, Lysaer stepped across the waxed boards of her parlour and caught her chapped fingers away from her habitual urge to fidget. 'Come sit,' he insisted.

He spun her gently to a chair. The shutters on the window were latched against the morning, the gloom pricked by leaked light through the cracks where the wood was poorly fitted. Clad in dark skirts and a laced bodice of brown twill, Jinesse looked more faded than usual. Her cheeks were drawn and her eyes as tintless as the palest aquamarine.

Memories of another prince in rough linen who had set her just as deftly on a woodpile dogged her thoughts as she sought once again to plumb royal character through a face. Where Arithon had shown her discomfiting reticence and a perception forthright enough to wound, Prince Lysaer seemed candid and direct as clear sunlight. His dress was rich without being ostentatious. The breathtaking effect of overpowering male beauty he countered in personal warmth that lent an effect no less awesome.

The study he flicked over the room's rude interior held detached interest, until the fired glitter of the fine, cut glass bowl on her dish shelves snagged his interest. His surprise was genuine as he crossed the room on a stride. The sculpted shape of his hand bore an uncanny resemblance to Arithon's as he lifted the Falgaire crystal from the shelf.

'Where did you get this?'

Jinesse's answer was cold. 'I received it as a present from a friend.'

Lysaer recrossed the floor, set the bowl on the chest by the window, then unlatched and flung wide the shutters. Sunlight streamed in, and the salt scent of breakers, cut by the shrill calls of the gulls. The facets of the crystal responded in an incandescent flare of captured brilliance.

'A lovely gift, Falgaire glasswork,' Lysaer said. He found the battered stool the twins liked for whittling and perched. 'I shan't hide the truth. I know you accepted this bowl from Arithon s'Ffalenn, though no doubt you would have declined his generosity had you known where he first obtained it.'

When Jinesse did not favour him with more than her stony-eyed quiet, Lysaer sighed and fingered the faceted rim. Broken light caught in the jewels of his rings, an icy point of cold at each knuckle. 'I know this piece well. It was granted to me during a state visit by the Mayor of Falgaire, then stolen in a raid by barbarians allied with the Shadow Master. You would do well to take heed. The man is a threat to every city in Athera, your own children even now at his mercy. You knew him well enough to receive his favour. Perhaps you also heard the name of the port that will come to shelter him next. Were this campaign in sole charge of Duke Bransian of Alestron, or my Commander-at-Arms, Lord Diegan, either one would use means to force the information from you. I shall give no such orders. Your collusion is a tragedy and I pity your twins. But I shall not try abuse to gain my ends. Your Master of Shadow held no such scruple with the man he took prisoner, who claims to have fired his shipyard.'

'Arithon kept no one captive,' Jinesse insisted.

Lysaer did not miss how her gaze stayed averted from the bowl. 'That's a falsehood most easily disproved. The wretch we saved off the *Shearfast* was left bound there to burn. Once we got him cleaned up, he was recognized as a former captain of Duke Bransian's, who had reason to bear malice toward your Master.'

'Why not go back and question him?' Jinesse said, a struck spark of iron in her tone.

Lysaer met her with patience. 'When the victim regained his wits, he talked well enough. He said he had torched the s'Ffalenn shipworks, and for that, suffered rough interrogation. The scars on his body attest his honesty.'

'Arithon never beat him,' Jinesse said.

'No.' Lysaer regarded her in level, brutal truth. 'Alestron's officers did that for what looks like mishandled justice. What Captain Tharrick received from your Shadow Master were burns, inflicted with a knife blade heated red-hot, then assault with a bludgeon that left knots in his sides from broken ribs. Not pretty,' he finished. 'The additional blistering he suffered from the flames before he was rescued from *Shearfast* cause him pain aboard an anchored galley. My healer says he needs stillness and rest. Therefore, I came to beg your charity. Let Tharrick come to your cottage to recover from his injuries. My servant will be sent to administer remedies as needed. After seeing this man's condition first-hand, you may reconsider your opinion on the criminal your silence comes to shelter.'

Too upright to feign horror, since every mark on Tharrick's body was already infinitely well known to her, Jinesse sat braced in her chair. The depths of her feelings stayed masked behind acid and painful politeness. 'Bring your injured man here. I refuse none in need. But lest you hope falsely, my kindness to an outsider will lend no more credence to your plotting.'

'Very well.' Lysaer stood in a frosty sparkle of disturbed gemstones. 'I see I've upset you. That was necessary. My concern for the dangers you refuse to acknowledge is no light matter for dismissal. Two of my guards will stand watch at your door. Having suffered the tragic consequences of s'Ffalenn cunning all my life, I realize the allure he can foster. Knowing, I stake no less than my personal assurance of your safety.'

'I wish no protection,' Jinesse said, obstinate.

Lysaer inclined his head in regal sympathy. 'I can hope you'll reconsider, if only to help your lost children. Have no fear. The ones in the village who disagree with your stand shall not be permitted to badger you. Should you wish to confide in me, you have only to send one of the men-at-arms. Rest assured, mistress, I will come.'

On the instant the Prince of the West had departed, Jinesse took the offending bowl of Falgaire crystal and shut it away in a clothes trunk. She banged the catch down and sat on the lid, then buried her face in her shaking hands and wept in painful relief.

Tharrick had survived the wreck of *Shearfast*.

By a stunning twist of fate, a misapprehension, and the sort of tangled handling Arithon left like moiled waters in his wake, Lysaer s'Ilessid meant to send him here, ostensibly to undermine her prior loyalties.

The sob in her throat twisted to a stifled gasp of irony. In fact, Tharrick under her roof would but tighten the villagers' resistance. They might have betrayed the exiled captain's collaboration with Arithon while he was aboard Lysaer's galley, but under her roof, he became as one of their own. Whatever ill intent they came to believe of the Shadow Master, Tharrick's interests would suffer no immediate betrayal.

The procession to deliver the invalid to her cottage arrived in the early afternoon. Jinesse had the bed in her

104

back room made up in clean linens to receive him. A brisk hour in the kitchen over pans of hot water and recipes for herbal poultices convinced the prince's physician that she was well versed in the treatment of burns. An indolent man and a scholar by nature, he was content to leave the convalescent in her care. Her dislike of outsiders left him distinctly unwelcome. He would check in, he assured, every few days to see that Tharrick's weals closed cleanly.

The litter bearers left, cracking crude jokes and laughing through the winter twilight that mantled pearly mist over the beachhead of Merior. As Jinesse closed the shutters against the sea damp and set about the chore of lighting candles, Tharrick stirred from the heavy sleep of drugged possets. He opened his eyes to the familiar sight of a pale-haired wraith of a woman with a profile like clear wax, underlit by the flutter of a tallow dip.

She saw him come aware. A still, pretty smile raised the corners of her mouth as she reached out to smooth the singed ends of his hair over his bandaged forehead. 'Don't speak.' Her look warned him silent as she whispered, 'Lysaer's men-at-arms wait without.'

Tharrick closed his eyes, unsure how he had come to be returned to the widow's care, but grateful for the comfort of her presence. That her cottage was kept under watch was not hard to believe. Lysaer and his officers had been demanding in their efforts at interrogation. Passion and urgency had driven them to dig for any clue to Arithon's intentions and location. Tharrick had withstood their pity and their blandishments. He had sweated in his sheets through their threats, and repeated himself unto tedium. His ignorance was no lie. Only the *Shearfast*'s dead captain had known their intended port of call.

Now, restored to friendly surroundings and the outward illusion of safety, necessity came hard to maintain the act that he and the widow were strangers.

Late in the night, when the thud of the breakers thrashed the spit at flood tide, Jinesse came to his darkened bedside. She brought water as she had when he was Arithon's charge, and tucked in the bedding tossed awry in his suffering.

'Do you believe the Prince of the West?' she demanded point-blank at a whisper. Fresh in her mind lay the morning's trip to the market, where a neighbour had refused to sell her eggs. Another wife pointed and insisted that she was a creature enspelled, drawn into wickedness to abet the Master of Shadow.

Tharrick studied the edge of her profile, printed in moonlight against the outlines of gauzy, high-flying clouds. 'That Prince Arithon is evil? Or that he's guilty of criminal acts in the north?'

The crash of the surf masked their voices. Jinesse bent her neck, her features blocked in sudden dimness. 'You feel there's distinction?'

Tharrick stirred from discomfort that had little to do with blistered skin. 'The accusations fit too well to deny. Don't forget, I saw what he caused at Alestron.'

'You'll betray him,' Jinesse said.

'I ought to.' Tharrick shoved aside the corner of the coverlet and reached out a wrapped hand to cup her knee. 'I won't.' Aware of her porcelain fairness turned toward him, he swallowed. 'Corrupt, evil, sorcerer he may be, yet I am not Daelion Fatemaster to dare stand in judgment for his acts. By my lights, he's the only master I have served who treated me as a man. For that, I'd take Dharkaron's Spear in damnation before I'd turn coat and pass blithe beneath the Wheel to Athlieria. If blind service to Prince Lysaer's justice is moral right, I prefer to keep my own honour.'

'What will you do, then?' Jinesse demanded. 'The peninsula's cut off by Avenor's crack troops. The duke's war galleys blockade the harbour. Lysaer's guardsmen watch every move I make. Sooner or later, demands shall be made of me. The villagers don't support my silence.' She finished in a bitterness on the trembling edge of breakdown. 'I cannot abandon my children.'

The tips of Tharrick's fingers flexed against her knee. 'I gave you my promise, mistress.' In short, snatched whispers, while the moonlight fled and flooded and limned the widow's form with silvered light, he told of the sailhands who rowed from the *Shearfast* for the shore.

'They were to seek sanctuary in the hostel of Ath's Brotherhood. It's my plan to go there and rejoin them, and take whatever facts I know concerning Lysaer's campaign plans. I'm telling you this, mistress, because I hold earnest hope that you will decide to come with me.'

'I can't.' The thread that held Jinesse to composure came unravelled, and her slender body spasmed to the jerk of stifled sobs. 'Fiark and Feylind are endangered. Lysaer insists he's concerned for them. But he cannot be everywhere and atrocities happen where armies march. I fear what might come if my twins were caught in the path of the bloodshed intended to bring down the Master of Shadow.'

The brimming, liquid tracks of her tears and the anguish in her voice caused Tharrick to shove upright despite his pain. He gathered her against his warm shoulder. 'I may have chosen to throw my lot in with Arithon. That doesn't mean I support the ruin of small children. Come away with me. I'll help see your young ones restored to you.'

'So he *did* tell you where he was bound,' Jinesse murmured. Her sigh of relief unreeled through a throat tight with weeping.

'No,' Tharrick whispered against the crown of her head. 'But as Ath is my witness, he must have told you.'

Interlinks

In striking unconcern for the Koriani plot to break the wards over Althain Tower, Sethvir sits dreamy-eyed over an emptied mug of tea, while his misty regard quarters sights far removed from the winter sky outside his casement: on Avenor's brick battlements, a desolate royal wife sheds lonely tears; two exuberant, blond-haired children laugh on a brigantine's decks in Southshire harbour; in Vastmark, wyverns ride the winds like blown rags, their reptilian eyes alert for strayed sheep, while below them, a laggard band of shepherds herd their flocks through the defiles to lowland pastures . . .

In the steppelands of Shand, a motley assortment of raided livestock stampedes through the wilds of Alland, herd after herd of mixed horses and cattle hazed westward by Erlien's clansmen . . .

In Merior by the Sea, patient as he waits out a widow's tortured silence, Lysaer s'Ilessid pens a letter to his wife tender in assurance that war is not yet in the offing, until his watch officer interrupts with the bad news that Jinesse and the man Tharrick have evaded the guard on the cottage, and a search of the village has failed to find them . . .

III. *VASTMARK*

On the morning that Lysaer's cordon across the Scimlade peninsula was tightened in brisk effort to block Tharrick and Jinesse in their flight out of Merior, Arithon s'Ffalenn put his sloop *Talliarthe* in at the trade port of Innish. There, he spent a busy brace of days playing for small coin in the taverns. He renewed select friendships and secured help from a merchant to arrange for a ship's crew to liberate the *Khetienn* from the rigger's yard at Southshire. Then he collected the messages left waiting for him in posthouses and taverns throughout the city.

In the bone-lazy mood brought on by a night spent in a first-rate brothel, Dakar watched the Shadow Master answer his correspondence in hagridden hurry. Since the threat posed by Lysaer's armies lay far removed from Innish, the Mad Prophet railed that the rush was a criminal waste. After more than a year lost to sea passages and the backwater boredom of Merior, only an idiot or a man possessed would not linger amid civilized comforts.

Arithon gave such complaint less weight than he ever had. On the following tide, he raised anchor again and set *Talliarthe*'s heading farther west. A rainy two-week passage brought her to landfall in the Cascain Islands.

Like everywhere else on the Vastmark coast, the shoreline was all hostile rock. Galleys made no ports of call there. Captains who plied the trade routes gave the chained islets with their reef-ridden narrows and foam-necklaced channels a nervous, respectful wide berth. Forbidding slate cliffs stabbed up through the froth of winter breakers, black, jagged-edged and desolate. Their knife-bladed faces, clean polished by storms, slapped back every sound in meshed echoes.

Assaulted from the moment the anchor splashed by the screeling cries of flocking gulls, Dakar puffed his cheeks in a sigh of relief. Today, he suffered no hangover. In a beady-eyed vigilance launched out of malice, he kept himself sober to see what Arithon would do next.

The loss of the shipyard in its way became as shattering a counterblow as the wreckage of the fleet inflicted upon Lysaer at Minderl Bay.

Never more patient, Dakar passed his days in cold-blooded discontent. Arithon caught out in ignominious retreat was novel enough to be fascinating. The options left to choice were all mean ones. Lysaer's warhost, so brilliantly reduced, now moved southward, pared down to its most dedicated divisions. Once the weather eased and more companies arrived to bolster the strike force at Merior, the Shadow Master dared not be caught cornered. No quarter would be shown by the specialized troops trained at Avenor for this war; Duke Bransian's seasoned mercenaries and the hotly partisan garrison divisions lent by Etarra and Jaelot would vie to be first to claim his head.

'Your tactics have only burned away the dross,' Dakar pressured as Arithon turned the sloop's second anchor line on a cleat and flipped in a sailor's half hitch. 'You now face the eastlands' most gifted commanders. They won't make misjudgments for the season and the supply lines. They'll know to the second how long they can expect prime performance from an army in foreign territory.'

Dakar fiddled with his cuff laces, a half-moon smile of anticipation masked behind his moustache. Against established officers and hard-bitten veterans, the live-stock raids made by Selkwood's barbarians would gad this war host no worse than stings by a handful of hornets.

'In case you hadn't noticed, Erlien's clansmen dance to their own mad tune.' Arithon straightened and wiped salty hands on his breeches. 'Am I meant to be grateful for your wisdom as a war counsellor? Lysaer and the duke won't find much satisfaction using crack mercen-aries to beat the empty brush at Scimlade Tip.'

Too wily now to rise to goading, Dakar listened and caught the fleeting catch of pain that even a masterbard's skill could not quite pass off as insouciance. Merior's abandonment to the whim of hostile forces stung, and surprisingly deeply. Just what the village had meant to Arithon, Dakar avowed to find out.

Asandir's geas bound his person to the Shadow Master's footsteps. Unless he wished to be crushed like furniture in the thrust of Lysaer's campaign, he must sound Arithon's plans, then use whatever vulnerable opening he could find to leverage influence over their paired fate.

But his nemesis acted first in that maddening, way-ward abandon that seemed designed to whip Dakar to fury.

Given the intent to embark on a foray into the moun-tains of Vastmark, the Mad Prophet blinked, caught aback. 'Ath, whatever for? There's naught in these hills at this season but frost-killed bracken and starving hawks. The shale beds in the heights get soaked in the rains, and the rockslides can mill you to slivers. Those shepherds with sense will have driven their flocks to the lowest valleys until well after the first spring thaw.'

For answer, Arithon packed a small satchel with necessities. He heated his horn recurve bow over the galley stove to soften the laminate enough to string. Then he fetched his lyranthe, his hunting knife and sword, and piled them into the dory.

'You'll need warmer clothing,' Dakar said in tart recognition that the shore excursion lay beyond argument. His dissent was ongoing as he squeezed his girth past the chart desk to delve in a locker and scrounge out a pair of hose without holes. 'There's ice on the peaks. How long are you planning to sulk in the hills if it's snowing?'

'If you wish warm clothes, fetch them.' Arithon checked the sloop's anchor lines one final time, then climbed the rail and dropped into his rocking tender. 'The yard workers I've retained won't rejoin us here for at least another two fortnights. If you stay, the wait could be lonely. I didn't provision to live aboard.'

Dakar almost lost his temper. No hunter by choice, he detested the stringy taste of winter game. Just how the Shadow Master proposed to maintain his team of experienced shipwrights lay beyond reason since the coffers from Maenalle were empty. Whatever else drew him to peruse the barren uplands that sliced like broken razors against the clouds, the principality of Vastmark was by lengths the loneliest sweep of landscape on the continent. The shepherds who wrested their livelihood from its wind-raked, boggy corries subsisted in wretched poverty.

In distrust and suspicion that Arithon's excursion must be plotted as a feint to mask a more devious machination, the Mad Prophet snatched up his least-battered woollens, crammed them in a wad in his cloak, and in a clumsy boarding that rocked water over a gunwale, parked his bulk in the stern of the tender.

His compliance did not extend to shouldering the work of an oar. Nor when the craft beached on the narrow, pebbled strand did he lift a finger to help drag the dory into cover above the high tide mark. Ferret insight into Arithon's affairs though he might through adventure into a wilderness, Dakar scowled to express his commensurate distaste. Open-air treks and clambering up scarps like a goat came second only to the mazes through sand grains once dealt him as punishment by Asandir.

The pace Arithon set in ascent from the strand was brutal enough to wring oaths from a seasoned mercenary. Breathless within minutes, aching tired inside an hour, Dakar toiled over rock that slipped loose beneath his boot soles, and wormed past chiselled escarpments which abraded the soft skin of his hands. The wind poured in cold gusts off the heights, freighted with the keen snap of frost. Chilled in his sweat-sodden woollens, raked over by gorse spines, and sliced on both palms from grasping dried bracken to stay upright, Dakar hung at Arithon's heels in an unprecedented, stalwart forbearance. The higher the ascent, the more stoic he became, until exhaustion sapped even his penchant for cursing.

By then, the divide of the Kelhorn Mountains loomed in saw-toothed splendour above; below and to the north-west, in valleys the sheenless brown of crumpled burlap, the black- and red-banded stone of a ruin snagged through the crowns of the hills. Once a Paravian stronghold, the crumbled remains of a power focus threw a soft, round ring through the weeds that overran the site. Had Arithon not lost access to the talent that sourced his mage training, he would have seen the faint flicker of captured power as the fourth lane's current played through the half-buried patterns. Since the site of Second Age mysteries posed the most likely reason for today's journey, Dakar's outside hope became dashed as the valley was abandoned for a stonier byway which scored a tangled track to the heights.

Once into the rough footing of the shale slopes, Arithon left the trail to dig for rootstock. He offered no conversation. The Mad Prophet spent the interval perched atop an inhospitable rock, undignified and panting.

The afternoon dimmed into cloudy twilight. Arithon strung his bow and shot a winter-thin hare, which Dakar cooked in inimical silence over a tiny fire nursed out of sticks and dead brush. Vastmark slopes were too wind-raked for trees, the gravelly soil too meagre to anchor even the stunted firs that seized hold at hostile sites elsewhere. The only crannies not scoured bare by harsh gales lay swathed in prickly furze. A man without blankets must bed down on rock, wrapped in a cloak against the cold, or else perish from lack of sleep, spiked at each turn by vegetation that conspired to itch or prickle.

Dakar passed the night in miserable, long intervals of chilled wakefulness broken by distressed bouts of nightmare. He arose with the dawn, disgruntled and sore, but still entrenched in his resolve to outlast the provocations set by his s'Ffalenn nemesis.

They broke fast on the charred, spitted carcass of a grouse and butterless chunks of ship's biscuit, then moved on, Dakar in suffering silence despite the grievance of being forced to climb while he still felt starved to the bone. Arithon seemed none the worse for yesterday's energetic side trips. His step on the narrow rims of the sheep trails stayed light and sure, the bundles slung from his shoulder no impediment to the steepest ascent.

'You know,' Dakar gasped in vain attempt to finagle a rest stop, 'if you slip and fall, you'll see Elshian's last lyranthe in this world crunched into a thousand sad splinters.'

Poised at the crest of an abutment, Arithon chose not to answer. Dakar sucked wind to revile him for rudeness, then stopped against his nature to look closer. 'What's wrong?'

Arithon shaded his eyes from the filtered glare off the cloud cover and pointed. 'Do you see them?'

Dakar huffed through his last steps to the ridgetop. His scowl puckered into a squint as he surveyed the swale below their vantage.

The landscape was not empty. Sinister and black above the rim of a dry river gorge, creatures on thin-stretched, membranous wings dipped and soared on the wind currents. The high mountain silence rang to a shrill, stinging threnody of whistles.

'I thought the great Khadrim were confined to the preserve in Tornir Peaks.' Prompted by a past encounter that had ended in a narrow escape, Arithon reached for his sword.

'You need draw no steel. Those aren't Khadrim,' Dakar corrected. 'They're wyverns; smaller; less dangerous; non-fire-breathing. If you're a sheep, or a leg-broken horse, you've got trouble in plenty to worry about. The Vastmark territory's thick with their eyries, but they seldom trouble anything of size.' He studied the creatures' wheeling, kite-tailed flight a considered moment longer. 'Those are onto something, though. Wyverns don't pack up without reason.'

'Shall we see what they're after?' When his footsore companion groaned in response, Arithon grinned and leaped off the boulders to land running through the gorse down the ridge.

'It's likely just the carcass of a mountain cat,' Dakar carped. 'Mother of all bastards, will you *slow down*? You're going to see me trip and break my neck!'

Arithon called over his shoulder, cheerful. 'Do that and you'll just have to roll your fat self off this mountainside. No trees grow within a hundred and fifty leagues to cut any poles to make a litter.'

Ripped by a bilious stab of hatred, Dakar spat an

epithet on each tearing breath until he slipped and bit his tongue between syllables. Sullen and sickened by the rank taste of blood, he hauled up panting beside the Master of Shadow and gazed over the brim of the cliff head.

The first minute, his eyes refused to focus. His head swam, and not from the pain; sharp drops from great heights infallibly made him unwell. Where the wyverns ducked and wove in fixed interest, the channel-worn rock delved out by a glacial stream slashed downward into a ravine. The bottom lay dank as a pit. More wyverns threaded through the depths. Their dark scales glinted blue as new steel, and their spiked wingtips knifed a whine like a sabre cut through updraughts and invisibly roiled air.

Arithon paused a scant second, then stooped and slung off his lyranthe.

'You're not going down there,' Dakar objected.

He received a look the very palest of chill greens that boded the worst sort of obstinacy. 'Would you stop me?' Arithon said.

'Ath, no.' Dakar gestured toward the defile. 'Be my guest. You're most welcome to crash headlong to your death. I'll stay here and applaud while the wyverns gnaw the bones of your carcass.'

Arithon stooped, caught a handhold, and dropped down onto a broken, narrow ledge. There he must have found a goat track. His black head blended with the shadow in the cleft. Dakar resisted the suicidal, mad urge to drive him back by threatening to hurl Halliron's instrument after him into the abyss. In the cold-hearted hope he might witness his enemy's fall instead, the Mad Prophet tightened his belt to brace the quiver in his gut, grabbed a furze tuft for security, and skidded downslope on his fundament.

The wyverns cruising like nightmare shuttlecocks screamed in piercing outrage, then flapped wings and arrowed up from the cleft. From what seemed a secure stance on an outcrop below, Arithon kicked a spray of gravel into the ravine. The pebbles bounced, cracking, from stone to stone in plunging arcs, and startled four other settled monsters into flight. The chilling, stuttered whistles they shrilled in alarm raised a dissonance to ache living bone marrow.

Dakar saw Arithon suddenly drop flat on his belly. He peered downward also, unable to gain vantage into the recess beneath the moss-rotten underhang. The Shadow Master's exclamation of warning came muffled behind a sleeve as he rolled, unlimbered his strung bow from his shoulder, then positioned himself on one knee and nocked an arrow.

Moved by danger to scramble and close the last descent, Dakar also spotted the quarry which held the wyverns in circling patterns.

In the deep shade of a fissure, on a ledge lower down, a shepherd in a stained saffron jerkin crouched braced at bay against the cliff face. One arm was muffled in a dusty dun cloak. The streaked fingers of his other hand were glued to the haft of a bloodied dagger. Heaped to one side like a sun-shrivelled hide, the corpse of a wyvern lay draped on the scarp. The gouged socket of the eye that took the death wound tipped skyward, stranded in gore like a girl's discarded ribbons between the needle teeth that rimmed the parted, horny scales of its jaw.

Another living wyvern perched just beyond weapon's reach, wings half-furled and its snake-slender neck cocked to snap. Its golden, round eye shone lambent in the gloom, fixed on the steel which was all that deterred its killing strike.

Arithon drew his horn recurve. The arrow he fired hissed down in angled aim and took the predator just behind the foreleg.

The wyvern squalled in mortal pain. Its finned tail lashed against the rocks. Torn vegetation and a bashed fall of stones clattered down the ravine. The leathery crack as its pinions snapped taut buffeted a gusty snap of air. One taloned hind limb raised to claw the shaft, then spasmed, contorted into death throes. The creature overbalanced. It battered backward and plummeted off the vertical rock wall to a thrash of scraped scales and torn wings.

The man with the knife jerked his chin up, his face a pale blur against the gloom. He cried in hoarse fear as another wyvern plunged from its glide in a screaming, wrathful stoop, talons outstretched to slash and tear whatever moved in the open.

Arithon nocked and drew a second arrow. 'I thought you said they never fought in packs!'

'They don't.' Morbidly riveted, Dakar watched the weapon tip track its descending target, the twang of release left too late to forgive a missed shot. Arithon's shaft sang out point-blank and smacked home. The wyvern wrenched out of its plunge. It cartwheeled, the arrow buried to the fletching beneath its wing socket.

His envy compounded with unabashed regret for such nerveless, exacting marksmanship, Dakar qualified. 'That was the mate of the one you killed first. The creatures fly paired. They defend their own to the death.'

'I believe you.' The edged look of temper Arithon threw back bruised for its knowing, poisoned irony. 'But if you happen to be wrong, you'd better do the same.' He thrust his bow and his unhooked quiver into the Mad Prophet's startled grasp.

Unable to mask his raised hackles, Dakar glared as Arithon hurled himself over the lip of the ledge. 'You think I'd bother? I don't care how often you're reminded. It's no secret I'll rejoice to see you dead.'

Arithon's reply slapped back in hollow echoes off the sheer walls of the ravine. 'I'm not quite the fool I appear. With eighty leagues of mountains between here and

Forthmark, if you don't fancy climbing, you're stuck. Unless you find the sea legs to single-hand my sloop.'

'That's not funny.' Dakar cast down bow and arrows in disgust and sucked in his paunch to give chase. If his descent was ungraceful, he was scarcely less fast. He dropped to the lower ledge in a shower of dragged gravel, yanked down the tunic left hiked up to his armpits, then spat out the inhaled ends of his beard to deliver a scathing retort.

His words died unspoken. A shudder of horror swept through him as he saw: the shepherd with the knife proved no man at all, but a boy not a year more than twelve.

The child stared at his rescuers in uncomprehending shock, eyes dark and round in a face of vivid angles, drained to wax pallor beneath its scuffed dirt. Straw tails of hair stuck in matted hanks to a bloodied shoulder. The stained, cloak-wrapped wrist used to fend off teeth and talons was rust with the same stiffened stains. His shirt was more red than saffron. The one bare foot visible beneath the ripped cuff of his trouser lay swollen beyond recognition.

'Daelion forfend, you're a very lucky boy to be alive,' Dakar said. Overhead, the wyvern pack whistled and dived in balked circles, too wary to close now their prey was defended.

While Dakar battled to contain squeamish nerves, Arithon bent, caught the child's knife wrist, and pried his sticky fingers off the grip. 'It's all right. Help has come. You aren't going to need that any more.'

The boy broke with a shuddering whimper. Arithon bundled his head against his chest and cradled him tightly, then used his left hand to probe the hot, swollen flesh above the ankle. The child flung back against his hold as he touched. 'Easy. Easy. We'll have you up out of here in just a minute.' But the jagged grate of bone underneath his light fingers belied his banal reassurance.

121

As if crazed by pain, the boy struggled desperately harder.

'Jilieth,' he gasped, the first clear word he had spoken. 'Look to Jilie.' He fought an arm free to tug at something shielded in the crevice behind his back: a second, more heartrending bundle splashed in scarlet.

'Merciful Ath!' Dakar dropped to his knees, his antipathy eclipsed. Closer inspection showed a face and a small hand inside the mass of shredded clothing. Behind the boy lay a second child, a girl no more than six.

'Your sister?' asked Arithon.

The boy gave a stricken nod.

'All right then, be brave.' While the Shadow Master shifted the injured boy aside, Dakar squeezed past with tender care and lifted the younger girl's pitiful, torn body into the open. She stirred awake at his touch. The one eye she had left fixed, brown and beseeching, on his bearded, stranger's face. 'Papa. Where's my papa?'

The Mad Prophet clenched his jaw in helpless grief. 'If I could command even half of what Asandir taught me, I could help.'

'Never mind that.' Arithon loosed the boy with a murmur of encouragement, turned aside, and cupped the girl's tear-streaked face.

'Papa,' she repeated as his shadow crossed over her.

'Your father is with you, believe it,' he assured in the schooled, steady timbre earned in study for his masterbard's title.

'Ghedair said he would come.' The girl gasped. Blood welled and trickled from the corner of her mouth. Her chest heaved against drowning congestion as she forced in another pained breath. 'It hurts. Tell my papa, it hurts.'

Arithon soothed back crusted hair to bare the mauled ruin a wyvern had left when its front talons had raked and grasped her face. The rear claw had sunk through her shoulder and chest; deep gashes had torn when it flew. Ends of separated bone and ripped cartilage showed blue through the shreds of her blouse.

'It wasn't Ghedair's fault,' the girl blurted. 'He *was* watching. But I ran off. Then wyverns came.'

'Hush.' Arithon added a phrase in lilted Paravian, too low for Dakar to translate. But the powerful ring of compassion in his tone could have drawn out the frost from ice itself. 'I know that, Jilieth. Stop fretting.'

In merciful relief, the child's one eye slid closed.

'Your bard's gift let her sleep?' the Mad Prophet asked.

Arithon soothed her cheek against Dakar's rough clad shoulder. 'That's the best I could do.' In the moment he glanced up, the deep empathy of his feelings stripped his face beyond hope of concealment. 'Keep her quiet if you can.'

Stupid with shock, Dakar clung to the girlchild while the Shadow Master bent to tend the boy. The blood on the torn saffron jerkin proved more the dead wyvern's or his sister's than his own. The arm, bundled out of its swathe of shredded cloak, bore deep punctures and gashes swollen to angry red. The break above the ankle was clean beneath the swelling. Arithon patted the boy's crown, arose, and in a fit of balked grace, kicked the rank, knife-hacked corpse of the other fallen wyvern over the edge of the outcrop. The implication was enough to stop thought, that somewhere lay another slain mate.

The resourceful boy owned courage enough to shame a full-grown man.

While the rest of the drake pack, in a squalling, stabbing squabble, glided down the gorge to scavenge the remains of their dead, Arithon disrupted Dakar's appalled stupor in brisk and fluent Paravian. 'We'll have to splint the leg first. Arrow shafts should do for the purpose. I'll tie them with my cuff lacings. The girl, we'll have to bind up as we may. I hate the delay, yet we've got no choice. They'll have to be moved. The herbs in my satchel and some of the roots can be pounded up to make poultices. But I can't brew the remedies without water and sheltered ground to make a fire.'

'There ought to be springs at the base of the cliffs,' Dakar said.

'Then we'll find a path down.' A leap and an athletic slither saw Arithon up to the ridgetop. He returned with his quiver and spare shirt. Before need that disallowed the indulgence of his hatreds, Dakar lent his hands to the grim work of splinting and binding.

The boy gave one full-throated, agonized cry as his shinbone was pulled into line and set straight. Arithon spoke to him, soothingly gentle, a constant barrage of reassurance. Whether his voice spun fine magic, or cruel pain claimed its due, when the ankle and knee were strapped immobile, the child lay quiet, unconscious.

'Pity them both,' Dakar whispered as he ripped linen to strap Jilieth's gaping lacerations. 'She must be half-empty of blood.' He need not belabour his certainty that the wounds beneath his hands were surely mortal. The grief in the Shadow Master's expression matched him in stricken understanding.

'There's hope. We might save her,' Arithon insisted as he tucked the shepherd boy into the folds of his cloak.

Dakar pushed back upright and trailed through the climb up the cliff path, the girl cradled limp in his arms. 'Are you mad? Five bones in her rib cage are separated from the cartilage, and one lung is filled up with blood!'

'I know.' Arithon draped the boy over his shoulders, clasped the small, unmarked wrist and one ankle, then set his weight to scale the last rise of rock. 'Just keep her alive until we find a spring. If she's still breathing then, try and find the forbearance to trust me.'

Dakar clamped his teeth. The Prince of Rathain had never asked his help; never before now bent his stiff royal pride to admit that other company was better than a burden to be managed in blistering tolerance. If Asandir's geas hounded Dakar to sheer misery, for Arithon, the bonding was a nuisance.

Tempted into a sympathy that felt like self-betrayal, Dakar ground out the first rude word to cross his mind. Then, stubborn in prosaic disbelief, he passed the doomed girl into Arithon's waiting grip and dragged his plump carcass back up the rim wall to the slope.

Two hours later, on a sandy bank beside a rock pool, Arithon prepared a heated poultice to treat the punctures and slashes on Ghedair's mauled forearm. His concentration seemed unaffected by the oppressive gloom of the site. Damp and streamered in green shags of moss, the gorge reared up sheer on two sides, the sky a hemmed ribbon between. Light seeped through the clouds, dim as the gleam off a miser's silver, while the breeze fluted mournfully through the defiles. Far off, the braided whistles of a wyvern pair screeled in bone-chilling dissonance.

Tired of feeling useless, set on edge by the spring's erratic plink of seeped droplets, Dakar gave rein to spite and prodded Arithon to elaborate on his earlier, misguided cause for hope.

'Jilieth's already failing.' The clogged drag of her chest seemed to worsen with each tortured breath that she drew. To distance the unaccustomed sting of pity, the Mad Prophet lashed out. 'You know full well there's nothing left to do but keep her warm and sheltered until she dies.'

Her face by then had been cleansed and swathed in the torn strips from Arithon's spare shirt. Outside the bandaging, the lashes of her undamaged eye remained, fanned like cut ends of silk against a cheek so colourless the freckles shone dull grey. To look at her at all, to see her child's hands so far removed from life they never twitched, was to suffer a sorrow past endurance.

Small comfort could be gained, watching Arithon's fine fingers wind and tuck smooth the ends of the dressing over the boy's poultice. That task completed, he settled Ghedair back in his cloak and plied him with herb possets until he slept.

Dakar could no longer hold out. The child in his arms gasped on the edge of suffocation; she was going to pass the Wheel within the hour. Her plight most ruthlessly tore away pride until no grudge was enough to maintain his sceptical rancour.

To Arithon, he ground out, 'If you think we can save her, say how.'

'Easily spoken, in theory. Not so simply carried out.' A wind-tousled figure stripped down to hose and shirt-sleeves, Arithon rinsed his hands. Water spattered off his reddened fingertips, shattered the pool into ring ripples that burst his reflection into a maze of jagged lines.

Dakar found himself pinned by a measuring stare that assessed him wholly without judgment.

'You've had longevity training,' Arithon said at blunt length. 'I've got a masterbard's ear for true sound. If you build the spell seals to initiate healing, I can link them through music to the signature vibration that defines Jilieth's life Name.'

If not for the hurt creature that burdened his arms, Dakar would have shot to his feet. 'Dharkaron's fell Chariot and Spear! You have no idea what you're asking.'

'You're most wrong.' Arithon looked away. 'I've a fair enough indication.' In unadorned phrasing, he described the time he had joined talents with the enchantress Elaira to reconstruct the mangled arm of a fisher lad. The result of that experience, coupled with the mage's schooling he had received from his grandfather, lent him full awareness of the implications. The aftermath had hurled his heart beyond peace; the woman had been driven to leave Merior.

Dakar shrank from revulsion that pealed like an ache through his bones. 'I might know your whole *mind*!' The unspoken corollary freighted his tension, that the shared course of such bindings could expose every facet of Arithon's warped character to the intermeshed weave of the link. No secret would stand between them; no subterfuge. If Dakar once lost his grip, he would find his awareness submersed in the quagmire of the other man's criminal nature, to the everlasting upset of his conscience.

'I don't want to be privy to your unsavoury intentions,' the Mad Prophet declaimed, afraid for what he might suffer.

The concept was abhorrent. His enemy's deadly aberrance; all the doomed, fell bindings of Desh-thiere's geas could backlash and imprint his private memory. Though he would not share Arithon's subjugation to the curse, the Master of Shadow asked him to risk first-hand knowledge of the hates that drove the war against Lysaer; the same amoral passions which had brought the bloody slaughter of eight thousand lives on the banks of the River Tal Quorin, then the burning of the trade fleet at Minderl Bay.

Those horrific burdens were none of his making, to assume for the sake of a child.

Rathain's prince at least had the decency not to stare while the Mad Prophet pondered the unkindly reach of later consequence. The faltering life held sheltered in his arms became tormented testimony to the list of his personal shortfalls. Dakar stood as a man on the edge of an abyss. One word in consent, one misstep in weakness, and his self-awareness might become forever skewed.

Worse, success could not be guaranteed. He could agree, and shoulder his whimpering fear, and still fail. The girl was far gone already. She could end a cold corpse beneath a shepherd's stone cairn, surrounded by her circle of weeping kinsfolk.

Dakar closed his eyes against a thorny barrage of selfish thought. He could equally well master the sacrifice and see Jilieth walk whole in the sunlight.

At his back, in drawn quiet marked off by the splash of the rock spring, Arithon awaited his decision. The understanding implicit in his stillness itself became a goad, until Dakar burst out in acrimony, 'There's no risk to you! All I have on my conscience is debauchery and vice. Every decadent trait you despise. You fear no remorse. Your self-restraint should scarcely be shaken.'

Arithon's reply was all steel. 'I stake a certain independence of mind. Nor am I Sethvir, to pick out every nuance of future impact.'

The child in Dakar's care shuddered through another racked breath; a wider patch of scarlet flowered through the layers of her bandaging. The spellbinder set his teeth and glared at rain-chiselled stone, that would endure through long ages, indifferent to the trials of mortal suffering. He measured himself in unprecedented cold logic, and understood, should he shy from the choice, the courage of a boy and a little girl's brown eye, beseeching, were going to haunt him forever. He bitterly dreaded to face their contempt in the dregs of every beer keg, to the ruin of his irresponsible pleasures.

There remained only malice toward the man who laid that irreversible crossroads before him. 'Damn you,' Dakar answered to Arithon s'Ffalenn in a tone very like the one Tharrick had used before swearing his oath in Jinesse's cottage. 'I cannot refuse, as you're fully aware. Ath's pity on us both when we come to regret this hour afterward.'

'There's always the chance that we won't,' Arithon said; but his pained snap of sarcasm showed his dearth of faith.

The fact such doubt was justified hurled Dakar over the edge. His consent was flung down like a duellist's challenge, as much to spite the scorn of an antagonist as to save a failing child from certain death.

'Make me the butt of your hatred all you like,' Arithon baited in maddening, nerveless composure. He fetched his lyranthe and in fierce, hard jerks began to unlace its fleece wrappings. 'But unless you wish to tempt disaster, let your feud with me bide until later.'

Dakar chose not to acknowledge the insult. Longevity alignment was no novice's lesson; five centuries of study made him far from incompetent. Any spellbinder apprenticed to Asandir would be well trained to put by his surface passions for the clear self-control demanded for acts of grand conjury. The practice had never been an exercise the Mad Prophet welcomed; the deep, still quiet required for fine spellcraft often fired his spurious fits of prophecy. If the Fellowship Sorcerers had insisted the gift could be tamed to control, the gut-tearing sickness that followed each episode had been Dakar's trial to bear. He preferred to escape in debauchery.

The fact hurt now with surprising venom, that he yet lacked the knowledge to initiate Jilieth's healing. Arithon might be damaged beyond conscious access to his talents; still, he owned the intuitive experience to explain how the trial should be approached. Dakar flicked up gravel in irritation. He had no option except to follow the plan, though trust gouged like sand against his grain. He had no wish to assume the reasoned risks of a man whose penchant for devious artifice held no limit.

Through the sweet, plucked run of his tuning notes, Arithon said, 'Merciful maker, Dakar. If we're going to be foolish and corrupt ourselves, let's not waste time browbeating the issue. Lay the child across your lap. Get comfortable. You may not be moving before nightfall.' The splashed descent of an arpeggio cut through his measured instructions. 'The theory should not be unduly complex. I can use music to build a bridge-link to Jilieth, then turn the discipline I learned at Rauven to open myself as a conduit. If you can conjoin into sympathy and thread your power through me, I can transmute the seals into sound and heighten their pull on the girl.'

As Dakar settled in capitulation, the Shadow Master cautioned him further. 'I can build upon your foundation. But I will be blind to the spell construct as it forms. You must be my eyes as well as the source of raw energy. I can only weave sound on what I hear and sense through my empathic gift as a bard. The result will be measured and limited by the depths to which you can release yourself into sympathy.'

Dakar chewed his beard in unalloyed apprehension as notes sprang and sparked like sprays of dropped crystal through the mournful moan of the wind. The browned tufts of sedges on the stream banks flattened and hissed and shivered. From the musician bent cross-legged with his instrument there came no hint of recrimination for the need to bare himself to an enemy.

Dakar swallowed back awe, unable to match such resignation. 'Why ever should you do this? You know how I hate you. Anything I capture in the backlash from your mind will later be turned hard against you.'

Arithon glanced up, his eyes deep and terrible with distance. 'You don't gloat for justice? I thought for certain you'd say I've a reckoning due for the young ones who died by Tal Quorin.'

Since no more vicious a subject existed to rip back in rejoinder, Dakar was caught short. Before he was ready, the last remaining bass string was fussed and brought to true pitch. Arithon feathered through an acid progression of major chords, then launched into dancing, sprightly melody.

For the tragedy of the setting, such vengeful, clean joy sounded blasphemous. Dakar felt his gorge rise.

Then the music's fierce honesty slapped him speechless.

For what Arithon described in the stunning command of his art was the signature pattern of a whole and healthy little girl. His melody captured Jilieth in her fabric of fresh innocence, extracted from one minute's fleeting, splintered view through the window of her sole remaining eye.

The bard's perception was an untamed awareness, unrestrained as the lofty flight of falcons; it did not judge, but accepted. It made no demand, but set free.

Dakar felt the small, contorted body in his grasp settle and ease across his knees. A tiny, stray smile bowed up the corners of colourless lips. Even through the fogs of unconsciousness, Jilieth met the song that was her living self and responded to the promise that lilted in light harmonics through each measure. In tripping runs, in fiery-sweet tangles of ascending and descending arpeggios, even Dakar could sense a glimpse of the woman she might become in the unfolded promise of later life.

The effect was to wrap the spirit spellbound.

Weakened as Jilieth had become, starved as her tissues were for air, she could not do other than rise above her affliction, then respond as the vital mirror image of herself looped and soared, and charged her fading spirit to delight.

Arithon played with half-lidded eyes. The intricate measures beneath his fingers flexed and flowed on a current of untrammelled intuition. Dakar had no space to marvel at his talent. Afraid for the cost of each second's delay, he poised in wait for the opening when the link would be offered to his use.

The awareness flowed over him like the plunge into glacial waters. Arithon dissolved his inner barriers without constraint, without fear, without regret.

The Mad Prophet steadied his concentration, slipped into trance and mage-sight. He let the spiralled structure of the music seize his mind and draw him inside the circle of the Shadow Master's consciousness.

The first contact all but disarmed him. Deflected and sent reeling by a vulnerability of shattering proportion, Dakar found his animosity disarmed, then submerged in a rush of expanding discovery: the forced gift of compassion lent to this s'Ffalenn prince a limitless capacity to forgive. Arithon owned no defence against hatred. He could do nothing before railing slights and prejudice except bare his heart in understanding. For a scion of his line, there existed no half measures; against misinterpretation and betrayal, even cold steel in the back, he had only temper to shield him. The pained patience that rooted his sarcasm became a lacerating revelation to upset Dakar's entrenched hostility.

Even through the sweet pull of the music spun for Jilieth, Arithon was not unaware of the Mad Prophet's distress. Solidly delicate as a wall of blown glass, constraints were offered to bolster him.

Against a lifelong assault to wide-open feelings, and the demands his own sympathy set against him, Arithon had learned to covet privacy. In the clear-cut solitude of a master's restraint, he carved himself space for peace of mind.

Stormed through by a tearing desire to weep, Dakar heard the lyranthe speak out in sharp dissonance. The note jarred him separate, lent him footing to salvage a grip on his drowned sense of self. He regained the presence to remember: his purpose was not to be overwhelmed by pity for the plight of an enemy, but to restore the ravaged body of a child.

He owned the knowledge to reverse mortal wounding inside a strict set of parameters. The foundation of his learning followed Fellowship precepts: all change must begin with consent. Jilieth herself must agree to her healing. In a girl too young to grasp adult implications, permission must be garnered in stages. The first step was easiest. Afflicted by wounds of fatal severity, she would seize at the chance to escape pain. Eyes closed, ears filled by the ringing dimension of spirit described by Arithon's lyranthe, Dakar laid light hands on the bandages that swaddled the wounds in Jilieth's chest. The tidal play of life force under his fingertips spun in whorled patterns across his mage-sight. Here, the current faltered, all but cancelled out; there, her energies burned in a frenetic, bleeding burst, punished out of balance by trauma. The structure had lost its given shape like candle wax set too near flame.

Dakar raised a fingertip and traced the seal for stability over the stained linen wrapping.

He summoned from himself to lend it power. A flare of illumination bloomed in the path of his touch. For an instant his cipher glimmered like calligraphy inked in light. Then Arithon's melody rang out in response and framed its pale resonance into sound. The construct glowed with fierce splendour, then dissolved in a shower of pinprick sparks and absorbed into the tracery of the girl's aura.

Arithon's deft progression of chords refrained the same vibration, then wove in an aching and beautiful counterpoint through the measures that framed the child's Name.

Tears streaked in earnest down Dakar's plump cheeks. For the span of an instant, nothing alive could withstand the tenderness expressed by the flight-dance of fingers across the length of a fretboard and fourteen silverwrapped strings. Arithon's talent held true as struck gold, commensurately brought beyond promise to potential by the gift of Halliron's teaching. Jilieth could do naught but respond. Beneath Dakar's hands, her next breath came easier. He dared another sigil for dampening pain, and the lyranthe's song soared through and answered him.

The influx of power fired an exhilarated rush. Dakar framed the next seal for mending torn tissue, awed yet again as pure melody resounded in polished clarity, an airy flight of chords as carefree as wind through the petals of budding flowers.

Immersed deep in trance, joined in lockstep with Arithon, the spellbinder no longer felt the chill bite of frost. The music wrung him deaf to the hunting cries of wyverns and the erratic splash of the spring. Try though he would, his precautions bled away. The allure of bright harmony meshed his mind in fair coils; swept him hapless into the interlocked dance of spelled mystery until the threads of defence and mistrust came unwound and slipped through his loosened grasp.

The most perilous moment of the binding framed for Jilieth had arrived. His heart held to no thing outside his craft and the lyranthe's uncontained joy. A smile on his lips, no shadow on his mind to trip and hamper him, Dakar initiated the twined cipher for renewal and ending that would link the spell's resonance to prime power.

Tied by the strictures of his training to the Law of the Major Balance, the child he sought to help possessed sole volition to close the first step. To open within her the conduit to enable grand conjury, to empower her to thwart death, Jilieth would have to embrace change. Her wilful young nature and the pull of heedless passion that urged her to go her headstrong way must yield to wisdom beyond her years and development. She must of herself be encouraged to accept the loving boundaries that skilled parents would instil upon offspring too young to protect themselves.

To recover and rise whole, a six-year-old girl must unmake the decision to flout her brother's care and run off to play alone among the rocks.

Jilieth heard the question that was asked of her. Enfolded in every protection a masterbard's music could draw to set her outside pain and suffering, her spirit shimmered in playful rebellion. She would dance, and court danger, even as her lost mother, who had cruelly abandoned her in childhood; who had ventured out on unsafe footing to save a stranded lamb, and perished in the grinding thunder of a rockslide.

Arithon cried out in sharp warning. 'Dakar, let her be! Don't pursue. She must be left free to turn back!'

But the spellbinder had already lost himself to frustration. His annoyance stained the seals and the sigils dull red, and the music, denied its clear channel, faltered one fractional beat off true rhythm.

The Mad Prophet despaired for his clumsiness. He scrambled to recover a patience he had never seen fit to cultivate. Jilieth needed the firm-handed guidance of a teacher. The censure and correction dealt out in restraint, that over and over, Dakar had refused from his Fellowship master.

For the first time in life, that failing cut through his thick-skinned obstinacy. He knew how to pleasure the most jaded of his whores; could wheedle his way to indulge in the worst forms of vice.

But in tragic revelation, he saw he owned no clue how to curb the same destructive urge in a child.

Arithon grasped the scope of Dakar's dilemma; his masterbard's empathy caught the jangled upset that flayed through the link holding Jilieth's attention to the course that would buy back her life. He extended his talent to its desperate limit in attempt to drive a clear opening across the spellbinder's flawed moil of indecision. When the cry wrung out in appeal from his lyranthe failed to win through, he opened his throat in a scream of wild hurt for the helpless, blind block that guilt had set over his mage-sight.

Arithon reached anyway, tried, his full will engaged in one piercing effort to break through and access his lost mastery.

Tapped into his talent, he could act in direct resonance and salvage the burst seals in the pattern.

But his attempt slammed against the blank barrier that fenced his inner vision like black glass. He floundered back, undone and crushed by untenable loss.

The shock tore him open, harrowed up his insufferable memories. Strangled afresh by the choices he had seen no moral avenue to escape, he had no control left to shield Dakar from the impact of shared sight.

All over again the children died on the field at Tal Quorin. Who else but he knew they had been spared a worse fate on the executioner's scaffold in Etarra? Their deaths had been sealed, along with the clan survivors he had sacrificed his integrity to spare from the misguided coil unleashed by Desh-thiere's curse when Lysaer had raised Etarra's army.

He lived with the guilt and annihilating fear for the sway the Mistwraith's geas held over him.

Cornered once again on the desolate sands at Athir, the humiliation bought at Minderl Bay a recent wound in his heart, Arithon had cried out in a despair that unmanned him. 'You wish my blood oath? *To hold me to life?* Ath Creator show me mercy! You can't know what you're asking!'

Then the Fellowship Sorcerer's unequivocal answer, 'I do know.' Through the Warden of Althain, Asandir was cognizant that one staunch liegeman's hold on an unmerciful duty had spared an untenable reckoning. 'It is all the more urgent that I ask. You've experienced the peril this Mistwraith represents. Whatever atrocities its curse may bring to pass, to spare humanity, your birth-born talents must be preserved for the future. Who dies and who lives cannot be made to matter before necessity as broad-scale as that.'

And so the knife to seal blood oath had bitten irrevocably, forging an unbreakable tie to a Sorcerer and a charge of responsibility to negate change of will. The sting of the steel shocked back the sundered currents of control.

Arithon wrung free of the past that tore his conscience, and Dakar snapped back to contained self-awareness with a gasp that rocked him like a blow. The link was severed, its purpose spent.

For Jilieth, the turning already lay behind. She was a wayward creature, heartset to go where she would, and for that she had met with her wyvern.

Her choice was made. In the wreckage of pride and the tatters of past pain, Arithon had no recourse left but to force back the semblance of dignity. He bent his head over wet knuckles and threw himself back into music; to loose his bard's bindings one by one and play the lost child through her transition out of life. He guided her last breaths in joy, in peace, to ease final passage in cherished sympathy.

The vision Dakar caught through the discipline of his mage-sight as she passed the Fatemaster's Wheel was of a carefree young girl, skipping through a golden flood of sunshine.

Day had long fled. The fire languished to ashes and the rags of the stormfront had dispersed. A night sky cold with stars cast ghost light into the ravine and spiked needles of reflection in the rock pool. Three bars after the girl's spirit aura dimmed and flickered into dark, Arithon cupped his strings into silence. He clamped his palms over the sharp bones of his face while the tears spilled unchecked through his fingers.

Still trapped in the fading remembrance of linked sympathy, Dakar could not bear the grief. He had no means at hand to assume the blame that was his, nor to ease his lapsed burden off the shoulders of the bard. Perhaps worst of all, Arithon in his boundless capacity for understanding turned no word against him in reprisal.

'You were all you could be for the one given moment,' the Prince of Rathain said at length. Never more Torbrand's descendant, he stared into the shadowy depths of the pool, too exhausted to care if his heart showed. 'There's no doubt in my mind. You gave all you had. The girl saw her chance and made her turning.'

But for the spellbinder, that absolution fell short. He was no more than five centuries of debauchery had made him. The compounded waste of every year he had squandered stung now in cruel regret for the price meted out to Jilieth as he failed her.

'What's left to be done?' Dakar asked, his canker of old spite set into eclipse by remorse.

'I suppose, take the children to their kinsfolk. Where should we look for their people?' Arithon set his lyranthe on the unfurled fleeces of its wrappings and pushed in numbed exhaustion to his feet. He scrounged by the fire, retrieved Ghedair's cloak, then gathered the cooling body of the sister out of Dakar's lap.

'There should be a shepherds' camp.' Dakar forced his numbed mind to start working. 'Their flocks would be moving down-country for winter. This one tribe must be delayed for some reason. Their young ones aren't usually left unwatched.'

'The fact this pair was deprived of one parent might explain that.' When the little girl was shrouded in the rags of her brother's garment, Arithon covered his lyranthe.

At some point Dakar recovered willpower to move. He packed up the satchel and wrestled to shed an unwelcome legacy of skewed viewpoint. The imprint of Arithon's consciousness clung to his thoughts like fine cobwebs. Dakar shrank from the coiled question in obstinate fear for another prince: the fair-haired s'Ilessid half-brother he cherished as his closest friend.

Discomfort gnawed him. He dared not re-examine the hour of Desh-thiere's revenge lest he encounter an unthinkable truth, that the past might no longer support his beliefs. The creeping thought answered, that nine years ago during the crisis at Etarra, it may have suited Prince Lysaer not to fight back against the wraith that had twisted foothold through s'Ilessid justice to seed its undying curse of enmity.

Later evidence lent credence. No Fellowship Sorcerer ever stepped back from human need without cause. There would be compelling reason why only one prince had been asked to swear blood oath at Athir.

In a cowardly need to plough past ugly doubts, Dakar resumed conversation. 'If we strike downslope, we ought to find the sheep.' He watched Arithon shoulder his share of their belongings, then hoist the unconscious boy across his back. The bard seemed as he always had, spare and assured in his competency.

On the strength of stolen insight, Dakar realized he could pierce that crafty mask of self-reliance. He was Lysaer's man, always, as Arithon well knew. What came to pass through tonight's unnerving partnership would not be simple, nor freely given. No law insisted that their bid to spare a child had occurred without the underlying subterfuge that trademarked the Shadow Master's style.

Dakar heaved the packed satchel off the ground and gathered up the corpse of the girl. The thought struck in fired clarity, that his splintered faith in Lysaer's decency could be restored but one way: by testing and prying until he forced out the proof that Arithon had exposed his royal gift of compassion for gain. The possibility existed. In cold calculation as Shadow Master, ruled by Desh-thiere's curse, he might have acted behind cover of Jilieth's need to disarm Dakar's enmity and twist a just hatred in diabolical change to complicity.

Ath's Adepts

Bored with the confines of the command galley, and fed up with dicing with sailors, Mearn s'Brydion paced in a rampaging temper across the carpets of Lysaer's campaign tent. 'Your Grace, it's a farce!' His thin fingers jabbed air by the tent flap, tied open to catch the sea breeze. 'The villagers we question hate talk worse than clams. Two men got snakebitten, beating the bushes. They found nothing else. Your officers at the cordon all swear by what hangs in their breeks that no fugitives have left Scimlade Tip. The only place we haven't searched is the hostel of Ath's Brotherhood. Have you ever questioned the adepts?'

Mearn cast a steely eye over the prince's settled calm. 'I see you haven't. Their kind don't deal in warfare or hostages. If they don't like your purpose, you may as well try to shift sand in a bucket with the bottom dinged full of holes!'

Unmoved by Mearn's ranting, Lysaer s'Ilessid pushed his lap desk off his knees, sat up straight, and tossed the dried nib of his quill pen across the clutter of dispatches spread in ranked piles at his feet. 'You want to send the galleys along the coastline, north and south, to seek the Shadow Master directly?'

'Yes.' Mearn gave a tight spin to glare over the darkened dunes, the braid on his oversleeves a stitched flare of sparks in the candles just lit to cut the grey fall of twilight. 'I hate sitting. We've no proof any sailhands survived *Shearfast*'s burning. If my duke's exiled guardsman or that village goodwife knew aught of Arithon's plans, they're not at hand to speak. Why stall for them? Catch a rat on the run, or wait and have the worse time digging him out while denned up.'

'Your rat is s'Ffalenn,' Lysaer said in forced patience. 'He'll be denned up already. You'd break the backs of your oarsmen in a needless, blind search.'

'Not blind. The villagers say he had dealings with a smuggler's brig called the *Black Drake*.' When this bit of news failed to move Lysaer from planted disagreement to enthusiasm, Mearn flicked at the salt a wet landing had left encrusted on his sleeve cuff. 'All right then.' Suspiciously triumphant, as though he had won some obscure point of argument, he grinned at the prince in a sparkling, new depth of malice. 'You can inquire at the hostel yourself, and welcome to the errand by my lights. Righteous types give me the creeps.'

Lysaer was inclined to avoid Mearn's tactless company on a diplomatic visit in any case. The man's nerve-jumpy habits could haze even Daelion Fatemaster to impatience. As the duke's youngest brother fretted in his haste to be away, the prince gave him gracious dismissal. 'I'll have a man row across to your galley in the morning to say what I've found.'

As the grooms were rousted to saddle mounts for himself and his escort to visit Ath's initiates for inquiry, Lysaer dismissed whatever bent of s'Brydion nature moved Mearn to prankish laughter.

* * *

Great torches burned in bronze brackets at the entry of Ath's hostel, sure sign, as Mearn s'Brydion might have cautioned, that a royal visitor was expected. Not born to familiarity with Athera's most time-honoured customs, Lysaer raised his hand and signalled his jingling guard to rein up. Shadows thrown off by twisted tree limbs inked crawling lines on the sigil-cut stones of the gate-posts. The horses seemed undaunted by the carvings, but their mazed shapes set the attendant groom on edge. The lad hovered close to the prince's large gelding, hands clenched white on his bundle of lead reins.

Lysaer dismounted, uneasy himself, but too much the ruler to falter. A full moon thatched behind clots of black leaves had made the ride down the lane an eerie traverse in patched light. The building past the gateway had no windows: bounded by the oppressive, rank growth of the Scimlade's oak hammocks and scrub forest, its shape and size were indistinct. The wind-ruffled scratch of dry weeds and the scrape of overgrown tree limbs against mossy walls lent an unsettled air of neglect. This site held no resemblance to the sacred ground Lysaer recalled from his childhood, bordered in trimmed hedges and crossed by brick walks and rows of flowering herb beds. Since the practice of the mysteries in Athera had suffered decline after the disappearance of the Paravians, Lysaer was scarcely surprised. The adepts here would inevitably lack funds to lavish on gardeners and grounds-keepers.

On brisk presumption his visit would be short, he bid his escort to wait, then advanced to the sigil-marked portal. The information he desired at worst case might be bought for a charitable donation to relieve the hostel from poverty.

'We have no use for coin,' said a velvet alto voice near enough to make Lysaer start. A figure in a full-sleeved, hooded white robe stepped from the night shadows to greet him. 'This place holds no threat unless beliefs in your heart make you think so.'

Nettled to a queer flutter of nerves, and startled to be approached from the side, Lysaer replied in jewel-edged diplomacy. 'Blessing on you, brother. When I wish the particulars of my faith to become your affair, I shall say so.'

A smile curved the lips beneath the snowy hood. 'Sister, in this case, may the light of the creator shine through you.' Hands with elegant, tapered fingers turned back the deep hood. The warm leap of torchlight dusted high, bronze cheeks, a regal nose, and eyes too direct for the comfort of a prince accustomed to royal rank and deference.

'Your will is ever your own.' Gently patient in correction, the adept gestured to welcome Lysaer and his escort into the sanctum of her hostel. 'Beyond these gates, the opinions you hold are not private. Ath's greater mercy will rule upon your petition and touch upon your actions.'

Lysaer kept his temper through statesman's reflex. 'I need not intrude on your hospitality, sister. I'm not here to petition, but to inquire after the presence of an injured man under my charge, and a woman I believe may be with him.'

'Tharrick and Jinesse. You may see them inside.' The lady initiate drew her hood back over her ebony coil of hair. She advanced like a sylph through the leaf-strained, shot beams of moonlight, self-possessed in stately grace. Her presence brushed all in the prince's party. Every man and servant received the same close regard until she passed through the archway and vanished.

Left cold by the torchlit gate, Lysaer faced the choice to leave, unsatisfied, or follow her inside. Since Mearn's rat hunt down the coastline seemed the more onerous alternative, he charged his escort again to await his return, then stretched his stride to pass within.

The concept never dawned that his authority would be upset, that when he entered the hostel's cavernous

143

stone edifice, his officers would dismount and disarm, then trail him into the anteroom. His order had been explicit; he had asked no one's company. And yet every member of his retinue came on. Undistressed at his heels, even the boy groom appointed to hold his horse stared in wide-eyed fascination at the seals and sigils chiselled in flowing bands around the walls.

The adept herself had invited them. If Lysaer wished to be annoyed by such presumption, his hostess smiled at him as a nurse might indulge an errant child. 'You have ventured inside of our precinct. Here Ath's law abides.' Her speech raised limitless echoes against high, groined ceilings, and her barefoot step fell soundless over floors of tessellated marble. 'Within our hostel, no man holds ruling privilege over any other beyond himself. Rest assured, the audience you ask will be private.'

'And our untended horses?' asked Lysaer in heroic effort not to snap. Despite all his care, the reverberation of his voice slapped back angry. 'They'll abide by Ath's peace and not stray in the bogs?'

'The creatures will do as their nature directs. Fear for nothing. They shan't hang their bridles. Claithen has gone to look after them.' In a swirl of white robes, the initiate sister breezed ahead through the rune-carved portal and led through to the inner sanctuary.

Behind her, alone, Lysaer slammed short.

The grand space beyond held anything but the run-down poverty he expected.

Lysaer entered a pillared loggia. An open-air courtyard stretched beyond with a fountain playing at its centre. Outside these grey walls with their coiling, queer incised sigils, the hour was night, lit by the risen moon and ruddy torches. Here, from no source the eye could discern, lay an ice-pale twilight, all silver and lavender and the deep leafy mystery of an enormous stand of trees. These were not scrubby, storm-tattered hardwoods, nor the palms of the Scimlade peninsula, but patriarch trees with towering, high crowns and trunks as broad as the reach of five men.

They were a living enigma, impossibly tall and wide; they should have towered through the roof of the building that housed them.

The air beneath their branches smelled of life, a tapestry of rich growing greenery bound to tension which reminded of the unseen power of a stormfront beyond the horizon.

'There,' said the adept, her hand on Lysaer's sleeve a feather-light, guiding touch. 'You may sit by the fountain for your interview.'

Lysaer took one step, two, and then faltered to a stunned halt. He braced one hand for balance against a pillar. The carved patterns beneath his palm seemed to emanate a profound sense of silence and harmony.

He blinked hard and shivered. The clothing on his body seemed to scratch and constrict, for no sane reason an intrusion on his flesh. The sensations struck through his being had no parallel inside his experience. Not when he had expected figurines in niches and verdigris brass lamps, and the painted gilt icons of Daelion Fatemaster and Dharkaron's Chariot. The cathedrals of Ath's Grace he remembered from his homeland held grand, groined ceilings shafted in stirred dust. Only echoes had filled them, as solemn robed priests made their way through devotions and prayer.

Here, beyond the pillars, spread a space with no walls, no roof, no lamps with lit candles burned for blessing. Before his amazed regard lay the creator's primal forest, its breathing summer foliage alive with animals and birds. Peace cloaked the loam-rich air, thick as drugged sleep, but sealed into clarity like crystal. Snapped to a razor's edge of awareness, Lysaer gave way to awe. No longer could he pay heed to the tinny voice of logic which insisted this place could not exist; or that he should show surprise at the dozing leopard he strode past as he resumed his way forward.

Past and future fell away from him. The crisp swish of grasses beneath his step held more meaning than remembered experience. A grazing hare hopped aside for his footfalls, unfrightened. Beyond lay the fountain, no carved edifice, but a natural spring that welled from a stepped scarp of rock. The glassine play of water sluiced away his last fragile hold on disbelief.

Mazed into wonder that pulled at the mind and cradled the heart in deep mystery, Lysaer lost touch with the waking awareness of his body. The forest of Ath's adepts held a limitless, expanded reality that extolled all life in celebration. Man's doings and causes outside came to seem a tawdry, overdressed dream, played out in gusty motion and senseless noise.

Exotic birds in rainbow plumage perched in the alders, nestled shoulder to shoulder with hawks and ocean shearwaters. They did not fly at the prince's approach, but watched him, bright eyed in fey wisdom.

'Where are the priests?' Lysaer whispered.

The woman beside him laughed, mellifluous as the water's voice, falling. 'We have no priests, no priestesses. That would imply a hierarchy where Ath's law bids none to exist. You come as a man, and as earth's balance dictates, the initiate who speaks will be female.'

'I need no one's counsel.' Lysaer rested his raised foot on the rim of the rock pool. Beneath his braced stance, rerendered in bled colours by the half-light, his reflection stared back at him, shattered as droplets rained down in random melody and scattered the illusion of his presence. Unable to feel alarmed, lost beyond reach of concern for that lack, the prince addressed his purpose. 'I came here to seek two others in your care, an exiled guard captain named Tharrick and the widow, Mistress Jinesse, from Merior. By the gate you told me I might see them.'

'So you might.' The lilted words were patience, not promise.

Lysaer broke his regard on the pool and stared at the porcelain-still figure beside him. She waited for him to give up something. The feeling pressed through his quietude with the force of solid touch or the chill of a storm-soaked shirt.

His hands were empty. The magnificence of this forest reduced his plan for a bribe to the basest form of insult. Lysaer regarded the white mystic in all her dusky-skinned beauty, and could not step back as he became watched in turn by a regard taintless silver as new rain.

An unprincely need stole through him to explain himself. The diplomat's training dunned into him since childhood failed to restore his focus, but instead sliced his mind into unmanageable disarray. One fragment insisted his concern stemmed from desire to protect the widow's twins from corruption. Another, unruly and traitorous, seized control: and that one urged answer first.

'The man, Tharrick, knows more than he's saying of my enemy's intentions, and the woman's part is crucial. She has no choice but to follow her children. When she does, she'll guide the way for my war host.' Against the plinked cry of springwater, over the feathered rustles as the birds ruffled and stared, the statement rang loud as a shout.

Ever proud of his grip on discretion, Lysaer shrank in dismay, in embarrassment; then, as the grasping manipulation in his words struck home, in disgraced and annihilating shame. He stared at the face of Ath's initiate, appalled.

Yet her ebon brows remained smoothed beyond censure. She said, 'The man and the woman you mention are guests here. They have their own will by Ath's law, and they desire not to be used so.'

Lysaer bit back impatience. He cupped his temples,

strove to reconcile his splintered self-unity and banish the mad play of hallucination. But the trickle of the fountain and the soft, fluting calls of the songbirds unravelled his intent to distraction.

Brazen and sharp, he was speaking again, this time from the half that was prince. 'Tharrick and Jinesse have been misled, even dangerously beguiled. For the good of all people, I *must* hunt down the sorcerer who corrupted them.'

The adept answered, brisk, 'To take his life!'

Lysaer felt hurled off centre once again, spun round and dizzied until he wanted to crack into crazed laughter. But only hot tears wet his cheeks. He clawed back to balance, but nothing was the same. By his elbow, the birds flapped alarmed wings and flew; the hare by his boot was already gone. The leopard, now alert and sprung to her feet, watched him with a huntress's glare, her verdigris eyes open and round as a pair of weathered copper coins. The initiate's edged speech had not upset the beasts from their peace; unsettled by chills, Lysaer understood that his refocused presence had triggered their sudden alarm.

He wished all at once to straighten, to walk, to leave. As he moved, the pool recaptured his gaze, cast a veil of magnetic attraction. Too late, he realized a trap had closed over him. The stilled peace of the trees pressed him into a deep well of lassitude.

At his side, the woman turned back her white hood. Her loosened hair gleamed in the pale, lucent twilight like ripples of dark-dyed silk. Her eyes were moonstone. Her lips framed the voice of Dharkaron Avenger, or the wheels of his Chariot as they turned on a thundering charge to claim the world's due redress.

'Arithon Teir's'Ffalenn is no enemy of yours.'

Lysaer felt a blistering cry rip from the depths of his throat. He felt strong, whole, and gloriously clearminded. 'Arithon s'Ffalenn would as soon see me dead, just as I would kill him. If you doubt his intent, he has toyed with you.'

'*Arithon Teir's'Ffalenn is no enemy of yours,*' the lady repeated. She stood tall before him. Her porcelain finger scribed a seal in white fire upon the air.

The flux of sudden light splintered between mind and spirit.

Riven by that rushing tide of power, Lysaer flung back, tripped on the rimrock, and found himself inexplicably turned around. Both hands splashed to the wrists in icy water. He gasped from the wet and the shock. Dizzied by the sensation of split personality, laced by pain that skinned through to his bones, he was embattled by irreconcilable truths: *of children trained to slit the throats of wounded men, and Arithon s'Ffalenn wholly innocent of the command that had sent them forth to cause bloodshed. Then the second, bleakly damning, of himself with his s'Ilessid gift of justice bent awry by the usage and possession of Desh-thiere's wraith.*

Lysaer screamed aloud in split voices. 'Ath and Dharkaron's pity on me! The deaths at Tal Quorin were none of my choosing.' But surcease was denied him. In the searing, deep mirror of the initiate's regard, amid the terrible mystery of the glade, he observed his past deeds recast in a mould that condemned him. *In turn, he beheld Arithon forced to the unwilling role of killer.*

The oddly skewed vision refused to relent: Lysaer saw himself, and wept for the deaths of clan wives and children brought through his given gift of light; *and* he saw himself in the stern role of prince, deluded by duty to enact an execution for an ignorant, blind claim of just cause.

Lysaer howled as the awful dichotomy ran him through like snapped glass, sharpened by razor-edged conscience.

'Who am I?' he cried to his tormentor, who was not mortal flesh, but steel which cut to lay him bare.

The adept's voice in answer was metal just quenched from the forge fire. 'Step back. Step into the pool. The spring will cleanse you. Ath's mercy will allow you forgiveness.'

The half of him that wept heard a haven in her words, and begged beyond pride for such release. The half of him that was prince saw no cleansing and no pool, but a whirling grey tide of Desh-thiere's wraiths, jaws agape and fanged mouths slashing in hunger to rip his bare flesh.

He cried out again, seared by the agonies of temptation. Desire made him ache to let everything go, to set aside strife and embrace his bastard half-brother in reconciliation.

Yet suspicion resounded in faint, far-off clamour, that the notes played by the fountain and the initiate's bright powers might lure in false promise to condemn him.

The words of his father lashed through his turmoil and damned him for selfish wishes. *'You were born royal, boy. A prince never acts for himself. No matter how hard, no matter how painful, regardless of how lonely the decision may be, you must rule in behalf of your people.'*

'Lady, there can be no quarter given in this war,' Lysaer gasped. To yield to belief that Arithon was blameless was to repudiate honour: to abandon justice for the unsuspecting cities bound under s'Ilessid protection and to endorse the full-scale ruin of hapless innocence.

'I will not suffer a peace to be built upon lies.' Whole once again, snapped back to self-command with the burning focus of a glass lens poised to seed fire, Prince Lysaer regained his feet and drew himself up to full height. He raised his wet palms and blotted skinned knuckles upon the dry silk of his sleeves.

His acts at Tal Quorin had not been misled choice. He was no man to take the lives of clan families without the most dire cause.

This initiate was no friend to believe he could be duped to embrace his half-brother in amity. Her uncanny powers and dangerous persuasion still threatened to besiege his unsettled grip on morality. Lysaer saw he must escape, else stand at risk of casting off his very honour as a ruler. Without his gift of light, the land had no protector from Arithon's insidious corruption.

'My lady,' he said, restored to flawless courtesy, 'I will be taking my leave.'

His statement seemed to rip a film off his mind, and the sanctuary's spell lost its hold on him. Lysaer turned from the pool. Free at last to move, he hastened toward the loggia through what seemed a dream gone to tatters. The grass beneath his step had turned a crackling, dry brown; the leopard and the birds had all vanished; the soft, twilight glow beneath the towering trees had become harsh and flat, like snow piled over cloudy glass. The air wore the stale, musty leaf scent of autumn on the heels of a killing frost.

Lysaer passed between the pillars, crossed the flagstone walk. As he stepped through the arched portal to the anteroom, a terrible shiver raked through him. For a dreadful moment, his knees went weak and his senses overturned into vertigo. He dared not look down at the sheened marble floor for the irrational fear that his body would cast no reflection. Then his men were beside him, talking, asking questions. He ignored them in his rush to be outdoors, to breathe bracing, chilly air under icy, ordinary moonlight.

The haunting unease flayed his nerves, even then. Surrounded by the company of his escort, he thrashed through uncertainty, still unable to tell whether his experience in the grove had been a vision brought on by a moment of weakness, or an assault of illusion, controlled by manipulative power.

Whichever reason answered, the implications were unpleasant. Should the adepts hold their sympathy with

Arithon, their mysteries posed a force that could not be ignored if the Master of Shadow evaded the new muster of his armed host. In sharp want of a drink and the refuge of his tent, Lysaer gave hoarse commands for immediate return to his war camp.

Behind him, in the sanctum the s'Ilessid prince had abandoned, the white-robed initiate sat in sorrow by the pool's rim. Falling leaves caught in her lap, scarlet and rust as two bloodstains set apart in time. The branches above her held a queer, still silence. The finches and the hawks had flown. She could sense their fading energy, soaring on spread wings to the source from whence sprang all Ath's mystery.

From beyond the loggia doorway, muffled very little by grey rock walls carved in sigils, the voice of the Prince of the West re-echoed back in mettlesome temper. 'Sithaer's Furies! We'll be the best part of the night recapturing those horses from the swamp!'

Then his officer's reply, hurt and sullen, declaiming, 'Your Grace, what did you expect to come mounted to a hostel of Ath's Brotherhood!'

'They always do this?' Lysaer blistered back. 'Take a man's stallion and turn it loose without leave?'

The altercation dwindled as the company passed on foot through the gate arch into the lane. 'Any beast in harness, your royal Grace. It's old custom. But surely you knew that . . . ?'

Within the desecrated sanctuary, the lady adept reached up with shaking hands and settled her hood in soft folds over her ebon hair. She waited in sorrow until Claithen's whispered step crossed to the pool's edge before her.

A moment he stood in communion. Mute in his grief, he mourned what he saw: the combined effects of a strong prince's will, and the insidious, warped legacy the

Mistwraith had made of the royal s'Ilessid birthright of true justice. The entangled ugly coil had stamped untold desecration upon a haven spun from dreams and prime power.

Such ruin augured ill for the future.

For the grove was not static, but a fluid play of forces susceptible to the influence of the mind and heart of any supplicant who entered. Out of need to restore a broken balance, to set right a kinked snarl in natural order, the sacred peace within had offered up its deepest well of mystery. The impact of Desh-thiere's curse against its current had torn like a hole into darkness, as a lamp expended before extremity. Since the loss of the old races, the order's fine knowledge was flickering, dying, reduced to mean sparks like candlewicks propped before a gale.

No adept alive could measure tonight's cost, nor number how many generations of strung sigils and gentle cycles of ritual had been tapped and burned away. Prince Lysaer had not been recalled to sane mind, but had only renewed the dedication which held him entrenched into blinded obsession.

The sanctuary would take many centuries to return to the glory of its former presence, if it could be restored at all. Those spirits called to wear the white of Ath's Brotherhood in recent years had been too few to replace ones who died.

Bowed to despair, the lady initiate regarded the unravelled decay of her hostel's inner sanctum. The tears that traced her face were not for the trees or the animals, but for a man royal born, warped so far outside the given pattern of his birthright, a compassionate summoning could not knit his life aura back into harmony and balance.

The sad fact confronted the enlightened at every turn: in the dead leaves, and the absence of beasts and winged spirits, and in the trickle of water grown lifelessly sterile.

The curse that afflicted this scion of s'Ilessid had become everything the Fellowship of Seven had warned and worse. The destruction of the grove offered tangible testimony: Lysaer could become a force in the land to unravel even basic, sacred order.

'I fear for the future,' Claithen murmured, a grainy, sad weight to each syllable. At his feet lay the harsh proof. The Mistwraith's geas as it afflicted the s'Ilessid prince was a fearful aberration, entrenched enough to cloud even the connection that linked the land to Ath's mystery. There were no precedents. With the Paravians vanished and the webwork of blessing they had invoked through grand rituals falling yearly into decay, the vital connection to prime power was fast becoming a forgotten art.

Claithen plucked the browned oak leaf from the initiate sister's lap and stroked its shrivelled length across his palm. 'Our course has never been more clear,' he sighed in resigned conclusion. 'We must interfere with the world's course, a little. Tharrick and Jinesse and the two sailhands who came for Ath's sanctuary must not be left to fall into the coil of coming war.'

The white lady laced her long fingers in agreement. 'By way of the mysteries, two of our brothers will be sent out with them to turn the eyes of the prince's sentries elsewhere. Ath's own grace will see the four safe past the cordon into the care of the *caithdein* of Shand.'

The High Earl of Alland, Lord Erlien, would not impinge on their freedom to choose their own course. In his hands the man and the woman would be spared from becoming a tool to hasten the onset of bloodshed.

Daybreak

The hike downslope to seek the shepherd children's family became a mutual contest of taut nerves. For the first time in Dakar's irresponsible life, the discomforts involved with bearing burdens like a pack-horse over inhospitable terrain came second to other concerns. He and Arithon cat-footed about each other's presence, the Mad Prophet in a brittle-edged, morbid fascination, and the Shadow Master, in the wolfish sort of reticence of a man who knew he walked weaponless.

Neither wished to test the effects of what they had shared in the ravine.

Midnight came and went. The stars above the Vastmark valleys scribed their set courses as pinprick sparks of scattered fire. The Kelhorn peaks rose sheer and fenced them in rim walls, etched like jagged, black glass, or spattered in hoards of midwinter ice, cupped like spilled silver in the clefts.

Off those high snowfields, the damp, uplands cold snapped in bitter, fretful gusts, tearing at dead grass and tossing the stems of browned bracken. Dakar clenched his jaw to stop chattering teeth and sorely wished he had carried a spare cloak. Between him and Arithon, every stitch of warm clothing had been lent at need to wrap Ghedair.

The boy rested in a makeshift sling across the Shadow Master's shoulders, bundled up like a carpet roll fringed with a shock of pale hair. The aching throb of his ankle kept him wakeful. He whimpered at each jar and slide caused by the uneven footing.

Tormented just as much by the sad, silent body in his arms, Dakar laboured down yet another dry gully that narrowed to a dim, dank defile. The walls were rotten stone, chinked in ferns whipped to thin, standing skeletons. Such a place might hold wyverns' lairs in caves higher up, where the ledges folded into gnarled rock. In darkness that in warmer months would have thrummed with bats and insects, Dakar picked a jinking path over beds of slipped shale, then swore a mighty oath over the leavings of livestock as he skidded and nearly sat down in fresh sheep dung.

From four paces off, Arithon peered at him, his guardedness loosened to amusement. 'By that, I gather we're somewhere near the flocks?'

Dakar ground out a last epithet and added, 'Stuff reeks like the vapours of Sithaer.'

'Careful.' Arithon's teeth flashed back a fast grin. 'Ivel the blind splicer won't know you any more. Or else he'll stop mistaking your presence for a beer vat left to dry in the sun.'

'The blind old coot did that?' Dakar shifted to juggle his load, then eased the lesser bite of the bowstring and the strap that hung Arithon's lyranthe. 'Dharkaron himself! If that filthy-tongued whoreson had eyesight to see his own face, he'd strike himself dumb, then spend all his days with his ugly mug stuffed in a sack.'

'Dakar! Where's your sense of fun?' Arithon threaded the gap through the gulch and reappeared, a burdened silhouette against the moon-washed floor of the valley. 'Ivel's foul gossip just happens to be the life of the shipyard. Nobody's spared. He sets great store by his honesty.'

'Ivel's grasp of truth would steam the scales off a snake!' Dakar tripped on a jutted chunk of rock, bashed his elbow against an outcrop, and emerged to more fluent curses onto open ground.

He needed a moment to notice why Arithon had stopped talking. A star of yellow light bobbed and wove up the furze-cloaked side of the corrie.

The Shadow Master gave a shout to guide the searcher, his effort broken into echoes against the inhospitable landscape. He then lengthened stride to close the distance as the flutter of the torch flame changed course.

Mindful such haste was an excuse to avoid his close company, Dakar pumped short legs to keep pace.

The torch bearer proved to be a young woman, armed with a short recurve bow and a quiver of steel-headed arrows. Lanky and agile as her nomad forebears, she crested the rise to meet them. Her caped, dun shepherd's cloak was flung back to free her long legs, her hood blown off in the wind. The rest of her was well covered in laced boots with tasselled cuffs and a skirt loomed in patterns of saffron and cream, strapped tight at the waist with yard lengths of thong kept handy to tie sheep in emergencies. She had a sharp-chinned face rubbed to colour by the cold. Her honey-pale braids jounced and jangled, hung with clusters of bronze bells strung on yarn through each end.

Dakar recalled vaguely that such trinkets were talismans, worn for some quirk of regional custom. Their notes tangled in dissonance as she flung up her brand and leaped the hooked bank of the streambed. 'Ghedair? Do you have Ghedair?'

'Dalwyn!' said the boy on Arithon's shoulder.

'Ath bless!' cried the woman on a broken, high note of relief. 'Child, Cait herdsman has searched half the night!' She thrust her cresset unseeing to Dakar, then pressed close to kiss the blond head which poked through the muffling cloaks.

'Easy, he's been injured.' Buffeted by the blown folds of sheep-pungent clothing, Arithon braced his stance and stayed patient. 'If you'll give me a moment, I'll lift him down. Are you kin?'

The woman named Dalwyn stumbled back, her brown-amber eyes gone wary and wide in discovery they were not tribesmen. The lilt of her Vastmark dialect emerged to a rush of embarrassment. 'Where's Jilieth? Did you find Ghedair's sister?'

The torch left abandoned in Dakar's hand did nothing to spare her from the bloodstained burden in his arms.

'Show me mercy!' she gasped, her chapped hands raised quickly in a gesture to turn the permanent settling of ill-luck. She glanced, imploring, back to Arithon, but his word was not needed. Already her hope ebbed away, redefining the bones that poverty and poor diet had left pressed sharp against the skin.

Dakar scarcely saw her. His attention stayed riveted by the insight that his antagonist was tired, or half-unstrung still, to have been caught aback; *else his masterbard's training should have stepped into the breach and broken bad news with better grace.*

Then action came, belated and too late: Arithon snapped the torch from Dakar's fist and spun his body to cast kindly shadow over the woman's crumpled stance and flooding tears. He said, 'We did all we could. The end, when it came, was light and painless.'

Born of a race well-seasoned to hardship, Dalwyn scrubbed her cheeks with calloused palms. 'The children's mother was my sister, dead in a rockfall two years ago.' Straightened to a sour chink of bells, she sighed, then stroked Ghedair's head to resettle him. 'More lasting, the sorrow of the father. He was crippled in the slide that took his wife. The children are his last family, and his only living hope for the future. Except for one bonded herdsman, he has none but me and the boy to tend his flocks.' She flung a discomposed glance toward the bundle held clutched to Dakar's chest. 'As you see, the three of us aren't enough by ourselves to mind the blessings we are charged with.'

Arithon briskly contradicted. 'Jilieth was headstrong, no fault of yours, and Ghedair did as much as a man could. Show us on, lady. If the father waits for news, we have a clear duty to see his son home to his side.' He pressed the brand back into the woman's shaky grasp, then waited for her to lead the way.

'*Druaithe!*' the woman swore in dialect. 'Here's me such a fool, I ran out without bringing a signal horn. Ill-thought, ill-luck follows. Cait will come in, I suppose, when he tires.'

They had not far to go. The corrie opened into a narrow, sheltered valley, monochromatic under moonlight, and aflood like moiled waters with the tight-packed, jostling backs of sheep. The air between gusts hung rank with the flock's musky odour, nipped by a darker tang of peat smoke. The angular contours of a shepherd's tent nestled amid the rim-lit scarps. A lamp burned inside, glowing dull red through the geometrical markings dyed into its oiled felt. The lore of the Vastmark tribes was extensive, as if elaborate customs and superstitions could replace their dearth of possessions. The banded patterns in each dwelling's weaving represented an inheritance, passed down through generations, to ward off a specific aspect of misfortune.

The movement on the slope raised a deep-throated bay from the guard dogs. Great beasts, broad-chested and sable with heavy white ruffs at the neck, they were bred to stand down the wyvern, and trained to defend sheep from winter wolves. At the approach of strange visitors, they burst from the flocks, unravelling order like blunt instruments through a burst seam. A fierce command from the woman halted their headlong charge. Tall as a man's waist, and fanned in a pack's closing circle, the dogs slowed to a stiff-legged walk.

'Come ahead, they won't trouble you.' Dalwyn's promise did little to reassure. The beasts sniffed at the arrivals, snarling low in their throats and glowering with wide-set, intelligent eyes.

The woman beckoned Dakar and Arithon uphill toward the tent through the bawling, packed mass of sheep. The dogs trotted after, hackles raised and still grumbling. She sent them off with a phrase in shepherd's dialect to bid them round up any strays, then pushed aside the painted entry flap. Light sliced the dark, yellow and blinding after black rock and grey moonlight.

'My tribe bids you joy and increase,' she said in formal welcome, a catch to her voice for the fact that her kinfolk this night lay diminished by a life.

Discomfited by the sudden brilliance, the visitors stepped over cushioning fleeces ingrained by the rancid tang of mutton fat and leather. Propped against a hassock stuffed with straw, the family patriarch waited amid a nest of woven blankets heavy enough to serve as a hearthrug. A man old and gnarled beyond his years, he had a drooping moustache and features quarried into slanting wrinkles by ongoing years and harsh weather. His eyes were gouged deep into bone-hooded sockets by the pitiless, strong sun which, summer and winter, burnished all that lived on the shadeless slopes of Vastmark.

Too proud to display his infirmity, too reserved to blurt anxious questions, the man regarded the strangers in iron patience, broken at once as Arithon crossed the light and lowered Ghedair onto the fleeces to clasp at his father's knee.

'*Druaithe*, boy, you gave us a fright,' the tribesman said gruffly, then cuffed the child with exasperated care with the back of a horny hand.

Dakar stood awkwardly through the stunned welcome, the stumbling, shocked questions, and finally, thankfully, the unbearable burden he had borne through the night was lifted from him by Dalwyn. A masterbard's given duty was to ease the hearts of the bereaved. Arithon was left to deliver explanation for an event too raw for anyone else to handle with grace or diplomacy.

The Mad Prophet sidled into a corner. No longer comfortable with the wastrel he had been, unwilling yet to measure the discontent which waited to poison his future, he peevishly wished the homes of Vastmark shepherds were not always wretchedly bare of furnishings. Not a stool or a cushion lay at hand to ease his need to sit down.

Winter cottages in the deep valleys might have a stone table or a few three-legged stools, but the tents taken upland to the flocks in high pastures held nothing that could not be packed and carried, or drawn on skids by a dog. Timber was scarce and precious. The most conspicuous item in any tribal household was always the bow rack, lovingly crafted with copper and bone inlay, hung with its indispensable rows of weapons: longbows for damp, inclement weather, and the powerful short recurves laminated from thin strips of horn, glue, sinew and wood, preferred for extreme range on dry days. Each unstrung weapon lay paired beside its quiver of barbed broadheads. Slung on thongs alongside were the ram's horns carried to call warning, each one an heirloom passed down from mother to daughter and father to son, with chased silver mouthpieces, and ciphers of blessing and guard etched into their flared rims.

The dwelling itself was cramped and close. Draughts eddied beneath the ridgepole under tugging fingers of wind, stirring the smoky reek of tallow, and sheep fleece, and the dusky must of felted wool. Dalwyn rummaged through some bundles tied with thongs and found a flawed hide to sew into a shroud. Then she stepped from the tent to heat lamb stew in the communal kettle over an outside fire. Still kneeling in his shirtsleeves, Arithon conversed with the old man. Dakar thrilled to find he could at last interpret the locked timbre of strain which burred his enemy's replies.

The Masterbard's eyes wore a look of glazed weariness when he stirred at last to reclaim his lyranthe. Caution marked that exchange also.

Arithon knew well to be chary of the hostility he had invited to stalk his naked back. Only his respect for the grieving family deterred him from the blistering stamp of dialogue he habitually used to distance himself.

All over again, at the shaken end of his wits, he wrung from his lyranthe the exquisite measures of the signature composition first played to speed Jilieth's dying. The catharsis left the old man bent and weeping into the blond hair of his son. Dalwyn sat in a crumple of patterned skirts against the tent's centrepole, her elfin chin pressed into whitened knuckles, and her braids with their belled ends silenced between her linked hands.

When Arithon at last set his instrument aside and arose to let himself out, no one stirred to deter him. The music had not lulled Dakar from subterfuge. Bound by knots of cold venom he lacked the subtlety to unwind, he chose to bide his time and revel in his stilled power. The day would arrive when he was not reamed to the marrow over the plight of a dead child. At his leisure, he could unpick his antagonist's wily nature now the barriers between them were fretted thin. The hour would be carefully chosen, when he became the one to strike and rankle the Shadow Master's sacrosanct poise.

The triumph would be sweet, as he mined through defences and exposed the mean motives which had to exist behind Arithon's deep layers of deceit. On that day, the Fellowship Sorcerers could surely be convinced to release Asandir's geas of binding. The miserable spellbinder would see himself freed from a service he viciously detested.

An hour passed before anyone sought to track the bard into the darkness. By then, the moon rode low in the west, a punched disc upon velvet. The stars had spun toward a dawn not far off, and the bowl of the valley lay under the huge silence of an upland Vastmark night. By contrast, the summers were alive with noise, the clicks of insects locked warp through weft with the thrum of swooping nighthawks.

Winters were ruled by the frost. Against the broad-vowelled whine of the winds, the yips of a herd dog after a strayed sheep and the restless bleats of the flock cut the vast air like fine spun scratches in crystal.

Arithon stood with his back to the tent, his tight-knit shoulders hunched from the wind against the rough slab of a boulder. The miscast healing for Jilieth had torn his heart wide open. He felt as if his bones had been pulled through the skin, then replaced, one by one, in flawed glass. The slightest of taps would see him shatter. The ritual of manners chafed too thin for constraint. His bard's gift of empathy and the compassion of his fore-bears had flung him too far out of balance. Should he go back inside to seek shelter, he would find no surcease. The lamentation of the tribesfolk for their lost child held sorrow enough to unstring him.

If not for the tearing, brittle cold that slowed the dexterity of his fingers, he might have fetched his lyranthe and sought simple solace in melody. Lacking that, he made do with solitude and ached for the companionship of another winter night, spent over the rags of fanned flames and birch embers, brewing tea for his master, Halliron.

'Oh, you'll know times when the music you bring is a boon to everyone else but yourself,' the old man had cautioned.

Now, in full possession of his bardic powers, when Arithon could pick out the chime of the far, distant stars, he missed his mentor the most sorely.

As many times as he had watched his predecessor play consolation for a death, Halliron had never taught him how to distance the racking grief afterward. No Fellowship Sorcerer lay at hand to advise whether the melancholy which clawed him now was inflicted by lingering exhaustion, or the unwanted burden of his ancestry.

Whatever knotty tangle he had spun for himself, he was not to have quiet to unravel it. A wind-caught chime of bells invaded his haven, followed by the grate of a footfall on the shale.

Arithon's shoulders stiffened in apprehension under his loose linen shirt.

No need to belabour his predicament, that the gullies were skinned over with glaze ice; as Dalwyn drew closer, she would see well enough. He was already violently shivering.

'I brought your cloak,' she ventured.

He faced around, murmured his thanks, and claimed his garment from her, then bowed to inevitable demand. After all, the mourning that simmered in her should not be left to fester in silence.

'How did you do that?' she asked of the song he had made which precisely recaptured the departed spirit of a child. 'Jilieth was exactly as you played her to be. How could you ever have known?'

Arithon's hands were numb from the cold. He fumbled with the oyster shell clasps to fasten his cloak at the collar, then gave up and settled for folding the fabric tightly around his crossed arms. 'I saw her die. No one keeps their secrets through a passage such as that.'

Her eyes regarded him, too wide and dark. Obligated still by his bard's responsibility as well as the onus of being the bearer of ill news, Arithon sensed a desperation in her that went beyond a mere loss.

As though attuned to the care in his listening presence, Dalwyn snapped all at once, like a stick bent back under pressure. 'I tried so very hard to restrain that child! But ever since she lost her mother, no one could make her hear sense.'

Arithon's response was pure reflex. He unfurled his cloak in a driven, fast movement and caught her into his embrace. The scratch of the wool he drew over her shoulders smelled of gorse and sea salt; of the herbal compresses he had made to treat Ghedair and faintly, of the lye soap he had last used for shaving. While Dalwyn dissolved into racking, harsh tears, he cradled her against his shirt.

Her warmth became an unpleasant reminder of how chilled he was, and how vulnerable. No matter how thin the ground he trod himself, the forced gifts of royal inheritance would not allow him to pull back; and so he did not try to unstring her remorse, but said only, 'I know the girl was headstrong. Not even my music could hold her.'

'Why should a man of your talent be wandering these hills?' Dalwyn raised her chin to the chink of a bell as her braid slipped over his elbow. 'Who are you? Why did you come here?'

'Athera's new Masterbard, and as you see, scarcely experienced with the arts that go with the title. I came for personal interests.' His fingers burrowed under the hair at her nape, an instinctive gesture to ease the cold. Yet Dalwyn, pressed full-length against him, could scarcely suppress the light, startled tension that wound through her frame as she reacted in female awareness.

Underneath her sheep-smelling woollens, she had a clean-limbed, athletic firmness that reminded him sharply of Elaira. Scorched through by unexpected desire, then a pain of loss so intense he could only gasp, he could do nothing to spare Dalwyn from the effort that followed, as he forced back his feeling and denied his response to crush her more tightly against him.

'You have no wife,' she whispered into the hollow of his throat. Her braid draped across his wrist and forearm, distinct as a brand against his skin.

'No.' He disengaged her hair in retreat to a petulant plink of disturbed bronze. 'Don't say any more.'

But his shaken, rough whisper unveiled too much. All the sorrow that burdened him since the denial of his love; the humiliation and fear he carried from the raid at Minderl Bay, patched overtop of the abiding hurt which harrowed him still, for the cost exacted in guilt that left him deprived of his mage-sight. Never whole since Tal Quorin, he felt set under siege. Tonight's effort to spare Jilieth had left him worn down and raggedly exposed.

He had small will to trample down his response to Dalwyn's need for human warmth.

His hesitation warned her as he groped for the strength to let her down. A sob of sheer misery ripped from her. 'Damn you to Sithaer, if you knew I was *nandir*, why ever did you touch me to begin with?'

The term was not familiar; Arithon's brows drew down in perplexity as his masterbard's lore fell short. The closest equivalent in old-style Paravian translated to mean '*without*'. He dared not ask her to interpret; before Dalwyn's baffling onslaught of pain, a wrongly put question could wound. He negated her rage in the only way possible: tightened his grip in helpless, trapped sympathy and soothed the belled end of her braid.

The bronze gave off metallic shimmers of sound as she yanked the hair from his fingers, then hurled her fury into his teeth in a burst of embittered loneliness. 'That means barren.' Dalwyn shook the braid to a stinging clash of bells. 'That's what these are: a warning. Our tribes hold that to touch a woman who cannot bear is to curse a man's sons to sour luck. But I thought you valley folk believed differently.'

'We do.' Arithon peeled her hard fingers off her honey

hair, then snapped the yarn ties in one pull. He dropped the bells, squelched them in the frost-rimed grass underfoot, and feathered her plait loose between his fingers. 'Whether you can bear children means nothing to me or the offspring I don't have.' Since the tremble in his touch betrayed his desire, she deserved the bared shreds of his honesty.

'You should know. If I took you in my arms to offer comfort, I admit my mistake. You are comely enough to arouse, but it is another woman's face that I see, and another's love I bear in my heart.'

Dalwyn gave a high, wild laugh for the flood of relief that washed through her. 'Is that all? Why is your lady not with you?'

'She can never be.' Arithon released her then, his face turned unseeing toward the flinty wall of the boulder. 'She took vows, you see. Her life is already dedicated as a Koriani enchantress.'

Against the comprehending pity that yawned into silence between them, he changed the subject. 'How can you be sure you are barren?'

Dalwyn stripped the bells from her other braid and let the wind tug that one loose also. 'Ah well. Does it matter? Tribal law on the subject is most strict.' Stiffened to wry strength by his private admission, she spoke in bald terms of her plight. 'After marriage, if a woman fails to conceive within two years and a day, she may choose five partners to share her bed. Each lies with her for the span of four seasons. If she bears to none inside that given time, she wears the bells for the rest of her life.' Her bravado wavered as she finished, 'Jilieth was the daughter I can never have. There are no words to repay what you and Dakar tried to do for her.'

Arithon let her come as she took a step forward, her hair fanned in waves across her shoulders and hood, spun silk against the coarse cloth. He regarded her face, fine-chiselled from hunger, and tipped up in entreaty, tinselled in tear tracks by moonlight. A queer thrill shocked through him, born out of clear truth and empathy. He saw that this once, he might indulge his raw need, and answer hers with the gift of his presence.

She was barren and had lost an irreplaceable child; and her woman's hurt ached for the ease of giving comfort forbidden within the circle of her people.

What else could he do but gather her in and nestle a sigh against the soft weave of her crown.

Her hands crept up and clasped behind his neck. As she began to worry out his harsh knots of tension, she murmured against the hollow of his throat. 'For what you have done for Ghedair, and for the sake of Jilieth's memory, I beg that you share what you know of your beloved. Can you bring yourself ease, I don't mind if you whisper every detail you remember of her face. On the contrary, the night is most cold and sad. I believe we should be doing ourselves a kindness.'

Crossroads

The day after his failed inquiry at Ath's hostel, Lysaer s'Ilessid releases Mearn's galleys to begin thorough search of the coastline, then moves his camp from Merior to Southshire, to winter until the larger body of his troops can complete their march to rejoin him; and his nettled thoughts circle, that since his encounter with the adepts, the threat he has dedicated himself to eradicate will but grow the more dangerously entrenched through the wait while his war host musters . . .

Far north, as the sun warms the ice on Avenor's brick battlements, Princess Talith packs her trunks and bullies her captain-at-arms to provide her a small escort, her wish to embark on a trader southbound across stormy Westland waters, and her intent to rejoin her royal husband . . .

In the water-worn cave of sandstone that serves as his winter headquarters, Erlien, *caithdein* of Shand, tosses aside a rolled sheaf of charts; over the scraping hiss as the parchment unfurls, he informs the man and the widow sent from Merior by the uncanny guidance of Ath's Brotherhood, 'Yes, my scouts can take you to Arithon, though I don't mind saying straight. I dislike your mistrust of him. His integrity is sound. But if the adepts saw fit to act for you, how can I shirk my part . . . ?'

IV. *THIRD INFAMY*

After the horror of the wyvern attack, Arithon recovered
his aplomb in snapping fast form, his vicious verbal style
grown the more barbed to drive back Dakar's encroach-
ment on his privacy. Whether he conspired in secret
toward some grand, subtle subterfuge became a point of
useless conjecture. He charted his days with the erratic
abandon of a swallow flying zigzags, and through the
course of three weeks made social acquaintance with
half the tribes in Vastmark. To the Mad Prophet's chagrin, his sojourn into obscurity included backbreaking
labour as he helped work their vast flocks of sheep.

Fed up with the rancid stink of wool beneath his nails,
and strenuous hikes in thin air, Dakar might have
wavered in his resolve not to drink. Except the herdsmen
stocked no beer or whisky. Unhappy past experience
kept him sober. The tribes brewed a spirit of unparalleled
potency, a noisome, sticky liquid hoarded in leather
flasks, fermented from wild honey and soured goat's
milk.

There were reasons why the barren slopes of Vastmark
were shunned by travellers and trade. A place of wind-
burnished scree and frost-chiselled peaks, the site was

only hospitable to wyverns and hawks, without roads or taverns or post stables. Since the nearest house of refined entertainments lay eighty leagues distant in Forthmark, the Mad Prophet dreamed at night of sweet-burning incense, and rouged doxies lounging in silk. By day, he bored himself silly, eating mutton stew and docking lambs' tails and enduring exhaustive rounds of archery.

By maddening contrast, the Prince of Rathain embraced such bucolic splendour as if he had worn greasy woollens all his life.

Wet snowfall and sheep leavings made a troublesome mix for a man in need of new boots. Dakar spent sullen hours by lamplight patching rotted leather and burst toe seams, while Arithon reeled out some vengefully cheerful dance tune from the strings of his lyranthe.

More clannishly isolate than the fishing enclave at Merior, and more forthright with their trust, Vastmark tribesfolk saw no harm in the Shadow Master's dry wit. They laughed when he bungled with the dogs and the sheep; their women chaffed him when he tangled the rough yarn they made with drop spindles while the talk circled the fires after dusk. His skill at the butts earned no chuckles at all, but only their sharp-eyed respect. For them, the bow was survival. Few outsiders could best their accuracy, acquired through lifelong practice.

'If they were sporting enough to make wagers, we could win ourselves a fortune in fleece,' Dakar said in ruffled petulance as they made breathless crossing over a ridge between settlements. 'By the tone of their boasting, a man would think nobody beyond these mountains had ever in his life touched a bow.'

Arithon paid no heed to the jaundiced glare sent his way.

'We're not staying on through the lambing season,' Dakar nattered on in hopeful, one-sided conversation. 'The herdsmen sleep in the meadows then. It's a sure-fire way to catch aches in the joints, with the ice still fast in the ground.'

The tail of Dakar's thought was too bold to gripe out loud: that further assignations with the belled woman, Dalwyn, were going to be difficult to conduct with any decency. The liaison flouted tribal mores on fertility and no elder would condone the ill chance of inviting a bane on the flocks.

On douce behaviour for the first time since puberty, the Mad Prophet gloated over each gleaned sign that his quips pricked Arithon to discomfort. For a man of self-contained habits, the close presence of an inimical observer had to rub like salt in a blister.

No clear purpose suggested why the Master of Shadow should bury himself in tribal hospitality or linger in these stony plateaus tending sheep. The inhabitants led lives too straightforward for subterfuge. Their poor tents and their half-starving children offered no prospects for wealth. Dakar chewed his lip and pondered afresh whether Arithon might immerse himself in directionless pursuits as a smokescreen. All the best theories led nowhere. Hobnobbing with shepherds would not stop Lysaer's war host. Nor would killing work defer the day of reckoning when the spellbinder bound to him by Asandir's will at last came to expose the deceit at the root of his affairs.

Yet the weeks stretched into a month. As the sun rode higher and brought thaw to the south slopes, and springs loosened into freshets that ran loud beneath the ice, balked logic fretted itself thin. Dakar lay awake at night on a bed of rancid sheepskins, listening as the Masterbard talked for hours, and the crawling flare of tallow dips lit circles of herdsmen and elders. A frisson of chill dogged the Mad Prophet's thoughts. It was easy to forget the plot he embarked on was dangerous: Arithon s'Ffalenn was many things, but never before this a man to shrink from confrontation.

Just when Dakar despaired of getting free before the flocks were driven to higher pastures, Arithon announced his intent to depart. The shepherds decided his send-off deserved a celebration. Since notice came too late to hoard brush for a bonfire, every herdsman felt moved to ransack his family tent and donate a flask of strong drink.

Dakar reaffirmed the fact he found the taste intolerable. 'Worse than white lye. Reams a channel from your gullet straight through to your liver. I've knocked myself down on that stuff before. You'd have to be daft to do it twice. Trust me. You'll bear the grandmother of all hurts come the morning.'

Reclined and obliviously comfortable amid the flea-scratching pack of huge shepherd dogs, Arithon regarded him and laughed. He wore a tribal shirt, patched at the elbows and none too clean, and if he had shaved the past dawn, his hair ran wild for want of cutting. Raffish and bright-eyed, he relished another swig and passed the liquor flask on to the next herdsman. The next thing he said folded everyone else into shrieking fits of mirth.

Convinced some ugly joke had been cracked at his expense, Dakar stalked off, disgusted.

By daybreak, in a queer change of roles, the Mad Prophet arose clear-headed. He found Arithon already wakeful, though rumpled, as if he had slept in his clothes. The rims of his eyes were angry red and his bard's voice held a pothouse husk as he made grumpy comment to one of the archers about the stones he had found in his bedding.

That brought a peal of hoots, which an avid and watchful Dakar gloated to see made him wince.

'*Druaithe*, man,' swore the archer. 'Last I saw, ye were sprawled by the spring, crooning some lovesong to a kelpie.'

Arithon gave an abandoned smile. 'You know, that's

174

the trouble with drinking. Come the morning, you can never remember their names.'

The herdsmen gathered to send him off jostled closer in camaraderie. His words shaped slowly to force precise diction, Arithon told them to relay his regards to his past night's drinking companions.

'Were ye nippy about it, ye could be back to say such yourself,' someone quipped. 'Yon laggards won't be stirring. Not even should the thunders and Dharkaron's Black Chariot come clapping about their sore heads.'

Another woman called in coarse awe, 'It's the creator's own miracle you're on your two feet after what you slugged down last night. I'd have wagered three ewes to a fleeced wether you couldn't make it to your knees, no matter how fierce you had the need to piss.'

Never more wickedly serious, Arithon shrugged. 'I had to get up. Else Dakar would have his revenge on me for the times I've kicked him when he was down. We really must be off.'

His circle of admirers parted, elbowing one another and chuckling. All showed regret at the leave-taking. One dog grown particularly fond of the Shadow Master whined on the fringes, morose. At the far edge of the circle, amid an isolate jink of bronze, Dalwyn awaited, her cloak hood pulled low over her face, and the anxious release of her half-held breath a feather of white in the cold.

'Will you come back?' she asked. 'Ghedair wished to know.'

Arithon regarded her through a careful pause, touched her cheek, then bent his gaze to encompass the high peaks, fired now like steel raised red from the forge in the first blush of sunrise. 'Lady, tell Ghedair to depend on it.'

The journey on foot to the coast took five days. Dakar grumbled to hide his relief that Arithon had lost his urge to dawdle. They wended a track through the valleys, slogging through peat bogs and crossing, rock to rock, over freshets risen with snowmelt. In the low country, the southland sun prevailed over the cold, which still mailed the peaks in ice. The hollows spread lush as new velvet, the scattered puddles skimmed into wind scallops that cupped turquoise glimmers of sky. The bracken on the hillsides lay stitched with new shoots. In the marshes, the springing tips of pale reeds were sliced by the cries of the curlews.

Dakar had not realized they had strayed so far inland, sharing migration with the herdsmen.

The sloop *Talliarthe* rode quiet in her anchorage, a bit mussed by storm wrack, her brightwork left gritted by roosting gulls and gannets, and her bilges in sore need of bailing. Still clad in his patched herder's smock, her master looked as neglected. Dakar made the painful discovery that slack grooming did nothing to blunt the edge from Arithon's tongue. If the Shadow Master had been scatheful company before, the affray over the dead child had peeled away even the pretence of manners in private.

Rather than suffer the satiric barbs slung at him each time his comments bit too near to the bone, the Mad Prophet chose the more peaceable labour of swabbing *Talliarthe*'s decks.

For a day, the sloop's rigging flapped like a farmwife's clothesline with laundry. Arithon whipped new ends on chafed lines and let the sunlight which sliced in gold blades through the cliff walls bleach the mildew from her stored canvas. Then, reclothed in a fresh tunic and a shirt with silk laces, his fingernails trimmed and his overgrown hair nipped back in a thong, he raised sail. *Talliarthe* threaded her way west in a dicey course through the reef-ridden waters that unreeled between the headlands and the tight, mazed shoals of the Cascains.

The channels between islets were too perilous to navigate by night. At anchorage each eventide, in the grim, shadowed mouths of a succession of remote coves, Arithon penned maps on new parchment. He sketched out the valleys and trails he had traversed through his winter excursion into Vastmark. He recalled those sites prone to slides, and which corries offered pasture, and how close the fodder could be grazed to support livestock at different seasons of the year. Trained to a masterbard's memory, he had amassed an impressive store of information from the course of the tribesfolk's idle talk.

'We're going to try sheepherding next?' Dakar asked, squeezing past to reach the companionway to dip a bucket of seawater to wash.

Arithon looked up as though he might answer, the flame in the gimballed lamp a ruddy glow over the upswept planes of s'Ffalenn features. Then his gaze brightened and his smile thinned to a scalpel's edge. 'You'll have to guess, if you can.'

The next day at noon, to Dakar's amazement, the *Khetienn* arrived in rendezvous, rigged out and completed on borrowed coin to the last fitted detail of her brightwork.

As her master saw her ghost between islands on the whispered breeze in her staysails, his expression lit to pure pleasure. Against the louring rocks of the shoreline, tanbark headsails crowned her in elegant curves like the flounces in a virgin's skirt. The brigantine was everything his design had intended, lean of frame, with the promise of a handy turn of speed in her grace, and the varnish on her spars glossy as polished citrine.

New canvas flogged up an echoing thunder as she backed her sails and dropped anchor. Arithon leaped to uncleat the *Talliarthe*'s tender, afire with joy and pride, as well he might be, Dakar allowed from his propped stance at the sloop's mainstay. Seafaring s'Ffalenn forebears in Karthan had time-tested that rapacious, long sheerline.

Then the shout of a child pealed through the clank of the anchor chain; Fiark's, Dakar determined with a wince at the sting to his eardrums.

Poised to thread oars in his rowlocks, Arithon looked around in dismay. His stunned glance locked on the pair of towheads butted over his brigantine's bowsprit. The boy's effusive peals of delight were predictably followed by Feylind's shrill hail to her dark-haired idol in the dory. 'Look sharp, all you lubbers! Your cap'n's coming aboard!'

The Shadow Master's flushed elation drained away into pallor and for a second his heart seemed to stop.

'Fiends plague!' Dakar crowed in righteous pleasure. 'If you hadn't meant to kidnap those twins, your fat's in the fire, regardless. Jinesse will tear you to ribbons.'

Arithon came alive as if pricked. 'She'd be far better off to warm the hides of her children.' His dilemma was unpleasant, with his formal promise given to guarantee the children's safety.

Their wayward presence here exposed them to risks he was powerless to avert. Merior was closed to him; the coasts were under search by s'Brydion galleys. He had no escort and no ship he could entrust to dispatch them home. The frustration in his anguish showed through his every movement as he slammed down his oars and squared his lean shoulders to row. The blades lapped deep and scalloped dark water to froth in the dory's agitated wake.

Too late, indignant, the Mad Prophet realized he no longer had hold on the painter. 'Wait! You're not going to leave me here!'

'In fact, I am.' The vinegar bite to the Shadow Master's smile chased a nasty chill down Dakar's back.

Unless the spellbinder undertook the fool's errand of swimming, he was stranded aboard the sloop until a longboat and crew were sent from the brigantine to ferry him. The creeping suspicion ate him to rage, that

Arithon might seize upon his absence to enact all his best covert planning.

By the time Dakar managed to commandeer himself a tender, the twins had been expertly chastened to silence and sent to bed in the first mate's cabin. Twilight sketched the high cliff rocks and the jumble of outlying islets in tones of poured lead and deep azure. A wind that nipped with the memory of winter slapped frisky waves against the hull. Belowdecks, the aft cabin was snug. A gimballed lamp warmed the grain of a generous chart table. Around the spread layers of maps and mismatched documents, a council of sorts was in progress. Angled so the best light fell over his shoulder, Arithon sat propped beneath the paned window, one knee raised, his hands kept busy cracking the seals on several thick packets of correspondence.

Dakar admitted himself without knocking, hungry, but too nosy to miss what might transpire through delay if he joined the crew in the galley for bean soup. Discussion trailed off in the stale sort of pause that marked a topic several hours old. The *Khetienn*'s paid captain filled one of the chairs. An opened wine bottle rested on a tray alongside several long-stemmed Falgaire goblets, once the property of Prince Lysaer. Cut crystal strewed focused arrows of light across the damp-riffled leaves of those letters perused and discarded. The Shadow Master's hair lay in light disarray, as if more than once the absorbed rake of his fingers had hooked loosened strands from the thong tie.

'So, a search has been launched to track my movements,' Arithon said, sparing no glance aside for Dakar's blundering entrance. 'Go on. Galleymen dislike these channels. The currents are treacherous and strong, as you saw. Every oarsman I drank with at Innish insisted the cliffs here were haunted by spirits.'

The captain was a hulking, solid man with square eyes and ruddy cheeks and an affable, hearty turn of speech.

At the mention of ghosts, his lower lip twitched into petulance. 'There's a Second Age ruin on the mainland causes the haunts, which are no rumour, mind, but plain truth. You'd be canny to listen. Ships wreck here too fast to count. These waters breed whirlpools to suck a keel under, stirred by the shades of drowned crews.'

Arithon leaned forward, caught up the carafe, and poured a goblet of wine, which he offered in friendliness. The grizzled man accepted, his hand faintly shaking, indication enough he found the shoals in the Cascains unsettling.

Dakar declined the same service. Arithon retained the second filled goblet for himself and flipped the string off his last stack of letters. A pair of dice clicked across the decking overhead; two sailors exchanged bets in low murmurs.

Eased by the wine, the captain resumed his measured review of the southcoast gossip. 'Word of your doings reached the taverns of Innish as we sailed. Best steer most softly if you dock there again.'

'The merchant who holds my notes won't be hurt.' The Master of Shadow snapped a thumb through an official city seal, apparently indifferent as Dakar forwent the empty chair and jockeyed his girth behind the table to assume a comfortless perch on the windowsill. There, he craned his fat chin this way and that, until, by design, he gained a clear vantage over the correspondence being perused.

'I intend to repay my loan and the interest to the last copper,' Arithon said.

'Your benefactor never showed a worry over that.' The captain seemed intrigued by Dakar's prying as he added, 'You'd warned us well enough what was coming. There are friends still at Innish who won't be turned, whatever has happened at Southshire.'

'What's happened at Southshire?' Dakar cut in, his

eyes meanwhile tracking, upside down, the curlicued script of a feminine hand. The seal had been a false cover. A connoisseur of scents, he judged the perfume that wafted off the thin, pastel paper to be from a brothel up the coast. Its message matched his hunch: *'The restoration of Avenor is nearly complete and no sorcerer has arrived to bring retaliation for the standing stones torn down. Prince Lysaer is considered a hero. With everyone's dread of the ruin laid to rest, and the roads reopened to West End, his stature has grown. The arrogance of the trade guilds weakens against him as they see their fears dissolved by the very royalty they deplored . . .'*

'Well, Southshire's in Prince Lysaer's pocket,' the hired captain obliged. 'The merchants were already primed to welcome the increased business drummed up by a muster for war. Plain avarice saw to that. Then Lysaer gave a show fit to blind Ath Creator when he entered the main gates of the city. The whole populace turned out to throw flowers in the street to salute his royal cavalcade.'

The tale emerged in full-blown colour as the vintage wine mellowed the captain's nerves; how Lysaer, Lord Commander Diegan, and the dandyish Mearn s'Brydion had swept into Southshire in grand state. The gems and bullion braid on the prince's horse trappings alone had impressed the merchant's wives to goggling awe. The live presence of old blood royalty, all chiselled, pale elegance and guileless good manners, had done much to enliven their winter parties.

While the captain rambled on through his narrative, Arithon finished the scented letter and refolded it, the faintest clipped tension to his fingers the only sign that the news it contained was all grim. The present trend against him would not be reversed; given time, the rumours would reach even the backwater villages like Merior. The day would come when he was going to find his welcome proscribed wherever he chose to go on the continent.

Never had his salvaged brigantine meant more to life and freedom than at this moment. Dakar read as much in the swift, searching glances directed at intervals around the white-painted cabin.

'I don't suppose the military interests in the city gave much thought to the fripperies,' the Mad Prophet interjected, pressured to a new and dogged turn of mind that set impatience on the dalliance of light gossip.

'Ah, that.' The captain helped himself to more wine and scraped an itch between his shoulders against the bulkhead. 'It was an easy enough conquest, so I heard. Lysaer paid for a festival match.' Details followed in humorous, wry satire. The city garrison had been reduced to blustering incompetence, first by the smoothly perfect drills of the royal officers, then by the hard-bitten mercenaries from Alestron. The shipwrights who had once dealt with Arithon, and received their pay in pale gold, had watched this latest byplay, reserved to nonpartisan silence. But as the coterie around the prince became outspokenly devoted, whispers over shadows and piracy began to circulate. The crisp efficiency that earmarked Arithon's transactions came to be regarded with suspicion in retrospect.

'That mightn't have mattered,' the captain summed up. 'Except the spurning of your interests by Merior's fishermen became the stone that tipped the balance. The folk who ply the nets there are a dour enough lot, but even the galleymen respect them. When those villagers chose to forsake their trust, their opinion was taken as testimony.'

Dakar shot a veiled glance to measure Arithon's response. But the elegant, bard's fingers had delved through the stack of papers and emerged with another penned in heavy, antique script. The front bore a cipher scribed in old Paravian; the seal in the splash of ruby wax was royal, slashed across by a diagonal bar, denoting correspondence initiated on kingdom business by Lord Erlien, Regent and *caithdein* of Shand.

'Daelion avert!' Dakar murmured in surprise. 'What possessed an old blood clanlord to commit his news into writing? I haven't seen that happen since before there were the headhunters' leagues.' He trailed off, not so much in embarrassment for his filching interest in Arithon's affairs as for the glower from the captain, interrupted from his meandering recount.

Since the *caithdein*'s missive contained nothing of interest beyond an inventory list of blooded livestock, the verbal news recaptured its due share of interest.

The captain related how the Prince of the West had waited until the city trade guilds and government were already moved to support him before offering a demonstration of the powers behind his gift of light. 'He stood himself up on a battlement in the dead of night and lit the damned sky afire. Whoever wavered after that was minded to take sides for sheer terror. No man alive ever saw such a show of raw might! Even ones who've claimed close acquaintance with sorcerers and Koriani witches.'

Only half as absorbed as he seemed by the particulars of hoofed booty lifted by clansmen out of Atchaz, Arithon said, 'When are the troops from the north expected to reach the south coast?'

'Post rider's report I heard last said by summer. That relies on support from the merchants, for galleys. Don't bet it won't happen. Damned fair-haired prince has a tongue like pure honey. He's charmed the harbourmaster at Southshire well enough. Gone and wheedled his vessels a free anchorage. That from an official who's married to a shrew who counts his shirt studs each morning in case the servants should steal one.'

Arithon arose in cat quiet, tipped the livestock list into the lamp flame, and twisted it to and fro to speed its burning. Shadows wheeled across his peaked brows and fanned a demonic caste to his features as he rose and leaned sideward to unlatch the stern window and toss the smouldering spill into the sea.

'Three months,' he mused. Only the Mad Prophet could detect his uneasy irritation as he stared out into the darkness; to the unschooled onlooker, his loose-fitted shirt well masked the tension in his stance.

Left to his own devices, Dakar succumbed before temptation and thumbed prying fingers through the left-over correspondence. He plucked up a missive addressed in a laborious, childlike script, and fishing for opening to provoke, said, 'Dhirken's written you. That's rather strange since you assured me she'd left your service.'

In sarcasm thin as ribboned steel, Arithon said, 'Are you going to play the secretary's part and enlighten us?'

Dakar required no more incentive. He snapped the smeared wax of the seal, sniffed the paper, then wrinkled his nose in disappointment. 'No attar of roses. She hasn't refined her female habits.' Quick at deciphering scurrilous facts, no matter how sprawling the handwriting, he skimmed over lines that wobbled as though they had been penned in the midst of a gale.

'Here's a rich little snippet.' He sniggered behind plump knuckles. 'Her Grace, the most exalted Princess Talith has inveigled some foolish young captain-at-arms to sail her to Alland to join her royal husband.'

'Lysaer doesn't know?' In a stunned turn of speed, Arithon snapped the smuggler's letter from the other man's avid grasp. He read in silence, his mask of pensive patience cracked to consuming attention. Then, in that inflection that infallibly raised Dakar to unease, he demanded point-blank of his captain, 'The hold is filled with scrap stock from the shipyard. I trust you also got the yew?'

Dakar sat up fast enough to bash his knee against the brace of the chart table. '*Yew!*'

'The wood's to be unloaded on the mainland,' Arithon continued, unmoved. He dug into the locker beneath the chart desk, straightened with hands filled with paper, ink, and wax, then began to pen a hasty missive. 'The craftsmen will hear my instructions tonight. Until we have coin to refound the shipyard, they'll use the scrap planks for small joinery: tables, stools, and maybe small chests and dogcarts.'

'Yew!' Dakar interjected again.

'You'll take my sloop *Talliarthe* and sail her to this cove by the Ippash river delta.' Arithon slid a chart from beneath his correspondence, stabbed at a dimple in the coastline, then turned his long fingers to folding the letter. He impressed the hot wax with the nondescript seal he had used for bills of lading out of Merior. While the captain studied his assigned destination, the Master of Shadow concluded, 'An associate of Erlien's will meet you.' The new missive changed grasp. 'Please see this reaches his hand along with the maps of the Vastmark valleys you'll find rolled with the charts aboard my sloop.'

'You cold-blooded bastard!' Dakar hurled at the dark head bent just beyond range of his fist. '*You planned to recruit here all along!* The horrible misfortune that befell those two shepherd children just gave you the opening to exploit. How Dalwyn would weep if she knew of your endless, twisted conniving!'

Pricked to explain before the captain's puzzled interest, Dakar spewed on in riled contempt. 'The scrap wood you've shipped in this vessel's hold is a priceless commodity in Vastmark.'

'What's there to gain?' The captain shrugged his broad shoulders, amused, but watching through hot, slitted eyes. 'Unless you want wool bales, the shepherds are poorer than field mice.'

'They have archers.' Dakar slammed to his feet and confronted Arithon. 'I should've guessed, when you shot

185

down those wyverns. *You jumped at the chance to finagle a welcome to bid for their fighting potential!'* The notion fit with a damnable perfection. Through sheer need for survival, the shepherds of Vastmark were the finest bowmen on the continent.

The quelled lash of temper in Arithon's carriage seemed proof that the sally struck home. His response came bracingly cool. 'The arrangement will be strictly mercenary.'

'Ath, but who'll pay them?' Dakar cried in emotional contrast. 'We know you're in debt. Or shall the tribes receive scrapwood and faggots for their loss when their young men lie dead on the field?'

Arithon countered in diamond-bright malice. 'Lysaer's going to pay them. Fine gold. When the tide crests at dawn, I'm going to ply the time-honoured trade of my family.'

'Piracy,' the hired captain drawled. He tossed back his wine, kindled to rich laughter, then sobered as fast to frank awe. 'Yon golden-haired prince had best look to his wife.'

'Lysaer, poor man, doesn't yet know it's necessary.' Arithon's straight glance drank the light like sheared tourmaline as he scorned Dakar's challenge in mockery. 'Did you think I launched the *Khetienn* as a berth for the freeloading barnacles?'

Born in the landlocked city of Etarra, acquainted with ships only as a notation in ledgers which outlined the cost of moving trade goods, Princess Talith of Avenor acquired a lasting distaste for sea travel. Her plan to rejoin her royal husband in Southshire had suffered rough setbacks since the grizzled veteran captain in command of the city garrison gave flat refusal to provide her with suitable escort.

Thwarted in her efforts to gain the deference which

should have been royalty's due, informed in blunt language that her prince's loyal officers would enforce his direct wish to keep her home, Princess Talith resorted to subterfuge.

Avenor's younger officers proved less resistant to her beauty, their tender sensibilities no match for her hand at connivance. The seedier vessels out of Hanshire had masters less enamoured of Lysaer's protective constraint. These were pleased to board her small party of servants and guardsmen, and take payment in gold to hide her plans. The princess changed ships three times to throw off determined pursuit. The men-at-arms who trailed her to uphold Lysaer's honour and drag her back into confinement could not follow across the border into Havish.

The vessel she engaged from King Eldir's port of Cheivalt was a dowdy merchant brig with scuffed paint and slack stays named the *Arrow*. Laden to her load line with baled fleece and hides from the Carithwyr steppelands, and barrels of tallow, wax, and rum, she reeked in the damp. Odours from the penned hogs that had been her last deck cargo seemed permanently ingrained in her planking. The sailhands were given to layabout habits and a hatred of the purser's watchmen, who caught them swaggering through the hold at odd hours, singing, or fist swinging, or morose, as the whims of stolen drink moved them. *Arrow*'s master was a rotund, cheerful man with pouched cheeks and a pug nose. He kept a rat-skinny mate who wore a fixed grin, even when prodded to mete out each morning's round of ship's discipline.

Lady Talith did not keep to her cabin as the captain of the *Arrow* clearly wished. The stupefying impact of her beauty fouled his sail drills. Amid the watchful presence of her liveried men-at-arms, and a handmaid with no stomach for coarse company, the princess strolled topside each day. The leers and the slangs she met unflinching, her Etarran bent for intrigue quick to sort out the byplay between those in authority and their underlings. The *Arrow*'s first mate was slack with the whip. His sailhands scarcely took his floggings to heart, but did as they pleased; another drunken sailor would stagger through his watch come the evening.

While this morning's yelling miscreant was unlashed from the hatch grating and hauled off to the forecastle by his commiserating friends, Talith set her elbows on the gouged and peeling rail and gazed astern. To the north, the horizon which masked the shores of Tysan met sky in flat jointure with blue waters. Through the tar-blacked cord of the ratlines, the high, golden headlands of Carithwyr etched the morning haze to the east. Talith pecked chips from blistered varnish with her nails, bored to mischief, while over the screeling complaint of diving gulls, the ship worked and drove her lumbering, creaky course southward. She was too staid a tub to throw off much spray, even when she wallowed through a trough. The vessel's plump captain trod an uncertain, hovering line between his royal passenger and his man at the helm, whose cow eyes kept drifting off the compass. The mate stalked the waist, his unctuous voice raised as he chivvied idle seamen to patch a holed sail on the maindeck.

The passage round the cape at West Shand stretched ahead, twenty days of punishing ennui, until the lookout called down from the masthead. 'Vessel bearing down off our windward quarter!'

'From the sea side?' The captain clumped over to the rail, his gawp of surprise like a fish which had spat something bitter. 'Is she damaged, do you think?'

'Damaged? No.' The lookout seemed awed. 'She's in mean fine trim and held sharp to her course like a cleaver.' Her lines, he resumed in admiring salty terms, were like nothing else seen in any port amid the westlands.

Surrounded by open air and full sunlight, Princess

Talith clenched her cloak through a sweeping, claustrophobic chill. She snatched back the skirts the breezes mired against her shins and said to the captain, 'We're in danger. Whatever defences you have on this vessel, I ask that you engage them immediately.'

Arrow's master blinked as though she had just taken leave of her senses. 'My dear princess, what's to fear? No renegade in these waters would risk the executioner for a haul of raw hides and wax.' His dimpled hand swept through a deprecating gesture that encompassed the broached locks amidships. 'Surely not for a few casks of grog. Not that I'd miss them. Malingerers and pilfering have left them a sorrowful sight less than full.'

'My husband has enemies,' Talith contradicted, chin raised as she balanced against *Arrow*'s nosing slog from the cresting roll of a swell.

Warmed to bated breath by the dazzling, amber slant of her eyes upon him, the captain straightened his doublet. The wrinkles tugged smooth above his lumpish paunch resettled in rucked curves beneath his belt, no more tidy, but at least past his view as he sniffed. 'These waters are under King Eldir's sovereignty and Havish is firm in neutrality. The Master of Shadow and his minions scarcely dare to turn their feud against a vessel under Cheivalt's flag of registry.'

He was wrong, Talith sensed. The oncoming vessel breasted the sea's edge to show taut-bellied, tanbark sails and a line as lean-waisted as a wasp. The heading she held was a falcon's stoop, straight for the isolated brig.

The captain chewed his moustache through a gusty, long sigh. 'It seems rather silly. Who would kill for a few crates of candles?' Yet he gave his grudging order for the crossbows to be fetched out of storage. Weathered covers were unlaced from the arbalests. The first mate had scarcely rousted his sailhands from their mending to man weaponry when darkness clapped down, soundless and dense as felted sable.

The first mate screamed in panic and pandemonium broke loose on deck.

The brigantine's prey was never chosen by mistake. Set after by shadows and fell sorcery, the *Arrow* floundered through the darkness like a wing-broken dove before a snake. Her mouldered chests of crossbows showed their dearth of handling, even for routine firing and maintenance to clean the rust off their latch pins. Lent no hope to repel boarders, afraid her person was the prize for an appalling set of stakes, Talith snatched her only chance. She must tuck herself away, and hope the *Arrow*'s loutish crewmen would establish through incompetence that they worked a cheap-rate hauler of no consequence.

Above the din of wild cries and running feet, Lady Talith gave orders to her bodyguard. 'Strip off your surcoats and disarm. Pretend you're common sailors when the Shadow Master boards us. Let no one mention my presence.'

'Go,' said her officer to the man posted nearest. 'Find her Grace's servants and tell them the same.' He gave a last, firm squeeze to his princess's arm before she left to grope her way below.

Two sailhands cannoned into her before she crossed the deck. Dishevelled, breathless, her lip bitten hard in an anger to scald her very blood, Talith fumbled through the aft companionway. Her guardsmen were well trained, but young, their ranks bolstered by five stout mercenaries hired in extreme circumspection from Havish; no match for the Master of Shadow in a raid. She feared to see them lose their lives in her behalf, when the most effective tactic was to stay hidden and pray that the louts who came to search delved no farther than the rum casks in the hold.

Talith fought her way through her cabin. She extinguished the lamps, at each step slammed and bruised where she fetched up against the bulkheads as the *Arrow*'s helmsman lost the heading. The brig rounded up, to wallow and roll and lose way. The thumping skitter of hurried feet and the oaths of scared seamen muddled through the thunder of loose canvas.

Her handmaid crouched in paralysed despair on her berth. 'Your Grace, we're to die. That cruel spinner of darkness will spill our poor blood for use in his unclean rites of magecraft.'

'Hush, that's ridiculous.' Talith grabbed her servant's wrists and bullied her onto her feet. 'I met the s'Ffalenn prince years ago in Etarra. He's wily, yes. A hard man to know, but no fool to murder a hostage who's of far better use to him alive.' Too late to regret that as a weapon to bend her royal husband from his purpose, her captivity would lend an edge without parallel.

'Come on.' Princess Talith towed her maid by touch through the darkened companionway and into the cramped starboard passage. On impulse, she elbowed the door to the mate's quarters open. The cubicle reeked of sweat-rancid shirts and the fishy exhalation from the bilges. Talith fumbled past the noisome berth, tripped on a discarded pair of seaboots, and crashed shoulder first against the hanging locker.

'Here,' she whispered to her maid. 'Get inside.'

Voices filtered down through the hatch grating amidships, shrill in contention over who kept the store of bowstrings. Through somebody's rapid-fire pleas for Ath's mercy, unseen hands winched to span an arbalest. The screeching ratchet of its corroded pawls set Talith's teeth on edge.

A muffled sneeze from the locker and a flurried crackle of oilskins marked the maid's attempts to burrow into cover.

'Hurry.' Talith squeezed into the cranny that remained, then swore like a mule drover as she skinned her elbow on the sharpened edge of the hinge. The closet was painfully small. Pressed full-length against her quivering servant, she sneezed from mildewed woollens, squirming to fold her skirts behind the mate's unsavoury garments. She scraped her wrist trying to claw the locker door closed, then cursed her gold bracelets when they hooked by ill chance on the jutting tang of the latch.

Then she had nothing else to do but wait in sweaty, breathing stillness and total darkness.

Through the slosh of waves against the weedy hull and the banging flog of canvas came shouts as the men blundered to take up arms. The princess strained to piece sense out of chaos.

The press of used clothing grew stuffy, then suffocating. The close air turned Talith dizzy. Terror caused her plump maid to snivel. On deck, something metallic fell over to a nerve-wrought rejoinder from the captain.

Then somebody bellowed in challenge and a bowstring twanged. The slap of the swell changed timbre as the attacking vessel closed to windward. Talith chewed her lip in unbearable tension, her jewellery clapped silent against her wrists by the shaking grip of her hands.

A crossbow discharged with a clipped ping of wire; the quarrel, released, thumped wood.

'Dharkaron show mercy, she's on top of us!' somebody cried.

Even through the planking, over the chafe of slackened gear, Talith picked out the thrum of the wind through taut rigging. Snapped orders filtered through while the enemy vessel wore ship; then the bang of crisp canvas as her sails caught aback and she shouldered the waves alongside.

Arithon's cloak of shadows must have lifted then, leaving *Arrow*'s crew bemused and blinded in full sunlight. A streak of illumination filtered through the chink in the deck beams and a command cracked across roiled waters. 'Heave to or burn with your timbers!'

Perspiration slicked Talith's temple. She repressed a stab of fear, aware even from the confines of the locker how the *Arrow* tempted fate through her tardy response.

Movement flurried topside. A bowstring whined. An eruption of shouted insults came whipcut by a hiss as an arrow creased the air. The shot struck to the sickening, dull thump of a broadhead into flesh. The planks overhead thudded to the weight of a fallen body. Wet gasps ripped through an unseen victim's torn throat.

Then the brig veered off station to a scream of freed cables as her wheel took charge, untended.

'That's a warning!' an incisive voice called through the bedlam. 'Deliver your passenger into my care and nobody else needs to die.'

The accent recalled memories from the Fellowship's failed king-making, except that spiked, cold ring of authority had never been heard from the prince brought for his crowning at Etarra. The tone prickled the hair at the nape of Talith's neck. She squeezed her eyes closed and drew a stifled breath. Any second, she imagined the brig's pudgy captain would give way and spill word of her presence. Defenceless and mute with apprehension, she waited alongside her trembling maid for the bargain to be struck for her person.

No word came. Only the groaning creak as the *Arrow*'s lines chafed. Perhaps struck witless by jelly-legged terror as the grapples clanged into her rails and barefoot enemies swung to invade her sorry decks, the fat captain made no overture of capitulation.

Instead, Talith heard Arithon snap in annoyance, 'Prudence, my good man. They'd burn you to your loadline for sheer pleasure. You're boarded and helpless. I'd say you'd best stop fussing and retire in comfort to your quarters.'

The captain went under coercion. Talith followed the shuffling, dragged steps of a man bound and prodded at weapon point. As captive and escort thrashed down the companionway but a plank's width from the bulkhead of the locker, she felt the jounced impact of fists and shoulders, then overheard a moaning complaint over lashings tied hurtfully tight.

'Aye well,' groused a sailor in a slurred southcoast accent, 'lucky for you it's not wire. You see the scars on yon devil captain's wrists? No? Somebody in his life maltreated him so. Fortune's with you, he's not one for grudges.'

'Pipe down!' a companion said in a clotted whisper. 'He hears you gossip, you'll rue it. Unholy fires o' Sithaer are nothing to the heat he can raise with his tongue.'

Talith swallowed. As nothing else had, those snatched lines of eavesdropping slapped home her plight, that the Master of Shadow had taken the *Arrow* with herself as his plotted quarry. While the ongoing jostles of captors and victim receded into the stern cabin, the brig groaned and rolled to the sucking slosh of her bilges. Splintery planks pressed the princess's hot cheek. The reek of dirty wool overpowered her. She had to fight in each breath. Her head spun, and her stomach had cramped from the tension that racked her in knots.

She could scarcely distinguish which thumps and commotion were made by *Arrow*'s crewmen being herded under guard into the forecastle, and others made by the searchers dispatched with lamps and candles to rifle cabins and loot the ship's hold.

The maid at Talith's back jerked in sharp, convulsive movement as the door to the mate's quarters wrenched open. Sounds leaped into clarity, foremost among them the grate of a trunk or laden box of cargo being dragged up the aft companionway. Its egress was marked by a rumble across the decking above. Nearer at hand came the squeak of a board, then the rustle of cloth as if someone explored the mate's berth.

Talith wished the intruder a pestiferous infestation of lice. To judge by the odours ingrained in the bedding, the mate had not bathed since his congress with the trollops back in Cheivalt.

The unseen brigand found a striker and swung down the gimballed lantern. The snap of the spark pocked the catcalls of pillagers busy ransacking the lockers farther forward. *Arrow* heaved with a splash through a trough. The motion wafted sooty smoke through the ill-fitted boards of the closet. Talith bit back an eye-watering cough. Then the latch to the hanging locker tripped up and gave, and its green, crusted hinges wailed open.

Talith bit her lip to stifle her reflex to scream. No man would be gratified by her cry as he touched her, she vowed in quaking silence.

Yet no prying fingers plucked back her curtain of oil-skins. No hand reached to prod, nor did any triumphant male grasp snatch through fusty woollens to expose her. Nothing happened. No intrusion, just a nerve-racked, punishing interval through which the rattling noises of invasion died back and reorganized into retreat.

The capstan's pawls thumped as the *Arrow* was warped alongside her pirate captor. Talith heard the cheerful calls of crewmen, vying with each other in colourful, coarse phrases as a halyard was rigged through a block on a yardarm to arrange the off-loading of spoils. Someone called orders to cast loose the bow lines.

To all appearance, the pirates were leaving.

Talith eased a sigh past her painfully constricted throat. Combed over by chills as the influx of fresh air fingered her crimped hair and dewed skin, she listened as the commotion abovedecks subsided. Soon nothing met her tense and waiting stillness but the slap of the waves against the hull, and the cranky, abandoned squeal as the opened locker door flopped on its hinges in time to the *Arrow*'s lugubrious wallow. No invaders seemed in evidence. Thin through the creak of timbers and the flap of freed canvas, she could hear the sorry moans of the captain, left bound and gagged in his quarters.

The miracle seemed possible, through one searcher's

negligence, that the Master of Shadow had withdrawn from his prize with the princess's cranny overlooked.

Threshed by a wave of sudden weakness, then by impatient struggles from the maid crushed breathless at her back, Talith wrestled to stay her impatience. She held until her last, savaged nerve gave way, and the hideous need to escape the stuffy locker became too overpowering to deny. She struck her arms through rank cloth and stumbled forward in blind instinct to claw free of confinement.

A courteous touch grasped her elbow and spared her a tripping sprawl onto her knees. 'I'm overjoyed, Lady Talith,' said a pleased, superb voice. 'Welcome to the company of your closest kinsman by marriage.'

Snapped erect by hot pride, eyes lambent with anger, Talith confronted the self-contained prince she recalled much too clearly from the tumultuous events that surrounded a failed coronation.

'You!' She jerked from his touch. 'Sorcerer! Defiler! How many spells did you invoke to discover my presence on board?'

'My dear!' Arithon said in the acid-wiped sarcasm he wore like an armour of enamel; then he laughed. 'Why trifle with sorcery? *Arrow*'s partridge of a captain would scarcely sport trunks of silk dresses. Profits from tallow were never so grand that merchants' mates should toss lady's bracelets on the floor. Nor do they wear scent like attar of roses.' This said, he tucked into her stiffened fingers the snagged links of gold the latch pin had torn from her wrist.

'This ship flies the colours of Cheivalt registry,' Talith flared. 'King Eldir's peace has been broken.'

'Quite the contrary.' Arithon s'Ffalenn drew her on in exquisite formality toward the open companionway. As checkered light from the hatch grating feathered across her flushed cheeks, he paused through a second of admiration. She had always been stunning, the more so now, with her fine hair tousled as though she had just arisen from tempestuous sport in a love nest. 'The King of Havish's subjects are unharmed. This brig and her cargo are untouched. Your jewels were enough to satisfy us all, and your company I've claimed for myself.' He cast a smiling glance behind as the oilskins rustled in the locker. 'Tell your handmaid to come out. Nobody's planning to abandon her.'

Talith narrowed her lashes in a glare to raise frost on hot iron. While her cowering servant emerged, softly sobbing, the princess bent in the douce, female pretence of smoothing down her rucked skirts. Mazed reflections sparked off a curved quillon. Her captor still wore the black sword she recalled from Etarra, paired now with a steel-handled dagger slung at an angle by his hip. Before she could snatch to seize either weapon, Arithon's hold tightened over her wrist with a force to grind the marrow from her bones.

'Manners,' he admonished through her gasp. 'King Eldir's vassals are blissfully unwounded and no one forced you from hiding. I'd much rather keep things civil. Bloodshed at this point would upset all the niceties.'

'You murdered the brig's helmsman!' Talith retorted.

Arithon smiled. 'Come and see.' He flourished an insolent bow, then handed her smartly through the passage.

Her pink-nosed, sniffling handmaid trailed after. The pirate prince allowed both women to pass into the open ahead of him. The courtesy was deliberate, as full sight of the deck brought Talith to a wrenching stop and shocked her distraught servant to screams.

Beneath the *Arrow*'s abandoned wheel lay the victim of that fatal, first crossbow bolt. Not one of the brig's indifferent seamen after all, but the untried young captain from Avenor that Princess Talith had persuaded to lead her escort. In an uncontrolled sprawl that seemed all boyish knuckles, he rested on his back. His chin was tipped to the sky. The chest which had no tan, that no fool could mistake for a sailhand's, forever stilled in its blood from the quarrel which had severed his life untimely.

The princess spun to confront her hysterical handmaid. 'Be quiet!' She struck the flighty woman on the cheek to stop the sobbing. Regal despite her extreme pallor, her every movement scored in light by the dazzle of gold thread embroidery, the princess went on to upbraid the Master of Shadow in stinging fury. 'What you have done is an outrage! I see no reason and no right for you to slaughter my guard captain outright.'

The dangerous, deep glitter to Arithon's eyes acquired a glint like a forge spark. 'Your captain at arms received his due, madam. You should have been proud. He refused to stand down with his fellows. Certainly my bolt was an easier death than the punishment your prince would mete out to an officer who allowed you to place yourself at risk.'

Before her fired, speechless rage could erupt, he cut back in withering irony. 'What? No scathing defence of the vaunted s'Ilessid justice? Should I write his Grace a letter absolving your other guardsmen of incompetence? Rusty weapons can't defend. Warped shafts in the hands of this brig's sorry archers are no use at all against shadow.' His voice whetted to a bard's stabbing satire, he added, 'Your young idiot of a captain got what he deserved, but the fault lies with you, princess, for your choice of a ship with slack discipline and ridiculously inadequate defences! With the rumour of your passage all over the south reaches, you're much more than lucky it's my hospitality you'll come to suffer for your folly.'

Taut in every tendon, Talith felt her cheeks flame pink. No male alive ever dealt her such a verbal public thrashing. The novelty made her strike out to slap for sheer insolence. Arithon could have ducked the blow with ease. He chose not to; her hand cracked his cheek and left stinging imprint, and his cold-cast expression never changed. Clad in a sailor's bleached cottons, his untrimmed hair tied back with a loop of leather thong, Arithon s'Ffalenn had never looked more the product of his heritage as the mountebank by-blow of a sea raider.

The trick was galling, that for one disjointed second, Talith thought she saw something more. Almost, she believed his barbaric sally was meted out against her as chastisement, as if he cared whether she took harm from ruffians for her rash impulse to rejoin her husband's company.

Then her hauteur came back like poured frost as she recalled just who this man was; what power he strove to gain in his bid to steal her as hostage. 'You won't get away with this.'

'Quite the contrary.' The nasty lilt of hilarity had returned. Arithon grasped her elbow again, his touch unnerving for its gentleness through the sheathing silk of her sleeve. He drew her past the corpse by the wheel, across sun-striped planking, his step cat sure against the rise of the swell. A board had been laid beneath the *Arrow*'s spooled rail to span the open slice of water to his brigantine. Two bronzed, grinning seamen knelt to steady each end.

Talith surveyed the uncertain bridge, then the heaving blue well that slopped and spat spray from the pinched-off motion of the wavecrests.

Before trepidation could weaken her pride, Arithon bent, caught her up behind shoulders and knees, and lofted her into his arms. They were matched in height and bone. The fact that her trimmed skirt and petticoats draped a choking froth about his knees had small impact on his balance. While Talith stiffened, then thrashed, he slung his thigh across the rail, perched to swing his other leg clear, then straightened, poised with her bundled over air. Unwilling to risk a wetting, Talith let him bear her, though she cursed like a sailor against his neck while he footed his way across to his vessel. He set her down as his prize on the deck, where her chests of belongings sat waiting.

She found herself greeted by a thunderous cheer from his crewmen.

Regal in arrogance, from the looped snags of hair unreeled like gold wire in the breeze, to her high cheekbones and milk-pale profile, to the tigerish, black-lashed eyes that no man could meet and not ache to possess, the princess snatched her skirts against the slap of the wind. She presented the leering men the stiff line of her back, while her shrieking maid was bundled across the gap by a sailhand and deposited unharmed beside her.

Despite every warning, the brigantine's seamen slacked off their duties to gawk at Lysaer's royal wife.

Arithon met their lapse with invective that sent men aloft like scalded rats. Others jumped at orders to fetch Talith's belongings to a cabin, then to retire back to the brig and cut one of the *Arrow*'s hands loose. In seamless, brisk discipline, the last lines that warped the brigantine to her quarry were cast off.

Arithon entrusted *Khetienn* in the care of his first mate to make sail and bear straight offshore.

'You're harsh with your crewmen,' Talith said as the plank was stowed away by a sailor still scarlet from his captain's raking rebuke.

Arithon turned his attention from the men on the yardarms and regarded her. Clear through the rattle of the mainsheet's slackened blocks, he said, 'I do no less than I must.'

His match for cool distance, Talith showed her contempt. 'Then what motive prompts my abduction, necessity or whim?'

Charcoal-dark eyebrows turned up, and a curl of amusement flicked his lips. No word did he say, but his study of her turned intent.

Talith stood firm. Beauty was her weapon, used to cut

or cajole or emasculate. She had handled randy suitors enough to welcome the edge. But this man's gaze traced her face for too long. She coloured; and his eyes raked down into detailed regard of her pearl-crusted neckline, jerked now to the heave of her breath. His study lingered over her fine shoulders, her breasts, her gold-cinctured waist, then travelled lower, where the arrowed folds of her airy silk skirts lay pressed to her thighs by the shameless play of the wind.

On a paper-thin edge of courtesy, Arithon struck. 'My motive is scarcely yours to question, is it?' He fingered a strand of her taffy gold hair and tucked it behind a loosened pin. 'The shame won't be mine, dear lady. You disobeyed your husband's instructions for your safety. Now you've no choice at all but to answer the ugly score.'

'You've no born right!' Talith stiffened, unable to resist his baiting innuendo. His eyes mocked her, drove her to a thoughtless, defensive step back. 'You dare not.'

'Dare not do what? Touch you? Who'll stop me? Certainly not your gullible young guardsmen.' Arithon caught her arm and swept her across the deck, through the jarring smells of tar and new varnish, and the stinging clean scent of the sea. He added, thoughtful, 'Aren't you going to claim the courtesy of kinship?'

Talith stepped beside him, her regard stony topaz with bored scorn. 'Do I look to be pleading you for mercy?'

'Magnificent as that sounds, it won't be necessary,' Arithon said in that maddening friendliness that defied all opening for riposte. 'You've merely been foolish. My need is for gold. To that end, you're nothing but a tool offered readily to my hand. Lysaer shall have you back, scolding and virtuous, but the ransom he shall pay for my forbearance will be to the coin weight what you're worth.'

Stabbed through by outrage, astonished that his callous, quick reduction of her allure to a flat price in bullion should sting her breathless, Talith ground her jaw, beyond speech. She scarcely heard, through her wrath, the instructions Arithon delivered to the clever little steward who served him. Nor did she find words as she was installed in lavish comfort in the nicer of the *Khetienn*'s two stern cabins.

Aware from the second the door shut behind her that the quarters were Arithon's own, and no refuge at all from the exacting mind left abovedecks, Talith snatched in a harrowed breath.

However hard she searched for some trait to revile, for some noisome proof of dire charms and dark sorceries, her effort was stymied by order. The tiny cabin was as bare of frivolous ornament as the man. The furnishings were selected for functional efficiency, in mirror image a forceful statement of a commander's expectations of performance from his crew and his ship. No trace could be found of carelessness in the rolled charts, the folded blankets, or the firmly inked lines of the logbook braced on the ledge by the locker employed for a desk.

Talith slammed the ship's record shut in savage irritation. A sparkle of silver hooked her glance in the gloom: the lined, taut strings of the Masterbard's lyranthe, lashed with soft ties to its pegs in a glass-fronted cabinet.

That one silent testimony to the art behind the pirate made the pain of her predicament intolerable.

'Damn your black heart to Sithaer!' she cursed her absent captor. For his subtleties were deep, and ever cruel. Talith knew he would apply every leverage her straits could inflict upon Lysaer. Love and hurt cracked her last veneer of poise. The princess hid her face, the unwanted tears she had held through the worst threading helplessly down her proud cheeks.

When she blinked and raised her eyes, she found her handmaid just arrived and staring in helpless, dumb misery. Laid open by the Shadow Master's reprimand, scared to anguish for the strain set against her new marriage, this last, ignominious breakdown grazed Talith's nerves like flung acid.

'Oh, get you gone!' she cried in snapped temper.

The maid started, gave a cry, then hesitated, uncertain where else she should go.

'Take your foolish face and get out of my presence!' Talith shouted. 'I'll not have you underfoot like some starving, stupid lapdog. Leave me alone, and at once!'

The handmaid only crumpled to her knees and dissolved into deep, injured sobs.

That moment, Lady Talith, Princess of Avenor, held the traitorous sharp wish that her own servants would respond to her orders with the fearful efficiency just witnessed on Arithon's quarterdeck.

Messenger

On the odd afternoon as whim struck him, the discorporate Sorcerer Kharadmon liked to drop by Althain Tower to chaff Sethvir in his isolation. Only on the rare day was the Warden found outside his library. The configured spells to ward the entrance seldom needed retuning or renewal, and yet Sethvir tended to check his arcane defences for soundness whenever he planned an extended journey from his tower.

Never before had anyone surprised him on his knees, curled in the draughty stone arch of the sallyport with his arms clutched around what ribs he could reach through the voluminous folds of his robes. The interrupted sigil left half-traced in the air trailed off in a jagged flare of scribbles. His eyes were squeezed shut in what looked like a fit, but was actually a paroxysm of laughter.

The likely reason for his lapse was no mystery to another Fellowship Sorcerer.

'Well, what did you expect after Athir?' Kharadmon chuckled. A sardonic flow of cold air, he breezed down the shallow stair from the level that housed the Paravian statuary and pooled into wry stillness. His presence cast a nip of frost through the passage, breathed through its murder holes and arrow loops by an incongruous fragrance of spring meadow grass. 'By any expedient, Asandir said, when he asked oath from our Teir's'Ffalenn to stay alive.' The errant spirit paused for what his colleague would take for a flamboyant grin. 'Granted such licence, and provoked against his grain, I'd expect any blood heir of Torbrand would seize the invitation to seed mayhem. What's he done?'

'Abducted Princess Talith. And the mayhem is moot. Prince Arithon's excuse was clear logic.' Sethvir struggled between muffled coughs to recover the semblance of composure. Settled on his hams, he caught back his breath and obligingly recited in a bitten, silver echo of the Masterbard's diction, '"*If my half brother plots to raise the countryside against me, I'd say that's fair reason to let him pay his share in the ongoing cost of my survival.*"'

Sethvir unfurled from his bundled-up posture, charged to a pixie's daft glee. 'Would you mind the errand to inform Lysaer? He's at Southshire plotting a campaign to storm the Cascain Islands.' Althain's Warden fluffed down the dishevelled ends of his beard, then gave an airy wave to unbind the malformed sigil left adrift by the outer portal. 'The ransom that's asked is five hundred thousand coin weight. Arithon wishes the exchange to occur on neutral ground under Fellowship auspices. We've settled on King Eldir's court at Ostermere.'

Which explained the Warden's preparations to leave his tower; the bundle of energies which comprised Kharadmon stirred from the fires of cogent thought. 'Luhaine won't like this,' he retorted in delight. 'I'm no sort of diplomat.' His tone rang devilish in provocation as he finished, 'Indeed, let Luhaine be sent as harbinger to Havish where his stuffy sense of etiquette will be appreciated. The s'Ilessid prince scarcely needs to be humoured. He should've known his own lady for a spirited creature too resourceful to be abandoned to neglect.'

Ruffled into disarray by the breeze of Kharadmon's departure, Sethvir remained in dustless gloom, a figure of blurred edges amid the grim scent of metal. The more acrid taint of his misspent spell figure spun between the hay-sweet emanations from outside. As he stood, his vivacious humour was replaced by the broad-scale, kaleidoscopic grasp of the earth link which tied him to Athera.

Unbidden, his awareness fanned out over distance to sound the movements of armies and the doings of men, tracing the ring ripple chain of circumstance the abduction of Lady Talith must set off. Vision revealed the milling march of armies through thawed mud on the scarp-shadowed road above Jaelot. Sethvir saw the beaked prows of galleys docked in rows beneath the city breakwaters, and heard the snap of ox drovers' whips as provisions and arms were rolled to the quayside for loading. Then that scene gave way to a thousand other views from which one yet to come stood out with jewelled clarity. On a ring of blue water in the Westland Sea, the Sorcerer saw a lone fishing smack sail, flamboyantly adorned with lettering; then in linked sequence, chest after chest of coins lying silted in gloom.

The bullion to redeem Lady Talith could do nothing else but underwrite a renewed round of violence.

Sethvir shook off further augury, his sigh impelled by the weight of all the world. The premonitions of conflict had increased relentlessly since the day the s'Ffalenn prince was driven from his refuge at Merior. Too many troops had been set on the march. Arithon's efforts of avoidance were not going to buy peace for much longer. Stirred to reminder of other pending problems, Sethvir returned to the purpose which left him woolgathering like some lunatic poet in the passage between Althain's paired defence portals.

Spring equinox was two days hence. From the time-worn flagstones where he stood, the Sorcerer sensed the stately turn of the stars, and beneath them a gathering dissonance: so tuned was his perception, he could hear and wince for the enslaved resonance of one hundred and eight individual quartz crystals. These were worn on silver chains by the Koriani enchantresses gathered to assist First Senior Lirenda in the task appointed by their Prime. The order's most skilled initiates trudged north in a body on the Isaer road, their destination Althain Tower. To Sethvir's jaundiced eye, the women's cloaked forms were less welcome than a flock of starving vultures.

He disliked very little underneath Ath's wide sky, but the affairs of Koriani were as thorns set under his skin.

Althain's Warden shrugged off the tatters of ominous dreams. Another sigh; then a prankish smile skewed his lips as he bent back to the task at hand, not, as Kharadmon had presumed, the retuning of the Fellowship's wardspells. Instead, he sought to strike a bargain with an older, darker power that stood sentinel beneath the tower's foundation. Its awareness had stayed quiescent through the centuries since the departed Paravians had bequeathed him his tenancy. If Sethvir gained the permission he sought, he intended to appoint his own style of ambassador to speak in his behalf when the Koriani circle came to call.

Night lay like dusky velvet over the torchlit spires and steep, shingled roofs of Southshire. Lysaer s'Ilessid stood with his hands on the alabaster railing of the Supreme Mayor's south-facing balcony. The distant dance of flames spat an imprint like sparks over his chased royal circlet. The nap of his state velvets swallowed his outline, deep indigo as midnight, pricked only at cuff and collar with the glint of fine jewels and seed pearls. This evening's banquet with the obliging southcoast guild ministers had raised the prince to gnawing discontent.

He sighed, stirred, and restlessly buffed his sapphire signet ring against the sheened silk of his sleeve. His affairs were in line; the cold in the northlands was breaking. The past week's couriers sent in relays through the posthouses had passed their dispatches without delays from late-season snowfall. The trained, élite core of his war host would rejoin him in fine time for Alestron's galleys under command of Mearn s'Brydion to smoke out Arithon's refuge. Every carefully winnowed scrap of hearsay and evidence, and several quiet rumours out of Innish pointed toward a site in the Cascain Isles.

A supremely frustrating target to attack; and a fiendish turn of strategy for an enemy hunted as a fugitive. The broken, rocky channels off the Vastmark coastline presented a mariner's nightmare. That reef-ridden shore was no place to risk a war fleet under threat of attack by sorcery and shadows.

The strike force sent to flush Arithon s'Ffalenn must be prepared to face the ugliest contingencies. Given any loophole, left even one unguarded cove, and their quarry would slip through their fingers again and make clean escape out to sea. The headland itself offered no less ready a haven, riddled as it was with scarps and ravines, and a thousand cliff-walled, hidden corries.

Lysaer massaged the creases from his forehead, disquieted each time he recalled the temptations which had besieged him inside Ath's hostel. The adept with her insidious web of illusions had nearly swayed him off course. Nagging, leftover doubts still dogged him, fuelled his unease to rank urgency, until staff meetings became an unsubtle battle of diplomacy against fawning city guild ministers who sought to profit from keeping his army in residence, and recalcitrant officers impatient to embark on campaign.

Unwilling to retire into sleep that would bring him fretful nightmares, Lysaer weighed the unpleasant, creeping facts. Only a fool could believe the delay would not work against him. Even as his trackers scoured bolt-holes, for each day his troops spent on the march to take their stand on the battlefield, his enemy would be busy weaving his unconscionable plots.

The encounter at Minderl Bay had taught a brutal lesson in caution. Lysaer would not let himself be baited into bloodshed until Arithon's demise could be undertaken with the least degree of risk.

Patience became an unsubtle form of torment. His elbow braced against the marble finial of the balustrade, the Prince of the West laced aching fingers through his hair. He took no joy from the mild, southland climate while his warhost wrestled the mud and the thaws on roads unsuitable for travel. His thoughts could but drift, and wonder how they fared, while around him, hanging smoke hazed the rooftops, tanged from the vats in the craft quarter sheds where resins were rendered into turpentine.

The raucous ebullience of the quayside pothouses never troubled the upper city, where the wealthy kept galleried mansions. Yet Southshire by night was never quiet. A gallant's carriage clattered through the cobbled lane behind the palace, iron-rimmed wheels throwing off yellow sparks. Its clamour roused a peacock's cry from a gilt-hooped cage in a matron's ornamental garden. The open-sided chamber adjoining the balcony wore the scent of stale incense, blended with citrus oils used to burnish the marquetry furnishings. A back stair creaked to a servant's staid tread, as the mayor's aged aunt sent for wine. On a floor lower down, a colicky baby wailed through the strains of a wet nurse's lullaby.

Nothing amid such ordinary sounds explained the odd suspicion that someone stood watching his back.

Lysaer raised his head, half-convinced the next second would bring a finger-light touch between his shoulder blades. Instinct before reason made him straighten and face about.

The figure that lurked in silhouette against the doorway gave him a violent start. Lysaer dropped to a crouch, his hand on his sword. Despite the late hour, there should have been a page and two guards on duty outside his suite to challenge visitors. The prince drew blade from sheath in a scrolled ring of sound, then stabbed to cut down what had to be an assassin.

His steel pierced the cloaked form at chest height and passed through with no resistance. The shape might have been an illusion wrought of shadow, except for the voice, which snapped in astringent irritation, 'I'm no fetch of your half brother's, and bare steel won't solve anything. My flesh perished five hundred years ago.'

But wild reflex overcame reason; Lysaer already called upon the power of his inborn gift.

Light flared in a blaze from his outspread hand. In a sheeting coruscation that carved up searing wind, he lit the narrow balcony until darkness lay banished, and the rose velvet hangings in the bedchamber cracked from their rods like burst sails.

Exposed for what he was in that white, actinic glare – unbanished and gloriously amused – the projected image of the Sorcerer Kharadmon advanced with a duellist's adroit step. Slim, fox-featured, and roguishly attired in a slashed and belted green doublet, he flicked narrow fingers over his spade black beard like a barrister served dubious evidence. 'If I were a bat or a mole, I'd be most impressively blinded. Since I'm not, you can desist. If the Mayor of Southshire's palace has cockroaches, they're certainly all scared to ground.'

Lysaer recovered his wits and quelled the outpouring brilliance of his talent. Too self-possessed for embarrassment, too annoyed to apologize, he showed the diplomacy of his ancestry and refused to let baiting raise his temper. 'You're certainly fond of dramatic appearances. I trust you've brought news of importance?' His sword filled the pause with a sullen ring as he slid it back in his scabbard.

Kharadmon pounced as the hilt snicked home. 'Your landing at Merior was restrained?'

'No one died,' Lysaer said, silkenly civil. 'For a village that harboured the works of a criminal, some would applaud my restraint. If you're sent here as a Fellowship messenger, I'll thank you to attend your proper office.'

Impervious to insult as a carp in a pool, Kharadmon raised an elegant, straight eyebrow. 'You've been tallying an impressive train of allegiances while your city goes to seed in your absence.'

'Go on.' Dense blue, Lysaer's eyes followed the image of the Sorcerer. The hand left curled on his weapon steadied in a vice grip of restraint, while against the winnowed glimmer of the indoor candles, the wheaten highlights in his hair scarcely shifted. 'You accuse me of neglect in Tysan?'

'Convict,' Kharadmon corrected crisply. 'While you raise your hound pack to run down the leopard, your quarry's played havoc in the henyard.'

'That *is* news.' Lysaer backed a half step, released hold on his sword hilt and arranged his palms behind him on the balustrade. The tailored breast of his doublet stayed firm, and yet, his pose held the violence of a lava flow masked under ice. 'The last message by post included nothing untoward.'

Kharadmon rebutted, 'The one which matters has yet to come through.' He paused to test a poise as contained in appearance as any shown by Halduin, founding father of the s'Ilessid royal line.

Lysaer stayed his grief. The sapphire collar laid over his shoulders flashed only once, the sparkle of his gemstones like frost against velvets rendered starlessly deep by the shadows.

He received the news in arrested silence as Kharadmon dealt the crowning blow. 'Arithon s'Ffalenn captured a merchant ship called the *Arrow*, engaged to bear your wife south. Evidently the princess grew bored with your absence. Your letters made your affairs in Alland sound tranquil enough that she believed a surprise visit would be safe.'

A flush scalded over Lysaer's cheekbones. His chest moved and restarted the interrupted rhythm of his breathing. The living moment when his royal gift of justice became fire and shield for the workings of Desh-thiere's geas stood clear as transparent glass to the watching eye of the Sorcerer.

The prince spoke at length, his words like sheared quartz, uncoloured by grief or compassion. 'She's light-headed as a dove, of course. When did this happen? I should know when to toast the bastard litter.'

Kharadmon's image intensified at the edges until he seemed a form etched in air by spilled acid. 'You're an ungenerous husband.'

'I have ungenerous enemies,' Lysaer cracked back. 'You forget. Begetting bastards on s'llessid wives is a time proven s'Ffalenn tradition.'

'There has been no congress between your lady and his Grace of Rathain!' As Lysaer surged off of the balustrade, Kharadmon's freezing anger snapped him short. 'Princess Talith has suffered great loss of pride at Arithon's hand. Nothing more.'

Dangerous in adversity as a wounded lion, Lysaer side-stepped the well of cold that bounded the Sorcerer's presence. He crossed the mahogany runner that braced the sliding doorframe and hurled a pretty, carved chair from his path. The wrathful beat of his footfalls fell muffled by the mayor's rich carpet. 'Let the blame fall where it's due. My wife was a *victim*.' He spun on his heel before the black lacquer clothespress, his features clamped still in a control unnerving to witness. 'What does he *want*?'

His venom left Kharadmon unscathed. 'Indeed, let's place rightful blame where it's due. For the year you've been away, you may as well have sent your half-brother a written invitation to exploit what he could from your absence!'

'*What does he want?*' Lysaer repeated, a snap to his tone few men would dare in the presence of a Fellowship Sorcerer.

Kharadmon blinked, every inch the disinterested courtier. 'Gold, five hundred thousand coin weight.'

'How very wise.' Lysaer matched him back in royal blandness.

'Had Arithon the effrontery to hold her as hostage to force my warhost to draw off, I should have picked apart the earth to spill his blood. No one life can absolve the hundreds of thousands set at risk by his threat to society.'

A cruel pause followed. While a stray cat yowled in the lane beneath the balcony, the Fellowship Sorcerer lent his silence to the quandary spurred by the Mistwraith's meddling. Spirit though he was, and irreverent toward sentiment, he could not but ache for the raw courage of this prince, who stanched his pain with the rags of his honour, and held firm in flawed mercy and conviction.

The entrapment tore the heart, that between Deshthiere's forced directive to kill, and the unrelenting coils of s'Ilessid justice, the life of Lady Talith of Avenor should ever come to be measured against the death of Arithon s'Ffalenn.

A gilt line of sweat streaked over his jawbone, Lysaer framed his reply. 'If coin is the sum of my enemy's demand, I will bargain for my princess's return.'

'Very well,' said the Sorcerer. 'Our Fellowship has been appointed to stand surety for the exchange. There are certain formalities both parties must observe. I'll require your royal word of honour.'

'Name the conditions to be met.'

'No act of bloodshed, on land or sea, and no violence

213

on neutral ground. Neither shall your armies invade or strike camp with intent to pursue feud or warfare. Arithon has sworn to the same. His brigantine *Khetienn* shall hold to peaceful trade for the time Lady Talith stays in his charge.'

Lysaer locked stares with the Sorcerer. Too bitterly well he understood that he owned no grounds on which to argue. The insufferable delay being demanded of his warhost could not be avoided, not without straining the loyalty of Talith's brother, who served as his Lord Commander at Arms. Diegan's heart-tied devotion to the cause against the Shadow Master could only lead to unbearable conflict, were his sister to be abandoned as a sacrifice.

One brief second, Lysaer shut his eyes in anguish for the lapse that had let him forge vulnerable ties. Ever and always, his s'Ffalenn enemy would seize on the chance to wring painful advantage out of sentiment.

The prince managed to sound steady as he answered. 'My word as given. No hostilities shall be opened against the Master of Shadow until Lady Talith is redeemed. But tell your pirate protégé this when you bring him news of my bond.' Dangerous, straight, a sheen like blued steel to his glance, Lysaer rounded off his ultimatum. 'Say I will exact from him, measure for measure, my personal retaliation for his action against my lady wife.'

'That's unworthy,' Kharadmon rebuked in dire warning. 'Send your own courier on matters of feud. When the ransom is raised, the exchange will occur at Ostermere under the hospitality of King Eldir of Havish. The peace will be kept under seal by our Fellowship, and be very sure, prince, that your conduct then befits your claim to royal ancestry.'

Kharadmon departed on a whirlwind of air that snuffed out his image like a flame.

Left to the night solitude of his bedchamber, impelled by a daunting, deep hurt that had no outlet but targetless anger, Lysaer pushed off from the clothespress. He grasped the delicate cane chair in his path and let fly in a fury he no longer tried to contain. The furnishing struck the panelled door to the corridor and cracked into an explosion of splinters.

Lysaer waited, each drawn breath half-forced from his chest. He coldly counted off seconds. When the bodyguards outside failed to stir back to duty, he raised a blistering shout and demanded their instant attendance.

The door clicked open, belatedly. Two mail-clad men-at-arms presented themselves for inspection, blinking off recent sleep. Since Lysaer could not fault them for a lapse more than likely the result of Kharadmon's meddling, he settled for running them like errand boys. 'Get me Lord Commander Diegan. If he's with a wench, I don't care. Just drag him out and tell his valet where to follow with appropriate clothing.'

Caught alone in his bed, less than pleased to be roused, Lord Diegan found himself met by stinging reprimand the instant he crossed the royal threshold.

'Which of your officers would dare to allow my lady to leave the security of Avenor? She's the most priceless jewel in the kingdom, and she sailed from port *with inadequate escort aboard a common merchant ship*! The most slipshod trader takes more precautions. Find the men who are at fault. For this grievous lapse in service, let them suffer public flogging and dishonour.'

Hastily clad, the trailing ends of his shirttails all that spared him from stares for the fact that his breeches were unlaced, Lord Diegan clenched his stubbled jaw. If the inference from this outburst meant that Talith was abducted, regardless, he was Etarran enough keep his reason. 'I'll flog no one before I've spoken to my sister.'

Lysaer stalked the breadth of the carpet, his eyes like sparks chipped off flint. 'How dare you gainsay me. She's in Arithon's hands. What in Athera could be worse?'

Lord Diegan hauled in a long-suffering breath, not

about to defend his sister's inclination to ignore good sense and sound counsel. While he marshalled his thoughts for the tact to intercede for the fates of his hapless officers, Lysaer spun away toward the rumpled hangings on the bed.

His words came back low and fixed, as if he spoke through his hands. 'Say *nothing* on behalf of the men! She's your sister. You know her stubborn nature. You're also well-versed with her illogical belief she's invincible and immune to all mishap. I'll not have her reputation sullied over this. The men who are punished for her sake must be made to understand. Try, if you can, to find willing volunteers to bear official blame in her stead.'

'Ath have mercy!' Lord Diegan stepped back and bashed his hip against a marquetry table. As small ornaments scattered and threatened to topple, he scooped with broad hands, then straightened, his rescued clutch of bric-a-brac cradled to his chest as if they were pricelessly sacred. 'You'd shield her from shame, that the subjects you tax to free her won't come to hold her at fault?'

'I must.' His hand on the knurled fitting that hooked the silk bed hangings, Lysaer shut his eyes. The wobble of failing candlelight cast deep brackets at the sides of his mouth. 'She'll be crowned one day as my queen. Tysan's people must respect her.' But the words rang hollow in the close, warm night, even to his best friend's ear.

Lysaer bent his head. A quiver rippled through him and roused a running shimmer over the rich fabric of his doublet.

Since the disaster to the fleet at Minderl Bay, Lord Diegan was unlikely to miss the details that sketched his prince's state of anguish. 'You truly love her, don't you?' He sidled, juggling glassware, and unburdened the collection on the seat of the overstuffed divan.

'Yes, Ath help me.' Through the fraught, high jangle

of discarded crystal, the admission sounded torn through the prince's teeth. The jewels on his collar yoke jerked once, twice, then shivered as he moved to collapse in a chair. Reduced at long last as the grief chased through him and shivered edged sparks in his rings, he admitted, 'I love her well enough to tear my own heart out. But Daelion make me strong, not over this. She cannot and must not weaken me now. I'd be no prince at all unless defence of my people came first. My cause against the Master of Shadow must take precedence, even before her life and safety.'

'Let it never come to that,' Diegan said in braced resolve.

Wrung by shared pain, Avenor's Lord Commander dared not touch his liege's shoulder lest one or the other of them break. Against the enemy's abduction of Princess Talith, action must serve in place of comfort. He could lend his prince's torment that much. 'Let me sail north to seek support from Tysan and raise the ransom for my sister in your name.'

Springtide

The hour before midnight on the equinox, a full moon licked the dry, tangled heads of dead grass stems like the skipped stroke of an engraver's awl across the hollow which sheltered Althain Tower. Outside the shadow of its sheer granite spire, frost rimed the edges of leaf and stalk, until each one seemed sculpted out of flint.

A smaller blot of darkness amid the meadow's flooded light, Lirenda, First Enchantress of the Koriani Order, regarded the bastion which had come to represent the Fellowship's inheritance of a power once the province of the Ilitharis Paravians. In First Age Year One, centaurs had forged the grand earth link, the tracks of their spells crossing and recrossing, until lands and seas lay webbed, warp through weft, in shining, linked self-awareness. When Desh-thiere had engulfed the last sunlight under mists, Sethvir had been ceded the grasp of that net by the last old race guardian to leave the continent.

Well aware she came to trespass, to steal, if she could, from the fastness of the tower's store vaults, Lirenda dared not deceive herself. The Sorcerer whose stronghold she intended to breach would be aware of her presence.

One could not shield and ward the footsteps on cold

ground of the one hundred and eight companion sisters who clustered like a hound pack called to heel. Every scuffed pebble, each frightened field mouse, even the small sprouts of the growing weeds crushed in the roadway: Sethvir could hear any and all of these at whim. It remained to be seen whether his wards were proof against a grand circle of enchantresses, raised to tuned power and fused into one will through the matrix of the Skyron crystal.

Lirenda presented her back to the fortress, her dew-drenched skirts clinging to bare ankles. Behind her, silent, the accomplices she had chosen awaited, their faces pale ovals cowled beneath dark hoods.

At her signal, the gathering dispersed.

The print of their unshod feet and the drag of their hems blotted the moisture from the weed tips and stitched the meadow across its length in dimmed swathes. Still wordless, the Koriani joined hands, their flesh pale as pearl in the ground mist. Not a few palms were clammy with unease; to challenge Sethvir in the seat of his own power was to call down unnameable peril. The women assumed their positions, undaunted. They were dedicated to reclaim their order's Great Waystone from the hands of the Fellowship of Seven, and for that cause, every last sister initiate stood prepared to offer her life.

Once the enchantresses formed a linked chain, they closed an unbroken ring around the base of the tower. Inside their joined figure, all iron determination, Lirenda knelt upon the earth before the locked grille of the portal and unsealed the coffer she carried. She unveiled the silk-wrapped crystal of Skyron and raised its faceted surface before her. The spring moon shone down, electrum and ice, and roused the gemstone's pale heart to splintered light.

The First Senior's dark, unpinned hair slipped from her hood to cascade over her forearms. Its warmth licked the ivory bones of her wrists, while her hands, cupped to crystal, felt bathed in ephemeral cold. The dire, stilled presence the stone wore while quiescent was as hostile to flesh as air breathed from a crack in a glacier.

Lirenda closed her eyes. She inhaled the scents of earliest spring, interlaced with the season's contradictions: the birth of green shoots cross-woven in the detritus of last year's dead growth, dank and rotted in the wake of the thaws. The First Senior's fingers traced steamed prints on the gem's surface as she settled her mind to begin.

The older the talisman, the more spells and scryings had been aligned into focus through its structure. The Skyron crystal had served in Koriani ritual for so long, no one remembered its origins. The patterns of its matrix were as water-crazed quartz, flecked like darkness in diamond with the coiled, spiteful residue of year upon year of used magic. If the most aged jewels became dependably stable, each flaw in their power fields long since tested and annealed by repeated trials, time lent them a querulous character. They did not tame with use, but grew ever more wayward and dangerous.

Lirenda cradled the Skyron gem warily, doused in soft chills by its aura of contrary malice. No stone for a novice, even Morriel Prime attuned its deep coils with caution.

No senior left alive had ever touched the amethyst Great Waystone. Since its loss had occurred three centuries before her birth, Lirenda could only postulate how difficult its matrix was to master. Excitement shimmered underneath her restraint, that tonight's work allowed her the coveted chance to find out. The Prime Matriarch alone recalled how to access the greatest of Koriani focus stones. While Lirenda's worthiness as successor for the post now hinged upon the Waystone's recovery, she refused to contemplate failure.

Poised in self-command, she aligned herself into light

trance and touched her mind to the Skyron jewel's centre.

Its icy presence pierced her, a sheeting rain of steel needles, there and gone before reflex could respond to cognition of elation or pain. For an instant her woman's outraged flesh shuddered in rebellion. Then discipline took hold. Lirenda damped back visceral, instinctive rejection, and embraced the stone's heart to compel its dread source to subservience.

Energies snapped forth in vicious protest.

Invaded by lightnings borne on winds of fired metal, she reversed the thrust on its axis, and claimed her place in rightful domination.

The moment often swept her to ecstasy as the raw powers submitted to her mind. Mortal frailty felt recast in quartz. Her inner spirit became a pearl window into moonlight, or old, stippled lace, shaken clean of blurred layers of dust. The Skyron matrix opened to her usage, balanced as the shaft of a lance. Through senses reamed open by self-will and training, the Koriani First Senior reviewed the poised powers of each sister initiate in the circle, stitched like ribboned knotwork through the small crystals each wore on a chain at her neck.

One by one, Lirenda reached out and plucked up the yielding threads of their consciousness. Through the aquamarine she bound them, sealed each in the halter of sigils granted to her as First Senior, and above her, known only to Morriel Prime. Tonight, Lirenda had no space to envy the secrets the order's matriarch held in store until her final rite of passage. Raised to refined vision through the power crystal's focus, she reeled in the gathered energies of each sister in the circle and joined them to the one source. The Skyron gem became the central hub, with the currents tapped out of the living chain of women like the ephemeral, starred spokes of a wheel.

Lirenda sketched her construct in runes of demand,

their drawing properties potent enough to leach spidery shadows from the moonlight. With the tip of her fingernail she skeined ciphers one upon another like fishhooks twined through sunken weed. The gemstone's gravid matrix responded and drew upon the linkage to each individual enchantress.

Power flowed like poured magma along the lines, then pooled into resonance until the awareness raised by one hundred and eight amplified to unified potential. In time, the crystal held a seamless reservoir of force poised between Lirenda's spread hands. Its aquamarine lattice transformed from a clear, waiting mirror to a smoky, dark nexus submissive to the First Senior's will. Its potency ran in fine tingles through her body. Her lips parted in anticipation akin to the heady, hot thrill of fierce sex.

Like addiction, the pleasure intoxicated. Lirenda revelled in the unfolding, exquisite rush of strength ceded to her sole discretion. Decades of training had shaped her for this office. She took pride in her disciplined awareness, that could rifle the secrets of the surrounding elements, then bid them to reshape at her whim. Within the Skyron nexus, the might and the trust of a hundred and eight colleagues became hers: she was the key to all the world's locks, and Althain Tower lay before her.

No older site of continuous habitation existed upon the continent. For century upon century, the rites worked by Paravians and Fellowship Sorcerers had channelled the natural powers. Here the earth's currents grazed very near to the surface of the land itself. To Lirenda's tranced awareness, the barren hills lay skeined in mercuric ribbons of energy, converging toward the balance point of equinox. In the instant when the transition between daylight and dark changed alignment, its force could be used to heighten spells. The impetus borrowed from natural sources must help her unstring Sethvir's wards.

Settled on her heels amid a field of weathered stones

and moonlight, Lirenda raised the Skyron focus. Her shadow pooled over the thread-tangled grasses. The granite shaft of the tower rose baleful and black as though chisel punched from the sky. Unquiet north winds spooled off the desert and hissed over its lichened walls, while the arrow slits of its chambers peered down on her, darkened and narrow as knife cuts.

To wrest the Great Waystone from Sethvir's wardship, Lirenda must first lay bare the defences her circle had been raised to unbind.

Where Koriani spellcraft held predictable structure, each summoned sigil paired to balance with strictures and stamped to submission by seals, Fellowship conjury held a random artistry that resisted mannered effort to decipher. The Sorcerers' bindings could seem enviably seamless, at times fashioned whole from one source. Their works were often Named into being, in complexity as unique as the branched veins of a leaf, no two under Ath's sun alike.

Paravian magecraft was wilder still: older, more primal, living and fluid as free-running water, or layered like a knurl in ancient oak. Few examples remained unfaded by the passage of time and the sunless decay lent by oppression under Desh-thiere's mists.

Conjecture suggested that Althain's defences would follow the patterning of other sites ruled by both styles of magic. Like a Second Age focus circle, or the crossing guards set into moss-hoary megaliths, Lirenda anticipated layers of interlocked spells, stitched like snarled knotwork over a span of many years.

Touched to unease, well warned that the scrying she undertook would try her to the limits of experience, Lirenda braced her nerves in determination. She raised her chin and engaged the Skyron focus. For a moment her form seemed to shimmer as if fused in an uncanny flame. Then she bent the driving weight of her mastery over the force at her command.

The latent play of current uncoiled with a snap. Power lanced out, a thin, scarlet ray honed into a stylus with which she scribed challenge above Althain Tower's grand portal. The spell she directed was a mere spark, an insolent static intended to tease the ingrained protections to display themselves in response.

With care, with persistence, as the wards in the stone wakened from quiescence, she could unriddle the secret of their structure.

Yet no kindly tangle of mismatched spellcraft glowed to meet her testing probe. Instead, a flare of savage, crackling light tore open the fabric of the night.

Clapped blind and deaf by the discharge, Lirenda recoiled. The Skyron crystal heated between her hands like a meteor. Snapped into reflex, she dropped it. The focus gem struck earth and grounded. Its moil of gathered powers dispersed without sound like ash winnowed off by a wind blast.

Fired to annoyance, the Koriani First Senior bent to ease her scorched palms in the grass stems. She stopped in mid-gesture, horrified. Around Althain Tower, the senior circle she had gathered stood lifelessly rigid. As if in one instant, clothing and flesh, each sister had been changed by a glassblower's art to a brittle, glittering replica.

The challenge which followed rang through the air and the earth. Its call was silent, and yet the more terrible for that. The ire battered against bones and teeth like concussion waves through tempered iron.

'Who meddles!'

Lashed into mindless reply, Lirenda cried out her name and rank.

The awful, ringing vibration she had raised brushed her answer aside with what felt like a bruising contempt, but in fact stemmed from power so sure of its place that, like sky, it existed without arrogance. *'Hear then, First Senior of the Koriathain! Your intent to trifle with the*

224

wards over Althain Tower has asked no sanction from me.'

Masked in the tumbled mass of her hair, Lirenda shoved erect, but failed to arise beyond her knees. If she could not subdue the shaking fear in her limbs, she could fall back upon sheer outrage. Yet her attempt at imperious protest came out as a mewling gasp. 'Who are you?'

A rumbling laugh split the night above her head. *'Daughter of merchants, do you claim to be bereft of your eyesight?'*

Against a wave of overwhelming apprehension, Lirenda clawed back her fallen locks. She dared to look. Black-haired, tawny-eyed, austere as midnight itself, she saw nothing at first. Only the coinface silver of the moon, now ridden high above the hills. Her first casting had provoked far more than she intended. The wards over Althain Tower were fully aroused, blazing in sheets of uncanny flame that threw no emanation, nor lit any feature of the surrounding landscape.

No sound intruded. Even the whisper of frost-gilded grasses had lapsed into eerie silence. The winds off the Bittern sands themselves had stopped speaking in a place where their sibilance reigned tireless.

Still trapped in their circle, one hundred and eight Koriani enchantresses stood planted and immobile. Not even the folds of their cloaks stirred. They were statues in time, as if breath and life had been reft away between heartbeats.

The static play of the third lane itself lay arrested, like a river snap-frozen into a vista of black ice. Shaken by a sweeping, savage chill, made aware she had stepped beyond her depth, Lirenda saw that Fate's Wheel itself had been halted on command by the entity she had wakened from quiescence. In ways she had no knowledge to fathom, it had set her outside the veil, while the world's very substance bowed, waiting.

Raised to etheric suspension, her altered eyesight

recorded the apparition with reluctance: a thing which appeared spun whole from a dust mote, translucent but never fragile. Its presence stunned the mortal mind to awe through an aura of unshakable quietude.

'Never doubt I am real,' the being admonished. Its speech held no sound, but cast an ache through living tissue like the tolling vibration of stressed earth.

Foursquare the being stood, like a beast, the boned pillars of its legs flared to silk-haired fetlocks that ended in hooves of cloven horn. Flank and chest were deep as a prize draught horse, but no equine neck arose from the flat-muscled sheen of its forehand. Lirenda tipped back her heart-shaped chin and gazed up, and up; the creature dwarfed her, its mass a tall man's height at the withers. A powerful torso and broad male shoulders reared above, feathered in a mane like flaxen gossamer. The face had human features, bearded like a king lion's, and royally crowned with the branching, tined antlers of a stag.

'Ath's infinite mercy,' Lirenda breathed, humbled before a majesty that reduced her green pride to dust.

The creature configured in spirit light before her made reason shudder and fail. Her heart leaped for joy and for pain, wrenched out of rhythm into paradox by a beauty beyond her five senses to encompass. Through the haze of her tears, Lirenda understood that she faced none else but the ghost of a centaur. One of the Ilitharis Paravian race, vanished from the continent since the advent of Desh-thiere's mists through South Gate.

The creature tipped its horned head. Stars and moon shot like sparks through its substanceless outlines. *'I am Shehane Althain, spirit tied to this place as prime guardian. My bones are this tower's foundation, as its wards are my charge for eternity.'*

Lirenda blinked, her dignity eclipsed by wonder for the first time since earliest childhood. 'You were a sacrifice?'

The centaur spirit glowered like a thunderhead. *'Never!'* His rebuttal rang in a bell tone too deep for hearing, but the frost-touched grasses underneath its planted hooves shimmered like thrown cullet in vibration. *'My life was a gift freely yielded for necessity, that the sanctuary you came here to violate should stand against trifling ignorance.'*

At this, Lirenda bridled. 'I came here, not through folly, but to reclaim from the Fellowship Sorcerers what was never theirs to begin with.'

The centaur bared its teeth in a wolfish snarl. *'The Seven are neither thieves nor hoarders!'*

Never less comfortable for being caught on her knees, Lirenda tried again to stand erect. No muscle in her legs would support her. Rankled to anger for the failing, she said in metallic acerbity, 'Your presumption is false. Or why should the Sorcerers keep our Waystone in their custody since the uprising five hundred years past? Had they deigned to return it, I should scarcely have come to raise a Koriani circle against them.'

'By our choice we have ceded this place into the care of those who swore to uphold the compact. The Fellowship has stood by their bond.' The centaur folded massive arms, its outlines pale quartz shot with stars. *'The granite blocks themselves gave consent to the bindings which protect what lies inside this tower. The stones' gift was no loan, to be reversed. They would crack and run to sand, ere they yielded their office. Go hither. Any violent use of force in this place is an offence.'*

Lirenda pushed back her hood, her hair a spilled fall of ebony over her back. Sarcasm chipped her reply. 'How else would you make Sethvir give back what is ours?'

A terrible, fey light glanced through the spirit's eyes. It stamped a substanceless forehoof, its movement dire elegance, and its strength beyond the pale of reasoned vision. *'Does your order spurn the grace of manners and hospitality? What else should you do but knock at the door? Why not make your request when Althain's*

Warden is present to admit you! Your timing is regrettable, since Sethvir embarked this morning for the court of King Eldir at Ostermere.'

Lirenda retorted in tart disbelief, 'What surety have I that the Sorcerer will listen?'

An electrum sheen of moonlight glanced off the crown of antlers as the centaur tossed its forelock; neat, flat ears with pointed tips nested like shells amid the strands. *'Did he refuse you, I should give you the door myself. Yet hear warning, mortal daughter. Try entry against my will at the risk of life and limb, and that of each one of your companions.'*

Its message finished, the apparition frayed at the edges, then dissolved like whirled flecks of salt.

Lirenda felt herself hurled out of altered vision. She knelt in crumpled skirts on a swathe of dank grass, broken and humbled and weeping. Such beauty as she had never imagined might exist drove her heart, thudding in bursts fit to bound through the walls of her chest. She struggled to compose herself, to shake off an awe that left her paralysed.

The Skyron crystal lay before her, stamped into scintillant reflection by the moon. She uncurled shaking fingers and reclaimed its dense weight. Time had cracked its unnatural suspension. The third lane's currents rang once again to the onrushing surge of coming equinox. Her confused, restored seniors crowded about her as she stumbled back to her feet. They asked, unaware why their circle of power had gone wrong. All were oblivious to Shehane Althain's hidden might, that for one perilous, hidden moment, had swept their breathing lives like cast-off thread cuttings into his realm on the spirit plane.

Lirenda clenched her jaw. She forced her spine straight, then clawed her hood up to hide the smeared tracks of her tears. Shamed and at a loss, she groped to find words to say why she had reason to dismiss the support of her colleagues, then stay on alone until Sethvir's return.

Morriel would be livid to know her successor had been forced to bend pride. Yet no choice remained. The latent power of one Ilitharis Paravian brooked no further argument. Lirenda must come to plead a sorcerer's indulgence, or else abandon her charge to return with the order's lost Waystone.

Ring Ripples

At Ostermere, ensconced in the royal kitchens over a plate of scones and jam, Sethvir pauses to chuckle over the success of his spell of illusion, that had tricked the Koriani First Senior to belief she had conversed with the spirit of Althain's dedicated guardian; her limited learning might never reveal the truth: that, had the tower's Warden lacked the foresight to beg a stay of tolerance, her meddling would indeed have raised the ward wrought from the bones of Shehane Althain, and neither she nor her ill-advised circle of accomplices would have escaped with their lives . . .

Over the coals of the bonfire lit to celebrate his wedding on spring equinox, Jieret s'Valerient, Earl of the North and *caithdein* of Rathain, stands with his bride to bid farewell to his war captain, summoned south to serve his prince in Vastmark: 'Be his shield, Caolle, and go with my blessing, for no other sword would I entrust to safeguard our liege in my place . . .'

* * *

Under a great cloud of dust, clan scouts sent out of
Alland drive a great herd of cattle and horses across the
Forthmark road; and bound into Vastmark in their company to recover the stowaway twins are the former
guardsman and the widow who had fled Lysaer's grasp
at Merior . . .

V. THREE SHIPS

Princess Talith weathered her forced passage to the Cascains with all the ill grace of a brooding goose in a pullet's crate. While she stayed immured in the stern cabin, her handmaid emerged at measured intervals for whining bouts that began with demands, and finished with piteous pleading. The *Khetienn's* brigand captain should order his vessel about and make port at Los Mar for the sake of her ladyship's health.

'She's seasick?' Arithon inquired. Poised at the mizzenmast shroud, his loose-fitted sailhand's shirt fluttered by the east breeze and his feet braced to balance the mild roll of the ship, he regarded the servant's handwringing affectations with rapt, disingenuous green eyes.

The recount of Talith's suffering filled a long and tiresome interval. At the finish, while the handmaid blinked in dewy-eyed expectancy, he shrilled a whistle through his teeth, then told the topmen who answered to break out staysails and flying jib. His brigantine came alive, slashing through the swell to a thunderous thrum of canvas, while the sheared spatter of spray sheeted rainbows off her sleek bow.

The princess's servant howled in complaint, and Arithon laughed, hands clenched to tarred rigging to ride out the buck of the deck. 'Be sure to take your ailing mistress my condolences. Tell her we'll make landfall that much faster.'

Dakar regarded this exchange with avid interest through the fringe of his dripping bangs. Curled like a damp hedgehog on a bight of rope, and determined despite his green face not to bolt for the leeward railing, he observed, 'You're a miserable, stone-hearted bastard.'

Arithon showed no change in expression. 'Indeed. Only the cook doesn't think so.'

Thereafter, the handmaid presented her daily complaints to Dakar's listening sympathy. Given to a startling, selfless turn of subterfuge, he would pat her damp hands, soothe her fears, then assure her he would speak in Lady Talith's behalf. To his credit, he never claimed his word could sway the Shadow Master from pursuit of his demanding offshore passage.

While the sniffling maid crept below to attend her mistress, the Mad Prophet retired to the galley. There, much too quiet, he peeled onions for the swarthy little desertman who claimed double pay for the roles of cabin steward and cook. The fellow had a face as inscrutable as a walnut. If a whistling lisp left by five missing teeth made him closemouthed enough for Arithon to tolerate his service, he was an adroit hand with the stewpots. Eager to win the man's contrary confidence, Dakar outdid himself as an unctuous, smiling toady.

The cook simply sucked in his crinkled lips and kept on dicing salt beef with a nasty, hooked dagger he had won playing dice with a fishmonger. For all that extended passages were a rarity since Desh-thiere's mists had repressed the finer arts of navigation, the nomads born to Sanpashir's black sands were wizards at knowing which seasonings and spices could sweeten the taste of turned stores. Caught out in chagrin, again and again,

Dakar found himself side-tracked from his probing to the chore of slicing lemons and garlic.

The cook was not forthcoming on his views of the Shadow Master's service. Exhausted from failed subtleties, Dakar lacked the nerve to ask outright. The princess herself was off-limits. His earlier brashness replaced by sullen wisdom, Dakar knew precisely when not to trifle with Arithon's affairs.

Lady Talith stayed belowdecks, supine and miserable and listless in her berth by the woeful account of her maid. The curtains across the stern windows were drawn closed night and day, until the sailhands grumbled for the need to ration lamp oil to indulge their passenger's overuse of stores.

Arithon silenced every whimper of complaint by meting out brutal work and sea drills.

By the energetic rush of feet across the deck, and the twanging clank of ratchets as the great arbalests were winched cocked and tested, Lady Talith was left in little doubt of the *Khetienn*'s trim readiness for action. Never once did Arithon disturb her, or trouble himself to visit and inquire after her health. Throughout the four-week voyage, his sailhands acquired a dangerous, smooth efficiency, and sharp new respect for his temper. Nothing else changed but the weather. The brisk, pranking winds and leaden rains of early spring smoothed into blue waters, too cold as yet to be thrashed by the squall lines brewed up in the heat of high summer.

The eastern horizon glowed gold and pink as the lip of a conch shell on the morning the *Khetienn* nosed in at slack tide, over glassy black waters to seek anchorage. The rock cliffs that hedged the twisty, narrow channel loured, lidded in fog, above her mastcaps; her sails sliced rust-red reflections through the bubbled trail of her wake. No one troubled to inform the princess of the landfall. Her only warning the sour reek of weed washed up by waves upon the rocks, Talith arose and called her handmaid to attend her grooming. Etarran to her core, enraged to frozen spite, she regaled herself in the magnificence of her most imposing court velvets. None who beheld her would fail to mistake the significance of her station. Beside her state jewels and her stylishly rich dress, her husband's half-brother would appear the insolent saltwater ruffian.

Talith timed her appearance to mesh with the clanging descent of the anchor chain. She swept toward the main deck, sure her adversary would be caught in busy disarray, with tar rimmed black underneath his chipped nails as he sent his men aloft to stow sails.

Instead she found him ready at the companionway to escort her, clad in a green doublet of impeccable light silk and a shirt of unwrinkled, pale lawn. The sable hair worn to sea in a sailor's club had been freshly trimmed; his hands were manicured, and his smile, bright mockery amid the tanned planes of his face.

The setback did nothing for Talith's brittle mood. She hung back in the shadows and swallowed a public explosion better suited to a dockside harridan. More ways existed to jab a man's pride; no male alive had ever dealt the last word. Against this one, she would need all her claws.

'You used lilac water,' Arithon admitted, amused by her venomous silence. 'My quartermaster's been fidgeting with his breeks all morning. He said his second-best mistress also favours that scent, and three sailors lost their month's wages at dice vying to be first to peer through the afterdeck hatch cover.'

Talith took his offered arm as though it were a snake, too urbane to rise to retort. No crewman had been spying, as Arithon knew best of any; else her maid's linen shift had gone to mildew for nothing, tacked up to block the gaps in the grating.

As she let herself be ushered into daylight, her captor made a study of her armour of velvets and jewels. A sardonic smile turned his lips. 'My dear, how lucky for you I keep such a tight rein on discipline. You might stall a man guessing to tell whether there's enough of you underneath to make the effort of stripping drapery worth a rape. But as you say, we're a desperate pack of thieves. If I ran my command like the *Arrow*, I'd break up a half-dozen fights just to see who got to cut your throat to loot your jewels.'

A matched glint of fight in the depths of her eyes, Lady Talith raised her chin another notch. The combed honey coil of her hair made her lashes and pupils seem a sooty, unnatural black. 'Trust a man to mistake discipline for crude intimidation,' she said. 'Am I meant to be impressed?'

'You're meant to be cowed,' replied Arithon, never more serious. 'But who expects that in a princess?' His critical regard raked her over again, to an exaggerated flick of amazement at the sparkle of her bullion chains, and the twisted strands of seed pearls caught like drizzle against the nap of her velvets. 'Are you truly as hot as you appear? At least shed your mantle. Indigo makes your colour look washed out.'

Talith returned a magnificent glare. 'Is my pallor not the fault of your beastly ship? If I'm kept in duress in trade for Tysan's riches, I'd expect you'd have some care for my well-being.'

Arithon handed her up the companionway. 'You'll have no pity from me for cooping yourself up like a broody hen. My cook assures me your appetite's been truly remarkable for an invalid. I scarcely need mention it's been calm enough for chess nearly every night you've been on board. Lady Talith, your beauty's enchanting, I admit. But you'll need to lie better to gain my respect for your wit.'

'I need no respect from a criminal,' Talith said, gratified now, in her element. 'Nor am I here for your coarse entertainment.'

237

They had reached the main deck. Several sailhands were staring. Talith swept past them as if they were insects. Dismay flushed her skin all the same; for the brigantine had made landfall upon no inhabited shore. The skyline meshed sheer into brooding cliffs, fretted in foam and dark water. No wharf and no gangway awaited. The rail lacked even a gate for the convenience of passengers in skirts.

Most maddening of all was the Shadow Master's wry joy at her side; then his words, touched in flint to spark her temper. 'My sweet sister-in-law, it's a delightful privilege.' His hands grasped her waist and slung her up in a frothed spill of petticoats until she rested face-down across his shoulder.

Talith jabbed her clenched fist in the small of his back and hoped her sharp rings tore his doublet. Burdened as he was, she could feel he was laughing. His hands through the muffling layers of her clothing fired outrage and thrilled her to tingling, combative heat.

'Damn you,' she whispered to the back of his belt. She thumped him again, then shut her eyes, dizzy, as he swung over the rail toward the longboat rocking below.

'Slippery as a marlin,' called the man at the oars. 'D'ye suppose she'll pinch?'

'Scratch, rather,' Arithon quipped back in good nature. He felt her fast snatch for the grip of his sheathed sword and jounced her weight onto her diaphragm. Her breath locked beyond speech, and the unsubtle, wrestler's twist to her knee brought a film of tears to her eyes. 'You don't want a swim in all these velvets, my dear. For the goldwork alone, you'd go down like a rock from a catapult. We'd have to drag the bottom for salvage.'

His foot touched the heaving gunwale and stepped down. There came a sinking jolt as he kicked to cast off. Then the princess was spun right side up and deposited in the stern like a muffled-up child in a bolster. Her coiffure had come loose. Through a wing of fallen hair and a jingling spill of diamond pins, she caught both hands to rough wood and waited for the jerk as four lout-fisted seamen slammed their full weight to the oars.

But the longboat glided shoreward like spilled oil on silk. Unresigned, prepared to lock wills with a master player, Talith rescued jewelled pins one by one from their slide toward the bilge. While the gulls screamed and shuttled in raucous patterns overhead, she hardened herself to cold cause. Born an Etarran, weaned on merciless intrigue, she would inveigle some way to thwart Arithon's bid for her ransom. For his slights to her pride and his callous turn of boldness, she would draw blood as she could, and see him humiliated before King Eldir and the Fellowship. However backwater the outpost where he had chosen to sequester her, he would find himself empty-handed when his vaunted exchange was set to occur at midsummer.

Talith clawed the last pin from her hair and smoothed wind-flicked strands from her lashes. Her velvets weighed her shoulders like cloths dipped in lead in the heavy, humid airs. A trickle of sweat licked her neck. She endured in damp poise while the bronzed and grinning oarsmen rowed the longboat through a notch like a gateway between islets. The splash of each stroke threw back glassine echoes; no sound of inhabitance cut their rhythm. Scarps of rock jutted on both sides like storm-chiselled barbazons. The breaking mists overhead framed a vista of desolation ruled by black and white birds and ragged clouds. Talith refused to give way and inquire where she was amid the wilderness.

Arithon took grave pleasure by informing her. 'These are the Cascains, off Vastmark, just east of South Strait inlet. Your stay won't be long and provisions have been made. Your handmaid will come ashore later with your boxes. She's already been told that you won't be quartered in the open.'

But despite this reassurance, the only human sounds

issued from behind, where the brigantine's indignant cook shouted lists of provisions to the crew who launched the second longboat. His thick desert dialect mixed with Dakar's deeper threats, should the craft be launched shoreward without him.

The argument fell away into distance as the craft bearing Talith rounded the spined jut of an outcrop. Along with screeling bird cries came the faint ring of mallets, and through them, with earsplitting clarity, a child's treble shout from a dory that bobbed among the rocks. 'The Master of Shadow is back!'

'Welcome to my den of iniquity,' Arithon said with a wicked, lazy grin.

The mallet strokes went ragged and died away, replaced by loud talk, then a man's whoop, followed by laughter.

'By Ath, he's snatched her after all!' someone pealed in an accent from Southshire's quay shanties.

Talith shut her eyes. Her hands clenched down on her cache of rescued pins until the gems pebbled marks in her skin. She endured while the longboat grounded with a grate on sea-washed stones. Cumbered in state velvets, she could not escape another round of ignominy as Arithon scooped her up like a trophy. He waded ashore and set her down for inspection before the uncouth pack of craftsmen on the strand.

His outpost held little beyond a scraggle of tents strung between what looked like the yard of a furniture shop. Small stools and benches and a vehicle that looked like a dogcart lay scattered about in various states of completion. The shoreline was littered in shavings of yellow pine, and the fishy, sour smell of the natural air twined through a cloying reek of resin. The chips were going to cling horribly to velvets.

Silent in distaste, her head still giddy from too many weeks on shipboard, Talith tried a mincing step. The narrow kidskin slippers on her feet were fashioned for carpets and paved walkways. On the rough ground, they slipped and wobbled. The flounces of her skirts obscured her footing. Unless she wished to walk like a crofter with her petticoats kirtled up, she would have to lean on Arithon for balance. Mortified that the sole slight in her power was to treat his courtesy as if he were a servant, Talith ground her teeth in forced patience. For the first time in her life, she wished to bundle her face behind her cloak as every sweating, shirtless labourer leered at her in wolfish interest. One or two with the shame of chastised boys dusted shavings off their forearms and chests.

Low and to the sidelines, somebody whistled. A man tried a coarse remark.

Arithon clipped through the lewd comment with a line like a forge-heated blade. 'May I present her Grace of Avenor. She is a princess, as you see. Every man in her presence may bow with the courtesy due her station, or else answer to me later for his insolence. And docked pay for all, a day for each minute the last of you stands idle.'

The gawking line of men melted clear of her path. They snatched up their tools to a few scattered laughs and a mild exchange of bluster. 'Kneel on such rocks, and ye risk a burst kneecap. Me, I'll take my blisters in the sawpit.'

A barrel-chested joiner spat sideward and chuckled. 'Man, don't fool us! Ye're old lady'd lash you to blisters wi' her tongue, did she hear you'd lost yer wage to ogle royalty.'

'Sithaer, then, who's for telling her?' The injured party shook a calloused fist. 'The jack who tries'll taste my knuckles for his breakfast and his teeth the next week, to the lifelong wreck of his digestion.'

'High drama and low comedy,' Arithon said, a pricking spark to his humour. 'We may not be refined, but you can't say you'll lack for entertainment.'

'And which sort is this?' Lady Talith stabbed back.

For as they crested the slope from the beachhead, one man had not moved on command. No sweat-drenched joiner, this one stood tall in a jerkin of thong-laced deer hide. He was armed with a bow, several bone-handled knives, and a deadly plain longsword with the handgrip wrapped in stained leather. The only flamboyance about him was the fox brush laced into the end of his braid. His eyes were alert and cool as dappled shade, and his body, a fit wild animal's. 'Your Grace of Rathain,' he greeted in the whip snap clean accents that tagged him immediately as clanborn. 'My Lord Erlien, High Earl of Alland and *caithdein* of Shand sends respects.'

Arithon inclined his head in greeting. A token changed hands. Talith caught the impression of a royal device before the disc was returned. 'I'm pleased to extend my hospitality.' Angled s'Ffalenn features showed inquisitive speculation. 'Why the formality? You've brought more than horses and cattle?'

'Fiends alive!' The clansman showed white teeth in a grimace. 'I've been in and out of every peat bog in these scarps, trying to soak that reek off me.' The barbarian softened to reproof as he fired back the gist of the question. 'The stock's your problem now, and a few other troubles along with them. Earl Jieret's cranky war captain, for one. He's got a temper like a stoat. But you know that since you asked for him, they said.'

'A sweet touch will scarcely train my mercenaries.' In tacit awareness of how the sun striking down through the defiles must feel on dark velvets, Arithon guided Talith forward and let the clan courier fall into step. 'What else?'

The scout hesitated, toyed with his fox brush, then shot a furtive glance toward the finery the prince wore like a townsman. A dubious brow twitched, for the slight, dapper figure seemed no match for the razor-tongued swordsman reputed to have bested his clanlord.

'I have two others with me, by Erlien's choice,' the messenger said to close out his business. 'A widow from Merior and a guardsman, once captain to Alestron's duke.' This last drew a nod toward Talith and a pause of evident uncertainty.

Arithon assured him, 'There's no secret. Jinesse and Tharrick are friends. Erlien expected some problem?'

The scout shrugged, his footfalls preternaturally quiet as he picked through the wood scrolls silted across the path by the wind. 'That's yours to determine. My lord bade me warn you. Both have fallen hard for Lysaer s'Illessid's opinion of your morals. The man's yours, despite his squeamish conscience. But the woman's a brittle, dry stick. She followed you only for her children.'

'High drama,' Arithon quipped. At the scout's flick of puzzlement, he gave a bitter laugh that raised the fine hair at Talith's neck. 'The matron's outraged, blind to reason, and expecting to be corrupted by slow inches? You just got here? Well then, let's not keep her waiting. Where is she?'

But there was only one place in his camp to quarter women that Talith could see. A ramshackle cabin perched at the cliff base, its unweathered wood a cry of light colour against rocks streaked by seeping, small springs.

Arithon dismissed the scout, then dispatched a nearby craftsman to find the twins. To Talith, he invited, 'Come along, your Grace. You might as well enjoy the fun.' His hand on her arm too firm for refusal, he towed the princess toward the doorway.

The hinges creaked open to reveal a room with a bare table and chairs. A blond, bearded man perched on the unglazed windowsill, his frame strapping and broad as a mercenary. He clasped the hand of a woman in a mousy brown dress who looked nervous and drawn, hair like fine flax tumbled in broken strands around her temples. She gave a timid start at the Master's forceful entry, reached her feet in a worried bound, then froze. Her eyes swept his person, plainly surprised by the rich sheen of silks that forced recognition of royal rank.

Unwilling and unwanted observer, Talith felt pity for her discomfort as Arithon swept aside her stammered greeting. 'Here I am, black as night in Sithaer and shedding blight like last season's leaves. At least, Erlien's scout tells me you believe all the fashionable rumours.' Lightly as he stopped, his tense stance presaged unpleasantness. 'If I'm evil, then make me repent.'

The male confidant in the window shot straight in protective shock. 'For pity, man! She's been worried sick for her children.'

'They're her offspring, not yours, Tharrick,' Arithon corrected. He took another step and leaned on fine knuckles against the tabletop. The faintest ring of horror shuddered through as he added, 'In Ath's name, you know me. What harm did you think I would do them?'

The pale woman swallowed. 'I don't care to survey the mire of your conscience. I came to fetch my twins clear of it.'

'Fetch away,' Arithon quipped on a thin snap of anger. 'Your children aren't infants. Place your boy in service to s'Ilessid, and he'll spend his next years polishing guardsmen's boots and eating table scraps. He'll learn the art of war. Obedience will be his only trade. If he's quick, if he kills well, he may become an officer. If he's not, two shirts, a sword, and an early death will be his lot. Will you be proud to weep at his grave site?'

He had managed to sting the mother to pale anger. She stiffened her spine; after all, she had never expected this confrontation to go easily. 'I had chosen an apprenticeship with a weaver in Shaddorn. That's honest, at least. My son would be free of your sorceries and no blind mark for your wiles.'

Arithon moved, sidestepped, and leaned by the door-post to lend Talith an untrammelled view. 'Ah, yes.

244

Looms and shuttlecocks for Fiark, whose gift is numbers, and who throws stones and strikes everything he aims at. Let's consider Feylind. She's no good with her hands. In fact, if you've noticed, she's farsighted. Her brother threads her needles when she needs to patch her breeches. She would blood you with her knife if she felt she had the need to, and she thinks of skirts like suffocation. Her talent is sailing and her trade is the sea. Hold her ashore, and you force her to a life of mediocrity.'

'Better that than see her claimed by Dharkaron for Sithaer,' Jinesse said in an obstinacy that won Talith's admiration.

That moment the latch rattled. Arithon spun and prisoned the bar with long fingers. 'Your son, mistress.' And he flung wide the door.

Fiark stood on the threshold, puzzled and motionless as he blinked to adjust to the gloom. The moment framed him, a gangling lad with overlarge fists and skinned knees, his spill of flaxen hair tumbled over a tanned, untroubled brow. Stronger and straighter than the day he left Merior, his direct blue eyes held a self-confidence as fresh as the sunlight at his back.

'Mother?' he said, reverted in a breath to boyish astonishment. He stepped into the shack with a heart-tearing mixture of restraint and joyous abandon.

Glad as he was to see Jinesse, he started as she knelt and swept him up, three months of worry compressed in an overpowering, tearful embrace. His high yelp of protest was smothered in brown muslin, and the wrestler's move he engaged to tear free was not at all couth or forgivable.

'I'm eleven!' he declared, defiant at her reprimand, his face stamped to square-jawed disappointment. 'Do you have to treat me like a baby?'

'She's your mother,' Tharrick chastened. 'You'll do as she directs.'

Fiark's sunny nature chilled over in comprehension,

his features rearranged to resentment beyond his years. 'You're here to take me away. You want to apprentice me to that weaver in Shaddorn.' Charged with the contempt, the young voice turned acid. 'Were father alive, he never would have allowed it.'

Stunned by the accusation's cruel candour, Jinesse gasped. The boy drew up and faced her. He did not, as she had feared, appeal to Arithon for protection, but waited in strait patience for her answer. When she could not speak for grief, he spun back toward the doorway. 'I won't go,' he threatened in a man's controlled rebuff, then bolted outside at a run. The panel banged shut in an unbridled blast of childish temper.

'Will you hear the bare truth?' Arithon said with a gentleness that pleaded for the boy. 'Not mine. Not Lysaer's, but Fiark's. He wants to be a trade factor. There's an honest house in Innish I know would be overjoyed to train him. The family is ageing and has no offspring to inherit.'

'You have no pity and all the answers,' Jinesse said through tight emotion. 'My son was always difficult, but Feylind was obedient. If she's changed, then you've warped her trusting disposition to your purpose. You turn the young, so they say. I saw you use my son against me now. I know your cause is bloody war. I am going to take my twins and leave this place, and never speak your name to them again.'

Arithon regarded her, opaque, wholly still; chillingly unlike the fair Prince of the West, who once came honestly and openly to her cottage in Merior to offer his clear-eyed consolation. Black-haired and shadowed, Rathain's prince said, 'Blame whatever you like on me if you can keep your peace of mind. But if you dare to know your heart, I rather think you'll find I'm a damned convenient crutch as a criminal. Condemn me out of hand, and you have the perfect reason to keep your children tied to your petticoats.'

He was right; even Talith as a stranger could see as much. The burly man by the window stared in anguish at clenched fists, while the widow stood erect in desperate anguish. 'Fiark at Innish would be safe. What do you ask for Feylind? Should she stay with you and suffer in the violence to come?'

Arithon expelled a soundless breath. He made two salient points. 'I alone can teach her the arts of offshore navigation. She already does star and sun sights, and is well on her way with reading charts. Against the war-host, I'll be truthful, I'm still seeking answers. But should you leave her, never forget. *You still hold my signet and my pledge.*'

The reminder hammered Jinesse like a visible impact. 'You know my twins were all that stopped me from sending Lysaer's galleys after you.'

Arithon shrugged. 'As a brother can love, so can he hate. Lysaer, also, will use what falls to hand.' Her shocked expression snapped him to a rust-grained turn of irony. 'You didn't know? He's my half-brother, and fittingly legitimate. He finds the attachment annoying, but I see no point in hiding facts. The Prince of the West has his own soiled linen, but you won't find me parading in the public eye to gain an army.' With lancing sarcasm, he ended, 'As Dakar will surely snatch his chance to tell you, *I snare children instead.*'

'That's enough!' Tharrick uncoiled from the sill and folded the widow into his arms. 'We came to fetch her twins. Why not decide their futures later? She's travelled three hundred leagues with a dusty herd of cattle. You don't have to tear out her heart!'

'He's sure if he doesn't I won't give my twins space to grow.' Distraught but not witless, Jinesse pushed away the needed offer of protection. 'Let me be. I have to think.'

'Feylind was out in the dory,' said Arithon on a start-ling break into tenderness. 'I asked a seaman to fetch her in. By now, she ought to be down at the landing.' He opened the door and allowed her to leave, her thin face bathed in tears, and her broken composure walled behind dignified silence.

Tharrick saw her to the threshold, spared a nod to the princess, then closed the panel behind, leaving darkness.

'I grant you the point about the children,' Talith said with quick contempt. 'What can we victims do but admire the diabolical cruelty of your lessons? You have no mercy in you. My husband is well justified to hound you to your death.'

'Lysaer's opinion is your affair,' Arithon fired back, then gave her his insolent laughter. 'Is winning or losing all you understand? Then I pity you. Whether or not you'll cede the match is quite moot. I charge you instead. Learn by what you saw and take fair warning.'

The day as it progressed became no less settled, although Talith's chests of belongings were off-loaded ashore, and she was given private quarters in one of the shanty's two rooms. Arithon afforded neither company nor sport for her scathing, sharp wit. He closeted himself away all afternoon aboard his brigantine in counsel with the grizzled and quick-tempered war captain called to serve from the clans of Rathain. The scout sent from Shand's *caithdein* received close instructions and left. The master shipwright and his least-skilled joiners were dispatched to *Khetienn*'s hold and asked to build stalls to confine livestock. The work would apparently be finished under way, to judge by the banty little cook's screeched invective as he bustled to reprovision the galley.

Time weighed on the princess, left alone in the company of her handmaid. Mistress Jinesse spent an hour with her daughter that ended in a tempestuous argument, young Feylind's responses turned filthy with sailor's vernacular she took care not to call out too loud. The guardsman Tharrick's stifled laughter affirmed the apt guess, that Arithon would make things unpleasant for the girl if he heard her use such ugly language to her mother.

Jinesse had no choice but to resign herself. Her twins had matured enough to have minds of their own. They held only scorn for the weaver's trade.

'Too dull,' Feylind said, cryptic. 'I hate sitting still.'

'The folk who have the fun trade the cloth,' Fiark added. 'I should rather count baled goods than threads.'

The widow had nothing to say to this. She ruffled the paired, leaf-gold heads instead. Feylind spoiled the gesture by twitching back from her touch; Fiark endured, but looked offended.

Jinesse also found herself at loose ends in a yard full of labourers. Wrapped in dense brooding since the Master of Shadow had so high-handedly intervened with her family, she had little to say to the princess. She looked to Tharrick for consolation and waited in pallid patience to demand the facts concerning the factor's family at Innish with interest in Fiark's future. On the topic of her daughter's wish to sign onto *Khetienn* as cabin girl, she pursed her lips in flat denial.

The day wore away to her fretting.

By dusk, the hammers fell silent, leaving the mingled sharps and flats of gulls skimming the tide line. The sea wind wafted the pungent resins of pitch pine, and the men ate boiled crabs from a pot, brought to smokeless heat by coal carried in on the brigantine. The small outpost embraced its evening routine with a certain rough tranquillity; except for the scouts sent in parties to sweep the rimrocks on patrol.

The council on shipboard broke up. By the damp rocks at the landing, Dakar's tones complained of perishing hunger, bitten through by Caolle, more querulous still, expounding on the need for more caution. 'So who's fooling whom?' he badgered to whoever lay in earshot. 'His Grace of Rathain is a hunted man in four kingdoms, and the chit he holds hostage is one an army would burn cities to win back.'

Feylind met the last dory, bearing Arithon. Oblivious to any need for tact, a swagger to her step meticulously copied from Captain Dhirken, she rushed through the falling dark and seized his hand. 'You said *Talliarthe* is due in with dispatches. Let me take her out when she arrives.' She tossed her head, insistent, the braid down her back like a glistening rope of oil in the flicker of freshly-lit torches. 'I must show my mother I can navigate and reef a sail. When she sees what I can do, she'll understand.'

The Master of Shadow let her tug at his fingers, standing thoughtful by the shoreline. 'You aren't strong enough to man the sloop by yourself just yet.' As she heaved straight to protest, he touched her lips silent. 'But that can be overcome. Here's what I think. You can captain her. Give all the orders. Fiark will go, and Tharrick, and one of the *Khetienn*'s sailhands for muscle in case a gale blows in out of season. If your mother gives consent, you can thread the mazes to the strait and come back. Fifteen days. After that, you understand, I can't do any more. What happens must become Jinesse's decision.'

'She'll let me go,' Feylind declared, her young face determined.

Arithon returned a grave shake of his head. 'She'll do what's best.' He worked himself free of her adoring grasp, a twist to his mouth that was wry and sadly tender.

A snag of light in a royal sapphire spun to sudden movement in the gloom; Lady Talith, as observer, whirled and fled. She had no desire, ever, to see this man vulnerable. He was her dedicated enemy, and Lysaer's bastard nemesis, a sorcerer born and bound to clever reiving. Her husband insisted he used children as a ploy.

If his compassion for the feelings of the little ones stemmed from falsehood, Talith would avoid the temptation to let his wiles sap the bastions of her hatred.

The princess invoked the privilege due her station and demanded her meal in the solitude of her cabin. She was not present to hear the widow consent to Feylind's trial aboard the sloop. Settled early in her bed of musty blankets, she lay wakeful to the brangle of the clansman, Caolle, and Tharrick, arguing over nuances of siege warfare. Interleaved through their gruff words and laughter, clear as the peal of flung coin, Arithon's meticulous, silver-tongued speech taught the twins the three-toned whistle used by the tribes at need to signal danger.

When sleep finally claimed the Princess of Avenor, it came laced with dreams of her husband's anguished pain for the assault by an enemy upon a vulnerable flank he had trusted in her good sense to guard.

The next day, Talith arose to find the Master of Shadow gone, and the yard in the moody care of his senior joiner. Astonished to be abandoned to her own devices, uneasy in hindsight for her flaunting show of jewels the day before, she stalked like a stork over the litter of shavings and asked imperious questions.

The sour fellow answered her, laconic, between powerful strokes of his adze. 'Ask Ivel what you will. I'm busy.' He tipped the haft of his tool toward a barrel where a shrivelled old splicer hunkered, chewing his breakfast of smoked cod.

Talith wrinkled her nose at the noisome stink borne downwind. Need for information overcame her distaste. The splicer, if blind, proved an addict for gossip, pleased to speak on any subject she wished.

'Master's off into the uplands. The clan war captain from Rathain's gone with him. That one came, you must know, to train mercenaries.' Ivel spat a cod bone and tucked meaty fists around the napped knees of his breeches. 'Once Caolle's established with the recruits,

Arithon's for the valley, where Shand's *caithdein*'s sent horses. They'll cull the herd, and select thirty to ship out for sale. The brigantine's to bide here at anchorage until the sloop brings in dispatches. She'll sail on the tide and rejoin him downcoast for loading.'

'He won't be coming back?' Talith could scarcely contain her surprise.

Ivel gave a teeth-licking grin. 'Now that's not a guess I'd set words on. The man's like the wind. In and out at his whim. The only engagement he's fixed on for sure is his plan to collect your ransom at Ostermere.'

'That's not until midsummer.' Talith tapped her foot. 'He'll keep me immured here until then?'

'Are you? I heard of no walls, no locks.' Ivel sucked the aftertaste of fish off his forefinger and rocked to a wicked, low cackle. 'I don't see,' he confessed with unnecessary relish, the shocking, white orbs in his eye sockets rolled up for her inspection. 'But say if I'm wrong. The young master didn't leave you any guards.'

He had not. The fact had chafed against Talith's confidence through every waking minute of the morning. Equally plain, the Prince of Rathain had not departed in an unplanned rush. Down by the landing a longboat rocked, where men loading wood for the livestock stalls poked fun at somebody's lame joke. Sounds of industrious hammering rang from the anchorage beyond the masking point of the barrier isles. Talith had noted the packet left for Jinesse, set with Arithon's signature and seal, papers drawn up with proprieties observed to present Fiark to the trade factor at Innish. Tharrick had spoken of being awake in the dawn to see the Shadow Master away. The stolid second mate from the *Khetienn* had his orders and his sea duffel off-loaded and ready. He had bathed and scrounged up a new shirt for the honour to crew on the sloop when Feylind sailed her passage through the straits.

In the dazzle of early sunlight, over odds and ends of

lumber pegged in dovetailed joints by muscular, half-stripped men, Talith moved off to search for signs of slackening, of inactivity. But the industry in the yard lapsed not a beat for Arithon's glaring absence.

'He's not human,' the handmaid ventured in a whisper, the rope-handled bucket she had borrowed to wash underthings clamped in her fretted, red fingers. She tipped her head toward the workers bent over the sawpit ripping out new planks. 'His men are trapped under spells, or why else should they sweat like slaves for an absent master?'

'Discipline,' Talith said, annoyed enough by the obvious to snap to her captor's defence. Despite her unforgiving hours of observation, no evidence had she found of fell powers beyond the use of his birth gift at her capture.

Behind her shoulder, she heard the splicer's rich chuckle. No doubt some clever repartee concerning her maid's beliefs would make rounds of the yard before noon. The old badger had a nose for dissent. His relentless, snide commentary on other people's problems kept half the yard in laughter, and the other half, fit to sling their chisels at him.

Talith ordered her servant to retire and resumed her covert study of Arithon's labourers. What talk she overheard was illuminating. The men appeared dedicated. They pursued their assigned tasks without complaint. The former guard, Tharrick, was no fool. Jinesse had confided, when asked of his ambivalence, the odd fact he had changed a lifelong allegiance in favour of loyalty to Arithon.

The Princess of Avenor twitched her skirts clear of a puddle and inclined her bright head to the man who stepped aside to let her pass. These folk were not honourless, nor were they lacking self-constraint; but in any group society, there would be factions. As Etarrans lived for intrigue, she should have small difficulty finding a weakness to exploit.

Two days passed. Talith bided in a stiff display of meekness until the sloop *Talliarthe* returned in due form with her dispatches. The paid captain who manned her disembarked, to reassume his former post aboard the *Khetienn*. Avenor's princess retired to her quarters while the graceful little pleasure craft was reprovisioned to set sail with Jinesse, Tharrick, and both twins, and the trustworthy seaman appointed for his strength, as guard against unforeseen weather. She embarked to Feylind's proud, shouted orders and vanished between combed, white reefs and black rock. The sloop's sister brigantine raised anchor at the crest of the same tide, three joiners on board still sawing timbers and banging pegs to refigure her hold.

Left to herself amid a yard of common shipwrights, and provided no comforts to divert her, Lady Talith arranged her hair and her clothing. She hardened her heart like sugar stirred in hemlock to test the temper of the Shadow Master's loyal following. The challenge lay before her, to subvert his given trust and make his men hers if she could.

In a dress cut down from its former state magnificence, unjewelled, but fitted at the waist, she ventured out as though to take the air. She gazed at the sky, the worked wood, and the workers' muscled bodies with all the sultry boredom she could muster; and was surprised.

None of them gaped in smitten lust.

What glances she received were not even curious, but snatched behind her back in irritation. Not every man was impervious; the rare few who were fidgety under her regard would redden and turn fumbling with their tools. One fled outright to take shelter in the privy. But even that fellow came back determined, and assiduously refused to look at her. Badger though she might with her stunning allure, like salt in a raw sore, if she lingered too long, or raised a skirt to rub her ankle, a tougher-willed

254

companion invariably came to ask her victim for unnecessary help with a measurement.

None returned her greeting by other than a nod. If she attempted conversation, she received a bobbing bow and some grumbled excuse or apology: that she was in the way, would she kindly move aside, her presence was a regrettable inconvenience. No one so much as met her eyes.

At noon, while the sun blistered down, except in the defile by the cliff wall, she presented complaint to the splicer. The blind man grunted, but at least gave her answer where he sat on an upturned barrel, at work amid a snake's nest of cordage. 'These know what their lives are worth, surely.'

His hands were like bear's paws, flat and short-fingered, but astoundingly deft at their craft. Talith watched his tacit touch on the tough, grey twine, half-mesmerized by the finish of a whip-smooth four-square sennit. 'Your master told his people to ignore me?'

Ivel tipped up his chin to roll his eyes, an affectation he enjoyed to shock the squeamish. 'Arithon told them to ignore the pride o' manhood in their breeches.' His fingers never faltered as he talked. 'You're a sight, so they say, to steal reason.'

Talith gave a low, metallic laugh. 'That makes them afraid to speak? Or were they forbidden?'

'Well now.' Ivel tilted his thatched, unkempt head and licked the pad of his thumb, then selected a new rope and twisted the plies open to begin work on a new hawser. 'Arithon said none was to touch you. It's the men, you see. They worried the issue amongst themselves.' The splicer twirled his marlinespike at the peaks which rimmed the sky all around. 'No whores here, you understand. Not even a pot-house to sell beer to numb the healthy itch. The men decided if they ignored you in a pack, they'd have a lighter time with the temptation.'

Talith blinked, set aback. 'Are they men at all, and

255

not animals, to so dread the loss of their manners? Or are they gelded by fear, to give over their male right to act as they please? Why should they cast off pride? It's for the whim of another they abstain from their basic human comforts.'

'Philosophy is it?' Ivel flipped the yarns back and in expert speed began to whip an eye splice. 'We're not much bent on refinements. Where's the profit? Best to leave such pompous rhetoric for the lazy rich and the scholars to chew over. The men here all work because the pay's good. Some are rootless. Some want better lives for their families. Arithon won't forgive a slacker. His demands can be hard, but he's fair.'

Talith gave a soft, scornful sigh. 'Is this paradise, that no one's discontent? I'm impressed. Will every living, unmanned one of you line up for his turn to lick a polish on Arithon's boots?' Her gaze fixed as a tiger's on Ivel's bent head, she took her chance and made her covert bid for subterfuge. 'I'd give every jewel I own, and all my gold braid, to escape such blissful false happiness.'

If the blind splicer was the sole spirit in the yard who dared speak to her, he had a mind inquisitive enough to ferret out any whispers of dissent. Her seed planted, her bribe offered, Talith turned on her heel. She walked on, her part now to wait and seem uninterested in case Ivel failed to take the bait. She would formulate a second strategy while she waited to see whether her effort bore fruit.

Three nights later, wakeful and agonized by circling thoughts, she heard a faint scratch at the window across from her pallet. Through the snores of the handmaid asleep in an unkempt heap that seemed all elbows and knees, Talith heard a faint whisper.

'Your Grace?'

She arose in her shift. Her unbound hair drifted like snarled floss over her bare shoulders, she crept to crack open the shutter. The unsanded floorboards creaked like the call of Dharkaron's doom under her barefoot step. She froze, taut and listening, while her maid groaned and stirred to a rustle of bed linen.

After a moment, the woman lay silent.

Talith stalked forward again, her lip caught between her front teeth. In the cool darkness, she heard nothing at all but the white splash of wavelets against the shore. The whisper of her title might have been imagined, a wishful echo of her desperate need.

She slipped the leather loop off the shutter peg anyway. A waning quarter moon drifted over the landing. The high, Vastmark cliffs sliced a line of sheared coal against summer's constellations, risen in a jewel-set tapestry as they had for three Ages to adorn the late hours of spring nights. Somewhere on the south coast, perhaps, Lysaer s'Ilessid regarded those very stars, and ached with the same loss that wore her heart.

'Lady Talith,' came a hushed whisper from the shadow below the sill.

The princess peered down, her breath sped by hope. She made out a furtive, crouched figure, then a nap of grey hair, and the raised, triangular features of Ivel the splicer, his blind eyes a glint of grey marble above the scooped hollows of his cheekbones. 'Lady, there are four men who have plans to leave the Cascains. They've decided to throw their lot with you. They've got a derelict fisherman's smack hove up in a cove behind an islet. She's being repaired in secret and made seaworthy as we speak. On the dark moon, she'll embark. The joiner who has the limp will come for you then. Have your jewels ready. If you can't keep your handmaid from making an outcry, don't fret if someone has to bind her. We all risk our lives. What Arithon would do if we're caught at your escape would drive a man witless to imagine.'

Talith still held the stinging, fresh memory of her youthful guardsman with a crossbow bolt through his neck.

Through the nerve-fired interval while the fishing smack was readied, she exerted her influence to improve on the plan. Her maid would stay behind and claim her mistress was indisposed, then pretend to look after an invalid.

'I'll cut my hair and leave it sewn around a bolster,' the princess slipped to Ivel in passing on her habitual morning walks. 'That should buy a few days without pursuit. I agree the stakes are desperate. My servant has said she'll do her part.'

Clandestine words blossomed into action more swiftly than hope had allowed. The cutting edge of competence so well enforced by the Shadow Master became strikingly effective, turned against him. The room in the shack grew confining as a cage. Talith and her maid purloined an eating knife and under cover of bland conversation, took surreptitious turns picking jewels and braid off the gowns and slippers in her clothes trunks. After that, Talith had nothing left to do but to pace and count the hours while the moon waned.

Wakeful on the night Ivel's man came to fetch her, she let him see the hoard, crammed like stashed plunder in a knotted square cut from a petticoat. The reward was deemed acceptable. She would pay out in port. That last detail agreed, she shook hands with her conspirator. Then, her head oddly light, the hacked ends of her hair feathered around her nape and ears, she wrapped up in a cloak of undistinguished colour and boarded the waiting dory. The shifty, pigtailed seaman at the oars rowed from the landing, fast, silent, his timed stroke kicking the small craft ahead in sharp spurts. For all his haste, their progress was silent. The brass rowlocks had been muffled with strips of torn silk much too fine for their usage as rags.

'The fancy shirt o' the Master's,' her conspirator supplied, his grin a bright nip of teeth against the dark. 'Fitting contribution, so Ivel says, the evil old louse.'

Talith stifled an enlivened burst of laughter. As the blackened span of shoreline with its wood stacks and trestles fell astern and slipped beyond sight, her Etarran heart thrilled to savage joy. The escape she engineered held a righteous sting of justice. Not only would Arithon's pride be put down before King Eldir and the vaunted Fellowship; the loss of her ransom would renege his promised payment to his mercenaries. Lysaer's campaign would become a bloodless triumph. This last little joke lent a crowning fillip: that for the sake of stealth, the s'Ffalenn bastard's very men had robbed his best shirt off his back.

'Fitting indeed,' she gasped back in low pleasure.

Then the fishing smack loomed ahead, her worn rails and spars ghostly grey against the bulking, jagged cliffs. As the dory slipped past her rudder, Talith saw a plate of wood with crude, chiselled lettering nailed to the side of her transom.

Her fellow conspirators had named their redoubtable little craft none else but the *Royal Freedom*.

'You're fools!' Talith cried in a pleased whisper as rough, friendly hands grasped her wrists and pulled her on board. 'It's begging discovery.'

But the four men who sealed their pact to betray the Master of Shadow emphatically refused to make a change.

'It's all fitting,' they told the princess between abashed smiles, then ushered her on into a tiny, cramped cabin infused by the gagging stink of cod. There, by the glimmer of a shielded lantern, the ringleader sat her down on a lashed cask and revealed the gist of his plan.

'The *Freedom*'s intent is to make port in Eldir's kingdom and beg sanctuary in your behalf.' The fellow wore a rough jerkin, half-unlaced at his throat. Sweat gleamed on his skin like molten copper as he traced a finger over his sea chart. 'We daren't ply the South Strait north to Redburn, though that's closest. *Khetienn*'s in the straits, and she can haul like Dharkaron's muckle Chariot, if things should come to a chase. Should wind of our passage reach Arithon, we'd see ourselves beached and flayed alive. Whole damned straits are a trap, too easily cornered and cut off.'

Talith could see as much, but patience lent her grace. She waited for the man to quit his fidgeting and finish.

'We've all thought it best to round the cape off West Shand and run due north to Los Mar,' he summed up. 'Mornos, as you see, lies too near to the border. We're too few to guard if an enemy caught our drift and snatched the chance to spirit you away.'

Talith examined the chart, her excitement too high to be daunted, though the outlined voyage was a long one.

'Won't be spit for comforts, your Grace,' the seaman finished in rough apology. 'Best we could do, given naught but a tub of an old smack. We've rigged quarters below in what used to be a fish hold. Smell won't air out. But if you can stand to wear canvas like a sailor, there's times we can let you pass on deck for a fisher's lad.'

Talith raked her fingers through the shorn ends of her hair, her eyes sparked topaz in the needle-thin spill from the lantern. She inhaled the reek of hot oil and rancid cod, and gave the man's anxious peering the most dazzling smile she possessed. 'I'm sure I shall do very well. For my husband's honour and revenge for Arithon's effrontery, in fact, I would endure a great deal worse.'

The sailhand gave her a roguish grin, gapped with missing teeth. 'That's it, then.' He winked a dark eye, leaned across the chart, and whispered into the night. 'Raise sail, lads. Our royalty's content.'

On Manners

While Lord Commander Diegan made port in Avenor to convene the high council and raise the ransom to redeem Princess Talith, on the distant shore of Shand, couriers mounted blooded horses and clattered through Southshire's land gates under a leaping flood of torchlight. Surrounded by a bristling armed escort to deter clan raiders out of Selkwood, they spurred north and west under the rippling silk of Lysaer's blazon. More often than not, the wax on the requisitions in their saddlebags had scarcely cooled from the candle. Already the highborn city officials in Alland languished in recoil from the driving, persuasive brilliance of the s'Ilessid request to quarter portions of his warhost at Atchaz and Innish. His Grace's tireless dedication through the weeks since spring equinox had ensured that no citizen in Shand remained uninformed of the Shadow Master's murderous history.

The prince, who had personally seen his cavalcade off, squared immaculately-attired shoulders and pushed open the grilled door that led from the gatehouse postern to the inner quiet of the palace gardens.

On the gravel path hedged by the fragrance of

primroses, his page met him. 'Your Grace, the galley bearing the delegation of ministers has arrived in the harbour from Innish.'

'Let the mayor's house steward find them guest quarters,' Lysaer said, not so distracted that he failed to find a smile for the boy, who was new, and as yet uncertain of his duties. 'Did their herald seem anxious?'

The child grinned and puffed his undersized chest to fill out the royal tabard. 'Your Grace, no. He said three were seasick. The rest were half-starved, the cook on the galley being unfit for his job. I told them to go ashore to the Marlin Tavern for dinner.'

'Well done.' Lysaer ruffled the boy's dark hair. 'We'll have my secretary write them a note to say I'll welcome them in the morning. Then tell the poor man he's excused. You too. I've kept you both from your beds.'

The page bowed and raced off to complete his last duty. Lysaer proceeded inside the palace, down wainscoted hallways to the Mayor of Southshire's cavernous study. There he anticipated a more difficult audience with an envoy who would wait upon nobody's pleasure.

Impatient under flittering candlelight, a note out of place amid gold-leafed panels and glossy, tessellated marble, Duke Bransian s'Brydion of Alestron paced, still jinking in rowelled spurs and a surcoat blazoned with his family arms. The cloth was fine silk, but stitched over in patches where hard campaigns had sliced rents in the weave. A man who only shed his mail at night to sleep, and then solely behind guarded walls, he faced the window as Prince Lysaer entered. The imprint of steel links bitten into the nap of the mayor's velvet padded chairs betrayed the number of times he had arisen and sat again. The waxed gloss on the floors showed scuffs from his trips to doorway and casement to peer out.

At the click of the door latch, he whirled about glowering like a bear baited onto its haunches. 'You do take your time, prince. I've been here an hour. Parrien should have been sent on this errand, except the virago he married would've knifed me had I ordered him off so soon. He can go, the hussy said, when she's bearing, which might not mesh with your war plans.'

Lysaer strode forward, smiling. 'Welcome. Parrien will miss nothing in pleasing his bride since my war plans have suffered a setback. If you won't sit, I must.' He grasped a chair for himself, by seamless reflex checking the tray on the side table to make sure his servants had been punctual with instructions concerning refreshments. Never finicky about accepting hospitality, Bransian had decimated the light meal to a wreckage of unjointed bones and scattered crumbs. The dark ale Lysaer recalled as his preference was untouched, sure enough indication tonight's meeting was earmarked for argument.

'I heard about your lady. A vicious shame.' Bransian's voice always rang too boisterous for even the largest room. His ice-flecked eyes swept a survey over Lysaer that could have counted scales on an adder. 'You don't seem shattered, I'm glad to see.'

The sheen on the prince's jewels shifted only to his unsped breath. 'I can't afford to be shattered. The man we both hunt is too dangerous, which is why I requested to speak with you, and not Parrien.' Unwilling to test the duke's impatience, he cut straightaway to the gist. 'I'm going to need help from Alestron to defend my supply lines.'

Bransian grasped a chair in his massive hands, spun it as though it were a toy, and straddled the seat, facing backward. His mailed limbs rattled over abalone inlay as he folded his forearms and leaned to an abused squeak of wood. 'Supply lines to where? Do you know yet?'

'The leads dug up by Mearn's galleymen all point to the Cascain Islands. We're near having proof. The wool traders out of Forthmark repeat rumours of unusual activity among the shepherd tribes.' Lysaer locked the duke's glance with steady, wide-lashed candour. 'Arithon's training the archers of Vastmark, at a guess. We'll have to prepare very well to wage a campaign in those mountains.'

The duke's furred eyebrows gathered over the bridge of his nose. 'That's a sharp move. Very.' The territory had no roads, no ports, no safe harbours; not even trees to break the weather or hide scouting forays and encampments. 'A defender's paradise,' Bransian allowed. 'You'll see your men get picked off like a lady's wing-clipped song sparrows.'

'We'll have the numbers to expend, if need be,' Lysaer said. His own hands, arranged in laced stillness on his knee, did not tremble a hairsbreadth. 'But if the losses become severe, our morale won't last if provisions aren't kept on schedule. I have other cities willing to shoulder the burden, but none who won't suffer the predation of Shand's clansmen. Any pack trains through those wilds will be moving bait for covert raids and ambush.'

Bransian uncoiled from his perch and circled the floor to a ringing slap of heels and chinked rowels. 'As clanblood, you think we're immune to attack?'

'As clanblood, I think you can speak the high earl's language,' Lysaer countered, more immediately concerned with the pitfalls of s'Brydion thorny temperament. 'Lord Erlien might not be overjoyed to have your troops trampling over his territory, but he'd scarcely kill your people out of hand.'

The duke reached the casement, parked his knuckles, and peered out like a caged animal. Mailed links shivered hot points of reflection as he moved again and clashed a closed fist in his palm. 'I'm Melhalla's liegeman, not Shand's.'

But Lysaer had studied his history. 'Melhalla has no surviving royal line and by legitimate birth I'm maternally descended from Shand's last crowned high king.'

Bransian laughed. 'Ath. Make that claim to Erlien's

face, you'll risk your twice-royal neck.' He swung his huge bulk from the casement, his bearded chin jutted in combative humour. 'You have steel, prince, I'll give you that. It's true. Lord Erlien's unlikely to wish a brangle between his fighting strength and mine. I'll agree to hold your supply lines with one promise from you as condition.'

He waited, predatory; poised to reject the whole matter out of hand if the prince, with his honey silk manners, misstepped or backed off a fraction.

Lysaer showed him a tolerant smile and said nothing, nor moved in impatience.

The silence stretched into brittle tension, then grew weighted. Bransian's eyes glittered. His quiet transformed to intangible, coiled menace, until the street noise beyond the casement and the cry of a late-going water hawker would have caused a lesser man to flinch.

'Dharkaron's avenging Chariot!' the duke said at length. His bristled poise departed in a strong, fluid stretch, then rebuilt as he cracked the knuckles in his sword hand. 'You haven't a live nerve in your body.'

'But I have,' Lysaer countered. 'It's been dedicated to the death of Arithon s'Ffalenn. Is Alestron with me, or against?'

'With you, of course.' Finished with popping his knuckles, the duke stamped in steel jingles to the side table, hefted the ale jug, and poured two foaming mugs. One he tossed off. The other he left filled and unclaimed, to test if the prince would rise to fetch it, or expect a liegeman's service.

Lysaer did neither one.

Deadlocked at his own strategy, Lord Bransian licked the foam from his moustache and gave way with cheerful grace. 'I'll hold your supply lines on express condition that my mercenary troops and half of my garrison shall battle at the forefront in Vastmark. Alestron's officers must share voice in your war councils. We're sworn to

Melhalla's royal charter, which means we don't serve. Never under another realm's prince. And my captains don't like nursemaiding pack trains. They'll have to be given some incentive to sharpen their troops back to form in a snapping, rough bloody fight.'

Amusement curved Lysaer's lips. 'You're not worried they'll be gutted like a lady's wing-clipped songbirds?'

'Sithaer, no.' All expansive good nature, now, Bransian refilled his mug, then passed the other as a courtesy to the prince. 'Any man of mine who gets his arse bested by some wool-spinning shepherd is no one I want to bring back. Drink to the Shadow Master's death,' he invited. His broad-handed toast encompassed the casement and implied vague direction to the north. 'I have to be gone on the morrow. The quarrymen in Elssine are cutting the blocks for a new drum tower. Keldmar's favoured stonemason's convinced if nobody checks the load, the granite they ship will be cut the wrong way for the grain.'

Since s'Brydion tradition held that toasts became a contest to see who wound up drunk beneath the table, Lysaer kept late hours in the mayor's study. When at last he wrangled his way free, Duke Bransian stood propped in the window, rollicking through tavern ballads at the top of his lungs, and setting the kennelled pack of tracking hounds to howling.

Several dozen casements had banged open, with citizens shouting protest over their disrupted sleep. Bransian ignored them. Large as he was, and cantankerous as a mercenary, the mayor's house steward crept outside the door, too petrified to intercede.

Lysaer gave the harried man a sympathetic shrug, then made his quiet way to his chambers.

There, in words that carefully masked his relief, he excused his last, hovering servants. Behind locked doors, alone, he threw off his restraint. He paced, hollow-eyed, across and across the rich carpets. No one, not even his personal valet, was permitted to glimpse the unquiet strain upon him since the day his lady fell captive. When he tired, but could not sleep, he sat long, aching hours, lacing together fraught nerves.

This night, like many another before, bled slowly away to cold light. A renewed spill of silver woven through by the stainless, sweet notes of birdsong heralded yet another dawn. Lysaer knitted back his façade of self-control and prayed that his stamina would last through the hours until he could retire again in solitude.

The fear never left him, that his hold on self-mastery might crumble. A chance word, a careless expression, a wrongly pitched word or inflection might reveal the buried depths of his anguish. The prospect was unthinkable, that anyone beyond Diegan should discover the true depths of his love for Talith.

Her captor was s'Ffalenn, and calculating as a fiend. Let Arithon have wind of what power he held to hand; let any clan enemy or nervous mayor discover how his feelings for his wife could bleed him to agony, and the risk was too real that such means could be used to pull him down.

His brave words to his Lord Commander were no better than a sham, his bravado before Bransian a player's mask. Lysaer understood the stakes in his vulnerable hour of risk. Prince as he was, he was also human. The threads of his sovereign responsibility could be weakened. He guarded, in desperation, that the people who relied upon his unassailable integrity should never guess how fast he might be broken; how for one woman's life and safety, he might be worn down to sell them out.

In the icy light of daybreak, Lysaer watched the tuck and dart of nesting martins. The art of fine statecraft was a cold man's game. Bitterly he understood this. Knowledge made fact no easier to bear, that through the month until the ransom on the solstice, he must bide, and stifle his passion to take punitive action. He had learned his lesson well through the attack at Minderl Bay: thoughtless response to provocation was his signal weakness. The Shadow Master knew too well how to pressure him beyond endurance, then strike to exploit the results.

Left an untouched bed and a brace of chairs indented with crumpled cushions, the Prince of the West stood at last and summoned his chamber valet to freshen his appearance for his audience.

He had no choice. Royal to the bone, he took what small solace his ruler's conscience would allow.

The misfortunes inflicted by the s'Ffalenn pirates throughout his childhood had taught him not to wallow in his losses. Unlike his father, who had vented his frustration in unconstrained rages, Lysaer sought his ease in the measured, reasoned calm of sound statesmanship. As a forced play of strategy, Talith's abduction must be turned to something more than a blow to his heart and pride. Handled with boldness, he might seize a backhanded advantage and turn the affair into the linch pin of his plan to win back crown rule in Tysan. One bitter spark of gain could be salvaged out of disaster.

Given the summer, through inspired diplomacy, he might bind a whole kingdom to allegiance.

On Mayhem

As the *Royal Freedom* and her fugitive passenger beat a laborious course upcoast, and Lysaer s'Ilessid's envoys raised gold for ransom, and armies for warfare in Shand, the Mad Prophet sat like a raisin swathed in burlap, his chin on his knees, on a sun-heated rock in Vastmark. For weeks, nothing had changed. Clear-minded as the sky that arched in cobalt glory above the serried summits, he bent his rapt and ruthless analysis upon Arithon s'Ffalenn, while under Caolle's experienced handling, shepherd archers were transformed into recruits. Since the men were natural marksmen, the clan war captain's efforts centred on teaching them discipline. From him, individuals learned the sly arts of concealment and the teamwork required for surprise action.

Dakar weighed all he saw; and like a hand misdealt to a cardsharp, his conclusions were never straightforward as circumstance made them appear.

Blunt as old nails, too tough to outface, Caolle earned quick respect through brute intimidation. His stentorian shout re-echoed up the slope as some green shepherd raised his head. 'Fiends plague, boy! Try that in battle,

and an arrow through an eye will be your last sight on
Ath's earth!'

The guilty party ducked a hairsbreadth too late.
Caolle's thrown sliver of shale sliced a punitive arc, then
struck to a howled string of curses.

Slit-eyed, brooding, Dakar gnawed at the calluses
acquired through the tedium of twisting bowstrings. The
clan war captain's rough nature held no mystery. His
competence lay beyond question, his years of brutal
experience an achievement few could stand down.
Caolle judged his applicants and chose which to train,
and which to send back to the sheep flocks. Women or
men matched the mettle he demanded, or he refused
them a place in the ranks.

Sharp skill with a bow was not the sole quality he
required of his trainees.

Arithon s'Ffalenn, with his masterbard's empathy,
need not haze tribesfolk to measure them. By turns acerbic and piercingly perceptive, he won their obedience
through fast wits and invective that could peel away
dignity like a scalpel. He shared his knowledge of field
healing, or assisted Caolle with lessons in close-quarters
fighting with sword and knife.

Like the cat crouched to size up its victim, Dakar
weighed words and actions, prepared to pounce on dis-
crepancy. The freedom he longed for required hard evidence. Asandir and the Fellowship must be shown the
unseen pitfall, if in fact the princely compassion displayed through a child's failed healing masked some
deeper subterfuge, a diversion to shield a manipulative
mind bound to a course of mass destruction.

If Arithon was by nature the criminal Prince Lysaer
had pledged to eradicate, Dakar would lay bare the truth.

Another dusty, wind-raked morning passed, while
shepherds practised the arts of stealth and ambush.
Dakar watched arrows raze into grass targets to Caolle's
peppery remonstrance. In the afternoon he trailed

Arithon's passage through yet another survey of Vastmark's deep glens and corries. By the dim, orange light cast by tallow dips, he saw the day's observations inked onto a growing sheaf of maps. Notations showed which valleys could shelter flocks and families as hidden refuge, and which narrow passes might serve to run covert relays of messages. Curled in an unnoticed heap on musty fleeces, Dakar feigned sleep, while the talk rose and fell and grew heated through unending revisions in strategy. The odd phrase would yield him the buried, racked strain that harried Arithon's composure.

Gone now, the ebullience which had won him the tribes' easy friendship; the lingering play with herdsmen and sheep stood replaced by unswerving competence. Steady as fine steel in drills with the archers, Arithon did his brooding in solitude. Dakar would see him walk the ridges in the silver fall of twilight, wrapped in deep quiet that masked thoughts. One attempt to follow was repulsed, first by words, then, when spoken daggers proved insufficient for the task, by the incontestable, bared length of a sword.

On the steep, dusty spurs that serried like knives above the meadows of Dier Kenton Vale, Arithon paced out the night alone, while the stars wheeled their high arcs across black Vastmark sky, and the sheep flocks pebbled the valley in fitful currents of movement. In the grey, dew-drenched dawn, Dakar retraced the same route. His dogged search discerned no trace signature of spellcraft. The layered, faulted beds of Vastmark shale remained as they ought, laced over in tough grasses and the tall, wind-combed stems of summer asters.

Unwilling to bow before gnawing frustration, Dakar twisted gut bowstrings until his fingers gained another set of blisters. Against his grain as a hedonist, he made no complaint of plain rations. He bided the hours as the adder waits, tight laced into stillness, while other nights in close company Arithon laid his case before the tribal elders gathered in yet another circle for counsel. The plans he laid out for the gold he would gain from Talith's ransom included scholars and books. Children would have learning, and their parents, new stock to breed sure-footed ponies. If the herdsmen could cover more territory, they could tend a much larger flock.

'We'll have a post courier,' Arithon proposed, 'then a trade wharf downcoast from Ithish. No more city factors and brokers to skim off their cut from your wool yield.'

At times acting as Arithon's secretary, his lines scratched out with a nib of the whippy, thin bone split from a wyvern's wing leather, Dakar could not help but admire the method. War would come to Vastmark and claim the lives of young men, but their tribes would be compensated, the grinding poverty of nomadic existence eased over by permanent change and improvement.

The bad years might cease to be remarked for their tragedies, the future set free from killing hardship. Babes would no longer grow stunted from malnourishment, nor lambs die from salt shortage, nor injuries mend badly for lack of sound treatment and healers. Dakar penned notations and pledges of agreement, unable to decide if the move stemmed from clemency or genius.

'Your lowland pastures could support blooded horses,' Arithon suggested. Thrown into relief by the crawling flames of tallow dips scattered on the rugs in clay bowls, his shoulders mantled in coarse saffron wool, he qualified in detail. 'The drifters in Tysan breed the best stock. I've already sent letters of inquiry. Choice studs can be imported, and the knowledge of husbandry brought in.' He scarcely need add that an ongoing climate of war must increase the demand for fine destriers.

The meeting broke up under starlight. When confronted by a snow-haired elder with sharp reservations, Arithon gave way to a moment of naked uncertainty. 'Your fears are all justified, grandmother. For the gains I have promised, the campaign must be won. No valley in Vastmark will be free from armed threat until Lysaer's warhost is vanquished.'

'Our tribes could be scattered,' the beldame said, her reproof rasped through the scrapes of night insects, and her gaze upon Arithon as keen as Dharkaron's last judgment.

Rathain's prince gave her truth, unflinching as rock, and strive as Dakar might, no flaw in the grain could be found in his masterbard's sincerity.

'We could lose.' Arithon clasped the woman's withered fingers, his entreaty mingled with humility. 'If that comes to pass, I can promise I'll be dead. Not only your tribes in Vastmark will suffer. The peril behind this curse is the Mistwraith's latent threat, which I'm bound by blood oath to answer. I must make my stand somewhere. The mountains here are too formidable for outright conquest. Of all peoples, yours are most needful of change, and through hardihood, the likeliest to survive.'

An interval passed, filled by the distant whistle of a wyvern pair. Then the grandmother worked free of his grasp. She arranged her layered shawls to close out the prying wind, but did not speak.

'Support me, or not,' Arithon finished before a censure that held him in contempt. 'I won't force you. If this warhost can be broken, the best I can hope is to win back a year's respite to seek the haven I'd hoped to find offshore.'

He gave no false assurance, Dakar took sour note, that the conflict would end here in Vastmark.

Eight weeks before summer solstice, Arithon consulted with Caolle to measure the state of their progress. Never empty-handed, the war captain hunched by an outdoor fire, burnishing rust from his byrnie. 'These are good people. They'll be ready to fight when you need them.'

The veteran campaigner was wont to hoard dissatisfaction as a weapon to ambush complacence; too clever to be victimized, Arithon waited.

'You'll need experienced men to bolster the ranks.' The mail chimed a querulous, jingled refrain as Caolle turned its bulk in broad hands. 'These troops are untried and wars are damned messy business. Shooting down wyverns is all well enough. Quite another matter when your target's a man who screams in bloody pain and pleads mercy.'

'You want to bring in clansmen,' Arithon surmised, his reluctance like flint struck to steel.

Caolle flicked out his polishing rag, methodical, then dipped up a clean dollop of river sand. 'Well, without them, I won't bet my second-best bootlace we can hold off the least of Skannt's headhunters. He's not Pesquil's equal for cunning, but the pair ran cheek by jowl for sheer, bone-headed persistence.'

'I'll hire in mercenaries, first,' Arithon said.

Caolle laughed. 'Erlien's clans will take issue with that, liege.'

To which Arithon had no choice but bend to plain truth; the Vastmark territory was a principality under Shandian sovereignty. If the *caithdein* of the realm elected to nose into his affairs, no scion of Rathain could deny the High Earl his given right.

Through the rasp of wet grit against worn links of metal, the familiar stillness stretched between Rathain's grizzled war captain and his liege lord, stiff with cutthroat pride and dissent. 'Caolle,' Arithon broke in at firm length, 'you'll send no appeal to Lord Erlien.'

'Don't need to,' came the bitten retort. 'The *caithdein*'s own scouts are scarcely blind. They've seen what I have. Lysaer's been recruiting in Shand. Headhunters' leagues from Forthmark and Ganish have added themselves to his ranks.'

The quality to Arithon's silence changed character, a subtlety Caolle at long last had learned not to miss.

'Liege,' he said in odd gentleness, 'this won't be the same sort of fight as Tal Quorin. This time, you're going to win.'

'To what use?' Arithon burst out in bitterness, and stopped. Too much thought would engender despair. For no matter what happened at Vastmark, regardless whose men were left standing, unless he or Lysaer fell as a casualty, the Mistwraith's curse would remain.

The Master of Shadow departed for the low country the next morning, Dakar puffing at his heels like a fat brown badger, a wilful bent to his stride. Under sunlight that blinded, while the gliding dart of wyverns flickered dappled shade over the rock-snagged folds of the fells, the pair left behind the raw design to break a warhost.

Ahead, in the roisterous care of a delegation of clan scouts, the fruits of the past year's livestock raids milled like a muddied river beneath the flanks of the crags. Driven in bunches from Orvandir and Alland, the four-legged booty reflected its forced trek across the steppe-lands of Shand. Angular hipbones and the sprung curves of ribs pressed through staring, bleached hides. Clouds of ochre dust churned up by sharp hooves silted unkempt coats in bleak monochrome.

Sun-browned, clear-eyed, as seethingly disgruntled as their charges, the force of young scouts from Selkwood had spent their spring in thirsty watches, turning wild-eyed stampedes, and swearing fell oaths over foaling mares and balked cattle. They had survived the full gamut of scrapes and escapes from harem-conscious bulls. Bound to their task by clan loyalty to a chieftain two hundred leagues distant, their continued adherence to the herder's role was fever pitched to last until that celebrated but unfamiliar stranger, the Prince of Rathain, should arrive to relieve them of duty.

As well for Arithon s'Ffalenn that he made his rendezvous three days early. A cry from the mounted sentries posted at the rims of the valley drew the riders from the herds at a gallop. In a flurry of noise and commotion, they drew rein and ringed the arrivals. Dakar had the instinctive good sense to step clear as the young clansmen eyed the prince like quarry closed on by wolves.

On foot, clad in a wide sash, knee breeches and a shepherd's shirt with tailored cuffs that Dalwyn had woven from wild flax, Arithon lent a disarming appearance of frailty. Beneath wind-flicked tangles of dark hair, his expression reflected the careless ennui of high breeding, the features, sharp-faceted marble. Disadvantaged by the glare, his gaze on the circle of herdsmen looked half-lidded and lazy.

Wide-eyed, peeling, and raffishly unshaven beside his immaculate detachment, the riders gave him their voracious study in return.

'Daelion's Wheel,' swore one in soft reverence. Black-eyed and lounging, muscled as an alley cat, astride a hammer-headed dun, he gave a low whistle. 'I've a small brother could span that pretty wrist with naught but one finger and a thumb.'

Alight with pure mischief, Arithon inclined his head. The glance he awarded rider and horse was brief to the point of insult. From his vantage on the sidelines, the Mad Prophet winced, his teeth set unpleasantly on edge.

'Your brother's not present?' Arithon asked, his politeness dipped to acid clarity.

The man who had challenged gave back a slow grin. 'He's not.'

'Well then,' invited Arithon, 'since you're no small fellow, why not show me in his stead?' He extended his forearm.

The clansman bent with a whoop of delight. Knuckles grey rimed with horse reached to snatch the limb in its immaculate, fitted ivory sleeve.

The moment of contact dissolved in a blur of fast

movement and a wrench. Square, dirty fingers convulsed upon air. While Arithon stepped clear with apologetic grace, his victim yelped in surprise and toppled headlong from his saddle.

Arithon loosed his hold. The scout struck earth still extended, randy oaths bitten off to a grunt. There he coughed up dust and struggled to rise, until a kick buckled his arm at the elbow. Dropped prone in the dirt, this time he stayed down. The prince who had felled him set foot between his shoulder blades and vaulted into his vacated saddle.

The sidling dun flung its nose once and settled to its new master. Then green eyes raked over the waiting ring of scouts in that scathing, distasteful directness which men learned fast not to question. 'I want the beef herds and the horses culled and sorted by sunset,' said Arithon s'Ffalenn.

His following strings of instructions reordered milling chaos to an oiled, brisk efficiency Dakar found detestably familiar. Companionable in sympathy, he crossed to the felled rider and helped him back to his feet.

Hawking up grit between curses, the man blotted a scraped chin. 'Fiends plague!' He grimaced in wry admiration. 'How was I to know I was set to shake hands with a snake?' He worked his jaw, discovered his lip split, and spat out the metallic taste of blood. 'Dharkaron's pity on me if that one treasures his grudges.'

'He doesn't,' Dakar volunteered.

The clansman stared, pity in his dark eyes. 'The claim of hard experience? Poor man! What binds you to his service?'

But the root of that question had grown tangled and deep beyond the pull of a sorcerer's geas. Caught without ready answer, Dakar retreated into silence.

* * *

277

By eventide, the horses grazed in three divisions, and the cattle in two, the herds held separate by hills and minded by those few unfortunates Arithon had caught slacking. The other clansmen gathered around Dakar's campfire, laughing, bone weary, and noisy with exuberant pride. They had all laboured like animals. The prince who had driven them sat in their midst, his elegant linen silted with dust and his voice burred hoarse from shouting. If he had broken their rebellion through merciless work, he had spared himself least of all.

Exhausted as they were, the clansmen were reluctant to retire. They sat picking shreds of hare stew from their teeth, and swapped stories of four-legged mishaps. More than one jaundiced glance was rolled toward the cooking pot, filled now with a bubbling concoction of urine, bark, and dried berries. Squat as a hedgehog in his frayed layers of tunics, the Mad Prophet stirred the ill-smelling brew intended for use as a dye.

'We'll need to mark the culls,' Arithon was saying. 'My archers need field rations to carry them through the winter, and your high earl's share of the spoils won't improve if the breeding stock's butchered for jerky.'

Across the fire, someone called a derisive comment. A log fell. The coals fanned up flame in a flying leap of sparks that lit the s'Ffalenn profile bloody red.

The sight caused Dakar to stiffen. A horrible prickle doused through his flesh, chased by a chill like needled ice. Stark sober, no kindly veil of alcohol to blur his awareness, he had no means at hand to evade the onset of his spurious talent for prescience.

A shudder rolled through him. Before he could make outcry, the next wave bent him double in a gasping fit of racked air.

The stick he used to stir up the dyepot toppled from his slack fingers. He felt his knees buckle. The vague impression grazed him, of someone's grasp on his forearm and a yank that spun him clear of the embers.

Then his senses overturned into vision.

He saw no fire, no clan scouts, no stewpot. His flesh stung and his ears roared. He beheld the sweep of a wintry hillside razed brown by bitter frost; and felled in dead bracken, that same royal profile, racked by the agony of a death wound. *The place was Vastmark. The season wept a dismal cold rain on the scene, and the water splashed lichened ground, stained from the blood that welled between Arithon's fingers. Around his prostrate, shuddering form, a fast-fading tracery of phosphor.*

Dakar's captive senses strained after the phantom glimmer of what might have been a dissolving chain of spell seals.

Then the place where Arithon lay dying folded and spun into itself. Darkness followed, ripped through by another strand of augury: *he received a whirled glimpse of Morriel Prime, matriarch of the Koriani Order, hunched like a web-making spider above the amethyst gleam of the Great Waystone.*

Then fey sight burst asunder, torn into sparks and white-hot, glass-edged pain. Dakar returned to himself with a choked-off cry. He lay on his side, hammered helpless by cramps and a nausea that ripped him like tissue. Somebody's hands supported him; *the same fine fingers that had worried at a bloodied arrow a scant second before in prophetic vision.*

'Ath forfend!' Dakar ground out. He coughed back bile and squeezed his eyes shut.

'Steady,' Arithon said above him. Another touch smoothed back the ruck of hair sucked against his locked teeth by his gasping. 'Steady. You're back with us now.'

Dakar mewled through another wave of sickness. Helpless as a baby, mauled by the aftermath of a talent he detested, he struggled for command of his dignity, and lost. 'Morriel Prime's no friend of yours,' he managed by way of crude warning, though in truth, the paired auguries might not be connected.

A soft burst of laughter came back. 'Well, that's no surprise. Can you sit? I've brought herbs. A tisane might settle your stomach.'

Undone by wretchedness, Dakar allowed himself to be shepherded back upright and propped with his shoulders against a rock. Someone's blanket flicked over his shivering limbs. Above him, limned in the fire's glow, he saw Arithon's face trained upon him in a sympathy that confounded all hatred.

That sight made Dakar weep curses. Pity he had no use for; all his life, his wretched fits had felled him as they chose, ever to the ruin of his happiness. At seven years of age, when he had foretold the fever that would come to kill his mother, his family had rejected him from fear. Maturity had brought him no succour. He had no way to avert the vision's burning grip, but could only flee into dissolute habits that blunted the impact and the pain.

At least while drunk to incapacity, he could escape the vice of moral dilemma that prescience ceded to his conscience.

Dakar flinched again for the future that awaited on that lonely, Vastmark hillside, where fate would resolve into happenstance.

Arithon dead, with no mind beyond his in all Athera to glean warning of the time and the place. The posited event framed a precedence. Somewhere, an enemy existed, who would spell-turn an arrow with the power to negate the longevity binding engendered by Davien's Five Centuries Fountain.

The Mad Prophet clamped his arms to his chest to still the waves of his shuddering. Not even Althain's Warden would expect the threat unearthed in the surge of tonight's surprise augury. Through fear and discomfort, a wicked thought bloomed: Dakar could have smiled through his sickness. For once in his born life, his wretched gift of prophecy had lent him an advantage he could act on. The power he had longed for, the means to escape an unwanted service, had been dropped at his very feet.

The life of the s'Ffalenn prince he was spell-charged to partner lay in his hands, to cast off or spare as he chose.

At a stroke, Desh-thiere's curse could be sundered. Another royal friend could be redeemed, his spirit won back from the meddling inflicted in the course of the Mistwraith's confinement. The tragedy of that hour could be reversed, when the Fellowship had chosen Lysaer s'Ilessid for the sacrifice to buy the fell creatures' captivity.

Across the fire, surrounded by the jostling clansmen won through quick wit and competence, Arithon rummaged through his satchel for the remedies suited to ease stomach cramps. Dakar watched through slitted eyes. One way or another, he would know Rathain's prince for what he was: compassionate bard, or the guileful master of subterfuge. Upon Dakar's sole judgment lay the power to forewarn, when winter sleeted rains on the sere hills of Vastmark and the Shadow Master faced his last reckoning.

Deep in the night, the Mad Prophet lay wakeful, wrung limp and ill from the aftermath of his seer's trance. Arithon had not slept, but sat wrapped in a blanket against the hazed coals in the firepit. At each turn of the breeze, the embers flared. Hot light fanned over his die-cut features, and the fine, musician's fingers laced in repose at his knee. The green eyes were stilled in fathomless thought, until Dakar stirred and ventured the question he had never before dared to ask.

'Why not take *Khetienn* and slip off to sea as you'd planned? Why this furore with ransoms and abductions? Why bother to close with this war host of Lysaer's at all?'

Arithon turned his head. He regarded his impertinent inquisitor, tucked into muddled bedding like a caterpillar lapped in a leaf. Then he sighed. His knuckles tightened against themselves, no longer content or relaxed. 'Your question has no straight answer.' A plangency to his tone suggested underlying anguish, as if the point circled to haunt him. 'There's a warhost, I could say, descended upon Shand and determined to wreak havoc to undo me. They'll march for their prince. They'll plunder bread from the villages and tumble farm girls whether I'm present or no. Could I sail on the tide and abandon hapless people to suffer their supply, and finally, the bloody price of their frustration?'

'So,' pressed Dakar, remorseless. 'You would lure those misguided thousands into Vastmark and ruin more lives for the cause of disbanding Lysaer's alliance?'

'Shand's villagers never asked to take part in this feud.' Arithon moved, reached, hooked a moss-grained stick of brush, and broke it in sharp, short cracks between his fists. He pitched the bits in fierce bursts at the firepit, and flames leaped up, greedy, to consume them. 'If you're wanting to weigh how much Desh-thiere's curse affects my decisions, I admit, to my sorrow, I don't know. I had friends at Innish and in Merior. Each one came to suffer for my acquaintance. Wherever I go, pain and trouble will follow. I can wear out my conscience trying to sort what's best until I've lost the will to keep living.'

Dakar waited, unrelenting; and the anger he expected bloomed finally and spurred the s'Ffalenn prince to his feet. 'Why not keep things simple,' Arithon said in that cutting malice that could jab, and distance, and raise hackles. 'Let's say when *Khetienn* sails, I'd rather know for certain just what sort of weapon I'll be leaving unsheathed at my back!'

The Mad Prophet closed his eyes, euphoric enough to feign sleep. After years of being bullied and made wretched through his shortfalls, he had gained his sweet

opening for revenge. His enemy's planned future lay proscribed by fate. Whether the brigantine built at Merior
ever crossed uncharted waters to buy a reprieve from
Desh-thiere's curse, she would never depart now, except
through Dakar's personal leave.

The next morning, the sheared edge to Arithon's temper
rousted comatose scouts from their blankets. The task
of marking out the herd's culls was framed as a contest,
the winning team to gain the task of delivering the prime
breeding stock to specified tribesmen in the Kelhorns.

'The losers will stay on as herdsmen until a task force
arrives to relieve them,' Arithon finished.

Eager for rough action after uneventful weeks away
from clan sweethearts and family, the scouts scrambled
to catch and bridle their mounts. They called jibes and
brandished sticks tipped in rags, and laced sticky jacks
of dye to their saddle packs. Insults flew freely as they
divided into teams, then swooped screaming through the
morning to roust their unsuspecting hoofed charges.

Amid bawling cattle and choking dust, and more than
one adversary unhorsed out of spite, many an animal
received more than its allotted blaze on the rump. Several riders returned splash marked. While the ecstatic
victors were engrossed in collecting wagers, and the
losers paid up, grumbling, Dakar and the Master of
Shadow saddled themselves fresh mounts. They
departed over the hills toward the coast with forty choice
mares from Alland and one stallion hazed before them
in a bunch.

The pair vanished before anyone mustered the presence to protest.

'Damn him to Sithaer!' cried an outraged scout, a
shocking, purple cheek turned toward his dumbfounded
companions. 'We've all been most foully enchanted!
Two days past, not even Dharkaron's fell vengeance

could have kept me here, and now look! We're stuck
nursemaiding cows through another blighted month for
a prince who holds none of our allegiance!'

Passages

Under dank evening fog in the straits of the Cascains, Arithon's trusted seaman awakens aboard *Talliarthe* to a gagging weight of blankets and the bruising clamp of fingers which pin him helpless. 'Go on, tie him,' whispers Tharrick to the widow, then adds rough apology to the victim: 'I'm sorry, man. You'll have the sloop to sail back. It's not fair to Feylind, but Mistress Jinesse wants her children beyond reach of Arithon's design . . .'

In another remote cove far north of Perdith, under cover of blown clouds, the brig *Black Drake* rides at anchor to take on fresh water; and the man on watch screams warning, too late, as against unlit shores, five armed galleys from Alestron sweep down, to close in and entrap her bold captain as the known cohort of Arithon s'Ffalenn . . .

One month prior to summer solstice, under fair winds and clear skies, a fleet of galleys flying the s'Ilessid royal star sails for King Eldir's court at Ostermere, and under bristling armed guard, locked chests belowdecks contain the named sum of five hundred thousand coin weight, fine gold, raised by Tysan's merchants to deliver Princess Talith from the hands of the Master of Shadow . . .

VI. OSTERMERE

Twenty-five days before the hour appointed for Talith's ransom, the fishing smack *Royal Freedom* tacked a harried course through the merchant vessels moored in the harbour of Los Mar. Her passage up the shores of the westlands had been rough, battered through the last weeks by squall lines. In salt-crusted stays and sprung caulking, in peeled paint and tattered sails, she showed the rough wear the angry sea could mete out as she reached the end of her voyage.

Mewed up in a hold still redolent of mackerel, and tired of salt meat and green cheese, Lady Talith knelt on damp blankets and combed her fingers through the dirty, cropped ends of her hair. By nightfall, she would be free. She could find a room at an inn, and ask for hot food and soak out her itches in a bath. To be clean again, to walk on plank floors that did not heave at each step; anticipation made her want to sing aloud. Laced through the taint of tar off the ships' rigging, fugitive gusts through the hatch wafted tantalizing scents of baking bread. She picked out heavy incense, and the ripe, earthy smell of dry land. Through the slosh of rank water in the bilges, she drank in the sounds of a harbourside beyond view. The indignant slang of fishermen vying for right of way wove through the wind-snatched cries of hawkers, each with his baskets of salt crabs, or trinkets, or ripe cherries, ferried between ships in oared lighters.

Los Mar was a worldly port built at the junction of a land route. Although the settlement had been but a fishing village at the time of the high king's downfall, when the royal port of Telmandir downcoast had been overset into ruin, the caravan trade brought in wealth. The city had libraries and scholars, and learned men from across the continent knew the beauty of its illuminated manuscripts.

A woman alone should have no trouble hiring horses and an escort, and finding suitable lodging at an inn.

The *Freedom*'s patched canvas at last rattled slack. When the splash of her anchor dragged the rode smoking through the hawse, Talith savoured her triumph. She had bested the Master of Shadow. By her own design she would see herself restored to her husband's side at Ostermere.

A thump sounded topside. The hatch cracked and the burly seaman who captained the *Freedom* slithered down the ladder into the closed space of the hold. 'Princess,' he greeted, and gave a small bow, 'we're secure in the harbour of Los Mar.'

'Well done.' Talith dug under her blankets and drew out her cache of jewels. 'With my thanks, take the payment I promised.'

The sailhand cupped the silk pouch in a calloused hand, picked open the drawstring, and peered inside. He gave an admiring whistle. 'My lady,' he said, 'the price is by far too generous.'

Before she could protest, he upended the hoard. Rubies, sapphires, citrines and pearls spilled in a tumbling swathe across the rude ticking of her berth. The uneven flare of the tallow lamp nicked sparks out of dimness, each stone a fleck of coloured fire as the seaman stirred through the collection. 'You'll need to hire yourself a retinue,' he chided. 'You can scarcely travel, either, clad in the pitiful rags of one gown.'

At Talith's exasperated silence, he gave a sly chuckle. 'Your Grace, for plain truth, we were leaving the Cascains anyway to try our fortunes elsewhere. Your plans fell in through sheer luck. We'll take due reward for the service, but not all the jewels you own.'

The snarls of gold braid, the thread ends which napped the strands of pearls that had once roped the sleeves and waistlines of her state gowns vanished back into the sack; the finer pieces set as jewellery in gold bezels; the rings, the pins, the gold wire bracelets and shimmering necklaces remained in a twinkling array on the blanket.

'Keep your baubles,' said the deckhand. 'For the leavings off your dresses, we're content.'

Touched by the unexpected sense of honour shown by the seafaring rogue, Talith scarcely minded that his hurried, last instructions involved patience and more waiting aboard the *Royal Freedom*.

'An associate of ours will come under cover of darkness, your Grace. He'll bring decent attire and see you safely on your way.'

So began the slow crawl of the hours. Shut in confinement until sundown, Talith fretted in the dimness. She endured the slosh of the bilge, stirred to noisome vapours by the swing of the *Freedom* on her cable. Too excited to rest, she counted the chime of the watch bells on the galleys. The dip burned low and smoked in puddled tallow until the weak, streamered flame flickered out. The needle of sunlight shot through a checked board in the hatch faded from gold to magenta, then faded with the glow of twilight.

Night fell over the harbour at Los Mar to the tireless refrain of wavelets slapping wood and the distant grind of drays. Nearer at hand came an off-key warble of lewd song, or the shouts of hired lightermen as sailors departed for shore leave.

The list of *Freedom*'s hull as a boarder caught her rail was scarcely more than the rocking tug stirred by the change in the tide. Talith started up from her berth, head tilted to listen. Soft footfalls crossed the deck: too regular for the burly joiner who had captained, and too assured for a common seahand. The next instant the hatch opened with all the deft speed of someone familiar with its fastenings.

The princess glimpsed a male figure in dark clothing pass in silhouette against the sky. Despite the encumbrance of a package beneath one arm, he slipped into the hold with a grace that stunned for its dreadful, uncanny familiarity.

Talith's foreboding exploded to viperish anger. 'You!'

'There's a greeting that could never be mistaken for a fish.' The intruder paused, his negligent fingers left braced on a rung as he sketched her a courtier's bow. 'Welcome to Los Mar, princess.'

Riled pink in humiliation, Talith snapped, 'You presume rather much, your Grace of Rathain! Tell me, what would you have done if I'd lacked the courage to escape?'

'Courage? Escape?' Arithon paused through a soundless breath of surprise. 'But the format was your own device. My men had simple orders. They were to bring you and your private stock of jewels here to Havish by my appointed date. Since they were bound to leave my service for reasons of their own, I asked them to take you willingly. Am I to blame if your enterprising nature made their crossing a joy to carry out? It's nobody's dark secret that Ivel's entertainment is snide observation and deceit.'

Masked in darkness though he was, his stifled ring of humour was unmistakable. 'Keep your driving obsessions as you like, lovely lady. But if you stay angry and hard bent on hatred, you'd best be prepared to become somebody else's ready tool.'

'Yours, do you think?' Stiffened back to coolness, Talith retorted, 'Your usage of people is ungenerous, if not unforgivably base.'

'I exploited what faults you presented to hand,' Arithon corrected, unruffled. He tossed his burden on the blankets, then moved on by touch and spiked a fresh candle on the dribbled bracket of the sconce. The new flame he kindled lined his lingering, wry malice as he added, 'I know of no ties that bind you to mistrust. Don't confuse me with your husband, my dear. I've never loved a weakness that can be nurtured into dependency.'

Stung deep by that unpleasant truth, Talith endured the stilted interval as her tormentor bent to her rumpled berth, retrieved his parcel, then slipped the knots of its wrapping.

Inside, folded neat from the tailor's, lay a dress of magnificent tawny silk, roped in sapphires and pearls. To the last gem and setting, the ornaments were the same ones she had paid to the seamen as reward for her passage. Arithon plucked up a fold of saffron fabric and let it slide in a sensuous ripple from his fingers. 'You'll receive the rest of your bullion and gems along with a wardrobe to replace the one you mangled. I will *not* be accused of petty thievery,' he finished. 'It's demeaning. Your ransom will cover the seamstress's fees, and leave plenty left for my mercenaries.'

Outflanked for the first time in her life, Talith had no words to strike back for this latest ingenious indignity. 'Am I allowed to bathe before I change?'

'But of course,' said Arithon s'Ffalenn, and gave her his arm without comment for the miserable, shorn state of her hair. Talith could do little else but bear up and allow his escort from her squalid accommodations aboard the *Royal Freedom*.

In quiet ceremony and impeccable style, she was

installed in quarters befitting her station back on the *Khetienn*. The brigantine lay anchored under s'Ffalenn royal colours to the restive, drumming thuds of the bloodstock loaded on at Vastmark.

On the flood of the next tide, she re-embarked to complete the last leg of her passage to Ostermere. Invited on deck, the princess watched the gabled slate roofs of Los Mar vanish into the haze of grey dawn. Given her first clear view of the harbour, an anomaly snagged her attention: the dilapidated fishing smack, *Royal Freedom*, had departed during the night.

A disagreeable chill ruffled her skin where she stood, hands clenched to the dampened rail. Her plight was sealed. There could be no further opportunity to exploit, not on an offshore passage. When next the *Khetienn* made port, her captivity would fall under the capable arbitration of the Fellowship of Seven. Upon neutral ground and in stylish hospitality, she and her abductor would become the guests of the High King of Havish.

Seven days before the summer solstice, under limestone cliffs snagged in fog, Arithon docked his brigantine at the central wharf in Ostermere. The rampant leopard pendant of the s'Ffalenn royal line slapped in plastered folds at her masthead, weighed down by smoking veils of drizzle. The crew of the *Khetienn* were no less handy in the wet. Brisk teamwork saw the heavy, tanbark canvas stripped from the yards and the lines dressed shipshape on deck. The gangway thudded into place, dripping silvered rungs from rope railings.

Present at the quayside, bunched under cerecloth awnings sagged awry by the damp, King Eldir's delegation waited to acknowledge the arrival. The young king had his pride. He maintained propriety despite unfavourable conditions. Beside the equerries attendant upon their liege, and the muscled bulk of the realm's champion in his ankle-length surcoat and mail coif, the welcoming party consisted of Havish's High Chancellor, lean as a hard run hound, and distinct in his disdain for sodden velvets. To his left, the ministers of Ostermere's trade guilds flocked in ruffles of wilted lace, three of them stiff as sticks, and the fourth, merry-faced and corpulent, but sniffling and blotting his reddened nose in the unkind gusts off the sea. The *caithdein* of Havish, Lord Machiel, stood a half pace aside. Least troubled by wet, he presented a broad-chested, imposing presence in the traditional unrelieved black. He had a wedged, balding head that once had been blond, and about him still the wary stance of a man unforgetful of his forests and the threat of stalking headhunters.

The sovereign he stood steward for was square-jawed and serious, a brown-haired young man of twenty-two. Eldir's straightforward nature set small store by the dragging weight of Havish's royal tabard, with its gold hawk blazon and embroidered pleats of scarlet silk. The king might have worn a labourer's woollens, for all the care he paid his massive jewels. An heirloom band of ancestral rank crowned an earnest brow, lined now in a faint, troubled frown.

To meet him, Arithon s'Ffalenn was clad in the costly restraint he had displayed for Talith's landing at the Cascains. Since he had not descended the switched-back thoroughfares from the upper citadel through the weeping, inclement morning, he was dry, his expression all scorching irony as he appeared with the captive princess on his arm.

They descended the gangway together, his step all but lost in the billow of the lady's lavish silk. Runoff from the awning fringed the air in between as he made his bow, acknowledged prince to foreign sovereign, before King Eldir's staid person. The pair could not have been more unlike: Havish's crowned ruler all stuffed finery and unpolished, granite directness; the Shadow Master

293

before him slim and poised as killing steel, his green eyes glinting with self-mockery.

At his shoulder, the Lady Talith, her beauty heightened by a carriage that made of any artifice an afterthought. Etarran-born, scornful of the courtesies exchanged by old blood royalty, she waited, a monument of victimized pride.

As Havish's High Chancellor cleared his voice to intone a memorized, formal greeting, the Master of Shadow met Eldir's level glance, then cut in with ice-breaking honesty. 'I think we can dispense with the language. Your weather has summed things up neatly. No doubt, given choice, I'm the last living spirit a king should welcome to his noble realm of Havish.'

Eldir's firm lips twitched in surprise just barely curbed. Too practical to hold the remark as anything less than plain truth, he did not smile as he said, 'My realm has survived the Mad Prophet's misadventures. What could you bring that's any worse?'

Arithon's smile turned wicked. He moved, swept the flat of his hand down the dripping fringes, and in the interval while the waterfall lessened, drew the lady fully under cover. 'I bring you the wife of Lysaer s'Ilessid.' He slipped her slender fingers into the hand of Havish's suddenly flustered young high king. 'Princess Talith, once of Etarra.'

State manners fell short of a counterthrust. Shoved headlong beyond his depth, Eldir lost his breath, eyes pinned to her tawny magnificence. His wild blush clashed with his tabard. He could scramble together no sharp wit to respond as Arithon admitted, regretful, that Dakar was included in Rathain's delegation, if currently in the hold overseeing the unloading of a royal gift, which thundered hooves in indignant fury against the *Khetienn*'s lower timbers.

Unable to stand upon dignity, King Eldir abandoned himself to a rare, deep burst of laughter. 'Welcome to my kingdom, Lady Talith. Though for the mountebank who brought you, I reserve the same grace until he shows better manners than to present you as potential trouble.'

The challenge floundered into awkward silence. The moment spun out to pattered rainfall while the ministers swivelled their hatted heads. The realm's champion craned his neck to peer past his coif, while, most perceptive, the *caithdein* closed a step toward his king. His cool regard surveyed Arithon's sudden, rigid stance. But the Master of Shadow had taken no umbrage. His glance had merely skimmed the delegation and fixed on the one wizened figure overlooked.

Crammed like wadded rag between the jewels and damp velvets of state panoply, Sethvir of the Fellowship stepped forward. If the Sorcerer had chosen to be last acknowledged, the effect of his presence was profound.

Arithon s'Ffalenn's veneer of manners cracked away. His face turned ice pale, and his movement, pure reflex, drove Eldir's ministers to fly back as though he jumped them with a knife.

But the sharp surge of speed that dropped him to one knee before that robed and bearded figure held no threat, but only abject humility. 'Warden,' said Arithon. 'Sethvir.' Then, Masterbard though he was, his throat closed; speech failed him.

The Sorcerer he addressed raised a fragile hand and traced his crown of black hair. As though the prince asked his audience in private, he spoke. 'We should fear, you think? Since your strike at Minderl Bay, the Mistwraith's geas has deepened its hold and grown worse. Your suspicion is well founded. At each encounter, its curse becomes more troublesome to manage.'

'You do see,' Arithon said, muffled. He looked up. The wells of his eyes were open and wide, his expression unmasked before horror. 'This exchange for the ransom could launch a disaster. If you ask, I could leave at the outset.'

Sethvir's crinkled features rearranged in reproof. 'We are guarded already. Ease your mind.' He thrust his other hand from the rim of his cuff and raised Rathain's prince to his feet. His glance held a glint like steel behind mist for the warning, not needed, that Arithon had voiced without heed for pride or witnesses.

Too late, if Rathain's prince now strove to mask how he cared, that the chancellor's glance turned cold in reserve, and Eldir's courtiers kept their marked distance. To Talith's trained eye, seeking weakness in an enemy, that incongruous moment of sacrifice rocked the very roots of her conviction.

King Eldir said something banal and polite. Sidelined from preoccupied thought, Talith answered, unmindful of the rain that clung, silver on gilt, in the cropped ends of her hair. She deferred to the royal wish and let herself be led from quayside. Solid in his duty, but without distinctive grace, King Eldir handed her into the dry comfort of his carriage. Footmen closed the lacquered door. She was left her peace and privacy as the coachman on the box took up the lines and set his matched team to a jingling, smart trot. Grooms brought a horse for the visiting prince, then the caparisoned mount of the king. Attendant men-at-arms clambered into wet saddles; the equerries retrieved banners sluiced to their poles from the deluge. Hazed by fog, peered at by curious, wet knots of bystanders from doorways and windows, and from archways spanned dark over puddles, the procession wound from the quayside. Enclosed by Ostermere's streaked limestone and tarnished copper brick, they ascended the tiered levels from the trade quarter to the high, buttressed citadel which guarded the seat of Eldir's council. Calls from the teamsters and the grinding of dray wheels and the slapping splash of boys running errands sounded thin, unreal, a fabric of noise webbed over scarce-buried tension.

The high officials of Havish completed their ceremonial entry in an edged, uneasy hurry for the creature of black hair and bare honesty and desperate, devious subtleties that their court had let into its midst.

King Eldir's monarchy at Ostermere embarked on its fifth year of office scarcely groomed to the ways of sovereign rule, uncertain in its unity as the threads of a tapestry quarrelled over by its commissioners. Factions were emerging, but not settled. The young ladies who vied for their liege's affection had yet to be sorted into favoured candidates, though ones with no interest in scholarly discourse were relegated to the hopeful fringes. The high king's justice subscribed to Havish's first charter, written at the dawn of the Third Age by the Fellowship. His taxes were fair. But since the edict against clan raids, and the repeal of bounties that disbanded the headhunters' leagues, his authority had been sorely felt. Royal guardsmen patrolled the trade roads in force. Day labour from the cities was collected on strict schedule to restore the dilapidated paving, the slate for which dated from Paravian times. Slowly, the isolated settlements in Lanshire were being won back and brought to the order of law and commerce.

On the central table in the king's close chamber, still subject to controversy, plans were being drawn to restore the clans from their centuries of wilderness exile. The ruins at Telmandir would be rebuilt for their habitation, and two lesser sites, reduced to weed-grown foundations that city records held no written name for, but that villagers and townborn alike still shunned in adamant dread.

Into that stew of unresolved power, of disgruntled mayors and town trade interests all vying in cutthroat ambition to hold their pre-eminence against ancient clan claims to position, came the person of Arithon s'Ffalenn. Neutral though Havish remained on the issue of Desh-thiere's curse, no royal edict could quell nine years of wild rumour. The court might absorb Princess Talith's hot pride and Dakar's wild antics in stride. But this was the prince who had helped restore sunlight and set seals of captivity on the Mistwraith; who was sorcerer, and pirate, and mountebank and Masterbard, that had folk in four kingdoms raised to arms.

The banquet to introduce his presence became a tilting ground of intrigue and curiosity. King Eldir received his gift of ten mares and a magnificent, silver-grey stallion to match them with the proper degree of cool courtesy. Known as he was for his indulgence in horse-flesh, he had a tenacious disposition for level thinking. Against Arithon's insouciance at the waterfront, Havish's liege exacted his grave style of revenge. He showed no favour, but settled in comfort on his dais and allowed his packs of courtiers to sate their voracious interests as they chose.

Princess Talith could have warned of the mistake. She had observed, front and centre, nine years in the past, when Arithon had been presented to Etarra's pedigree élite as the prince sanctioned for Rathain's sovereignty. If he looked no day older for the years that had passed, his skill at evasion had sharpened. The finery he chose, then as now, was expensive, but simple to the point of severity. He wore no jewels; no leopard device. Rathain's royal colours of green, black, and silver commanded no aura of respect. He had grace, but no majesty; no overweening presence of muscular height or size. This caused the men, infallibly, to underestimate him. Their more observant women disregarded his slight stature, but looked instead at the way he filled his clothes.

For their fawning, their advances, their unwelcome prying questions, they discovered too late the word, the fast quip, deployed in small malice like the sting of a briar masked in ivy. They found that Arithon could move through a crowd like shadow itself and shame his clumsier pursuit to embarrassment. Inside of three hours, his wishes were made clear. He invited no close acquaintance, no female company, no circle of wishful admirers. Of his gifts of shadow or his upbringing by mages on Dascen Elur beyond West Gate, he would make no display for entertainment.

Eldir regarded the blunt failure of his retaliation and the stunning rebuff of his courtiers with his cleft chin parked on steepled fingers. His eyes stayed peat brown in thought. 'Your prince is dangerous,' he said in outright judgement to Sethvir. 'He has no heart in him at all.'

'Do you think so?' The Warden of Althain moved veined knuckles and set a bread crust to one side, unmindful as his transition from vagueness left the ends of his beard in peril of wicking up gravy. 'I should venture, instead, what you see is a man too long hunted.'

'My *caithdein* Machiel's not like that.' Eldir gestured with his meat knife as Arithon came to rest in a particularly dim corner, his back to a tapestry and his lips flat set in distaste.

Sethvir's reply was very quiet. 'Your clan steward only stood guard for his life. This prince lies under siege for his spirit. Look, you shall see.' The Sorcerer crooked a hand and beckoned.

Insignificant as the gesture appeared, Arithon saw. For the Warden of Althain, he came in willing, incongruous respect.

'Ostermere's court has established no patronage,' said Sethvir as Arithon paused beneath the dais. 'The treasury's too scant and the trade ministers are uncultured. His Grace has no titled bard in residence.' Althain's Warden finished in a bracing rebuke that startled Eldir to attention. 'If you won't make conversation, I charge you by your office. You owe this court the music you were made and trained to share.'

Arithon's carriage hardened to chiselled anger.

In the face of s'Ffalenn rage, that a half-breath might

trigger, Sethvir gave a smile that unstrung his victim for sheer pity. 'It hurts. I know this. I ask in Halliron's memory. This realm is neutral, and I believe the old master would not have your name be reviled on false grounds. You will play and leave nothing to the mercy of unkind hearsay.'

To the king's page who hovered in mouse quiet to one side, the Sorcerer said, 'Fetch a lyranthe from the gallery.'

Arithon accepted the beautiful, varnished instrument with a word for the boy, but no bow for the king, and scarcely a glance at Sethvir. He was shaking; no one close at hand could fail to notice. A stool was fetched. He sat mute and tuned each silvered string.

This was not the exquisite instrument left under glass in the captain's cabin aboard his brigantine. Only Talith and Sethvir shared past knowledge of the other lyranthe, smashed in Etarra by Lysaer's hand in a fit of curse-driven violence. Here, where mishap might turn the best-laid plans, Arithon chose not to risk the treasure inherited from Halliron. The princess was aware he held rank as a bard, but had never before heard him play; like Eldir and his courtiers, the experience took her by storm.

His skill tore their hearts, bled them white, and then bound them, effortless as wind, in haunting sweet resonance like coins thrown down through a rainfall. He made them cry tears for sheer joy. His was a talent not seen on Athera for more than a thousand years, Sethvir admitted through the salt-damp folds of his napkin. When at the last, silvered string was damped still by the bard, the court had been wooed and won over.

They had seen the jewel in their midst in all its rare splendour, and no matter how thankless its cutting edge, nothing could make them give it up. Rathain's prince would have no surcease now, however he bristled and snapped.

He snatched what refuge he could in rough sports.

Hunting, hawking, matches at arms, then contests with bows on horseback: Arithon showed them a competence that humiliated, and won back his right to reserve. He handled a sword with a killing polish even the softest trade minister could respect. If Sethvir's intent was undone by a fraction, no one any longer risked baiting Rathain's prince to plumb the mettle of his intellect.

Four days before solstice and the arrival of her ransom, Princess Talith perched in the gallery above the high king's main hall, looking down on candlelit tables and the tossing press of courtiers who languished replete from the feast. The air smelled of lilies, almond sauces and lavender, almost too cloying to breathe.

Talith had climbed the stair to clear her head. Beside the bench she chose for refuge, swathed in borrowed cleric's robes, the Mad Prophet stood with his elbows stubbed against the marble rail and his knuckles matted through his beard. The irony caught the princess's notice, that the man the pair of them tracked like choice prey was the inimitable Prince of Rathain.

Like Talith, Dakar seemed to ache for a fact intrusively, even desperately denied: that Arithon's viciousness stemmed not from cruelty but from too terrible a gift of compassion.

'He strikes out because of his vulnerable heart,' Talith shared in dismay to the rotund prophet propped by the cushions where she sat, silk skirts fanned about her like frost over glass in stilled shimmers of pearls and embroidery. 'Why should you wish to pull him down? I have my husband's royal honour to defend. What reason do you have to hate?'

'The same, nearly.' Dakar hunched his shoulders, her perception unwanted as the prick of a rapier at his back. 'Prince Lysaer has been my best friend.' He ducked his spaniel head, palms ground into fists for his inadvertent slip into past tense. That brush with conscience was too painful. Revile his nemesis though he would, a small girl's dying had branded itself into memory. Whatever Arithon was, or was not, his care for one child had been genuine.

'If he's acting,' the Mad Prophet promised, 'if he takes just one step awry, he shall receive the full measure he deserves.'

Whatever veiled threat lay behind Dakar's statement, Talith found she had no wish to find out.

Three days before solstice, while the candlemakers bent over their moulds through short nights to meet the demand for the festival, and children in the merchants' mansions cut paper talismans to hang behind windows and eaves, the poor quarter folk wove baskets of osiers to set on their doorsteps for alms. Wood for the dancer's bonfires was unladen from farm wagons in Ostermere's wide public squares. Through the racketing snarl of traffic as the royal kennelman took his hounds to exercise, Asandir of the Fellowship rode through the restored north postern, slick as a needle through fleece. He was flanked by a blast of unseasonal chill air which contained the entities, Kharadmon and Luhaine.

Traithe remained downcoast in Cheivalt, aboard Lysaer s'Ilessid's state galley.

Among the Fellowship Sorcerers, agreement was unanimous long before Arithon's warning. Through the supervised exchange of Princess Talith's ransom, the half-brothers must not come face-to-face. For the cursed pair to enter the same city, even for the span of one day, would require the most stringent precautions.

The Mistwraith's blighting geas could not entirely be curbed. At each confrontation, its drive to seed destruction intensified. The best the Fellowship Sorcerers could expect was to lace the walls and the harbour in safeguards, then hope to shift one or the other prince to safety if unforeseen mishap should occur.

Over tea in a squat tower keep that overlooked Ostermere's notched rooftops, spread in tiered steps to the seaside, Sethvir shared counsel with his discorporate colleagues, while Asandir stitched a silvered veil of wards over the mansion Lysaer was to occupy once his half-brother embarked a safe distance offshore in the *Khetienn*.

'You've measured the hard evidence in the Shadow Master's aura. Arithon suffered far worse than a slip of control at Minderl Bay. Our theory's borne out,' Althain's Warden said sadly. 'At each encounter, the curse will unstring a little more of the grip the Teir's'Ffalenn holds on his sanity. He has implored us to require his s'Ilessid half-brother to send a delegate to receive the Lady Talith from his hand. We must listen. Wards are not enough. The risk of further damage must not be left to chance.'

'Lysaer won't like it,' Kharadmon cracked. The restless vortex of his presence riffled over the tapestries and caused the glass in the leaded casements to sing at odd moments in stress-caught tones of vibration.

'Lysaer's wishes don't matter,' Luhaine countered, tart with the worry they all felt. 'The harrowing of Shand is going to unhinge quite enough of the peace as things stand.'

For no opening remained. Even Arithon's ingenuity could no longer forestall the brunt of Lysaer's muster in the south. Once the princess's ransom was accomplished, bloodshed must inevitably follow. Armies massed on the borders of Vastmark, thick as the lines of summer anvil heads. Caolle's shepherd archers set stone breastworks in the passes, and prepared points of ambush to stall the mighty army that threatened any day to roll over them.

As a miniature wind devil upset Sethvir's quill pens

for the second time in an hour, Luhaine upbraided his rival colleague. 'You're worse than an ill-mannered child! We'd all be most grateful if you could restrain your excessive energy.'

'Oh, indeed?' Kharadmon loosed a whiplash breath of mirth. 'My excessive energy scarcely signifies.' His nasal retort a dead ringer for Luhaine's style at lecturing, he ended, 'Certainly not when your reference is childish rampaging.'

Outside the latched-back casement, over the sullen flap of royal pennons on the walls, cracked the high, thin snap of a whip. Someone shouted. A thunder of hooves erupted from the meadow by the tiltyard, swelling to galloping crescendo.

Arithon s'Ffalenn had fastened his interest on Eldir's blooded chariot teams, and no one had found a deterrent in time to keep him from trying the reins.

'The last of Rathain's princes could get himself dragged and mangled, and you've the gall to waste your nattering on me.' Kharadmon huffed across the tabletop, scattering stray leaves of manuscript. 'Well, I'll stop fretting when someone makes that idiot prince give up his foolish fascination.'

No fellow sorcerer volunteered for this office. Luhaine ventured his stuffy opinion that Arithon s'Ffalenn milled over by chariot wheels was by far not the worst that could happen, against Davien's longevity binding.

While Sethvir watched the butterfly that alighted on his knuckle with eyes as vacant as glass, his discorporate colleagues turned on each other, haggling. Outside, beyond reach of reproach, the sore point at issue pursued his wild antics to the palpable alarm of half a dozen court onlookers.

Havish's master of horse was himself too busy to worry. With his legs wrapped around a fast, handy pony, he bent low in his saddle, calling volumes of steady instructions.

His pupil, though royal, was not too proud to ignore sense. Arithon steadied the ribbons to a flying whirl of wheels. In the delicate reverence of a man who loved horseflesh, he guided the team of jet horses through a wide, sweeping turn. The chariot, a lightweight affair of laced leather and wood, bounced and rocked like a chip hurled helter-skelter through a millrace. The rattle of singletrees and the creak of its oak shaft against the yoked collars of the team raised a riotous racket, not quite enough to drown out its driver's exultant whoop.

Atop the limestone wall which bounded the mowed edge of the tourney field, the Mad Prophet sat tucked like dough in a beer keg, picking at runners of ivy. Unlike the young king who stood with shaded eyes to one side, he refused to glower at the flat-out run of the horses. His brow stayed unfurrowed by worry. Arithon s'Ffalenn would not perish crippled by mishap, as his talent for augury offered surety. Freed to ponder more devious possibilities, Dakar made spiteful comment, 'What do you suppose are the war plans behind this morning's diligent apprenticeship?'

He received King Eldir's most penetrating gaze for the unbroken span of a minute.

Perspiration slicked the Mad Prophet's brosy face. 'Could you expect any less, your royal majesty?' he defended, if only to escape the measuring weight of those too-level, too-grave brown eyes. 'Arithon gathers knowledge like s'Brydion collect weapons, and always for the same reason.'

King Eldir still said nothing, but waited until his master of horse and the errant driver of the chariot had pulled up in exuberant noise. While liveried grooms rushed forward to grasp the lathered team, and three ladies released bated breaths, Arithon leaped down, his hair spiked in tangles from the heat and the play of the wind.

The royal inquiry which met him concerning military

usage of chariots was direct as a hammerblow to rock.

He stopped, the laughter stunned from him, and regarded the young king who barred his path like an immobile post of scrap iron. 'Was that a jest?' he asked, and got no answer.

Eldir held his ground. Better at tolerance than temper, his patience seemed drawn to snapping. The lazy summer fragrance of meadow flowers and grass seemed crushed out by the martial tang of leather, and hot horse-flesh, and oiled steel.

A flick of irritation shot through the Prince of Rathain, just as swiftly quelled. 'Forgive me, your Grace. I see you inquired in deadly earnest.'

Arithon gestured his dismissal to the grooms, who led the blowing team away for stabling. A suspect sparkle of enjoyment crept back. 'Even if the Vastmark valleys were not seeded over with boulders, I scarcely think chariots would be useful on a field of war. Three ransoms in bullion would be needed to buy the collective guts to man them. Fiends alive, those vehicles aren't just fragile, they're treacherous. Wilful as a half-swamped longboat, never mind that quantities of horses hitched in harness manage to agree with one another a hopeless portion of the time.'

An accurate enough summary, Eldir reflected later in private, as his valet muddled over his wardrobe for his afternoon audience to hear complaints. A ruler who liked puzzles, and who never shied off from perplexing, obscure twists of subtlety, the king made mental note of Dakar's warning. Then, he ploughed on to mull over Arithon's peculiar choice of phrasing concerning ransoms in triplicate.

A prince who was also Athera's Masterbard would not be given to slipshod use of language.

Eldir tugged off his royal fillet with a curse. His hair stuck up in hanks and his temper was ruffled, but the other loose end was what rankled. Where the Master of

Shadow was concerned, any implication of trouble posed a peril too dire to ignore. Stray elements of chance amidst a tangle of diplomacy induced by the Mist-wraith's curse offered too grave a potential for disaster. In his tousled shirt and a tunic still redolent of horse, against the plaintive, hobbled protests of his valet, the King of Havish thrust aside propriety. He marched his suspicions up three breathless flights of stairs to cast into the laps of the Fellowship Sorcerers.

Asandir answered his knock. Brisk, imperious, and impeccable in his court dress, he heard Eldir through in a bottled impatience that woke baleful light in his eyes. 'You were right to bring this to me.'

To Kharadmon, invisible, he demanded, 'Find Arithon. We'll have his explanation.' Then, in an irony sheared to suspicion, he spun in the doorway and glared at Sethvir, who perched on the window seat with one of the stable kittens batting at loose threads on his cuff. 'You knew about this?'

Through the uncanny, stabbing chill as Kharadmon drifted by, Eldir saw Althain's Warden give an abstracted blink. 'The ransom?' he said presently. His hands stroked the kitten, which retracted tiny claws and yawned. Then insane glee bent the Sorcerer's mouth, half-masked in the bristles of his beard. 'You don't know? The gold has been stolen, of course.'

'What!' Eldir advanced into the sun-drenched tower chamber, bristling with royal antagonism. 'Do you mean to say while I've been running fool's circles to keep your Teir s'Ffalenn from making mincemeat of my courtiers, *he has raided an armada and made off with five hundred thousand coin weight in gold!*'

'Did I mention any name?' But dissembling was wasted; Eldir only glowered until Sethvir gave way with a shrug. 'That's the part of his personality that makes us all feel like we've been kissing coiled vipers for a penny bet.' On the far side of a table cluttered with books, across the candles that had dribbled the faces of the wrought-silver nymphs who upheld them, he unfolded into a stretch, mild as milk before the high king's outrage. 'You can rein in your fuming and thank your creator for the favour of Arithon's resourcefulness. Else our peril before the Mistwraith would be redoubled. There's no space left for diplomacy. Only force can prevail against the war host that's gathered in Shand.'

'His Grace of Rathain gave his oath to keep the peace,' Eldir persisted, unmoved. 'Does your Fellowship condone his act of thievery?'

'Certainly not.' Asandir was unequivocal. 'If Arithon's accounting fails to satisfy, the issue will be taken to trial under Havish's royal justice.'

Out of pity for the redoubled apprehension behind Eldir's straight stance, Sethvir set the kitten on the floor, pulled out a cushioned chair, and swept the seat free of papers. 'Sit,' he urged gently. 'Let the miscreant answer for his own acts.'

A step echoed up the turnpike stair. Long before it arrived, the postern swung open to admit the icy, poured draught that heralded Kharadmon. Arithon followed, damp from his bath, and wearing little but trunk hose and a shirt still half-unlaced. A pace inside the doorway he stopped. His sharp glance swept the assembled Sorcerers, then Havish's king, united in postures of annoyance.

His dark brows flicked up, but not in surprise. 'You've heard the ransom was waylaid,' he surmised without pretence of apology.

'Dharkaron avenge!' Asandir exclaimed. He snatched a chair for himself. 'You had better have your reasons, prince, for no one of us will spare you from punishment.'

'My royal oath,' Arithon gave back in rapid-fire reply. 'The one I swore in blood at Athir that avowed I would do anything in my power to survive.'

Eldir, amazed, saw Asandir of the Fellowship succumb

to a wine-deep flush. The words he forced out were beaten metal. 'Go on.'

Under that scouring scrutiny, Arithon broke into sweat; but never from nerves. He sucked in a vexed breath. 'The gold was to be surrendered into your hands as soon as may be, though not to ransom the lady. I sought the diversion –' He broke off, shook his head, then resumed in quick anguish, 'Ath show me mercy, *I needed a delaying tactic*.' Green eyes held steady under interrogating glares as the last of his appeal was flung in desperation toward the one Sorcerer who might be disposed to listen. 'If you've looked in on Vastmark, you'll know why,' he told Sethvir. 'Put baldly, I had to buy time.'

Althain's Warden gave back an arch censure that cracked before a glimmer of interest. 'You've bearded the lion in a way you can't be implicated?'

Arithon inclined his head in careful respect to Eldir of Havish. 'When the ploy is discovered in public, that will be for the king's grace to decide.'

'Well,' said Sethvir, nonplussed. 'The law's well and good, but you'd better have made a clean job of this. A term of incarceration for grand theft would scarcely work with Lysaer's war host of a size to level any stronghold to see you dead.'

'I pay my debts,' Arithon said, clipped. 'The Royal Justiciar of Havish and his sovereign can be the judge of my case.' He bowed to Eldir, spun on his heel, and left, while the strapped oaken door thudded home in its frame with force enough to crack plaster.

'Torbrand's temper!' Sethvir shook his head, bemused to commiserate despite Asandir's thunderous affront. 'He has a way, Rathain's prince, of letting us all know what his given oath at Athir cost his dignity.'

'S'Ffalenn dignity be damned,' Kharadmon rapped out from his unseen place by the casement. 'Whatever the cost, there's too strong a chance that blood pledge may become all we have against threat of Athera's total ruin.'

On the eve of midsummer, the armada sent from Tysan made port to a blare of trumpets and a flying, wind-snapped panoply of banners and sapphire pennons. They docked at the quayside, surrounded in the swoop and dive of swifts, and white gulls chased by the noise from their nests in the cliff caves. Bristling with weapons and smartly turned men-at-arms, enfolded amid her escort of warships, the royal galley seemed unmolested. No officer came ashore crying tales of piracy on the high seas.

Mistrustful despite the atmosphere of pomp and decorum, Luhaine went to investigate. He brought the incredulous bad news. 'Lord Commander Diegan doesn't know, nor is any other officer on board aware. But the strongboxes on the flagship hold no coin. They contain soggy bags of ballast sand. The secret can't be kept. Once the lightermen lift the first coffer ashore, they're going to notice something wrong.'

King Eldir took charge before the scandal broke, and in venomous ill temper, asked his valet to regale him in his robes of state. He dispatched his seneschal to the harbour with forms of requisition. Lysaer's senior officers were summoned from their vessels for a manda-tory royal audience.

The close council took place in the small, panelled study where the harbourmaster filed his accounts. The room smelled of dried ink and salt-musty carpets. Its paned casements were curtained in green gloom from the grape arbours left to run riot without. Jackdaws nested in the cornices. The sleepy twitter of their fledglings chirped through the creaking scrape of chairs as men in clothing too hot for the season shifted their weight in impatience.

King Eldir presided, long-suffering in resignation as a muzzled mastiff. His mood was familiar to his justiciar and his chancellor from his first years of crown rule, when he had stood down his council and his crabbed city mayors as a lad just barely eighteen. 'You will say if anything unusual happened on your trip down my coastline.'

The ranking captain of the armada blinked, his narrow head tipped like a fishing heron. 'Your Grace, nothing at all untoward —' His hesitation rocked the silence like a hiccough. 'Except for one disabled fishing smack. She was left adrift, flying distress flags. We boarded and took her in tow, since her crew had abandoned ship. The hull was sound enough, though her rigging had suffered damage from a squall. We sold her to the island villagers south of Torwent.'

'How long did you drag her on a cable?' asked the justiciar in his grainy bass.

'Three days,' came the puzzled answer. 'She was a vessel of no account.' The galleyman stroked his beard, careful to remember in detail. 'Twenty-six coin weight was all she was worth. Dharkaron's Horses, her planks were half-sprung. We were grateful enough to be rid of her. If her owners lodge complaint, our salvage was fair. We've witnesses will swear she was abandoned.'

'No one questions your integrity,' Eldir assured. He arose, solid in his royal trappings, and rankled enough to snap as he called for Arithon s'Ffalenn to present himself.

Lightly made as fine steel before a battle-axe, the Master of Shadow made his bow. When questioned on the subject of fishing smacks, he produced two legitimate bills of sale. The first was scrawled across with the armada captain's signature and doucely sealed under Tysan's official blazon; the second one, of folded, cheap paper, showed the plain capitals of a country scribe.

'The villagers made a profit,' Arithon finished off. 'For

311

myself, I only bought her for the ballast under her bilges.'

Irony within irony played like sunlight through clouds behind his masking grave smile as the justiciar perused the ribboned documents and noticed: the fishing smack's name was *Royal Freedom*.

The boat herself could not be presented for inspection. 'An accident with a lamp,' Arithon said with a true ring of regret. 'She burned at her mooring the day after she was purchased.'

If Sethvir knew aught of the false planking which must have concealed a thieving crew; whether his earth-linked senses had seen furtive moves at the dark of the moon when men must have crept hand over hand up the fishing smack's cable, to steal into the galley's hold to exchange the gold in the strongboxes for their ballast sand, he proved to be immersed in one of his vacuous dazes. No matter who addressed him on the subject, he stayed patently deaf under questioning.

Signal

While the theft of Princess Talith's ransom set sorcerers and officials seething like stirred ants at Ostermere, and the bonfires in celebration of the solstice blazed for masked dancers across the continent, a much smaller snag in the world's affairs sat huddled beside a bed of embers twelve leagues downcoast from Shand's lesser trade city of Ithish.

Feylind had never known such low spirits in all her young life. She sat with her chin cupped in dirty palms, unresponsive to her mother's pleas for reason, and well practised at glaring when Tharrick, who had betrayed her, spoke in rebuke for her rudeness. The summer rasp of crickets and the thrummed wings of nighthawks skimming over the thickets were of more interest than adult persuasion. No one alive could force her to believe the sea she was leaving was no loss.

Her three attempts to steal away by night met with failure, even the last, when Fiark abetted her by groaning through a theatrical display of stomach cramps. Always Tharrick tracked her down and dragged her back. By now, the little sloop with Arithon's second mate would have sailed too far downcoast to overtake. Feylind brooded. She reviled her fate in inventive, filthy language. Most sorely, she wished she shared her brother's nasty talent for throwing rocks. Just now Tharrick's leather-clad backside posed a tempting target, while he stooped to clean the coneys he had snared for their supper.

Darkness stole over the stepped shoulders of shale where the dwindled spine of the Kelhorns gave way to low pine scrub. The vetch-tangled meadows caught between lay flecked in seasonal white asters. Posies of wildflowers were not Feylind's passion. She watched the stars kindle the arch of the zenith, heartsore as she named off the ones she had learned for navigation.

The sliver of new moon reminded her of Dhirken's bright cutlass. Fingers locked around her skinned knees, Feylind longed to steal the curved knife Tharrick used for dressing game, then pretend it was a sword like the captain's.

Fiark ached for his twin's unhappiness; his long, grave look spoke more than words. While Jinesse busied herself cutting herbs for the stewpot, he leaned into her side and whispered, 'If Mother binds you to that weaver as apprentice, I'll help you slip off to sea afterward.'

'I heard that,' Jinesse snapped. 'Trade galleys don't take girls into service. Their backs are too weak for the oar.'

'Galleys!' Feylind spat. 'I'm not such a simpleton. Sail is where the future lies.' Small use to argue how deepwater keels would offer faster, safer transport when coupled with new knowledge of navigation. Her mother was not minded to listen.

Stung afresh for the reversal that had torn away her dreams, the girl blew a strand of fair hair from her lips and raised her voice in loud song. The chanty she chose was salty and lewd, learned at the dockside in Southshire while the *Khetienn* had rolled mastless at her anchorage.

Jinesse tossed wild onions in the stewpot, her lips a pursed ridge of determination. 'Feylind, be still.'

But she did not insist. Worn down from contending with her daughter's wayward spirit, she cast a shamed glance toward Tharrick. Feylind saw, and sang louder, clever enough to guess the appeal for stronger discipline would rankle the former guardsman's sensibilities.

'Such caterwauling will just make you sore in the throat,' Tharrick chided, his heart in sympathy with her. 'If it makes you feel better, keep on till you're hoarse. You'll only wear yourself out.'

Jinesse hunched her shoulders in tormented unhappiness and stirred the thin gruel of meal with a peeled stick while her daughter sang seventeen exhaustively long ballads. No one gave a thought that the racket might come to draw notice.

Supper was a cheerless affair. Through much of the night, Feylind lay sleepless and weeping. When dawn came, Tharrick commented that three days more would see them through the downs to the trade road. The girl overheard, stole her chance, and tried to bolt again.

The chit could dodge like a hare through the pine brakes. Engrossed in headlong pursuit through the scrub, ducking through deer trails and skinning under branches, Tharrick laboured against the slap of green branches. He swore and gained a mouthful of needles. His bow snagged a bough and nearly jerked him off his feet. In heated annoyance, he discarded it, then the quiver of arrows which jounced and clattered against his thigh.

The most damnable aspect of this morning's chase was the pitiful truth that he had no choice but to catch the girl. A hundred and fifty leagues of deserted coastline distanced her from Arithon's outpost in the Cascains. No child could survive such a journey alone. Even if she could find an adult guide to assist her, the encampment on those shores was not permanent. By now, very likely, the site lay abandoned. Too many galleys flying enemy colours threaded in search through the islets. Arithon s'Ffalenn was never such a fool as to set roots in one location for too long.

Tharrick crashed down a rocky gully and followed its winding bed to a draw. Sticks snapped ahead; a whorled thrash of grasses marked Feylind's panting progress through the clearing. He called her name.

An insolent whistle floated back. He recognized the piercing trill of notes for the call that Arithon had taught the twins on the eve of his departure.

'See sense, by Ath's mercy!' Tharrick tripped over an edge of shale, just escaped a turned ankle, then ripped his palm like blistering vengeance on a thorn branch as he floundered to recoup his balance. 'Girl, will you listen? There's nothing in these wilds to win your way back to Prince Arithon.'

'Is there not?' cried a voice in rebuttal.

Tharrick snatched back his bleeding hand and cast a startled glance ahead. Several archers in stained buckskins stood foursquare in his path. Their bows held steel broadheads nocked and ready to draw, and their expressions were inimical as death.

Wise enough to know when he was beaten, Tharrick raised his arms from his sides and uttered the rudest phrases he knew from his years in the mercenaries' barracks. When he ran out of breath, he swore fresh oaths at Feylind, then glared in black chagrin at his captors. 'You're tribesfolk?'

'Sheepherders?' A grey-haired man returned a sharp laugh. 'Never. We're Erlien's liegemen. Yon whistle's a clan signal. We take it the girl is discontent with your company?'

Feylind crawled out of a brush brake, green twigs caught in the sailor's braid that tumbled half-undone down her back. 'They want to drag me off to a weaver

316

in Shaddorn. But I would rather learn the sea, under Arithon.'

The elder scout gave her an uncle's stern scrutiny. 'He'll have taught you that whistle himself, then?'

Feylind nodded. She tipped a grin in apology to Tharrick, still pinned under threat from the archers. The angle of her chin, the set lift of her jaw, and the gleam in her eyes as she seized her moment to claim her due destiny showed through her unfinished, child's form like blued steel.

She would make a formidable person, Tharrick saw. No weaver's wool-musty shop could ever contain her in safe bindings of yarn and soft thread.

He needed no threats from armed clansmen to accept the final outcome, that the widow must be made to see reason, to untie the apron strings and let this twin go. 'Take her,' he said to the scouts. 'See her safely to his Grace of Rathain.' Then, to Feylind, man to woman, he added, 'Girl, sail the seas with my blessing.'

The smile that lit her fair face became worth all the world, even if it broke her mother's heart.

Tharrick shut his eyes against a desperate swell of emotion. When next he looked the draw was empty, sun dappled and serene, except for the squall of a jay. He raked back his damp cuffs, twitched a bristle of evergreen from his shirt laces, then retraced his steps to reclaim his dropped bow and quiver.

Then he looked ahead and discovered in complaisance that the future was going to be simple after all.

War was a rotten, grinding misery of a life. The brothers s'Brydion and the Master of Shadow in their separate ways had weaned out his taste for professional violence. Tharrick's muddled wants resolved then and there.

He and Fiark would take the road to Innish. The factor sympathetic to Arithon was bound to need a stout hand to guard the gates of his warehouses. For Jinesse, a whole man could give a shoulder for her tears. Though it took him all the days he had left to live, Tharrick vowed he would rebuild her broken home, and her hearth, and her misplaced contentment.

Sorrow

The scandal of Talith's lost ransom resulted in strings of hot horses, hard-pressed in fast passage as royal couriers spurred up smoking trails of dust. They crossed and recrossed the forty leagues of roadway between Ostermere and Cheivalt. For two months, the post stables did brisk business in remounts. Every outbound galley bore letters north to Avenor, or dispatches southward to Innish with news and fresh orders for the mustered warhost.

Prince Lysaer's strapped mood ran counter to summer's languid rhythm. Never had Lord Commander Diegan seen any man held so severely in check, his smallest move calculated, his every word tempered like hot steel quenched into patience. The mansion provided for the royal delegation was exquisite, the finials of pillared doorways gilded or adorned with marble borders of carved leaves and beasts. The tessellated floors and groined ceilings were polished agate, veined in gold, or jade green, the majesty of stone laid in patterns to soothe the nerves. Wide, arched windows fronted the sea and scooped the breezes. They framed the lapis tints of Cheivalt's harbour, the painted sails of fishing fleets splashed against the squall lines massed above the horizon.

But the ocean held too recent a recollection of s'Ffa-lenn piracy for Lysaer to appreciate the view. Inland, the wide, rolling hills rippled under ripening barley: Chei-valt's true wealth lay in her acres of farmlands. Yet the old thread still wound, deep under earth, remnant of the mysteries that had been before man. In black hedgerows where the wild lilies bloomed, the moonflower vines and bindweed twined to a less-ordered rhythm, when the grasslands grew unscarred by the plough, and unicorns had run in a beauty that burned across the wilds of Carithwyr.

Under starlight in the grainfields, from the corner of the eye, a man might glimpse their dancing ghosts.

For Lysaer, the pastoral peace of Cheivalt sawed like the cut of a canker. He might go out with the ladies and their gallants to dance in the masques held by torchlight, but the laughter and the gaiety rang hollow. For him, in that summer of Talith's captivity, the city was a cage in which he was fed a steady diet of bad news.

To raise the second ransom, every man in his retinue had stripped himself of wealth. His lady's chests of personal jewellery and the coffers in the armada's galleys had been emptied. Men-at-arms forwent their pay.

On the heels of such sacrifice came Arithon's insolent refusal: payment in gems was unsatisfactory when terms had been set in gold coin weight.

Through the crystalline, hot days, and wearing delay
•as factors were engaged to sell royal sapphires for bullion, Lord Commander Diegan reined back his temper, time and again shamed by the impeccable decorum of Avenor's fair-haired prince. Buyers who could afford even the least of Talith's pieces were rare; to hurry their sale was to sacrifice her jewels at far below their fair value.

Yet haste was what Lysaer required. For each day that passed, by diplomatic constraint, his massive war host stayed paralysed in Shand. Summer reached its splendid fullness and mocked him: each day that passed shortened the interval left before autumn when unfavourable weather would force him to disband his hard-earned troops. Royal officers fretted every minute. The alliance with s'Brydion threw strain in the weave, as Duke Bransian's vociferous letters urged action despite the thorns of statecraft.

'I'm aware large campaigns can't be fought in the mud,' came Lysaer's reply, consonants pinned through vowels like welded rivets. 'Nonetheless, I gave my royal word.'

The scribe who sealed his missive packed his pens in quaking haste, then fled with the dispatch to the harbour.

Except in close council, Lysaer spoke and moved in a patience that captivated hearts; he attended the mayor's private socials. He kissed the hands of ladies and discussed rare books in the gardens with the highborn of Cheivalt. Their children adored his indulgence, clamouring at his knee for the games he had learned in his birth world beyond West Gate.

Diegan alone was not fooled. Behind masked blue eyes, the royal temper raged and flared like leashed lightning.

The setbacks at Valleygap and Minderl Bay had imprinted their harsh lesson. The season for active campaigning was slipping away, precisely as the Shadow Master intended.

Into that sticky honeycomb of pretence, of statecraft woven in threads that looked effortless to a webwork of larger strategy, Asandir of the Fellowship of Seven brought word from the king's court at Ostermere. His arrival made a stir in a city unaccustomed to living visitors out of legend. At his side walked the Mad Prophet, as the Prince of Rathain's appointed spokesman.

In the airy chamber shown them by trembling

servants, Dakar made his bow before the royal half-brother whose company was more to his taste. 'Your Grace of Avenor, I bring joyful news.' He straightened up, smiling, stone sober and tidy in his best brown broadcloth. 'Your last chest of gold lies secure in King Eldir's treasury. At long last, your princess's hour of deliverance lies at hand.'

Lined in the spill of sun through the window, Lysaer bent his golden head. He could have been a statue etched out in pure light, or the motionless figure of a white guardian from Athlieria, come in male form to spin song in the hour of creation.

'Ath bless!' The spell broke to his whispered catch of breath. Lysaer regarded the pair of streamered stick puppets clenched in his hands for the amusement of the Mayor of Cheivalt's dimpled daughter. His fair, straight profile stayed hard set, as though against nature the dolls' painted faces might turn animate and utter a curse on him; as if night after night in the torment of nightmares, he had heard the same news, only to waken to another cruel setback.

Yet the uncanny stance of the Fellowship mage in Dakar's company became assured proof of reality. The girlchild's openmouthed awe was no dream, as the Sorcerer's forceful presence made her shrink behind the marquetry furnishings.

'My liege,' murmured Lord Commander Diegan from the sidelines, 'grant me leave to assemble your retinue.' The chests of state finery, the banners, the appointments of the royal galley had long been held in readiness. 'You need only meet us at the quay. The docklines can be cast off inside the half hour.' Pressed at full stroke, the oarsmen could work in shifts and see their prince northward to Ostermere inside of two days.

'Post-horses through the night would be more direct,' Dakar blurted, his past ties renewed to a surge of thoughtless sympathy.

322

'I know,' said Prince Lysaer in a patience that shamed. 'But my retinue could never match the pace.'

He roused back into himself. The stick puppets between his ringed fingers had tangled, their ribbons wrapped by nerves until the merry figures lay noosed into strangling partnership. Lysaer smoothed the streamers back to order. Gravely he placed the toys in the hand of the little girl who lingered, still shy, behind his chair. 'I'm sorry, sprite. I have to leave Cheivalt. Please find your mother and father for me. I owe them my thanks for hospitality.'

His pat on the head sent the child skipping off. No longer overmastered by the moment, Lysaer s'Ilessid looked up and gave the Mad Prophet the recognition he craved from a friend he had missed for nine years.

The royal features now were a shade less serene, the stainless, clear flesh remoulded over bone to a leaner, stronger beauty. The blue eyes remained unflawed by shadow. Despite Desh-thiere's curse, their gaze held direct in a way that pierced a man's heart. Only the most searching study could unmask in turn the burden such honesty entailed. The lines traced by private grief and self-sacrifice were masterfully eased over; the relentless, lonely imprint of a fair-handed sovereignty contained in majestic reserve.

Dakar turned aside, torn by regret that duty denied him free choice. 'I'm sorry,' he whispered.

Lysaer's formality thawed into smiling, sunny pleasure. His warm regard noted the neat clothing and anxious care Rathain's envoy displayed in his behalf. 'You look properly bludgeoned into the role of a courtier.' He arose and clapped Dakar on the shoulder. 'By this, I presume I see a man in crying need of a drink. What's your preference in this heat? Ale? Beer? Fine claret?'

Struck speechless that footing still existed for amity after four years in liaison with an enemy, Dakar allowed himself to be swept into step as Lysaer gestured for his bodyguards to stand away and allow them a moment of intimacy. 'You have my promise, the stores on my galley will admit you to paradise without pain. Indulge yourself as you please while I see to my leave-taking. After that, we'll find time to talk.'

Dakar swallowed back discomfort, his love of rowdy drinking a dangerous habit to encourage on the occasion of Talith's ransom. 'You don't ask of your wife,' he said, stung to more sharpness than he meant.

Lysaer stopped, spun, faced him in all his matured splendour of restraint. 'She's healthy and unharmed?' At Asandir's spare nod, he produced a magisterial smile. 'I can lodge no complaint, then. As a hostage, her needs would seem adequately met.'

Shamed to embarrassment, Dakar kicked himself for a fool. As Arithon's envoy, he was no likely candidate for Lysaer's easy confidence; yet the emotionless language of statesmanship rankled. Unthinking as the first, sliding step through a pitfall, he recalled Arithon at the wharfside in Ostermere. On his knees, Rathain's prince had voiced warning to the Warden of Althain, his horror and fear in full public view without care for political expediency.

Cross-grained, viciously defensive when imposed upon, Arithon s'Ffalenn masked no secrets behind mannered complaisance.

Dakar fell to brooding. Unaware of Asandir's speculative interest upon him, he endured through the seamless courtesies as Prince Lysaer discharged his debt to the mayor's household. He found he could not smile at the quips. Nor did he feel drawn into the camaraderie that bound Prince Lysaer's retinue. The poisonous, creeping, new suspicion refused to be dismissed, that old ties could be used to exploit his recent connections. Strong liquor might be offered to encourage a loose tongue.

The chance to test Lysaer's intentions became lost in

the whirlwind as Avenor's guard and servants assembled for swift departure. Pushed aside by the parade of officers seeking direct orders from their prince, Dakar found in distaste he had adjusted too well to Arithon's astringent independence. The fawning adoration of young page-boys; the scrambling bustle of chamber steward, valet, and bodyguards, all tripping over the ship's crew as they vied for position, abraded Dakar's sensibilities. He sought a calm corner where the chatter and commotion would leave him a clear space to think.

Asandir had no moment to spare for sympathetic counsel, absorbed as he was in strong magecraft. When the royal galley set sail for Ostermere, she drove through the sunset wrapped in wards of concealment and protection. The Fellowship would extend its full surety that mischance could not strike through the Mistwraith's curse while the two half-brothers stood in perilous proximity.

Lysaer travelled in state befitting a prince. Food was fresh and plentiful, and the wine of the finest vintage. Two musicians played a lyrical counterpoint in the galley's cushioned salon to ease the hours of passage. But touched to unwonted and maudlin melancholy, Dakar avoided the avid circle of Avenor's officers.

While the night unreeled its spill of summer moonlight, he leaned on the weather rail and watched the frothing, black heave of breakers tear themselves against a quiet shoreline. The headland's high cliffs threw back sound in rhythmic thunder, perfumed in the green scents of orchards. Dakar missed the brigantine, where the gusts combed over the bow unstained by the taint of sweating oarsmen. The crew belowdecks were not chained convicts, but free men who laboured in shifts. Lysaer's speech to fire their hearts for swift passage had done little to lift Dakar's spirits. He saw no need for rush, that war could be closed to exterminate a band of Vastmark archers before the onset of winter.

As the beat of the oars thrashed white tracks in the swell, Avenor's Lord Commander at Arms emerged on deck to join him. Diegan parked his muscled height, unfamiliarly altered, his dandy's silk and jewels replaced by steel mail that licked his torso in chains of silvered highlights.

'Don't take appearances too much to heart,' he said in reference to his prince. 'He's bled every night since my sister was taken, but in private. No one sees his grief. His Grace refuses the self-indulgence lest his people find cause to lose heart.'

'Cause?' Dakar straightened, surprised by his own vehemence. 'I can't embrace bloodshed clothed over in a mantle of false righteousness. This is no clash of morals you will fight for in Shand, but the drive of the Mistwraith's geas.'

'Do you think so?' Steel jingled as Diegan stretched through a wolfish shrug. 'Then you should be pitied. How dare you overlook the destruction that happened to innocents in Jaelot? Was Desh-thiere's curse the provocation for seven wanton deaths at Alestron? Condone those events and what else have you become but Arithon's lackey after all?'

Dakar swore. The truth raised his gorge and half-choked him, that both incidents in their way had been prompted by his own brash faults. Remorse followed, damning him in guilt: for far more than a shepherd child's forfeited life, Arithon had forborne to condemn him. Glad for the night that masked his wretchedness, Dakar took leave of irksome company. The first servant he found he sent scurrying to fetch Lysaer's strongest spirits from the hold.

The Mad Prophet crawled away with a cask and a jack and sat with his back against the chain locker. There, settled pounds of cold iron damped back the singing ache of Asandir's layered defence wards enough to spare him the rank bite of nightmares. In stubborn pain, he applied himself to stun his busy conscience into oblivion with drink.

Like the draw of ebb tide, the stupor he desired slipped his grasp. Entangled instead in punishing insight, he pleaded aloud for escape. Despite hatred, through an unwilling service that encompassed several attempts at cold murder, the years he had suffered in Arithon's company had irremediably changed him. Even sunk in his cups, he could howl for pure gall. His abrasive unhappiness yielded no ground to the blurring ambiguity of peach brandy.

Truth chafed through and sprang stark to the eye. Lysaer bound his following to love and devotion. He was the honed sword, the just light, and the high star to follow. Without the bedazzling example of his strength, like Lord Diegan, the company he gathered to his banner were as men lost. Dakar hiccuped behind a closed fist. He hated deep thoughts when his head pounded. But his maudlin mood kept its terrier's hold; he could not shrug off his conclusion.

A puzzle of subtlety set in absolute contrast, Arithon rejected dependency, spurned even his sanctioned claim to royal ties. He discouraged without mercy the weak spirits who sought to cling. The likes of Jinesse and Tharrick found their need turned around in painful, brisk handling that left them whole and contained in themselves; and enemies found their hatreds used against them.

The spirit who followed the Shadow Master's course in the end acted by informed choice, freely sharing loyalty and respect.

As sorely as Dakar longed for the undemanding warmth of Lysaer s'Ilessid's close company, his yearning came flawed as he played through the temptation of false steps. To take refuge with his friend was to embrace a wrong cause, and hunt down in turn another prince who was innocent at heart of self-blinded delusion.

Desh-thiere's curse had bent Arithon to private subter-fuge and flight, not as Lysaer, to raise a public cry to take arms for a misdirected justice.

Long before the brandy cask was emptied to the lees, Dakar threw aside his cup, bent his head on soaked wrists, and wept. For the means to win Lysaer's salvation from the blighting morass of Desh-thiere's curse remained his, to use or discard as he chose. His augury at Vastmark held good. He need only stand aside and let an arrow fly its course, and leave Arithon s'Ffalenn to meet his fate.

The set hour for the princess's ransom arrived like the crowning play of a chess match, each major piece allotted its place for a carefully arranged set of moves. Asandir and Luhaine kept Lysaer and Avenor's royal galley swathed under wards at the quayside. The force of their labours skewed the eye and shimmered the outlines of rail and rambarde like heat waves. Passersby and tradesmen backed off in stiff fear, making signs against evil. Though the spellworks in no way upset the sensibilities of draught animals, commerce recoiled. Carters snarled the side streets with vehicles to avoid the avenue by the docks.

Arithon remained in King Eldir's state apartments, Sethvir and Kharadmon in attendance.

Despite every safeguard and surety, each member of the Fellowship sensed the sliding, straining pressure as self-seeking energies within each half-brother strove to slip through restraint. Air itself held an unquiet tension. The limestone and brick of Ostermere's keeps became wont to spring stress cracks in the old, crumbled mortar. The Sorcerers had long suspected no forcible separation of the princes could quiet Desh-thiere's geas of enmity. Now, as they played subtle threads of constraint through layered curtains of spells to deflect the immediacy of its force, they saw their dread theory borne out.

'There's a radius of proximity, do you feel it?' Kharad-mon fumed in the hour the royal galley tied up in Ostermere's harbour. 'Despite all our seals and protections, this curse is a self-aware thing. There's a low-grade current that cross-links the princes beyond any power to subdue.'

'Unnatural,' Sethvir agreed, too immersed in defences to review the dire worry: that the passing of time intensified the danger. The princes' opposed gifts of light and of shadow, the world's best line of defence against the peril still active beyond South Gate, could not help but erode farther beyond reach of reconciliation through each successive encounter. The smallest mistake now would exacerbate the problem, until even Luhaine's fussy nature did not argue with necessity.

The exchange of Lady Talith for her ransom must be handled with consummate speed.

The event took place without fanfare or ceremony in Eldir's grand hall, the parquet floors cleared of carpets for the summer, and the galleries empty of curious courtiers. On the red baize dais, his state chair flanked by two dozen men-at-arms and six kingdom officials to stand witness, the High King of Havish presided. Ten coffers of gold lay piled by a counting table, where his *caithdein*, his royal seneschal, and the justiciar of the realm oversaw the tally of the ransom; then, the coin count confirmed, each box was set under lock and sealed with ribbon and wax impressed in Eldir's winged hawk blazon.

The borrowed carriage and retinue to bear the princess pulled up under guard at the inner gate. Through another postern, unarmed and unattended, Lord Commander Diegan was admitted by the oldest of the royal pages. As Avenor's ranking officer and Lady Talith's blood sibling, he would stand through due process as Lysaer s'Illessid's representative. Slitted light through the lancet windows by turns drowned and spattered the splendour of his white studs and velvet as he knelt by old custom and paid his respects to the high king.

On his carved chair, his knuckles splayed over the paired, crested heads of the gryphons carved rampant beneath his wrists, Eldir inclined his head. Composed as he seemed, he wished he were elsewhere, the princes departed, the startling blue snap of static that leaped off his fingertips from too close an acquaintance with ward fields banished from his city of Ostermere.

'Lord Commander Diegan,' he opened, 'I ask your oath on behalf of your prince that no violence will be presented to Arithon s'Ffalenn inside the bounds of my realm.'

'I so swear,' Lord Diegan intoned. 'Dharkaron as my witness, strike my liege dead if a sword under Avenor's banner should be first to raise bloodshed.'

'You have leave to proceed.' Eldir signalled his page, who accepted a heavy key and unlocked the door to a side chamber.

Prince Arithon entered, Lady Talith on his arm. Before the blinding magnificence of her finery, his simpler dress seemed a cry of sheenless dark against a scintillance of gold and white silk.

The only glint of light about the Shadow Master's person was the circlet of royal rank pressed over his black hair. He crossed the waxed floor in measured steps, Dakar at his shoulder, and Sethvir just behind in a new maroon robe banded in jet braid interlace.

Lord Diegan felt himself bristle, astounded to find how his memory had faded. Almost, he had forgotten the slight stature of Rathain's prince, and the insolence the man flaunted toward propriety. Overwhelmed by the intensity of his desire for revenge, the Lord Commander had to tear his gaze away to spare proper attention for his sister.

Talith looked in good health, if a trifle drawn. Dark

eyebrows and lashes framed eyes without artifice, tawny as glints off new brass. Her steps paired Arithon's with unwonted deference, Lord Diegan noticed. Too haughty to be meek, her cream features did not soften to the slightest hint of welcome.

If her spirit was unbroken, her stay with the enemy had not left her unchanged.

Lord Diegan clenched his hands in weaponless, bound rage for the misfortune which had turned his sister to a flesh-and-blood pawn, caught in the breach between enemies.

Then the party bringing Talith swept to a halt, the presence of the Master of Shadow scarcely a knife's thrust away. Frigidly clear, green eyes flicked up and met Lord Diegan's inimical features square on. 'My lord, your lady sister.' And he passed Talith onto the arm of her brother.

Her touch was ice, and her face, a marble mask. The cut glass brooch at her collar shimmered to her rhythmic breaths. Etarran to her core, her poise never wavered, yet her fingers on the sleeve of Diegan's court finery bit a death grip into the damask.

Forced to stifle his simmering anger, Avenor's Lord Commander delivered the message his liege lord had charged him to bestow on the Master of Shadow. 'The fortune you receive for your unconscionable act is an ill thing for our people in your hands. Along with the gold you've extorted, my prince includes this small token.' Diegan opened the wallet at his belt and handed over a slim leather packet.

By design, its strings were not tied. A crescent edge of brass snicked a slice through the gloom as the wrapping fell open. The contents became exposed to the recipient in full public view of the court. Colour left Arithon's face in raw streaks. He needed no second glance to identify the exquisite, engraved cross-staff last seen on the decks of the brig, *Black Drake*. Off Farsee, for repayment of passage, the instrument had been his free gift to Captain Dhirken. 'You had better say quickly how you came by this.'

'It tells its own story,' Lord Diegan answered in soft malice. 'Another of your collaborators was executed.'

'By whose order?' Too stunned for finesse, Arithon closed anguished fingers over the shining, fine lines of Paravian engraving. He seemed unaware, yet, of other eyes upon him, or of Sethvir's sharp attention just behind. 'Captain Dhirken owed me no loyalty. Her vessel was a hired charter I signed on for transport.' Unable to contain his incredulous anguish, he ended, 'As Ath is my witness, she'd have told you if she could. My affairs were never her sworn cause.'

'She made that claim in the hour she surrendered her command. Mearn s'Brydion believed her, until your token gave the lie to her testimony. She meant something to you,' Lord Diegan insisted, fired to elation to realize his liege had scored an astonishing victory. 'Or why bestow so priceless an heirloom on a stranger?'

'If I cared for her, your allies could have tested your case.' Arithon looked up, his voice like ground glass against the stilled tableau of the chamber. 'Mearn might have petitioned me for ransom. I could have brought evidence and witnesses to show the plain truth. Dhirken was not my close associate.' The facile, glib sarcasm he used to buy distance this once seemed ripped beyond reach.

Talith looked on, startled to a horrified glimmer of epiphany; Dakar hung suspended, while Sethvir raised a hand to forestall King Eldir from a disastrous order to deploy his poised men-at-arms. Yet the ripples of unrest in the background scarcely touched the Master of Shadow.

'I knew the *Drake*'s captain well enough,' he admitted. The steel of his masterbard's discipline unlocked his tongue at last; let him temper useless fury into sorrow.

'If she surrendered her brig, she showed her good faith in the expectation of fair treatment. Your justice betrayed that trust. The ruling which condemned her lay outside of mercy. I repeat, Captain Dhirken had no cause to die for any hired charge I laid on her.'

The Lord Commander of Avenor inclined his head, the sheen of his hair like rubbed onyx in the flame glow and his expression alight in flushed triumph. 'Then, your Grace, take care you befriend no more innocents.'

Diegan turned on his heel and departed, annoyed beyond words for the fleeting look backward his sister cast toward her former captor. For himself, he held no regret. Nor would he deny the implicit accusation, that Dhirken's life had been claimed for no better cause than to inflict small revenge on an enemy.

While Arithon's brigantine *Khetienn* slipped her cable and sped seaward before winds coaxed to favour by Kharadmon, Lysaer s'Ilessid accepted King Eldir's hospitality to spend the night ashore in joyful reunion with his lady. The couple were given private chambers behind guarded doors, with Fellowship protections to shield them until the active threat of Desh-thiere's curse dwindled back into quiescence.

'Not just yet,' Lysaer murmured in response to Talith's urgent need to speak. 'Let me look at you.' His warm hands roved over the lace that clothed her shoulders, then rose to cup the slant of her jawline. He tipped up her chin and trained a devouring gaze on her face. 'You're more lovely than I ever remembered.'

A tear swelled and slipped through the fringe of her lower lashes. Lysaer caught it on his knuckle, then began in awed reverence to explore the shorn ends of her hair. Strand after gilt strand sifted through his fingertips, to frond the smooth skin of her neck.

Talith began, 'I should never –'

Lysaer stopped her words with a brush of his lips. 'What's past is done. Don't trouble with regrets.' He closed his fingers over her nape and drew her into his kiss.

The months of separation had been too long, too strained; emotion charged the moment beyond bearing. Talith locked her arms around her husband for fear her knees might give way. 'My love, forget Vastmark. Leave the pursuit of useless war. I beg you instead, return home. Let us build a sound kingdom on the city you've raised at Avenor.'

Lysaer stroked his thumbs through the silky, short locks that curled against her temples. Temptation beckoned him. Her warmth in his arms made him feel restored, as though every fissure in his life could be closed into balance by the simple balm of her presence. 'My lady,' he answered in heartsore regret, 'there can be no peace anywhere until my warhost in the south ends the life of the Master of Shadow.'

'He's not worth your pursuit,' Talith murmured. 'His associates are craftsmen, sailhands, a half-starved band of shepherds. They support him for no grand cause.'

'My enemy would have you think that.' Lysaer disentwined his fingers from their sleek netting of hair, took her hand, and drew her across the floor, a mosaic interlace of dolphins and sea foam in shades of pastel blue and grey. A bed with silk hangings and blankets of spun cashmere had been left turned down by the servants. To one side, a table inlaid with lapis lazuli held wax candles in stands carved of sandalwood, a tray of sweet grapes and white wine. Pink roses shed fragrance from a vase. No need or small comfort had been omitted.

Lysaer swept his beloved in his arms and enthroned her amid the scented sheets. Neither drink nor fresh fruit were half so tempting as what swelled to each breath beneath the laced closure of her gown.

The prince decided to make a ceremony of her

undressing, and assuage their need to talk through the process. His unhurried hands began to unstring gold eyelets, while his eyes, shaded turquoise, drank her form. 'You weren't at Merior to see, my beloved. But a widow there had her twin children stolen away. A guardsman who lost his rank in the destruction of Alestron's armoury was held captive and horribly tortured. This Master of Shadow you wish to pardon used heated knives to mark his victim.'

'But I did meet Tharrick.' Talith could scarcely forget the scars. 'He told me himself. Arithon had no hand in what befell him.'

A bow slithered undone under Lysaer's ministrations. He worked a finger beneath the fabric and stroked. 'Enspelled by the snake, does the mouse tell the truth? We speak of a sorcerer who corrupts little children and lures them away from their mothers.'

'You speak of Jinesse's twins? Fiark and Feylind?' Talith sat up, the sweet, languid shudder coaxed from her by dalliance cancelled out by distress. 'But Arithon was right. The woman lost her husband. For need and for grief, she wanted her children tied to her apron strings.'

A small thread of chill curled through Lysaer's happiness. He propped his weight on one elbow and regarded his wife, whose allure left him breathless in her unstrung billows of dress lace. 'Lady, beloved.' He sighed, his forbearance framed in gentle patience. 'The Prince of Rathain is nothing if not subtle. You must recall as much from his byplay in Etarra. As well, he's a master at appearances. In ways without parallel, his wiles draw people in.'

Talith let her bodice slide from her bare shoulders. She shrugged the ribboned cuffs off her wrists. 'His mind is difficult to fathom. I'm not convinced he's a criminal.'

They were going to want the wine, after all. Lysaer fetched the carafe and filled two crystal goblets. He closed his lady's fingers upon the stem and watched her drink, his sapphire eyes dark with sympathy. 'I was taken in myself once, almost to my ruin. I never told you what I saw in a poor quarter alley the day before the Fellowship Sorcerers tried to crown the man as high king.'

Lysaer set his back against the headboard, then drew her to lean on his shoulder. The hand not tied up with the wineglass cupped her hip as he rested his chin on her crown. 'Arithon once built a miniature ship out of shadow to amuse a pack of knacker's conscripts. They were children, underfed and ill-used. His clever little sorceries made them laugh. I was led to believe he thought no one was watching, and his pity for the young ones made me love him.'

Lysaer spun the fluted crystal in slow turns between his fingers, his eyes fixed in memory, and fine sweat on his brow for a burden that still held the power to chafe him. 'The mask was designed,' he said, deadened by remorse. 'We marched into Strakewood and were slaughtered by traps, by subterfuge, by unspeakable nets of black sorcery. The killing was started and finished *by children*. They were the bait by which seven thousand townsmen came to die. Too late I understood how this Master of Shadow played upon my sympathies. In deliberate purpose, he made me believe he had a heart and a conscience. Then when the time suited, he used me as a dupe to further his bloody-handed slaughter.'

Talith set aside her emptied goblet. Silk slid on silk as she nestled against her husband, her hands working through his shirt to ease the tense muscles in his chest. 'There's a chance your intuition wasn't wrong,' she suggested, haunted to self-honesty by thought of Arithon's blanched features as the mask had slipped, once before Jinesse, again for Sethvir; and not least, today in the public presence of an enemy upon the hour he heard news of Captain Dhirken's death.

'Perhaps what you saw in that alley was real, and the

rest sprang from the meddling of Desh-thiere,' Talith said.

A bar of late sunlight sliced through the casement and illuminated Lysaer's face. Melted by his magnificence, Talith scarcely noticed how he studied her in turn, rapt as a man who laboured to unravel hidden meaning from a torn page of manuscript. In belief that he listened, she added, 'If the Fellowship Sorcerers are right, and the Mistwraith's curse forced this enmity to set your paired gifts of light and shadow at odds, why ruin our lives to pursue it?' She stroked the nap of gold stubble on his cheek and leaned into his solid comfort. 'Why not withdraw your warhost and wait? The truth will out soon enough. Either we'll see your half-brother raise arms against Tysan, or Arithon s'Ffalenn will go his own way and bloodshed can be avoided altogether.'

'Do you honestly believe this campaign is misguided?' Lysaer asked without emotion. 'What made you lose faith in my cause?'

'I saw Arithon s'Ffalenn go down on his knees to plead Fellowship protection from the curse,' Talith admitted. 'I was wrong, before. The crown prince I knew and hated in Etarra was a man I never understood.'

'He's bewitched you,' Lysaer whispered. 'Even you.' He pulled through the clasp of her arms and arose, his gaze still locked to her face. 'Sithaer's blind furies! I don't believe this happened. How many nights did he whisper in your ear to convince you of his innocence at Jaelot? Did he have an excuse for the seven men who burned in the destruction of Alestron's armoury?'

Talith's temper flared at her husband's shocked anguish, and for his assumption as well. 'Arithon s'Ffalenn made no such claim! Nor did he admit me to his confidence. Quite the contrary. We were enemies. But as a woman caught in the conflict between you, I could scarcely hide my eyes and stop my ears! The judgement I've drawn is my own.'

'But of course,' Lysaer said. 'His traps for the innocent are never any less than diabolically perfect.'

Talith surged erect in a flushed, magnificent rage. 'How dare you!' Her half-discarded gown bared her perfect, rose-tipped breasts. The necklace of white glass at her throat fanned a sparkle at each breath. Unconscious of her charms in the throes of her conviction, she was powerfully seductive, temptation enough to freeze a man's reason and undo him.

Lysaer stepped back, mortally afraid. He longed to stay lost, then trembled for the urge. His honour as prince seemed a strident, dry duty, fed to ripe weakness by the strangling ties of love already spun about his spirit.

In his wife's presence, he beheld his own downfall, and his shocking self-revulsion must have showed.

'Merciful Ath, what are you thinking?' Talith raised her arms. 'Do you imagine I was sent back to corrupt you?'

Again Lysaer retreated from her touch.

'Daelion save us both, you infer a base congress!' Shattered beyond pride, Talith resorted to entreaty. 'Your enemy laid neither hand nor tie upon me!'

Quite the opposite was true. Once she had surrendered to recognition of his assets, Arithon had been scrupulous to avoid her company. Yet the damage had happened regardless: beyond all salvation, the poison of mistrust raised a solid wall between the affection and forgiveness two people required for future happiness.

'This wasn't meant to be,' Talith protested, the first break of heartache in her appeal. 'The ransom was done for gold, to pay for the defence to meet the allied might of your war host.'

'Truth or subterfuge, what does it matter?' Lysaer braced his weakened stance on the back of a stuffed chair. 'My nemesis has spoiled your belief in me.'

Her beauty was changeless, unforgettable. The tender need that had made her long months of captivity a living misery to endure coalesced to sharp pain, as a scalpel might open living flesh. The extreme, harsh strength Lysaer engaged to keep from breaking turned his face to a mask of white ice.

Unstrung, not yet unmanned, he clung raggedly to principle. His heartbreak was terrible to witness as he strove to overmaster the bitter fruit of this betrayal. Royal as he was, raised to hold judgement in the face of self-sacrifice, the burden of bloodline had never before shackled him so harshly. Every line of his elegance was racked out of true, his self-belief shaken by mortal passion.

'Oh, my dear!' Talith cried, unable to bear the gulf she sensed as it widened. 'Nothing has changed in my life or my love that ever mattered between us.' She moved again, begging the embrace that promised affirmation, to refound the basis of their union.

Lysaer cried out. He shoved the chair in her path, one hand raised, while the other fumbled blindly for the latch. Then he reached the door, dragged it open.

He was going to step through. Talith pressed her hands to her lips and pleaded through tears for one word in reconciliation. 'I implore you, don't leave this here. Don't let an enemy stand between us.'

The sight of her, broken-spirited and begging for his sympathy, and yet still firm in her defection, snapped the last of Lysaer's pride. 'Before Ath, how I loved you!' he cried in strangled sorrow.

Then the door thudded to. The latch plinked and caught. Sheltered on the far side, the Prince of the West pressed his cheek against the painted panel, punished to a vista too harrowing to admit the balm of tears.

His suffering made the moment too real. The scent of waxed wood; the startled flight of two maidservants caught idle and gossiping in the corridor; tiny things, each burned in bleak imprint that ripped away hope of self-denial.

Lysaer squeezed his fists closed. The dig of his nails into flesh gave no surcease. Memory harrowed him in every vicious detail; still he saw Lady Talith's appalled shock as her loss shredded the last tissue of her hope. He saw her skin lose all tint; the blushed tips of her breasts a cry of colour the more punishing for the surge as desire remained to hound his flesh before a need that made him quiver like an addict.

For of course, he could not entrust her now to bear his heir. He could never again treasure her unsullied company, nor allow her inside his defences. Not without suffering her suborning influence and the deadly, real chance she might seduce him to abandon law and justice.

Once passion escaped reason, a man could go mad.

Lysaer cursed his weakness. If one fool had been blind enough to lose himself to love, the blame for the turned weapon was an enemy's. Through tears of hurt for his wife's tragic usage, like a litany against demons, the Prince of the West recited the lethal chain of logic that undid him.

'Never gold, you inhuman, soulless bastard. The ransom and the raid, they were all smoke and ruse. Your purpose with Lady Talith was *this*, and no other: to pierce and to weaken and to level by storm the only exposed place within my heart.'

Ways and Means

Sethvir returns to Althain Tower after an absence of five months and on his doorstep finds Lirenda, First Enchantress of the Koriathain; and to her tartly-phrased demand for the return of her order's Great Waystone, he replies, 'I've been wondering for the past five hundred years when you ladies would trouble yourselves to ask. Why not come in for tea . . . ?'

Spurred on by outrage over the piracy that has caused Talith's ransom to be paid twice over, a delegation of Tysan's city mayors and trade ministers gather in council at the crossroads city of Erdane, and the document they thrash through in state language is the draft of a charter to acknowledge Lysaer's right of succession to Tysan's high kingship, underwritten by town law . . .

While Avenor's royal galley rows north bearing Princess Talith back home to the towers of Avenor, her husband drives south with all speed; and like darkening storm, his armies mass on the borders of Vastmark to wreak vengeance and death upon the Master of Shadow before the onset of winter . . .

VII. *GRAND AUGURY*

Dawn broke in a spray of high cirrus over the Westland Sea. Tossed like a chip on the royal blue swell, the brigantine *Khetienn* ploughed southeastward in an offshore course, her bowsprit hazed under plumed sheets of spray, and her stretched canvas bent to the force of each following gust. Dakar the Mad Prophet sat on a bight of rope, a woeful stream of water frayed by the wind off the screwed ends of his hair. He was not seasick.

'I wish I'd had a sword,' he said in black vehemence. 'So help me, someone should have paid for Dhirken's death.'

The voice of Kharadmon flung back through the keening air. 'To what use? Vengeance won't bring her back. Arithon told you the same.'

'Then went ahead and vented his scalded nerves on his seamen.' Dakar rolled his eyes at the creaking gear aloft, while behind him at the wheel, the quartermaster and two sailhands wrestled oaths through clenched teeth, straining to man the rank helm. 'Fiends plague, we're risking every stick in this tub to a gale, and not one sail with a reef tied in!'

'I do have more finesse than to rip out her canvas,'

Kharadmon said in reproof. When his accuser failed to return an apology, the discorporate Sorcerer added a breezy remonstrance that tweaked the untidy hems and untucked laces of the Mad Prophet's sodden state garments.

'We're in a hurry because *Khetienn* has debts against her at Innish,' someone said in unwarranted explanation. 'I want them cleared before the notes come due.'

Dakar's sullen brooding gave way to awareness that Arithon s'Ffalenn stood behind him, and had probably overheard his last comment. Braced for unpleasantness, he spun to look.

State doublet and silk shirt had been changed for a sailor's smock with several generations of tar stains. Beneath wind-snatched dark hair, the Shadow Master's expression showed no stripped edge of reprimand, but a self-haunted directness Dakar had never seen.

Arithon addressed a query to the invisible presence of the Sorcerer. 'If Dhirken could be condemned for the honest charter of her brig, what in Ath's mercy will befall Talith?'

'Do you really wish to know?' Kharadmon's interrupted appeal to the winds whirled into a small eddy that chased droplets over the deck.

'I must,' said Arithon in stark demand.

'Why care?' Dakar broke in. 'Talith was insufferably arrogant. She flaunted her looks outright to manipulate an opening for intrigue.' To the Fellowship spirit which arrowed above the brigantine's masthead, he added, 'I watched the whole thing. Arithon kept his distance from the lady as though she were fiend-plagued and venomous!'

'So he did,' Kharadmon agreed. Wind screamed through stays, and the brigantine slammed smoking through another swell. A green swirl of waters slapped across her rails, to drain in throaty gurgles through her scuppers. 'Despite that care, Talith came to recognize

Arithon's compassion. She was too proud to play false with her husband. And she believed Lysaer's judgement was not impaired. Desh-thiere's curse showed her the error of her trust, but too late.'

'Her marriage is ruined,' Arithon concluded in an anguish that begged against hope for contradiction.

Kharadmon was not wont to soften the impact of cause and effect. 'Lysaer will never lie with her again. He'll honour her position and not flaunt a mistress. But his liaison with his wife until the day of her death will be kept to a state formality.'

'He'd put her aside?' Incredulous, Dakar shoved up straight. The *Khetienn* rolled. Braced through a particularly virulent dousing, he became torn into conflicted interests by Arithon's precipitous departure.

'Believe it,' Kharadmon finished. 'The lady came back having seen too much. The marred gift of s'Ilessid justice won't let Lysaer abide the ambiguity.'

Ice-cold, shivering in suspicion that rang clear through to his bones, Dakar laced stubborn, red fingers over his streaming knees. Fellowship Sorcerers were ever subtle players. The distinct possibility could not be ignored that Kharadmon might play his sympathies against Lysaer for a purpose; particularly if Sethvir sensed any echo that he harboured a secret augury on Arithon's life.

Dakar lacked the straight courage to confront the matter outright; and at an indeterminate point inside the next hour Kharadmon left the *Khetienn* to make her way south on the world's winds.

The seamen changed watch at nightfall before the Mad Prophet caught the startling anomaly: Arithon had made no other appearance on the brigantine's deck since his disjointed inquiry after the fate of Princess Talith.

The weather had eased with the sunset. *Khetienn* sailed large, rocking to a fair weather swell. Her course bent due south, and wind off her quarter flapped the royal pennon no one had troubled to run down from the masthead. A game of dice was under way in the galley; the whoop of a winner and the pound of a fist against wood drummed up from the trestle belowdecks. Topside, sails and rigging carved the starry sky in neat order; too neat, the Mad Prophet surmised. As if the mate on watch had tidied the *Khetienn*'s lines and spars in the expectation no adjustments would be asked.

'Himself went below,' the quartermaster answered in laconic response to Dakar's concern. 'Said, let him bide. He didn't want to know if the wind changed. Steward was turned off, also. No food and no service before morning.'

Dakar's pulse quickened in alarm. Adamant as Arithon could be when he desired solitude, he was an irreproachable captain. Never before had he failed to oversee every nuance of sail trim and course. His slackened attentiveness now made no sense, not when the *Khetienn* was engaged in a race to reach Shand ahead of Lysaer's galley.

'Fiends,' swore the quartermaster, his brow creased with disbelief for the determined set to Dakar's stance. 'Oh man, you're not going down after him. The fool who tries his temper, I swear on my hindparts, is fair askin' to get the gizzard knifed out o' him.'

But like the misfortunate princess, Dakar had been too far and seen too much. From an altered perspective he scarcely knew for his own, he lashed out at the helmsman in anger. 'Did you never think? Arithon's not indestructible, however hard he tries to act the part. He's just been told another friend passed the Wheel. The upset can't help but aggrieve him.'

The staid old quartermaster looked wary, his eyes knurled in wrinkles like walnuts. 'True or not,' he allowed, 'I'd rather you twist the snake's tail than me.'

Dakar returned an epithet, not cheered by the thought

that for once in his born life, Asandir would have praised him. 'I've been a dimwit since the second I drew breath.' Still grousing under his breath in sad misery, he squeezed his girth down the companionway. 'Even a dog has the good sense to know when it's too old and simple to change.'

The sterncastle door lay ahead, an unlit square of dark varnish. Dakar weighed his outright cowardice against his unspeakable fear; and terror won. He stepped forward, entered, and bumbled against the heave of the vessel down the narrow corridor to the captain's quarters.

His knock went unanswered. The door, unsurprisingly, proved locked.

'Open,' snapped Dakar, out of tolerance with unease. 'If you don't, so help me, Arithon, I'm going to break the latch. And not by neat sorcery, either.'

No sound came from the far side. To a half-snarled oath, then a rushed prayer to Ath, the Mad Prophet lowered his chin for a bull's charge, prepared to crash his shoulder against the wood.

The latch tripped and the panel whipped open to reveal Arithon in his shirtsleeves. 'I asked not to be troubled,' he said in ruthless annoyance. 'The quartermaster warned you. Is this loyalty, Dakar? Or, Sithaer forbid, an attempt to shepherd my conscience?'

'None of those.' Dakar straightened up, dusky as a plum. A self-control he never knew he possessed held him steady as he raked his attention over the prince who opposed him. The clothing and hair, faintly dishevelled, and green eyes acute in their focus gave him scant grounds for reassurance. He planted himself amid the opened doorway in outright, stubborn intent.

'By all means,' cried Arithon in explosive antagonism. 'If you're going to make an occasion of my mistakes, you might as well come inside. The whole blighted crew doesn't need to share in the happy exhibition.'

As the Shadow Master cleared the passage, Dakar saw

347

beyond to the damning array of items laid out in the spill of the lamp on the chart table.

'You were going to break in,' Arithon said by way of rough defence for the small stone pipe, and the opened cap of a canister whose spice-scented contents snapped Dakar's foreboding into dread.

'Ath's own infinite mercy!' The Mad Prophet spun to face down the Prince of Rathain, unmindful of temper, uncaring how he meddled, this once in his life a Fellowship spellbinder upbraiding a fellow mage for sheer idiocy. *What were you thinking to do?* You can't try an augury under influence of tienelle. *You've blinded your talent!* The poisons in that herb will run their course beyond control. If the toxins don't land you stone dead, you'll end up crippled or witless.'

'That can be argued,' Arithon said, his fury burned down to rankling sarcasm as he twisted the key in the lock. 'Davien's works and the Five Centuries Fountain should put your unpleasant point to the test.'

Dakar fell back and sat with a thud on the cabin's lower berth. True to his own form when high stakes left him shaky, he forgot the most salient details.

As Arithon regarded him in nasty hilarity, he resisted with mulish annoyance. 'You've got longevity protection, no more than that. It doesn't make you immortal. The Fountain's effects might keep your body alive, but nothing about the Betrayer's handiwork can guard you from going insane. Lost to mage-sight, your mind will be undone and naked.'

'Well then, one way or another, I won't be self-blinded after this,' the Shadow Master said. He sought the tienelle scrying for more than just augury. Plainly he intended to use the same means to smash down the blocks which disbarred his access to his arcane perception.

'I've never known you to be such an outright fool.' From Dakar, the censure fell bitter.

Arithon crossed the cramped cabin, turned before the dark panes of the stern window. The confined space snapped his temper, and he spun; slammed a fist in cornered force against the bulkhead.

'Listen,' he said in breaking desperation. 'If I keep on making errors of judgement and see every friend I have come to grief, I'm going to be driven mad anyway.' The fallow glow of lamplight lined his shoulders and the suffering, stark edge of an expression kept turned beyond view. 'Tharrick was tortured. Dhirken and Maenalle were executed. Merior's now the bound outpost of Avenor, and Talith –'

'*Stop this!*' Dakar cracked. 'You aren't responsible for everybody's lives! You can't let yourself be ruled by their choices, no matter how much the s'Ffalenn royal gift leaves you exposed to their hurt.'

Arithon whirled, his eyes defenseless in pain as few ever saw, and terrible for the depth of their vision. 'Ath preserve, we're not talking about individuals this time. If I make a miscall against this warhost in Shand, the Vastmark tribes will be scattered. Erlien's clansmen are also involved, and outside my sovereignty to forbid. Do you think I can live with a repeat of Tal Quorin, but on a scale to make that massacre seem an exercise? Save us all! My feal clans in Rathain were all but destroyed the last time Etarra marched to war.'

'I'm sorry,' Dakar said, still obstinate as a dog caught lounging muddy in silk sheets. 'I can't stand aside and let you take such a risk.'

Arithon gave way to a laugh that cut off in abject disgust. 'I only meant to drive you *out* of my affairs. What I've gotten instead is an interfering ally, and Dharkaron witness! I'd rather you stayed drunk.'

'No ally at all,' Dakar amended, crisp above the thunder of the wake as the brigantine nosed through a swell. 'You forget. We're eighty leagues from land and I don't know the first wretched rule of navigation.'

'All right.' Arithon pushed from the bulkhead, his tension rueful in capitulation. 'You've won your right to berate my choice of timing. If we're going to argue, at least use your powers as spellbinder to set a minor binding on that door latch. There could be other crewmen with the interfering guts to break down my joinery and investigate.'

Dakar shoved up, staggered, caught a handhold, and banged his head in the ridiculous train of mishap that passed for locomotion on a ship. When the heave of the deck let him reach the companionway, he bent to the door lock and cast the spun thread of his consciousness through his fingers to engage the rusted dregs of his training.

The Name of the wood answered him, clean as new song. He had never felt so fired to self-awareness. As he marvelled at the change, he scarcely heard the step behind him. Nor could he react, lost in trance as he was, or feel aught but the pain of the hard, sure blow that slammed into his nape and felled him.

Dakar awoke, limp as a slit meal sack, and sprawled out prone in the cramped little corridor outside of *Khetienn*'s master cabin. His mouth tasted like baitfish. The lump on the back of his neck flamed his skull and his shoulders into a jellied mass of aches. These exploded to white sparkles of shot pain the instant he tried to move. With his cheek pressed to oak, and his fists crimped under his breastbone, he groaned a string of oaths that came out all vowels against the battering effects of s'Ffalenn temper.

For a racked span of minutes, he lay slack before a hurt that undid his desire for survival.

Forward, through the sluice of parted waves and the creak as a sheetline tugged through a stiff block, the click of ivory dice and laughter drifted back as a sailhand finished a joke about a whore and a belaying pin. The talk turned to gossip. Someone else joined in comment that made laughingstock of Dakar's lame-brained effort to butt into Arithon's business.

'Coldcocked the interfering fool, right enough,' came the excited baritone of the bosun. 'You didn't see him? He's sprawled out flat beyond the aft companionway, senseless as a skinful of sausage. We've got us a wager that says he won't stir until the midnight change in the watch.'

The Mad Prophet mumbled another oath to the deck boards, though, in fact, he bore the sailhands small rancour. Rather, he wished he had a bet of his own on. The pull of the stars against his bludgeoned awareness showed he was awake against all the odds. The least he deserved was a round of winnings for his troubles since the pain scarcely let him keep breathing.

In natural complication, Arithon s'Ffalenn would have gone on to try the unthinkable.

The breath Dakar drew to fortify himself came burdened: the frost-clean bite of tienelle fumes trailed from the crack underneath the stern cabin's door. He understood he had no choice but to burst in and measure the extent of the damage. A dead prince was an altogether safer prospect than Arithon bound insane in a prescient trance while entangled in the geas of Deshthiere's curse.

As if in response to that surge of jagged fear, something in the cabin crashed over to a scream of splintering wood.

Jolted to hurry, Dakar took a jelly-legged step and thumped into the door panel. The latch had been wedged from the far side and the key left turned in the lock.

'Dharkaron's Spear and Chariot!' Working magecraft in the pinch of a thumping headache was his particular hated pastime.

His palms printed sweat marks on the varnish as he leaned on the lintel alongside the fastenings. He moaned, shut his eyes, then let his awareness filter like fingers of light through the layered grain of the wood. Fused within its substance, Dakar sensed the kissed warmth of summer and the rainfall that had nourished the cut tree. Against the airy grace of its substance, the latch stood out, a bright cry of resonance wrought screaming in hammer strokes and forge fire. The pin was brass, and had been braced with a rolled leather map case. The hides of its making, to mage-sense, still reeked of the stock pens where the bullock had been slaughtered before skinning.

In need of a moment to resettle his nerves, the Mad Prophet measured his options.

The imbalance required to tip the obstruction and cause it to skid out of place was infinitesimal. A busy sea surrounded him with inanimate energy his powers could tap without the encumbrance of permissions. Dakar reached out, borrowed force from the brigantine's laggard roll, then deflected a random twist of motion. The bracing map case clattered clear, which left the lock, a grim, black lump of opaque vibration stamped in the acid tang of wrought steel.

Dakar cradled his head before a sharp flash of pain behind his temples. He had no skill with cold iron. The secret of its mystery always twisted through his grasp; chased reason into knots that left him gasping. Battered to a mood of monumental ill temper, he tried the unbinding anyhow. The guttural command to raise the signature of steel passed his lips. Then he asked the permission, and stunned himself witless when the lock sang back in vibration and answered.

The mechanism turned; the bar slipped aside, and the door gave, creaking, and swung open.

The lamp on the table within had burned down to a sickly red glow. Its faltering flame winnowed as the brigantine tossed her course through the swell, silting the blue gloom of smoke which overhung its glass cover. The pungency of narcotic spice stung Dakar's nostrils.

Even spent to dilution, his first coughing breath spun a flick of raw fire through his nerves. The aches in his body incinerated with a scintillant flash of heat. His senses whirled, teased to a half-glimpse behind the veil of wider consciousness, not unlike the sickening plunge into vertigo that preceded his prophetic visions.

But this was no moment of augury. Too well, Dakar recognized the wretched first kick of the drug that initiated a tienelle trance. Its perils at least framed a dance he was well schooled to master. He huffed the air from his lungs and grounded his senses, then closed down his mage-sight behind a blank barrier of will. He would see only what was traced out in common flame light, and hear only what sound grazed his ears.

The confines of the cabin swam clear once again. The lamp panes glinted ruby gold. Fanned in hot light lay the stone pipe, discarded and cold, its crumbled ash scattered from the bowl. Black flecks remained where the strayed cinders had cooled, pitting scorch marks in the varnish. The canister rested open on its side, its treacherous dregs upset. A stipple of silver-grey leaves strewed in patterns across the board, winnowed and licked by the draught.

Arithon's chair stood empty. The blankets on his berth were rucked into snarls, the sheets half-torn from the mattress. Chart chest, hanging locker, cabinet, and logbook, all were closed and still neatly latched, which left only the well of gloom on the deck, buried in attenuated shadow.

Sweating through apprehension, Dakar resumed his search. He scanned past a jumble of upset quills, the smashed veneer of a lacquered coffer; beyond these, a hand in faint outline, spread out and locked, the tight-fitted bones of a face pressed into a cradling forearm. Arithon lay curled on his side beneath the bowed curve of the stern window.

Too clumsy to move with the heave of the deck, Dakar crashed past the chart table and dropped to one knee beside the prince. His drug-heightened hearing drummed to the din of white foam off the wake, unreeling across starlit ocean a yard beneath the sill. He firmed his control against a dread that made him cringe, reached across darkness, and touched.

The bared nape of Arithon's neck was ice-cold and beaded in sweat. A shudder jarred from the contact. Dakar heard the saw of an indrawn breath over the squeak of steering cables as the *Khetienn*'s helmsman took up a spoke to ply the rudder to weather.

Dakar gave the unresponsive shoulder a shake. 'Arithon?'

No movement answered.

The lantern flame on the table wobbled and dimmed, its spill of bloodied light tremulous in recovery. Opened to options by the narcotic in the air, Dakar extended his spellbinder's knowledge into a feather of inquiry; and power answered. The lantern wick spurted up in false brilliance, enough to let him measure the prince's life signs.

Under their blued lids of flesh, his pupils were expanded black wells. Arithon's limbs were dangerously cool, the reflex that spasmed the muscles to burn off deep chill reduced to intermittent, thin shudders. His pulse was erratic and fast, his skin drenched, and his tissues scoured to a dangerous, toxic dehydration.

The symptoms of tienelle poisoning were multiple and savage, a rigour no practising mage would undertake at less than the peak of mental fitness. Warmth and fluids were immediate needs. Given water, the body could flush some of the effects.

Dakar scrambled to the berth, tore off a wadded blanket, and tucked it over Arithon's still frame. The lantern on the chart table started shuddering in wild spurts, its oil reservoir plumbed dry. The Mad Prophet let the flame go out. By touch and by mage-sight, he found the cask and the cup laid at hand to counter the tienelle's initial side effects. A brazier stood readied, but unlit, to prepare infusions of herbal tea.

Afraid the debilitating symptoms had progressed past the reach of simple remedy, Dakar knelt with Arithon's fine-boned fingers cradled between his two hands. A pang rocked through him for the musical legacy Halliron had left Athera, set into irrevocable jeopardy.

For the physical damage was not yet severe. A fatal poisoning by tienelle took hours to run its due course. Worse peril threatened the defenceless mind, spiralling uncontrolled through a visionary trance without access to sighted guidance to stabilize the vaulting flight of expanded awareness. The trained mage who offered help for the floundering spirit was as prone to stray and drown in the selfsame nightmare vortex.

Here was proper work for a Fellowship Sorcerer, not for any bumbling apprentice who had wasted his centuries of instruction chasing whores and getting paralytic drunk. Dakar held no pretence. Since he lacked the practised skill to send a distress call over leagues of open ocean, the best he could do was seek contact with Sethvir through the earth link bequeathed by the Paravians.

The Mad Prophet shoved his bulk upright, clawed open the lid of the chart table, and scrounged out the flake of slate kept for windy days to weight the pages of the brigantine's logbook. He rummaged through drawers for a candle and a penknife. The ritual he employed was simplicity itself: scribe a distress rune in blood on the rock, set the mark in new flame, then unlatch the stern casement and let the construct splash overboard into the sea.

The rune, the blood, and the imprint left by fire on the extreme staid energies of stone would disrupt the patterned resonance of saltwater. If Althain's Warden was not too preoccupied, he would detect the anomaly and send aid.

Crouched on his hams, his elbows jammed against the sill, Dakar waited, while the minutes crept past and the brigantine's wake unreeled like crochet on dark silk under starlight. The flake of slate by now should have settled to the sea bottom. Arithon's prone form lay unmoving, all but unbreathing, a discouraging sign. Dakar would rather have seen him thrash in nightmares. Convulsions, screams of delirium, the most unpleasant twitch of life would have been better than such stark, disoriented stillness.

Dakar fidgeted, desperate. The wait had extended too long. Sethvir was not going to respond. Any of a thousand small crises might preoccupy the Sorcerer's attention; or he might hear clearly enough, but be hard-pressed with other trials, and have no discorporate colleague available to dispatch help.

When a quarter hour passed, Dakar had no choice but to confront the dire prospect that the problem was his own, to master or fail on his merits. The ghost of Jilieth haunted him still for shortcomings he had not sought to remedy. Guilt racked him. The alternative was to do nothing, to risk Athera to the unleashed effects of Arithon's madness, whipped on to who knew what lengths by the driving hatreds engendered by Desh-thiere's curse.

Dakar closed the casement and bent over the prone form at his feet. He firmed hold on his mage-sense and cast a shallow probe into the veils of unconsciousness to try and raise the Shadow Master back to primal awareness. His effort met and drowned in a velvet layer of darkness. He felt battened in shadow, adrift. The surface currents of Arithon's mind were untenanted, blank and reflectionless and still as an unrippled lake.

Dakar roused and opened his eyes. Forced by need to an unkind choice, he cursed Daelion Fatemaster to be left alone at the crux of such crisis. With *Khetienn* at sea, he could scarcely engage the services of a herb witch to spin him small talismans of protection. If the volume of saltwater beneath the ship's keel would buffer his effort from the unshielded presence of the sailhands, the blessing came mixed. Bedamned if he would try a deeper sounding while wedged beneath the chart table, and the unkind roll of a following sea rattled his bones like a string puppet. Since Arithon was built small enough for even a fat man to heft, Dakar shouldered to the effort, half dragging the Master of Shadow across the deck.

Movement and disturbance roused a flicker of tension in the unconscious man's frame. His lips moved in whispered entreaty, '*Are they safe yet?*'

A static flash of mage-sight closed the contact between them: some leftover channel from the link forged through the child's failed healing in Vastmark, raised active by the tienelle fumes. From Arithon, the Mad Prophet snatched the tattered image of trees burning. Against that flashfire rage of white heat, sword-bearing figures reeled and cried, entangled in the light-caught contortions of a desperate, killing struggle.

Sickness shot through Dakar's belly. He knew what he saw: the memory reborn in Arithon's mind, of the war that had ruined eight thousand lives on the banks of the River Tal Quorin. The blank darkness encountered in his earlier probe had been nothing else but a Shadow Master's mesh of defences, set nine years past to smother all Strakewood and quench out the reiving flame loosed by Lysaer's gift of light.

Overturned into dread, Dakar rolled his limp burden onto the wadded bedding on the berth. The tienelle visions had not led Arithon's awareness outside of himself. Instead, he was lost in relivings, damned by his own pity and unable to win reprieve from his burden of s'Ffalenn conscience as perception turned inward to unstring him.

Dakar sat and laid the prince's sweat-soaked head in his lap. Nerves he never knew he possessed recoiled in trepidation as he steadied himself into balance. He had nothing in that poised moment to suggest the best way to begin. With a whimper of fear, he smoothed back damp black hair and closed his eyes. He let his awareness unreel into stillness, then turned down to plumb the racked depths of the mind beneath his hands.

The last thing he recalled was a scream to pierce the *Khetienn's* very timbers; perhaps his own. Horror closed over him, *worse than nightmare,* for the pain he came to suffer in rapport with the Shadow Master became real with the impact of unalloyed experience . . .

Dakar shared the fell massacre at Tal Quorin, not as retelling described it, nor even in the history rerendered by art to the majestic tragedy of Halliron's ballad. Instead, first-hand, he heard the screams spawned by rapine, as Pesquil turned headhunters loose to despoil mothers and young girls; he beheld the flash-burned remains of the women and children Lysaer had annihilated in one blast of cold strategy, to draw Arithon's allies in a hot rush of vengeance, to be entrapped and slaughtered in their turn. He cried in terror for the tearing forces that had burned through Arithon's hands, as the Master of Shadow undertook the unthinkable to achieve the impossible: as he bent his knowledge of grand conjury to kill to spare Deshir's clans from annihilation.

The harrowing went beyond even this, as in wounding pain that could find no atonement, Arithon walked the battleground in the deeps of the night. Again and again over the corpses of slain victims, of townsman and clanborn, of woman and child, he called power through the Paravian ritual to reweave their violent deaths. Beyond the dregs of his strength, on the shining, wilful force of spirit alone, he had absolved the shade of each lost and grieving victim and set them free to find Ath's highest peace.

Repulsed on a wave of untenable pain, Dakar reacted from reflex, cried Name to reaffirm self. Stunned separate from reeling confusion, he wove over torn thought a stinging hedge of screens to isolate the thread of his consciousness. His defences unfurled like sparkles of spun light, then shimmered before an answering counterforce.

A blow hammered down out of nowhere. Dakar felt his fragile defences smashed and then winnowed like metal exploded under heat to a glittering, scintillant shower of spent force. In the instant before blackness roared over his focus, he realized his intrusion had raised Arithon's reflexive protections.

Then, spinning, twisting, battered to sickening vertigo, he was flung off into rarefied, airless darkness that burned him all over in stinging pain.

Dakar came to retching, flattened on his side in the salt-musty cabin aboard the brigantine. He was weeping, wrung; scarcely himself. His back was wedged at a horrible angle against the leg of the chart table. Bruises and wrenched joints combined to a fiendish chorus of aches. Slats from the broken coffer dug into his thigh. A spilled bin of quills winnowed under his right cheek, tickling his nose at each breath. Warning viced over his tissues, prickling prelude to a violent reflex to sneeze.

He batted the feathers away and sat up, engrossed in black curses. His glare pierced through darkness and found the Master of Shadow, roused now to jerks and small thrashes in the hellish grasp of nightmare where he lay, still unconscious on the berth.

'Damn you, prince. Of course, you'd be guarded, even past the gates of unconsciousness.' Too late, in pungent resentment, Dakar recalled a comment of Asandir's that had outlined the very effect.

A simpleton should have recalled. Arithon's was a

brilliant and forthright discipline. While life lasted, and self-will, he was too much the trained mage to stop fighting to reassume his control. His grandfather's early schooling had instilled rigorous defences against possession, the telling, likely reason why he had managed to resist the wide-reaching effects of Desh-thiere's curse.

Lysaer s'Ilessid had owned no such advantage of protection. First-hand, in sorry clarity, Dakar had to recognize why the Fellowship Sorcerers had chosen the fair-haired half-brother for the sacrifice through the Mistwraith's battle to confinement.

Had Arithon been risked, had the wraiths reached and turned him, the result could have spun his very strengths and trained power outside of all sane restraint.

Broken to fresh grief for old cruelties, Dakar sat in a cold sweat and chewed over the quandary ceded to his unwilling judgement. He could not heal this tienelle poisoning without inner consent from a mind that had already ranged far distant, vaulted on the drugged tides of vision to inflamed reliving of the past. Feeling battered, the Mad Prophet mumbled mixed lines of invective and self-pitying prayer. He lacked the stomach to suffer the private layers of Arithon's anguish. Yet his limited frame of knowledge allowed him no other means of access.

For his moment of rapport had revealed what was wrong. He had traced the channels of Arithon's lost powers, seared first by misuse, then racked, forced, compelled to overextend beyond the wise limits of talent and strength. The scars of past experience had healed over time, but not into functional recovery. Guilt remained, a bleak, damning barrier locked fast by the royal s'Ffalenn gift of mercy.

Dakar saw too clearly, and the damage made him weep. Too easily, the power to raise grand conjury for destruction might fall sway to the Mistwraith's directive to kill. Arithon feared beyond life to bear the result. The very compassion of his bloodline intervened, to blind and to deafen; to block off beyond even irrational reach all the fires of bright power born in him.

The hour grew late. Silted in shadow, the stern cabin rocked in twisting violence as the brigantine plunged with a crash of spray through a trough. The swell was building. Jounced to the shudder and thrum of rising gusts through the rigging, aware of vibration singing down through the hull, Dakar sensed the first warning of ill weather.

As if hazed by the creaking distress of his vessel, Arithon's fingers spasmed a tortured grip in the blankets. His head arched back, and he groaned. His nightmares of old bloodshed had begun to fray into delirium and tear at his living spirit.

The progression would grow worse. Dakar knew for a clammy, cold surety that the tienelle's effects had not peaked. He dared not try to face Arithon's devils, nor attempt to partner the blazing expanded consciousness of a drug vision unless he assisted his paltry perception as well.

'Damn you to Sithaer,' he groused as he arose to grope after the discarded stone pipe. Being milled under by the wheels of Dharkaron's Chariot was a kindness beside the wretched discomfort of withdrawal from a tienelle trance.

Dakar packed the bowl with the dry, silver-notched leaves, set the stem between his lips, snapped flint to striker, and inhaled.

The next instant, the deck of the brigantine seemed to swoop and rock from beneath him. His senses smashed under a starburst of white fire and dropped him spinning into vertigo. Wherever Arithon had collected his plants, they were of rarely stringent potency. Dakar squeezed his eyes shut, alarmed through the unfolding climb of his higher awareness. Before he smoked, he should have counted the hours since the last time he had eaten; in punitive proportion, he would know how wretchedly he could expect to be sick.

Then that detail whirled from his mind as the narcotic bit into the core of his being and vaulted him to visionary prescience.

He steered back to the berth without stumbling *because he sensed in advance* how the wind would gust. Sucked into a multiple, overlaid perception, he could forecast cause and effect, every natural force laid against sail and bolt rope and frail wood. The tienelle's scouring coil showed him *which way the deck would come to roll.* In a scalding burn of clear sight, his mind spiralled outward to trace how wind and sea would braid and spin cloud into a cyclonic axis of black storm.

Dakar grabbed the bulkhead, gasping in deep, aching breaths. His feet felt rooted straight down through the ship's hull. Beyond the abyss, icy fathoms beneath, he could have counted each grain of sand on the sea's floor. His head floated, wrapped in the singing bands of energies that were stars. The startling clarity of his insight went beyond prior experience, even through scryings under Fellowship auspices at solstice convocations. Whether his heightened powers had been induced by stress, or by the clean state of living he had embraced since Vastmark, he had no chance to determine.

Necessity required every nuance of art he could manage to cobble together.

The Mad Prophet sank to his knees, one hand on the Shadow Master's forehead, the other placed over his chest. Outside of fear, threshed beyond doubt, he forced a grip on his drug-widened consciousness. He sealed himself inside an inviolate stillness, then dropped like an arrow shot off a high arc into the heartcore of Arithon's mind.

Maelstrom sucked him under, white-hot and merciless, the effects of the tienelle redoubled as the physical torment to Arithon's body rocked him off-balance into cramps. Then vision sliced him through like silver-bladed knives.

Dakar mustered flayed resources. This time when mage-trained reflex sought to fling him wholesale into the dark, he cried Arithon's Name, tuned into a key of compassion.

Careful as he was, his personal feelings leaked through and coloured the weave. What secrets he hoarded allowed no false pretence; he was anything but impartial where the Prince of Rathain was concerned. As the fires of reaction roused to hound him once again, he sensed the futility of further effort. He could batter himself silly in attempt to weave an access, and only buy repeated failure. He was not as Asandir, powerful enough in wisdom and strength to intervene without force, and call spirit to respond from within. The final conclusion was unpleasant in the extreme. The herb had entangled Arithon in the same guilt which blocked off his mage-sight. Only one means existed that Dakar was aware of, to reverse the process and storm through.

He groped back to the table, too ragged to weep. Nothing, nothing at all, had prepared him for what he must endure. Whether he despaired or he howled, whether he emerged irrevocably changed, he had no other means to stem the remorseless tides of the tienelle's dissolution than to hurl Arithon's own guilt back against him.

Dakar scraped up the spilled remains of the herb, then gathered pipe and striker and flint. He bore the items back to the floor by the berth, heartsick for what must follow.

'You difficult, cross-grained, shadow-binding bastard,' he murmured to the heedless prince as he repacked the stubby little pipe. 'If I do this, I'll never be quit of your memory.'

Dakar glared at the stilled form on the berth in a malevolence of sick misery as he fumbled the striker and managed at last to light the bowl. Bitter fumes bit the back of his throat as he inhaled. The far more likely truth was that Arithon s'Ffalenn would kill him stone dead for interference.

The Mad Prophet drew on the smoke, deeper and deeper until his awareness whirled like motes of dust through a starfield. He was going to have to overdose just to stay ahead of the other man's blinding fast reflex. The tienelle's narcotic was unforgiving. If he misjudged by a fraction, he would lose himself with the prince, with no man aboard the *Khetienn* trained to the mysteries to lend either one of them succour.

Settled into drug-heightened mage trance, tight-laced in control like a spear tipped in adamant, Dakar readied his assault. Then he arrowed a stinging cry of awareness across the mind of Rathain's prince.

Defences lashed back, a peal of meshed force that Dakar had no skill to match except by a shield of stark vision: in the graphic detail impelled through heightened prescience, he shaped Arithon's own pernicious memory of the townsmen his act of grand conjury had cut down on the field by the River Tal Quorin.

Sight collided with s'Ffalenn remorse. Dakar *saw* the silver-bright flare of imposed power as royal compassion stung the prince into flash point recoil. Arithon's defences shuddered into disarray. Through that momentary gap, Dakar rammed force tempered like a killing blade. He struck without mercy, armed in ruthless, unsheathed power.

Arithon's mage-sight had been poisoned by guilt; therefore, in judgement more pitiless than Ath's angel of vengeance, those deeds that stung conscience would be turned, reft beyond reach and veiled from recall. Dakar was relentless. He ransacked what memories he knew in ruthless succession: the grand failures at Tal Quorin; Steiven s'Valerient and his lady, now mouldered bones beneath a stone cairn in Deshir Forest; for one boychild spared, a generation lost in bloodshed; then

Dhirken; Lady Maenalle; and nine other hapless innocents in an armoury; Talith's lost marriage; all these griefs, Dakar swept into the fiery ring of his ward.

At each turn, Arithon's awareness protested his presumptuous meddling. The fight in him would not be quenched. This violation of his innermost privacy roused a vehement storm of prideful temper. Dakar ploughed on, beleaguered. His instinct to show mercy for need must be utterly stamped out. He held all the weapons. He was inside the Shadow Master's deepest defences. Any of a thousand thorny fragments of happenstance were his to seize and turn, to cut off resistance, no matter how brave, and to break down spirit and courage into reeling pain.

And even stung and stung again to inward howls of agony, Arithon's nature would not give way in submission. The man who intervened in the effort to spare his sanity could do nothing else but meet each tortured obstruction, then use grief and sorrow to unbalance.

Dakar plumbed layer upon layer of guarded record, through events he had not shared through experience – memories that extended back to Arithon's time as Karthan's heir beyond the West Gate, where moral ideals and the fresh hopes of youth had culminated in an unspeakable interval as a prince in captivity under another s'Ilessid king. Laid out like tapestry, the Mad Prophet beheld the foundations for all that Arithon had become. Through each turn of event which had shaped a master of shadow rose the silver-gilt blaze of Fellowship intervention, the instilled gift of Torbrand's compassion. Its influence laid an unmistakable trail to follow: a father's death of an arrow upon the flame-racked decks of another brigantine; a kingdom lost to blood feud; a beloved grandfather whose every warning and principle had been disregarded and finally betrayed.

Dakar dug in and occupied, and cut like a scalpel until at long last he recoiled against the black, entwined web that entrenched the poisoned work of Desh-thiere's curse. There he turned at bay. That tangle, not even the Fellowship Sorcerers dared disturb.

And waiting for him there, still armed with enough power to stun, was Arithon's trained awareness, enraged to stabbing malice for an unconscionable violation of self.

Dakar knew despair. He had achieved no master's training at magecraft: in born talent, in training, in knowledge, the other man outmatched him. He was in beyond his depth and pinned with no avenue of retreat. The straits were not forgiving. Through the mage's reflex that disbarred his try at rescue, he could sense the ongoing pressure as the effects of the tienelle coursed through Arithon's body. Should his hold slip, should the diversion of his presence become unseated, the guilt in the visions he defended would resume their inflamed sequence and spur on the unwinding descent into madness.

A course of sheer folly remained. The personal bindings of selfhood, which Dakar for expedience had broken, but that a master's exacting reflex in defence must be instilled to respect; aware of only that one barrier that Arithon's counterthrust would hesitate to cross, Dakar reacted. He claimed the burden of remorse he had stolen and assumed the full coil as his own.

As he conjoined borrowed memories with the signature pattern of his Name, the bleeding roots of the other man's compassion became his personal inheritance. Along with the guilt came every wounding twist of fate that had arisen to separate a masterbard from his born calling to shape music.

A heartbeat, and the victim was freed from his crippling guilt. Reason returned, and full cognizance. In a rush fired to bounding expansion by the tienelle, Arithon's mind unreeled through sharp, unfolding vision into the lost power of his mage talent.

For him, a wondering, peaceful miracle of insight; for Dakar, a stab of dark agony the likes of which ground and shattered his being through a paroxysm of change.

'*Do what you must*,' he charged the prince he sought to salvage. '*Transmute the drug's poisons and pull yourself out of this!*' He need not remonstrate that his spellbinder's resource was finite. Nor could he sustain the weight of Arithon's conscience for one second longer than shocked nerves could withstand the strain. He was not royal, nor tempered to mastery, nor disciplined to a masterbard's empathy, but only a fat man born to a spurious gift of prophecy whose burdens had driven him to drink.

'*You are more than that, truly*,' Arithon's reply sang back through the terrible, twinned link. '*Else I would be mad, and you would be drunk, and the Mistwraith would have its fell triumph.*'

But a darker deception lurked hidden behind the spellbinder's barriers. The threat that awaited when winter browned the bracken in Vastmark, the prescient secret held guarded, stayed sealed away, along with the paralysing ties to memory Dakar had locked beyond reach. Then, as though the blast of s'Ffalenn conscience was not enough to flatten him, he saw the intent of his sacrifice repudiated.

'*Ah, you scheming, clever bastard!*' the Mad Prophet cried.

For Arithon did not use the reprieve he had been given to restore his taxed faculties to safe limits. Instead, he shouldered the restored scope of his self-command, grasped the reins of the tienelle's powers of expanded vision, and launched through a nerve-stripping sequence of augury. As he had done before the battle at Tal Quorin to buy the survival of his clansmen, he tried now for the forthcoming débâcle at Vastmark.

Dakar was drawn in as hapless witness. Meshed still in the wards that had stood down mage-trained defences, he had no resource to exert his own control as Arithon imposed his chosen test of cause and effect to trace a sequential array of probability. The spellbinder was forced to follow to its bloody finish each traced-through combination of strategy. In an agony paired with Arithon's, he counted, in sorrow and blood, the bodies fallen on the field. The battering ordeal imposed a cruel order. Through a horrific train of posited futures, Dakar came to realize that the Master of Shadow did not replay each ugly nuance with the sole intent to save his own.

At each turn, through every crafty twist of projected circumstance, the deployment of shepherd archers and clan scouts was replayed to sound for alternate tactics. Arithon broke rules. He trampled morality. He stretched every resource to unconscionable limit, and spared nothing of himself. At every turn, his exhaustive effort sought openings to disarm conflict. Dakar sensed the driving will to create ways to demoralize, and frighten, and haze back the enemy; to allow men misled for false cause the free option to retreat, and live, and return to their hearthstones and families.

Through the terrible course of the auguries made to steer the war in Vastmark, the Mad Prophet came to know that *nothing concerning the massacre at Tal Quorin confirmed his past set of assumptions*. Arithon had acted in perfect consistency, start to finish, each predetermined move done for mercy. He had not, after all, struck out in wanton fury, but used destruction as his most calculated tool, the sole means he had at his disposal to turn the scope of much wider disaster.

And so he would do again at Vastmark, over terrain most ruthlessly chosen to disadvantage a warhost. If Lysaer's troops closed to fight, they would march into ruin. Arithon's scryings were unequivocal. His light force of archers and clansmen would give way and strike from ambush. They could beat swift retreat into the mountains and lose themselves, or turn and cut down pursuit from the high cover of cliff walls while their enemies blundered, unable to find the hidden tracks to scale the cruel rocks and retaliate.

In spilled blood and in resource, for Lysaer, the campaign against the Shadow Master would be a terrible, drawn-out waste of life.

And still, *even still*, Arithon remained unsatisfied.

Dakar sensed the drawn interval, the gathered moment of preparation. Through the harrowing unpleasantness he sustained to impound conscience and hold open the Shadow Master's mage-sight, he felt the stripped-down, silverpoint discipline Arithon called into play to engage yet another course of augury. The tienelle's influence by then was nearly spent. Through the friable webs of inner consciousness, Dakar sensed the poisons eroding his tissues to dissolution. Arithon would suffer the same awareness, and yet, his grip was as granite, and his assurance new steel as he raised his will to carve out his planned line of prescience.

'What are you doing!' Dakar wailed through the pause. He had no strength to spare to expound on the dangers.

'I'm seeking a way to turn them,' came Arithon's reply. *'If the warhost never marches, there won't be any bloodshed. Lysaer may have a weakness in his resolve to seek my death. If he does, I'm going to find it.'*

The task was impossible. Dakar tried to protest. He knew the Prince of the West, had watched him at Cheivalt and been forced through sorrow to an unwanted evaluation. Best of any he understood how the prince's morality had been wrenched awry and used by Deshthiere's curse. The royal gift of s'Ilessid justice would never let Lysaer back down.

Arithon saw the same, but was undaunted. *'There's one way we haven't tried yet. Make the stakes too punishing for even Lysaer's staunch morals to endure.'*

By then, Dakar had seen all there was to know of the

mind of the Prince of Rathain. In a burst fired out by the
tienelle, he guessed the horrific intent. 'You can't do
this!' he cried. 'Don't try, for your heart's sake.'

But his warning was hammered aside.

Written in blood and in razed human lives, the desperate deterrent unreeled. Arranged for maximum
impact and effect, Dakar was given a raw vista of twisted
corpses and fired ships as fruits of a merciless slaughter.
Alongside the handful of witnesses chosen by intent to
survive, he beheld the utter death of hope.

The horrible, harrowing reverberation of their pain
snapped his hold on concentration.

He had no second's warning, no moment to prepare,
as his senses overturned into an untimely, drug-fired
augury. His birth-gifted talent sundered his control and
ripped through, and like a cascading fall of dominoes,
chaos stormed the breach.

Dakar cried out, racked over by truesight: *of Lysaer
s'Ilessid, brought weeping to his knees in a field tent,
while a shaken, white-faced captain received orders:
that the warhost was to turn in retreat.*

*'There's no foray worth the cost of forty thousand
lives!' Lysaer said. 'I'll not see my men lured in and
toyed with just to be needlessly broken. The conclusion
is plain: the Master of Shadow has made Vastmark a
trap. He cannot be run to earth over ground he has
chosen. We must pull back now and rethink our strategy
until other ways can be found to destroy him.'*

'It's going to work, what you plan,' Dakar gasped.
'When Lysaer receives word of the carnage, his warhost
will be turned and disbanded.'

The next moment, his whole edifice of wards
crumbled down. Protections cobbled together at need
dissolved into scouring static. His grip on Arithon's store
of conscience slipped free to slam up the old barriers and
lock off all access to his mage-sense.

Aware of disaster, hurled into pain as his inner sight

crashed into darkness, Arithon grasped the fast-fading edge of knowledge. He wrung from the dregs of his failing talent a last twist of craft to effect a swift cut of unbinding.

Dakar had no moment to measure the effect. Darkness howled down like battening felt and drowned his last spark of awareness.

While dawn threw light like old ice through the stern window, the Mad Prophet reawakened to the gut misery of withdrawal, made worse by the slamming toss as the brigantine bucked over storm swells. The weather had gone foul with a vengeance as dire as the descent of Dharkaron's Chariot. Rain flung in spatters on the mullioned casement. The reefed gear aloft crashed and shrilled to the shrieking swoop of rank gusts.

Arithon lay on the berth, limp to the jostle of the ship's roll and scarcely conscious. The shivering spasms had left him wrung weak; his body had ceased its attempt to expel the raw poisons his lost powers could not transmute.

Dakar said the first rude word to rise to mind. Stripped by the ache of overextension, in no grand fettle himself, he understood by the hollow ring of sound in his ears that he was going to require a terrible effort to move, far less to begin a dangerous course of healing to ease Arithon back to recovery.

'Are you all right?' came a ragged whisper from the berth.

The Mad Prophet paused in his effort to swear. He peered across the creaking gloom of the cabin to where Arithon lay, eyes slitted in pain, but watching him closely all the same.

'I have a headache that could kill,' Dakar answered. 'And balance so wrecked, I doubt I could manage to make a puddle in a chamber pot without missing.' He refused

371

to address the rest, or confront the meat of the question's intent. For of course, he would never be quite right, nor be able to resume his past carefree ways. Stitched into memory beyond his power to dissolve, he held the pure recall of everything in life that Arithon s'Ffalenn had ever suffered.

The sting of conscience was unrelenting, and twofold for the parts where his personal lapses had added impetus to the burden: the scouring devastation of pride at Minderl Bay, the betrayal at Alestron's dungeon, the loss of Halliron at Jaelot. Remorse was too paltry a concept to encompass the wretchedness he shared with Rathain's prince. Pretence was ripped away. The conclusion he had to bear forward was forthright in simplicity: that Arithon s'Ffalenn was no criminal at all, but a creature of undying compassion whose natural bent was to celebrate an irrepressible joy for life.

Music could free that hidden aspect, had the burdens of royal bloodline and the Mistwraith's curse between them not forced his nature away from his birth-born inclinations.

Dakar looked up, touched to sorrow, to find Arithon's weighted gaze still fixed in stilled patience on his face. 'You're going to go through with this,' he said in choked reference to that unspeakably lethal last augury outlined for a small, coastal cove called the Havens. 'Ath show you pity.'

'No choice.' Arithon looked sick white for the knowledge that his chance was now lost, to recheck and sound for a full set of sureties. For his trouble he held only one frail thread of hope behind a proposed action that courted the edge of cold murder. 'I have your scried proof. The tactic of terror alone will turn Lysaer. What are five hundred deaths in exchange for the lives of forty thousand?'

'You take a great risk. The whole plan could go wrong.' Dakar pressed pudgy palms to his thundering temples, magnified and made worse by the pound of the ship's timbers, hurled working against contrary waves. He was too reamed with weariness to define nuance, that his auguries manifested two ways. The ones he saw as visions were always mutable, subject to change or reverses if subsequent circumstances intervened. Others came in blind fits of spoken prophecy, beyond his recall when he awoke. These alone held pinpoint accuracy, and if the content of their riddles held opening for change, only the Fellowship had seen proof.

The vision of Lysaer recalling his troops had borne no such terrible certainty. 'Arithon, what if the purpose of your killing field fails?'

Curled into a reaming fit of dry heaves, the Master of Shadow closed tormented eyes. He answered with no change of position as soon as he was able to command speech. 'I'd be forced to follow through, as you saw. Ath's pity has no part. By blood oath to Asandir, I'm charged to survive. If the ploy fails and I draw the wrath of that warhost into Vastmark, I can't let my allies come to die for it.'

The Mad Prophet hung mute, unable to refute that tortured course of logic.

As if the dread in that moment were shared and transparent, Arithon ended, 'I've made the issue no longer your concern. You haven't felt the change? You're no longer bound to me by duty.'

And Dakar understood in wild exhilaration just what that desperate, last unbinding had achieved.

Arithon had made a gift in return for his sacrifice: had broken his Fellowship master's geas and ceded back his unimpaired freedom.

Except for Asandir's verbal charge of service, Dakar's free will was once again his own. He drew breath to speak, then coughed through his beard, crestfallen. For the issue was no longer simple. The changes to his person had been driven too deep; and an arrow's fatal role in the Shadow Master's affairs remained yet to happen in the winter.

Dakar took stubborn hold, pushed himself to his knees, then shot a poisoned glare at his nemesis. 'You won't be rid of me so easily, and anyway, you're going to need a nurse who knows how to draw you clear of a tienelle poisoning.'

He was Arithon's man, that much could not be changed, at least until after the campaign was turned in Vastmark. Only then could he measure the impact of what he had become. He had until equinox to weigh the warning impact of his augury and decide whether he should abandon Lysaer to fate and stay involved with the Master of Shadow.

Strike at the Havens

Summer's end saw Lysaer's proud warhost in their closing march upon Vastmark. They came from the north, through the passes beyond Thirdmark, under snapping pennons and sunlit lances and scudding clouds. From the walled city of Ganish, they came on by road, then by river, to march in dusty columns over the parched stems of the late summer grasses into the wilderness beyond. They skirted the lower foothills of the Kelhorns from Forthmark, the brilliant banners, polished armour, and glittering, gilt harness of pedigree commanders flung like hoarded jewels against the dusty landscape, bleached to the duns of sun-faded velvet by the pitiless southern latitude.

Their orders were simple: to cordon the territory in a living noose, then to engage and clean out any ally of the Master of Shadow.

Like the closing fingers of a gauntleted fist wrought of forty thousand dedicated lives, they came also by galley and fishing boat to crush out an enemy they well knew for an author of dangerous sorceries. Into the stiff, shifty winds that presaged the first change in season, uncounted small fleets nosed up the shadowy narrows of

South Sea and through the twisted straits into Rockbay Harbour. Each had decks packed to the gunwales with armed men. On shores north and south, headhunters and town garrisons converged on the peninsula of Vastmark, to land on stepped shingle and ledges of moss-rotten rock, and to invade the high ramparts of its twin walls of mountains, arrayed like jutted battlements toward the sea.

Among a hundred such landings, one was singled out.

Flattened amid a fractured clutch of shale on the brim of a cliff, his black hair stirred to a clammy breeze off the inlet known as the Havens, the Master of Shadow lay cat still. He wore no armour, but only a grass-stained shepherd's jacket and tunic; on his person he carried no weapon beyond a knife. His intent study encompassed the cross-weave of rigging and yardarms of a fleet of merchant brigs and fishing sloops, recently anchored.

'They're lazy as well as careless,' he murmured, for the haphazard way the sails on the vessels had been left brailed up to the yards.

'Well,' said Caolle in sour censure behind his shoulder, 'you wanted a place where they'd play straight into your design.'

'Killing is killing,' Arithon said, flat bland. 'Are you faint? I'm surprised. After all those murdered couriers out of Jaelot, I didn't think you had any tender spots left to offend.'

The barb shamed Caolle to stiff silence; a contrary and difficult service he had of this prince, but one he was forced to respect. Bloodshed had never balked him for the sake of his clans in Deshir. If Arithon's proposed tactics lay outside his approval, there were headhunters' devices amid the town pennons which streamed from the mastheads below. Except for the odd fishing sloop out of Merior, these men marked as prey were not innocent or harmless, but professionals as dedicated as he.

Reduced to black specks by height and distance, four

companies of troops seethed up from the feet of the cliffs. They seemed insignificant as wingless insects against that vast landscape, but for the chance-caught glitter of sunlight on mail or the coloured threads of yarn that were banners. The occasional shouted order spiralled up, half-masked by the clicks of summer crickets in the broom.

Minutes became an hour, with only the formless shadows of clouds fanned in movement across the upper scarps. To the invaders who toiled upslope, the scabbed old ridges their advance scouts searched seemed bare, tenantless; raked over by winds, and too steep to harbour any trees or small scrub, far less an outpost for ambush.

What their maps did not show, and their legends had forgotten, were the caves stitched between the seamed ledges, for which the Havens had been originally named.

A clan scout emerged from such a crack to pause at Caolle's shoulder. Words passed between them, low and hurried; then the scout slipped back into the brush.

To Arithon, the clan war captain said, 'The headhunters' advance foray has given their officers safe signal. The garrison divisions have started up the rocks. If you're bent on going through with this, you won't be getting better timing.' Then, to shrug off the leftover sting of rebuke, he added, 'My liege, let me have the honour. I ask to fire the first signal.'

'No.' Just that one word; royal claim to a responsibility no other would be suffered to share.

Arithon s'Ffalenn slid back from the precipice. He took up the strung bow of black-lacquered horn set waiting against a rock, then chose the first of three marked arrows arrayed in a row in the dirt. The red streamers affixed to its head flicked over his shoulder as he knelt and nocked the first. Slight, thin-tempered, dwarfed by the bowl of the Vastmark sky, he made a drab figure against its surfeit of colour as he drew and took aim.

The hammered look of anguish his features showed then gave even his war captain pause.

Then the bowstring sang into release. The arrow arced up, poised, tipped into irrevocable descent. Ribbons unfurled behind in a snapping tail of bloody scarlet.

Men tucked in concealment in the crevices of the cliffs saw the flagged shaft's passage. It plunged seaward like the fall of an evil portent, harbinger of an unnatural steel rain, and sure death for the troops below.

The stakes were unrelenting: clan archers with long-bows and years of skill hunting game in the lean north-ern winters to feed their families; tribe marksmen with their powerful, horn recurves, unerring at bringing down wyvern, a prey they could spit through with pinpoint accuracy as it spiralled on the high thermal currents. The hundred and twelve bowmen chosen for this foray had been ruthlessly selected for steady nerves and unfail-ing obedience. As the red-tagged signal snapped earth-ward, all drew their weapons. They took aim, and shot from the sun-scoured cliffs into ranks who toiled in strewn formation over uncertain footing on the moun-tain's flanks.

The wasp hiss of air over fletching became all the warning human targets received.

Then the hail of barbed shafts struck. The first casual-ties wrenched and went down, sprawling, rattling, writh-ing uncontrolled in their death throes down the baked, stony slopes. Living companions flattened back against the rim walls, only to become transfixed as they stood, blades drawn in hand. They were helpless to strike back. The enemy who slaughtered was beyond reach, beyond view. In vain, townbred archers squinted upward against sun-glare to seek retaliation against invisible targets. Trapped helpless, they died, while flight after enemy flight sleeted in and pared their ranks, remorseless.

The dust-dry stone became ribboned in blood. Broadheads took men seasoned at war and raw recruits with no discrimination. Men scrabbled to seek cover in terrain that showed them no mercy. They crumpled, buckled at the knees, or jerked over backward with arms outflung at the shock of impact, crying in pain and cruel rage.

Ones not broken outright on the rocks thudded onto the shingle, where their blood ran and mingled and sullied the salt breakers which ruffled the shoreline, uncaring.

On the clifftop, Caolle knuckled his fist to closed teeth, raked over by a sudden wash of cold sweats. He had seen war; had fought and inflicted ugly carnage in his time. This was not battle, but a living, tearing nightmare that made him want to cringe and block his ears.

Below raged a chaos tripped off and arranged, coil within coil like a clockspring. Hazed beyond grief, officers cried orders over the screams of mounting casualties. The fallen were beyond hope to rally; the terrified had lost wits to heed. Retreat became a mêlée of panic, a desperate, zigzagging rush from cleft to outcrop that invited the slip, the missed footing, the rocking, final plunge into air. As many men succumbed to falls as to bowfire; smashed onto rocks and buttresses of shale like knives, no less agonized, no less dead for the fact the Wheel took them in accident.

'Turn them back! Ath's pity, get them down to the boats!' cried a garrison commander from the beachhead. Erect in dedication, he wore the black-and-gilt surcoat emblazoned with Jaelot's gold lions. As a man who had once matched companionable bets over bows with the conniving imposter, Medlir, he knew beyond fear what he faced.

Help came to his cry. In the narrows between the cliff heads, captains screamed for longboats to be launched; for crewmen to unbrail canvas and man capstans to weigh anchor. Headhunters and town troops alike were in flight, and still, the marksmen in the heights main-

tained their incessant barrage. This was not war, but
unconscionable slaughter. Men shook their fists, or scattered and ran, or huddled in clusters under targes that
failed to protect. Arrows raked the clear air and pinned
their scrabbling, yelling figures like flies, whether they
struggled in mad flight, or stood ground in a vain effort
to cover their comrades' retreat.

Jaelot's guard captain dropped in the shallows, clawing
at an arrow in his thigh. Two sword-bearing headhunters
leaped to assist, cut down on the next flight to share the
watery cradle of his agony. The next crest dashed their
dying convulsions against the pebbled shale ledges.
Amid the heaving, shouting knot of survivors pinned
under fire on the strand, boats were relaunched into surf.
Men rammed the keels against the unravelling foam in
frenzied haste, trampling over wounded and bumping
over bodies to escape a rain of shafts no defending troop
could hope to cut back with cross fire. Cries of terror
and mortal pain rang thin over the screams and the
echoes shot back by walling rock.

'They're well beaten,' Caolle murmured. Another
scout poised at his elbow, pale with raw nerves, his
appeal sent by fellows who begged for permission to ease
off the force of the attack.

If Arithon was aware of the plea, he said nothing. Nor
did he turn from the seething scene below as, made
miniature by height and distance, oarsmen bent their
bronzed backs and grappled their laden craft in toothpick
strokes across waters lapped blue-green in shade. Bowfire
harried their progress. The relentless rain of shafts clattered over rib and seat and gunwale to bite off white
splinters from the wood. Live men used bristled corpses
as cover, or cowered behind living shieldmates, moaning
prayers to a deaf deity.

The crack of sails being set and sheeted home
rebounded from the imprisoning cliffs, then spiralled on
the breeze to the heights. Every vessel in the anchorage

turned her helm down to flee, but for the one plucky fishing sloop from Merior. Manned by a captain too dour to stand down, that one wore ship in a neat turn of seamanship and tucked up underneath the ledges. Shielded by rock, she launched off her dories, while her stubborn master bellowed orders to evacuate the wounded from the shingle.

His bearing like a puppet chiselled out of ivory, Arithon plucked the second signal arrow from the earth, set nock to string and prepared to fire again.

Chilled in his liege's shadow as he bent the black bow, Caolle urged the shaken scout, 'Go back. Now, I say! The wrong word will doubtless raise the royal temper. Let me speak in behalf of your men.'

Horn and lacquer snapped in recoil. The arrow hissed out. A flight of yellow ribbons unreeled across the sky of the Havens.

In the caves lower down, bound to obedience, the archers tipped the lids off ceramic pots of coals. They changed from broadheads to shafts tipped in tallow-soaked lint, then touched them aflame one by one. Their next shots were fired in high arcs across the water, their targets the billows of unbrailed canvas. The air rippled, first singed into distortion by brown smoke and fat-fed flame, then cut by hissing arcs and the heartrending, treble shouts of panic. The ships nearest to the shoreline sprang into fire like toys. Men jumped clear of burning rigging. They escaped the scything crash of fallen yard-arms into water, to thrash in frantic circles until they drowned. Or they swam back onto the blood-slippery beaches, into the directionless mêlée that drove the trapped garrisons hither and yon, while the arrows fell and fell and served lethal end to their struggles.

The more fortunate ships on the outer line ran up headsails, and let their bows fall off toward the free waters of Rockbay inlet. Tiny figures scrambled up rat-lines, packed the footropes on the yardarms to unbrail more sails to draw against the gusting onshore breeze.

The lead vessel scarcely caught her wind when the *Khetienn* rounded the headland, tanbark sails like old wounds against the clean shear of the water, and her gear in fearful trim. An order cracked out. The arbalests mounted on her maindeck loosed more bolts, fiendishly tipped in fire. Other bowmen stationed in her crosstrees released strings.

Inside of a second, the channel between the cliffs became transformed to a death trap. The narrows to the sea were bottled in. Outbound ships had the wind against their favour, their attempt to return fire robbed by the gusts of full range.

The first flights snatched short, flames quenched in small plumes by the sea. Through the unreeling first billows of smoke, Lysaer's captains read their fate: no single vessel in the Havens was going to manage to claw free. They could wear ship and run, to slam aground on sharp rock, or they could hold course under barrage from the arbalests and burn with their vessels to the waterline.

From the clifftop, the Master of Shadow watched his works, drawn like glass under heat, then hardened into a brittle finish subject to shatter at a tap.

Caolle edged a step toward him, while urgency warred with reason. Every instinct of command that let him measure men shrilled an internal warning.

The fool who intervened now might upset a dire balance, fragile as the tension in a water drop.

'The Havens,' Arithon ground out in a whisper. The peal of laughter that followed caused Caolle to stiffen. He raised a hand, decisive, to deal a swift slap to break hysteria.

Moved by swordsman's reflex, Arithon spun to block the blow; and the icy, pitiless sarcasm fixed into his expression checked his war captain cold.

'I'm not going to snap,' Arithon said, his tone incised

like a sheared scrape of crystal over yelling and the harrowing echoes of the screams. 'My half-brother may. Pray to Ath, if you know how, that he finds the cost of his blighted justice high enough to break his princely nerve.'

A choking drift of smoke fanned the defile. The windborne cinders from consumed wood and canvas arose in towering, tainted columns, incense from an evil sacrifice, to mask the too-bright gaze and features stamped still as chipped quartz. A gust tore through. Like an opening between a stage curtain, a tableau framed in carnage: the little sloop backed sail and bid for freedom, her decks laden down with prostrate wounded.

'Dharkaron avenge,' swore Caolle. 'Give me the bow.'

When Arithon made no move to comply, the war captain snatched the last signal arrow from the earth, the one with white ribbons for cease-fire. He reached to pry the weapon from his sovereign's grasp by main force and met a blinding fast recoil.

A demonic flare of irony lit the depths of green eyes. 'Ah no,' said Arithon. 'No mercy. Not now. You'll spoil my intent. There are men down there alive still, and in no mood for charitable action.'

'Daelion himself!' cried Caolle. 'Let the wounded go! Ath forbid, she's just a fisher sloop! This isn't war you wage now, but pointless slaughter.' He drew a scraping breath. Never had he foreseen the hour he must argue for mercy against a prince who, before this, had been too soft to sanction the necessary harsh measures.

'You'll do nothing,' Arithon said, distant, tuned in to some altercation arisen on the water down below.

Over the noise, raised through the crack of flame by some fickle trick of the rock, sound winnowed upward from an argument in progress aboard the *Khetienn*. One of her crewmen was a sailor born in Merior, pleading exception to the order to blockade. 'For mercy, let them by. That's no soldier on that sloop, but a captain I've known since my birth!'

Then the brigantine's commander, in diminished rebuttal. 'Our orders stand. *Get back to your post!* Our liege was plain. We dare not cease fire until the signal.'

And Arithon gripped the black bow, a very statue of indifference. He did not ask back the white arrow while the sloop clawed bravely against the wind. His delay sealed her fate. On the *Khetienn*'s deck, the tinny clang of an arbalest sang sharp in release. Its quarrel arced out, and fire raged through the fishing craft's sails like Sithaer unleashed. The screams as her burden of wounded burned alive racked the air, cut by a south shoreman's curses for a prince who had once claimed false refuge in his village.

Caolle gripped the white shaft in locked fingers. 'The clansmen are mine. *I could pull them off, despite you.*'

'Do that!' cracked the Prince of Rathain. 'Then stand and endure the taste of my *sanctioned* royal justice. I'd take the heads of the ones who obey you for treason.'

No threat, but hard certainty; Caolle read as much. He spat in revolted disgust.

'So many deaths,' Arithon mocked him, vicious. 'You say they're enough. *Well, half measures won't serve.* We're not fighting against a man, or a moral, or a principle.'

'Desh-thiere's curse is your justification? Then I'm questioning that.' As much as Caolle knew of the reasonless hatred and inspired lust to kill from what Jieret had related after past events at Minderl Bay, this act at the Havens broke the mould.

His hand on his sword grip, Caolle quivered to a chill that ran him through. He wondered how much of today's slaughter was based any more on clear sanity.

Arithon saw Deshir's war captain waver and redoubled his savagery to compensate. 'Lysaer won't stop for my mercy. I dare not stop for his. *Step back, Caolle!* I'll not be gainsaid, nor buy a cheap failure for the sake of one bleeding heart. The cease-fire will not be given, do you hear? *Not for as long as one man under Avenor's Ath-forsaken banner remains standing.*'

'If they're all dead, who takes Lysaer the warning?' Caolle cried.

Arithon gave back a nasty smile. 'I'll pick the envoys I need from among the least-hacked survivors.'

Caolle could not contain the rise of his gorge. He hurled the white signal arrow to Arithon's feet, eyes inimical as black steel boring into his prince as his sword sang clear of its sheath. 'You may not be sick,' he said in a low, taut rage he had never before felt toward any man. 'But by Ath, I am. For both of us.'

Arithon's lip curled. 'Don't worry,' he taunted before that steady, levelled blade. 'If my foray here doesn't raise enough terror, you'll have your chance to shoulder the larger sacrifice. You'll stand front and centre, *up against forty thousand*. I'll watch you direct the bloodbath to stop the next wave when the warhost mounts the vale at Dier Kenton.'

Which urgent bit of viciousness slapped Caolle short. He did not challenge a madman, but encroached instead on a naked and tortured vulnerability.

The carnage at Tal Quorin had been done in heated battle, over the freshly gutted bodies of clan women and children. The Havens was a tactic wrought out in calculated cold blood to break nerves; to raise by brutal storm the very reasonless upset a seasoned man of war would never imagine he could fall victim to.

Stung too late for the impulse that had made him question his liege lord's timing, Caolle recoiled against the uttermost cruel paradox: Athera's Masterbard was no spirit to be forced to command here. Yet the half of him that was Rathain's born prince was too much the man to relinquish the unendurable weight of sovereignty.

'Ah, Ath, I can't fight you.' The war captain stood down, abashed. 'Not over this. Not when you're like to wish yourself dead over what you believe is stark necessity.'

Spared the searing coil of guilt and conscience, touched to a pity he could not bear, the seasoned campaigner turned his back. He hunched over his blade in staid misery and endured through the cries, the soft whine of bowstrings, the drifts of stinging smoke, until the assault upon the ships played itself out into soaked carbon. In time, naught remained beyond timbers quenched into steam and the pale, drifting knots of the bodies entangled by the incoming tide.

When at the last the white signal flew to end the bowfire, Caolle was unashamedly weeping.

The men who descended to walk the scene of slaughter were hand-picked, all clansmen, veterans of the past butchery in Strakewood Forest. Arithon chose ones still bitter from the loss of their families in the grottos of Tal Quorin, who would not balk at unrelenting vengeance. The young officer with them was one of Jieret's Companions, no stranger to dealing a mercy stroke to a man moaning helpless in fresh blood.

Others went along to bear litters for the lucky few chosen to survive.

Arithon led, still swordless. Under the merciless sunlight, he descended the gore-streaked stone, past men lying sprawled with eyes and mouths opened to sky; past others who were little more than boys, curled in agony over the slow pain of lacerations; the torment of an arrow in the gut. He did not hurry. The scouts selected to carry the wounded trailed at his heels, half-sickened by the stench of sudden death and hazed by the circling buzz of flies. They listened, struck mute, for their liege lord to speak; to point to the grey-haired captain panting in the half-shade of a niche, a broadhead pinned through a wrist. 'That one.'

Two scouts peeled off, bent to the cringing victim, and lifted him, to bear him away in a drawn-out, jouncing passage up the cliff face to the ridgetop.

Downward, the party passed, into the shadowed throat of the Havens inlet. Now the air reeked of char and the tide-bared weed on the rocks. Arithon pressed footprints into a shingle fouled in the stains of dying men; past corpses piled like drift wrack. He stepped over discarded swords and slackened fingers, and once, a face blistered to featureless meat where canvas had fallen, still burning, upon a swimmer. Amid the carnage and dead, a young boy who had been a banner bearer sat, crying over blistered hands. 'That one.'

The lad screamed as the scouts caught hold of him.

Arithon never turned his head. Straight as cold steel, he pressed onward, around the upset shell of a longboat, prickled with arrows. Two men underneath were alive and unmarked. 'Those also, if they surrender without fight.'

One died on a clansman's knife. The other, dazed and sobbing and out of his wits, was herded back up the cliff trail, past the first, settling flap of black vultures; the croak of feeding crows; and the inevitable, sinuous, circling flight of the wyvern pairs, sailing the breezes to scavenge.

'That one and that one,' to a couple of seamen adrift on a plank, one with an arm half-torn away, and the other supporting his companion.

Not every face was a stranger's. Nearby a sailhand off the doomed fishing sloop from Merior lay on his side, scarcely alive, his laboured breaths in low venom reviling the name of the Master of Shadow whose merciless act had brought him, crippled and blistered, on a shingle heaped over with corpses. Arithon passed him, wordless, his gaze straight ahead. From another group lying arrow struck, one mortally, he pointed, 'Take the one with the slashed shoulder.'

When the chosen man-at-arms was forced away from his fellow, he cried out, 'For pity, what's to become of my friend?'

Arithon did not answer, but walked on. The litter bearers who manhandled the weeping townsman to separate him from his prone shipmate knew in cold surety, but said nothing. Ones their prince did not designate were to die where they lay, a swift mercy stroke to end their suffering. The scouts followed a scant pace behind with their bloodied knives. By strict royal orders, they did their grim work unabashed before the horrified eyes of the few winnowed out to survive.

The strand at the Havens was emptied of living men inside of three hours, the unburied skeletons discarded for the wyverns to pick. *Khetienn* ceased her blockading patrol, braced around, and slipped seaward, to draw clear of trammelled waters and air sifted dim with spent smoke.

Shepherd archers and clan scouts who had never descended to witness the charnel ruin on the beachhead were broken into small groups, then sent under Caolle's direction to sites elsewhere. The men who had borne the litters, who had dispatched the fallen in stone-hearted, deafened efficiency, stood guard over an open-air camp. Their perimeter was centred by the sun-faded felt of a shepherd's tent set up for use as a hospital.

The wounded brought away from the Havens were treated there by the same black-haired man who had designated who should be spared. He made his rounds, quiet, self-contained, and versed in the arts of healing. The remedies in his satchel had no witcheries in them. He spoke no unnecessary word.

'What will the Shadow Master do with us?' gasped a boy with a broken arm, held flat by two scouts as the bones were splinted. 'Why were we saved, except for some fate more terrible?'

His plea received no answer. The small, dark man in still patience just finished wrapping the splints, his sure hands astonishingly gentle. Through air pressed close with the scents of stirred dust and the herbal pastes brewed to make poultices, he went on to bind a compress on the next man in line, who lay moaning in pain on a pallet with a gaping shoulder wound.

Behind, the instant the clan scouts released their constraint, the boy laid his forehead on his drawn-up knees to hide his face and weep in silenced fear. No one came to comfort him. The eyes of the clansmen who guarded the tent held no mercy, and the one who brought healing and succour for pain seemed deaf to any outcry of the spirit.

When the last wound was treated, the last shattered bone strapped straight, and the final posset doled out to ease suffering agony into sleep, the imprisoned wounded from the Havens were left to themselves. Late day sun slanted down from the heights, adding the scent of rancid felt to the reek of astringent herbs. Breezes bowed the tent's door flap and billowed the saffron and rust patterns encircling the fire-blackened ridge post. In whispers thrummed to fear, those men still awake began to speak. They compared observations and quickly came to realize that, except for the fact no man in their present company bore a leg wound that would impair his ability to walk, neither rhyme nor reason attended their selection. Some had been taken in acts of rank cowardice, playing dead beneath the bodies of fallen victims. Others were singled out who had fought in cornered courage in some small grotto or tide-washed ledge.

'Why were we spared?' they asked, haunted over and over by the five hundred and forty of their fellows who had at one stroke been most pitilessly dispatched beneath the Wheel.

They numbered twenty-five, that had braved the landing at the Havens and lived.

For his spree of unbridled killing, the Master of Shadow had lost one, taken by surprise when a headhunter knifed him from under a splintered shelter of beached planks. Two other scouts had suffered slight wounds in the course of their murdering work among the fallen. Those had been left to wait, bleeding in stoic patience, until the dark-haired man finished his ministrations to the enemy.

'What if we're to be sacrificed in some ugly rite of magecraft?' said a veteran with a crippled hand. In the dimness of the tent as the day failed, eyes flashed and looked away while the boy in the corner, in tearing, sad sobs, finally wept himself into exhausted dreams.

Night fell over the Vastmark coast before Dakar the Mad Prophet mustered the courage to emerge and walk the site where the fighting company camped at the Havens. Amid the banked, rocky corrie set back from the cliffs, he threaded amid the cookfires of the clan scouts mustered to serve their liege lord. He overheard the talk, the coarse jokes, the jagged intervals of quiet someone always jumped to break with a laugh, a story, or a boast. The day had been won. In the spectre of widespread death, men celebrated and affirmed their ties to life. Being clansmen well hardened to the hatreds of entrenched feud, the odd complaint arose amid the brosy glow of satisfaction.

'There were fourteen other inlets like this one,' someone grumbled. 'It's a living oddity, why our prince should've left those alone. We had enough archers. Raids could have been launched on all of them, with three thousand murdering townsmen left lying as wyvern bait tonight.'

'Good thing his Grace is beyond earshot,' somebody

else ventured from the sidelines. 'Mood he's in now, he'd be like to knife you on reflex for loose talk.'

Dakar edged off from the circle of scouts. He checked, unsurprised to find the fire where Arithon had knelt brewing remedies deserted and burned down to ash. The battered brown satchel remained, its canisters of herbs, its neat rolls of bandaging, and glass flasks of tinctures and elixirs undisturbed where they had been left. The straps that fastened the flap were tied shut, sure sign the prince was not making rounds to check the injured.

Dakar paused. He rubbed the itchy bristles of his beard, filmed in the bitter dust that at summer's end seemed to coat everything. While the crickets scraped in their hanks of dry grass, he stood in troubled thought and pondered where to look for a man who would at this moment hold a virulent aversion for companionship.

His memory of Ath's shrine at Ship's Port came back, on the night of Halliron's death.

After the first moment of fainthearted hesitation, Dakar turned away from the campfires, where the jokes rang a fraught pitch too shrill. He walked under starlight, the heads of seed-tipped grasses tapping his cross-gartered calves, and the lichens on their beds of exposed shale crumbling under his step. He wound through gorse and bracken and the crushed fragrance of wild thyme until he reached the scarp overlooking the sea.

A half-moon threw needled light across waters pooled deep indigo between the knees of the headlands. The winds combed the wild rocks, cleanly freighted with salt. Insects clicked their frenzied last mating song before the killing autumn frosts. A man who had access to mage-sight could pick out the blue-white dance of their life energies, like tiny constellations of stars strewn amid the tangled briar stems and the rustling, forked stands of bracken.

A man trained to vision could see also the hazed burn of life force undone and ripped into untimely death; the animal magnetism released with spilled blood, that fanned like a taint of ill-spawned fog on the airs overhanging the Havens. The shocked blur of light would fade slowly with the passage of days, until only the rock would retain any trace of the vibration. There, the faint resonance would stay preserved like a cry in deep darkness, to remind of a violence long past. Once, when Ilitharis Paravians had walked the land, their song had eased such haunted strains of burdened energies into peace. The silver fall of rain would perform the same office, but over time, through the thousands of years that framed an age.

A prince with his mage talent blinded would see no mark at all; but his masterbard's ear might hear the wails of the spirits caught in shuddering confusion, who had yet to refind themselves as whole spirit in completed transition out of life. He might ache in despair for his lost powers, that in this time and this place could effect no ritual of release for his unforgiven toll of dead.

Touched to concern, Dakar hurried his step. He trampled through late-season asters, flecked like floating lace amid the broom. Before he was ready, he came upon a steep promontory, isolated from the land by the knife-edged slope of a trail. And on that battered height, a balled outline against sky, he made out a figure hunched into itself, arms wrapped over knees as if such a posture could bind an unwilling spirit into its vessel of bruised flesh.

Another moment only, Dakar balked on the ridge. Then, steeled against whatever rebuff might await him, he set foot on the scarp and edged forward.

Arithon s'Ffalenn remained still as the intruder he did not want stopped to a chink and scrape of boot leather over crumbled shale. He spoke through his fingers in stabbing, sudden venom. 'I suppose you couldn't resist the chance to come and meddle.'

Unpractised at minding the affairs of others, Dakar

392

ventured the first words to cross his mind, just to fill in the silence. 'You'll gain nothing by brooding.'

The awkward moment came anyway, while wind patted fingers through his unkempt hair, and twisted and untwisted the cord lacings on the other man's suede herder's jacket. 'You have no choice now and there'll be none tomorrow. The blood's been let. Accept what's finished and have done.'

Fine drawn in malice, Arithon stirred. 'You'll not put the cloak of suffering martyr over me. I fight because I will it, remember? Else I'd be aboard *Khetienn* and far from these shores. The remorse tonight must be Lysaer's.' He uncoiled further to disclose a leather flask cradled in the crook of his elbow, then jerked out the tasselled cork to an unmistakable sweet scent of strong spirits. 'Drink to my half-brother's tears with me?'

Dakar ripped the proffered flask out of strong fingers and threw it, gurgling in protest, over the cliff face. Without heat, he said, 'You damned fool. I know you too well not to guess the exact measure of your feelings.'

'And curse you for that, while I think of it,' Arithon said. The words clipped short in a cough. His hands moved in a blur to shutter his face and he twisted aside in the grass.

Aware of what was happening, Dakar dropped to his knees. He caught the prince's racked shoulders in a grasp that clamped bone, and held on through a horrible interval. Arithon lost grip on every nerve all at once, bent helpless in a vicious, heaving nausea that seemed to go on far too long.

'Have you eaten anything since morning?' Dakar asked as dry retching let up enough to allow an attempt at speech.

Spent in a shivering huddle, Arithon assembled sound into speech with great effort. 'Ask Caolle. He's been the tireless nursemaid.' He was too beaten even to set sting to his tone.

Familiar with overwrought nerves from the course of his prescient fits, Dakar knew such sickness. The shudders that wrung the other man were not going to subside until total exhaustion forced collapse.

Belated and thrown out of his depth, he came to understand worse: the prince beneath his hands had lost himself into a wilderness of grief. Arithon was weeping in harsh, unbridled bursts that had everything to do with a mind-set unsuited for cruelty.

'Think of the forty thousand,' the Mad Prophet murmured like a litany. 'Take hope for the ones you may have saved.'

The words fell thin, whisked away by the sea wind, their impact reft of meaning by an unpardonable truth. Logic, morality, justice, or reason could not stay the cut of s'Ffalenn compassion. And it came to Dakar, through the channels of his rage and an unaccustomed stab of anguish, that in fact, he was not helpless after all.

He asked and received from Arithon a ragged assent, along with the unequivocal understanding that if anybody else had dared the intervention, they would have been harried off the clifftop.

His unpractised spell of deep sleep required time to take effect. But when those terrible, dry sobs of remorse finally stilled, the Mad Prophet crouched on his knees on sharp stone, a prince he had never believed he could pity cradled in his arms like a brother.

The fine hands that had drawn a terrible lesson upon the bodies of Lysaer's troops lay undone in dreams, sealed into peace for a little while.

Alone under stars, Dakar bent his tangled head to Arithon's shoulder and mourned. He could scarcely cry for the wasted lives, torn as he was by a tragic remorse geas-cursed to outlast them. Desh-thiere's ills were not ended. He knew, as no other, that the day's burden of horror could never in life be lifted from the spirit of the man who slept enspelled in his arms; even if, under the shadow of Dier Kenton Vale, forty thousand other misled troops abandoned the war to return alive to their families.

Field of Thorns

Day broke over the Havens to the screeling calls of feeding wyverns, dipping and gliding and snapping in sharp squabbles over ledges mercifully masked behind fog. The camp atop the cliffs was broken down in cracking efficiency by the clan scouts, the dazed survivors of Lysaer's decimated companies given plain fare before they were banded together to be marched under guard into the hill country.

To the boy with the splint who still snivelled, a fellow hostage gave bracing reprimand. 'Lad, if we're to be knifed by barbarians inside the next hour, they'd scarcely waste their bread and jerky keeping us fed. Be still now and bear up.'

The more stoic veterans among the prisoners kept better grip on raw nerves, but few held much store by quick platitudes. Between snatched glances at the clansmen, who went about their duties with brisk indifference, they watched until the black-haired healer whose word had delivered them from the carnage on the strand reappeared in the company of an unkempt fat man.

His grass-stained jacket of the day before had been changed for a clean tunic of the same dusky dun that blended with the napped lichens underfoot. He spoke in words too quiet to overhear to the archers, distinguished amongst their burly frames by his slighter build. The cloak he wore was the same coarse wool. He carried no weapon, just his battered satchel of remedies slung across one shoulder.

Only when he stepped close to check bandages and poultice wraps could a man see the marks on him of a haunted, uneasy night. He looked harrowed. Beneath his every movement lay a hunted, flinching tension that startled at slight sounds, and turned listening for voices only he seemed to hear. As if he were dangerous, or chancy to cross, all but the fat man maintained their wary distance.

As different from the clanborn killers he walked with as a hawk's quill cast among broadswords, still, no man among the captive wounded dared to break his aggrieved silence to inquire why he should be here so obviously against his given will.

The company started off slowly. The pace was set to accommodate the slowest and most infirm, winding inland between peaks snagged like spindles in white cloud, or silvered in dustings of thin snow, sublimated into air the moment the sun burned through. So began an arduous trek through the high passes that lasted for fifteen days.

Townbred men who were strange to the rugged Vastmark landscape grew to hate beyond measure the whine of the winds through broom and stone and escarpment. They cursed the treacherous, uncertain shale that crumbled underfoot without warning, to skitter fragments in shattering bounds downslope. The squall of the wyvern and the hawk filled the day, and the chorus of insects by dark. Peat for fuel was dug from the marshes and borne into the heights by hand, which made cookfires cheerlessly small and short-lived. The available heat through the bone-chilling nights was limited by necessity to those sapped by blood loss who needed it most. The clansmen made no complaint. Inured to outdoor hardship, practised at setting tents out of the wind's prying fingers, they clustered together under blankets, or stood guard in the lee of lichened outcrops, scouring rust from their bone-handled weapons.

Awakened each pallid dawn to the cry of the wyvern and the accented consonants of the night watch reporting, some of the captives found their dread for the future fed and deepened. Others, seated still while the healer tended their hurts and changed their dressings, were deeply disturbed to find they were not. Their time amid clan company had shown them no evidence of the Shadow Master's inhuman witcheries. Carefully as they watched for signs of evil or corruption, nothing arose beyond the competence of superior leadership and an unbroken teamwork, well versed to maintain its cutting edge.

No matter who asked, whether in the grey-haired veteran's tactful phrasing, or in the young boy's pleading fear, none of the survivors could pry a clue from their keepers concerning the destiny awaiting them. The fat man proved deaf to all questions.

The clan scouts said in blunt dismissal, 'That's for his Grace himself to say, when he wills,' often with a fast glance over the shoulder, as if they feared someone watching.

From the healer who gave them no name, they had the soft promise, 'You will live.'

But for what sorcerous usage, or what turn of fate, every man of them dreaded to imagine, and dreamed worse in racking bouts of nightmare. In time, they arrived at the mouth of a broad meadow, dropped like a green twist of silk between the mounded debris of two rockslides. A spring-fed stream cut the swale like a scar.

Black-footed sheep grazed amid stems of goldenrod on the banks, guarded by bristling, brindle dogs. Tucked into shadow, unnoticed at first glance, three herders' tents lay pitched against the ridge of the north slope, loomed in broad, tribal patterns of saffron and sienna, sun faded to the tints of weak tea.

The advance party of clansmen were challenged by a sentry, unseen among the scree until she spoke. Of Vastmark stock, she wore her loose trousers cross-gartered to the knee and a dusty tunic hooked ragged by thorns. Her pale hair was knotted in braids. A handsome, lacquer-worked recurve bow lay slung at her shoulder. The horn at her belt had a patterned, silver rim, and she carried a sheep crook beside the quiver with her broad-bladed arrows. Those seasoned men-at-arms among Lysaer's captive wounded took her measure, and could not miss the trained squint as her eye measured distance, or the muscled, alert manner that showed the stamp of a skilled command.

After the slaughter just endured at the Havens, the appearance of a young shepherd girl indoctrinated to the arts of war chilled their blood. The hospitality they received in the larger of the tents failed to allay their unease, as they were served mutton stew and goat cheese by a tribal grandmother who muttered in dialect and made signs against the evil eye behind their backs. Over jugs of cold water and coarse biscuit, the survivors huddled, their whispered speculation cut to stark quiet as a scarred older clansman snapped the entry flap open. He announced that the Prince of Rathain would address them.

Silenced by dread, every captive faced the small man who entered, armed with a black lacquered bow and a sword of unnatural, dark steel. His neat frame glittered to the muted wash of light through the canvas, the sable and silver leopard of Rathain stitched rampant upon a green silk tabard. Under trimmed hair and the circlet of royal rank, the face was one grown familiar through the past fortnight.

Here stood the Prince of Rathain, called sorcerer and Master of Shadow. He was also none other than the healer whose hands had dressed their wounds and splinted their broken bones in a compassion whose memory became overturned into stunned disbelief at the moment his captives identified him. The irony dismembered reason, stopped thought, that *this same man's whim had sown broad-scale, indiscriminate death at the Havens.*

'Ath preserve,' gasped the iron-haired veteran. On reflex, he thrust the boy with the splinted arm behind his bulk for protection.

Green eyes flashed a glance in aggrieved recognition for a fear that drove even the bravest to edge back, and the most openhearted to cringe from too close a contact. 'I'm here to appoint you all as my sanctioned envoys,' said the Master of Shadow into the hostile quiet.

Here was none of Lysaer s'Ilessid's forthright appeal. This prince's features stayed shuttered. His voice, crisp and light, made no bid for close loyalty. Without fire, stripped to its thread of bald conviction, the fate Rathain's liege held in store for the chosen twenty-five he had selected was forthright to the point where no listener dared to believe him.

'You'll be given an escort to the central valley of Vastmark to rejoin the main body of your army.' Through a murmur of astonished voices, Arithon cracked, 'I want a spokesman. You.' His gesture singled out the senior officer, a captain from the city of Perlorn, whose fealty by old kingdom charter should have been subject to Rathain. 'Step forward.'

The appointed man stood forth, too straight in his ripped hauberk, the wrist healing clean through an enemy's faultless care clenched to his breast as he suffered a scrutiny that seemed to strip him skin from bone.

'I want the news of your ruin at the Havens to reach your master before the week's end,' Arithon said. 'Find Lysaer s'Ilessid. Spare him no detail of your report. I wish no mistake, no attempt to dismiss your defeat at the inlet as unlucky.' A pause, while the wounded captain sought some simple way to unravel the contradictions and discern what moved the slight enemy confronting him.

'Know this,' Arithon cut him off before he found nerve enough to question. 'If this allied warhost under Lord Commander Diegan takes arms in Vastmark, I stand prepared. You've tasted the mettle of my archers. What tactics you suffered at the Havens can be made the more deadly through sorcery or shadows. I warn. Numbers make no difference, nor morals, nor dedication. Any who march here to take me will suffer disaster on a grand scale. The men you lead back are my witnesses. Be sure they are heard. Make the officers of Lysaer's warhost understand that if they seek bloodshed in Shand, I will not stay my hand.'

'You want us to sap our men of courage,' the gaunt captain accused.

Green eyes flicked up to match him, stung to a frost spark of irony. 'Daelion as my witness,' Arithon flared back in pure anger. '*I want you to save their sorry lives.*'

Lord Diegan had rediscovered in his service to Lysaer how much he detested open-air camps and chill rain. For three days, while the central body of the warhost laboured on its closing march into Vastmark, the peaks lay roofed over in cloud. Drizzle dulled the landscape to pewter, the broken slate slopes snagged into overcast like the layered slabs of scrap lead in a glassworker's yard. The poor, stony soil glistened with runoff, or gave way to black bogs where a horse could mire to the brisket. Dry ground was non-existent. Tents pitched on gravel became wet and unpleasant as the ones staked into the peat-reeking mud.

The wool factor's man recruited as a trail guide had no opinion for ill weather beyond a glance tipped through bushy eyebrows toward the silted grey sky. 'Blighted Vastmark clouds could shed wet for a week. Thank Ath Creator. In this benighted country, that's the only damned thing puts good wool on the sheep.'

Dismounted to the spitting flare of torches, his boots gritted with gravel on the inside and mud caked to stretched leather without, Lord Diegan clenched perfect teeth and cursed everything connected with fleeces and sheep. Provisions were an ongoing devilment. With flour and oats wont to mould, any flock caught in the path of his troops would find itself slaughtered for mutton.

Flagged down before he could surrender the reins of his destrier into the care of his groom, the Lord Commander of Lysaer s'Ilessid's warhost blessed fate that the s'Brydion brothers held the supply lines. Without their bull-stubborn efficiency, the campaign would have bogged in its tracks.

'Lord, there's a man arrived from the fringe patrol with news,' interrupted his equerry, a scrappy little man who regarded inbound scouts and the intrusion of inept servants alike on his list of life's nuisances.

Routine problems never disrupted the command tent; the scout, still mounted, had no word to say beyond, 'My lord, I think you should come.'

'Bad news?' Diegan hitched his shoulders to relieve the rub of his mail shirt and soaked hauberk, caught back the reins of his horse, and set his foot into the stirrup. 'You can report just as well from the saddle.'

As the pair rode past the picket lines, dodging grooms, and crossed the outer ring of sentries to press into the rainy darkness, the scout related the raw gist: an engagement with the Master of Shadow at the Havens had left five hundred men dead. The shock that threatened upset were the twenty-five survivors, held apart in a small glen beyond the camp perimeter by the patrol of four who had encountered them, stumbling down from the high passes toward the lights and the fires.

'They claim they were brought from the coast by the enemy's feal clansmen,' related the scout as he rounded a last rock spur, flanked in dark skirts of dripping bracken. 'When you hear what they say, you'll see why we held them. Their story's going to rip morale to bloody ribbons.'

This far outside the lines, there could be no torches. The hollow tucked beneath the jagged shoulder of the hill was cheerless, filled with the moan of the wind and trickle and drip of water. There, the wounded from the Havens pressed in a huddled mass beneath the partial shelter of an outcrop, a blurred jumble of pale hands and featureless, rain-blurred faces.

Lord Diegan pulled up, dismounted, and said, 'Wait here.' On presumption the scout would catch his tired mount's bridle, he strode over loose stone into the shallow defile. The jingle of his spurs drew a heave of movement in the pathetic, wet knot of refugees. They surrounded him like schooling fish to crowd close, inquiring.

An older veteran captain with a north country accent presented himself as their spokesman. Recognition of the Lord Commander's rank brought a respectful hush, cut by the cry of a night heron from some unseen marsh down the ridge.

'I've been told you suffered an attack by the Master of Shadow,' Lord Diegan opened, then demanded to hear what had happened.

From the first account, the surrounding night seemed to turn fearfully colder. His pulse quickened, the skin beneath his soggy gambeson shivered into chills, the commander of Lysaer's warhost listened as men rendered nameless and faceless by the night gave their bare description of a trapped cliff and a relentless toll of dead, fallen to arrows and fire. The voices held the ragged stress of reliving; all the stifled, helpless rage of men who had watched comrades die, and questioned their right to keep breathing. The clenched fists, the soft curses, the coarse tears of the boy with the splinted arm brought back hateful, ugly memories.

Lord Diegan stared away into shadow hazed grey with rain, bedevilled by the raised spectre of another drenched field, and the mud-silted, tangled dead on the banks of Tal Quorin in Strakewood.

'What took place was no battle, but a planned execution,' the veteran captain summed up. 'Lucky we are to have reached your ear swiftly, my Lord Commander. For we survived by design to carry last warning to Prince Lysaer. The Master of Shadow has sworn his oath on our blood that what happened at the Havens was no accident. He's promised if the warhost advances to engage him in Vastmark, we shall be snared in disaster.'

'That's no news to be handled lightly,' Lord Diegan agreed, too urbane to reveal his blazing rage. 'Before we go the next step, I'll have your report set in writing. A scribe will come here to take statements under my seal before witnesses. I'll send guards, a tent, food and blankets, as soon as they can be arranged. The rest must wait until morning, since our prince has retired for the night.'

Brisk in distess, the Lord Commander took his leave. He strode up the rise, waded through bracken feathered in droplets to the gulch where his scout remained with the horses. Careful to keep his voice low, he said, 'The rest of your patrol are Etarran?'

A soft word confirmed from the dark. 'All trained under Pesquil, rest him. Why, you have need for discretion?'

Diegan let go an imperceptible sigh of relief. 'Near

enough.' His scouts were well seasoned. Already they grasped the sensitive problem posed by these survivors. If measures must be taken for expediency, he need not grind through tedious explanations to convince them to follow his orders. 'I'm going to send servants from my personal train. They'll set up two tents, one to serve a cold meal. When the refugees have eaten, you'll bring each in singly, but not to make the written statements they've been told to expect.'

Bit rings jingled as Diegan's horse butted a damp nose against his chest. Knocked back a half-step by the antic, he slapped the animal off, clammy where the water ran off his black hair and soaked steady, cold runnels down his gambeson. 'Your men will bind and gag the refugees and hold them there,' he added to the scout. 'No noise, no fuss. Nobody speaks with them. Word of the slaughter at the Havens must never leave this hollow. In time, a team of headhunters will come to relieve you. Gather your party then and return to the main camp. I'll see the man dead who asks questions. This matter will be handled to my satisfaction, and your part is to keep your own counsel.'

'You won't want an escort back?' the scout asked, Etarran born, and well accustomed to the clandestine intrigues men of power engaged for necessity.

Lord Diegan set foot in his stirrup, swung himself astride to a grinding jingle of metal. 'I need time to think by myself.'

He turned his weary mare and spurred her to a trot through the darkness, while the heron cried like a lost spirit over the marshes, and the rain tapped chill tears against his face. Until Arithon s'Ffalenn lay dead, the horrors enacted at Tal Quorin, at Minderl Bay, at the Havens, were bound to repeat and compound.

Burdened now by the need to avert the vicious stress which had nearly unstrung Prince Lysaer at Werpoint, Lord Diegan weighed his options, alone in the Vastmark night. Bluff and cleverness were entrenched s'Ffalenn tactics. No doubt the bloodshed at the Havens had been wrought as a weapon to tear the heart from the warhost. Worse, the strain incited by the horrific rout was expressly designed to chafe at Lysaer's moral conscience. Well warned that the nightmares and the driving remorse still suffered by his Grace since the fleet burned at Minderl Bay would make the affray at the Havens loom large, Lord Diegan measured his alternatives.

By the time he threaded his horse through the mucky lanes between the bonfires of the war camp, he had determined tonight's news of an unspeakable carnage was a provocation his prince must be spared. Lysaer had been living on nerves and determination since his break with Talith at Ostermere. His mood had run sharp and brittle as eggshells, and through the nights he scarcely slept. The risk must not be taken, that the calculated slaughter of five hundred men might become the excuse to turn the army from its purpose in Shand.

To avenge the cruel usage his sister had suffered, perhaps to mend her sadly scarred marriage, Diegan resolved to take fate in hand. By himself, he would make certain the campaign proceeded to corner and claim its due quarry. For the Havens was a bluff, a last brazen effort on the part of Arithon to buy escape. No man with a motley force of shepherd archers, even given the strengths of wielded shadow, could rout a warhost forty thousand strong.

Settled by hard logic that the odds lay in his favour, Diegan dismounted before his tent, tossed his reins to his groom, and meted out swift strings of orders to the equerry on duty. His body servant arrived, wide-eyed and nervous, to strip off his surcoat and mail. Hard at heel came his secretary, rousted from bed by his summons.

'I'll want privacy and the loan of your lap desk,' Lord Diegan said. Without another word, he stepped out of the rain, into the dense, clammy gloom of his command tent.

The lanterns engaged in pallid war against the dark creaked and tossed on their hooks as the wind slapped over laced canvas. Water ran, dripping in broken arpeggios, from seams long since soaked through. A particularly virulent leak had sprouted over the blankets on his cot. Resigned to sleeping in puddles, Diegan rubbed a wrist stained in oil and rust across his brow, then threw himself down on a camp chair. He took the lap desk from the thin-shanked scribe, who trailed at his elbow like a hound. 'Come back for your things in the morning.'

'Yes, lord.' The little man departed, tripping over his large feet in his haste.

'Later,' Diegan barked in dismissal to the servant who hovered by his clothes chest, a towel in hand to clean his boots. He yanked open the lap desk, rummaged out pens and ink and two pristine squares of parchment.

By the time Skannt's headhunters reported for their assignment, he had the necessary documents signed and sealed with his personal cipher.

To the sinewy, weathered captain who entered the tent for instructions, he said, 'Outside of camp, due northwest, you'll find a pair of tents guarded by four Etarran scouts. There are twenty-five men with them, all deserters from a minor skirmish with the enemy that took place on the upper coast. They've been duly judged and sentenced. I ordered them bound. Your knife work should go quick and quiet.'

Diegan arose. His hand did not shake as he proffered the ribboned, official documents, though even he was unsettled by the man he had engaged. The captain's presence carried a miasma like the reek of old blood; whether real or imagined, few would draw near enough to determine.

'Here's proper writ for arraignment, and here, the order

407

of execution.' The warhost's Lord Commander finished off, 'See the shirking dogs beneath the Wheel, then burn the bodies. We need no reminders lying about to undermine the morale of our other steadfast troops.'

'Ath!' The steel studs on the captain's jerkin caught baleful light as he stuffed the rolled parchments through his belt, then peeled off a gauntlet to test the edge on his dagger. 'Should've guessed, at this hour, the duty'd be a messy one. We getting scalp pay to clean up your bothersome details?'

'Ten silvers a head,' Diegan affirmed. 'Two of my servants will ride with you to inform me when the deed's been done.'

The headhunter gave a silent, wheezed laugh as he snicked his steel in its sheath. 'Assassins' guildsmen?' He squinted askance at his Lord Commander, a sneer on his full upper lip. 'You know we don't need any pandering witnesses to make sure of our kills.'

Diegan gestured his dismissal without comment. When the tent flap cracked closed after the headhunter's stalking stride, he bellowed for his servants to return and attend to his interrupted comforts.

He was too hardened, too practical, too much the survivor of ambitious years of city politics. His dreams would be troubled by no screams at all, as Arithon's fell tactic was foiled, and the twenty-five died in cold blood.

Endings

As the sun rises over the pastel drum towers of Innish,
and the light falls gold and pink through the sandstone
arches of a portico facing the harbour, Jinesse and
Tharrick stand with linked hands before the robed
figure of an adept of Ath's Brotherhood; and as each
swears the vow of marriage, their thoughts dwell with
ambivalence and regret upon the enigmatic, black-
haired prince whose fate brought their two lives
together . . .

In a purple-carpeted chamber in the Koriani orphanage at
the coastal town of Firstmark, Lirenda lays the amethyst
Great Waystone into the hands of Morriel Prime with
the words, 'Matriarch, rejoice, for my mission to Althain
Tower has brought the success you required . . .'

In a high, guarded tower in the city of Avenor, Princess
Talith sits on velvet cushions in a south-facing window
seat to stare out over the sea; and through a weight of
unbearable sorrow, she aches for the absence of her

beloved, pledged to lead a warhost to kill a single enemy whose cursed destiny has come to poison everything in life she held dear . . .

VIII. *STRIKE AT DIER KENTON*

The dawn over Vastmark came in smothering white mist, threaded by intermittent rainfall. Against air textured thick as unpressed felt, and the eerie shrills of flying wyverns, the cluster of shepherds' tents set on the lip of the scree came and went from view, their primal, dyed patterns like an herb witch's talismans scribed in old blood and rust. Before them, furled in damp clothing where he crouched stirring peat embers with a gorse twig, Dakar the Mad Prophet brooded in silence, his hair and beard screwed into rings.

Behind him, standing, the hood over his mail dull grey as the landscape, Caolle tested the edge of his newly oiled sword, a squint to his eye that boded trouble. Since the Havens, he had lost flesh. The skin pressed like cured leather over the craggy jut of his face bones, and his hands, never wont to pause between tasks, turned the blade in forced deliberation. 'The tactic last fortnight has failed,' he said, flat. 'Lysaer's warhost is coming despite us. Please Ath, don't make me be the one to break the news.'

'His Grace already knows.' Dakar gave a particularly fierce jab at the embers and the sparks flurried, red-gold

411

on the colourless air. 'Arithon said last night he could feel the stir of the Mistwraith's curse.' For Lysaer pressed his march forward, not back. His army had closed, and harried, and set cordons, until the vale of Dier Kenton lay bottled in, each goat track and pass leading over the peaks sealed off by hostile troops. 'Arithon said we have until noon before the pull of the geas builds to unmanageable proportions.'

Caolle sheathed his blade without sound by wary habit, then flicked a swift glance at the tent. 'He's sleeping?'

'No.' Dakar looked up, his pudding-round features all misery. 'But he's reasonable, and trying to rest.'

'Let him bide, then,' Caolle said. 'We won't need his final orders before the mist starts to lift.' He strode off from the fire, disgruntled for the first time in his life by a bellyache before the onset of battle.

The mists that presaged autumn in Vastmark could hug the land like raw silk, impenetrable, then part without warning to some unseen caprice of changed air. The vale at Dier Kenton emerged out of stainless, cloaking white like an uneven bowl draped in furrows of burlap left out and beaten by weather, then salted with dirty flecks of shale. Mountains arose around the rim. The mild range of hills which invited easy access from the west built ever higher as the pitch of the valley steepened. The east wall swept up, a sheer face of grim scarps that speared blue-green shadow across the knoll where Caolle stood. Around him, pitched as a decoy to draw Lysaer's main force, an array of steel helms set on stakes presented empty eyeholes toward the lowlands. Planted on a pole in their midst, the lazy slap of standards flicked a buffet of silk on leather against the war captain's shoulder. Clan custom dictated their arrangement: the purple-and-gold chevrons of Shand uppermost; then the black-on-grey wyvern, sigil of the principality of Vastmark; and lowest, the green, sable and silver of Rathain's royal leopard, symbolically set in deference to the sovereign rule of the southland.

The irksome rains had ceased. Today's clear morning held a fresh crispness and tension like an indrawn breath. Across the saddle at the vale's far rim seethed the frontal body of the allied host to bring down the Master of Shadow, particoloured as sweepings from a tailor's shop, spiked like stray pins where early sun flicked the metal of a helm or a sword blade. The landscape was vast, and the men, an unnatural, living carpet a league and a half in width.

'Such bother for one life,' Caolle murmured. 'It's not canny.' The nerve-fraught awareness he was surrounded by foes ranked many thousands strong made his skin feel harried by itches. He cleared his throat, then finished his instructions to the runner scout waiting at his elbow.

The clansman slipped off. The knoll remained pressed in grim silence, while the mists ebbed and came in white-footed waves like ranked ghosts. The swirl of moisture and the presence of the peaks funnelled disjointed sounds in queer patterns. A rider's horn call might ring in deceptive, close clarity, or make some distant officer's snapped word to correct a laggard man in formation seem close enough to touch. Other times the breeze blew muffled in drifts, as if broken stone and desolation were all that had ruled since Paravian times.

Then the fog would clear again to reveal the army's advance a disquieting furlong closer. The front lines were near enough now to mark divisions, each city's garrison ranked out in squares. Rowed pikemen trickled like ants around the boulders left strewn by old slides. The stream of ribboned banners, the snorts of fresh horses, the snatched strains of voices raised in song to hold the tempo of the march as helms bobbed, disappeared and crested the banks of gullies, formed an inexorable flow of greyed steel over uneven terrain.

Easier to regard them as a leaden wave, Caolle thought, a mindless, cutting tide of sharpened weapons. Details only served to tear at the heart, that defined the ragged edge of the advance as single men who had lives and human fears.

Caolle shut his eyes, aching inside for what must come. For the stakes were no longer malleable. Each side would kill in defence of its prince; the living would mourn and the slain would stay dead. As Arithon had most cruelly foreseen, the recent blood spilled at the Havens in the weight of this moment seemed a pittance. A man could stand atop the knoll at Dier Kenton where the trap would be sprung and wonder if five hundred planned casualties had been enough; whether more than one raid and a thousand more corpses could have stemmed the flood of tens of thousands. Then if not a thousand, how many more, until the goading question of if and if again caused the mind to shudder off its wretched track and embrace the plunge into despair.

For the first time since childhood, Caolle felt haunted by his ghosts: from a few dozen caravan drovers and couriers in Jaelot livery with slit throats, to the wyvern-picked corpses on the shoreside ledges, to the current warhost still living, still marching in deafened belief of a just role in a grand destiny.

A stranger to himself, to feel harried by a young man's uncertainties, Caolle found the prospect of drawing steel abhorrent. Nor did any cause under sky seem reason enough to claim another life. In the wrong place, years too late, he realized his pride and his skills as a killer led nowhere.

'I have no one else I trust to see this through,' husked a quiet voice near his elbow.

Caolle started, spun, and met a face as haunted as his own. His liege lord had arrived without sound at his side, the change in him since the Havens the very epitome of heartbreak.

Too thin, too pale, too worn, Arithon met the mirrored anguish in his war captain's glance. Again he answered the unspoken shock for the changes to his appearance. 'It's as much Desh-thiere's curse and the draw upon my will as Lysaer approaches our position as any single burden from the past.'

Caolle bunched helpless fists at his sword belt. 'Lysaer's a murderer beyond compare, to mislead so many for the effort of buying your life.' A sweep of his arm embraced the advancing lines, now darkening the vale's western end like an infestation of blight. 'Your tactic at the Havens was a mere pittance before this.'

'No.' Arithon studied the overwhelming, massive deployment, unable to mask his expression. Or perhaps the strength in him was too self-absorbed to spare any token thought for privacy. While the wind flicked his loose sable hair, the compassion that in this moment lacerated him from within showed in scraped pain through his words. 'Lysaer's not yet blinded to mercy. I have to believe that. Our twenty-five survivors never got through, nor had their chance to deliver fair warning.'

No argument remained; the weeks since the Havens had seen their shepherd archers surrounded. Nothing else could be done except embrace grim reality and follow the final step through.

After one bitter lesson at Merior, Arithon's decision was fixed. He would abandon no ally to suffer the curse-twisted influence of his half-brother.

Caolle regarded his prince with an uneasy mix of pity and wary apprehension. 'You have a will Dharkaron himself should fear to cross,' he said, then spun on vexed reflex to meet a scrambling disturbance at his back.

Dakar crested the rise, wheezing like a holed bellows. Beneath his tousled hair and the wiry bristle of his beard, his complexion showed the blued pallor of half-congealed candle wax. 'Nothing alive should be standing here,' he gasped. An expressive roll of his eyes encompassed the surrounding peaks, this moment clogged under clouds. As if chased by a thought, his brows furrowed underneath his woolly bangs. 'Fiends plague, Arithon. So *that*'s what you were doing mooning about, walking this place over and over again at night throughout the spring.' He turned an impossible shade paler.

'Listening to the pitch of the stone,' Rathain's prince admitted, steady enough for all that he looked as if the touch of a finger might shatter him.

'Dharkaron's tears!' Dakar cried. For since the seep of the autumn rains had rinsed the heights, even his limited mage-sight could detect how the shale was faulted. 'Don't anybody sneeze. I want for nothing except to be finished my work and hunkered down on high ground.'

'Well, his Grace said the scarp would slide and close the passes,' Caolle said, never impressed with histrionics.

'A bard's prize understatement,' Dakar groused beneath his breath. Then louder, 'Both of you, move. You're standing on the site I need to enhance my spell pattern.'

Caolle edged aside as though faced by coiled snakes. Magecraft and mystery lay a rung below cheap trickery in his opinion, but he knew better than to waste breath arguing points of honour with a madman.

'Dakar adheres to Fellowship teaching,' Arithon reassured. 'Any spell he works upon life or substance must be founded upon free permission.'

'You say!' The war captain snorted his disbelief, dark eyes squinted down the valley out of habit to mark tactics as the warhost began its last stage of deployment. 'So, they're smart enough after all not to charge their light horse over stone. You'll face pikemen in squares with archers at the centre. Slow but sure. The gullies will hamper their advance, but not much.' The war captain paused to slice a glower up the rise, where Dakar paced off a slow circle around the banners and helmets, his head tucked in frowning concentration. 'And I don't believe yon soldiers all chucked you a grin and bent their stupid necks to be witched.'

The Mad Prophet paused between steps, his offence expressed in a crafty glint of teeth that might have been a smile behind his beard. 'Not in so many words. But Lysaer's soldiers, to a man, allowed themselves to be deluded. The mesh I weave here will only cause them to see exactly what they believe they should find.'

'A sorcerer, a vile killer, a corrupter of innocent children,' Arithon finished in shaded, soft sorrow. 'They will behold what my half-brother has led them to expect and react as they have been trained.'

'Which means, prince, you'd better have distance between and a blindfold on when it happens,' Dakar retorted.

Arithon did not respond, but held his regard on the warhost below in cat-eyed concentration. The Mad Prophet glanced at him, sharp, then spun to the war captain in a high-strung concern that was strikingly out of character. 'Caolle, for the love you bear Rathain, *get your liege lord out of here, now!*'

The sun climbed another two hours higher and the mists fled before warmth, leaving a sky matted in haze the colour of bleached bone. Ruled by perversity, the wind died until the banners of the royal warhost draped limp on their poles. The hemmed ranges at the head of Dier Kenton Vale reflected every sound back, until the snort of a horse, the dull plink of mail, the jangle of harness held a hemmed-in, unsettling intimacy.

Puddles had dried, but the stubborn mud lingered, turning each step to sucking misery. The horses slid and sweated and cast shoes off damp-softened hooves.

417

Grateful for the one coarse mount in his string too tough to pull up lame, Lord Diegan leaned over its unstylish, thick crest to tighten the strap on his helm. He lowered a sweaty wrist tinged in rust and swore. Armour polished inside of three days already showed attrition from the damp. No longer the dandy to fuss over appearances, the soldier he had become reviled the neglect to his gear.

At his side, a figure bright as a gilt-trimmed icon in a steel cuirass edged with gold chasing, Lysaer s'Ilessid turned blue eyes spiked to a baleful charge of humour. 'Why mind the rust? Your gear's sure to need scouring tonight just to clean off the bloodstains.'

'I don't care how many shepherds' tents our patrols counted out on the heights. Those tribesfolk can move like wind itself and today's shown no movement to report.' Diegan lifted his chin to scan the peaks which ringed the vale like the glistening, crusted teeth of a wolf's jaws. 'Either nothing's up there, or they're holed up like stoats, just watching us work up a lather.'

Lysaer smiled. 'Did you truly expect this would be easy?'

'Never.' But through the past weeks, riding in exhausting zigzag patterns up and down rocky corries as strike teams were dispatched to drive Arithon's lighter forces before them like scrap sweepings chased by a broom, Diegan found his temper worn to breaking. Too many of the unseasoned garrison men boasted on their successes, that the archers always broke and ran under attack. If today the prince's troops held the Shadow Master's encampments surrounded, the creeping suspicion lingered that they were for a surety being led.

Lord Diegan held no illusions. When his warhost was finally permitted to close, when the shepherds and clansmen stood their ground, courage and armed might were not guaranteed to bring victory. Arithon s'Ffalenn would not be cornered without an ugly fight. His blood would

418

be bought in fallen bodies, his sorceries crushed at last under the weight of sheer numbers.

'Well, we haven't long to wait,' Lysaer finished in frigid certainty. 'Our enemy is near. I can sense his presence.'

A staccato rattle of hooves on shale marked an inbound scout, who crested the rise ahead of the advance army. Pressed flat to the neck of his mount, he thundered straight for the cluster of command standards and reined his hill pony to a head-shaking halt. 'Your Grace, my Lord Commander, we've made contact.' He unfisted a hand from his reins and pointed up the vale toward the stony rim of the knoll which divided the swale of the valley. 'We've seen royal banners there. A band of armoured enemies lie entrenched in ambush behind.'

'Halt the columns,' Lysaer said to Lord Diegan. As the ranks around him shuddered still to a magnified creak of harness, and horn calls repeated the command down the vast length of the line, he snapped his fingers to the page boy who trailed on foot by his stirrup. 'Hand me my glass.'

His eyes, cold sapphire, stayed fixed on the crest of the knoll as he accepted the brass casing and snapped its segments open. Trained upon the summit, the eyepiece yielded a grainy view of silver-pebbled helms, a ranked thicket of pole weapons, then the standards of Shand and Vastmark, accompanied in presumptuous arrogance by the leopard device of Rathain.

Lysaer felt a sharp sweep of heat cross his skin. His eyesight seemed to blur momentarily out of focus. A half-sensed brush of cold that might have been magecraft prickled the hair at his nape. For an instant, he *almost* saw a black-haired figure lift a mocking, triangular chin to taunt him over the blade of a black sword.

The animal snarl that arose in his throat was nearly too savage to repress. Fired to white fury, Lysaer clenched his fingers on brass and fought a blistering, sharp battle to retain his grip on self-command. Wise in restraint since the disaster provoked at Minderl Bay, he jerked down the glass and snapped it shut. 'He's there. There's a fighting force behind him.'

Which statement required no name to qualify; his steely majesty hammered over in tight anticipation, the Prince of the West met his Lord Commander face on. 'In my name, for the deliverance of all people, lead the advance. Let right prevail over darkness.'

Diegan's salute held matching eagerness. 'Mine the honour, highness. In your name and for the memory of Etarra's city garrison sacrificed on the banks of Tal Quorin.' And, he added inwardly, for the dishonour of my lady sister.

Then he filled his lungs, raised his shout. The trumpet notes of his staff officer relayed the signal to attack down the lines.

The Prince of the West and his personal bodyguard relinquished their place in the advance guard. While one chosen company peeled away to stand with them on a vantage lent by high ground, the main body of the royal warhost juddered into motion, to sweep up the throat of Dier Kenton Vale and close upon the knoll, and lay waste to the Shadow Master's allies. At their backs, a figure of inspiring magnificence on his gold-maned war-horse, Lysaer raised his fist. He threw back his head and shouted in glad satisfaction as his gift swelled and answered. Then he opened mailed fingers. Raw light slapped forth, a blinding hot fireball hurled skyward to carve a scalding arc across the heavens.

The elemental burst exploded in blinding force at the zenith to a blast of distant thunder. Visible for leagues, the signal would alert the supporting forces from Jaelot and Alestron in position beyond the mountains of the rim wall. These would enact a simultaneous advance up the far slopes of the cliffs. The steel ring that hedged Dier Kenton began its closing march to crush the trapped quarry, over ground too stony for pit traps, too bare for ambush or cover. This time, the ragtag dregs who defended the Master of Shadow would be left no direction to run.

While the central deployment of the warhost rolled in dust and noise up the broad spread of the valley, Lysaer unclenched locked fingers and passed the glass to the most keen-eyed of his scouts. 'Keep watch,' he commanded. 'If you spot any sign of the enemy, tell me.'

Not for nothing had the prince practised with his gift through the years of preparation at Avenor. Bowfire and shadows had been Arithon's key defences at Tal Quorin. Lysaer bared even teeth. Praise be to justice, now, he had the finesse to forge his gift into a countershield for both. A silky, sure smile curved his lips. If need be, he would fire the very spine of the mountain, burn out the entrenched bands of tribesmen and archers, and light the way for his troops to advance and claim victory.

Tucked into a rocky declivity in the rimrocks above Dier Kenton Vale, the Mad Prophet stood at Arithon's back, his plump hands pressed white against the royal shoulders that had not stopped trembling since Lysaer's signal bolt had roared aloft.

'Steady,' he murmured. 'Hold steady.' Then, as the distant glitter of the s'Ilessid bodyguard settled on station behind the rear ranks amid the low hills to the west, 'For the love of Ath, don't look now.'

Arithon gave a choked-off smile. Balled in a crouch with his hands locked around his knees, his eyes swathed under a black binding tied off with spell-turned knots, he was most effectively blinded to the movements of his enemy. Dakar and his war captain must serve as his eyes. Since the botched tienelle scrying aboard the *Khetienn*, the spellbinder had earned the clear

421

right to ask permissions of him even a Fellowship Sorcerer might hesitate to impose.

The time was past for uncertainties, beyond all reach of regrets. Meshed into the pattern traced out through cold auguries, Rathain's prince could only hope his unreserved consent would lend Dakar the leverage to help him if the mad onslaught of the curse became too great to endure.

In the event such constraint let him down, in final threat, his black sword Alithiel lay unsheathed and waiting.

The chance shrank his heart, made his nerves flinch in dread, that the terrible, edged beauty of the Paravian starspell might be turned against him again. He dared not frame the possibility that one day even this measure might fail him. The sweat which ran down the slant of his jaw arose as much from that fear as from grief for the trap set in the path of Lysaer's warhost.

The spread of thin sun on his shoulders, the smell of wild thyme and wind-caught evergreen held the untrustworthy peace of a drug dream. Needled by circling thoughts, Arithon shifted.

A firm, bearing pressure thrust him down as Dakar said, 'Damn you, prince, not yet.'

Yet a masterbard's ear could pick out the spellbinder's cranked tension, and know: the platitude masked the surety that the advance ranks drew within bowshot of the cluster of banners on knoll. The circle of illusionary spellcraft that had lured twenty-eight thousand to advance would not hold together in close proximity.

An outraged shout of discovery floated up, sliced by the peal of a horn call.

'Lord Diegan's troop?' Arithon asked, a thin tug of humour tilting one corner of his mouth.

'The very same. Their scouts just brought word of the helmets.' Dakar snorted back a laugh at the snarled disarray as the proud centre companies from Avenor converged, yelling outrage. The banners, the staked ranks of armour and pikestaffs seemed a pitiful ruse to have made grand fools of them all.

'I tell you,' cried the foray's captain, his humiliated anger shaved brittle by distance. 'That knoll is bare of any enemies! There is no ambush, no hidden strike force at all.'

Yet Lord Diegan had learned deadly caution under Pesquil. Tenacious as a lashed mastiff, he deployed a half-company to quarter the ground to be sure. The knoll swarmed with movement. A foot soldier rendered toy-sized against the span of the vale raised a sword and in a fit of silent fury hacked down the royal leopard standard.

That flash of bare steel and the wind-caught shreds of green silk for some unnamed reason ignited Dakar to slow rage.

'Now,' he ground out in a whisper.

Arithon stilled underneath his grip, locked for a second against the horrific inevitability of the moment. Then, as he had once loosed a bowstring to launch an arrow streamered in red ribbons, he deployed his gift in unreserved signature of his presence.

Shadow ripped out and battened Dier Kenton under implacable darkness.

Cries of terror ripped up from the valley, followed in fated sequence by Lysaer's defending counterplay of light. The burst of illumination sheeted through to create a flickering, sulphurous twilight. No longer the green fool, the Prince of the West would not fire blind strikes at an enemy which offered no target. His response came tempered, sufficient in force to provide his troops with the illumination they required to close and fight.

'More,' Dakar whispered.

Arithon spun his darkness thicker, deeper, smothering his half-brother's effort in what seemed an effortless parry.

In direct touch with the tension which knotted the muscles beneath his hands, Dakar was not deceived. 'Lysaer's gotten stronger with his gift, has he not?'

A nod snapped back in response. Arithon braced through a hard shudder, and the dark coiled out like steel bands, laced warp through weft in anchored struggle.

The impact of Lysaer's bolt was less seen than felt, a fan of hot wind burdened in a cracking scent of ozone. The report followed, a smothered whump of compressed air that shivered the stone underfoot.

A sound escaped Arithon's lips. His hands locked into sweaty fists as he deepened his shadows yet again. Lysaer's next counterburst bowled a crescendo of thunder across the heavens. The thrust came straightforward in control, directed skyward, its aim to sear off the unnatural night and reclaim an untrammelled field for battle. Yet even expended without solid target, the princes' paired gifts clashed in violence.

The booming concussion of shocked elements hammered earth and air like a physical blow, then recoiled off the walls of the peaks.

For an instant, the mountains seemed to quiver in echoed, resonant response.

Caught in a flickering, flaring, tainted wash of daylight, Dakar followed with mage-sight the wrenching scream of force as the unstable faults in the shale slopes below surrendered their last ties to gravity.

A tortured rumble rocked bass echoes down the vale. The grumble built, compounded into a grinding, full-throated roar as the shoulders of the mountains front and centre buckled and let go, followed like unravelled crochet work by the slopes on either side. Soil and vegetation sliced away from the scarp. Half-glimpsed through torn thickets of shadow, lit lurid by the unnatural tangle of sheared light kinked like sword cuts through absolute dark, the slow-motion crumple of boulders and torn soil gained frenetic speed in a race to meet the exposed valley. As if ploughed to rolling chaos by the impact of a giant's fist, the mass surged in a wave down the steep rims of the vale.

The vanguard of Lord Diegan's troops glimpsed their doom through the sickly yellow twilight, their panicked screams battered under and lost in the roaring complaint of outraged earth. Horses reared on shaking ground. Pennons dipped, cast out of nerveless fingers. Ranks of pikemen compressed in raw terror, their weapons juddered into recoil like a tailor's pins in crushed cloth.

Then the caroming breaker of rock and soil smashed down from the middle, and on both flanks. The companies in the vanguard were sprayed aside, then harrowed under like shell soldiers abandoned to the muddied teeth of flood tide.

The rearguard array became chewed, then engulfed, mashed under the surge in the moment they wheeled in hopeless flight. If any screamed, their cries were drowned out. If any prayed, none were answered. Where an army had marched like steel-studded velvet over grass, within a heartbeat and a breath, of living soldiers, there were none.

The peaks channelled between them a racked furrow of turned stone and puffed dirt. The titanic, roiling thunder of debris milled on in a mindless torrent that dwarfed human works and consumed all things in its path.

Minutes passed, while the mountains shook to their roots from raw noise.

Then, in slowed force, the barrage dragged thin and slackened, spent into a last, dying tumble of stray boulders. Fanned like a rucked, brown train in its wake, a flayed span of ground wide enough to stun reason was left to settle into dust and racked stillness. Stabbed through by the distress of displaced birds, the thinner wails of human survivors offered up ragged refrain: those few set by luck on the unfaulted rise where the hills were too mild to slide, and one isolate group in the swale, protected where the shoulder of the knoll had parted the riven marrow of the earth.

Separate from the advance, the company of the prince's personal guard was also untouched. Spared only by distance, the men in their immaculate surcoats stared in dumb shock at the site where their comrades had marched. The demarcation was a cruel one. Like a ripped edge in cloth, the scar ended and whole grass flicked in breezes silted with grit churned up by the mass of downed stone.

Strewn at Lysaer's very feet, in disembowelled earth and crushed hope, a mass grave site: ploughed into irretrievable oblivion the pulped bits of tissue, wood and dented steel of what once had been twenty-eight thousand dedicated men.

The howl of the Prince of the West clove the morning, shrill with grief and wild pain. The light of his gift left his fist. A flashfire bolt of distilled energy shrieked across distance and slammed against the summit of the knoll. Impact carved up a flying gout of rocks, an eruption of dead matter that yielded his rage no balm of satisfaction.

Lysaer wept for his impotent strength. The Shadow Master's spelled decoy of banners and empty helmets flamed and melted under impact of his grief, leaving the site razed bare.

Thrown off his berserk mount when the slide boomed past, then knocked flat a second time by the light bolt's raw thud into the hillcrest above, Diegan, Lord Commander of the royal warhost, struggled up from his knees. Around him, spent thunder cracked and slammed in flat echoes against the changed face of Dier Kenton. His hip and one shoulder flamed protest, the joints wrenched and bruised from his falls. Since the knoll had blocked his view as the cataclysm struck, he cast a dazed glance at his surroundings. On all sides, he saw harrowed earth. The day hung dimmed with dust, the sky itself stained grey-brown. Limned in murk, the headwall of the vale on three sides lay cloven into a barrier of raw cliffs, floored over in acres of rubble. Where scant minutes before his brave army had marched under order and flocking standards, there remained only knife-point shards of splintered shale, struck and jumbled and stirred by mad forces across a valley dismembered into waste.

The vista was one to numb the mind.

Diegan heaved in a strangled breath, half-mad from shock and disbelief. He felt delirious; light-headed. As if through the ordinary course of an eye-blink, firm rock had exploded and rearranged itself into some diabolical landscape out of Sithaer.

Sick white, shaking, he scrubbed grit from a skinned forearm, then resettled the rucked weight of his mail and adjusted his sword from blind habit. Through air hazed with pulverized rock, he sensed other movement and belatedly found he was not alone.

The handful of survivors sheltered by the knoll were regaining their feet, coughing dust. Some, crazed beyond reason, had drawn swords. A few were unmanned by fear. One lay moaning in misery, trampled or kicked by someone's panicked horse. The blue-purple pulp of his gutted abdomen established at a glance that he would not be rising, nor would another, apparently thrown onto the impaling point of a pole weapon. Nearby, someone's squire crawled on his hands and knees, sobbing the name of his mother.

The first flame of rage licked through Diegan's horror. His throat was too dry to swallow, and his tongue, too thick to curse the name of s'Ffalenn. Avenor's Lord Commander choked on the tainted taste of soil and shrank in guilt for the warning a band of condemned men had entrusted to his hearing one dismal night in falling rain.

'Dharkaron avenge!' he strangled through a seizure that hooked like a sob in his throat. For the gut-wrenching horror of his straits all but felled him. The diabolical threat sent by Arithon, that he had brushed aside from expediency, had been, every word, meant in earnest.

Unknowing, the Prince of the West had marched his forty thousand into jeopardy.

Thrown headlong into wholesale ruin, Lord Diegan beheld the Master of Shadow's promised vengeance. The scope of the disaster saw every justification to silence the testimony of twenty-five men remade into a fool's play. A brother's self-serving passion for retribution for his sister had cost Lysaer's allies tens upon thousands of lives.

The full toll remained yet to tally. Diegan forced himself to think beyond blinding self-pity. Twelve thousand men in the flanking divisions dispatched by Lysaer's signal to spearhead the assault beyond the ridges might already suffer as dire a peril. Fear spurred his nerve to face downslope, to see whether his sovereign prince's company had been spared at the mouth of the vale. His first sweeping search caught the flash of moving metal. Faint through the haze, the last company under Lysaer's direct command could be seen, still standing, and engaged in a steady advance.

Some trap would be waiting. That ripping, stark certainty shocked back Diegan's stumbling wits.

He took swift stock, did his best to confront the inconceivable extent of his losses: scarcely a handful from the centre ranks of his company were alive. Forty-two solid veterans, one of them a wiry, tough sergeant bent already on what he could salvage. When his frustrated effort to unclog the turf lodged in the mouthpiece of his horn met with failure, he snapped off a curse, then raised a gritted shout to rally. Bruised, dirtied, a scarecrow pack of men responded. More stragglers picked themselves up off the grade of the only unscoured hillside about, the remains of the foray dispatched at the whim of black rage to quarter the knoll for hidden enemies.

Those left unhurt showed the mettle of their training as they stumbled to rejoin the truncated remnant of their company.

Lord Diegan spat out small bits of gravel, flicked grass chaff off his surcoat, then limped in hurried steps down the rise to reassert his authority.

He had but one purpose, now, and that to reach Lysaer in time to reverse what damage he might. Another light bolt could be fired to signal swift retreat. If the warning was timely, the flanking companies across the ridgetops might still have a chance to seek safety.

The beleaguered little sergeant caught sight of his Lord Commander. 'Ath bless!' He mopped his sweating lip with the back of a bleeding wrist, squared his shoulders, and awaited fresh orders.

'Retreat,' Diegan said, his voice split with urgency. 'Now! The prince is behind, left one company to defend him. Dharkaron's truth, I don't think we've seen the end to the Shadow Master's offensive.'

'What of the wounded?' The sergeant gestured to a scattered few figures still prone. 'We've got no wood to make litters.'

Lord Diegan shut his eyes, every scuff and bruise and wrenched tendon combined to one screaming ache. Upslope, the decoy of pole weapons left by the enemy had been razed to charred carbon by Lysaer's light bolt. Even had alternate materials been at hand, a fast review showed what the sergeant already knew: the loosened footing and turned rock in the scar of the slide would be lethal enough without burdens. A man might break his legs on a misstep, or tumble through loose dirt into cracks and crannies where the churned-up debris had mounded over air pockets.

'Whoever can't help themselves, leave them,' Diegan

429

said. 'Our prince is riding into unspeakable danger and his need must outweigh all else.'

Under the dust-smeared face of the sun, the men mustered. One dragged the sobbing squire away from the casualty with his innards torn out. Over the intermittent crack and rumble as unstable rock gave and settled, or loose boulders tore away from the knife-edged wall of sheared cliffs, his weeping appeal rang shrill. 'I won't leave him! I can't.' On a fresh note of torture, 'He's my *brother*!'

'Force him,' cracked the sergeant to the man-at-arms who importuned the boy. 'If he doesn't straighten up in a hundred paces, leave him behind for carrion. Our prince's safety comes first.'

In a saddle between summits on the north spur of the vale, Caolle squinted through silting layers of dust to assess the moves of the enemies left standing since the landslide had razed Lysaer's first wave advance. Isolated men clustered on the fringes, battling now to regroup their ranks on firm ground. Scattered across the heights, Caolle had archers to prevent them from gaining a defensible foothold. His tight squads of clan scouts and tribesmen had the simplest of orders: shoot to kill where possible, and give ground in retreat the instant their positions became threatened.

At this critical juncture, while Arithon and the Mad Prophet abandoned their vantage overlooking Dier Kenton and shifted the thrust of the assault against the flanking enemies beyond the ridges, Caolle remained. His assignment was to track the movements of Lysaer. He must stand as his prince's rear guard and act to forestall any unforeseen event. No chance could be left to swing the odds in favour of rousing the uncontained drive of Desh-thiere's curse.

Having survived the decimation of his frontal assault,

the Prince of the West would be dry tinder for rage.

If Arithon s'Ffalenn became cornered, if he lost grip on his constrained set of tactics, the plan he had formulated through augury to halt the war in Vastmark could all too easily come to naught. Enough townborn enemies remained still at large to outnumber their disparate bands of archers by a factor of eight to one.

If Lysaer was kept pinned in Dier Kenton, the other companies from Jaelot and Alestron could be hazed off their course; once they learned their main force had been laid waste in the vale, their desire to fight could be harassed and worn away into debilitating frustration and despair.

At present, Caolle concerned himself with the ragged remains of the centre division, a struggling, determined knot of survivors picking a reckless, hurried path across the field of rubble. Like Lysaer's élite company, advancing, these men had discovered the perils of the footing the hard way. Two of their number lay screaming behind them, pinned by a shifted mass of boulders. The scar from the slide was unstable enough that even a stray tap could dislodge the loose fill and trip off a grinding, settling thunder of crumbled shale. One mishap convinced even the most brave to make for the broken seam beneath the cliff face, where the march could be made with greater safety.

The plan was sound enough, had shepherd archers better versed in the perils that arose after rockfalls not dogged their progress from concealment.

Keen of vision from his years leading raids, Caolle assessed each tiny figure in turn, then paused, cut back, and singled out one whose muddied surcoat bore the gold star on white of Avenor's élite garrison.

A low whistle hissed through his teeth. 'Fiends alive. That's Lord Commander Diegan himself.'

A rustle of rapacious movement swept through a team of archers downslope. Some were tribesfolk, content to bide time and wait. The others were clanborn, their young officer one of Jieret's Companions, scarred since his boyhood with the undying grief left by the family slain in the débâcle at Tal Quorin. He would not miss who approached their embankment; the enemy officer who had led Etarra's divisions into Strakewood would be sighted and marked for easy prey.

Moved by sharp instinct, Caolle swore. He carried no shepherd's horn. Any shouted order could not carry against the wind. Stabbed by keen urgency, he scrambled up from the rocks, sprang out of cover in a sliding, futile dash to intercept.

For the Lord Commander's straggling refugees, the moment could not have been worse for a barrage of enemy arrows. Exposed amid perilous terrain, left unable to run for fear of a misstep upon uncompacted ground dangerous as dropped knives with silvered shale, they were hedged in by boulders tilted at hair-trigger angles that had already proven as lethal. Lord Diegan shouted. Around him, the men sought to fling themselves behind whatever screening cover they could find.

He knew as a shaft bit the gravel by his foot that Lysaer was too distant to know he had allies under attack. There would be no screen of light cast to spare them.

Diegan sought for inspiration to save his last men when the shaft thudded into his side. Its broad-bladed head pierced his surcoat and mail, ripped through the gambeson beneath and drove the last air from his lungs in a wordless, half-vocal gasp. He stumbled forward, clawing at rock to stay upright.

The message of desperate urgency he carried must at all costs reach his prince.

Dull, tearing pain turned him dizzy. Diegan swayed, kept his grip on broken stone until his fingers split with the effort. Weeping tears for the punishment, he managed to stay on his feet.

The wasp whine of the second shaft grazed through the beat of his agony. Its splintering strike caught him to the right of his breastbone, ripped him backward until the world fell away into a shimmering view of a Vastmark sky bleached with haze.

Shock and pain winnowed him into sick dizziness. He strove to roll over, to find his knees and try to rise. If he failed, twelve thousand men stood at risk, most beloved of them all the life of Lysaer s'Ilessid.

'Daelion preserve,' he moaned through locked teeth, though he had never been one for praying.

Nearby, a gruff voice was shouting. 'Ath save us all, let him not be dead!'

The accent was barbarian, Diegan noted in self-mocking surprise. An odd twist, he thought, that his foot soldiers should affect a clan dialect.

'That was the Lord Commander!' returned a younger man in ringing protest. 'It's he, I say. The townborn who raised Etarra's garrison for the massacre that undid us all at Tal Quorin.'

Damned, Diegan muddled in thick confusion; he was condemned for the carnage, but not for Tal Quorin, never a deed so straightforward as that. Daelion Fatemaster would see him in Sithaer for the dead killed untimely at Dier Kenton. Ironic, if he passed the Wheel in their company.

He struggled again to rise, felt the saw of the arrows bite deeper. His breathing came laboured. Through a fearful, sucking rush of faintness, he realized the strength had bled out of him.

Then a blurred face shadowed the blank vista of sky. Someone grey-haired and gruff shoved a supporting arm beneath his shoulder. He heard the chink of steel studs from the man's wrist bracer grind against the links of his mail. Through dust and blood, he caught the martial smells of sweat and oil, and decided his saviour had to be the sergeant who had survived the shale slide beneath the knoll.

'Merciful Ath, you came back,' gasped Diegan. 'For my spirit, for my prince, tell them all to retreat.'

'Don't talk,' the other replied, his consonants still stubbornly bitten. 'You've already lost too much blood.'

Diegan resigned himself. The barbarian accents were surely cruel dream or delirium. He coughed through a hot rush of fluid. 'There was a warning,' he pressed, laboured now, desperate to get his words out. Sight came and went in tides of blackness, and the pain was spoiling thought. 'Twenty-five men brought me word from the Shadow Master. I ordered them dead lest they tell. But my prince . . . he must hear . . . there's grave danger. Tell him. The light signal . . . retreat, before it's too late.'

'Ath forfend!' cried the man who held him, anguished. 'That accursed misdeed was your doing! Had those twenty-five survivors from the Havens reached Lysaer, you must know. By my liege lord's clear augury and Dakar's prophecy, not a man would have marched on Dier Kenton to die.'

Diegan gasped, unable to command fading vision to bring the face above him into focus. 'Who are you?'

'The very last man in Athera your prince would allow a live audience.' A bitter cough of laughter presaged answer. 'I'm war captain to your sworn enemy, his Grace the Prince of Rathain.'

The last syllable fell away, bringing horror which unravelled into a horrible, jerking spasm. Diegan squeezed his eyes closed, undone.

'Daelion pity,' he wrenched out. The final breath past his lips ripped through tears of regret, for his bequest could never reach Lysaer s'Ilessid now. His dedicated love and devotion, every pain he had tried to spare his liege and his friend, had all passed for naught.

'Fatemaster witness, that was ill done,' murmured Caolle. He raised the coiffed head of Avenor's Lord Commander from his knee and laid him to rest on turned earth. Habit let him dash the wet blood from his knuckles on his leathers; no stranger to death, he watched in resignation as a fly settled on the trickle of bright scarlet that bled through teeth and lips, still twitching in spasm from a desperately fought passage out of life.

The swathe of shadow across his shoulders shifted as the Companion scout who cast it stepped aside to spit in the dust. 'How was I to know the murdering dandy was planning to call the retreat?'

Caolle twisted aside from Diegan's body. His hard gaze bored up into a face too young, too bitter, too scarred by early carnage to embrace the concept of mercy. 'You couldn't know, lad. Now it's too late.' Drenched in sweat and scraped in a dozen places from his mad rush down the scarp, the clan war captain completed a reflexive tally of the slain, shot down in their wretched scrabble over wrecked earth to gain firm footing. One in a squire's tunic barely showed the faintest first shading of a beard. Caolle sighed. Ath knew, he'd seen worse in his time.

But the ending an arrow had bought his townborn counterpart now left him bitter. Burdened by queer regret, Caolle straightened up to leave.

'I only pray you learn how to pity,' he said to Jieret's Companion. 'It might one day save your life from becoming what mine has, a futile pursuit of old hatred.'

'You always said it's the hate that keeps us alive,' the scout returned.

'Once, I believed that was true.' In the sad recognition he faced a younger version of himself, Caolle raked back a stickied tangle of slate-coloured hair. 'I've since learned there are better ways.' But sooner than any, he knew: if not for his service to the Prince of Rathain, the lesson would have slipped his grasp entirely.

The war captain who had survived the brutal massacre at Tal Quorin, whose very tactics had helped decimate those ranks of Etarrans, found a priceless irony in the thought that, at the end, his hope and a citybred Lord Commander's last wish should be alike to the very bone.

He, too, felt that if his liege came to die, everything he had struggled to accomplish in life would be rendered brutal and meaningless.

Arithon s'Ffalenn was young Jieret's legacy. Without him, hope died for the northern clans. Rathain's old blood could never emerge from their lives as hunted fugitives to reclaim their heritage if no prince lived to be crowned under Fellowship auspices at Ithamon.

To the scout still stiffly awaiting orders, the war captain said in tart dismissal, 'Unless you want to become a cinder in yon upstart princeling's accursed fireballs, we'd best take cover on the ridge.'

Late day threw slanting, orange light across the vale of Dier Kenton. A blue-tinged, premature twilight lapped the scoured face of the scarp, cloven down to its steely flanks of shale. The surface offered only brittle footholds. All the known, safe trails to the passes were utterly scoured away.

Of five teams of scouts sent out to seek an alternate route, two came back not at all. One pair limped in with losses and the others brought relentless bad news.

They reined in lathered horses before Prince Lysaer s'Ilessid, chalk-faced and hawking up dust. 'No path, your Grace. The day's lost. We've been blocked in by the slide.'

Climbers on ropes might make the attempt on the precipice, but no means existed to move armed men and eighty spent mounts over the cliffs to find the passes. Lysaer s'Ilessid regarded the sheer walls, deaf to the echoes of stamping horses, the murmurs of complaint from the ranks. No matter how determined, no matter how brave, his defeat at Dier Kenton Vale was complete.

All the powers of his gift could not offer a way to reconnect the royal company with the troops who fought to win through, who even this moment pressed the attack to pin Arithon's forces against the mailed teeth of a war-host which no longer existed.

One hundred men and the ninety-six odd survivors who had straggled in after the rockslide were all he had left at hand. The prince reined back a raw need to swear. A troop of a thousand in fit form would have been too few to cover such a broad sweep of open territory. The enemy could slip through their lines at whim after night-fall; Lysaer could not be everywhere with his gift, to safeguard each sentry from archers.

The horses were spent; the men, heartsore and grieving. The bare dell where the company gathered offered neither water nor safety to pitch camp. Lysaer knew this, just as he was aware of the surreptitious glances of his officers, who fretted and watched him, but dared raise no voice to address him.

The look on his face hammered iron, he sat his saddle in stillness before the razed face of the rim wall.

Never in his life had he dreamed of a downfall on this scale.

The campaigns and the ships his royal father had wasted to s'Ffalenn predation on Dascen Elur were insignificant before today's toll of dead at Dier Kenton. Worse, perhaps, was the way his given gift of light had been hobbled and rendered helpless. Throughout, he had been unable to act in defence of his troops. Rancour stabbed deep, for that. Somewhere beyond these rotten scarps of shale, for cold surety, Arithon s'Ffalenn still worked shadows and sorcery. His heart knew no word for mercy. With total impunity, he would wreak what ruin he could upon the rest of the allied warhost.

Diegan would have understood his liege lord's smouldering rage; Avenor's bold Lord Commander, found dead of a clan scout's arrow on the same violated earth, when

Ath's own miracle had spared him untouched from the first fury of Arithon's rockfall. Lysaer felt as stone, beyond tears or regret. If this moment of grim impotence made him burn for revenge, he was never the fool to show weakness before the eyes of disheartened men.

'Turn about,' he said, his voice burnished level, and his trappings filmed over with bitter dust. 'We must withdraw altogether from Dier Kenton Vale. Tomorrow we'll seek another route past the ridge to regroup with Lord Keldmar s'Brydion and the garrison divisions out of Jaelot.'

Lysaer wheeled his cream charger, every inch the unconquered prince. For Arithon s'Ffalenn had not won the day, never so long as his s'Ilessid enemy was left alive to take the field and men sworn to rid the land of evil remained whole enough to muster and march.

The officer of the royal guard had the temerity to ask whether the beaten remains of the warhost could be assured of retreat back to Forthmark.

His question received the freezing glare of Avenor's prince front on. 'We shall not be going back. *Never as long as we have living allies from Jaelot and Alestron left to fight*. What happened here was no accident.'

In a candour that held no apology for the turned ground, the razed stone, the doom of all his proud warhost, Lysaer added in terrible quiet, 'Twenty-eight thousand men died because one sorcerer lured them onto trapped ground with clever tactics, then pulled down a mountain to kill them. There will be no retreat and no safety. Not until this one ruthless criminal has been overthrown and cut dead.'

As his weary war-horse stumbled over a loose fall of shale, the prince gave on the reins from numbed habit. Above the metallic skitter of hooves and the rattling chink of loose rock, he summed up in ironclad resolve. 'Had I the same number to spend over again, I would do so for the same cause. Our losses here prove the true scope of the danger. With all of Athera set at risk, how dare I count a few thousand deaths as anything less than worthwhile? There can be no end. Never until Arithon s'Ffalenn is fully and finally brought down.'

Field of Fear

Assured by Caolle's scouts that the slide had effectively
bottled the remains of Lysaer's assault force behind the
cliffs of Dier Kenton, Dakar the Mad Prophet rolled his
eyes heavenward and mumbled a disjointed prayer of
relief. At least one aspect of Arithon's damnable scrying
had seen itself through without mishap. With the
frontline threat of Desh-thiere's curse thwarted through
natural barriers, there now remained only the two garrison companies the Prince of the West had appointed to
corner Arithon's forces from behind. These were engaged
in mounting a sweeping advance on the slopes behind
the rim wall of the vale.

The commander entrusted with one arm of the flanking assault hailed from the city of Jaelot. Shadows and
archers would hamper his bid to close access to the
corries from the south.

To Dakar fell the joy of dispatching the north wing of
troops, led onto the field by Keldmar s'Brydion, brother
to the Duke of Alestron.

Since the morning's first signal to march, the hard-
bitten mercenaries had pressed in remorseless formation
over gullies and fractured ground, harassed by spurious

440

ambushes upon their scouts, and picked off singly by tribal bowmen. These would pause in the brush brakes and loose their one shot, then slip unseen through the scree. The duke's seasoned captains had been stung by small losses until even the most stolid of veterans were wont to fire crossbows into the furze when wind roused a ruffle of movement. They thought back on the thundering interval while the ground had quaked to some distant, cataclysmic disturbance and swore as uneasiness chewed their nerves. Through the shadeless afternoon, they fought and bled and advanced, hating the empty furlongs of baked moss and tough scrub grass, grazed the incongruous green of new velvet in the hollows where sheep had been pastured.

The rise toward the north pass from Dier Kenton Vale raked up in forbidding, open rock, razed clean of brush by leaching summer winds and harsh gales. Cover was non-existent. Each step a man took scattered rattling shale, and the lowering light steeped every pocket of rock with shadow which could mask concealed archers. Alestron's men-at-arms met the challenge in grim confidence, determined in discipline as the landscape was hostile to their presence.

Curled like a dried leaf in a cleft near the summit, Dakar admired the drill as ten polished companies of pikemen re-formed to begin the last ascent. Their sharp, block phalanxes rearranged into wedges, with fanned lines of armed bowmen and skirmishers sent ahead to clear the gulches before them.

Keldmar disdained the finicky use of horns. His orders rang out in bullish shouts, interspersed with oaths and obscenities. Despite his pungent temper, the s'Brydion army moved into place like oiled clockwork. Their staff sergeants were brutes with a deathless love of fighting, to whom the noise and gut effort of war was the very sinew of life.

The cohorts seethed upslope like boiled vengeance.

Dakar puffed flushed cheeks until his beard bristled up like a blowfish. Beyond the passing malice of a bar brawl, he had small love for risks that favoured the chance of getting maimed. At drinking or dice, or for charming paid wenches, he would have had a fair contest against Keldmar s'Brydion. On a field of battle, the odds made a fool's wager, unbalanced enough that the Fatemaster's furies would laugh themselves stupid in prostration.

The ultimate bungle, the Mad Prophet thought. A crazed man's machinations had ensconced him here with an armed band of clan scouts whose lives all relied on his wits. His Fellowship master would have buried his face in his hands and groaned for their faith in the ridiculous.

A scuffle over rock, then a clipped password to a scout. The last tribal archer scrambled in, breathless for respite. To the Mad Prophet, in passing, he threw the tired comment, 'It's high time you came. We can't stay them on this slope. No cranny a strayed sheep could hide in.'

Dakar rolled him a grimace, then said to the clansman who lingered, prepared to become the bearer of return messages, 'Tell Arithon to allow me two hours.'

'That's sundown,' the scout said, his wolfish eyes on the immense force of mercenaries who tackled the scarp in practised order. 'You've cut things damned fine. If the advance isn't stemmed before nightfall, our people are going to start dying.'

No matter how skilled, shepherd archers could not use bows in the dark. Once cornered in hand-to-hand battle, the s'Brydion mercenaries would hack their small numbers to ribbons.

'Well, here's thanks in advance for your proud vote of confidence,' Dakar said, morose and punch-drunk with fatigue.

He scrubbed sweaty palms upon his tunic and chafed. At the moment he felt good for nothing beyond craving for pillows in a cathouse beside some sultry doxy. The

442

wistful heat of wishes could scarcely stir him to desire, not with hard Vastmark shale chewing dents in his backside, and the withering sun limning the hungry steel teeth of the s'Brydion warhost.

No imagination was required to picture how Keldmar would rejoice to see one plump, dishonest gem peddler impaled arse down on a pike.

Inspired to a wicked bent of afterthought, Dakar smothered down a chortle. To the dubious scout who awaited, he said, 'Take my message. If you don't want to spoil your humourless thinking, don't for a second look back.'

The clansman went his way, dour and unmollified, while Dakar gazed with fresh interest downslope.

The troops from Alestron could scarcely be pleased. Theirs was an honourless assignment, to labour in sweating files to scale a face of stripped rock, then engage a sneaking band of shepherds scarcely worth blisters to dispatch. Sun-baked and footsore from a punishing day in full war gear, pricked at each step by whining, small tempests of hostile arrows, many of their number would be inwardly longing to quit the field for missed comforts.

Others would be irksome and cantankerous, hot for a thumping bloody skirmish with living foemen they could hack to twitching rags to relieve a lethal measure of frustration.

Dakar bit his lip, his eyes half-closed in anticipation. The spells which exacted the least effort were fashioned illusions, the inconvenient, tangled little bindings designed to hook a man's thoughts and sow from them the dreaming recreation of whatever lust held his heart.

From the ground underfoot, the Mad Prophet selected a stub of shale to use as a stylus. The runes he scribed like tiny seeds upon the air broke into motes, a haze fine as spider's silk caught to a sheen of dimmed silver. The light sparked and multiplied and strewed on the wind, a scarcely visible dusting of energies that by their drawn nature would gravitate and form to the dictates of human desires. For effect, and by way of fair warning, the Mad Prophet laced his finished work through the blank coils of the fogbanks which gathered to descend and girdle the heights after sundown.

In typical fashion for all his maligned practice, some permission or small cantrip skimmed awry. The spell assumed an unruly life of its own and unreeled like blight to gnarl the peace of Ath's order.

Downslope, the men-at-arms under Alestron's banner marched squinting against the stabbing glare off scoured shale. Their feet were blistered, their backs sore from the rub of gambeson and chain mail. Thirsty and sweating, held to position by short-tempered commanders, their cohorts of mercenaries ploughed ahead in dogged competence. The first startled shout from the skirmish line bristled them into close shield rings, ranked fifty abreast and three deep down the rise.

Which snapping, precise discipline did them small good as an uncanny mist fanned across the mountainside before them. It engulfed the rocks just ahead of their position, glutinously thick and glimmering a sickly, pale green.

While men murmured and shrank and fingered talismans bought for small silver from dealers in arcane charms and herbals, Keldmar took a brash step forward. Just shy of the gesticulating vanguard he poised, hooked out his broadsword, and sliced at the yielding green mass.

Nothing happened. He repeated the move, then added a whistling swing, yanked off his left gauntlet, and skimmed bare fingers down the steel. The metal proved neither hot nor cold to his touch.

'Sorcerer's illusion,' he pronounced in contempt to the staff officers attendant on his orders. 'Foolish, to think we'd be cowed.' He hailed the veteran in charge of the advance scouts. 'Send in your best team for a look. If they find nothing and return, we press on as planned.'

The wait passed in uneasy fidgeting. Men checked their weapons, tightened straps on their helms, or shrugged to rub pressure sores under the shoulders of their mail. No sound creased the quiet beyond the distant whistle of a wyvern; no movement beyond the heat waves rippling off day-warmed rock. Twitching off the hunch that they were as sitting targets, captains reviewed their divisions and watched Keldmar, who scratched his chin and with rankled impatience eyed the mist that never moved.

The scouts returned, unscathed and puzzled. 'My lord, we found nothing. Just more queer fog and sharp boulders. The sun's out and clear just four hundred yards higher up.'

'Well then,' said Keldmar, satisfied. He strode forward in bearish distaste, first reduced to a hulking outline, then to a blurred shadow within the bilious green mist.

'Step lively, soldiers!' shouted the captain by the standard-bearer. Too brave to abandon their lord to his own devices, the whole mass of the army had no choice but to muster shrinking nerves and try to follow.

The mist had no scent, no texture beyond the expected clammy pall of heavy moisture. Tinged gruesome colours in its sickly embrace, men started and swore and made grumbling complaint to bolster their faltering courage. The lack of visibility masked their officers' view of the flanking phalanxes. If some soldiers flinched from odd flickers of light, half-seen at the edge of strained vision, if now and again the chink of loose rock beneath someone's step raised an infinitesimal spark of glimmerance, soon enough they decided the uncanny gloom was harmless. Their talk lapsed to jokes and their thoughts drifted off into boredom.

Dakar's insidious tangle of seals fixed on longings for

distant wives and wenches; of dinner at a trestle and a foaming draught of ale in the camaraderie of a warm taproom; of a soft feather mattress after a hot bath, and uninterrupted sleep. Reality blurred and daydreams became manifest. The next thing men knew, they *saw* what they craved, in powerful, alluring fits of vision.

Someone exclaimed, 'Fiends plague! There's my wife.' If her smiling, buxom beauty was brighter than reality, and if she appeared, beckoning, to swim through green air, the spiralling pull of magic caused the man to pay details no mind. He slammed to a stop and threw down his weapon to kiss his beloved on the lips.

The first gap in the ranks was joined by another, as a second man dropped smiling to his knees, stuffed his mouth full of dirt and chewed with groaning relish. The horrified shieldmate who grabbed his shoulder was cuffed away and chastened. 'After hardtack for a month, my bowels are jammed. Bedamned if I'll leave a basket of pears here to rot!'

One man hugged his helmet and murmured endearments. Another raised the butt of his dagger to his lips as if he swilled wine from a bottle. One quarter of the middle company simply plonked their arms down for pillows and snored. The bloodthirsty few who wanted to gut enemies screamed bull-throated war cries, whipped swords from their scabbards, and determinedly began hacking rocks.

Buffeted amidst the unravelling chaos of Alestron's best troop of mercenaries, Keldmar stared about, red to the ears with flummoxed rage. '*Have you all gone crazy?*'

The scant few who heeded were mystified as he, as discipline came wholly undone. All but the most strong-minded veterans abandoned their march and fell victim to the allure of Dakar's spell. Like a jerked tear in a knit, neat drill undid into knots of rollicking celebration. Pikes clattered from emptied hands. Men whooped in abandon and threw themselves into ribald frenzy, stripping off armour and moaning prone on bare rock as if they lay coupled with their lovers. The banner bearer became engrossed in a weepy, long dialogue with his belt buckle. Around his curled form, the troop's most trustworthy captain leaped in tight circles, stabbing at gravel and shrieking about snakes in the grass.

Keldmar lost his temper, kicked his staff officer in the flank, and received back a murmured endearment. He jabbed another man-at-arms with his boot toe, was ignored, then progressed through obscenities to blistering threats.

'It's no use,' said a scarred old campaigner who had fought with the troops for twenty years. 'They've been spell-turned. If we take out the sorcerer, they'd recover.'

Too irate to credit even sensible suggestion, Keldmar peered through the virid gloom. Perhaps a hundred men remained unaffected, ones who lacked imagination, or whose heartfelt desires were too weak or uninspired to spring the snare of ensorcelment. Some cursed and exhorted their afflicted companions. Another dedicated sergeant swiped at laggards with the flat of his sword, then got himself flattened by a burly pikeman, who howled a shocking profusion of epithets, then accused, 'Bedamned to you, man! Keep on clodding about and you'll upset the ale barrel for certain!'

The next instant, a swirl in the soupy fog disgorged the commander of the second division, his flushed face running with sweat that dripped off the knurled ends of his moustache. 'Ath preserve! This madness gripes your troop, as well? We're fair paralysed. Every ninny in our ranks who pines for a wench seems bollocksed witless on some spell of illusion.'

Keldmar cast a jaundiced eye after a battle-scarred campaigner who danced mother-naked over the engrossed forms of his fellows. 'Damn me, we'll get even. March any man you have who will listen. We've got to press on and skewer the sorcerer who's doing this.'

'With pleasure!' The commander lent his shout to Keldmar's bellows to muster any standing soldier who could be hazed back to coherent action.

A cobbled-together company of seventy-five regrouped and resumed the advance. Outrage drove them, and fierce thirst for revenge to punish the indignities visited upon their companions. They unlimbered swords and pole weapons, swore dire oaths at the mists, and resolved on their course to hack the first mage they found into whimpering meat.

The advance scout they passed in amorous attempt to couple with his discarded byrnie gave their industry no second glance.

'Useless,' groused a soldier who knew him. 'Spends all his silver in the bawdy house, does Gundrig, then sleeps while the whores rob him blind. Ten years, I've watched. Some things never change.'

Someone else loosed a raw gust of laughter. 'Keep on like that, he'll hang his fool bollocks in his mail and bend the rest of himself beyond using. Habits are bound to change quick enough then. Most ladies don't like their fun kinked.'

'Quiet!' snapped Keldmar.

Something whined through the mist. A man four paces off crumpled at the knees and sprawled with a shattering, coarse cry. Blood spread across the breast of his surcoat, and his fingers raked the ground in grasping agony. Then the air came alive with a hail of shafts fired in terrible accuracy.

'How can they see to take aim?' The troop commander ducked as men dropped from his ranks. 'Dharkaron himself couldn't cast his ebon spear and hit any sinners in this murk.'

'It's got to be sorcery. Scatter!' Keldmar shouted. 'Fan out in skirmish lines and move!' He plunged up a low rise, felt bright sun splash his face. Through a dazzle of glare, he blinked, astonished to see the lance streamers of his strike force casting thin, smoky shadows over the top of the fogbank. No fool, he dropped flat. The marksman's shot dispatched to take him whizzed over his helm and smacked into stone downslope. He rolled out of reflex and escaped a second shaft, launched in an arc from above. Impact splintered into the lichens where he had lain a scant second before.

'Jam your pole weapons upright as decoys and run!' he screamed. 'The tips are piercing through the mist and every man with a pike's a walking target!'

The troops who had the presence to obey shed their pole arms and charged up the mountain, swords drawn and lips peeled from their teeth as they sucked burning breaths to ease exhaustion. The ground pitched and dipped, then rose again, steeper, and green mists gave way to clear air.

A grey-clad line of clan archers threw down bows and quivers and drew swords to check them in a screaming clash of steel.

These were Erlien's clansmen, tenacious and skilled. They had done battle with mercenaries before, and arrows had levelled the odds. Up and down the scarp, small knots of combat raged to curses and threats, snatched between clangs as blade bit blade in a lethal exchange of parry and feint and riposte. Men fell. Their blood slicked the shale in treacherous, slick patches. The clansmen pressed in, relentless.

Keldmar found himself engaged, surrounded, then deliberately worried separate from his men. The enemies who pressed him took consummate care to drive him off-balance and corner him. Their swordplay was fresh, skilled, and agile enough to sting the grip of his hand through his heavy, leather gauntlets. Sliding on gravel, outnumbered beyond recourse, Keldmar fought and blinked through the sweat that burned into his eyes. His throat was rasped raw, his chest laboured. He knew no sound but the whistle of his own breath, and the sour, metallic shock of punished steel. Hazed backward until he could scarcely swing to parry, he found himself at bay against the side of a weed-tangled gully.

'You can fight until you drop,' one antagonist baited in the butter-soft vowels of Shand. 'Or by our high earl's invitation and Prince Arithon's preference, we'll take your weapons and your word in surrender.'

'You have my word,' Keldmar said through gritted teeth. As son of an old blood duke, he could rely on the code of ethics his ancestors shared with these descendants of the displaced clans. He tossed his sticky broadsword with a ringing, flat clash at the feet of the swordsmen who pinned him. Stubborn he might be, but never the fool to die for pointless bravado. 'I'll have my satisfaction. Your earl's fiend-plagued ally, the Master of Shadow, will curse the hour he left me alive.'

A clansman carried word of Keldmar's capture to Dakar in his cranny seconds later. 'We have him, blazing mad, but unharmed. We'll need time to get him clear before you raise the mist and let his troop find out he's gone missing.'

Tucked between rocks like an uncombed hedgehog, Dakar swore with disgruntled lack of heat. He had a snarling headache, result of stressed concentration and too much sun without any beer to ease his paralysing thirst. The diversion he had spun over the s'Brydion garrison had decidedly grown out of hand. The spell-laced green mist had lured the more imaginative men-at-arms over the threshold of delirium. The air down the rise had spawned schools of pale mermaids with alluring long tresses and shell bracelets. They drifted above the incline like displaced succubi, to strains of wild music that sounded sawed from an instrument an excruciating half-pitch too flat. The occasional yelling brawl erupted

through the murk as men crazed by visions of unbridled
lust vied for the favours of Ath knew what sort of female.
Pikes poked up at odd angles through the turbulence.
The lance tip of one was festively streamered with what
looked like some strumpet's scarlet petticoat.

Dakar might have thought the sight uproarious if
his skull felt less like an anvil pounded silly by a
blacksmith.

The scout who reported raised a sceptical eyebrow and
burst into whooping amusement. 'You do have a touch,'
he commiserated, then jumped back as Dakar swung
chubby knuckles at his middle.

'You'd better clear out,' the Mad Prophet warned.
'Those revellers down below won't stay so friendly when
their women change back into rocks.'

'You say,' gasped the scout. He slithered back to leave,
all but knocked aside by an inbound runner streaming
sweat from a sprint across the ridge.

'Word from the Shadow Master,' the newcomer forced
between breaths.

'Trouble?' Dakar pushed fallen hair from his eyes, and
squirmed to face the tired messenger.

'Jaelot's divisions are stubborn as rock.' The scout
braced his hands against the buttress of shale and panted
through the rest of his message. 'Our archers are gutting
their ranks like damned sheep. Still, they won't turn.
Even stark blind in shadows, they plough up the crests
and attack. We could let the whole murdering mass of
them slaughter themselves on our weapons, but the
tribesfolk are running out of arrows. Arithon's asked,
can you clear out an opening so our people can turn in
retreat?'

Dakar stubbed a finger into his cheek and rolled
spaniel eyes in forbearance. 'He's that desperate?'

The scout straightened up, affronted. 'Need you ask?
That garrison commander from Jaelot became laughingstock over something our prince exposed in a satire.

Whatever the scandal, the man's mad for revenge. He'd kill his whole company out of spite just to even the score.'

'The general of Jaelot's garrison?' Dakar smirked in sly malice. 'His prick wilts in bed. The wife scratched her itch with every footman and stableboy she could lure to try out her favours. She's had six sons and four daughters, no two of them by the same father. And it was Halliron Masterbard's ballad, not Arithon's.'

'Well, for our part, that's a fine point scarcely worth standing ground to die for.' The clan scout peered at Dakar in sharp concern. 'Can you help? You look washed as a bucket of old curds.'

'I can pray for an almighty miracle.' The Mad Prophet appended his graphic opinion of the garrison general's tartish wife.

'Well the old wheezer could have saved himself a skinful of trouble,' the clan scout agreed in scornful earnest. 'Should've just had done and tossed the bitch off the nearest battlement.'

'It's nobody's secret the citizens of Jaelot invented the tradition of bloody grudges.' Dakar drew in his undone shirt laces to ease the chill, since the low sunlight lost warmth to his memory of the garrison commander's treatment of the city convicts condemned to labour on the seawall.

A harrowing yell from a victim downslope recalled his diverted attention. His spell-turned spread of mist was wearing away, torn in wide patches and thinning. That first boggled shout was followed by cried curses as several of Alestron's crack mercenaries recovered mazed senses, clinched in loving poses with buttressed chunks of knife-edged Vastmark shale. A mermaid with blue hair puddled into a haze of spent light. Then the pike flying the lacy furbelows cracked with a bang into a blackened explosion of fragments. Dakar knuckled the hair at his temples in dismay. The gnat swarm of sigils set loose to wreak havoc had gone unstable, most likely because of a seal of protection laid infinitesimally awry, or some tiny, incompatible property of nature neglected in the heat of inspiration.

The spellbinder cringed to imagine how his Fellowship master would reprove his shoddy turn of conjury. Worse, his spreading green fogbank scarcely established a sound base for permission to ensorcel the enemy, since the duke's paid soldiers could not refuse to enter without rejecting orders from their officers. The lapse in proprieties left the spellbinder unrepentant. The only way he knew to divert the troops now was to twist the dregs of his dream binding into a mass hallucination. That Asandir might come to punish him later for chaotic intervention was a point he shrank from examining. The offered stake was the Shadow Master's life.

Then the choice became moot. A shepherd woman scrambled in, soaked and breathless and bearing desperate news. 'The enemy's broken through from the south. We're routed and running. Arithon's thrown up shadow to screen our rear guard from bowfire. But that's not protection. We're going to need space, and quickly, to open the way to escape.'

A breeze sharpened to a flaying, unseasonable cold snapped down off the heights, pressing damp braids to her neck and streaming the thong ties of the emptied quiver at her hip. She glanced over her shoulder, worried, and Dakar shivered. More aware than she, he knew that Arithon was driven to binding his gift of shadow with unsubtle malice. Those enemies holding a steel-handled sword, or touching bare skin to their armour were probably finding their flesh flash-frozen to chilled metal.

The woman spun back to him, urgent. 'If you're planning to help, we haven't much time.'

'There are some six thousand mercenaries down there!' Dakar cried in protest.

His quandary raised not a murmur of sympathy. At

the crest of the rise, frantic shouts rode the wind, twined through the belling play of steel. Shepherd archers were fleeing the ridgetop, their grey-and-dun clothing scarcely visible amid falling twilight. The Mad Prophet uttered a scatological curse upon every mother's son born in Jaelot, balled up his fists, and screwed his eyes shut.

He ripped out three summonings, scribbled runes in cold air, then threw his vivid, disordered imagination into a vision to raise terror.

His unpremeditated jumble of forced power cast a baleful snap of fire across the zenith.

Dakar embellished this with his most evil remembrance of nightmares brought on by cheap gin. In garish, deafening splendour, an apparition burst from the glare, made manifest through an irresponsible explosion of spells.

His finest rendition of Dharkaron's Chariot roared into the arc of the sky.

The visitation was drawn in sable splendour by the Five Horses of Sithaer, harnessed in lightnings, their coats polished ebony and their nostrils flared to expose dark red linings. White-stockinged hooves struck sparks off the very roof of heaven. After them rocked the dread chariot of black lacquer and bone inlay, its narrow, spoked wheels a whirl of steel rims which sliced clouds in their path like spent smoke.

Ath's avenging angel grasped the lines in his gauntleted fist. Not by accident did the face beneath its raven hair bear resemblance to Rathain's sanctioned crown prince.

Dharkaron opened tapered lips and laughed against the winds that streamed his silvery cloak. The blazoned Wheel of Fate spread blood scarlet on his breast as he straightened to full height and checked his steeds' wild rush. They reared in trumpeting splendour. The silhouette of their bellies darkened the afterglow of sunset. Then the Avenger brandished his ebon spear. He howled

454

a curse of damnation upon the dream-fuddled mercenaries strewn across the shale slopes below. His team flung down, snorting. On a whipcrack shout from their master, they launched into a pounding charge straight for Alestron's disordered battle lines.

Torn in rude fear from lascivious dreams, roused up naked and weaponless, some shaken out of sleep or raised staggering from improbable, drunken fits of gluttony, Keldmar's companies of mercenaries wailed in abject terror. They leaped up to flee, tripped and fell flat, then scrambled off hands and knees in blind panic to escape. Barefoot and shod, they trampled over shucked mail and snagged heaps of clothing, discarded boots and dropped shields. Swords and pikes were abandoned where they lay. Seized by mass fear, every war-hardened man-at-arms scattered before Dakar's unholy illusion and bolted flat out for low ground.

None looked back, even when the chariot and horses dissolved in a flat slam of thunder over the vacated slope.

Arithon's bands of shepherds and clan scouts were freed to slip away and disperse into the seamed hills and corries where nightfall and spun shadow could hide them.

Severance

Behind a locked iron door, the Prime Enchantress of the Koriani Order sat amid a bare stone chamber in the battered shell of a signal tower within the coastal city of Thirdmark. The lancet windows which commanded a strategic view of the headwaters of Rockbay harbour were masked off in stiff felt. Old dust stirred in the mouse feet of draughts. The stone smelled of mildewed mortar and sea salt, and the curtains like fusty woollens rinsed in old sweat and bog water.

In that place, the time could have been midday or the deepest hour of night. No chink of outside sky showed through. Sound was muffled to resentful, dull silence, feathered in the subliminal resonance of old wars when the tower had withstood the battering assault of nameless, forgotten sieges.

Morriel preferred the ambivalence. Her skin the yellow of aged, crumpled linen in the light of a single candle, she rejoiced for the freedom restored by the Great Waystone cradled in her lap. Never again need she leach borrowed energy from the diurnal rhythms of the earth. The passage of days and seasons no longer ruled her arcane might.

The Prime Matriarch of the Koriathain traced an ivory nail over the cold arc of the stone's surface, aware as a strained current of vibration awakened to even that slight touch. The Fellowship Sorcerers had not tampered with the jewel. Its freight of stored energies, every perilous, layered contortion ingrained by generations of past spells remained twined through its shadowy depths. Any unshielded handling of the great amethyst required rigorous discipline. To command its focus demanded far more than a mastery of mind and will. The stone was deadly dangerous. The wielder who failed to channel its bright focus could be enslaved, her self-awareness broken by gibbering nightmares until her mind became consumed in madness.

Morriel had cared for past victims during her girlhood as a novice. Left those disquieting memories, she abjured a course of unwise haste. Time and practice would be needed before the Koriani Order could remaster and wield the Waystone's full might. Perhaps a decade of exacting instruction lay ahead, before First Senior Lirenda dared the trial to engage the jewel's deep focus without the Prime's partnered guidance; years Morriel could ill afford to squander if her chosen successor proved unfit.

Against this added demand of power and responsibility, the Prime sought her own private sureties. If the Great Waystone's properties had lent her some surcease from the crippling pain which hounded her overtaxed body, it could not extend the span of her life by even as much as one day. The burden of breathing had grown little less for the promise of the order's restored influence. Closed alone in the airless stone room, her hair unbound in waves over shoulders clothed in a robe of bleached silk, Morriel cupped the melon-sized amethyst between her spidered fingers. Her decision was set. No anomaly would be left to risk. Against the gnawing host of her doubts, she would engage a deep scrying to map the last steps to secure Lirenda's transition into prime power.

Unlike the properties of the Skyron focus, the great amethyst met the mind which sought dominance in vast and ominous quiet. Morriel closed lightless eyes to strain her thoughts clear of distraction, then linked her awareness to the crystal. Swallowed into smothering darkness, undermined by the old, familiar dread that the Waystone's pooled malice might slip her control and unstring the coils of her sanity, she held her mind in balance. She was too old, too wise to be baited to insecurity. Neither did she ease her guard as the stone's vast quiet gentled into seductive invitation.

The jewel she bid to master had been wielded by a thousand prime enchantresses, its latticed structure over time compounded into a vicious labyrinth of tricks.

Morriel bided in chill patience. Ancient, she was herself well tempered in the power of stillness. She outwaited what green youth would challenge, her strength kept hidden for the moment the crystal's random currents would align themselves against dominance.

Always the change struck without warning. Morriel gasped under the first onslaught. Pinched by a rising, twisted mesh of resistance cruel as the rake of barbed wire, she grappled. Any tapped access into the heart of the stone's focus forged a gateway into its centre; and like any portal kept guarded too long, the unquiet detritus imprinted by spent spells boiled up in charged effort to escape.

Its hot, resentful force sieved through her sealed consciousness like a raking barrage of slivered glass. The stone's near-sentient presence probed for weakness, any flaw, any breach in her character, any bastion of self-awareness left untended. Should such opening exist, no matter how small, the pent malice of the Waystone would reach through and devour her alive. The wrong response, and she would be lost in a maelstrom of nightmare, wrought from the latent shame and guilt sown by her own past mistakes.

Morriel stamped down the perilous instinct to flinch. She was mistress of her pain. Flesh, thought, and viscera, her body was thralled to her will. She cut through the stone's clamour of resurrected hatred, firmed against the warped cry of crystal enslaved. Her consciousness darted and thrust deeper into the web's meshes. To chain the flared spite of the Waystone's dark aspect was like using bare flesh to quench magma. Against a revulsion that raised the hair at her nape, into the rage of the jewel's matrix the Prime rammed the frigid counterspells of mastery. Hers was the sure knowledge of the primal seals to impose unconditional domination.

As she shaped the runes and sigils in ritual configuration, she suffered the fragmented echoes of past uses to which the great amethyst had been turned: scryings of fire and smoke and bloody battle. In fleeting imprint, she smelled the putrescent reek of corpses scythed down by plague. She felt again the clean flood of healing spells raised to stem the tides of human pestilence; knew the scream of faulted earth pressed down and called to heel; the howl of tempests reined back from assault upon merchant fleets and settled shorelines. Bone and nerve thrummed to the echoes of past conflict and sweeter surcease. Morriel exalted to the might of compassion and humanity, pitted broadside against the unquiet force of nature's cruelties. For a heartbeat her inner sight was battered under the white lick of deluge and chaos.

Struck deaf and blind to the world beyond the tower, she fought and closed the last seal.

The scream as trained will collided with elemental bare force slammed a cry through every synapse in her mind. Momentary agony thrummed in recoil through the marrow of her bones, flicked each nerve down to her fingertips.

Then the threshold was past, the stone's focus subdued. The Prime was no longer tied to a weakened vessel of aged flesh, but freed to pluck the currents of the world's winds and demand them to bend in submission. She was the thought to crack the heart of wild stone, the sand grain to drink the sea to dust. Sun and moon and stars were her servants, to yield their silvered secrets on demand.

In that moment of ascendancy, the crone's form glowed in scintillant outline, framed in the same violet light which kindled the depths of the Great Waystone. Alone, Morriel spun the mighty axis of its focus to delve into the shadowy future.

She expected problems. The path to prime succession was fraught with snarls, each derived from flaws in a candidate's development. No aspirant could succeed, nor survive the last test without submitting to an exhaustive, ever-narrowing course of study to cleanse her character of imperfections.

Lirenda's training was far from complete. Scrying clearly mapped those weaknesses yet to be conquered. Morriel tracked them, methodical: the small ambitions that blinded in tomorrow's imperfect handling of a dispute between two novices; then the annual placement of boy wards in craftshop apprenticeships evincing a stubborn prejudice still ingrained from an overly privileged childhood. Envy of the Fellowship's sure grasp of grand conjury would give rise to a critical inattention. And like a chained snag in knit, that moment yielded in turn to a faulty understanding of a minor sigil which, another day, would fail to halt an affliction that caused stillbirths.

For each shortcoming, Morriel marked out the corresponding lesson to enforce the desired correction. She sounded the sureties to discern which seal spells to use to impose subtle influence to curb, then realign and hone the last rough edge from Lirenda's self-awareness.

At the last the Prime reviewed the most glaring of all

drawbacks, given into her attention as warning through a long past scrying at Forthmark. The pitfall most likely to spoil Lirenda's bid for primacy was her persistent, drawing fascination for the compassion which ruled Athera's last Prince of Rathain.

Aware of shimmering danger in that single thread, Morriel Prime traced the span of coming happenstance with the delicate care of a spider spinning webs above a waterfall. Her augury took hold, unreeling in fierce energy to yield a scene set in falling sleet against the shadowy postern of a coastal city's back alley.

There, the vision of Lirenda, lost in Arithon's embrace, a flush to her cheeks, and her hair a fall of spilled sable down the violet cloak of the order.

For this startling glimpse of lapsed vows, Morriel was caught in blank astonishment. Before she could ponder, the sequence reeled on, inexorable, a lightning strike partnered by thunderclap.

A fired burst of passion, then heartbreak stanched in ice; this followed in sequence by a second, clearer vision: *in a bleak tower dungeon, and the same prince, bound captive in iron and spread-eagled upon a stone slab. The s'Ffalenn features were stamped to mocking irony. In contempt for his helplessness, Arithon spoke a phrase whetted to a glib stab of satire.*

Then an ugly revelation, a shattering break in continuity; the ongoing chain of future event overset to smash more than First Senior Lirenda's overblown pride. For Morriel, presaged ending came in a deranged explosion that built to a keening, savage force. Her will was milled under. Self-control ripped away, snagged into sparks and white agony. She saw the Wheel's turning; then the etheric veil; then the awful, sharp snap which would sever final connection to the withered husk of her flesh.

The matriarch's outcry fell dampened by the muffling felt curtains as the stream of her prescient image impelled off its known course. Scalded in the mind,

461

seared to blisters where her palms held contact with the great crystal, she gasped, crumpled over and shivering.

Cast headlong out of disciplined trance, she opened her eyes, disoriented. Blackness imprisoned her. A burst of raw terror lanced through her until she cried out a cantrip and grounded her awareness in the stale, cold stone of the tower.

The candle by her knee had knocked over or snuffed out. In darkness, she forced a steadying breath. The copper-tinged aftertaste of fear stayed with her, rank as the pound of her heartbeat. For branded in memory was the promise of her own sudden death.

What circumstance she could garner from the shreds of smashed augury stabbed like old rust through her inner mind: because of Arithon s'Ffalenn she would meet her passage uncelebrated, unprepared, long before Lirenda's succession to prime power was transferred and sealed to completion.

The instrument of her successor's downfall and her own annihilation was no mystery: beside Arithon's role, the Waystone itself would play a part. Morriel hissed through locked teeth. Her blood rushed through thin veins to the pressure of her rage.

The chance was inconceivable that she should come to die through the meddling intervention of one mortal.

Perspiration sealed her grasp to the faceted sphere of the Waystone. Its matrix remained roused. Spiked to dangerous, slipped vectors since her lapse in control, stray spurts of faulted power spun sullen patterns through the elements. The air sang with peril. Dissonance chimed from dead dust and rock like the wasp-thin clash of dropped steel.

The Koriani matriarch forced control over terror. She steadied the crystal's riled focus. Adamant before an overwhelming surge of fury, she struggled and failed to regain either equilibrium or objectivity.

In harsh fact, this one setback could hurt too much.

For the imbalance was no longer so small as Lirenda's starved craving, or her female fascination with male attraction. If Arithon s'Ffalenn was left a free hand with fate, Morriel faced a permanent failing. She could become the single matriarch since the first to break the chain of inherited power. The deepest of mysteries, the keys to prime inheritance itself, would pass the veil with her, forever lost from the Koriani Order's living store of knowledge.

A moist brush of her palm and a steel-hard seal of binding severed the Waystone's roiled focus. While shivers of dread raked Morriel's weary flesh, she stroked the sweat-printed surface of the amethyst.

Her choice was plain. Unless she risked an immeasurable disaster, she dared not suffer the Prince of Rathain to live.

Beloved of the Fellowship of Seven he might be as the last of a chosen royal line, nonetheless he was born a mortal man. His days would have a thousand artless moments of pregnability. Morriel's forehead fretted into pleats as she pondered the thorns of her dilemma. The Koriani code forbade murder, an inconvenience she had ways to circumvent. Evading the Fellowship's interest would be harder. Any trap to take Arithon must be spun in dire subtlety to escape prying notice from Althain's Warden.

An outside hand must act as her catspaw to accomplish the killing in her stead.

Sealed in the icy chamber with the flat scent of dust and the taint of moth-rotten felt, Morriel Prime released a scratchy sigh. In her hands, the Great Waystone spiked a glimmer of cold violet against the masking darkness. Through its grand focus, she held the power to comb all Athera and align the precise junction of motive with its matching opportunity.

Somewhere there lurked an unguarded mind with the passion to wish Arithon dead.

Her task was to ferret out that individual, to assist just one bitter enemy to couple the means with the moment. If she spun her desire through subliminal suggestion, her bit of small meddling would never be traced to link her hand or her order to a plot of assassination.

Interventions

Hazed into deep-water swells by a scalding attack from a brigantine flying Arithon's blazon, Alestron's fleet of galleys is forced to jettison supplies of flour and hardtack to keep waves from crashing through the oarports; and as the last battered vessel limps into sheltered waters, their captains discover their proud flagship missing, with Mearn s'Brydion lost with her . . .

As the autumn rains resume their dismal fall on Vastmark, and mists seep white through the valleys, a supply train out of Forthmark is waylaid by northern clansmen feal to Rathain, who strike in a whirlwind attack, leaving upset wagons and hamstrung oxen, and only when the officer of the guard seeks the duke's brother to deliver report of the incident does he hear that Parrien s'Brydion is nowhere to be found . . .

In a chilly tent drummed by hard rainfall, surrounded by a war camp churned into thick mud, Lysaer s'Ilessid paces past guttered candles, his calm line of dictation closing a letter to be sent under seal to Duke Bransian of Alestron, *'You have my sincere grief, and my royal regret, that your brother Keldmar was not found among the living after your mercenaries became routed on the slopes behind Dier Kenton Vale . . .'*

IX. COUNTERPLOYS

The rains returned colder, musked with the scent of dying bracken which presaged the dismal turn of season. Autumn came to Vastmark in shades of ochre and brown, then burst into a short-lived, false green as the hills sprang new shoots after summer's dry winds and drought. Each year, life in the low country seized one last frantic chance to throw off seed heads before the first killing frost.

Like the doomed industry of the grasses, the remnants of Lysaer's brave warhost regrouped. Reduced to one-quarter of their original strength, wedded to their cause in grim tenacity, they drove on with their effort to send the Master of Shadow beneath the Wheel.

The losses at Dier Kenton had convinced the last doubters of Arithon's broad-scale ability to sow ruin. If the Prince of the West could endure the decimation of his recruits from Tysan and Rathain and stay unshaken, his allies from Jaelot and Alestron, and the supporters garnered from Shand, took fire from his example. They poured out their hearts to meet his demands and match his unbending dedication.

But now the shortening days turned the weather against them.

Soaked peat made poor fires. The brick ovens for baking bread stayed dismantled, the wrapped iron pots corroded in mouldering canvas. Flour stores spoiled and cheeses grew rinds of sticky mould. The days dawned the same, dim under spun webs of mist that wisped and coiled through the corries; only now the fogs lingered, shedding silver drizzle and a miserable, pervasive clinging damp.

Chain mail and weapons lost their shine despite polishing, and the tents grew streaks of black mildew. Men slept on wet ground and donned byrnies splotched with rust to ride out and scour the uplands for the fugitive enemy.

Arithon's motley force of shepherds melted before their patrols, elusive as wind. Or they lurked concealed in ambush, to rain down their killing flights of arrows. No day passed without casualties. If Lysaer still commanded a force eleven thousand strong, they were not enough to cordon off Vastmark's wild territory, with its seamed peaks and dim ravines and steep-sided, rock-scarred ranks of ridges. The best a scourging army could effect was a headhunter's aim, to pocket small groups of skirmishers, or scour the vales for flocks or unwary settlements, then close in and leave nothing alive.

Against their armed numbers, the nomad tribes were pitifully few. Each death brought the Master of Shadow a loss he could ill afford, a life that left the shepherds one foothold less on the land to preserve family ties and survival.

Lysaer laboured, tireless, to reforge the knit of troop morale. No matter what the hour, he arose to meet the sentries at every change of the watch. He heard each report from inbound scouts, unfailingly at hand to number their dead or credit their diligence, or acknowledge their smallest success. Thin and tired and regaled in soaked finery, he stood in chill darkness and engaged his gift of light to warm the garrison troops dispirited by the cheerless, dreary nights.

Each dawn, while camp followers called coarse encouragement from damp wagons, the patrols rode out to sweep the mist-cloaked crags and comb the ravines for the sign of the Shadow Master.

'He's out there,' Lysaer insisted, his confidence a balm to fuel faith. Nights he awakened to the tug of antipathy that bloomed into sweating, harsh nightmare: the sense of a step on the earth, or a current in the air, raised to a distinctive stab of awareness that warned of his half-brother's proximity.

The hours when the feeling burned strongest, he dispatched Skannt's headhunters, backed by squads of Alestron's leaderless mercenaries. No few of these rode refitted to arms at his personal expense. Since the gear cast off in the rout behind Dier Kenton had vanished to tribal looters, Keldmar's divisions gave their loyalty in redoubled diligence to atone. No one berated them for giving way before a barrage wrought of sorcery. Prince Lysaer's direct word silenced any loudmouths who jeered. Still Alestron's men stung for shame that the enemy's escape had been accomplished through the break in their lines.

They raked the hostile hills and splashed through the grabbing reeds of the bogs that spread like virid stains along the bottomlands. At nightfall, most foray teams returned empty-handed, unblooded, chilled to the bone, and disheartened.

Others suffered a lightning-swift attack, played through and finished before they could fight back. Their fallen died unavenged as they seethed in grim circles that netted them no target to strike back.

For each paltry triumph garnered by the headhunters' tactics, shadows and sorceries claimed their ongoing toll. No matter how well-disciplined, the outlying skirmish lines became swallowed at random by unnatural dark. Arrows killed them. As often, the inbound supply trains straggled off their known route, bewildered and misled by illusion. Patrols later found them, bogged down in mud, or wandering lost, parted from their livestock and wagons.

The sorry truth persisted as the cook tents thinned their gruel and shortened rations. Through a fortnight of blood and sweat and selfless effort, the manhunt launched after the Master of Shadow gained Lysaer no measurable results. By small nips and bites, his ranks were whittled by losses.

Lord Commander Harradene of Etarra became a familiar sight, splashing from the puddled muck of the picket lines in his oversize boots and a cerecloth cloak which flapped off his broad shoulders like the hunch-backed plumage of a vulture. He was at hand to quell the upset when a pike rack beset by iyats brought a tent down in tatters, then sent the contents of the armourer's tool chest kiting through the high bracken, mallets and nails tumbling and tangling ahead of the men who raced to snatch them.

'Your Grace, such misfortunes won't let up,' Lord Harradene importuned once the last errant tool had been netted in chain mail, and four shelterless men crouched on their hams in the rain, stitching up rents in soaked canvas. 'Any time troops suffer sour spirits, their angst will lure in the stray fiends. In this benighted country, Ath's adepts keep no hostels to drive the accursed creatures off. We could send to the Koriani hospice at Forthmark for talismans. But if our couriers drive their remounts any harder, they're going to break legs in the bogs. Another fortnight will pass before word of our need gets through.'

Lysaer was seated on a camp stool sharpening a dagger. His hair beaded silver with wet, and his blue-and-gold surcoat a cry of unnatural colour against the unremitting gloom of wet hillsides, he looked up at the towering officer given rank as Lord Diegan's successor. 'You know such vexations are precisely how our enemy hopes to weaken us.' His mildness a mask over iron determination, he added, 'A whole lot worse than iyats will plague the five kingdoms if the Master of Shadow escapes alive.'

Lord Commander Harradene gave back no comment.

The Prince of the West laid aside whetstone and knife. He arose, snapped his fingers to his page, and received the cloak with Tysan's star over his shoulders. Then he waited, silent also, until the burly man of war who balked with folded arms could no longer sustain his level gaze.

'Are you suggesting Etarra should withdraw?' asked Prince Lysaer.

Flushed red by the implication that the allies from Jaelot and Alestron were more staunch, Lord Harradene gave way. 'Persistence is a credit, but it cannot stay the weather, nor lift the gloom of defeat off the troops. The hunger they suffer isn't helping. If this campaign's to win us aught but despair, our quarry had best be drawn and cornered quickly.'

'See to your men and he shall be,' Lysaer pledged.

An approaching jingle of steel, a man's bitten laugh, then the squelch of a fast stride through mud heralded the courier with the report from Skannt's last patrol. 'Mount a foray team,' the headhunter called, wringing out his cloak. 'We've seen more circles of flattened grass left by tents, and three pits of warm coals. Tracking dogs are out. There were tribesfolk watering a flock by a spring. By the sheep slots in the muck, they just barely departed.'

'The men who take them get the mutton,' Lysaer promised on a smile as Harradene's gruff mood brightened to immediate enthusiasm. With the latest supply train three days overdue, the contest would spur chafing troops.

In the dank flood of puddles, under misted wind and drizzle, the teams saddled horses and rode out in high heart.

Although the lure of fresh meat spitting hot fat over their fires held the men to the trail through weary hours, the herders vanished into the crags, untraceable. Skannt's tracking hounds circled and sniffed for scent on rinsed gravel until their pads bled. Squads of riders charged up and down the foggy glens, lured on by the echoed barking of herd dogs, or the chance-caught glimpse of sheep filing through a break in the mists. They would arrive in sweating fury to find the site vacant. Whatever notched pass had let the herders slip by, the most diligent scouts found their war bands no path through the scarps to give chase.

'Sorcery,' some of them muttered as they gave winded horses rein to breathe. 'The stones themselves could be witched.'

Others argued over which routes were safe. The slides at Dier Kenton had undermined their trust in the steep-sided corries. The grain of high ledges rose grooved in wet like sheared lead, their walls etched in guano from eyries of wyvern, and their weed-choked, ruffled brown gulches gouged out by the scars of old rockfalls. Men took fair warning from the runes scraped by shepherds to mark where the ground was unstable.

The more suspicious captains complained the placement was deliberate strategy. 'What are such signs if not decoys to divert us? Pay too close attention, and we'll ruin good mounts in the sinkholes or break our necks climbing boulders in the gullies.'

On one point, weary men agreed in creeping, hoarse whispers behind their officers' backs: Vastmark was a fiend's place, and the Shadow Master a genius in choosing the battleground upon which to break their hearts and spirits.

That night, past firepits clogged with soggy ashes that had signally failed to roast any haunch of captured mutton, a rattling pound of hooves raised trail-weary men from their tents. The cry of Alestron from the sentries and the blazon worn by the outriders raised a swift flurry of expectations. But no wagons of supplies were forthcoming. Instead, a company of fifty lancers on sweat-lathered horses pounded into camp under the ducal banner.

A splendid figure in his scarlet-and-gold surcoat, Lord Bransian s'Brydion vaulted from his saddle in a singing clash of war gear. He tossed his reins to a skin-wet royal squire and called in his boisterous bass, 'I've come to speak with Prince Lysaer.'

A thin-faced equerry in Avenor's blue livery stepped out with a smoking torch. 'His Grace is in council with the division captains.'

Duke Bransian ripped off his gauntlets, shedding wet in a pattering deluge to add to what drizzled from the sky. 'Which tent?' At the servant's fractional hesitation, he resumed in a blast of irritation, 'I don't give a damn if your liege is stark naked in his bath with six mistresses! I didn't ride forty leagues over Ath-forsaken gulches to stand in a downpour, waiting.'

'I'll take you,' offered one of the sentries on guard before the drapes of the royal pavilion.

Bransian grunted, then barked for his troop captain to stay at his side. 'The rest of you, commandeer a space and pitch camp. I'll join you when I've had my audience.' He followed the royal guardsman to what looked like a supply tent, then burst through its sagging entry without pause for a servant to announce him.

The ongoing murmur of voices inside wavered into sharp silence. Lysaer s'Ilessid looked up where he stood at the centre of a torchlit trestle. His arms were braced on a tactical map, his pale hair and circlet a patch of brightness gouged gleaming out of the shadows. He was attended by his ranking senior officers, clad in splotched mail, or surcoats still mud-spattered from the field. The tallest and most imposing of these was Alestron's own commander of mercenaries.

Aware of whose presence loomed at the entry, that one straightened up from close council. 'My lord!'

'Duke Bransian s'Brydion, accept my welcome,' greeted the Prince of the West. 'You have my condolence. By your arrival, I presume you received my letter concerning your brother, Keldmar?'

The royal candour caused the mercenary who knew the duke to cringe.

Bransian strode nearer, the clink of his spurs marking time to a tautened span of stillness. 'A scribbled word of sympathy would scarcely draw me here. And your sentiment's wasted.' He ripped off his mail coif. As though the steel were featherweight, he tossed it in a jingling arc. The captain who trailed at his shoulder fielded the catch with long-suffering familiarity. Over the sour clash of links, the duke added, 'I came because of *this*!'

He raked a crumpled square of parchment from his breast, impaled it on his unsheathed dagger, then hurled the weapon across the crowded tent.

The yellowed page fluttered, impelled by its missile of angry steel. The men-of-war nearest the trestle jostled clear, while the blade impaled with a choked-off clang through the centre of the flattened map.

'Go on, read,' Bransian snapped, while the pins and counters representing men tumbled in rattling disarray. The ducal face flushed over the wet pelt of his beard. 'Your men want to know why their supply train is late? You can tell them that murdering bastard of Shadow has trapped my three brothers as his hostage.'

Lysaer slit the parchment down its length rather than work the dagger free. His eyes, hard blue, scanned down lines of bold writing that strung him to rage of his own.

'. . . the well-being of your brothers now held as forfeit. If you wish them to live, you will cut the supply lines across Shand that sustain the great warhost in Vastmark.'

Over the outraged, incredulous murmur of the gathered senior officers, Bransian shouted, 'By my very name and lineage, the insult to s'Brydion is one I'll not suffer to bear!'

His fury clashed with Lysaer's tempered calm like the testing tap of crossed sword blades. 'Are you telling me eleven thousand dedicated men will be abandoned to hunger because of a threat to three lives?' The prince yanked the knife from the map, while the upright markers which outlined proposed patrols scattered in ironic retreat. 'You know if you give way to this, our last chance of victory will be ruined.'

Every man in camp knew the politics: the s'Brydion clan name was all that held the Selkwood barbarians from plundering every wagon to cross the wilds of Shand.

Bransian's eyes glittered like sheared iron as he shouldered his way to the trestle. 'You bear the blood of Tysan's *caithdein* on your hands, an affront no clanborn dares forgive. If your enemy is my enemy, that's no binding tie. The lives you would sacrifice are my brothers'!' The parked bulk of his frame set torches and candles into flickering eclipse. Amid the lick of wild shadows, his stance seemed as rock, implacable before royal sovereignty. 'Did you forget? Half of your vaunted eleven thousand are my own. How dare you presume my close family is worth less than the neck of one shadow-bending fugitive!'

Lysaer faced that lion's burst of temper in outright, scornful censure. 'For Maenalle's just arraignment for execution, I owe no living man apology. And while I share sympathy for the plight of your kinsmen, to measure their lives against the death of the Shadow Master is a mistake that could threaten us all.'

475

His hands locked to the dagger and parchment in restraint, Lysaer gave Bransian's hard-breathing ire no space at all to reply. 'This Teir's'Ffalenn's end is worth any cost, as your mercenaries here have stood witness. Even hungry, even abandoned by their lord, they will stay.' He finished in passionate entreaty to hook even the most grieving heart. 'Our effort must not fail here. Innocents rely on our protection to bring this fell sorcerer down.'

'Oh, he'll die for his effrontery, never fear.' Bransian held out his huge hand, received back his knife, snapped it home in the sheath at his wrist. 'I'll kill the slinking spy myself, not only for Alestron, but to see my brothers safe. Yet before my arrow or my steel takes his life, or until Mearn, Keldmar and Parrien are won free of his hands, no more of your supply wagons will have my escort across Vastmark. No troops from Alestron will march alongside your banner.'

'Add to our cause, or weaken us all,' Lysaer warned.

Bransian spat. 'I'll take back our field troops and plough apart these mountains. What you've failed to accomplish with a warhost, I shall finish alone with Keldmar's remaining six thousand.'

'Then issue your orders,' Lysaer flung back in brittle challenge. 'See if your fool's cause can draw them to abandon my side.'

'His Grace is right,' ventured the mercenary captain in rooted, unnerving conviction. 'My lord, even for Keldmar, we cannot agree to desert.'

'Desert?' Bransian bristled. 'What cant is this? Fiends plague! It's my treasury serves up your pay. Our people never joined this campaign for the pretty scruples! Take care how you speak. The one you pay lip service with royal title is no prince to command the fealty of any man born in Melhalla!'

The captain held ground in granite calm. 'You were not here for the murder of twenty-eight thousand, nor did you see your own seasoned troops undone by illusion and sorcery. The Prince of the West sees a danger in this Shadow Master that runs beyond blood ties or kingdoms. His gift of light is promised to guard us. Any troop riding against this enemy without protection is begging a fool-hardy end.'

'Sithaer! You speak of the rockslide that mauled Dier Kenton Vale?' The tawny spikes of Bransian's moustache lifted into a sneer. 'Everyone knows this countryside's unstable. Your prince's warhost died of plain tactics. Any cornered fugitive would've chosen faulty ground to save his skin when a mass of armed might fit to flatten a whole kingdom came trampling in to seek his death.'

'Nonetheless,' the captain insisted, 'Avenor's gold replaced our lost arms. We stand as the prince's men now.'

'Starve with him then, for his morals.' Bransian poised, eyes glittering, and regarded the Prince of the West, who had not moved. Eye-to-eye, the pair faced off, Alestron's duke furious, and Lysaer, detached in regal sadness.

'I see nothing I say will convince you.' Magnanimous, Lysaer creased the ripped parchment. To a sparkle of rings, he laid Arithon's missive across the rucked map on the trestle. 'Go in grace, my lord duke. Your brothers have my prayers for safe deliverance.'

A laugh ripped from Bransian's throat. 'Don't trouble the creator over them. I can kill an enemy and spare my born kin without any plea to Ath's grace for assistance.'

His captain of horse still hard at his heels, he stamped outside, immersed in rapid-fire orders. 'Tell my escort, and any of our mercenaries who might listen, to pack up now and resaddle. We've better things to do than to bed down with ninnies who breathe righteous principle and snivel in shrinking fear of shadows!'

The noise and the shouting disrupted half the night, as the Duke of Alestron gathered up his banners and his men and clattered into the darkness. At the end, some four hundred of Keldmar's command broke away and rode with him. The cavalcade was lost from view before dawn, swallowed up by the mists and the drab rains of Vastmark as if they had never existed.

In Lysaer's command tent, by the dribbled stubs of stale candles, the prince's scribe folded and sealed the last of a thick stack of dispatches. While the scent of hot wax curled through the reek of mouldered leather and the martial tang of oil and filed steel, the courier held waiting to ride scraped his stubbled chin with the back of a gloved knuckle. 'Do you think any of those deserters will survive?'

Exhausted, immersed in deep thought, Lysaer speared his quill pen into the throat of the inkwell. 'They're not deserters.' Regret weighed his shoulders beneath the trim tabard, with its gold bordered edges and the embroidered star of Tysan tarnished a bit green from the damp. 'Any foe of Arithon's is our firm ally. Let no man dare make the claim that Duke Bransian didn't ride out with my blessing.'

'You don't fault him for abandoning help with the supply train?' asked the guard by the door flap. He took liberty for the fact this prince never disparaged lowly rank, but would indulge his curiosity with clear answer.

Lysaer smiled as though the sun had come out and tapped the sealed pile of dispatches. 'I've inherited some five thousand of Alestron's best mercenaries. Duke Bransian may have withdrawn his family banner. We'll just have to see that Erlien's barbarians don't hear the same men are now taking pay from my coffers.'

To the courier's stifled awe, the prince laughed outright, a balm after hours of stiff protocol as officers came and left with terse orders. 'I'm assigning the mercenaries to resecure our supply lines from the coast,' Lysaer affirmed in that logic which could banish raw fear. 'What did you all think? That I'd stand down and leave because one old blood duke threw a tantrum? No. That would be a tawdry epitaph for the brave men who died, and small excuse to others who rely on us.'

Under the mists, as electrum veils of drizzle gave way to a colder, heavier thrum of rain, the Vastmark valleys crawled with armed men. For the shepherds under Arithon's protection, despite the hard-fought illusion of success, patrols were getting harder to avoid. Sheep and non-combatant families with young children were suffering under the strain. They slept in coiled nerves for the breathless word brought by scouts in the deeps of the night, then the hasty, rushed moves under cover of darkness, with babes muffled silent, and dogs nipping the skittish heels of panicked sheep.

In an open ditch choked with gorse, Dakar swiped dripping hair from his eyes and numbered the aches of exhaustion. The unscrupulous urge became plaguing temptation, to abandon the tenets of the Law of the Major Balance. How he itched to conjure a forbidden set of seals, draw the separate parties of enemy scouts to mistake each other for Arithon's archers, and let them noisily demolish each other. Certainly if he had to spend another day seeking permissions of sheep to seal illusions to make them look like rocks; or the same for rocks, to make them wear the semblance of sheep, he would beg for a mad fit of prescience just to escape his miserable boredom.

The clan scout sharing his guard post expressed the same sour view. 'Stubborn as a beggar's biting lice.' Below them, spread out like a stream of plugging ants, a line of troops scoured the gulches. Although worn and hungry on shortened rations, they ground on with their task in obdurate zeal, and unshaken belief in Lysaer's cause.

Yet faith could not reduce their real suffering, or the rain, and each day with its grinding weight of losses. Four bands of scouts had been diverted from the insignificant, rugged seam that led to the glen Dakar guarded. He watched amazed as a fifth party laboured up the rise, a spatter of pebbled silver against the gloom.

The leader's voice carried in surly complaint through the cleft. 'Damned rocks. Fit for nothing but turning a man's ankle.'

'Pleased to oblige and the more fool you,' Dakar breathed on a whisper. For the nature of stone was to absorb and reflect the influence of its environment. The wards the spellbinder had left strung like latticed light across the hillside now compounded the boulders' propensity to align to their surrounding energies. They were keyed to awareness, letting malediction and injury become turned back in kind.

Throughout the day, the switched-back little sheep track had become adept at shrugging off scouts who expressed their weary hatred of patrols.

A second later, to a grate of slipped shale, the man-at-arms who maligned the ground where he trod lost his footing and sat. A high-pitched curse left his lips. 'Fiends plague! My leg's wrenched. This place is Sithaer itself!'

'Better and better.' Dakar coughed back bursting laughter and wormed from his niche, neglecting to wince as the wet funnelled trickles down his hood. 'Best to leave,' he urged Caolle's scout. 'We don't want to witness what that harebrain's unleashed. Trust me, gravel never forgets an insult, and if iyats are near, they'll delight to play along for the malice. Nobody's going to use the path through this notch for a ten-day without risking a broken neck.'

The Mad Prophet scrambled upright behind the ridge, soaked and dishevelled, and marvelling still for the new-found acuity to his mage-sight. With each passing day, he realized afresh how much earth and air had forgiven his clumsiness through the years he had studied with

480

Asandir. The old platitude was no fable, that the world's luck walked in a Fellowship Sorcerer's shadow.

More cautious with his oaths of displeasure, Dakar shivered under soggy clothing. 'How are we holding?'

'There's fighting, northside of the fissure,' the scout admitted, his braid fallen loose and fanned in plastered ends to his leathers. 'Duke Bransian's guard,' which meant a show of muscle by men who were fresh and well fed. 'They shouldn't break through now. Arithon's there.'

'To draw them, or maze them in shadow?' Dakar asked in concern.

The scout shrugged. 'Whatever's needed. He promised the tribe.'

'Take me.' Dakar skidded downslope over grass choked in gravel and loose scree. The day had become an exercise in frustration, repeated sweeps by foray teams blundering to penetrate a glen where a tribeswoman laboured in childbirth. Made helpless by her time, she was attended by two midwives in a herder's shelter. Until the babe was born and her condition could withstand a litter, archers and clan scouts had dedicated themselves to divert enemies and seal off the passes.

That the affray had come to open fighting offered the worst of ill news. Bransian's company would press hard to gain ground defended by Arithon's allies. The duke's lancers had been scavenging the countryside like dog packs, shooting the wyverns off corpses and lying in ambush around springs in search of his captive brothers, to no avail.

More archers could die in one hour, here, than on the slopes behind Dier Kenton Vale. That Arithon s'Ffalenn should spend lives for a promise to the young mother's kinsmen was a folly no one dared argue. The shepherd tribes of Vastmark might lie under Lord Erlien's sovereignty, as vested *caithdein* of Shand, but for their help against Lysaer's warhost, and the use of their pastures for his battleground, the Prince of Rathain had made them his personal trust.

Dakar laboured through a gully, then started up the flank of the hill on the glen's farther side. 'If word reaches Skannt's patrols, his Grace could die for the sake of that mother and babe.'

'I said so.' The scout hunched, face turned against a dismal slash of rain. 'Ath Creator can't make our liege listen when his mind's fixed.'

'Then hurry.' Head down, Dakar ploughed through a hollow choked with stunted evergreen. Through branches crippled into tangles by the abuses of weather and poor soil, he heard arrows whine from the ridgetop, then the low, clipped accents as a clansman maligned a snapped bowstring. Past a crest of lichened boulders, the Mad Prophet collided with a herdsman whose dun frieze blended with the landscape.

'We're friends!' he yelped, before a dagger thrust on reflex could skewer him. 'How can we help?'

The offending blade tipped expressively up the slope, and its wielder said in dialect, 'Wish Alestron's stamina to Sithaer.'

'That's his sister, in labour,' Caolle's scout informed Dakar. 'How much longer do we need to keep them off?' He began to extricate his bow from his cloak, kept wrapped against his body to spare the string from the wet.

'She's delivered an hour ago. A fine son. They're moving her now.' A clash of steel past the rise caused the shepherd to wince. 'Arithon's said he'll hold the lancers off himself so our people aren't pinned in the gulch.'

'No.' Dakar shoved ahead. His hood blew back to free hair screwed in rings against the plump flesh of his neck. When an arrow creased the wind and just missed him, he flung himself flat and crawled. In a cleft of puddled shale the defenders grouped, beleaguered, the rain in their eyes, and the gloom falling fast, to rob their slim advantage of height.

Arithon was with them, wrapped in someone's borrowed cloak. Where his own had gone was anybody's guess; Dakar had seen him strip his shirt to cover a man struck by a mace, that his kinswoman not be haunted in her grief by the memory of his shattered face.

'You have to pull back.' Dakar shoved through the press and spoiled the aim of a bowman to make his point. Through curses in tribal vernacular he insisted, 'Skannt's got patrols out. Use shadow, and they'll pin your location.'

'Darkness is closing.' Arithon straightened, a strip of hide he had sliced off his boot cuff in hand. He tossed the leather to an archer who had welted his wrist on his bowstring, the result of a bracer clawed off in a climb. 'I can make the defence look like nightfall.'

'That's a fool's risk and you know it!' Dakar need not belabour the frightening facts: Lysaer's encampment was scarcely a league down the valley, and any use of shadow would provoke the lawless forces of Desh-thiere's curse into play.

The shepherd he had jostled knelt, drew, and loosed. Downslope, a man screamed to a sliding clash of metal while the Mad Prophet threatened, 'If you stay, I fight beside you.'

'Dakar, you can't.' Arithon looked up, his dismay blurred in streamers of mist. 'Your talents are needed to clear the way to the pass. Caolle's sent word. There are headhunters entrenched to cut off our retreat to the high country.'

'My duty to Asandir was to defend your royal life, and for no light reason.' The Mad Prophet met and strove to hold that fierce stare, then flushed and gave way before the obvious. Any sally by headhunters could create a vicious standoff, see their small force trapped between the blundering aggression of two disunited sets of enemies.

'You do see.' Arithon dashed rain off his stubbled chin, then sheathed his dagger. 'For that, I owe you everything.'

Dakar broke away, unwilling to speak. The storm was driving harder, and downpour raked the mountainside in sheets. Morning could see the summits sheathed in grey sleet, with the north face of the passes glazed in shining, glass ice. His mage-sight could sound the elements for what the most vigilant scout would miss. He would know if the trail lay safe to cross, or sense early warning of an ambush.

Bad enough to suffer the cruelties of nature, far less the driven fury of thwarted men-at-arms whose commanders were too righteous to let them quit.

Bone-weary, stinging and bloodied where he had raked himself in the scrub, the Mad Prophet huddled in the lee of an outcrop while the band he was to guide gathered at the head of the glen. Five brindled sheep dogs padded anxious circles through the legs of tribal archers, who gnawed on smoked jerky and tested wet weapons in worried regularity. The beautiful horn and lacquer recurves they preferred were packed away in dry leather. Heavy wet would ruin them. During squalls, they favoured the same indestructible yew longbows as the woodland clansmen.

Over the common woe of bowstrings that stretched, Rathain's scouts exchanged phrases in stilted tribal dialect.

No one made jokes. Hungry, half-frozen, they waited for twilight, then set out in gloom under silver-bellied cloud. Ahead lay the Kelhorn's worst cliff walls and precipices, where soldiers unfamiliar with the territory could only follow at severe disadvantage.

Needled half-blind in cold rainfall, cloaked in smoking drifts of mist, the men in Dakar's party picked their slow way, with the sheep dogs flanking to scent out the presence of enemies. The endless hiss of runoff over rock could not always hide the chink of slipped shale, or the sliding rattle of a misstep. Inside the first furlong, a pack of tracking hounds picked up their backtrail. The deep-voiced bay of man-hunting mastiffs was answered by the cry of a horn, then by shouts as their handlers fanned out in search.

'Skannt's band,' said the rearguard scout who raced up to deliver breathless warning. 'Watch the ground ahead. He'll have an ambush waiting. On my mother's grave, that's his style.'

A whicker of attacking bowfire stuttered off the boulders where the shepherds had flattened into cover. Someone cursed in dialect. All shared the sharp frustration: they could see no target to aim at.

Plagued by the crowding sensation of raw fear, Dakar peered into the night. 'They hope to pin us in place.' Mage-sight yielded intermittent pulses of life aura through the stippled fall of precipitation. The staid form of stone was always more elusive to pick out when he had little stomach for patience. He persisted, though the interference thrown off by running water harried his nerves and made him queasy. Their party held position on a windswept rim of shale. He could sense the scarlet-tinged bloodlust of enemies entrenched where the scarp met the mountain.

'We could loose our dogs to stall the trackers,' a herdsman offered.

Dakar shut his eyes to steady himself through a moment of clawing dizziness. 'Do that.' If he could stand off the chill enough to concentrate, he could set a spell to magnify sound, create enough echoes to make the animals seem more fearsome than they truly were. The hounds might not stay fooled. But men in the dark in strange country would be vulnerable to unsettled nerves. For the ambush entrenched ahead, he had no recourse.

Clan scouts with their knowledge of infighting must battle every step of the way.

Caolle's men sorted themselves into a skirmish line and slipped up the ridge through the dark. The herdsman stroked muzzles, his soft-vowelled dialect sharpened by regret. He fingered the luck talismans twined to the dogs' ruffs, then released his beloved animals with the trained commands to drive off wyverns or wolves.

Eager whines, a bound of motion, a gale-flung scent of wet fur, and the sheep dogs hurtled down their backtrail. While their growling charge diminished in the storm, Dakar mustered tattered skills, fumbled his first wardspell, then lost the thread of the second to a shimmering, redoubled fall of rain. Cloudbursts played havoc with conjury, could mute wards and cancel out his most reliable constructs of spells. The Mad Prophet fought through lethargy, shook off numbing cold, and finally succumbed to bright anger. He wove the elemental chaos of the deluge into his next effort and the bindings grabbed, then like fell vengeance.

In the darkness, the snarls became magnified as the herd dogs launched into attack. Yowling hounds and the fall of kicked shale pocked the night as the two packs collided in conflict. Men's shouts clamoured through the uproar, faint and scared against what sounded like the very wolves of Sithaer, set reiving by the hand of the Fatemaster.

'Go,' urged the herdsman, torn to tears by his pride. 'As long as my dogs live, they'll keep fighting.'

But immersed in a webwork of glass-edged spells, Dakar shook his head. 'Arithon's people need this trail after us. The headhunters will have to be routed.'

Bloody swords were going to get bloodier, and on the black spine of the mountain, strafed by howling winds, weather would hamper both ally and enemy. Pouring sweat off cold skin, Dakar clamped down on a vicious twist of nerves. How simple if he could pit the pack of

486

Skannt's headhunters against Bransian's lancers, and as a herb witch did with vermin, let them hack at each other, bemused under spells, until the way to the passes lay open.

The front rank skirmishers returned, wiping sticky knives, their numbers pared down by half. In typical fashion for clanborn, they showed no sentiment for losses. 'Trail's cleared ahead.'

Behind, the guttural snarling of dogs echoed back, cut by the yelps of one wounded. Steel clashed on rock, and men exchanged shouts in townbred accents. Through a gap in the drizzle, Dakar saw Caolle's clansmen lock glances.

'Headhunters aren't fools enough to give way. They'd just track us from behind. Daren't leave them,' said one, bearded and very young. No doubt one of Jieret's Companions, he spat on his blade in salute. 'That, for the blood of my sister.' A grin and one step saw him vanished amid the storm, older clansmen in formation close behind.

'Come on.' Dakar rallied the huddled band of shepherds. 'If we don't make the high country, Caolle will get worried and send another party down.' He hoped against chance that Arithon would be quick; rough conditions were not going to slacken.

Two dogs rejoined them as they pressed up the ridge, both torn at the ears and one limping. The rank taint of blood stained the rainswept air, leaving Dakar gut sick and gasping. The trail up the scarp cut back on itself, draped with the throat-slit corpses of ambushers, dangling head down from wet rocks.

By midnight, the winds drove a barbed slash of sleet. Dakar flexed numbed toes in his waterlogged boots and shouldered head down against the blast. A cold yet more bitter rode the back of the storm, and a chill raked him through his wet clothing. The shepherds seemed inured to the discomforts of the climate. They made no sound

in complaint. Dakar was aware of them only as movement, the tap of a bow against a silver-chased horn, or
a soft, slipped step in total darkness. They relied on his
mage-sight to feel out the path. His senses were over-
strung and tired.

Enough that he misread his own vision.

When a flare of thin light glanced at the edge of his
perception, and his nostrils picked up what could have
been a faint, sheared trailer of ozone, he stopped. He
unreeled his awareness into howling dark until he could
taste the rank density of the night. He found nothing.
The flare had not been lightning. Flat clouds spread over
the mountains in a fabric of random motion.

Nowhere did he encounter the latticed energies of
charged spellcraft. Hazed to uneasiness, he could pinpoint no reason why the blank elements should feed his
spurt of alarm.

A shepherd blundered into him and spoke soft apology.
Poised on the trail, his straining skills immersed in the
web of natural forces, Dakar bludgeoned tired wits for
some clue to prompt whether he had imagined that trace
flicker of strayed energy. Nothing remained but the ugly
recognition that this cold snap would turn the grass and
bracken. Winter had crept in, all unnoticed, while one
fragment of prophecy had unforgivably slipped his attention. As his pause grew prolonged, and the shepherds
voiced uncertainty, for need, he reassured them and
pressed on.

Once his party was safe, at the soonest opportunity, he
must turn back and tell Arithon of his prescient vision
concerning an assassin's posited attempt to claim his
life.

Dakar tripped on the scarp, slammed his knee on an
outcrop, and bit back his urge to cry curses. Ath knew,
if Rathain's prince was to die of a strike from covert
ambush, these hills held the gamut of his enemies to
choose from.

The arrow foreseen on that sere, rain-bled slope would be frightfully simple to arrange.

In an agony of doubt, the Mad Prophet struggled on to the upper vale settlement. The archers by then were staggering on their feet from the punishing climb against the tempestuous gusts. A biting drop in temperature made the last league a terror of slick rocks, glazed over in snap-frozen ice. As desperate as the men for the chance to get warm, the Mad Prophet crawled into the first shelter he was offered, hurting to his bones from too many hours with his mage-sight cranked to heightened focus. In a dank tent on a gale-whipped hillside, he accepted hot soup from a shepherd child with huge eyes, wrapped in some grandmother's tasselled shawl.

Wet, weary, the archers shed quivers and unstrung yew bows. Given loaned blankets, or hunkered down in fleeces, they slept where they sat. By the light of a swinging lantern, two herd girls treated the dogs with a salve made from herbs and mutton fat. The air smelled of meat and fresh blood and wet sheep. Dakar strained reddened eyes through the smoke-thickened air, unsurprised to find a ewe who had lambed out of season, legs folded and dozing in the corner. A younger child lay curled between her kids, tucked asleep amid their grey-fleeced warmth.

Outdoors, the gale shrilled and rain fell, and sheep milled in plaintive, wet knots. A sentry reported. Caught nodding over his meal, the Mad Prophet snapped straight and snatched his bowl as it tilted. He need not have troubled. The broth had cooled off and congealed. Too tired to swear, he asked the grandfather who tended the peat fire. 'Arithon. Has he come in?'

'No.' The answer was given by a clanborn scout, just arrived in from the passes. 'Caolle's gone out. There's been some delay down the trail.'

'Not more headhunters?' Dakar raked back his bangs, winced to the sting of a scabbed wrist, and fought against

the ache of abused muscles. His boots had stiffened like
cold iron around his ankles and he was sitting in a
puddle.

'If enemies were lurking, we couldn't see them.
Night's like the black heart of Sithaer.' The scout peeled
his soaked cloak, then surrendered the dry linen he had
saved to tend his sword to bind up a gash on a sheep
dog.

Cold to the bone, warned by the creak of the ridgepole
on its pins and the thrummed slap of canvas of a wind
still sullenly rising, Dakar shook off paralysing tiredness
to ask the grandfather for a blanket to replace his soaked
clothes. While the tribesman stepped out to borrow from
a neighbour, the Mad Prophet lost his battle against
exhaustion. Sleep overcame him, and in misplaced kindness, no one saw the need to roust him out.

He woke to the gut-sick, upset sense of something gone
terribly wrong. As if power had stirred just beyond his
awareness, or a prescient tremor had shot through his
dreams before he could grasp its significance. The first
thing he heard was Caolle's voice, declaiming, in a tone
unwarrantedly jubilant.

Someone else answered, laughing. Then a scout's
buoyant whoop shook droplets from the ridgepole onto
Dakar's face. He spluttered and sat up, stiff enough to
groan and blinking to clear bleary eyes. The tent was
empty, the fire gone out. Startled by the lateness of the
hour, he ploughed through dank fleeces to the door flap.

Cold air slapped his face, no improvement. His wits
were too sleep-clogged to think. The view met his vision
in blinding whiteness. He squinted, picked out thin
mist, grey rock, and dead bracken, dusted over with
hoarfrost.

Dawn was hours gone and a shepherd had filched his
cloak.

He groped through a dimness muddled in the smells of rancid food and peat ash until he found a garment to pull over his shivering shoulders. Emerged like an otter out of water into cold, he gasped, 'What's happened? Where's Arithon?'

Caolle stood by the cracked ice of a spring, slapping caked sleet from his sleeve cuffs. He turned a face with rimed eyebrows toward the tent. 'You slept through the news? Jaelot's garrison's finally had enough. This morning, they're folding their camp. Columns are marching east as we speak. They've started to pull out of Vastmark.'

To Dakar's continued stiff silence, he added, 'Not to worry for the others. They've delayed for good reason, to be sure the retreat matched the rumours.'

'Where's Arithon?' Dakar repeated.

His plaintive note of fear cut through at last and snapped the war captain's complaisance. 'Why?' Caolle strode over, his raw knuckles clamped to his sword hilt. 'His Grace is down the trail. Asked for time to himself.' He swept a glance that bit over Dakar's dishevelment. *'Fiends alive, what's wrong?'*

The Mad Prophet never broke his own absorbed study: of cliffs that felt skewed out of balance; over a wilderness of mist, raked like tufted fleece across the valleys; and under sky capped in lead-bellied clouds. The steep rake of rock where the tents clung like lichens dropped away into sparkling white, spiked in frost that cased stone and grasses in ethereal, glassine beauty.

Through the brutal cold, Dakar cried, 'Caolle, get your scouts! Tell them to look for an assassin!'

Then he was off at a limping run toward the narrow trail that snaked down the slope. Shouting erupted behind him, sliced by the sliding, steel ring of blades from wet scabbards. Clansmen were running at his heels, fanning out to scour the ridges.

Too fat to sprint, Dakar skidded down a shale face to cut off one bend in the trail. White plumes of moisture streamed past his lips. He moaned at the stab of icy air. There was no rain, he thought, desperate. His prescient dream had shown rainfall, dead bracken, and lichened boulders, not the naked, scoured rock he traversed at a windmilling scramble.

The track cut to the right. Past the rim of the hill, the trail jagged like a kinked cord into a ravine *sheltered from the winds, and grown with stands of grass and russet fronds of killed bracken.* The cold of high altitude had turned the plants early. Dakar gasped as dread plunged in a rush through his vitals. The site was the same. He had passed the place, unrecognized, unknowing, last night in the darkness.

Here lay the location his prescient prophecy had revealed for the Shadow Master's death.

The last, outside hope became dashed at next breath. There the prince stood with his back turned, absorbed by something farther down the trail. Arithon wore leathers streaked dull from foul weather, the black hair uncut since his court visit to Ostermere knotted back with a deer hide thong. A quiver of arrows hung near empty at his hip, the yew bow he had borrowed set aside, still strung, against a scaled shoulder of rock. His bearing held the loose-limbed, enviable grace seen so often on the tranquil sands of Merior.

Then a rattling fall of pebbles shattered his moment of solitude. Arithon spun, his wild start of tension eased to a welcoming smile.

'Dakar,' he shouted. 'It's over. The warhost has broken to march east.'

Even from a distance, his face looked shadowed. The hollows left chiselled by sleepless nights and strain had yet to soften, though the killing, the risk, the deadly danger presented by Desh-thiere's curse grew less for each minute that passed. He might have no time to celebrate the fact he had survived with his integrity intact and his tribal allies unharmed.

Dakar swore and kept running.

Time slowed. Vision acquired a rending brilliance of detail; again he saw the brown skeletons of bracken, the eerie sense of framed stillness in the half-breath before frightful tragedy.

Then the last hope, ripped away as the sky opened up into downpour. The final facet of the vision given months before fell inexorably into place. Two steps, and Arithon would complete the angle of that image. Some assassin's arrow would fly and strike, and all they had accomplished would be lost. All; Dakar howled for the waste. The Mistwraith's dire threat would acquire free rein through his own colossal carelessness and a tardy, selfish hoarding of a loyalty he had almost rejected for blind prejudice.

He tried to shout. The wind snatched his words. He could not make himself heard for the drumroll of rain on rock, nor cry over the unbroken trickle of runoff guttered over bare ledges. By some cruel trick of nature, a fickle gust from behind, he heard very clearly the twang of a bowstring from cover higher up the scarp. Then the hum of the arrow as it launched toward rendezvous with its living target.

Dakar had no time to frame spells to command steel, to bend air and arrest wood and feather. His desperate effort to warn Sethvir slipped awry in the chaos of the deluge. The fleeting second for preventive action slipped past. Arithon closed that fatal, last step, to stand isolate at the crux of fate and prophecy.

There was nothing else left under earth and sky one labouring, fat spellbinder could do.

The Mad Prophet launched his ungainly body in between to offer himself as Arithon's shield.

A split second he had to flinch from folly, to ache for the likely fact the archer in hiding could simply fire a second spelled shaft and complete the diverted work of the first. One heartbeat he raged against the futility

493

of his act and ached for obligations left undone.

Then the arrow struck. Impact pitched him forward onto his face and pain sliced his regrets to screaming ribbons.

Dakar hit gravel rolling, primed with the counterspells he needed to engage his longevity training. His first effort was waylaid and poisoned inside. Slashed through the scald of his blood by something more sinister than steel, he locked his jaws and groaned. Had he not been spellbinder to a Fellowship Sorcerer, he might not have recognized the distinctive bite of arcane energy; the crystal driven resonance of a Koriani seal, furtively set to ensure the arrow's wound would be mortal.

He gasped. Rain fell in his eyes. Every muscle in his back and abdomen cramped, and agony drove him to whimper. He could feel the bleeding. Instinct insisted he must engage *this* sigil and *that* binding to stem the gush; to close torn tissues and claw back a firm foothold on life.

But a rank tide of dizziness sucked through his awareness. He could not think, could not concentrate, could not snatch back the threads of self-discipline. Five hundred years of arduous study, and he lacked the means to unwind the fugitive work of a solitary Koriani death seal.

He had time to taste irony along with the blood. The spell-turned arrow intended for Arithon hurt a thousand times worse than the knife thrust taken from an irate husband for his stolen kiss from a kitchen wench, the signal bit of folly which had bought his unwanted term of service.

Then darkness blanked his sight. Tears of remorse wet Dakar's cheeks, striped by the cold fall of rain. He understood he was not going to pull himself together, was not going to staunch the ebb of his life force in time. He would pass the Wheel and suffer Daelion's judgment without seeing whether Arithon survived.

Of all disappointments, that sparked his anger. He

could not even snatch the awareness for the handful of minutes he needed to know the outcome of his train of mistakes.

The last thing he felt were hurried hands on his shoulder. Then a voice, perhaps Caolle's, in gruff and distant protest. 'Name of Ath, there's no justice in the world if he dies . . .'

But therein lay the unkind twist of fate. Had Dakar any breath, he would have railed against paradox, that for all his inept living, his one selfless act should seal his end. He wondered if Sethvir's histories would name him hero, or if his Fellowship master would appreciate the contradiction; and then he had no thought but silence.

For a very long time, there was nothing. Darkness, stillness, utter cold; then a point of blue light, etching a fretted course to close patterns a trained mage should recognize. Meaning that tantalized reason grazed the edge of labouring consciousness. The mind knew nothing, felt less. Just an invidious lassitude and a quiet more profound than winter's grip of black ice.

Then a powerful voice pierced the chill and cracked the shackles of freezing blankness. Dakar heard his Name twined in power that could have raised the earth's molten core in fiery summons.

A question followed, demanding a permission. Dakar felt tears prick the insides of his eyelids and a ghostly sense of flesh he had forgotten he still possessed. His thoughts imprinted an awareness of Asandir's presence, then gave free consent to what was asked.

Someone he could not see cried out in relief.

Then a burst of white light scoured through him and pain rushed back like a shriek torn through perfect vacuum.

Weeping for the return of bodily sensation, gasping

breaths that seemed drawn in pure flame, the Mad Prophet opened his eyes. Rain and clouds; a bitter wind snapped his cheek. He saw Asandir's face, drawn in weathered lines and a fearful, patient concentration.

Then Caolle's voice, surly with concern. 'Shouldn't we get him to shelter?'

No one answered. Dakar felt the Sorcerer's hands in tender strength turn his body. He rolled prone on sharp gravel, rinsed over in running water. Blood trailed from his mouth. The taste made him gag. Too depleted to shiver, he felt the chill spear clear through him as fingers gently cut the tunic from the broken off arrow shaft struck on an angle through his back.

'Steady,' said Asandir.

Then, as Dakar struggled to ask what crisis should bring a Fellowship Sorcerer to his side, and to warn of the Koriani plot against Arithon, his master said, inarguable, 'Don't speak.'

Dakar felt the burn of a sigil drawn in warm fire against his skin. The pain bled away, stilled from a thundering scream to a murmur.

'Sleep, Dakar,' said the Sorcerer in that tone no mortal man could summon the wits to disobey.

The time was much later. Night, Dakar sensed as he clawed through mazed wits to reclaim his smothered awareness. He opened his eyes to the ruddy glare of a tallow lamp. Spidery legs of shadow stalked across the woven patterns of a shepherd's tent. He smelled rancid fleece and the hot reek of fat. Scapegrace that he was, he longed for cheap gin to obliterate the upwelling emotion that threatened to rip up his guts.

Against every blundering mistake in creation, his master had seen fit to assist his survival. The result promised punishment and joy.

A swathe of firm bandaging constricted his chest.

Every breath jerked an ache through his back. He still did not know; he feared above all to ask if his foolhardy act had won reprieve.

Then the voice he most wanted to hear this side of the Wheel spoke in gentle censure at his bedside. 'For the armoury at Alestron, I'd say we were quits.' Lean hands closed over his palms and pressed something sharp and metallic into his strengthless grasp.

The Mad Prophet rolled his eyes to find the Prince of Rathain propped on crossed arms against his bedside.

Too hurt to move, Dakar traced the razor-edged metal between his fingers. 'A clan vengeance arrow?'

Arithon recited the inscription on the flange, unblinking, his grave features lent an unwarranted sense of majesty by the uneven play of the light. '"*From the hand of Bransian s'Brydion, for the seven who died in the armoury.*" You know you saved my life.'

Against more than the Duke of Alestron, Dakar struggled to say. A banespell from Morriel Prime had sped the s'Brydion vow of enmity; and now, most dangerously, her guile had ensured that no trace of evidence would remain. Had he not taken the arrow in the Shadow Master's stead, not even Althain's Warden could have known of a plot in progress. Except for his testimony as living witness, the magic had left no aura.

Arithon answered his urgent concern. 'Asandir found out about the Koriathain as he healed you. No one knows why their order should wish me dead.'

Dakar expelled a scratchy sigh. 'If the Fellowship saw, why didn't my master do something earlier? Where has he gone now?'

Above him, etched in motionless tension, Arithon weighed his reply. A masterbard's exacting intuition let him say, 'Sethvir picked up your distress on the ridgetop and passed on the warning. But Asandir made no intervention until you had accomplished the errand he set you on course to complete.'

'Ath!' Dakar whispered, too weak for heat and vehemence. He coughed out the rancid reek of mutton fat. 'Don't ever run afoul of a Fellowship Sorcerer. Their ways are devious and tangled in a manner even Daelion couldn't fathom.' But hindsight showed his assigned service to Arithon was no penance, after all; just a difficult lesson brought to full circle.

'You can rest,' the Master of Shadow said in rueful sympathy. 'Asandir has ridden on as my envoy to inform Lysaer s'Illessid of another ransom. Thanks to your timely call to action, Caolle's scouts took Duke Bransian prisoner in my name.'

'You've got *all four brothers s'Brydion*?' Dakar's beard twitched to his lopsided grin. 'A bloody plague of fiends would be simpler to banish. You'll let them go for Lysaer's gold?'

Green eyes flashed to a gem-cut glint of bright humour. 'Stay and find out. Asandir left his wish that you choose your own road from this place.'

The Mad Prophet grabbed the blankets to shove up on one elbow, then groaned. Felled by a stab of wretched agony, he surrendered to prostration while spinning senses settled. 'I can go with him or make my own way?'

In dreamy disbelief, Dakar pondered this, a frown furrowed under the hair left screwed into a cockscomb nest of wild tangles. Beyond doubt he felt unready to resume the disciplines demanded of a Fellowship spellbinder. The willing burden of responsibility was too fresh, too unwieldy a yoke upon shoulders still far from self-reliant.

The prince he had spilled his blood to preserve had opened his mind to new venues. Their relationship intrigued him like some razor-edged puzzle he could not resist the urge to challenge.

'I'd stay in your service, if you'll have me.' Reddened in diffidence, Dakar tucked his bearded chin beneath the coverlet. 'If after Jaelot and Merior and yesterday's blunder, you can imagine me becoming something more than a damned liability.'

Across from him, Arithon raised eyebrows in surprise. 'My service of itself is a damned liability. Has an arrow in the back taught you nothing?' Then his lips flexed and dismissed his rare smile. Unmasked by deep warmth few others came to witness, he added, 'In truth, Dakar, I'd be honoured. Three times you've proven your worth and your caring. I'd be the world's greatest idiot to turn your offer of friendship aside.'

Overset by embarrassment, Dakar stared up at the worn weave of the tent, pricked with holes at the roofpole. 'I'll still get drunk,' he warned. The light swam around him, bright beyond bearing, and the air felt too thick to draw past the lump in his throat. Against a maddening, sleepy urge to drift beyond thought, the Mad Prophet mumbled into the fleeces. 'I'll not give up whoring, no matter how horribly you plague me.'

Somewhere far off, the s'Ffalenn prince was laughing without satire. 'If five centuries of apprenticeship with a Fellowship Sorcerer failed to break your decadent habits, who am I to dare try?'

Last Defeat

Rain fell over Vastmark in cold, autumn torrents, and the valleys lay pooled in pewter puddles. In a war camp half-dismantled, undone into chaos, and up to its ankles in churned mud, Lysaer s'Ilessid stood in the open, bareheaded, while the Fellowship Sorcerer, Asandir, took his leave after bringing word of Duke Bransian's captivity.

The moment was not private or friendly. Around the site where prince confronted Sorcerer, wet ox teams drew the great drays. Spoked wheels sucked over the moiled ground to a creak of stressed timbers, laden beds heaped with war gear and furled canvas. The drovers goaded their beasts and stared in furtive fear as they passed. No few marvelled over the proud courage of their liege lord, who dared the attempt to stand down a mage of the Fellowship.

'You are not welcome here,' Lysaer said in stiff anger, while the Sorcerer regarded his stilted reserve in a stillness that marked them both as figures set apart. 'Not only for the fact you speak for the Shadow Master, and not just for the misfortune that Arithon demands another ransom from me for a hostage.'

Asandir regarded the s'Ilessid prince unabashed, while

the water channelled off his silver hair and through the grooves scored from the corners of his eyes over cheekbones like weathering on old granite. His answer, when it came, held restrained sorrow. 'That's a very large statement, made from a very closed heart.'

He offered no advice, no wisdom, no platitude, but smiled to the trembling royal page who brought his black horse to hand him the reins. He patted the boy's shoulder before he mounted. 'Did the soldiers say something to frighten you? You're a bigger man than that. You have my promise, there's no truth behind whatever tale of horror you've been told.'

The boy looked uncertain. 'You take no babes from their mothers for sacrifice?'

'Never.' Asandir flicked his silver-bordered mantle off his horse's steaming hindquarters, draped it back over his shoulders, then set his foot in the stirrup and settled into his saddle. The stud snorted under him. Its ghost eye rolled white in eagerness to be off. Asandir held his restive mount and looked down at the fair-haired royal scion his Fellowship could not sanction for inheritance. 'Neither do my kind intervene with mortal lives unasked. You do your followers no service to foster that misapprehension.'

'Should I lie?' Lysaer rebutted, his attention already strayed ahead to the needs of the people beneath his banner. 'Men have every right to fear the forces of sorcery for as long as the Master of Shadow is free to terrorize their towns, and slaughter their comrades by the thousands on the field.'

In aggrieved awareness that no words of reason could pry through the implacable beliefs engendered by Deshthiere's curse, Asandir lent the statement no endorsement. 'Would you sentence a criminal without hearing both sides of a grievance? I leave you with a challenge, that you make the chance to ask your half-brother's allies for their view.'

'I shall, if you deliver him to my court for judgment in chains,' Lysaer countered.

But the Sorcerer had already set heels to his mount. The stallion shouldered ahead, an apparition of night and shadow against the drab heave of men's industry and the leaden, unending fall of rain. The servants and squires collapsing tents or loading the bone-skinny backs of the pack mules scattered uneasily before that dark rider's passage. A few gave way with extreme respect. A camp follower in trailing, muddied skirts curtsied to the ground, more deferent than she would have been toward royalty.

Asandir checked his mount. His gentle request to spare him her adulation left her smiling like new morning as he resumed on departure.

No one watching could fail to acknowledge the power in the Sorcerer's capacity to care for detail. The fact that his Fellowship had twice stood as Arithon's envoy fed a steady and latent uneasiness.

Lysaer damped back a sullen flare of resentment.

Alone, unsupported amid the dismembered wreckage of his hopes, he fought back despair as the seep of grey weather and the measure of his losses sank their grip on his heart and squeezed. The shame of his defeat at Dier Kenton Vale would weigh on him all of his days. Nearest to the heart, on the heels of his wrenching estrangement from Talith, he must bear home the news of her brother, killed on the field by barbarians.

Beyond life, the mark of ignominy would endure, indelibly set in Third Age history.

A thousand lesser sorrows surrounded him. Soldiers who had set faith in his march to claim due justice slogged through chill puddles to dismantle the field tents. They moved with bent heads, and cheeks grown hollowed with hunger. Their voices as they attended their duties rang dispirited, except in reference to their longing to return home. Under the leaning, bare poles of a cook shack, the wounded and the sick waited to be carried to wagons on litters. In a field pavilion nearby, in sombre, lowered voices, Lord Commander Harradene conferred with other captains on how they should handle the inevitable illness that must sweep through the ranks as the weather worsened.

Pain became anger, that all the brave efforts of three kingdoms' muster had come to naught.

Ravaged by the effects of his enemy's unrelenting cleverness, Lysaer had no choice but accept his bitter defeat at the hand of the Master of Shadow. Yet he was too much the prince to leave the matter here in Vastmark, or to let the ruins of another campaign become an uncontested victory.

Chilled through his rich surcoat, the prince called his page to send for Avenor's captain-at-arms. Then he instructed his steward to tell his officers to wait an hour before striking his command tent.

'Your Grace,' the servant murmured, troubled as he arose from his bow for the sharp expression still stamped on the features of his prince.

The captain of the royal guard arrived, his surcoat brushed clean of mud, and the gold braid against all odds still kept shining. His sallow, axe features were a fixed mask to hide disappointment as he presented himself to hear what he expected would become his liege's last order to retreat. 'My prince, your cause is just. Never would we have betrayed you, though the last of us died in these hills.'

Lysaer turned away from his study of the mists that masked the cut rims of the mountains. 'This war is not finished. No defeat is ever final. My mistake, always, was to fight the Master of Shadow on his own chosen ground.'

No warhost could close every bolt-hole in a continent. Nor could a galley fleet scour every cove in the shoreline.

'We lost,' Lysaer admitted in full surety, 'because indeed, I demanded the impossible.'

'No prince could have done more,' protested Avenor's captain. He had tears in his eyes for a pride beyond reach of mortal heartbreak.

Inspired by recognition that he had cast his net too small, Lysaer gave a smile of encouragement to rival a Fellowship Sorcerer's. 'We return to Avenor, not to accept what has happened, but to become the supreme example for all other cities on the continent. If every man comes to hear of this campaign, if every village learns of our enemy's threat and guards itself against corruption, there will be no roof anywhere under which the Master of Shadow can find shelter. We can make certain, the next time he strikes, that no one alive gives him haven.'

And there lay the answer, Lysaer determined as he watched his captain straighten tired shoulders and stride off to attend his men in revived spirits.

Arithon s'Ffalenn could never succeed again if he was stripped of his welcome to delude backward settlements and win allies.

Lysaer stepped into his command tent, sent his page to find his secretary, then pondered the formidable obstacles confronting the seeds to restore his grand plan. Avenues of support still existed for Arithon, whose powers could never be vanquished: Fellowship Sorcerers and adepts of Ath's Brotherhood were unmoved in corrupted belief that his shadow-bending deeds were tied to innocence. To make way against such uncanny force and mystery, the influence of initiates and mages must become undermined or supplanted.

To crush an enemy who commanded the fell powers of the dark, an armed host must be raised that was willing to die for the cause. One bound to unity through beliefs too strong to be routed by old superstitions or illusions of Dharkaron's legendary chariot.

Lysaer settled into the damp velvet of his camp chair. Knuckles pressed to his temples, he frowned as logic vaulted him through avenues of fresh thought. To bring down a criminal who manipulated men's fears as a weapon would require soldiers who would march on command to outface the very essence of evil.

To lead such a force, Lysaer perceived he would have to be more than a Prince of the West, more than Lord of Avenor, greater than the ancient royal bloodline of Tysan.

He must stand before people of all kingdoms as a presence beyond mere flesh and blood. Only then could he raise the inspiration to fire men to offer themselves in sacrifice.

His talent with light gave him birth claim to power. Davien's fountain lent longevity. Should he not stand as the servant of innocence to rid the land of Arithon's malevolence?

A light cough at his shoulder returned the prince to awareness that his secretary awaited his instructions. 'I'll need a letter written,' he said, brisk in restored habit of command, 'a requisition to my council in formal language to raise the gold to redeem the four brothers s'Brydion.'

A mousy, worn man, the scribe made a sound in surprise.

Lysaer regarded him, sobered to attentive sympathy. 'What were you thinking? Did men dare to presume I'd forsake my sworn allies over a conflict between blood family and loyalty?'

'Some say so, your Grace,' the secretary whispered in diffidence.

'Well, they must be made to see otherwise.' Lysaer surged to his feet, charged to magisterial vehemence. 'The name of no man who fought here shall be forgotten. No ally shall go unsung. The s'Brydion brothers will be ransomed by my treasury, and every survivor who leaves here shall go as my vested envoy. We who survive must spread word of the wiles and sorceries that led our best

505

companions to ruin. Our cause is unfinished until this whole land has been raised against the Master of Shadow. When all cities stand against him, how can this Spinner of Darkness win aught but misery and failure? Our work must be diligent. Until every heart lies barred against his wiles, our enemy will have foothold to seed ruin.'

The secretary bowed, sat, and opened his lap desk. Refigured by hope, the proud scion of s'Ilessid began his energetic dictation. The missive he sent, penned and sealed beneath his sigil, was signed, 'Lysaer, Prince of the Light.'

When the captains were given orders to strike the royal tent, they were asked to see if Avenor's men could raise the spirit to sing through their task.

'Become the example,' Lysaer exhorted, his stance unbowed, and his voice a ringing call of inspiration. 'If we show no despair, all others will take heart.'

Between the collapse of the camp and the dismal, chill fall of night, the secretary spread his story of the letter written for his liege lord. His reverent account gained fresh impetus as Lysaer walked the common ranks, clad in shining gold and surrounded in a nimbus of summoned light. Where he passed, he left laughter behind him. The first, hopeful whispers of rumour began to spread. By the hour Avenor's staunch captains dispatched their sentries to stand guard at the war camp's perimeters, the password they used became the slogan, 'light over darkness'. Talk around the smoking, half-drenched embers of the firepits bandied a hopeful new title. Men found their warmth in a litany against cruel grief and despair. 'The Spinner of Darkness will one day come to fall before Lysaer, Prince of the Light.'

Avenor's fair prince heard the murmurs. He caught the furtive, awed glances his servants bent his way when they thought his back was turned. In that moment, he realized that a greater truth could be built from the deaths at Dier Kenton. Shame and loss could be reforged into a shining beginning, as the men who looked up to him foresaw.

The prince pledged then never to fail their brave belief. In fierce fervour, a beacon of hope against the ill-turned machinations of an enemy who had no claim to principle, Lysaer s'Ilessid rededicated his life. More than prince, greater than king, in a faith beyond mortal limits, he would labour all his days to become the example of a higher truth.

Of all men, he alone held the gifts to lead, and to rid a helplessly pregnable land of exploitation born from misuse of sorcery.

When the hour arrived, and the Master of Shadow was at last brought down, Lysaer resolved to leave something brighter, more enduring, than a history of war to reward the faith of his followers. Straight in his chair, his eyes alight as the concept took fire in his mind, he let a small smile turn his mouth.

From defeat would come a monument of shining strength. His work would bequeath the five kingdoms a benefit beyond the cost of Arithon's death, and bestow upon Athera a structure of permanent protection to outlast all creeds and boundaries. For as long as men kept records and built cities, his name would be remembered for justice.

Last Victory

Mewed for several weeks in a shepherd's stone hut with no company except his two brothers, Keldmar s'Brydion at last gave in to boredom and agreed to shoot dice with Mearn. The breadth of his folly became apparent inside an hour when the grimy twist of paper that represented his best yearling colt was lost to a rocky round of luck.

Gambling with Mearn was cutthroat business, an irrevocable, terrible mistake.

Keldmar hooked a knuckle through his itchy growth of beard and hissed in glum fury at the hand-scratched symbols faced up at him, mocking, from the dice on the packed earthen floor. 'By Dharkaron's immortal arse, I swear you always cheat! No man born wins sixteen turns without losses!'

Mearn showed his teeth in a cadaverous grin, linked his fingers above his head, and stretched until his knuckles popped. 'It's all in the flick of the wrist.'

'Huh!' Keldmar grunted, still regarding his losing throw askance. 'The robbing way you toss?'

'No.' Mearn twitched straight in miffed disdain, a black eye and the yellowing bruises on both cheekbones making him look more mournful than usual. 'The way I set my luck.'

'What in Sithaer's fury is the difference?' Parrien grumbled from his posture of prostration upon the hut's sole amenity, a heap of pallets made of grass ticking. These were piled against the wind-driven draughts of high altitude and spread with aged sheepskins with half the fleeces rubbed off. On nights when the weather stilled, a man could lie awake and drive himself silly listening to the rustle of the nesting population of beetles in the straw. Vermin had spun webs in the rafters, too. Parrien had poured his corrosive impatience with captivity into knocking them down with shale pebbles, until one frigid night had seen them dead.

Most days passed in fierce bickering, with Keldmar and Parrien as deadlocked rivals, and Mearn wont to take umbrage at everything. The tribesmen assigned to guard the hut proved thick-skinned as their sheep, too patient or too dull to rise to insult themselves. They only intervened with the brothers when their fracases threatened dismemberment.

Extracting information on their captor's intentions, the brothers had found, was like trying to pierce armoured steel with a straw stalk. After three weeks of incarceration, deprived of their daggers, all three sported flamboyant beards like the duke's. Keldmar was cursing their dead mother's wisdom for giving his two siblings birth, and Mearn was strung to a quivering storm of nerves that threatened any moment to drive him to burrow tunnels through Vastmark shale with his teeth.

Parrien, on the pallet, waited slit-eyed for another ripping fight. Always, his younger brother's glib insults set Keldmar into a rage. In idle, seething boredom, Parrien wondered if the archers outside would use arrows through the hole in the shutter again to stop Keldmar from bashing Mearn unconscious with his fists.

But the slimmer of the pair of combatants only sprang

erect with his head cocked askance. Perceptive as a weasel, Mearn fastened on something he heard outside the door. 'Listen,' he said, urgent, and fanned a splay-fingered gesture for his other two brothers to keep quiet.

They all heard, then. On the slope outside, blustering curses through the milder lilt of a southern clansman's accents, rang the voice of their brother, the duke.

Parrien shot upright and coughed through a whirlwind of shed fleece. 'Ath! They've got Bransian!'

'Better hope not,' Keldmar rebutted, chin still outthrust like a bulldog's. 'He's all that's left to get us freed.'

The outer bar on the door was shot back. Then the massive panel wrenched open, blocked at once by the bulk of the eldest brother s'Brydion.

'What's happened?' cried Mearn. 'Are you prisoner? Have you been mistreated?'

Reduced by the gloom to a shadowy presence, the Duke of Alestron finished his absorbed string of oaths and crossed the threshold.

They had a hoarded stub of candle in one corner. Mearn, who was nearest, struck a spark to the wick, his blunt fingers sheltering the quiver of new flame against the tireless draw of the draughts. Wavering light played off Bransian's bristled, tawny beard, his pebble grey eyes, and the raffish, wild fringes of a shepherd's cloak thrown over what looked like a sling. Closer study revealed a linen bandage, stained from beneath by old blood from a gashed forearm.

'*What have they done?*' demanded Parrien in a grating, low whisper.

The duke sucked in a huge breath. Dulled light caught on the scored links of mail through the gaping rents in his surcoat as he announced with bemused interest, 'They've done nothing.' His beard twitched to reveal a flash of teeth. 'That's just it, I can't fault their judge-ment, though Ath knows, for our folly, I've been unforgiving as the Fatemaster himself. We've been lied to. A tidy division of our mercenaries have been thrown away for a false cause and an idiotic misunderstanding.'

'*What?* Are you mad?' Mearn knocked into the candle, snatched left-handed before it toppled, then stood, the flame whipped down to a sullen, red spark as he rose with the light in his fist.

'I didn't suffer a head wound,' Bransian protested, stung. 'Brothers, we've been fighting this war on the wrong side.' ·

'You *have* been addled!' Parrien coiled back onto the pallet, his hot gaze fixed on his kinsman, while Keldmar, his arguments stilled to perplexity, stared openmouthed at his older brother.

'Explain,' snapped Mearn, moving closer.

'I say, we've been trying to kill the wrong man.' Before the fire thrust in his face torched his whiskers, Bransian snatched the candle away. 'Did you know Lysaer s'Ilessid is half-brother to Arithon s'Ffalenn?'

Mearn started.

Keldmar's square face showed interest. 'Who says?'

'Erlien's clansmen told me.' Bransian tipped the wick above the nearest stone windowsill, dribbled off melted wax, then fixed the shaft upright in the puddle. 'Others from Rathain knew a good deal more besides.' He waited for hot liquid to congeal.

In silence as the tormented flame steadied, the incarcerated brothers noticed the telling fact that their sibling still possessed all his weapons. They exchanged a long glance, while Mearn rounded back, eyes mean as a ferret's, and furious. 'Why aren't we fighting our way out of here?'

'I gave my word,' Duke Bransian admitted. The candle had stuck upright. Undershot in gilt light, he threw off his coif and let the mail fall discarded to the floor. Then he rubbed the stiff fingers of his uninjured hand over a graze on his temple and glared at the fish-eyed suspicion

511

of his brothers. 'You aren't listening. I've said outright. We've got reason to rethink our position.'

'You'd *forgive* the blast in our armoury?' cried Mearn.

'Forget our total rout at Dier Kenton?' echoed Keldmar, while Parrien, out of character, set his chin on his fist and looked thoughtful.

'I don't for a second discount what's been done,' Bransian said. 'But this is a high prince sanctioned for inheritance we're speaking of! Our formal protest through the Kingdom of Melhalla's appointed regent was given over to Shand. By the laws of the realm's charters, justice was served when Lord Erlien fought the Teir's'Ffalenn at swords for our honour. Arithon bested him. The fight was a fair one. The *caithdein* of Shand has pardoned the grievance, satisfied.'

Not one of three younger brothers looked reconciled. Understanding their perplexity, Bransian poked about for a stool or a chair. When he found none in evidence, he folded his giant's frame and perched on a corner of the pallet. 'Just hear this through,' he insisted. 'Lysaer ran a trumped-up campaign to finagle us into alliance.' Then he talked, while the candle burned down and grew hunchbacked in its dribbled spills of wax.

The bloody encounter at Tal Quorin was recast to fit a less lofty pattern. By Bransian's retelling, the clansmen of Strakewood had made no attempt to vindicate the ugly details. Nor did they grant the violence born of Desh-thiere's curse with anything less than cold truth.

'Etarra marched first. The Master of Shadow used grand conjury in defence of his feal following. He has answered for his misdeeds in the north.' In fact, by clan account, Bransian had been given to understand Rathain's prince kept no tolerance at all for masking his acts behind false ideals and self-sacrifice.

The flame fluttered out in a drowned reel of smoke by the time Duke Bransian summed up. 'We hated the man and desired to break him because he destroyed our best armoury.'

'So why did he?' Somewhere in darkness, Mearn spun from his pacing, twitchy as a tempered rapier blade. 'We lost men there. Our keep became gutted by sorcery, and where was the Mistwraith's provocation for that?'

'I say, we ask him,' rumbled Bransian, emphatic. 'What's a weapon or a thousand weapons, and seven of our guardsmen? Arithon's attack on us was forthright. Lysaer inveigled our trust, then enticed men from our banner into his personal service. He used all we gave to further a cause little better than a private vendetta.'

'Well it can't be so easy, this wish you have to parley,' Parrien broke in, doleful for the time the war had kept him from the bed of his pretty new wife. 'We've been here three weeks and never once seen this slinking royal sorcerer show his face.'

'We will.' Bransian sounded most certain. 'His Grace will come by in the morning.' Then, as he realized the significance of what Parrien had just said, he slapped his knee with one hand and chuckled outright. 'You've been mewed up in this place for all that time? And you haven't smashed one another's skulls? Dharkaron's living bollocks, I believe I've just witnessed a true miracle!'

Warned by a frost-sharp tension among the clansmen standing guard on the hut, Mearn broke off his pantherish pacing and poised himself behind the door lintel. Bransian set down his crust of biscuit untasted, and Keldmar kicked Parrien awake.

Then the panel swung open, and a neat, small-knit man stepped through. Keldmar took a guess at the number of throwing knives that might be concealed beneath the caped wool of his shepherd's cloak, and decided against trying to rush him. No strait of confinement could make him forget the quick reflexes of the spy who had demolished Alestron's armoury.

Bound by no such reservation, Mearn sprang, seized the right arm of the prince who stepped in, and bared palm and wrist to the daylight.

Half-blind in transition from dawn to the peat smoke dimness of the hut, Arithon offered no resistance. While the disfiguring welt left by the light bolt that had delivered Desh-thiere's curse suffered Mearn's devouring scrutiny, he said in slightly strained greeting, 'A sensational birthmark, I agree, but there could be a more polite way of admiring it.'

Mearn released the royal wrist as if stung. 'That's no birthmark.'

Arithon twitched down his cuff, reached under his leathers, and produced a brace of fresh candles. Silent, thoughtful, he proceeded to light them in succession, while the brothers s'Brydion regarded the sorcerer who had fired their keep three years before. Seen under flame glow, removed from the harried press of action, the face beneath its ink-dark hair retained an unforgettable severity. More tired, perhaps, more drawn from wear and strain, the features held the reticence of cut glass. Plain shepherd's dress masked a highly bred frame that lent a deceptive impression of fragility to what was actually tough and murderously agile: the brothers s'Brydion had excellent cause to remember.

'What moves you to keep us trapped here like flies?' Menace edged Mearn's accusation. 'We already know you're practised at skulking. If you took this long to raise the courage to face us, how long will you take to arrange our release?'

Arithon wedged the last candle beside the wreckage of Bransian's breakfast, then stepped back to assume an unruffled stance by one wall. Without thought for insult, he said, 'First, I need your advice to curb your lordship's strayed guard of lancers.'

Taken aback, Mearn maintained silence, but the duke

blew crumbs from his beard, stabbed his dagger in the earthen floor, and peered up in bearish irritation. 'What's the problem?'

Arithon met the huge man's agitation with a shrug. 'It's scarcely urgent. But since my war captain managed your capture, they've been picking the very mountains apart. The herdsmen are tired of stampeding their flocks clear, and my clan scouts are getting out of sorts running fools beneath the Wheel who persist long beyond the point of folly.'

'Why shouldn't our lancers fight you?' Parrien demanded. 'Prince Lysaer's got a warhost here to back them.'

'I forgot,' Arithon admonished. 'You're behind on the news. Erlien's clansmen weren't fooled for a second, once your duke pulled Alestron's support from the supply lines. Rather than starve, Lysaer's captains have been forced to withdraw. If you want any crofters left to tend your barley next season, we'll need to pack your lancers off home. They're scouring the hills with determined thoughts of your rescue, but of course, until the last allied divisions have left Vastmark, the tribesfolk can't afford to see you freed.'

Unshaken from the subject, Mearn glared at the impassive face of the s'Ffalenn prince poised before him. 'Our men-at-arms never farm.'

Arithon showed bland surprise. 'Well, since Lysaer has appropriated your best band of mercenaries, you're going to need to restore your city's field troop from somewhere. You can either train lancers who spin, sew, and wear skirts, or else you'll have to settle for mustering up recruits among your farmhands.'

Mearn snarled an obscenity.

Parrien broke into bull-chested laughter. 'Fiends! You've got a brass tongue, for a mountebank. I admit it's refreshing after Keldmar swooned like a dupe over Prince Lysaer's pious mouthings at Etarra.'

While his rival shoved off fleeces to defend this rank insult, Parrien flushed to blustering purple. 'Well, you admit we never fought for the mealy-mouthed scruples. It's been feud for our armoury all along.'

Before abrasive slanging could compound into fisticuffs, Arithon stepped in between. 'I came to discuss terms for your ransom,' he cut through in his masterbard's diction.

'Ransom!' Now Bransian uncoiled from the floor and spat. 'You're still an enemy, but Alestron no longer serves Lysaer. The sooner that's noised abroad, the better.'

Arithon raised expressive, dark eyebrows. 'Who spoke of service?' From under his cloak, he drew out a parchment tied with official layers of ribbons and crusted by a weight of royal seals. He slapped the document into the duke's calloused grasp with the insouciant comment, 'I merely thought Alestron's coffers deserved compensation for the losses imposed for misplaced causes. How much can we wring from Avenor's lord treasurer to have you back hale and whole?'

'Dharkaron!' yelled Keldmar. 'You'd give us the gold?'

While Mearn snatched the document from the duke's fist to read, Arithon grinned at the stupefied faces of the older brothers s'Brydion. 'I thought to keep half, for my troubles. But yes. If you've decided to withdraw your support from the invasion here in Vastmark, do everyone the favour of calling your stray lancers back to heel.'

'We can do that,' Bransian said in that tar-slow deliberation he saved for touchy points of state. 'But after you've answered for the destruction of our armoury.' He had about his stance the immovable sort of grudge that could eventually wear mountains down to sand.

Arithon sighed, crossed his hands behind his back, and leaned in neat grace against the windowsill. 'That was Fellowship business, given over to their spellbinder, Dakar. A record exists. Apparently the Warden of

Althain suspected some kind of foul play. You'll recall, an inspection Asandir asked of your steward was summarily refused. Your keep was to be searched, and I lent my help, with my shadows and Dakar's ploy with the emeralds used to gain covert entry. To the sorrow of us all, there was unexpected violence in the outcome. No one thought to warn us that you stored some sort of fire spell inside those barrels in your dungeon.'

'We don't use any sorceries, stuffed into casks or otherwise,' Mearn pealed in mercuric protest.

Keldmar and Parrien flushed matching shades of deep puce. Their simultaneous charge was stood off by Bransian, who stepped into the breech and planted a knee into one brother, and a massive fist against his other sibling's breast.

From the corner, volatile as fanned flame, Mearn said, '*Now* you've told us a lie. We saw your spells wreck our keep!'

'Mine?' Touched to queer sorrow by denial, Arithon shook his dark head. 'But that's not possible. Jieret's Companions can testify. I lost the trained use of my mage talent since my abuse of grand conjury on the field of blood at Tal Quorin.'

'That's what your clansmen *did* say,' Bransian lowered his leg to free Keldmar, then shook Parrien off with a sharp backward thrust. 'Also, Erlien's scout confirmed. He told me he saw you fight nearly to a standstill, and yet you called down no shadows, even when you thought you'd end up maimed. This doesn't sound to me like a sorcerer given over to carelessness.'

Arithon said nothing. The light let through the cracked shutter left his green eyes disturbingly clear.

Mearn, in steamed movement, began to pace. 'Well if the sorcery wasn't yours, who would've dared interfere with us? Some enemy must have planted arcane seals in our dungeon, if you say you happened by and set them off.'

'Sethvir could have been trying to find that point out.' Bransian sighed, grinned, then shrugged like a rawboned hound, beaten often but never quite housebroken. 'We were rockheads and obstructed his investigation. For not heeding the Fellowship, likely we deserved all we got. But if we misplayed things then, we need not add to the problem. There's a bigger injury over the theft of our mercenaries and the misuse of our clan honour. I'd say we have cause to apologize for one wrong, and help Rathain to bloody Lysaer to right the other.'

'I don't want any support,' Arithon interrupted. 'When the shepherds are settled, the Vastmark lands will belong once again to their flocks.'

Keldmar brushed aside protest. 'Lysaer's no man to give up his grudges. Over beer at Etarra, I found out. Yon prince recalls every slight, even to the ones your dead father dealt his family during his childhood beyond the West Gate. That's obsession, his pretence at justice. You didn't just break Lysaer's warhost here in Vastmark. You stuck a thorn in his family pride.'

'I don't want your alliance,' Arithon insisted, shot straight to emphasize his point.

'By Ath, man, don't spit on good fortune!' Bransian towered over the smaller, dark prince with his arms crossed and his eyebrows bristled down like the boss of a bull set to charge. 'After what you accomplished in Dier Kenton Vale, you have to know you're going to need us.'

'Ath forfend!' Arithon melted back into laughter. 'I should hope not! At least, not for a very long time. Besides, if we're both plotting to get rich off your freedom, the peace might last longer if Lysaer was left to believe you're still loyal in support.'

Bransian scratched his head. 'You know,' he said in dawning and devious joy, 'that misapprehension might be a useful thing to foster. Serves the canting liar right.'

'Do you think so?' An answering spark gleamed in

Arithon's eyes. 'I'd never presume to ask, but truly, the warning could be useful, next time, to know what sort of counterploy my half-brother's got brewing inside his closed city councils.'

'I like this.' Keldmar grinned like a wildcat. 'It will be my born pleasure to make that yellow-haired pretender pay our ransom, then use his private trust to strike him back. It's fitting. He got me drunk to mislead me as Alestron's envoy, a cold-handed breach of hospitality. And the blood of his own *caithdein*'s on his hands. No one's made him answer for that.'

'It's the classic mistake.' Parrien finished in bleak ire. 'We're clansmen, and always those cityborn upstarts forget, and try to treat with us under town law.'

'Then it's settled.' Bransian yanked out his dagger, spat on the blade, and grinned through his frizzled nest of whiskers. 'You've got allies, your Grace. If you want them or not's a moot point. Sure as you're born the sanctioned Prince of Rathain, you have no vested sovereignty in Melhalla. Nothing's to prevent us from acting in your favour. Not unless you want to challenge my authority with bare steel and send me to the Fatemaster unrepentant.'

'I wish to challenge no one.' Arithon looked up in chagrined impatience. 'And we won't need the services of any divine office. I asked your authority, as I said, to stop your belligerent company of lancers from scouring the hillsides to skewer shepherds.'

Still smiling, Arithon s'Ffalenn leaned aside and raised the door latch. The panel swung open to reveal the anxious faces of several tribesmen waiting in worried clusters outside. 'The war's over. Duke Bransian s'Brydion and his brothers have agreed. Our purposes lie in accord.'

Then he stepped out, the weight on his shoulders lightened at last, and the way to his freedom at hand.

Propped up in bandages amid the group of shepherds, Dakar the Mad Prophet saw a flare of rare joy transform the face of Rathain's prince. After horrors and pain, here lay a moment of precious victory.

Vastmark could be left to its wild, bucolic splendour. Beyond the winter peaks of the Kelhorns, wide oceans awaited, with the *Khetienn* already provisioned to sail where no enemy could navigate to follow her.

Views

At Althain Tower, Sethvir resifts a triad of auguries made upon winter's solstice to unriddle the bearing axis which turns future threat from the Mistwraith: the split arc of mass faith, undermined by s'Ilessid from the guardianship of Ath's adepts; the resurgence of Koriani interference upon recovery of their Great Waystone; then at the crux point of all, the life of Rathain's prince, and twined through his Name, to help him stand or bring his downfall, the Koriani healer who stole possession of his heart since Merior by the Sea . . .

In Tysan, while snowfall dusts the roads, Lady Talith watches from a tower window as Avenor's surviving garrison marches in, battered, from Vastmark; and though she sits at Lysaer's side when Tysan's city delegates present their official charter, sealed under ribbons of blue and gold, to grant a high king's office to its steadfast defender, the fair-haired Prince of the Light, she is no longer privy to her lord's gracious smile, nor does she share his royal bed . . .

*   *   *

Elsewhere, on an unbroken circle of ocean, a lone brigantine bowls ahead of the winds toward the forgotten Isles of Min Pierens, marked on a Paravian chart; and the hand at her helm is that of a young girl, grown lean and sun-browned and angular; and beside her, his black hair blowing loose, his clothing a sailor's simple linen, the Master of Shadow stands content . . .

Glossary

ADRUIN – coastal city located in East Halla, Melhalla. One of two at the head of a sea inlet, at odds with the brothers s'Brydion of Alestron, usually over the setting of blockades to interfere with trade.

    pronounced: ah-druin like 'add ruin'

    root meaning: *adruinne* – to block, or obstruct

AL'DUIN – father of Halliron Masterbard.

    pronounced: al-dwin

    root meaning: al – over; *duinne* – hand

ALESTRON – city located in Midhalla, Melhalla. Ruled by the Duke Bransian, Teir's'Brydion, and his three brothers. This city did not fall to merchant townsmen in the Third Age uprising that threw down the high kings, but is still ruled by its clanblood heirs.

    pronounced: ah-less-tron

    root meaning: *alesstair* – stubborn; *an* – one

ALITHIEL – one of twelve Blades of Isaer, forged by centaur Ffereton s'Darian in the Second Age from metal taken from a meteorite. Passed through Paravian possession, acquired the secondary name Dael-Farenn, or Kingmaker, since its owners tended to succeed the end of a royal line. Eventually was awarded to Kamridian

s'Ffalenn for his valour in defence of the princess Tali-
ennse, early Second Age. Currently in possession of
Arithon.

    pronounced: ah-lith-ee-el

    root meaning: *alith* – star; *iel* – light/ray

ALLAND – principality located in southeastern Shand.
Ruled by the High Earl Teir's'Taleyn, *caithdein* of Shand
by appointment. Current heir to the title is Erlien.

    pronounced: all-and

    root meaning: *a'lind* – pine glen

ALTHAIN TOWER – spire built at the edge of the Bittern Desert, beginning of the Second Age, to house
records of Paravian histories. Third Age, became reposi-
tory for the archives of all five royal houses of men after
rebellion, overseen by Sethvir, Warden of Althain and
Fellowship Sorcerer.

    pronounced: al like 'all', thain to rhyme with 'main'

    root meaning: *alt* – last; *thein* – tower, sanctuary

    original Paravian pronunciation: alt-thein (thein as
in 'the end')

AMROTH – kingdom on West Gate splinter world,
Dascen Elur, ruled by s'llessid descendants of the prince
exiled through the Worldsend Gate at the time of the
rebellion, Third Age just after the Mistwraith's
conquest.

    pronounced: am-roth (rhymes with 'sloth')

    root meaning: *am* – state of being; *roth* – brother
'brotherhood'

ANGLEFEN – swampland located in Deshir, Rathain.
Town of same name at the river mouth with port to Gulf
of Stormwell. One of the six port towns that link sea
trade routes with Etarra.

    pronounced: angle-fen

    root meaning not from the Paravian

ARAETHURA – grass plains in southwest Rathain; principality of the same name in that location. Largely
inhabited by Riathan Paravians in the Second Age. Third

Age, used as pastureland by widely scattered nomadic shepherds.

  pronounced: ar-eye-thoo-rah

  root meaning: *araeth* – grass; *era* – place, land
ARAITHE – plain to the north of the trade city of Etarra, principality of Fallowmere, Rathain. First Age, among the sites used by the Paravians to renew the mysteries and channel fifth lane energies. The standing stones erected are linked to the power focus at Ithamon and Meth Isle keep.

  pronounced: araithe, sounds like 'a wraith'

  root meaning: *araithe* – to disperse, to send; refers to the properties of the standing stones with relationship to the fifth lane forces.
ARITHON – son of Avar, Prince of Rathain, 1,504th Teir's'Ffalenn after founder of the line, Torbrand in Third Age Year One. Also Master of Shadow, the Bane of Desh-thiere, and Halliron Masterbard's successor.

  pronounced: ar-i-thon, almost rhymes with 'marathon'

  root meaning: *arithon* – fate-forger; one who is visionary
ASANDIR – Fellowship Sorcerer. Secondary name, King-maker, since his hand crowned every High King of Men to rule in the Age of Men (Third Age). After the Mistwraith's conquest, he acted as field agent for the Fellowship's doings across the continent. Also called Fiendquencher, for his reputation for quelling iyats; Stormbreaker, and Change-bringer for past actions when Men asked to settle upon Athera.

  pronounced: ah-san-deer

  root meaning: *asan* – heart; *dir* – stone 'heartrock'
ATAINIA – northeastern principality of Tysan.

  pronounced: ah-tay-nee-ah

  root meaning: *itain* – the third; *ia* suffix for 'third domain'

  original Paravian, *itainia*

ATCHAZ – city located in Alland, Shand. Famed for its silk.

    pronounced: at-chas

    root meaning: *atchias* – silk

ATH CREATOR – prime vibration, force behind all life.

    pronounced: ath to rhyme with 'math'

    root meaning: *ath* – prime, first (as opposed to *an*, one)

ATHIR – Second Age ruin of a Paravian stronghold, located in Ithilt, Rathain. Site of a seventh lane power focus.

    pronounced: ath-ear

    root meaning: *ath* – prime; *i'er* – the line/edge

ATHERA – name for the continent which holds the Five High Kingdoms; one of two major landmasses on the planet.

    pronounced: ath-air-ah

    root meaning: *ath* – prime force; *era* – place 'Ath's world'

ATHLIEN PARAVIANS – Sunchildren. Small race of semi-mortals, pixielike, but possessed of great wisdom/ keepers of the grand mystery.

    pronounced: ath-lee-en

    root meaning: *ath* – prime force; *lien* – to love 'Ath-beloved'

ATHLIERIA – equivalent of heaven/actually a dimension removed from physical life, inhabited by spirit after death.

    pronounced: ath-lee-air-ee-ah

    root meaning: *ath* – prime force; *li'era* – exalted place, or land in harmony; *li* – exalted in harmony

ATWOOD – forest located in East Halla, Melhalla.

    pronounced: at-wood

    root meaning: *ath* – prime vibration/Ath's wood

AVAR s'FFALENN – Pirate King of Karthan, isle on splinter world Dascen Elur, through West Gate. Father of Arithon; also Teir's'Ffalenn 1,503rd in descent from

Torbrand, who founded the s'Ffalenn royal line in Third Age Year One.

 pronounced: ah-var, to rhyme with 'far'

 root meaning: *avar* – past thought/memory

AVENOR – Second Age ruin of a Paravian stronghold. Traditional seat of the s'Ilessid high kings. Restored to habitation in Third Age 5644. Located in Korias, Tysan.

 pronounced: ah-ven-or

 root meaning: *avie* – stag; *norh* – grove

BECKBURN – market in the city of Jaelot, on the coast of the Bay of Eltair at the southern border of Rathain.

 pronounced: beck-burn

 root meaning not from the Paravian

BITTERN DESERT – waste located in Atainia, Tysan, north of Althain Tower. Site of a First Age battle between the great drakes and the Seard-luin, permanently destroyed by dragonfire.

 pronounced: like bitter

 root meaning: to sear or char

BLACK DRAKE – a brig often hired to run contraband, captained by a woman named Dhirken.

BLACK ROSE PROPHECY – made by Dakar the Mad Prophet in Third Age 5637 at Althain Tower. Forecasts Davien the Betrayer's repentance, and the reunity of the Fellowship of Seven as tied to Arithon s'Ffalenn's voluntary resumption of Rathain's crown rule.

BRANSIAN s'BRYDION – Teir's'Brydion, ruling Duke of Alestron.

 pronounced: bran-see-an

 root meaning: *brand* – temper; *s'i'an* – suffix denoting 'of the one'/the one with temper

BWIN EVOC s'LORNMEIN – founder of the line that became High Kings of Havish since Third Age Year One. The attribute he passed on by means of the Fellowship's geas was temperance.

 pronounced: bwin to rhyme with 'twin', ee-vahk as

in 'evocative', lorn as in English equivalent, mein rhymes with 'main'

    root meaning: *bwin* – firm; *evoc* – choice

CAILCALLOW – herb that grows in Athera's marshes, used to ease fevers.

    pronounced: rhymes with 'kale-tallow'

    root meaning: *cail* – leaf; *calliew* – balm

CAIT – herdsman of a declining tribe of shepherds in Vastmark.

    pronounced: kate

    root meaning: to herd

CAITH-AL-CAEN – vale where Riathan Paravians (unicorns) celebrated equinox and solstice to renew the *athael*, or life-destiny of the world. Also the place where the llitharis Paravians first Named the winter stars – or encompassed their vibrational essence into language. Corrupted by the end of the Third Age to Castlecain.

    pronounced: cay-ith-al-cay-en, musical lilt, emphasis on second and last syllables; rising note on first two, falling note on last two

    root meaning: *caith* – shadow; *al* – over; *caen* – vale 'vale of shadow'

CAITHDEIN – Paravian name for a high king's first counsellor; also, the one who would stand as regent, or steward, in the absence of the crowned ruler.

    pronounced: kay-ith-day-in

    root meaning: *caith* – shadow; *d'ein* – behind the chair 'shadow behind the throne'

CAITHWOOD – forest located in Taerlin, southeast principality of Tysan.

    pronounced: kay-ith-wood

    root meaning: *caith* – shadow 'shadowed wood'

CAOLLE – war captain of the clans of Deshir, Rathain. First raised, and then served under Lord Steiven, Earl of the North and *caithdein* of Rathain. Currently in Jieret Red-beard's service.

  pronounced: kay-all-e, with the 'e' nearly subliminal

  root meaning: *caille* – stubborn

CARITHWYR – principality consisting primarily of a grasslands in Havish, once the province of the Riathan Paravians. A unicorn birthing ground. Currently used by man for grain and cattle; area name has become equated with fine hides.

  pronounced: car-ith-ear

  root meaning: *ci'arithiren* – forgers of the ultimate link with prime power. An old Paravian colloquialism for unicorn.

CASTLE POINT – port city at the eastern terminus of the Great West Road, located in the principality of Atainia, Tysan.

CAMRIS – north-central principality of Tysan. Original ruling seat was city of Erdane.

  pronounced: kam-ris, the 'i' as in 'chris'

  root meaning: *caim* – cross; *ris* – way 'crossroad'

CHEIVALT – coastal city south of Ostermere in Carithwyr, Havish. Known for its elegance and refined lifestyle.

  pronounced: shay-vault

  root meaning: *chiavalden* – a rare yellow flower which grows by the seaside

CILADIS THE LOST – Fellowship Sorcerer who left the continent in Third Age 5462 in search of the Paravian races after their disappearance after the rebellion.

  pronounced: kill-ah-dis

  root meaning: *cael* – leaf; *adeis* – whisper, compound; *cael'adeis* colloquialism for 'gentleness that abides'

CILDEIN OCEAN – body of water lying off Athera's east coastline.

  pronounced: kill-dine

  root meaning: *cailde* – salty; *an* – one

CILDORN – city famed for carpets and weaving, located in Deshir Rathain. Originally a Paravian holdfast, situated on a node of the third lane.

    pronounced: kill-dorn

    root meaning: *cieal* – thread; *dorn* – net 'tapestry'

CLAITHEN – an adept of of Ath's Brotherhood in the hostel south of Merior.

    pronounced: clay-then

    root meaning: *claithen* – garden, earth/soil

CORITH – island west of Havish coast, in Westland Sea. First site to see sunlight upon Desh-thiere's defeat.

    pronounced: kor-ith

    root meaning: *cori* – ships, vessels; *itha* – five for the five harbours which the old city overlooked

CRATER LAKE – small body of water with an island at its centre, located in Araethura, Rathain. Where the Fellowship Sorcerers made landfall on Athera.

CRESCENT ISLE – large island located east of Minderl Bay in Ithilt, Rathain.

DAEL-FARENN – Kingmaker, name for sword Alithiel; also, one of many Paravian names for the Fellowship Sorcerer, Asandir.

    pronounced: day-el-far-an

    root meaning: *dael* – king; *feron* – maker

DAELION FATEMASTER – 'entity' formed by set of mortal beliefs, which determine the fate of the spirit after death. If Ath is the prime vibration, or life force, Daelion is what governs the manifestation of free will.

    pronounced: day-el-ee-on

    root meaning: *dael* – king, or lord; *i'on* – of fate

DAELION'S WHEEL – cycle of life and the crossing point which is the transition into death.

    pronounced: day-el-ee-on

    root meaning: *dael* – king or lord; *i'on* – of fate

DAENFAL – city located on the northern lake shore that

bounds the southern edge of Daon Ramon Barrens in Rathain.

pronounced: dye-en-fall

root meaning: *daen* – clay; *fal* – red

DAGRIEN COURT – market in the city of Jaelot, on the coast at the southern border of Rathain.

pronounced: dag-ree-en

root meaning: *dagrien* – variety

DAKAR THE MAD PROPHET – apprentice to Fellowship Sorcerer, Asandir, during the Third Age following the Conquest of the Mistwraith. Given to spurious prophecies, it was Dakar who forecast the fall of the Kings of Havish in time for the Fellowship to save the heir. He made the Prophecy of West Gate, which forecast the Mistwraith's bane, and also, the Black Rose Prophecy, which called for reunification of the Fellowship. At this time, assigned to defence of Arithon, Prince of Rathain.

pronounced: dah-kar

root meaning: *dakiar* – clumsy

DALWYN – a clanswoman of Vastmark; aunt to Jilieth and Ghedair; friend of Arithon's.

pronounced: doll-win

root meaning: *dirlnwyn* – a specific aspect of misfortune; to be childless

DANIA – wife of Rathain's Regent, Steiven s'Valerient. Died by the hand of Pesquil's headhunters in the battle of Strakewood. Jieret Red-beard's mother.

pronounced: dan-ee-ah

root meaning: *deinia* – sparrow

DAON RAMON BARRENS – central principality of Rathain. Site where Riathan Paravians (unicorns) bred and raised their young. Barrens was not appended to the name until the years following the Mistwraith's conquest, when the River Severnir was diverted at the source by a task force under Etarran jurisdiction.

pronounced: day-on-rah-mon

root meaning: *daon* – gold; *ramon* – hills/downs

DASCEN ELUR – splinter world off West Gate; primarily ocean with isolated archipelagoes. Includes kingdoms of Rauven, Amroth, and Karthan. Where three exiled high kings' heirs took refuge in the years following the great uprising. Birthplace of Lysaer and Arithon.

pronounced: das-en el-ur

root meaning: *dascen* – ocean; *e'lier* – small land

DAVIEN THE BETRAYER – Fellowship Sorcerer responsible for provoking the great uprising that resulted in the fall of the high kings after Desh-thiere's conquest. Rendered discorporate by the Fellowship's judgment in Third Age 5129. Exiled since, by personal choice. Davien's works included the Five Centuries Fountain near Mearth on the splinter world of the Red Desert, through West Gate; the shaft at Rockfell Pit, used by the Sorcerers to imprison harmful entities; the Stair on Rockfell Peak; and also, Kewar Tunnel in the Mathorn Mountains.

pronounced: dah-vee-en

root meaning: *dahvi* – fool, mistake; *an* – one 'mistaken one'

DEARTHA – wife of Halliron, Masterbard of Athera; resident in Innish.

pronounced: dee-ar-the

root meaning: *deorethan* – sour-tempered

DESHANS – barbarian clans who inhabit Strakewood Forest, principality of Deshir, Rathian.

pronounced: desh-ans

root meaning: *deshir* – misty

DESH-THIERE – Mistwraith that invaded Athera from the splinter worlds through South Gate in Third Age 4993. Access cut off by Fellowship Sorcerer, Traithe. Battled and contained in West Shand for twenty-five years, until the rebellion splintered the peace, and the high kings were forced to withdraw from the defence lines to attend their disrupted kingdoms.

pronounced: desh-thee-air-e (last 'e' mostly subliminal)

root meaning: *desh* – mist; *thiere* – ghost or wraith

DESHIR – northwestern principality of Rathain.

pronounced: desh-eer

root meaning: *deshir* – misty

DHARKARON AVENGER – called Ath's Avenging Angel in legend. Drives a chariot drawn by five horses to convey the guilty to Sithaer. Dharkaron as defined by the adepts of Ath's Brotherhood is that dark thread mortal men weave with Ath, the prime vibration, that creates self-punishment, or the root of guilt.

pronounced dark-air-on

root meaning: *dhar* – evil; *khiaron* – one who stands in judgment

DHIRKEN – lady captain of the contraband runner, *Black Drake*. Reputed to have taken over the brig's command by right of arms following her father's death at sea.

pronounced: dur-kin

root meaning: *dierk* – tough; *an* – one

DIEGAN – once Lord Commander of Etarra's garrison; given over by his governor to serve as Lysaer s'Ilessid's Lord Commander at Avenor. Titular commander of the warhost sent against the Deshans to defeat the Master of Shadow at Tal Quorin; high commander of the warhost mustered at Werpoint. Also brother of Lady Talith.

pronounced: dee-gan

root meaning: *diegan* – trinket a dandy might wear/ornament

DIER KENTON VALE – a valley located in the principality of Vastmark, Shand.

pronounced: deer ken-ton

root meaning: *dien'kendion* – a jewel with a severe flaw that may result in shearing or cracking.

DRUAITHE – Vastmark shepherds' dialect. An epithet applied to emphasize stupidity.

pronounced: drew-ate-the

root meaning: Vastmark dialect for idiot

DURN – city located in Orvandir, Shand.

pronounced: dern

root meaning: *diern* – plain/flat

DYSHENT – city on the coast of Instrell Bay in Tysan, renowned for timber.

pronounced: die-shent

root meaning: *dyshient* – cedar

EARLE – Second Age ruin, once a Paravian stronghold, located on the southern tip of the peninsula in West Shand. Site of the defences that contained the Mistwraith's invasion prior to the uprising incited by Davien the Betrayer.

pronounced: earl

root meaning: *erli* – long light

EAST BRANSING – city located on the shore of Instrell Bay at the south border of Tysan.

pronounced: east bran-sing

root meaning: *brienseng* – at the base, at the bottom

EAST HALLA – principality located in the Kingdom of Melhalla

pronounced: hall-ah

root meaning: *hal'lia* – white light

EASTWALL – city located in the Skyshiel Mountains, Rathain.

EAST WARD – city in Fallowmere, Rathain, renowned as a port that served the trade route to Etarra from the Cildein Ocean.

pronounced: ward

no Paravian root meaning as this city was man's creation

ELAIRA – initiate enchantress of the Koriathain. Originally a street child, taken on in Morvain for Koriani rearing.

pronounced: ee-layer-ah

root meaning: *e'* – prefix, diminutive for small; *laere* – grace

ELDIR s'LORNMEIN – King of Havish and last surviving scion of s'Lornmein royal line. Raised as a wool-dyer until the Fellowship Sorcerers crowned him at Ostermere in Third Age 5643, following the defeat of the Mistwraith.

pronounced: el-deer

root meaning: *eldir* – to ponder, to consider, to weigh

ELIE – name of a newlywed woman in Merior. Short for Elidie, which is a common southcoast girl's name.

pronounced: ellie (long form, el-ed-ee)

root meaning: *eledie* – night-singing bird

ELKFOREST – wood located in Ghent, Havish; home of Machiel, steward and *caithdein* of the realm.

ELSHIAN – Athlien Paravian bard and instrument maker. Crafted the lyranthe that is held in trust by Athera's Masterbard.

pronounced: el-shee-an

root meaning: *e'alshian* – small wonder, or miracle

ELSSINE – city located on the coast of Alland, Shand, famed for stone quarries used for ships' ballast.

pronounced: el-seen

root meaning: *elssien* – small pit

ELTAIR BAY – large bay off Cildein Ocean and east coast of Rathain; where River Severnir was diverted following the Mistwraith's conquest.

pronounced: el-tay-er

root meaning: *al'tieri* – of steel/a shortening of original Paravian name, *dascen al'tieri* – which meant 'ocean of steel' referring to the colour of the waves

ERDANE – old Paravian city, later taken over by Men. Seat of old Princes of Camris until Desh-thiere's conquest and rebellion.

pronounced: er-day-na with the last syllable almost subliminal

root meaning: *er'deinia* – long walls

ERLIEN s'TALEYN – High Earl of Alland; *caithdein* of Shand, chieftain of the forest clansmen of Selkwood.

pronounced: er-lee-an stall-ay-en

root meaning: *aierlyan* – bear; *tal* – branch; *an* – one/first 'of first one branch'

ETARRA – trade city built across the Mathorn Pass by townsfolk after the revolt that cast down Ithamon and the High Kings of Rathain. Nest of corruption and intrigue, and policy maker for the North.

pronounced: ee-tar-ah

root meaning: *e'* – prefix for small; *taria* – knots

FAERY-TOES – a brown gelding Dakar won dicing with mercenaries.

FALGAIRE – coastal city on Instrell Bay, located in Araethura, Rathain, famed for its crystal and glassworks.

pronounced: fall-gair, to rhyme with 'air'

root meaning: *fal'mier* – to sparkle or glitter

FALLOWMERE – northeastern principality of Rathain.

pronounced: fal-oh-meer

root meaning: *fal'ei'miere* – literally, tree self-reflection, colloquialism for 'place of perfect trees'

FARL ROCKS – standing stones located in Daon Ramon Barrens, Rathain; site of a rendezvous between Jieret Red-beard and Caolle. These markers once channelled the earthforces for the Paravian dances at solstice and equinox.

pronounced: far(l)

root meaning: *ffael* – dark

FARSEE – coastal harbour on the Bay of Eltair, located in East Halla, Melhalla.

pronounced: far-see

root meaning: *faersi* – sheltered/muffled

FATE'S WHEEL – see Daelion's Wheel.

FELLOWSHIP OF SEVEN – sorcerers sworn to uphold the Law of the Major Balance, and to foster enlightened thought in Athera. Originators of the compact with the Paravian races that allowed Men to settle in Athera.

FEYLIND – daughter of Jinesse; twin sister of Fiark; inhabitant of Merior.

    pronounced: fay-lind

    root meaning: *faelind'an* – outspoken one/noisy one

FIARK – son of Jinesse; twin brother of Feylind; inhabitant of Merior.

    pronounced: fee-ark

    root meaning: *fyerk* – to throw or toss

FIRST AGE – marked by the arrival of the Paravian Races as Ath's gift to heal the marring of creation by the great drakes.

FORTHMARK – city in Vastmark, Shand. Once the site of a hostel of Ath's Brotherhood. By Third Age 5320, the site was abandoned and taken over by the Koriani Order as a healer's hospice.

    root meaning not from the Paravian

GANISH – trade city located south of Methlas Lake in Orvandir, Shand.

    pronounced: rhymes with 'mannish'

    root meaning: *gianish* – a halfway point, a stopping place

GARTH'S POND – small brackish pond in Merior by the Sea, on the Scimlade peninsula off Alland, Shand.

    pronounced: garth to rhyme with 'hearth'

    root meaning not from the Paravian

GHARMAG – one of the senior captains in Etarra's garrison.

    pronounced: gar-mag

    root meaning not from the Paravian

GHEDAIR – Vastmark shepherd boy who stands off an attack by wyverns.

　　pronounced: sounds like 'dead air'

　　root meaning: *ghediar* – to persist

GHENT – mountainous principality in Kingdom of Havish; where Prince Eldir was raised in hiding.

　　pronounced: gent, hard 'g'

　　root meaning: *ghent* – harsh

GNUDSOG – Etarra's field-captain of the garrison under Lord Commander Diegan; acting first officer in the battle of Strakewood Forest; died in the flooding at the River Tal Quorin.

　　pronounced: nud-sog to rhyme with 'wood log'

　　root meaning: *gianud* – tough; *sog* – ugly

GREAT WAYSTONE – amethyst crystal, spherical in shape, once the grand power focus of the Koriani Order; reputed to be lost since the uprising.

GREAT WEST ROAD – trade route which crosses Tysan from Karfael on the west coast, to Castle Point on Instrell Bay.

GUNDRIG – a mercenary in Alestron's field army, best known for his womanizing.

　　pronounced: gun-drig

　　root meaning: *giunud-erig* – a coarse suitor

HALDUIN s'ILESSID – founder of the line that became High Kings of Tysan since Third Age Year One. The attribute he passed on, by means of the Fellowship's geas, was justice.

　　pronounced: hal-dwin

　　root meaning: *hal* – white; *duinne* – hand

HALLIRON MASTERBARD – native of Innish, Shand. Masterbard of Athera during the Third Age; inherited the accolade from his teacher Murchiel in the year 5597. Son of Al'Duin. Husband of Deartha. Arithon's master and mentor.

pronounced: hal-eer-on

root meaning: *hal* – white; *lyron* – singer

HALTHA – Senior enchantress of the Koriani Order; assigned to keep watch on Avenor at the time of the city's restoration.

prounounced: hal-the

root meaning: *halthien* – white aged

HALWYTHWOOD – forest located in Araethura, Rathain.

pronounced: hall-with-wood

root meaning: *hal* – white; *wythe* – vista

HANSHIRE – port city on Westland Sea, coast of Korias, Tysan; reigning official Lord Mayor Garde; opposed to royal rule at the time of Avenor's restoration.

pronounced: han-sheer

root meaning: *hansh* – sand; *era* – place

HARRADENE – Lord Commander of Etarra's army at the time of the muster at Werpoint.

pronounced: har-a-deen

root meaning: *harradien* – large mule

HAVENS – an inlet on the northeastern shore of Vastmark, Shand.

HAVISH – one of the Five High Kingdoms of Athera, as defined by the charters of the Fellowship of Seven. Ruled by Eldir s'Lornmein. Sigil: gold hawk on red field.

pronounced: hav-ish

root meaning: *havieshe* – hawk

HAVISTOCK – southeast principality of Kingdom of Havish.

pronounced: hav-i-stock

root meaning: *haviesha* – hawk; *tiok* – roost

HAVRITA – fashionable dressmaker in Jaelot.

pronounced: have-reet-ah

root meaning: *havierta* – tailor

HIGHSCARP – city on the coast of the Bay of Eltair, located in Daon Ramon, Rathain.

* * *

ILITHARIS PARAVIANS – centaurs, one of three semi-mortal old races; disappeared at the time of the Mist-wraith's conquest. They were the guardians of the earth's mysteries.

    pronounced: i-li-thar-is

    root meaning: *i'lith'earis* – the keeper/preserver of mystery

IMARN ADAER – enclave of Paravian gem cutters in the city of Mearth, who dispersed in the times of the Curse which destroyed the inhabitants. The secrets of their trade were lost with them. Surviving works include the crown jewels of the Five High Kingdoms of Athera, cut as focus stones which attune to the heir of the royal lines.

    pronounced: i-marn-a-day-er

    root meaning: *imarn* – crystal; *e'daer* – to cut smaller

INNISH – city located on the south coast of Shand at the delta of the River Ippash. Birthplace of Halliron Masterbard. Formerly known as 'the Jewel of Shand', this was the site of the high king's winter court, prior to the time of the uprising.

    pronounced: in-ish

    root meaning: *inniesh* – a jewel with a pastel tint

INSTRELL BAY – body of water off the Gulf of Stormwell, that separates principality of Atainia, Tysan, from Deshir, Rathain.

    pronounced: in-strell

    root meaning: *arin'streal* – strong wind

IPPASH DELTA – river which originates in the southern spur of the Kelhorns and flows into the South Sea by the city of Innish, south coast, Shand.

    pronounced: ip-ash

    root meaning: *ipeish* – crescent

ISAER – city located at the crossroads of the Great West Road in Atainia, Tysan. Also a power focus, built during the First Age, in Atainia, Tysan, to source the defence-works at the Paravian keep of the same name.

pronounced: i-say-er

root meaning: *i'saer* – the circle

ISHLIR – coastal city located in Orvandir, Shand.

pronounced: ish-lear

root meaning: *ieshlier* – sheltered place

ITHAMON – Second Age Paravian stronghold, and a Third Age ruin; built on a fifth lane power node in Daon Ramon Barrens, Rathain, and inhabited until the year of the uprising. Site of the Compass Point Towers, or Sun Towers. Became the seat of the high kings of Rathain during the Third Age and in year 5638 was the site where Princes Lysaer s'Ilessid and Arithon s'Ffalenn battled the Mistwraith to confinement.

pronounced: ith-a-mon

root meaning: *itha* – five; *mon* – needle, spire

ITHILT – peninsula bordering Minderl Bay, located in kingdom of Rathain.

pronounced: ith-ilt sounds like 'with ill'

root meaning: *ith* – five; *ealt* – a narrows

ITHISH – city located at the edge of the principality of Vastmark, on the south coast of Shand. Where the Vastmark wool factors ship fleeces.

pronounced: ith-ish

root meaning: *ithish* – fleece or fluffy

IVEL – blind splicer hired by Arithon in his shipyard at Merior.

pronounced: ee-vell

root meaning: *iavel* – scathing

IYAT – energy sprite native to Athera, not visible to the eye, manifests in a poltergeist fashion by taking temporary possession of objects. Feeds upon natural energy sources: fire, breaking waves, lightning.

pronounced: ee-at

root meaning: *iyat* – to break

*   *   *

JAELOT – city located on the coast of the Bay of Eltair at the southern border of the Kingdom of Rathain. Once a Second Age power site, with a focus circle. Now a merchant city with a reputation for extreme snobbery and bad taste.

    pronounced: jay-lot

    root meaning: *jielot* – affectation

JIERET s'VALERIENT – earl of the North, clan chief of Deshir; *caithdein* of Rathain, sworn liegeman of Prince Arithon s'Ffalenn. Also son and heir of Lord Steiven. Blood pacted to Arithon by sorcerer's oath prior to battle of Strakewood Forest. Came to be known by headhunters as Jieret Red-beard.

    pronounced: jeer-et

    root meaning: *jieret* – thorn

JILIETH – girl from a Vastmark shepherd tribe.

    pronounced: jill-ee-eth

    root meaning: *jierlieth* – to be stubborn enough to cause pain; a thorn of worry

JINESSE – widow of a fisherman, mother of the twins Fiark and Feylind, and an inhabitant of Merior by the Sea.

    pronounced: gin-ess

    root meaning: *jienesse* – to be washed out or pale; a wisp

KALESH – one of the towns at the head of the inlet to Alestron's harbour, located in East Halla, Melhalla, and traditionally the enemy of the reigning s'Brydion duke.

    pronounced: cal-esh

    root meaning: *caille'esh* – stubborn hold

KARFAEL – trader town on the coast of the Westland Sea, in Tysan. Built by townsmen as a trade port after the fall of the High Kings of Tysan. Prior to Desh-thiere's conquest, the site was kept clear of buildings to allow the second lane forces to flow untrammelled across the focus site at Avenor.

pronounced: kar-fay-el

root meaning: *kar'i'ffael* – literal translation 'twist the dark'/colloquialism for 'intrigue'

KARMAK – plain located in the northern portion of the principality of Camris, Tysan. Site of numerous First Age battles where Paravian forces opposed Khadrim packs that bred in volcanic sites in the northern Tornir Peaks.

pronounced: kar-mack

root meaning: *karmak* – wolf

KARTHAN – kingdom in splinter world Dascen Elur, through West Gate, ruled by the pirate kings, s'Ffalenn descendants of the prince sent into exile at the time of the Mistwraith's conquest.

pronounced: karth-an

root meaning: *kar'eth'an* – one who raids/pirate

KARTH-EELS – creatures descended from stock aberrated by the *methurien*, or hate-wraiths, of Mirthlvain Swamp. Amphibious, fanged, venomed spines, webbed feet.

pronounced: car-th eels

root meaning: *kar'eth* – to raid

KELDMAR s'BRYDION – younger brother of Duke Bransian of Alestron; older brother of Parrien and Mearn.

pronounced: keld-mar

root meaning: *kiel'd'maeran* – one without pity

KELHORN MOUNTAINS – a range of shale scarps in Vastmark, Shand.

pronounced: kell-horn

root meaning: *kielwhern* – toothed, jagged

KHADRIM – drake-spawned creatures, flying, fire-breathing reptiles that were the scourge of the Second Age. By the Third Age, they had been driven back and confined in the Sorcerers' Preserve in the volcanic peaks in north Tysan.

pronounced: kaa-drim

root meaning: *khadrim* – dragon

KHARADMON – Sorcerer of the Fellowship of Seven; discorporate since rise of Khadrim and Seardluin levelled Paravian city at Ithamon in Second Age 3651. It was by Kharadmon's intervention that the survivors of the attack were sent to safety by means of transfer from the fifth lane power focus. Currently sent to the worlds cut off beyond South Gate to explore the Mistwraith's origin.

pronounced: kah-rad-mun

root meaning: *kar'riad en mon* – phrase translates to mean 'twisted thread on the needle' or colloquialism for 'a knot in the works'

KHETIENN – name for a brigantine owned by Arithon; also a small spotted wildcat, native to Daon Ramon Barrens, that became the s'Ffalenn royal sigil.

pronounced: key-et-ee-en

root meaning: *kietienn* – small leopard

KIELING TOWER – one of the four Compass Points or Sun Towers standing at Ithamon, Daon Ramon Barrens, Rathain. The warding virtue that binds its stones is compassion.

pronounced: kee-el-ing

root meaning: *kiel'ien* – root for pity, with suffix added translates to 'compassion'

KITTIWAKE TAVERN – sailors' dive located in the city of Ship's Port, Melhalla.

KORIANI – possessive form of the word 'Koriathain', see entry.

pronounced: kor-ee-ah-nee

KORIAS – southwestern principality of Tysan.

pronounced: kor-ee-as

root meaning: *cor* – ship, vessel; *i'esh* – nest, haven

KORIATHAIN – order of enchantresses ruled by a circle of seniors, under the power of one Prime Enchantress. They draw their talent from the orphaned children they

544

raise, or from daughters dedicated to service by their parents. Initiation rite involves a vow of consent that ties the spirit to a power crystal keyed to the Prime's control.

pronounced: kor-ee-ah-thain (thain rhymes with 'main')

root meaning: *koriath* – order; *ain* – belonging to

LANSHIRE – northwestern principality of Havish. Name taken from wastes at Scarpdale, site of First Age battles with Seardluin that seared the soil to a slag waste.

pronounced: lahn-sheer-e (last 'e' is nearly subliminal)

root meaning: *lan'hansh'era* – place of hot sands

LAW OF THE MAJOR BALANCE – founding order of the powers of the Fellowship of Seven, as written by the Paravians. The primary tenet is that no force of nature should be used without consent, or against the will of another living being.

LEINTHAL ANITHAEL – great Paravian navigator who was first to circumnavigate Athera.

pronounced: lee-in-thall an-ith-ee-el

root meaning: *lienthal* – direction; *anithael* – to seek

LITHMERE – principality located in the Kingdom of Havish.

pronounced: lith-mere to rhyme with 'with here'

root meaning: *lithmiere* – compound word with the meaning 'to preserve intact, or to keep whole', as in maintain a state of perfection

LIRENDA – First Senior Enchantress to the Prime, Koriani Order; Morriel's intended successor.

pronounced: leer-end-ah

root meaning: *lyron* – singer; *di-ia* – a dissonance (the hyphen denotes a glottal stop)

LOS MAR – coastal city in Carithwyr, Havish. Once a

fishing village; grew into a caravan crossing after the Mistwraith's invasion. Known for its scholars.

pronounced: loss-mar

root meaning: *liosmar* – letters, written records

LUHAINE – Sorcerer of the Fellowship of Seven – discorporate since the fall of Telmandir. Luhaine's body was pulled down by the mob while he was in ward trance, covering the escape of the royal heir to Havish.

pronounced: loo-hay-ne

root meaning: *luirhainon* – defender

LYRANTHE – instrument played by the bards of Athera. Strung with fourteen strings, tuned to seven tones (doubled). Two courses are 'drone strings' set to octaves. Five are melody strings, the lower three courses being octaves, the upper two, in unison.

pronounced: leer-anth-e (last 'e' being nearly subliminal)

root meaning: *lyr* – song, *anthe* – box

LYSAER s'ILESSID – prince of Tysan, 1,497th in succession after Halduin, founder of the line in Third Age Year One. Gifted at birth with control of Light, and Bane of Desh-Thiere.

pronounced: lie-say-er

root meaning: *lia* – blond, yellow, or light; *saer* – circle

MACHIEL – steward and *caithdein* of the realm of Havish. In service under King Eldir.

pronounced: mak-ee-el

root meaning: *mierkiel* – post, pillar

MAENALLE s'GANNLEY – steward and *caithdein* of Tysan.

pronounced: may-nahl-e (last 'e' is near subliminal)

root meaning: *maeni* – to fall, disrupt; *alli* – to save or preserve/colloquial translation: 'to patch together'

MAENOL – heir, after Maenalle s'Gannley, steward and *caithdein* of Tysan.

pronounced: may-nall

root meaning: *maeni'alli* – 'to patch together'

MAIEN – nickname for Maenalle's grandson, Maenol.

pronounced: my-en

root meaning: *maien* – mouse

MAGYRE – scholar who discovered the secret of black powder. In accordance with the Fellowship Sorcerers' compact, he was forced to give up his studies, but a copy of his papers survived.

pronounced: mag-wire

root meaning: *magiare* – a chaotic force

MAINMERE – town at the head of the Valenford River, located in the principality of Taerlin, Tysan. Built by townsmen on a site originally kept clear to free the second lane focus in the ruins farther south.

pronounced: main-meer-e ('e' is subliminal)

root meaning: *maeni* – to fall, interrupt; *miere* – reflection, colloquial translation: 'disrupt continuity'

MARAK – splinter world, cut off beyond South Gate, left lifeless upon creation of the Mistwraith. The original inhabitants were men exiled by the Fellowship from Athera for beliefs or practices that were incompatible with the compact sworn between the Sorcerers and the Paravian races, which permitted human settlement upon the continent.

pronounced: maer-ack

root meaning: *m'era'ki* – a place held separate

MARL – Earl of Fallowmere and clan chieftain at the time of the battle of Strakewood Forest.

pronounced: marl

root meaning: *marle* – quartz rock

MATHORN MOUNTAINS – range that bisects the Kingdom of Rathain east to west.

pronounced: math-orn

root meaning: *mathien* – massive

MATHORN ROAD – way passing to the south of the Mathorn Mountains, leading to the trade city of Etarra from the west.

    pronounced: math-orn

    root meaning: *mathien* – massive

MEARN s'BRYDION – youngest brother of Duke Bransian of Alestron.

    pronounced: may-arn

    root meaning: *mierne* – to flit

MEARTH – city through the West Gate in the Red Desert. Inhabitants all fell victim to the Shadows of Mearth, which were created by the Fellowship Sorcerer Davien to protect the Five Centuries Fountain. The Shadows are a light-fuelled geas that bind the mind to memory of an individual's most painful experience.

    pronounced: me-arth

    root meaning: *mearth* – empty

MEDLIR – name carried by Arithon s'Ffalenn while he travelled incognito as Halliron's apprentice.

    pronounced: med-leer

    root meaning: *midlyr* – phrase of melody

MELHALLA – High Kingdom of Athera, once ruled by the line of s'Ellestrion. The last prince died in the crossing of the Red Desert.

    pronounced: mel-hall-ah

    root meaning: *maelhallia* – grand meadows/plain – also word for an open space of any sort

MELOR RIVER – located in the principality of Korias, Tysan. Its mouth forms the harbour for the port town of West End.

    pronounced: mel-or

    root meaning: *maeliur* – fish

MERIOR BY THE SEA – small seaside fishing village on the Scimlade peninsula in Alland, Shand. Site of Arithon's shipyard.

    pronounced: mare-ee-or

    root meaning: *merioren* – cottages

METH ISLE KEEP – old Paravian fortress located on the isle in Methlas Lake in southern Melhalla. Kept by Verrain, Guardian of Mirthlvain. Contains a fifth lane power focus and dungeons where *methuri*, or hate-wraiths, were held temporarily captive before transfer to Rockfell Pit.

> pronounced: meth isle
> root meaning: *meth* – hate

METHLAS LAKE – large body of fresh water located in the principality of Radmoor, Melhalla.

> pronounced: meth-las
> root meaning: *meth'ilass'an* – the drowned, or sunken ones

METH-SNAKES – crossbred genetic mutations left over from a First Age drake-spawned creature called a *methuri* (hate-wraith). Related to iyats, these creatures possessed live hosts, which they infested and induced to produce mutated offspring to create weakened lines of stock to widen their choice of potential host animals.

> pronounced: meth to rhyme with 'death'
> root meaning: *meth* – hate

METHURI – drake-spawned and iyat-related parasite that infested live host animals. By the Third Age, they are extinct, but their mutated host stock continues to breed in Mirthlvain Swamp.

> pronounced: meth-yoor-ee
> root meaning: *meth* – hate; *thiere* – wraith, or spirit

MIN PIERENS – archipelago to the west of the Kingdom of West Shand, in the Westland Sea.

> pronounced: min (rhymes with 'pin') pierre-ins
> root meaning: *min* – purple; *pierens* – shoreline

MINDERL BAY – body of water behind Crescent Isle off the east coast of Rathain.

> pronounced: mind-earl
> root meaning: *minderl* – anvil

MIRALT – port city in northern Camris, Tysan.

> pronounced: meer-alt

root meaning: *m'ier* – shore; *alt* – last

MIRTHLVAIN SWAMP – boglands filled with dangerous crossbreeds, located south of the Tiriac Mountains in principality of Midhalla, Melhalla. Never left unwatched. Since conquest of the Mistwraith, the appointed Guardian was the spellbinder, Verrain.

pronounced: mirth-el-vain

root meaning: *myrthl* – noxious; *vain* – bog/mud

MORFETT – Lord Governor Supreme of Etarra at the time the Fellowship sought to restore Rathain's monarchy following the captivity of the Mistwraith, and during the muster for the warhost against Arithon.

pronounced: more-fet

root meaning not from the Paravian

MORNOS – city on the west shore of Lithmere, Havish.

pronounced: more-nose

root meaning: *moarnosh* – a coffer, specifically where a greedy person would hoard valuables

MORRIEL – Prime Enchantress of the Koriathain since the Third Age 4212.

pronounced: more-real

root meaning: *moar* – greed; *riel* – silver

MORVAIN – city located in the principality of Araethura, Rathain, on the coast of Instrell Bay. Elaira's birthplace.

pronounced: more-vain

root meaning: *morvain* – swindlers' market

NANDIR – Vastmark tribal dialect word for a barren woman who is considered unlucky. To become involved with a *nandir* woman is to curse one's sons to ill fortune. These women wear bells on their braids. Since life among the tribes is unpleasant for them, they often end up as prostitutes in coastal cities. In the southcoast trade towns, specifically Ithish and Innish, belled women are generally considered available; hence the custom of bawds wearing bells to attract customers.

    pronounced: nan-deer

    root meaning: from Vastmark dialect ancient term for 'without'

NARMS – city on the coast of Instrell Bay, built as a craft centre by Men in the early Third Age. Best known for dyeworks.

    pronounced: narms to rhyme with 'charms'

    root meaning: *narms* – colour

NORTHSTOR – city located at the northern tip of the East Halla peninsula in Melhalla.

    pronounced: north-store

    root meaning: *stor* – summit, or apex of a triangle

NORTHSTRAIT – narrows between the mainland spur of northern Tysan, and the Trow Islands.

ORLAN – pass through the Thaldein Mountains, also location of the Camris clans' west outpost, in Camris, Tysan. Known for barbarian raids.

    pronounced: or-lan

    root meaning: *irlan* – ledge

ORVANDIR – principality located in northeastern Shand.

    pronounced: or-van-deer

    root meaning: *orvein* – crumbled; *dir* – stone

OSTERMERE – harbour and trade city, once smugglers' haven, located in Carythwyr, Havish; current seat of Eldir, King of Havish.

    pronounced: os-tur-mere

    root meaning: *ostier* – brick; *miere* – reflection

PARAVIAN – name for the three old races that inhabited Athera before Men. Including the centaurs, the Sun-children and the unicorns, these races never die unless mishap befalls them; they are the world's channel, or direct connection to Ath Creator.

> pronounced: par-ai-vee-ans
>
> root meaning: *para* – great; *i'on* – fate or 'great mystery'

PARRIEN s'BRYDION – second youngest brother of Duke Bransian of Alestron; older brother of Mearn, younger brother of Keldmar.

> pronounced: par-ee-en
>
> root meaning: *para* – great; *ient* – dart

PASYVIER – meadows in Korias, Tysan, where clan-blood drifters raise horses.

> pronounced: pass-ee-vee-er
>
> root meaning: *pas'e'vier* – hidden little vale

PERDITH – city located on the east shore in East Halla, Melhalla; known for its armourers.

> pronounced: per-dith
>
> root meaning: *pirdith* – anvil

PERLORN – city in Fallowmere, Rathain on the trade road midway between Etarra and Werpoint.

> pronounced: pur-lorn
>
> root meaning: *perlorn* – midpoint

PESQUIL – mayor of the Northern League of Headhunters, at the time of the battle of Strakewood Forest. His strategies cause the Deshir clans the most punishing losses.

> pronounced: pes-quil like 'pest-quill'
>
> root meaning not from the Paravian

PRANDEY – Shandian term for gelded pleasure boy.

> pronounced: pran-dee
>
> root meaning not from the Paravian

QUAID – trade city in Carithwyr, Havish; inland along the trade road from Los Mar to Redburn. Famous for fired clay and brick.

> pronounced: quaid to rhyme with 'staid'

root meaning: *cruaid* – a specific form of clay used for brickmaking

RADMOORE DOWNS – meadowlands in Midhalla, Melhalla.

    pronounced: rad-more

    root meaning: *riad* – thread; *mour* – carpet, rug

RATHAIN – High Kingdom of Athera ruled by descendants of Torbrand s'Ffalenn since Third Age Year One. Sigil: black-and-silver leopard on green field.

    pronounced: rath-ayn

    root meaning: *roth* – brother; *thein* – tower, sanctuary

RAUVEN TOWER – home of the s'Ahelas mages who brought up Arithon s'Ffalenn and trained him to the ways of power. Located on the splinter world, Dascen Elur, through West Gate.

    pronounced: raw-ven

    root meaning: *rauven* – invocation

REDBURN – city located in a deep inlet in the northern shore of Rockbay Harbour in Havistock, Havish.

    pronounced: red-burn

    root meaning not from Paravian

RENWORT – plant native to Athera. A poisonous mash can be brewed from the berries.

    pronounced: ren-wart

    root meaning: *renwarin* – poison

RIATHAN PARAVIANS – unicorns, the purest and most direct connection to Ath Creator; the prime vibration channels directly through the horn.

    pronounced: ree-ah-than

    root meaning: *ria* – to touch; *ath* – prime life force; *ri'athon* – one who touches divinity

ROCKFELL PIT – deep shaft cut into Rockfell Peak, used to imprison harmful entities throughout all three ages.

Located in the principality of West Halla, Melhalla; became the warded prison for Desh-thiere.

    pronounced: rock-fell

    root meaning not from the Paravian

ROCKFELL VALE – valley below Rockfell Peak, located in principality of West Halla, Melhalla.

    pronounced: rockfell vale

    root meaning not from the Paravian

s'AHELAS – family name for the royal line appointed by the Fellowship Sorcerers in Third Age Year One to rule the High Kingdom of Shand. Gifted geas: farsight.

    pronounced: s'ah-hell-as

    root meaning: *ahelas* – mage-gifted

SANPASHIR – desert waste on the south coast of Shand.

    pronounced: sahn-pash-eer

    root meaning: *san* – black or dark; *pash'era* – place of grit or gravel

SAVRID – merchant brig chartered to transport armed men from Minderl Bay to Merior.

    pronounced: sahv-rid

    root meaning: *savrid* – thrifty

s'BRYDION – ruling line of the dukes of Alestron. The only old blood clansmen to maintain rule of their city through the uprising that defeated the rule of the high kings.

    pronounced: s'bride-ee-on

    root meaning: *baridien* – tenacity

SCIMLADE TIP – peninsula at the southeast corner of Alland, Shand.

    pronounced: skim-laid

    root meaning: *scimlait* – curved knife or scythe

SEARDLUIN – drake-spawned, vicious, intelligent cat-like predators that roved in packs whose hierarchy was arranged for ruthless and efficient slaughter of other living things. By the middle of the Second Age, they had been battled to extinction.

    pronounced: seerd-lwin

    root meaning: *seard* – bearded; *luin* – feline

SECOND AGE – Marked by the arrival of the Fellowship of Seven at Crater Lake, their called purpose to fight the drake spawn.

SELKWOOD – forest located in Alland, Shand.

    pronounced: sellk-wood

    root meaning: *selk* – pattern

SETHVIR – Sorcerer of the Fellowship of Seven, served as Warden of Althain since the disappearance of the Paravians in the Third Age after the Mistwraith's conquest.

    pronounced: seth-veer

    root meaning: *seth* – fact; *vaer* – keep

SEVERNIR – river that once ran across the central part of Daon Ramon Barrens, Rathain. Diverted at the source after the Mistwraith's conquest, to run east into the Bay of Eltair.

    pronounced: se-ver-neer

    root meaning: *sevaer* – to travel; *nir* – south

s'FFALENN – family name for the royal line appointed by the Fellowship Sorcerers in Third Age Year One to rule the High Kingdom of Rathain. Gifted geas: compassion/empathy.

    pronounced: fal-en

    root meaning: *ffael* – dark; *an* – one

s'GANNLEY – family name for the line of Earls of the West, who stood as *caithdeinen* and stewards for the Kings of Tysan.

    pronounced: gan-lee

    root meaning: *gaen* – to guide; *li* – exalted, or in harmony

SHADDORN – trade city located on the Scimlade peninsula in Alland, Shand.

    pronounced: shad-dorn

    root meaning: *shaddiern* – a type of sea turtle

SHAND – High Kingdom on the southeast corner of the Paravian continent, originally ruled by the line of s'Ahelas. Device is falcon on a crescent moon, backed by purple-and-gold chevrons.

    pronounced: shand as in 'hand'

    root meaning: *shand* – two/pair

SHANDIAN – refers to nationality, being of the Kingdom of Shand.

    pronounced: shand-ee-an

    root meaning: *shand* – two/pair

SHEHANE ALTHAIN – Ilitharis Paravian who dedicated his spirit as defender and guardian of Althain Tower.

    pronounced: shee-hay-na all-thain

    root meaning: *shiehai'en* – to give for the greater good; *alt* – last; *thain* – tower

SHIP'S PORT – town on the coast of the Bay of Eltair located in West Halla, Melhalla.

SICKLE BAY – body of water located inside the Scimlade peninsula in Alland, Shand.

s'ILESSID – family name for the royal line appointed by the Fellowship Sorcerers in Third Age Year One to rule the High Kingdom of Tysan. Gifted geas: justice.

    pronounced: s-ill-ess-id

    root meaning: *liessiad* – balance

SITHAER – mythological equivalent of hell, halls of Dharkaron Avenger's judgment; according to Ath's adepts, that state of being where the prime vibration is not recognized.

    pronounced: sith-air

    root meaning: *sid* – lost; *thiere* – wraith/spirit

SKANNT – headhunter captain, served under Pesquil.

    pronounced: scant

    root meaning: *sciant* – a lean, hard-run hound of mixed breeding

SKYRON FOCUS – large aquamarine focus stone, used by the Koriani Senior Circle for their major magic after the loss of the Great Waystone during the rebellion.

pronounced: sky-run

root meaning: *skyron* – colloquialism for shackle; *s'kyr'i'on* – literally 'sorrowful fate'

SKYSHIEL – mountain range that runs north to south along the eastern coast of Rathain.

pronounced: sky-shee-el

root meaning: *skyshia* – to pierce through; *iel* – light ray

s'LORNMEIN – family name for the royal line appointed by the Fellowship Sorcerers in Third Age Year One to rule the High Kingdom of Havish. Gifted geas: temperance.

pronounced: slorn-main

root meaning: *liernmein* – to centre, or restrain, or bring into balance

SORCERERS' PRESERVE – warded territory located by Teal's Gap in Tornir Peaks in Tysan where the Khadrim are kept confined by Fellowship magic.

STEIVEN – Earl of the North, *caithdein* and regent to the Kingdom of Rathain at the time of Arithon Teir's'Ffalenn's return. Chieftain of the Deshans until his death in the battle of Strakewood Forest. Jieret Red-beard's father.

pronounced: stay-vin

root meaning: *steiven* – stag

STORLAINS – mountains dividing the Kingdom of Havish.

pronounced: store-lanes

root meaning: *storlient* – largest summit, highest divide

STORMWELL – Gulf of Stormwell, body of water off the north coast of Tysan.

STRAKEWOOD – forest in the principality of Deshir, Rathain; site of the battle of Strakewood Forest.

pronounced: strayk-wood similar to 'stray wood'

root meaning: *streik* – to quicken, to seed

SUNCHILDREN – translated term for Athlien Paravians.

SUN TOWERS – translated term for the Paravian keeps still standing on the site of the ruins of Ithamon in Daon Ramon Barrens, Rathain. See Ithamon.

s'VALERIENT – family name for the Earls of the North, regents and *caithdeinen* for the High Kings of Rathain.

    pronounced: val-er-ee-ent

    root meaning: *val* – straight; *erient* – spear

TAERLIN – southeastern principality of Kingdom of Tysan. Also a lake of that name, Taerlin Waters in the southern spur of Tornir Peaks. Halliron teaches Arithon a ballad of that name, which is of Paravian origin, and which commemorates the First Age slaughter of unicorn herd by Khadrim.

    pronounced: tay-er-lin

    root meaning: *taer* – calm; *lien* – to love

TAERNOND – forest in Ithilt, Rathain.

    pronounced: tear-nond

    root meaning: *taer* – calm; *nond* – thicket, copse

TAL QUORIN – river formed by the confluence of watershed on the southern side of Strakewood, principality of Deshir, Rathain, where traps were laid for Etarra's army in the battle of Strakewood Forest.

    pronounced: tal quar-in

    root meaning: *tal* – branch; *quorin* – canyons

TALERA s'AHELAS – princess wed to the King of Amroth on the splinter world of Dascen Elur. Mother of Lysaer s'Ilessid, by her husband; mother of Arithon, through her adulterous liaison with the Pirate King of Karthan, Avar s'Ffalenn.

    pronounced: tal-er-a

    root meaning: *talera* – branch or fork in a path

TALITH – Lord Diegan's sister; betrothed lady of Lysaer s'Ilessid.

    pronounced: tal-ith to rhyme with 'gal with'

    root meaning: *tal* – branch; *lith* – to keep/nurture

TALLIARTHE – name given to Arithon's pleasure sloop by Feylind; in Paravian myth, a sea sprite who spirits away maidens who stray too near to the tidemark at twilight.

    pronounced: tal-ee-arth

    root meaning: *tal* – branch; *li* – exalted, in harmony; *araithe* – to disperse or to send

TAL'S CROSSING – town at the branch in the trade road that leads to Etarra and south, and northeastward to North Ward.

    pronounced: tal to rhyme with 'pal'

    root meaning: *tal* – branch

TASHAN – elder on Maenalle's clan council, present at the raid on the Pass of Orlan.

    pronounced: tash-an

    root meaning: *tash* – swift, quick; *an* – one

TEAL'S GAP – pass in the northern spur of Tornir Peaks in Tysan, which passes through the Sorcerers' Preserve.

    pronounced: teel's gap

    root meaning: *tielle* – ravine

TEIR – title fixed to a name denoting heirship.

    pronounced: tay-er

    root meaning: *teir's* – 'successor to power'

TELMANDIR – ruined city that once was the seat of the High Kings of Havish. Located in the principality of Lithmere, Havish.

    pronounced: tell-man-deer

    root meaning: *telman'en* – leaning; *dir* – rock

TELZEN – city on the coast of Alland, Shand, renowned for its lumber and saw millworks.

    pronounced: tell-zen

    root meaning: *tielsen* – to saw wood

THALDEINS – mountain range that borders the principality of Camris, Tysan, to the east. Site of the Camris clans' west outpost. Site of the raid at the Pass of Orlan.

    pronounced: thall-dayn

root meaning: *thal* – head; *dein* – bird

THARIDOR – trade city on the shores of Bay of Eltair in Melhalla.

    pronounced: thar-i-door

    root meaning: *tier'i'dur* – keep of stone

THARRICK – captain of the guard in the city of Alestron assigned charge of the duke's secret armoury.

    pronounced: thar-rick

    root meaning: *thierik* – unkind twist of fate

THIRD AGE – marked by Fellowship's sealing of the compact with the Paravian races, and the arrival of Men to Athera.

THIRDMARK – seaside city on the shores of Rockbay Harbour at the edge of Vastmark.

TIENELLE – high-altitude herb valued by mages for its mind-expanding properties. Highly toxic. No antidote. The leaves, dried and smoked, are most potent. To weaken its powerful side effects and allow safer access to its vision, Koriani enchantresses boil the flowers, then soak tobacco leaves with the brew.

    pronounced: tee-an-ell-e ('e' mostly subliminal)

    root meaning: *tien* – dream; *iel* – light/ray

TIRANS – trade city in East Halla, Melhalla.

    pronounced: tee-rans

    root meaning: *tier* – to hold fast, to keep, to covet

TIRIACS – mountain range to the north of Mirthlvain Swamp, located in the principality of Midhalla, Kingdom of Melhalla.

    pronounced: tie-ree-axe

    root meaning: *tieriach* – alloy of metals

TORBRAND s'FFALENN – founder of the s'Ffalenn line appointed by the Fellowship of Seven to rule the High Kingdom of Rathain in Third Age Year One.

    pronounced: tor-brand

    root meaning: *tor* – sharp, keen; *brand* – temper

TORNIR PEAKS – mountain range on western border of the principality of Camris, Tysan. Northern half is actively volcanic, and there the last surviving packs of Khadrim are kept under ward.

pronounced: tor-neer.

root meaning: *tor* – sharp, keen; *nier* – tooth

TORWENT – fishing town in Lanshire, Havish, where the smack *Royal Freedom* was sold.

pronounced: tore-went

root meaning: *tor* – sharp; *wient* – bend

TRAITHE – Sorcerer of the Fellowship of Seven. Solely responsible for the closing of South Gate to deny further entry to the Mistwraith. Traithe lost most of his faculties in the process, and was left with a limp. Since it is not known whether he can make the transfer into discorporate existence with his powers impaired, he has retained his physical body.

pronounced: tray-the

root meaning: *traithe* – gentleness

TYSAN – one of the Five High Kingdoms of Athera, as defined by the charters of the Fellowship of Seven. Ruled by the s'Ilessid royal line. Sigil: gold star on blue field.

pronounced: tie-san

root meaning: *tiasen* – rich

VALENDALE – river arising in the Pass of Orlan in the Thaldein Mountains, in the principality of Atainia, Tysan.

pronounced: val-en-dale

root meaning: *valen* – braided; *dale* – foam

VALENFORD – city located in Taerlin, Tysan.

pronounced: val-en-ford

root meaning: *valen* – braided

VALLEYGAP – pass on the trade road between Etarra and Perlorn in the Kingdom of Rathain, known for shale slides and raids.

VALSTEYN – river which springs from the Mathorn

Mountains in Rathain, and which crosses the Plain of Araithe.

    pronounced: val-stain

    root meaning: *valsteyne* – to meander

VASTMARK – principality located in southwestern Shand. Highly mountainous and not served by trade roads. Its coasts are renowned for shipwrecks. Inhabited by nomadic shepherds and wyverns, non-fire-breathing, smaller relatives of Khadrim.

    pronounced: vast-mark

    root meaning: *vhast* – bare; *mheark* – valley

VERRAIN – spellbinder, trained by Luhaine; stood as Guardian of Mirthlvain when the Fellowship of Seven was left shorthanded after the conquest of the Mistwraith.

    pronounced: ver-rain

    root meaning: *ver* – keep; *ria* – touch; *an* – one; original Paravian: *verria'an*

WARD – a guarding spell.

    pronounced: as in English

    root meaning not from the Paravian

WARDEN OF ALTHAIN – alternative title for the Fellowship Sorcerer, Sethvir.

WATERFORK – city located in Lithmere, Havish.

WERPOINT – fishing town and outpost on the northeast coast of Fallowmere, Rathain. Muster point for Lysaer's warhost.

    pronounced: were-point

    root meaning: *wyr* – all/sum

WEST END – small merchant town in Korias, Tysan. Once was a great port, before the Mistwraith's invasion, but the loss of navigational arts set the city into decline.

WEST GATE PROPHECY – prophecy made by Dakar the Mad Prophet in Third Age 5061, which forecast the return of royal talent through the West Gate, and the

Bane of Desh-thiere and a return to untrammelled sunlight.

WESTLAND SEA – body of water located off the west shore of the continent of Paravia.

WESTWOOD – forest located in Camris, Tysan, north of the Great West Road.

WHITEHOLD – city located on the coast of the Bay of Eltair in East Halla, Melhalla. Once saved from storm surge and flooding by a circle of Koriani seniors.

WORLDSEND GATES – set at the four compass points of the continent of Paravia. These were spelled portals constructed by the Fellowship of Seven at the dawn of the Third Age, and were done in connection with the obligations created by their compact with the Paravian races which allowed men to settle on Athera.